TRICKSTER

LIBRARY OF CONGRESS CATALOGING-IN-PUBLICATION DATA

TRICKSTER : NATIVE AMERICAN TALES : A GRAPHIC COLLECTION / EDITED BY MATT DEMBICKI.

P. CM.

ISBN 978-1-55591-724-1 (PBK.)

1. INDIANS OF NORTH AMERICA--FOLKLORE--COMIC BOOKS, STRIPS, ETC. 2. TRICKSTERS--NORTH AMERICA--COMIC BOOKS, STRIPS, ETC. 3. TALES--NORTH AMERICA--COMIC BOOKS, STRIPS, ETC. 4. GRAPHIC NOVELS. I. DEMBICKI, MATT.

E98.F6T73 2010

741.5'97--DC22

2009049668

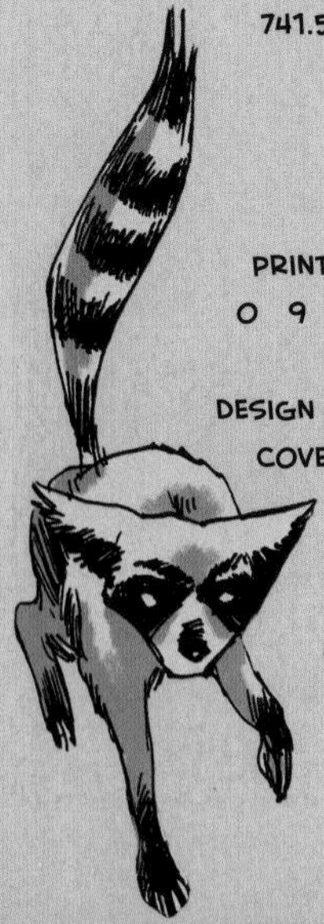

PRINTED IN THE UNITED STATES OF AMERICA

0 9 8 7 6 5 4 3 2

DESIGN BY JACK LENZO

COVER IMAGE © BY JACOB WARRENFELTZ

FULCRUM BOOKS

A DIVISION OF FULCRUM PUBLISHING, INC.

4690 TABLE MOUNTAIN DR., STE. 100

GOLDEN, CO 80403

800-992-2908 • 303-277-1623

CONTENTS

COYOTE AND THE PEBBLES 5
DAYTON EDMONDS AND MICAH FARRITOR

RAVEN THE TRICKSTER 19
JOHN ACTIVE AND JASON COPLAND

AZBAN AND THE CRAYFISH 33
JAMES BRUCHAC, JOSEPH BRUCHAC,
AND MATT DEMBICKI

TRICKSTER AND THE GREAT CHIEF...47
DAVID SMITH AND JERRY CARR

HORNED TOAD LADY AND COYOTE...55
ELDRENA DOUMA AND ROY BONEY JR.

RABBIT AND THE TUG-OF-WAR.......63
MICHAEL THOMPSON AND JACOB WARRENFELTZ

MOSHUP'S BRIDGE 71
JONATHAN PERRY, CHRIS PIERS,
AND SCOTT WHITE

RABBIT'S CHOCTAW TAIL TALE........79
TIM TINGLE AND PAT LEWIS

THE WOLF AND THE MINK 89
ELAINE GRINNELL AND MICHELLE SILVA

THE DANGEROUS BEAVER..............103
MARY EYLEY AND JIM8BALL

GIDDY UP, WOLFIE 111
GREG RODGERS AND MIKE SHORT

HOW THE ALLIGATOR GOT
HIS BROWN, SCALY SKIN 123
JOYCE BEAR AND MEGAN BAEHR

THE YEHASURI: THE
LITTLE WILD INDIANS................137
BECKEE GARRIS AND ANDREW COHEN

WAYNABOOZHOO AND
THE GEESE 143
DAN JONES AND MICHAEL J. AUGER

WHEN COYOTE DECIDED
TO GET MARRIED 149
EIRIK THORSGARD AND RAND ARRINGTON

PUAPUALENALENA, WIZARD DOG
OF WAIPI'O VALLEY....................161
THOMAS C. CUMMINGS JR. AND PAUL ZDEPSKI

ISHJINKI AND BUZZARD................173
JIMM GOODTRACKS AND DIMI MACHERAS

THE BEAR WHO STOLE
THE CHINOOK 185
JACK GLADSTONE AND EVAN KEELING

HOW WILDCAT
CAUGHT A TURKEY....................194
JOSEPH STANDS WITH MANY AND JON SPERRY

ESPUN AND GRANDFATHER...........203
JOHN BEAR MITCHELL AND ANDY BENNETT

MAI AND THE
CLIFF-DWELLING BIRDS 215
SUNNY DOOLEY AND J CHRIS CAMPBELL

FROM THE EDITOR................................225

CONTRIBUTORS..................................226

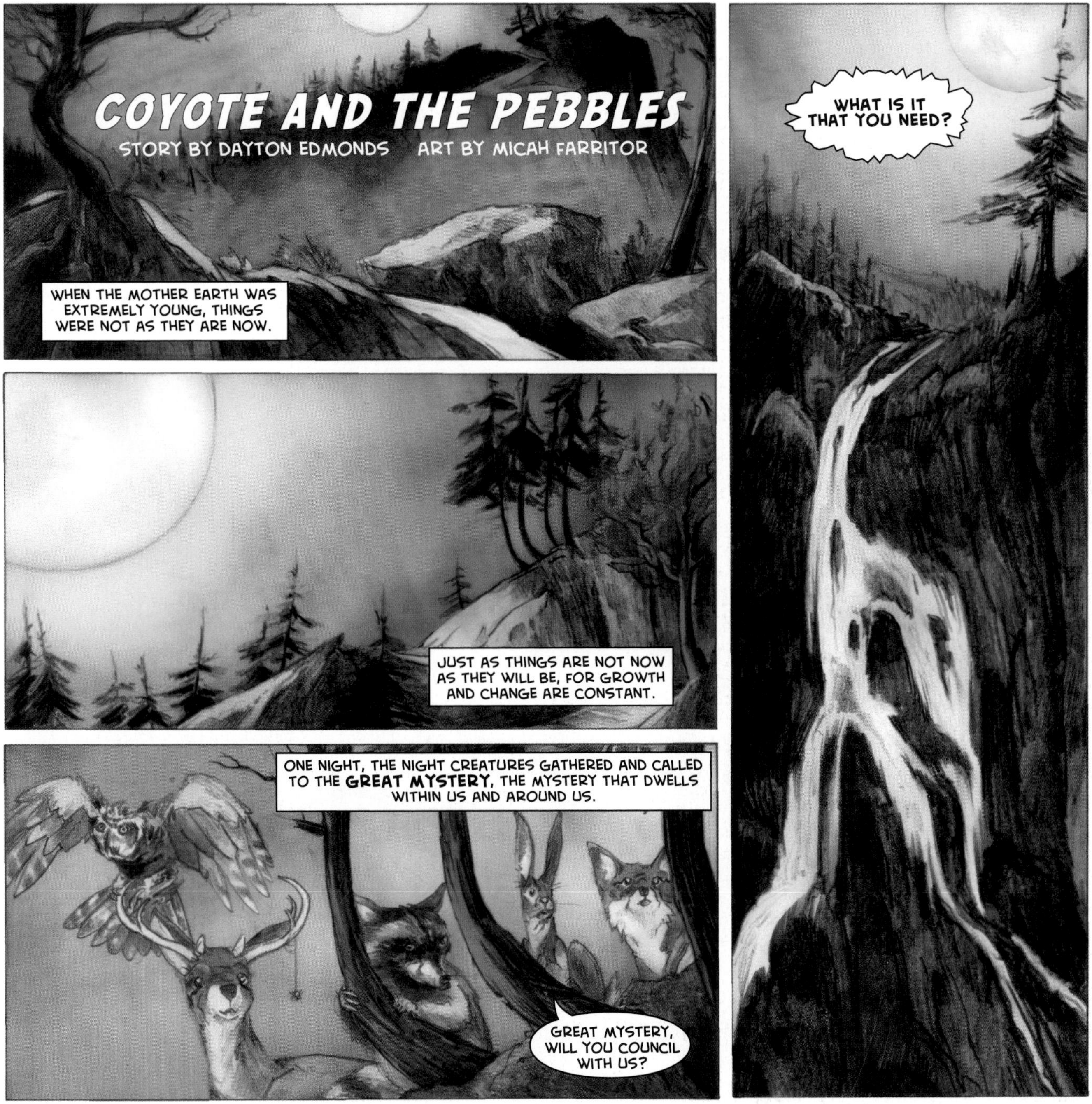
COYOTE AND THE PEBBLES
STORY BY DAYTON EDMONDS ART BY MICAH FARRITOR
WHEN THE MOTHER EARTH WAS EXTREMELY YOUNG, THINGS WERE NOT AS THEY ARE NOW.
JUST AS THINGS ARE NOT NOW AS THEY WILL BE, FOR GROWTH AND CHANGE ARE CONSTANT.
ONE NIGHT, THE NIGHT CREATURES GATHERED AND CALLED TO THE GREAT MYSTERY, THE MYSTERY THAT DWELLS WITHIN US AND AROUND US.
GREAT MYSTERY, WILL YOU COUNCIL WITH US?
WHAT IS IT THAT YOU NEED?

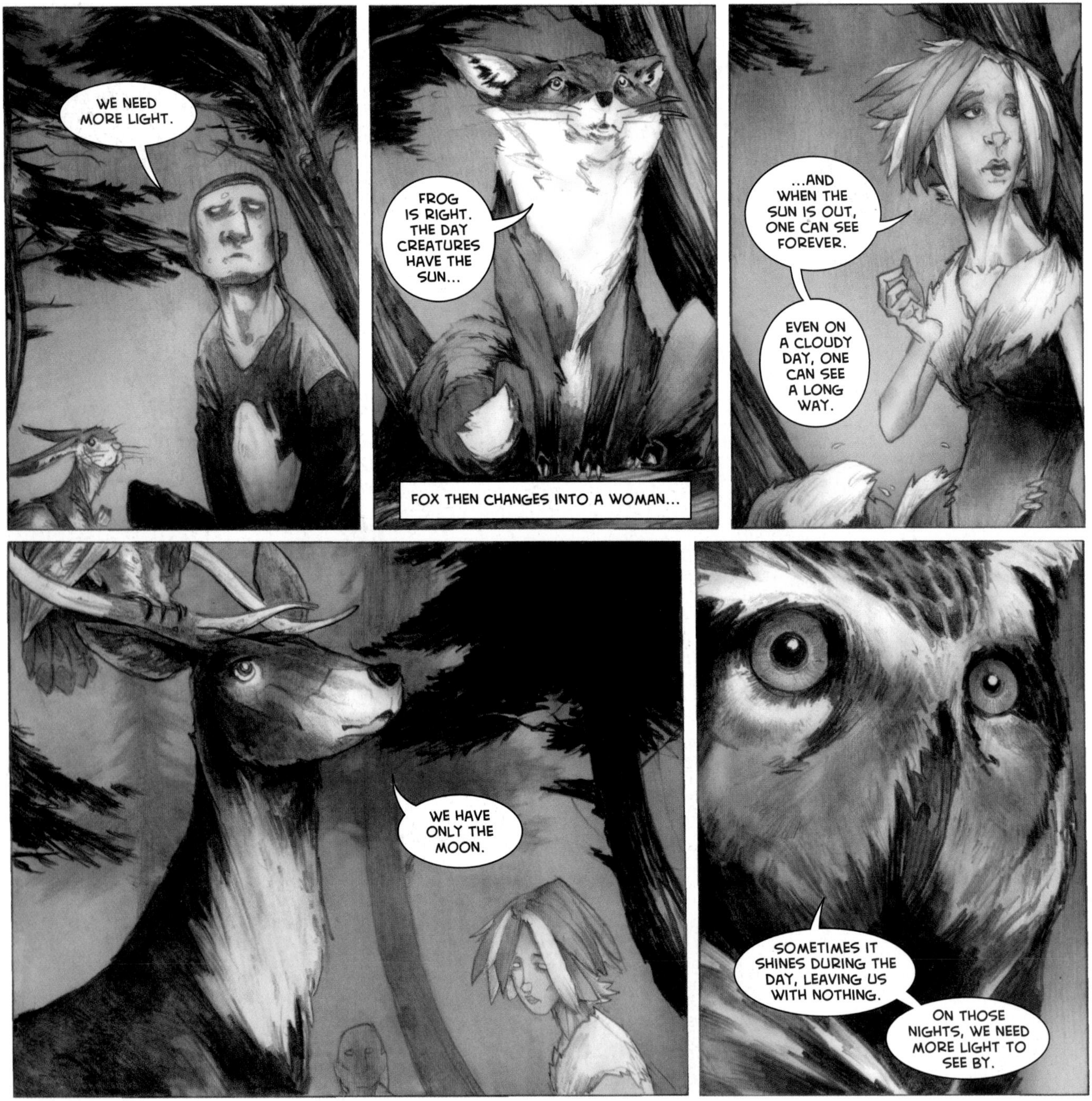
WE NEED MORE LIGHT.
FROG IS RIGHT. THE DAY CREATURES HAVE THE SUN...
FOX THEN CHANGES INTO A WOMAN...
...AND WHEN THE SUN IS OUT, ONE CAN SEE FOREVER.
EVEN ON A CLOUDY DAY, ONE CAN SEE A LONG WAY.
WE HAVE ONLY THE MOON.
SOMETIMES IT SHINES DURING THE DAY, LEAVING US WITH NOTHING.
ON THOSE NIGHTS, WE NEED MORE LIGHT TO SEE BY.

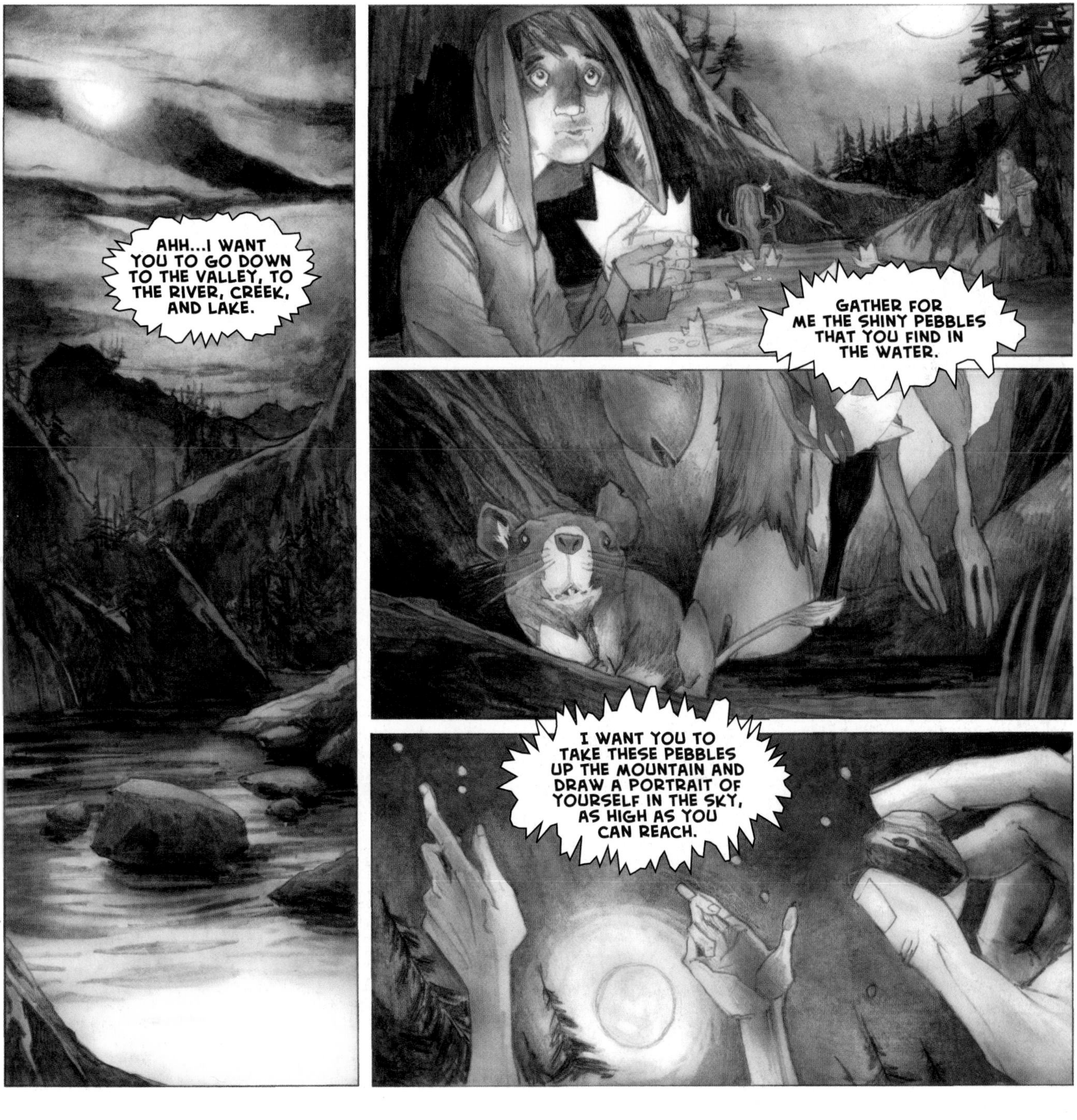
AHH...I WANT YOU TO GO DOWN TO THE VALLEY, TO THE RIVER, CREEK, AND LAKE.
GATHER FOR ME THE SHINY PEBBLES THAT YOU FIND IN THE WATER.
I WANT YOU TO TAKE THESE PEBBLES UP THE MOUNTAIN AND DRAW A PORTRAIT OF YOURSELF IN THE SKY, AS HIGH AS YOU CAN REACH.

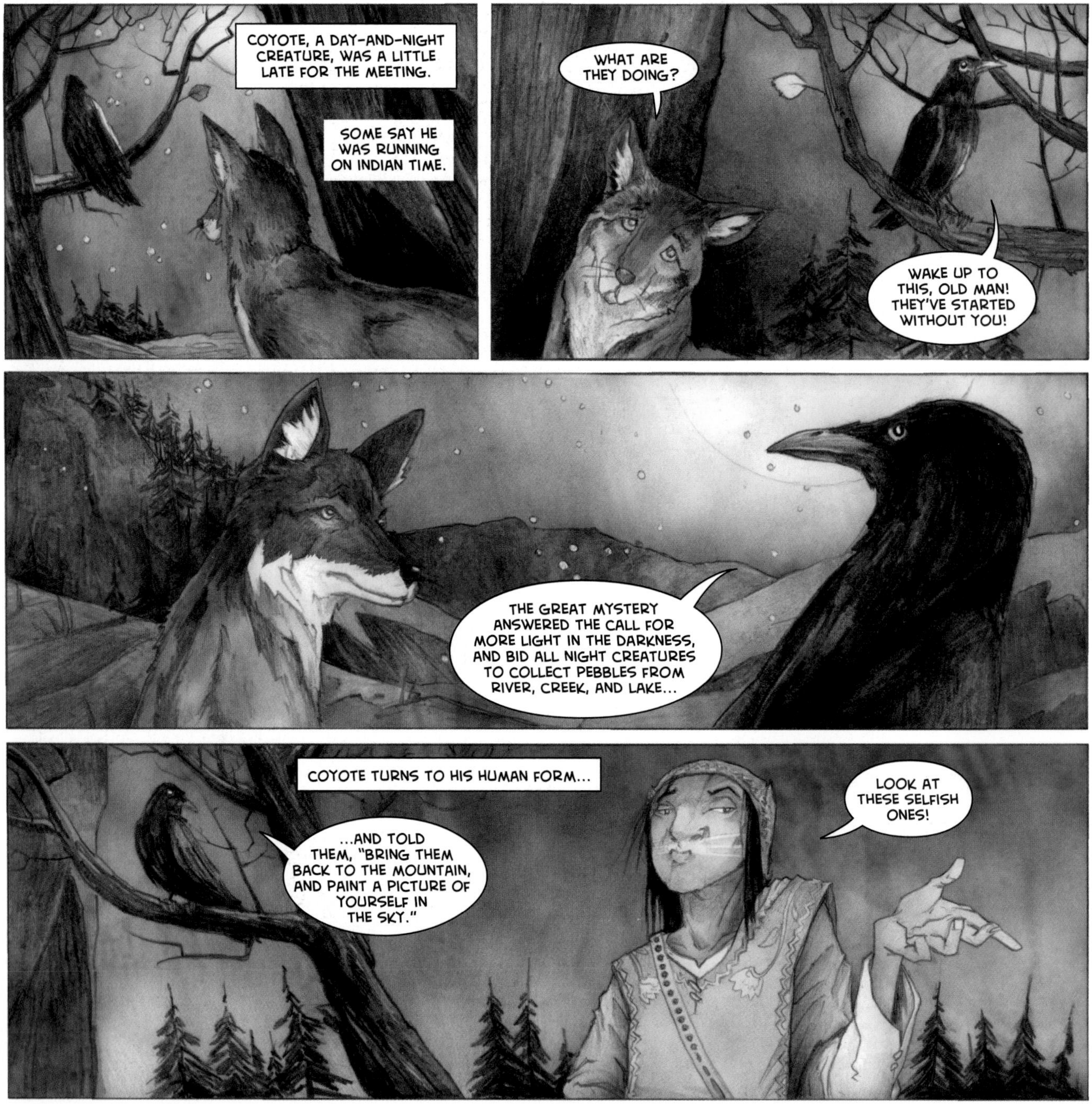
COYOTE, A DAY-AND-NIGHT CREATURE, WAS A LITTLE LATE FOR THE MEETING.
SOME SAY HE WAS RUNNING ON INDIAN TIME.
WHAT ARE THEY DOING?
WAKE UP TO THIS, OLD MAN! THEY'VE STARTED WITHOUT YOU!
THE GREAT MYSTERY ANSWERED THE CALL FOR MORE LIGHT IN THE DARKNESS, AND BID ALL NIGHT CREATURES TO COLLECT PEBBLES FROM RIVER, CREEK, AND LAKE...
COYOTE TURNS TO HIS HUMAN FORM...
...AND TOLD THEM, "BRING THEM BACK TO THE MOUNTAIN, AND PAINT A PICTURE OF YOURSELF IN THE SKY."
LOOK AT THESE SELFISH ONES!

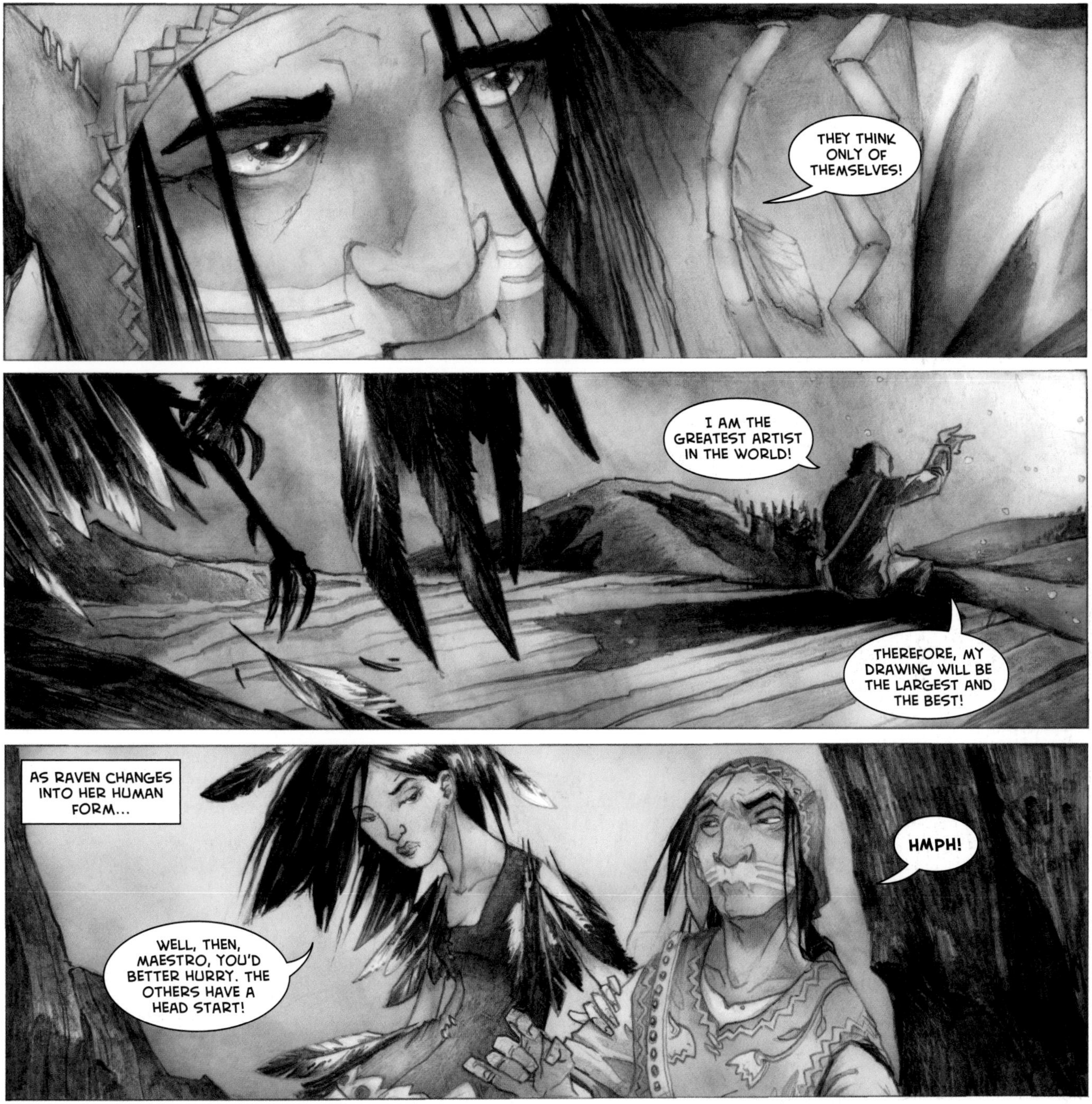
THEY THINK ONLY OF THEMSELVES!
I AM THE GREATEST ARTIST IN THE WORLD!
THEREFORE, MY DRAWING WILL BE THE LARGEST AND THE BEST!
AS RAVEN CHANGES INTO HER HUMAN FORM...
HMPH!
WELL, THEN, MAESTRO, YOU'D BETTER HURRY. THE OTHERS HAVE A HEAD START!

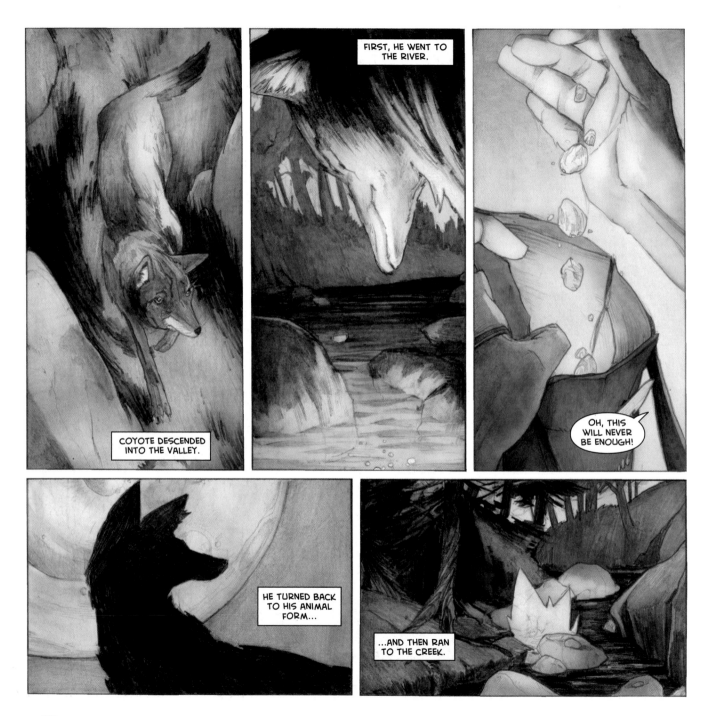

COYOTE DESCENDED INTO THE VALLEY.

FIRST, HE WENT TO THE RIVER.

OH, THIS WILL NEVER BE ENOUGH!

HE TURNED BACK TO HIS ANIMAL FORM...

...AND THEN RAN TO THE CREEK.

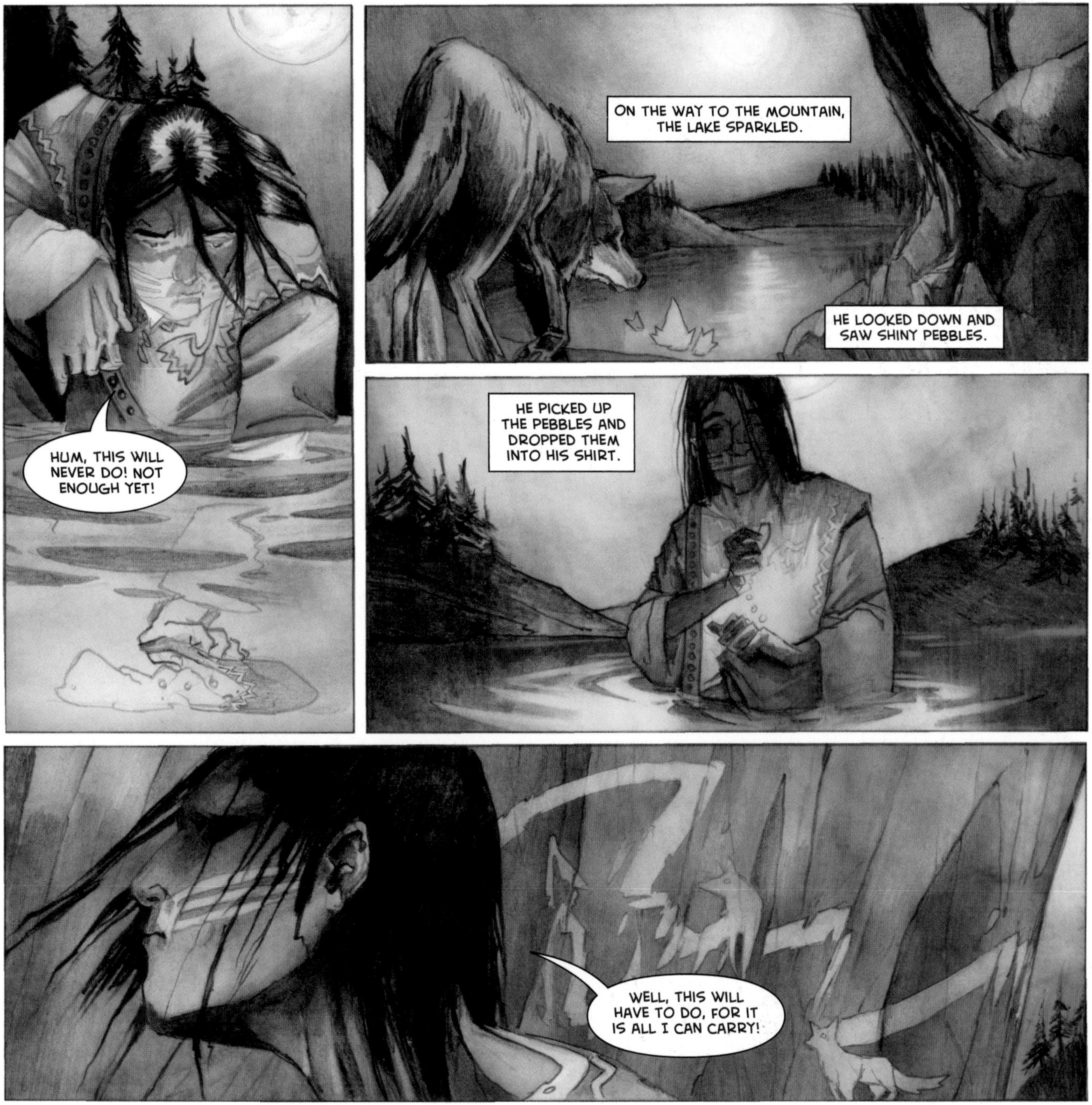
HUM, THIS WILL NEVER DO! NOT ENOUGH YET!
ON THE WAY TO THE MOUNTAIN, THE LAKE SPARKLED.
HE LOOKED DOWN AND SAW SHINY PEBBLES.
HE PICKED UP THE PEBBLES AND DROPPED THEM INTO HIS SHIRT.
WELL, THIS WILL HAVE TO DO, FOR IT IS ALL I CAN CARRY!

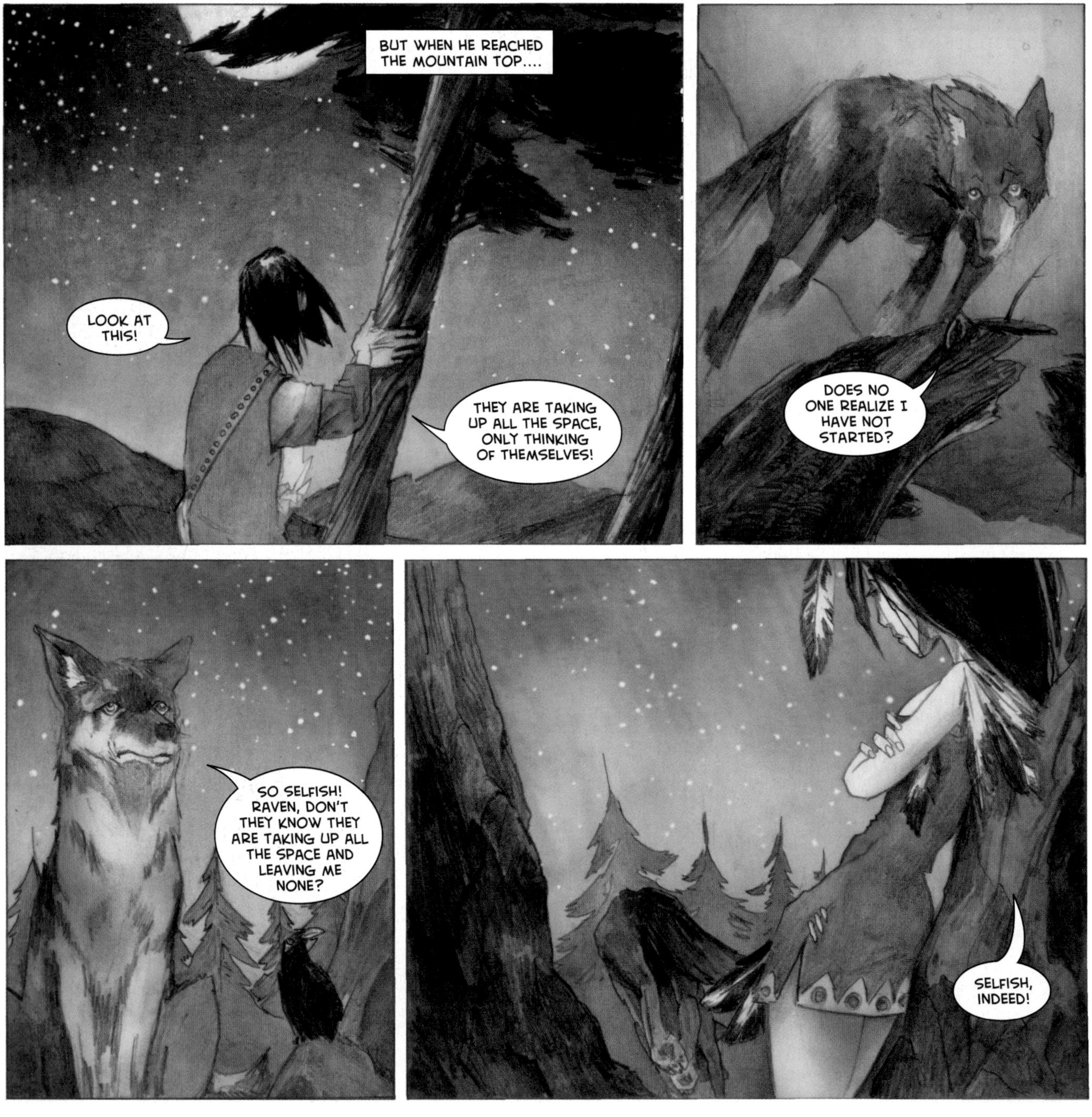
BUT WHEN HE REACHED THE MOUNTAIN TOP....
LOOK AT THIS!
THEY ARE TAKING UP ALL THE SPACE, ONLY THINKING OF THEMSELVES!
DOES NO ONE REALIZE I HAVE NOT STARTED?
SO SELFISH! RAVEN, DON'T THEY KNOW THEY ARE TAKING UP ALL THE SPACE AND LEAVING ME NONE?
SELFISH, INDEED!

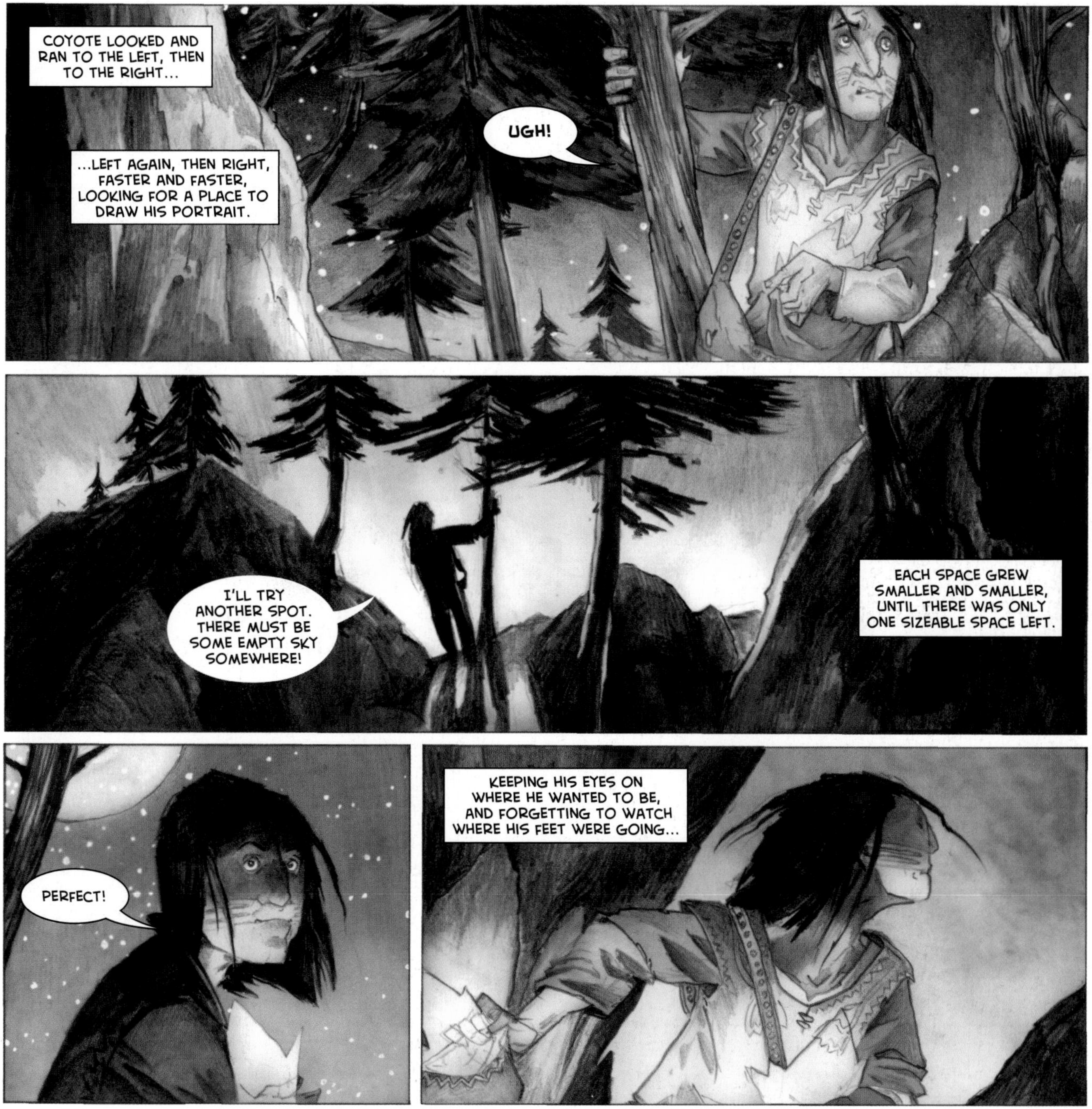
COYOTE LOOKED AND RAN TO THE LEFT, THEN TO THE RIGHT...
...LEFT AGAIN, THEN RIGHT, FASTER AND FASTER, LOOKING FOR A PLACE TO DRAW HIS PORTRAIT.
UGH!
I'LL TRY ANOTHER SPOT. THERE MUST BE SOME EMPTY SKY SOMEWHERE!
EACH SPACE GREW SMALLER AND SMALLER, UNTIL THERE WAS ONLY ONE SIZEABLE SPACE LEFT.
PERFECT!
KEEPING HIS EYES ON WHERE HE WANTED TO BE, AND FORGETTING TO WATCH WHERE HIS FEET WERE GOING...

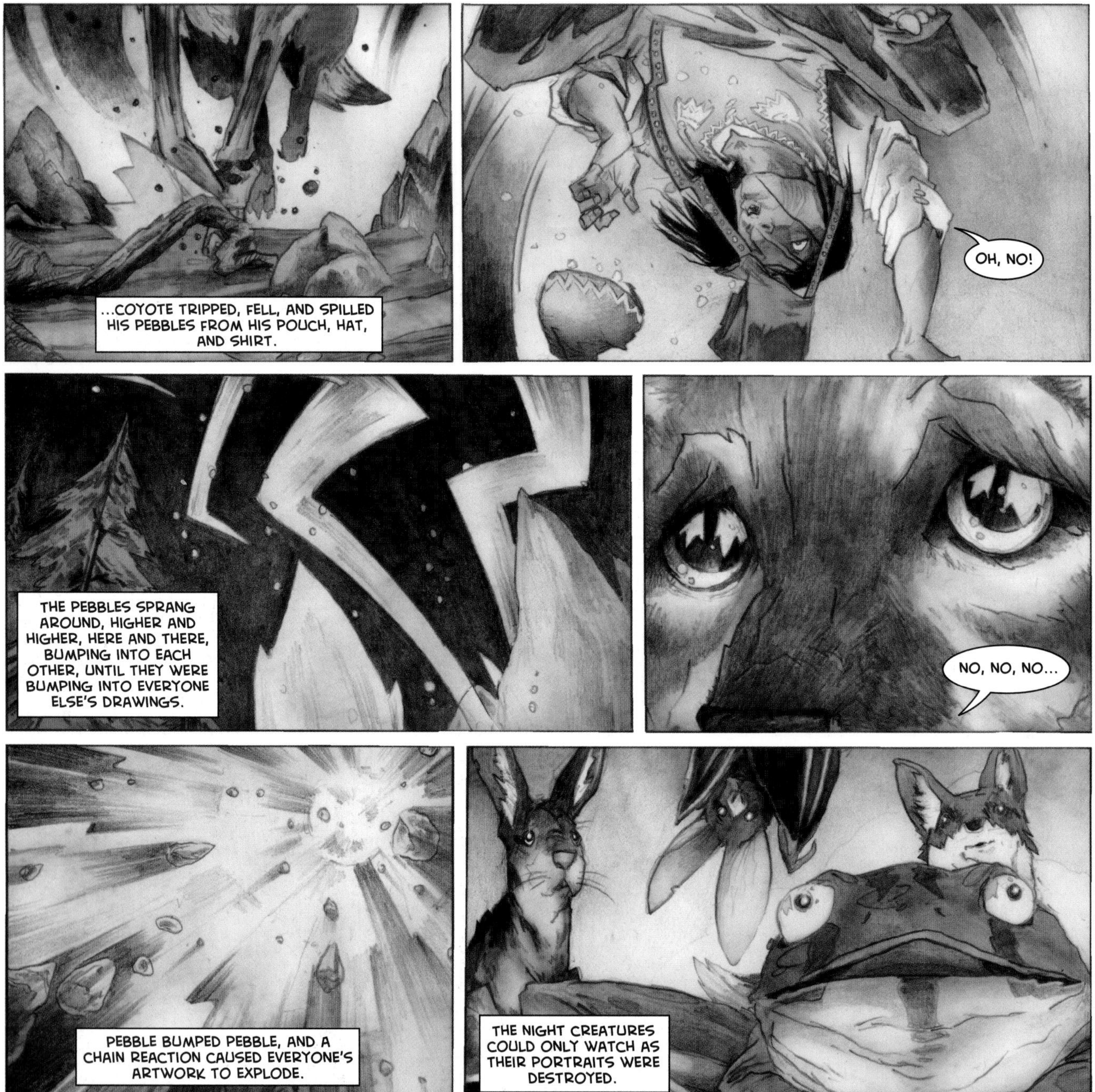
...COYOTE TRIPPED, FELL, AND SPILLED HIS PEBBLES FROM HIS POUCH, HAT, AND SHIRT.
OH, NO!
THE PEBBLES SPRANG AROUND, HIGHER AND HIGHER, HERE AND THERE, BUMPING INTO EACH OTHER, UNTIL THEY WERE BUMPING INTO EVERYONE ELSE'S DRAWINGS.
NO, NO, NO...
PEBBLE BUMPED PEBBLE, AND A CHAIN REACTION CAUSED EVERYONE'S ARTWORK TO EXPLODE.
THE NIGHT CREATURES COULD ONLY WATCH AS THEIR PORTRAITS WERE DESTROYED.

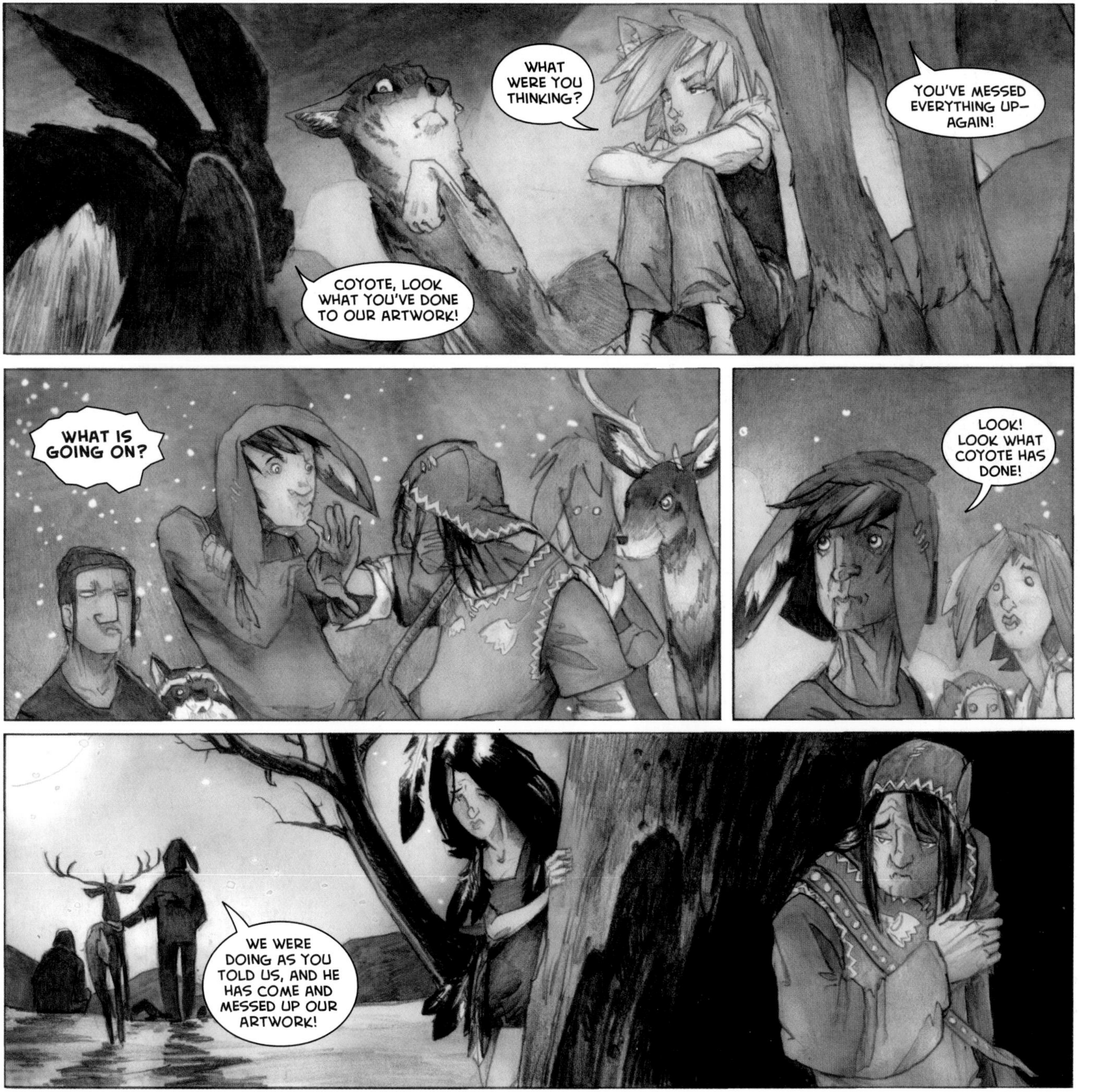
WHAT WERE YOU THINKING?
YOU'VE MESSED EVERYTHING UP— AGAIN!
COYOTE, LOOK WHAT YOU'VE DONE TO OUR ARTWORK!
WHAT IS GOING ON?
LOOK! LOOK WHAT COYOTE HAS DONE!
WE WERE DOING AS YOU TOLD US, AND HE HAS COME AND MESSED UP OUR ARTWORK!

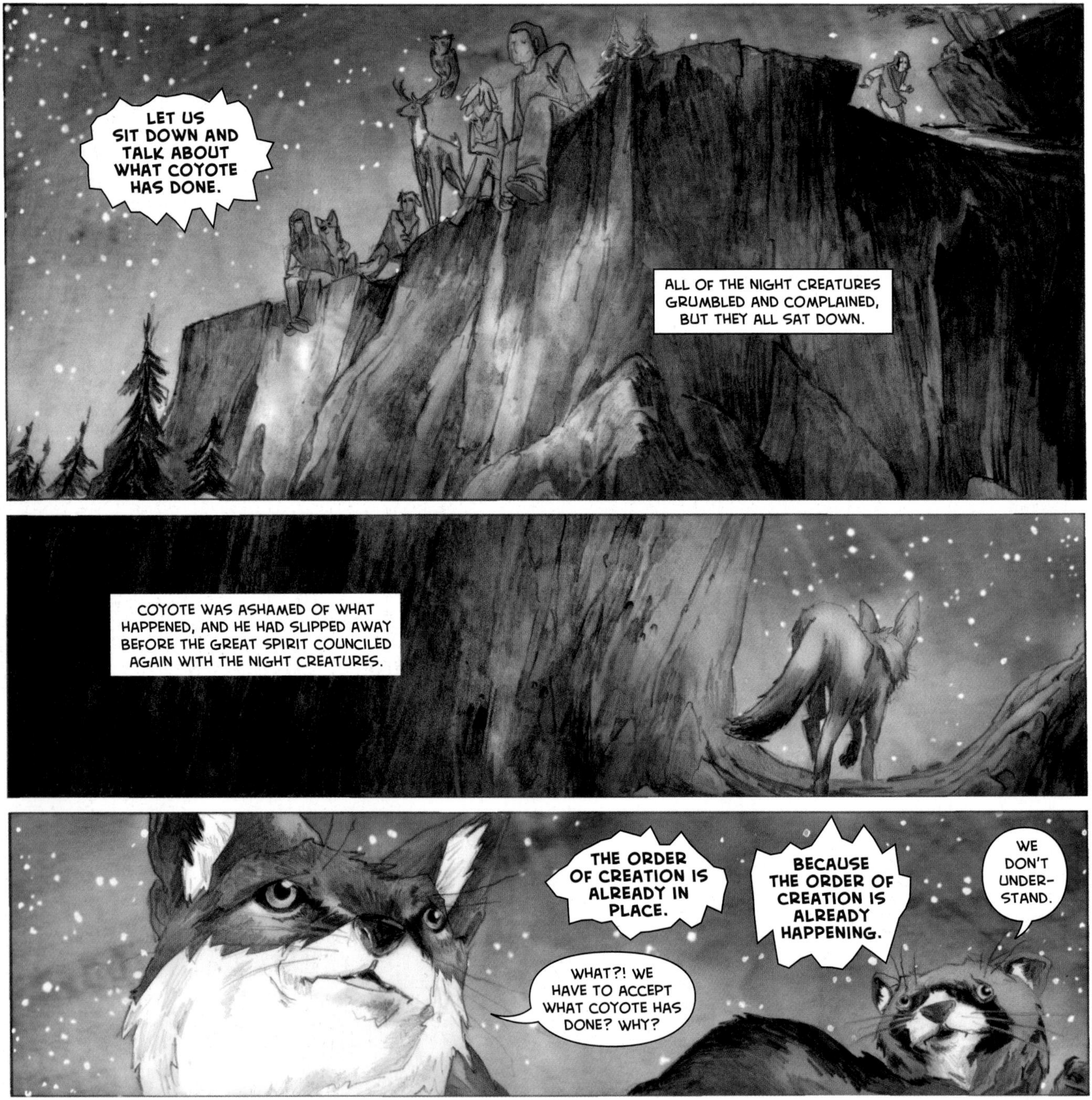
LET US SIT DOWN AND TALK ABOUT WHAT COYOTE HAS DONE.
ALL OF THE NIGHT CREATURES GRUMBLED AND COMPLAINED, BUT THEY ALL SAT DOWN.
COYOTE WAS ASHAMED OF WHAT HAPPENED, AND HE HAD SLIPPED AWAY BEFORE THE GREAT SPIRIT COUNCILED AGAIN WITH THE NIGHT CREATURES.
WHAT?! WE HAVE TO ACCEPT WHAT COYOTE HAS DONE? WHY?
THE ORDER OF CREATION IS ALREADY IN PLACE.
WE DON'T UNDER-STAND.
BECAUSE THE ORDER OF CREATION IS ALREADY HAPPENING.

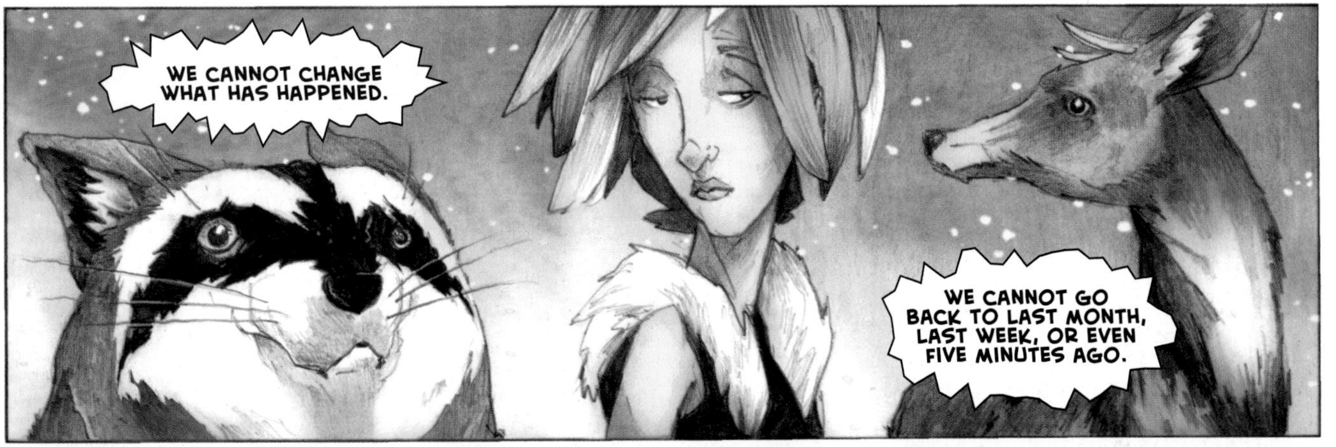
WE CANNOT CHANGE WHAT HAS HAPPENED.
WE CANNOT GO BACK TO LAST MONTH, LAST WEEK, OR EVEN FIVE MINUTES AGO.

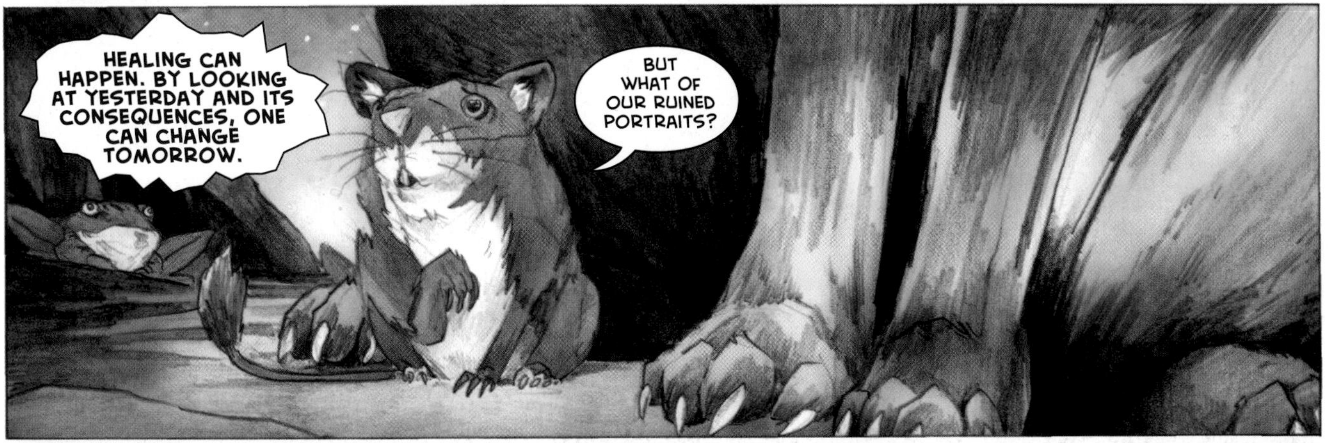
HEALING CAN HAPPEN. BY LOOKING AT YESTERDAY AND ITS CONSEQUENCES, ONE CAN CHANGE TOMORROW.
BUT WHAT OF OUR RUINED PORTRAITS?

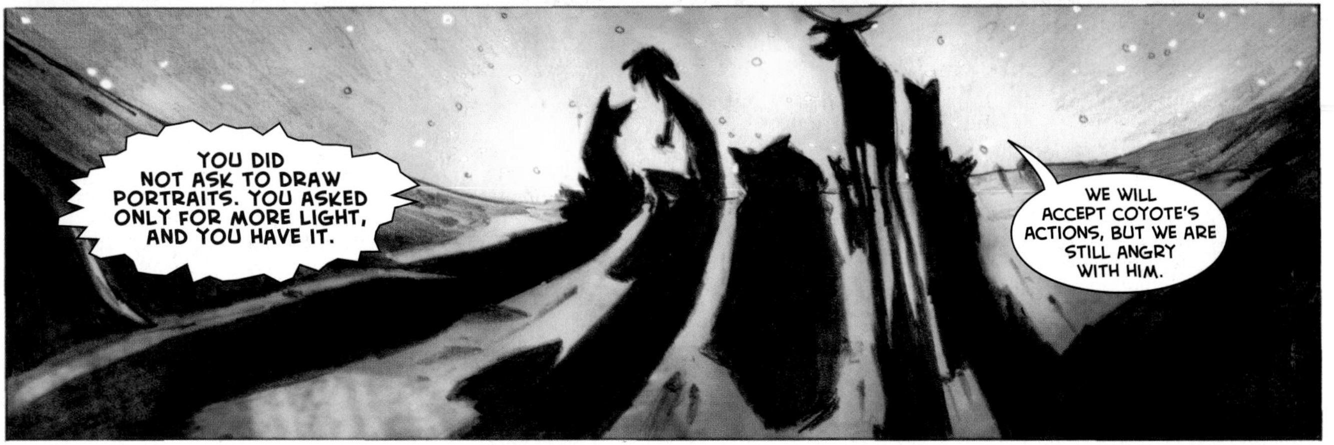
YOU DID NOT ASK TO DRAW PORTRAITS. YOU ASKED ONLY FOR MORE LIGHT, AND YOU HAVE IT.
WE WILL ACCEPT COYOTE'S ACTIONS, BUT WE ARE STILL ANGRY WITH HIM.

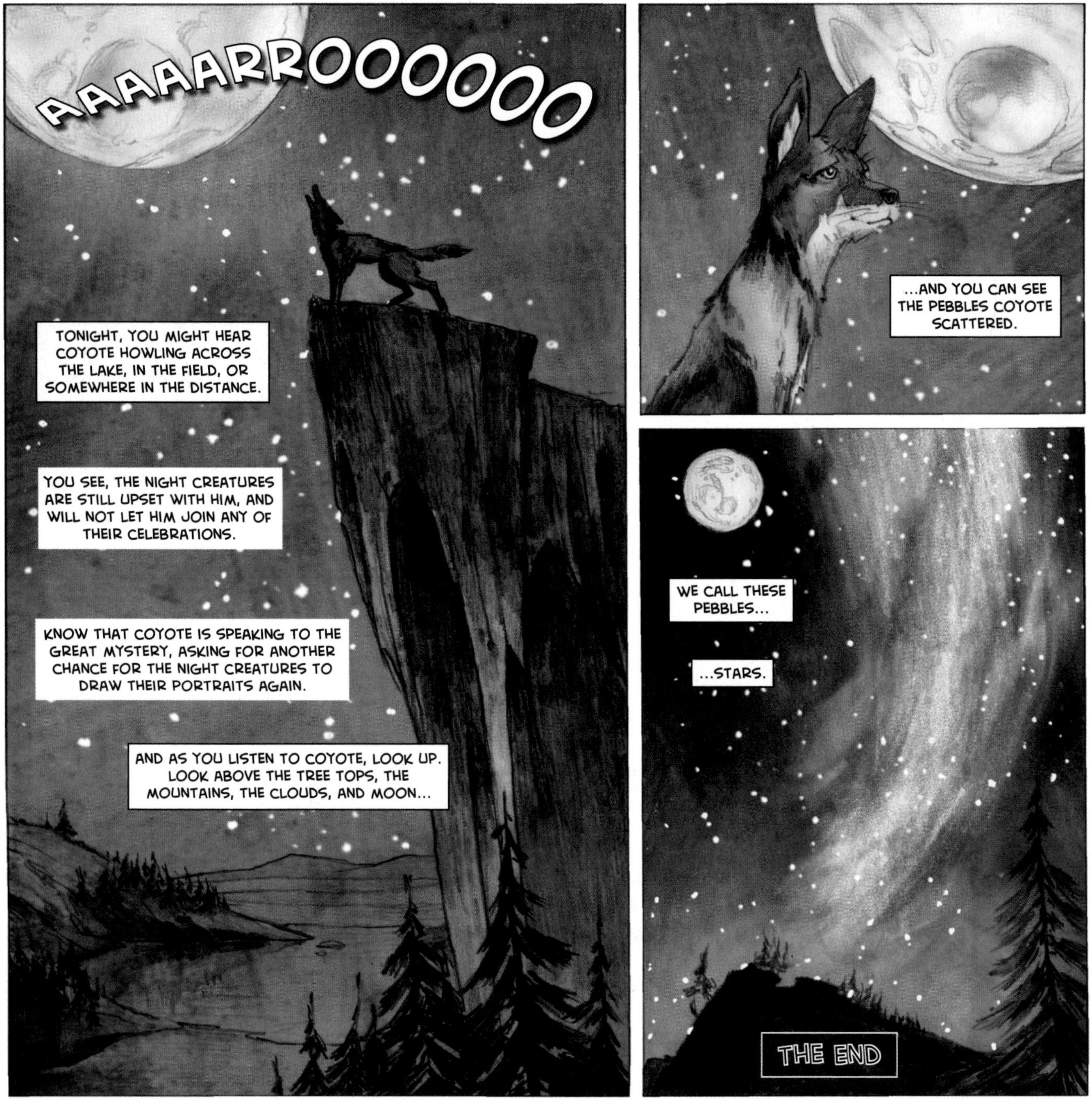
AAAAARROOOOOO
TONIGHT, YOU MIGHT HEAR COYOTE HOWLING ACROSS THE LAKE, IN THE FIELD, OR SOMEWHERE IN THE DISTANCE.
YOU SEE, THE NIGHT CREATURES ARE STILL UPSET WITH HIM, AND WILL NOT LET HIM JOIN ANY OF THEIR CELEBRATIONS.
KNOW THAT COYOTE IS SPEAKING TO THE GREAT MYSTERY, ASKING FOR ANOTHER CHANCE FOR THE NIGHT CREATURES TO DRAW THEIR PORTRAITS AGAIN.
AND AS YOU LISTEN TO COYOTE, LOOK UP. LOOK ABOVE THE TREE TOPS, THE MOUNTAINS, THE CLOUDS, AND MOON...
...AND YOU CAN SEE THE PEBBLES COYOTE SCATTERED.
WE CALL THESE PEBBLES...
...STARS.
THE END

RAVEN THE TRICKSTER

STORY BY JOHN ACTIVE   ART BY JASON COPLAND

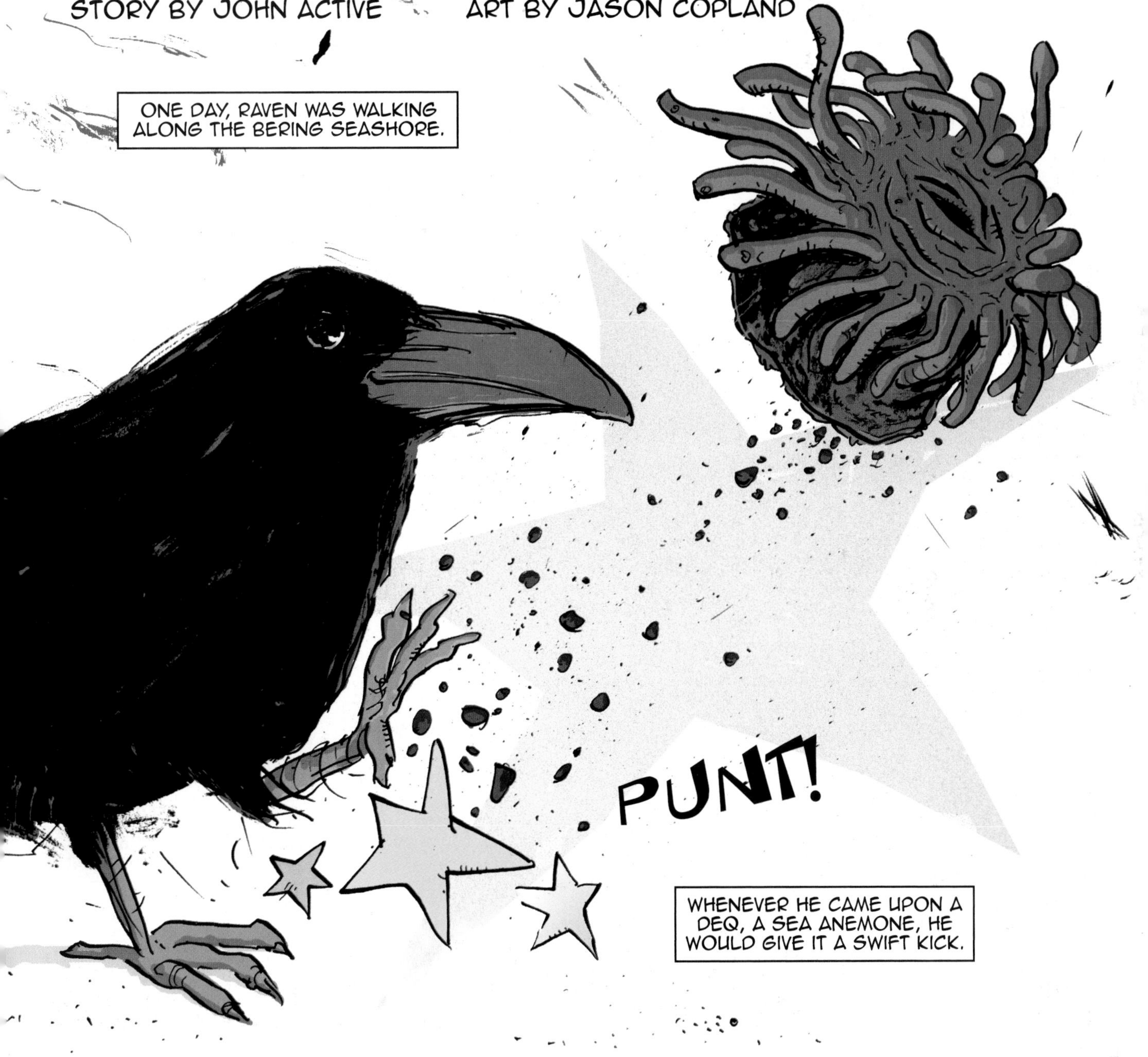
ONE DAY, RAVEN WAS WALKING ALONG THE BERING SEASHORE.
PUNT!
WHENEVER HE CAME UPON A DEQ, A SEA ANEMONE, HE WOULD GIVE IT A SWIFT KICK.

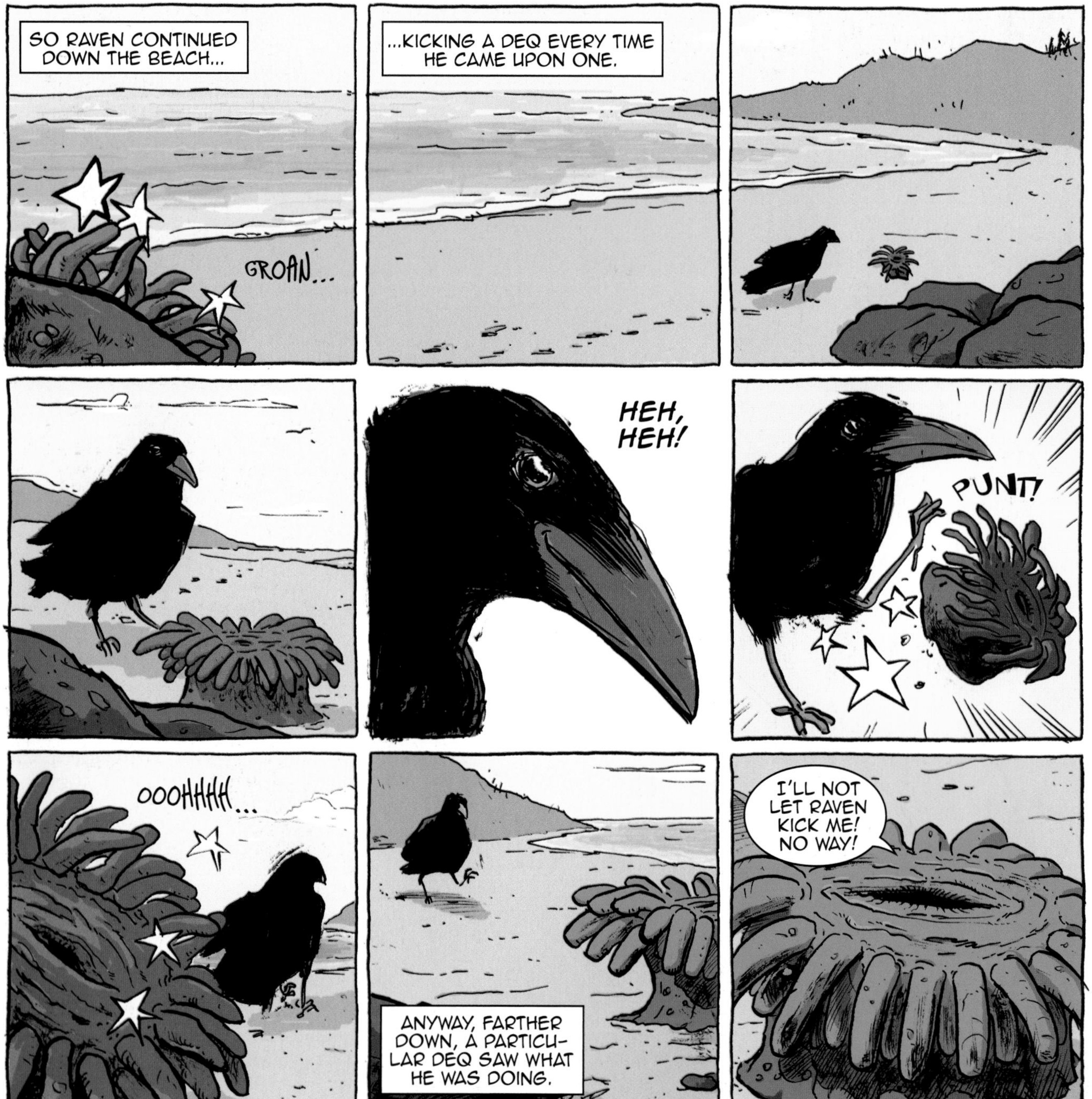
SO RAVEN CONTINUED DOWN THE BEACH...
GROAN...
...KICKING A DEQ EVERY TIME HE CAME UPON ONE.
HEH, HEH!
PUNT!
OOOHHHH...
ANYWAY, FARTHER DOWN, A PARTICULAR DEQ SAW WHAT HE WAS DOING.
I'LL NOT LET RAVEN KICK ME! NO WAY!

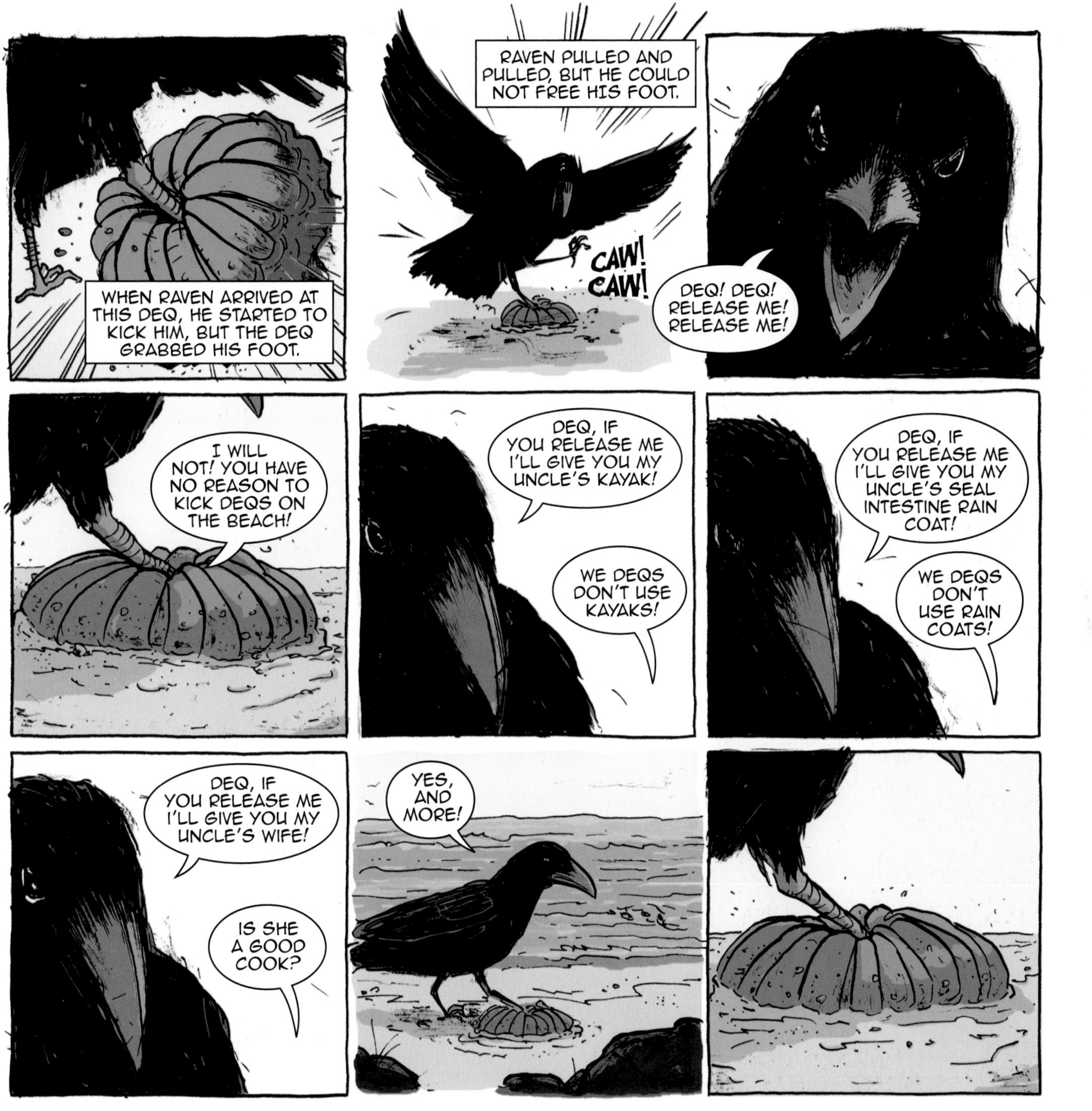
WHEN RAVEN ARRIVED AT THIS DEQ, HE STARTED TO KICK HIM, BUT THE DEQ GRABBED HIS FOOT.
RAVEN PULLED AND PULLED, BUT HE COULD NOT FREE HIS FOOT.
CAW! CAW!
DEQ! DEQ! RELEASE ME! RELEASE ME!
I WILL NOT! YOU HAVE NO REASON TO KICK DEQS ON THE BEACH!
DEQ, IF YOU RELEASE ME I'LL GIVE YOU MY UNCLE'S KAYAK!
WE DEQS DON'T USE KAYAKS!
DEQ, IF YOU RELEASE ME I'LL GIVE YOU MY UNCLE'S SEAL INTESTINE RAIN COAT!
WE DEQS DON'T USE RAIN COATS!
DEQ, IF YOU RELEASE ME I'LL GIVE YOU MY UNCLE'S WIFE!
IS SHE A GOOD COOK?
YES, AND MORE!

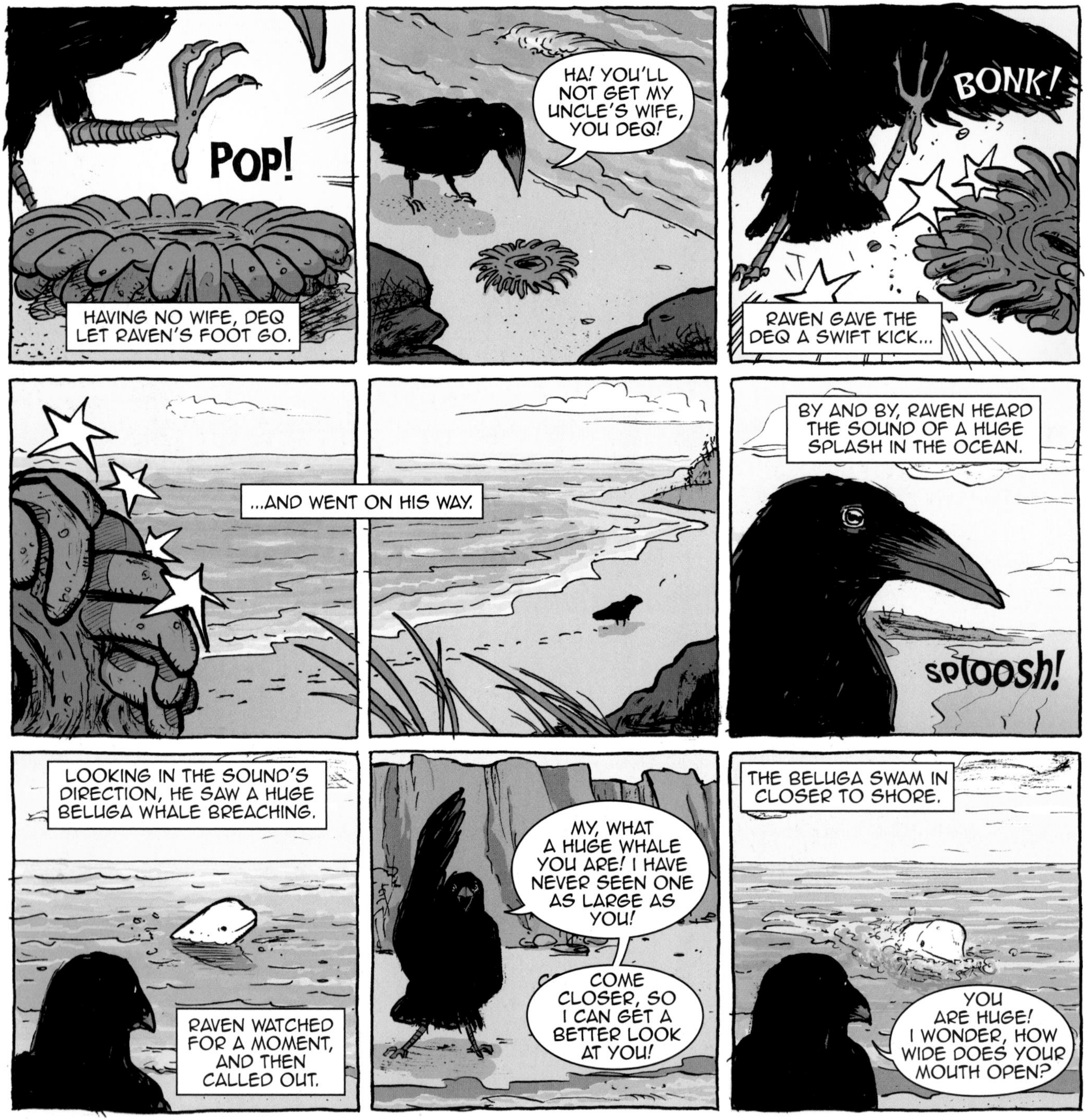
POP!
HAVING NO WIFE, DEQ LET RAVEN'S FOOT GO.
HA! YOU'LL NOT GET MY UNCLE'S WIFE, YOU DEQ!
BONK!
RAVEN GAVE THE DEQ A SWIFT KICK...
...AND WENT ON HIS WAY.
BY AND BY, RAVEN HEARD THE SOUND OF A HUGE SPLASH IN THE OCEAN.
SPLOOSH!
LOOKING IN THE SOUND'S DIRECTION, HE SAW A HUGE BELUGA WHALE BREACHING.
RAVEN WATCHED FOR A MOMENT, AND THEN CALLED OUT.
MY, WHAT A HUGE WHALE YOU ARE! I HAVE NEVER SEEN ONE AS LARGE AS YOU!
COME CLOSER, SO I CAN GET A BETTER LOOK AT YOU!
THE BELUGA SWAM IN CLOSER TO SHORE.
YOU ARE HUGE! I WONDER, HOW WIDE DOES YOUR MOUTH OPEN?

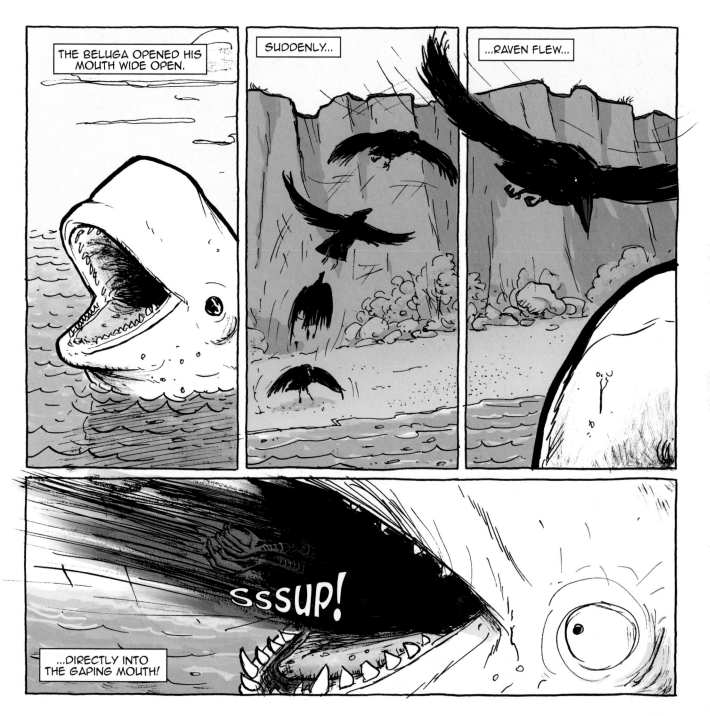

THE BELUGA OPENED HIS MOUTH WIDE OPEN.

SUDDENLY...

...RAVEN FLEW...

SSSUP!

...DIRECTLY INTO THE GAPING MOUTH!

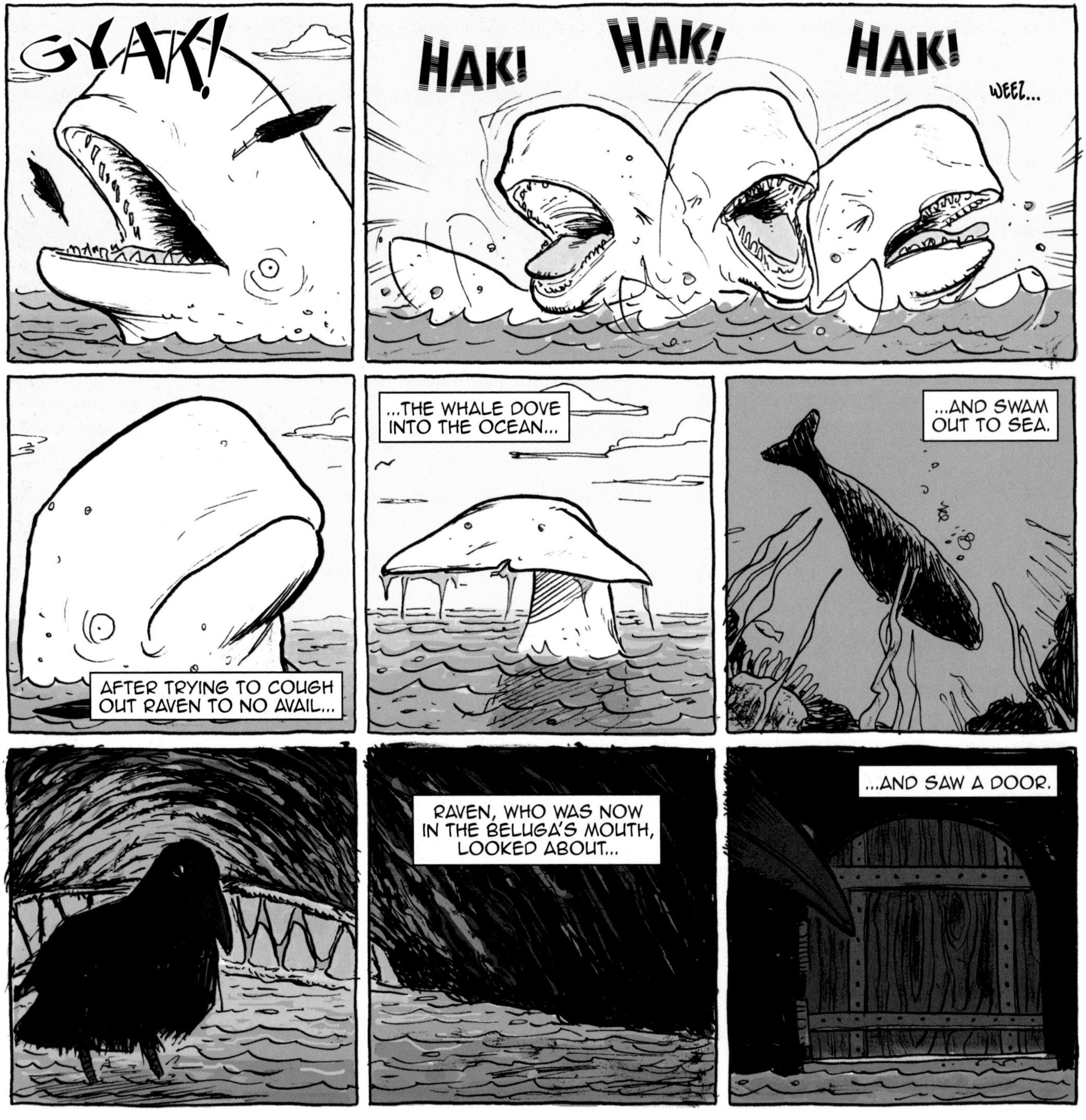
GYAK!
HAK! HAK! HAK!
WEEZ...
AFTER TRYING TO COUGH OUT RAVEN TO NO AVAIL...
...THE WHALE DOVE INTO THE OCEAN...
...AND SWAM OUT TO SEA.
RAVEN, WHO WAS NOW IN THE BELUGA'S MOUTH, LOOKED ABOUT...
...AND SAW A DOOR.

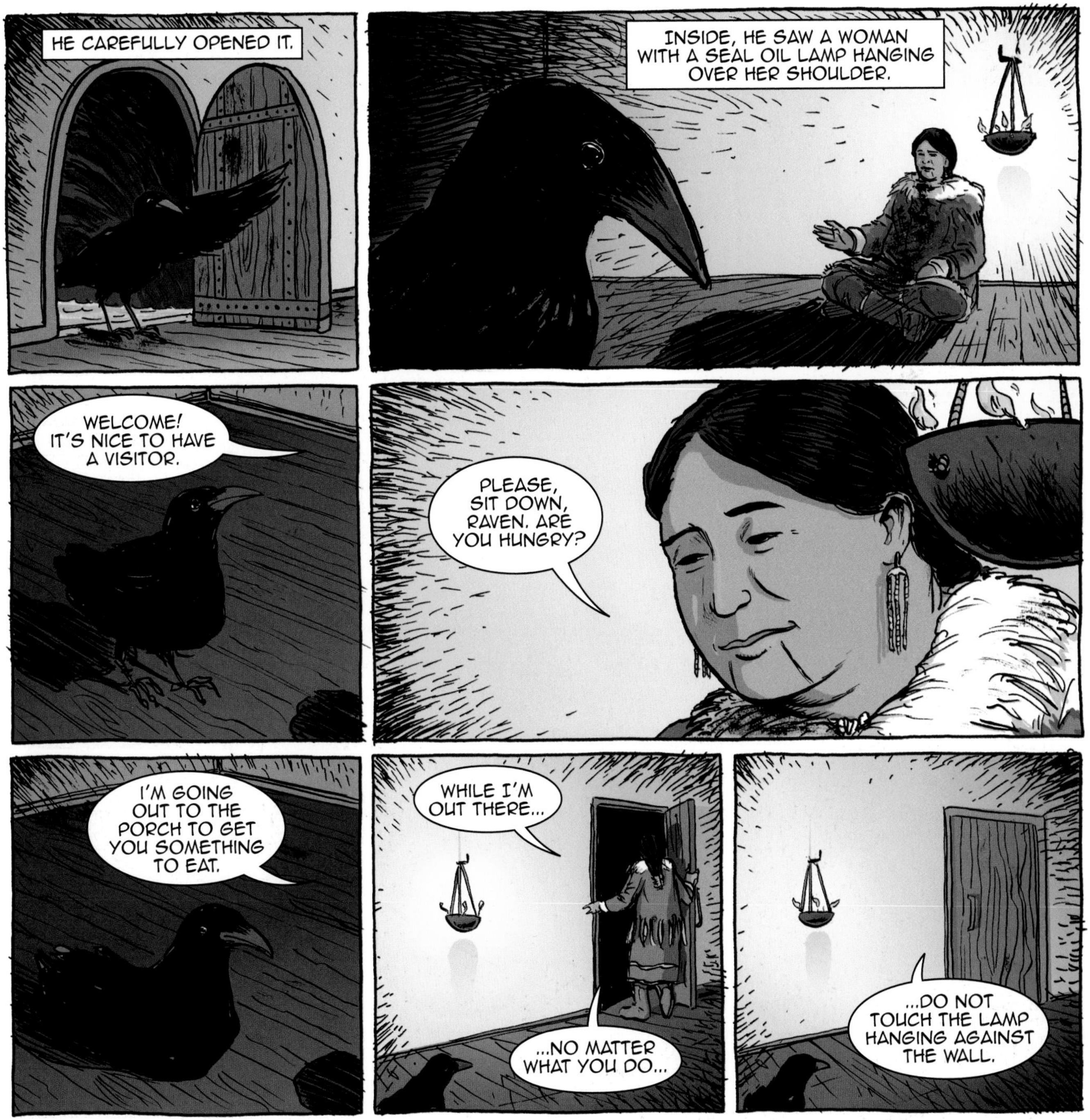
HE CAREFULLY OPENED IT.
INSIDE, HE SAW A WOMAN WITH A SEAL OIL LAMP HANGING OVER HER SHOULDER.
WELCOME! IT'S NICE TO HAVE A VISITOR.
PLEASE, SIT DOWN, RAVEN. ARE YOU HUNGRY?
I'M GOING OUT TO THE PORCH TO GET YOU SOMETHING TO EAT.
WHILE I'M OUT THERE...
...NO MATTER WHAT YOU DO...
...DO NOT TOUCH THE LAMP HANGING AGAINST THE WALL.

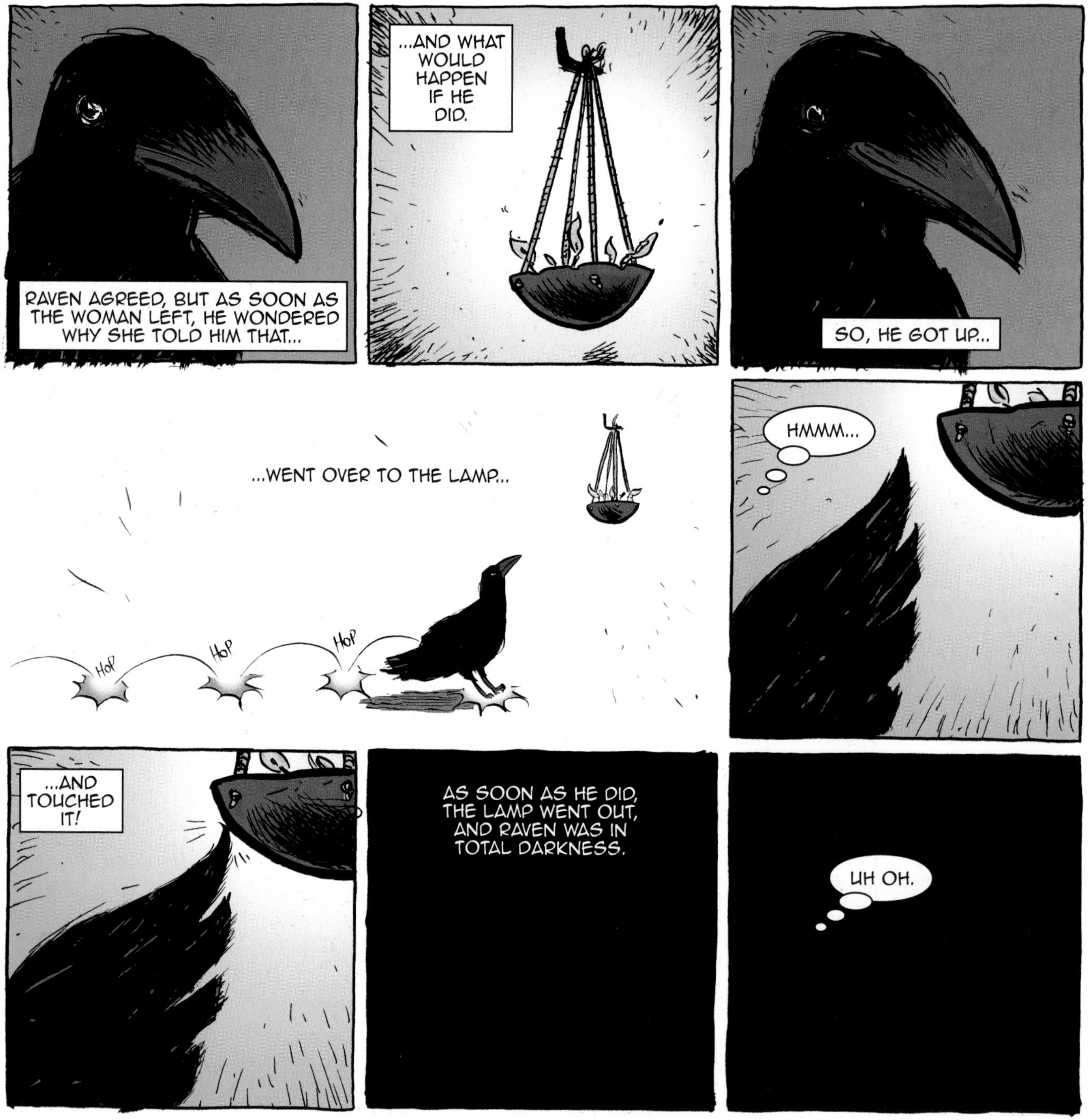
RAVEN AGREED, BUT AS SOON AS THE WOMAN LEFT, HE WONDERED WHY SHE TOLD HIM THAT...
...AND WHAT WOULD HAPPEN IF HE DID.
SO, HE GOT UP...
...WENT OVER TO THE LAMP...
HOP
HOP
HOP
HMMM...
...AND TOUCHED IT!
AS SOON AS HE DID, THE LAMP WENT OUT, AND RAVEN WAS IN TOTAL DARKNESS.
UH OH.

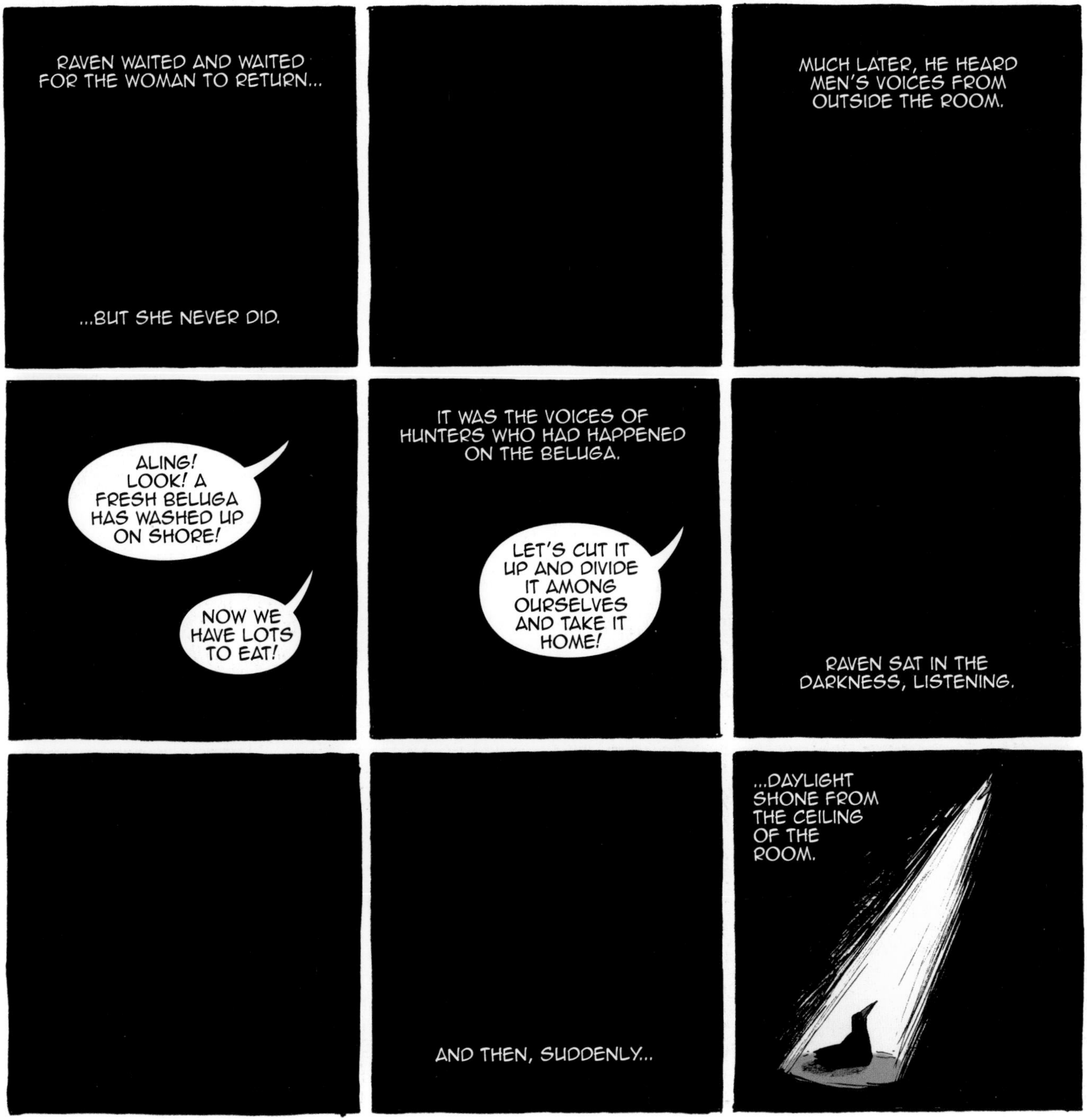
RAVEN WAITED AND WAITED FOR THE WOMAN TO RETURN...
...BUT SHE NEVER DID.
MUCH LATER, HE HEARD MEN'S VOICES FROM OUTSIDE THE ROOM.
ALING! LOOK! A FRESH BELUGA HAS WASHED UP ON SHORE!
NOW WE HAVE LOTS TO EAT!
IT WAS THE VOICES OF HUNTERS WHO HAD HAPPENED ON THE BELUGA.
LET'S CUT IT UP AND DIVIDE IT AMONG OURSELVES AND TAKE IT HOME!
RAVEN SAT IN THE DARKNESS, LISTENING.
AND THEN, SUDDENLY...
...DAYLIGHT SHONE FROM THE CEILING OF THE ROOM.

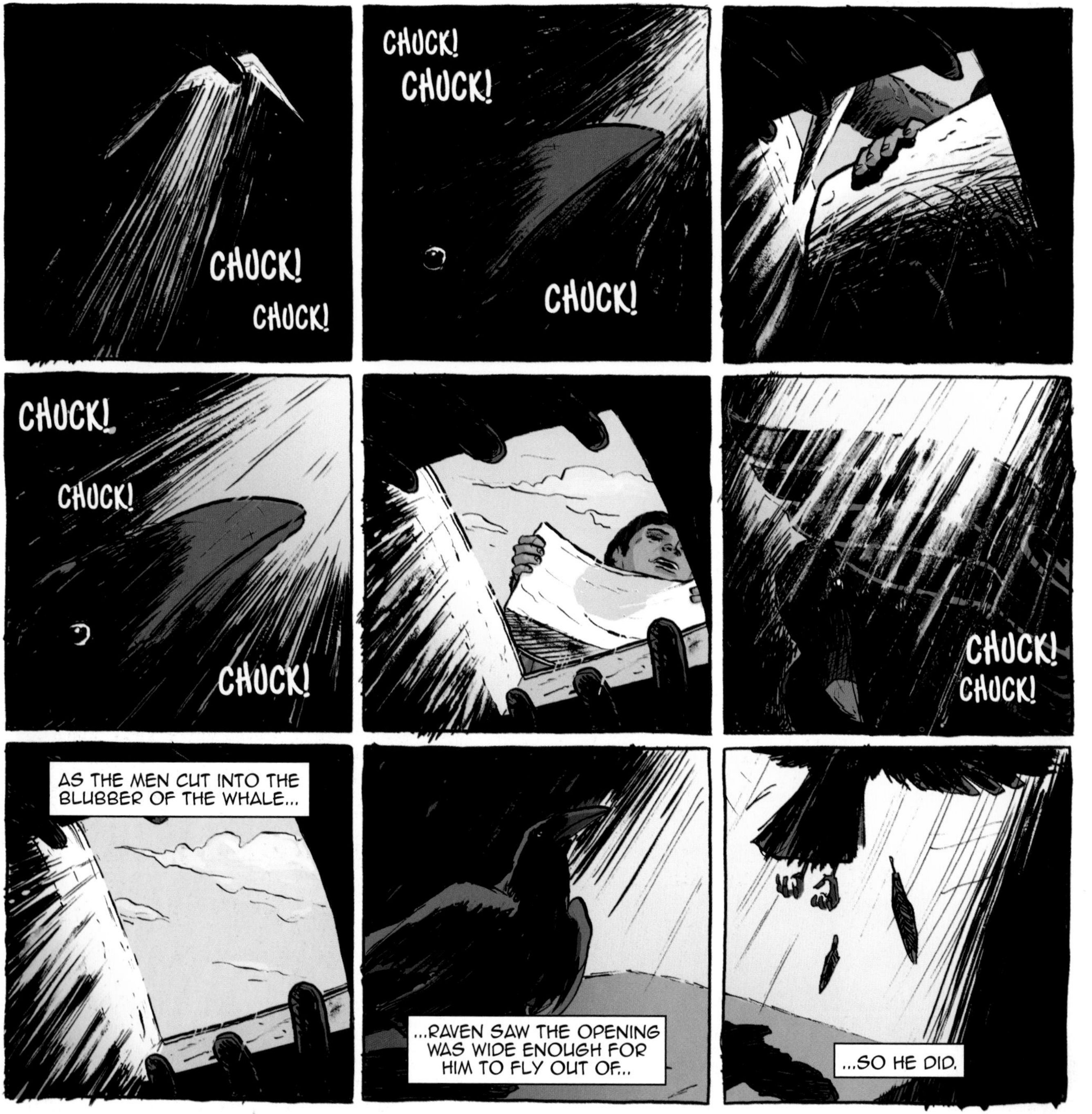
CHUCK!
CHUCK!
CHUCK!
CHUCK!
CHUCK!
CHUCK!
CHUCK!
CHUCK!
CHUCK!
CHUCK!
CHUCK!
AS THE MEN CUT INTO THE BLUBBER OF THE WHALE...
...RAVEN SAW THE OPENING WAS WIDE ENOUGH FOR HIM TO FLY OUT OF...
...SO HE DID.

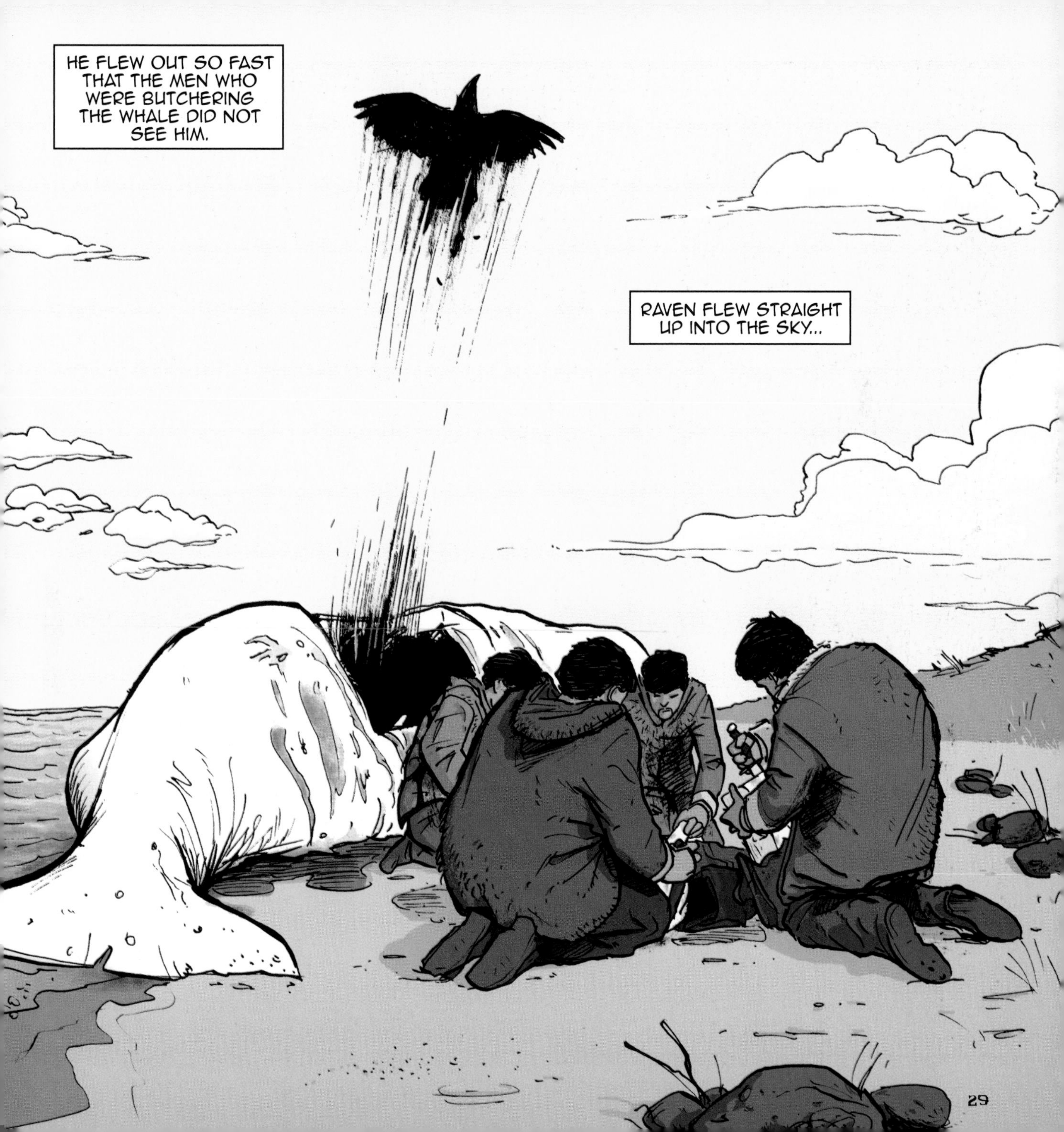
HE FLEW OUT SO FAST THAT THE MEN WHO WERE BUTCHERING THE WHALE DID NOT SEE HIM.
RAVEN FLEW STRAIGHT UP INTO THE SKY...

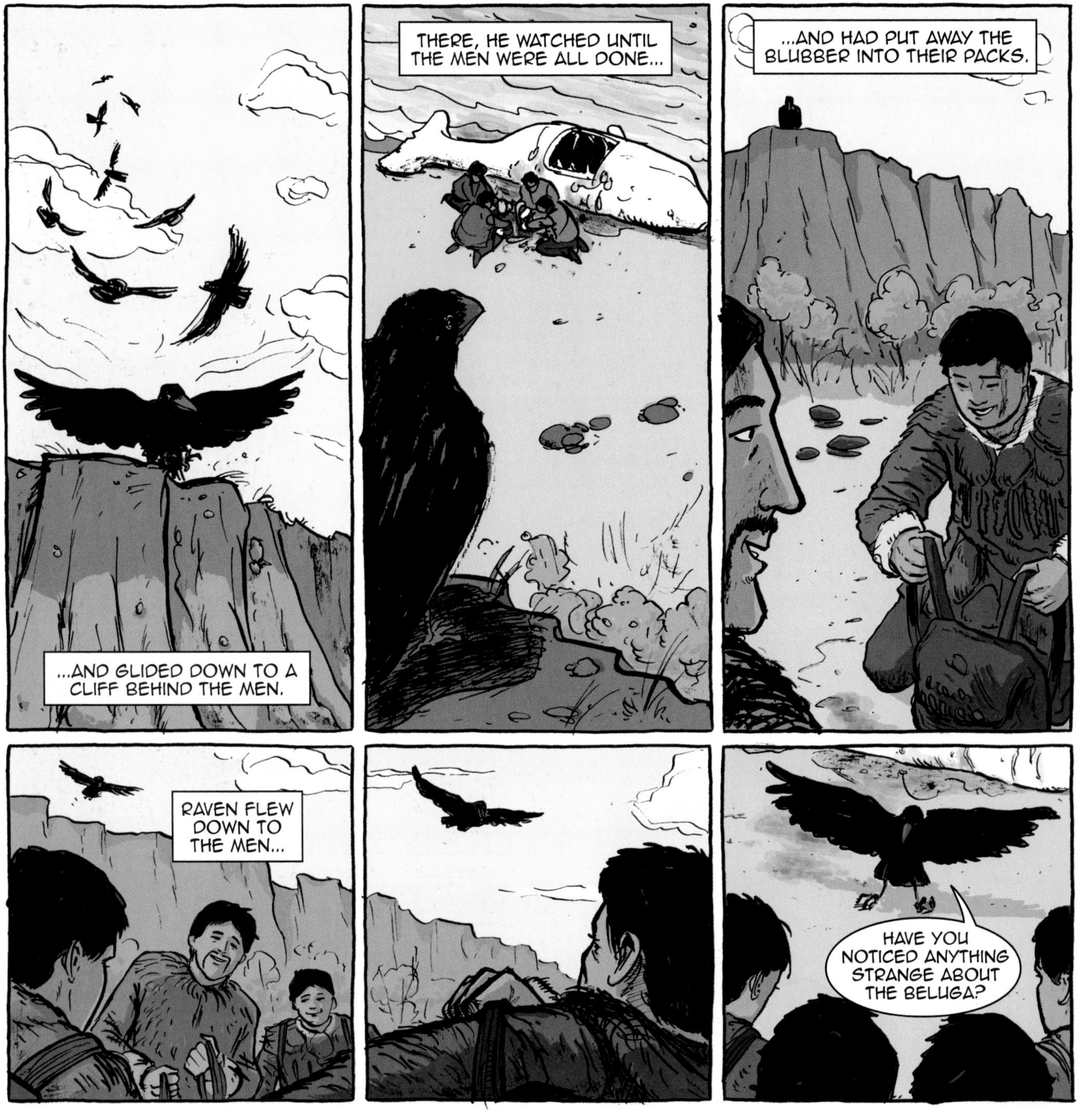
...AND GLIDED DOWN TO A CLIFF BEHIND THE MEN.
THERE, HE WATCHED UNTIL THE MEN WERE ALL DONE...
...AND HAD PUT AWAY THE BLUBBER INTO THEIR PACKS.
RAVEN FLEW DOWN TO THE MEN...
HAVE YOU NOTICED ANYTHING STRANGE ABOUT THE BELUGA?

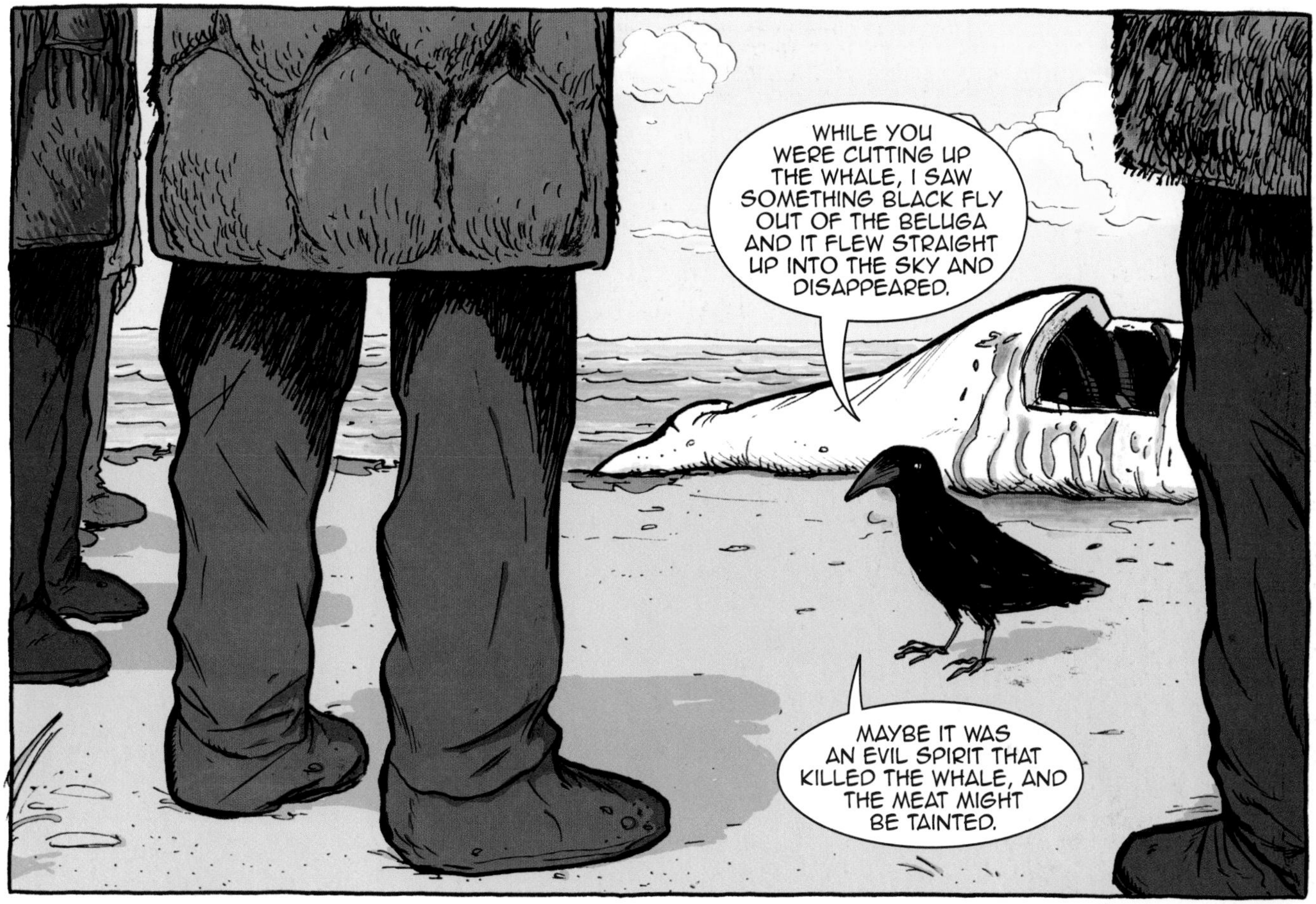
WHILE YOU WERE CUTTING UP THE WHALE, I SAW SOMETHING BLACK FLY OUT OF THE BELUGA AND IT FLEW STRAIGHT UP INTO THE SKY AND DISAPPEARED.
MAYBE IT WAS AN EVIL SPIRIT THAT KILLED THE WHALE, AND THE MEAT MIGHT BE TAINTED.

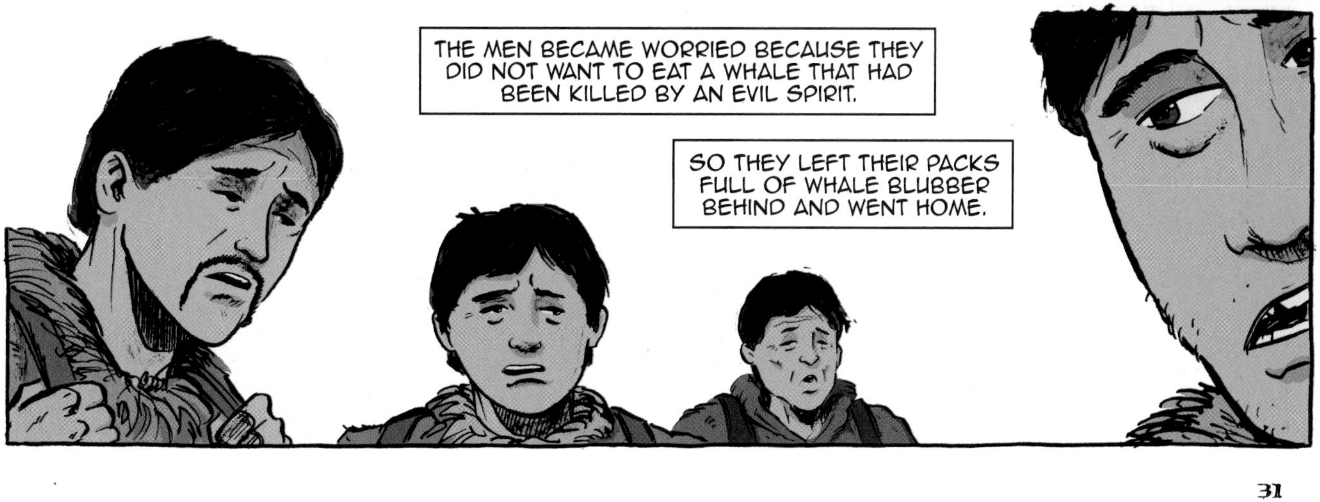
THE MEN BECAME WORRIED BECAUSE THEY DID NOT WANT TO EAT A WHALE THAT HAD BEEN KILLED BY AN EVIL SPIRIT.
SO THEY LEFT THEIR PACKS FULL OF WHALE BLUBBER BEHIND AND WENT HOME.

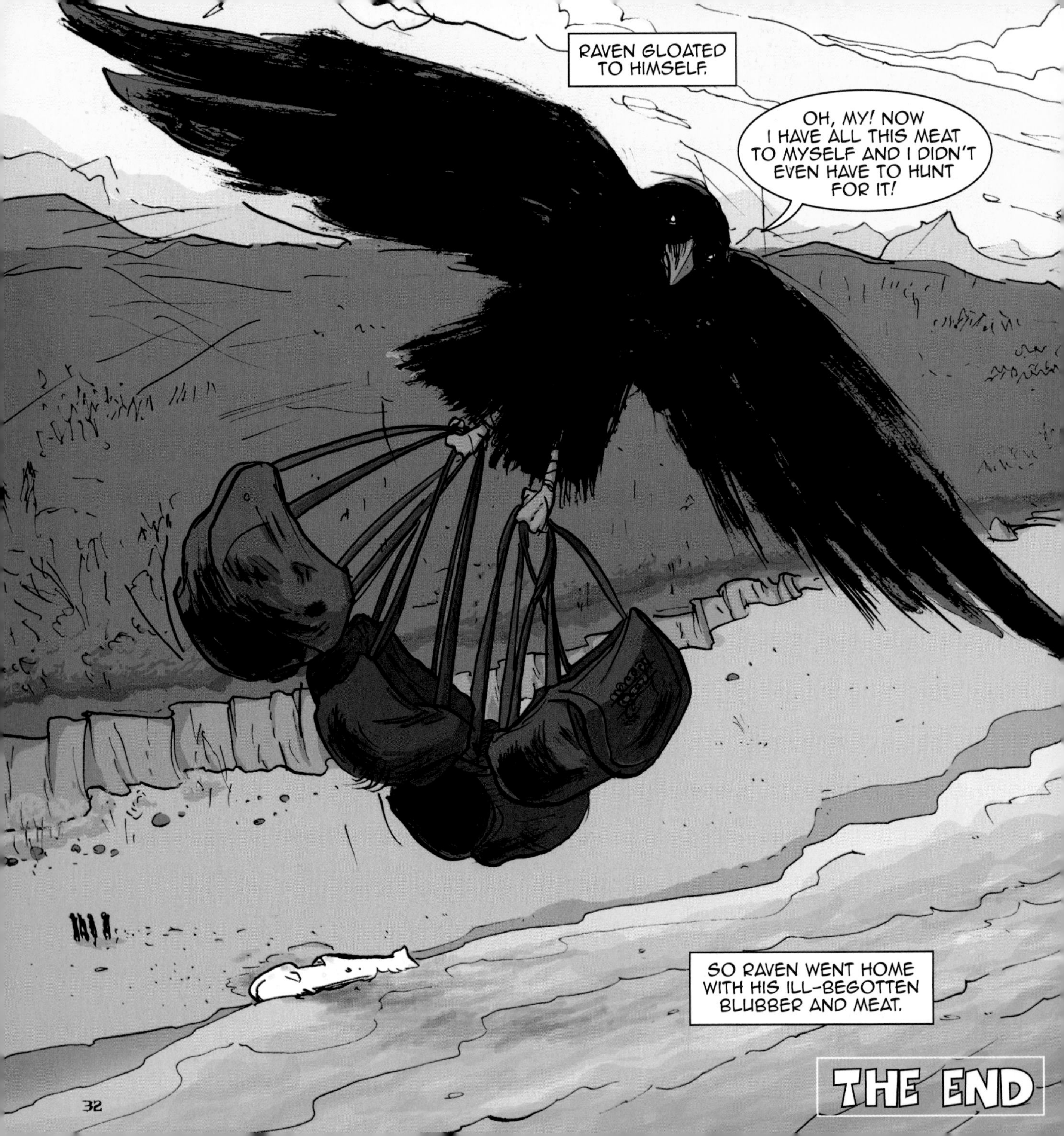
RAVEN GLOATED TO HIMSELF.
OH, MY! NOW I HAVE ALL THIS MEAT TO MYSELF AND I DIDN'T EVEN HAVE TO HUNT FOR IT!
SO RAVEN WENT HOME WITH HIS ILL-BEGOTTEN BLUBBER AND MEAT.
THE END

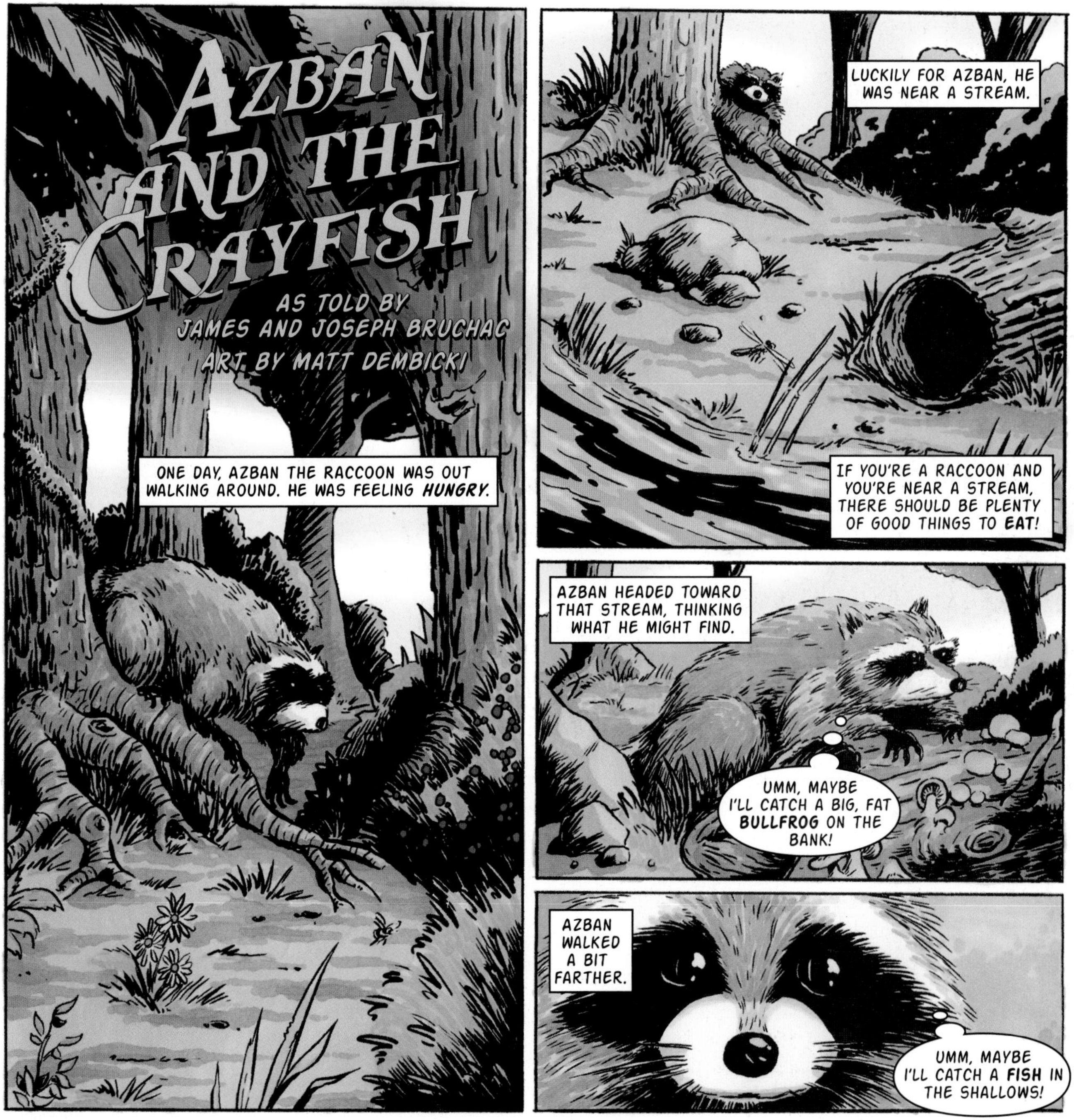
AZBAN AND THE CRAYFISH
AS TOLD BY JAMES AND JOSEPH BRUCHAC
ART BY MATT DEMBICKI
ONE DAY, AZBAN THE RACCOON WAS OUT WALKING AROUND. HE WAS FEELING HUNGRY.
LUCKILY FOR AZBAN, HE WAS NEAR A STREAM.
IF YOU'RE A RACCOON AND YOU'RE NEAR A STREAM, THERE SHOULD BE PLENTY OF GOOD THINGS TO EAT!
AZBAN HEADED TOWARD THAT STREAM, THINKING WHAT HE MIGHT FIND.
UMM, MAYBE I'LL CATCH A BIG, FAT BULLFROG ON THE BANK!
AZBAN WALKED A BIT FARTHER.
UMM, MAYBE I'LL CATCH A FISH IN THE SHALLOWS!

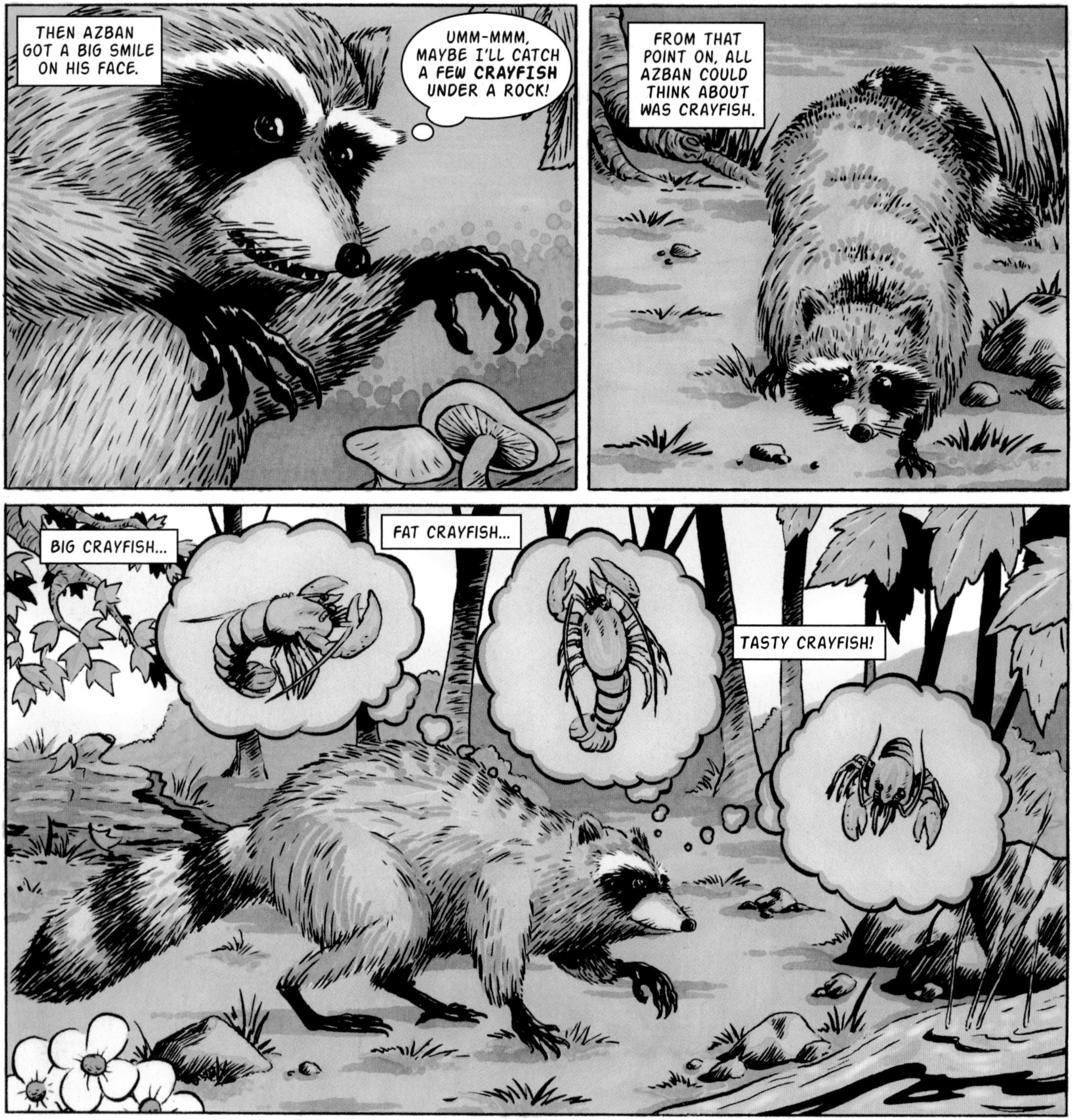
THEN AZBAN GOT A BIG SMILE ON HIS FACE.
UMM-MMM, MAYBE I'LL CATCH A FEW **CRAYFISH** UNDER A ROCK!
FROM THAT POINT ON, ALL AZBAN COULD THINK ABOUT WAS CRAYFISH.
BIG CRAYFISH...
FAT CRAYFISH...
TASTY CRAYFISH!

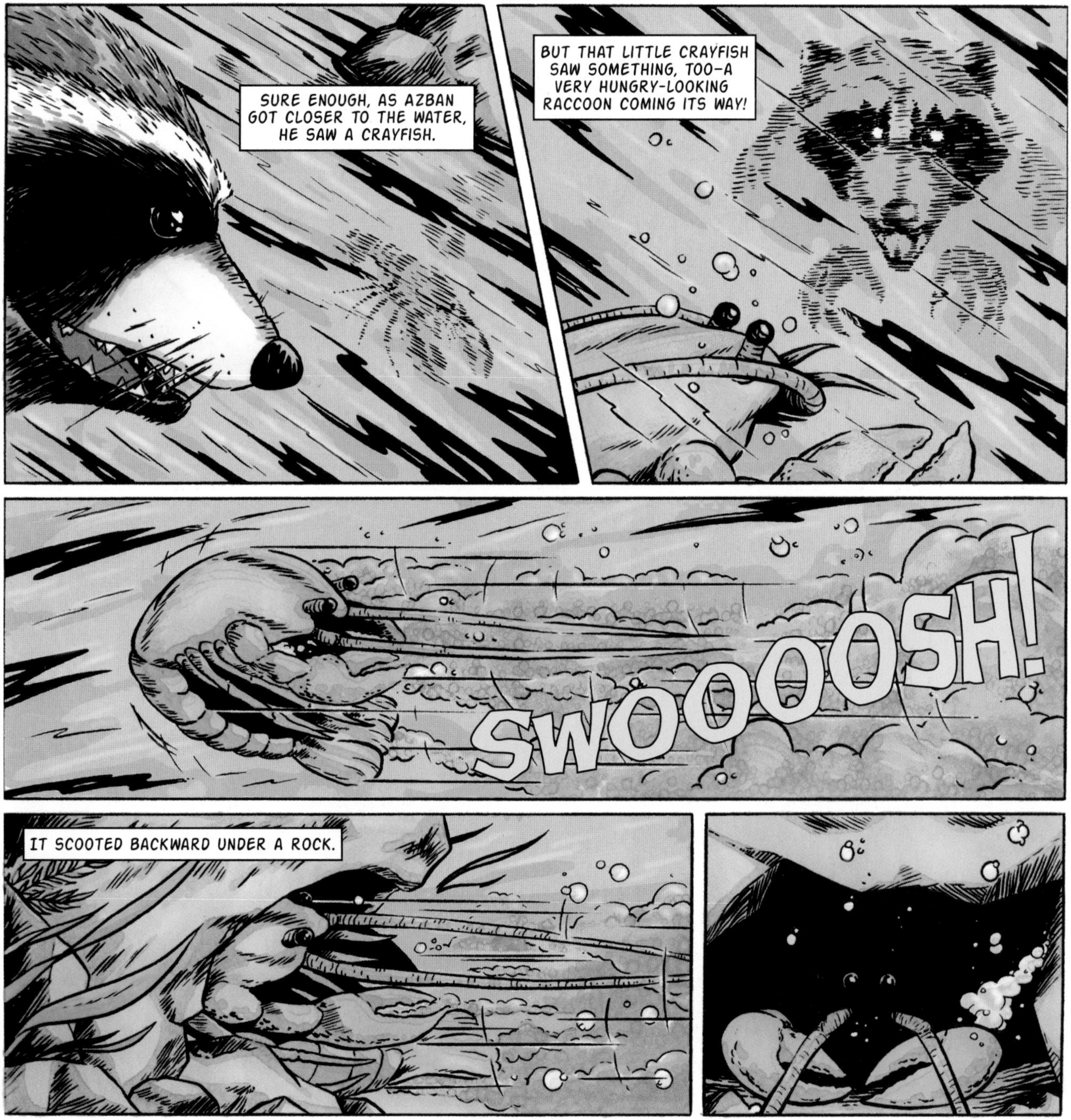
SURE ENOUGH, AS AZBAN GOT CLOSER TO THE WATER, HE SAW A CRAYFISH.
BUT THAT LITTLE CRAYFISH SAW SOMETHING, TOO—A VERY HUNGRY-LOOKING RACCOON COMING ITS WAY!
SWOOOOOSH!
IT SCOOTED BACKWARD UNDER A ROCK.

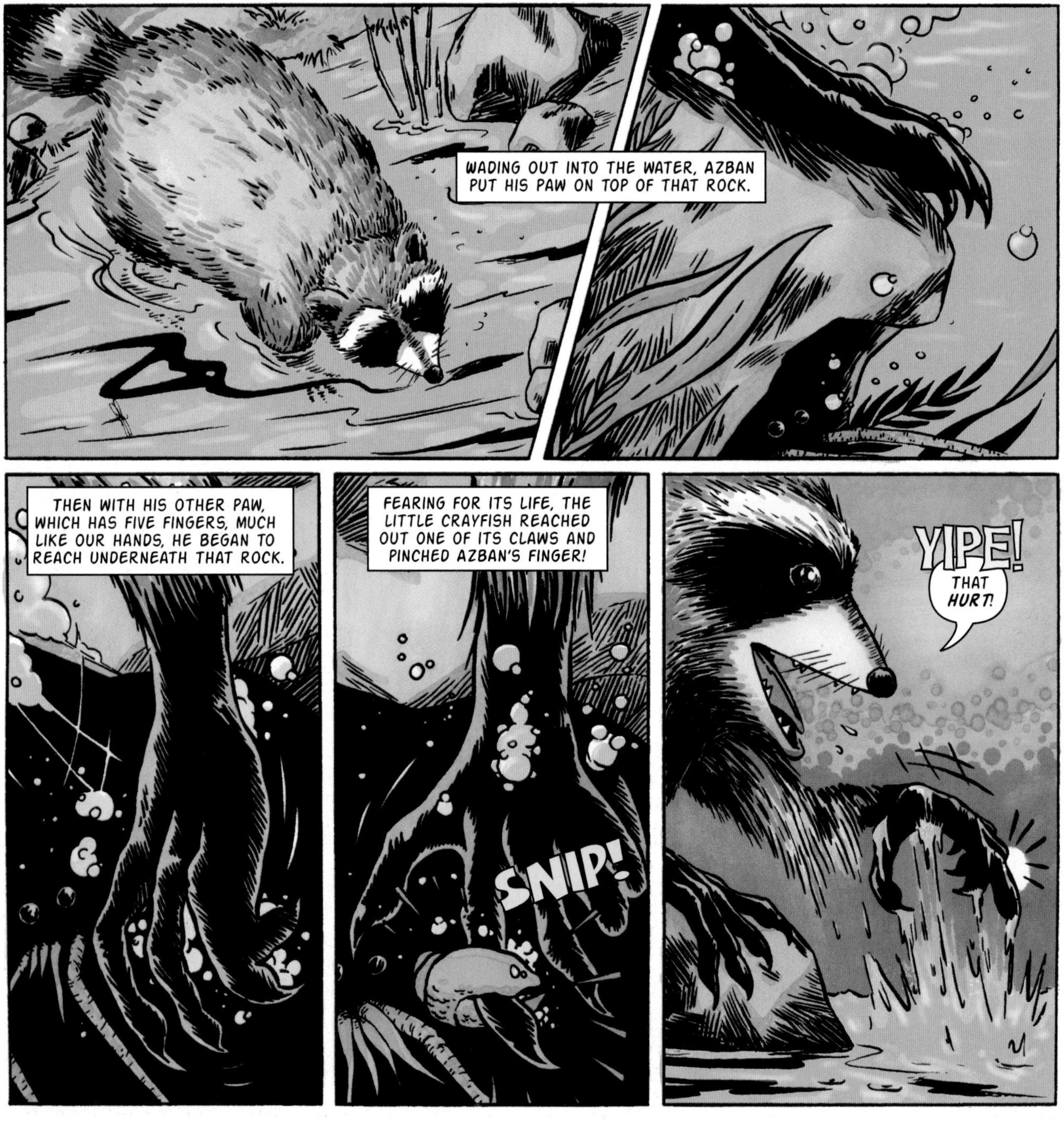
WADING OUT INTO THE WATER, AZBAN PUT HIS PAW ON TOP OF THAT ROCK.
THEN WITH HIS OTHER PAW, WHICH HAS FIVE FINGERS, MUCH LIKE OUR HANDS, HE BEGAN TO REACH UNDERNEATH THAT ROCK.
FEARING FOR ITS LIFE, THE LITTLE CRAYFISH REACHED OUT ONE OF ITS CLAWS AND PINCHED AZBAN'S FINGER!
SNIP!
YIPE!
THAT HURT!

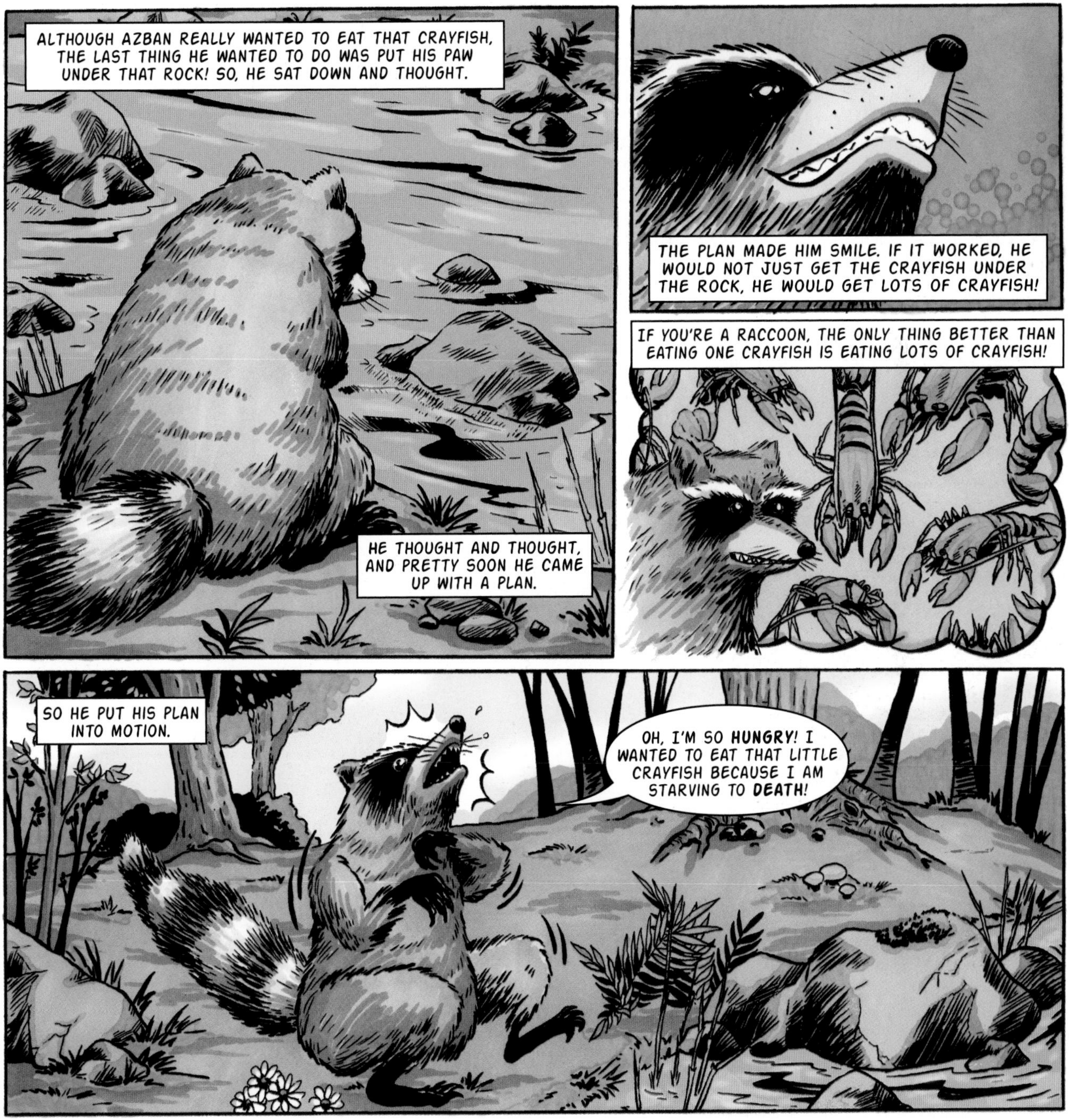
ALTHOUGH AZBAN REALLY WANTED TO EAT THAT CRAYFISH, THE LAST THING HE WANTED TO DO WAS PUT HIS PAW UNDER THAT ROCK! SO, HE SAT DOWN AND THOUGHT.
HE THOUGHT AND THOUGHT, AND PRETTY SOON HE CAME UP WITH A PLAN.
THE PLAN MADE HIM SMILE. IF IT WORKED, HE WOULD NOT JUST GET THE CRAYFISH UNDER THE ROCK, HE WOULD GET LOTS OF CRAYFISH!
IF YOU'RE A RACCOON, THE ONLY THING BETTER THAN EATING ONE CRAYFISH IS EATING LOTS OF CRAYFISH!
SO HE PUT HIS PLAN INTO MOTION.
OH, I'M SO **HUNGRY**! I WANTED TO EAT THAT LITTLE CRAYFISH BECAUSE I AM STARVING TO **DEATH**!

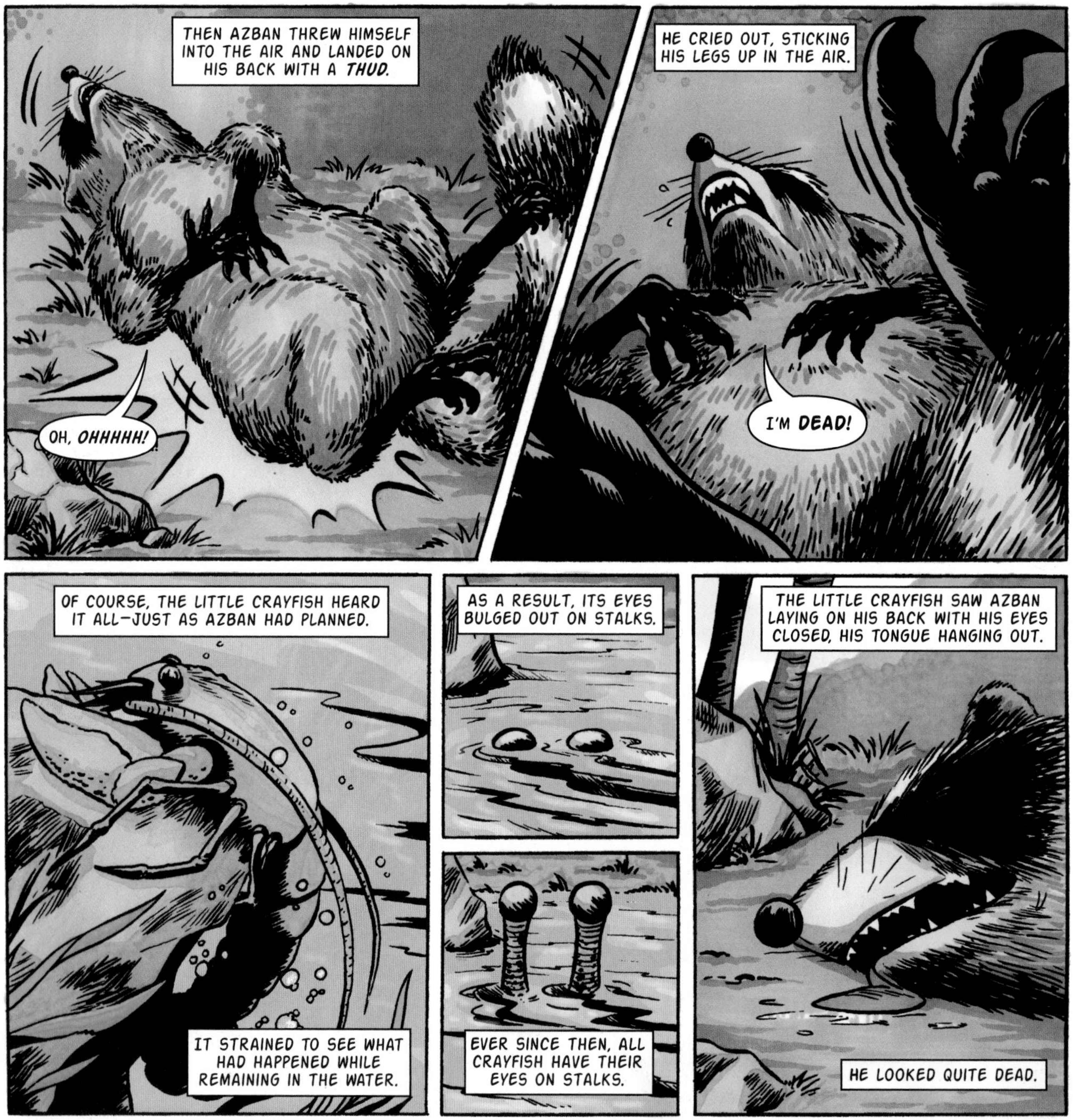
THEN AZBAN THREW HIMSELF INTO THE AIR AND LANDED ON HIS BACK WITH A *THUD*.
OH, *OHHHHH!*
HE CRIED OUT, STICKING HIS LEGS UP IN THE AIR.
I'M **DEAD!**
OF COURSE, THE LITTLE CRAYFISH HEARD IT ALL—JUST AS AZBAN HAD PLANNED.
IT STRAINED TO SEE WHAT HAD HAPPENED WHILE REMAINING IN THE WATER.
AS A RESULT, ITS EYES BULGED OUT ON STALKS.
EVER SINCE THEN, ALL CRAYFISH HAVE THEIR EYES ON STALKS.
THE LITTLE CRAYFISH SAW AZBAN LAYING ON HIS BACK WITH HIS EYES CLOSED, HIS TONGUE HANGING OUT.
HE LOOKED QUITE DEAD.

It's true! It's true! The man-eater is dead! The man-eater is **dead!**

I must go tell my chief!

Then, scuttling as fast as he could along the bottom of the stream, the little crayfish headed for the crayfish village and the home of his chief, leader of the crayfish.

It was a long journey. As he traveled along, the little crayfish began thinking up a good story, a story that could make him look really good.

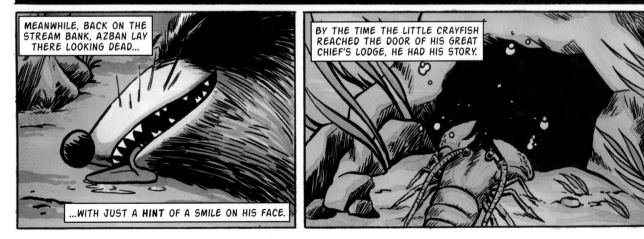

Meanwhile, back on the stream bank, Azban lay there looking dead...

...with just a **hint** of a smile on his face.

By the time the little crayfish reached the door of his great chief's lodge, he had his story.

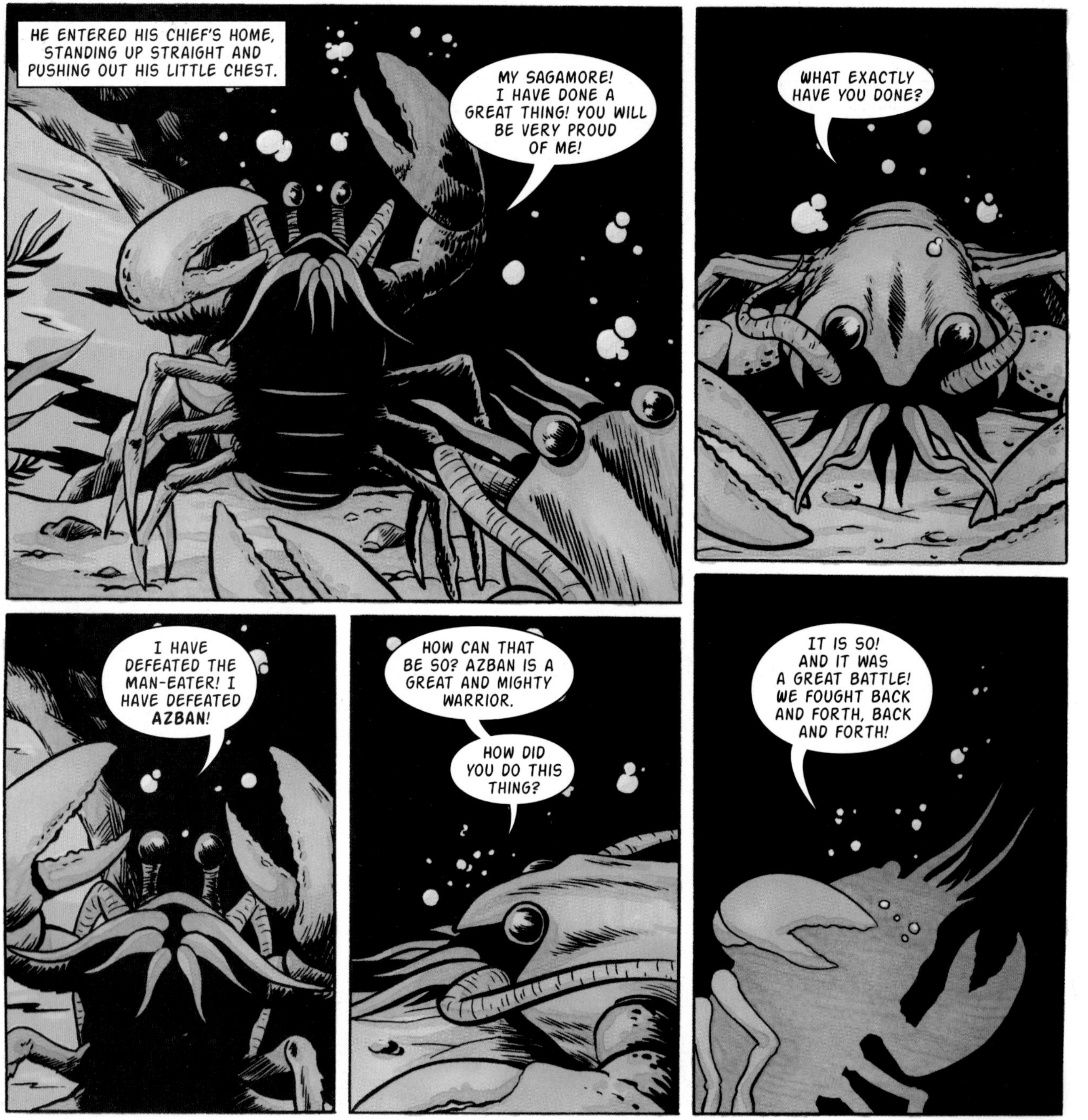
HE ENTERED HIS CHIEF'S HOME, STANDING UP STRAIGHT AND PUSHING OUT HIS LITTLE CHEST.
MY SAGAMORE! I HAVE DONE A GREAT THING! YOU WILL BE VERY PROUD OF ME!
WHAT EXACTLY HAVE YOU DONE?
I HAVE DEFEATED THE MAN-EATER! I HAVE DEFEATED **AZBAN**!
HOW CAN THAT BE SO? AZBAN IS A GREAT AND MIGHTY WARRIOR.
HOW DID YOU DO THIS THING?
IT IS SO! AND IT WAS A GREAT BATTLE! WE FOUGHT BACK AND FORTH, BACK AND FORTH!

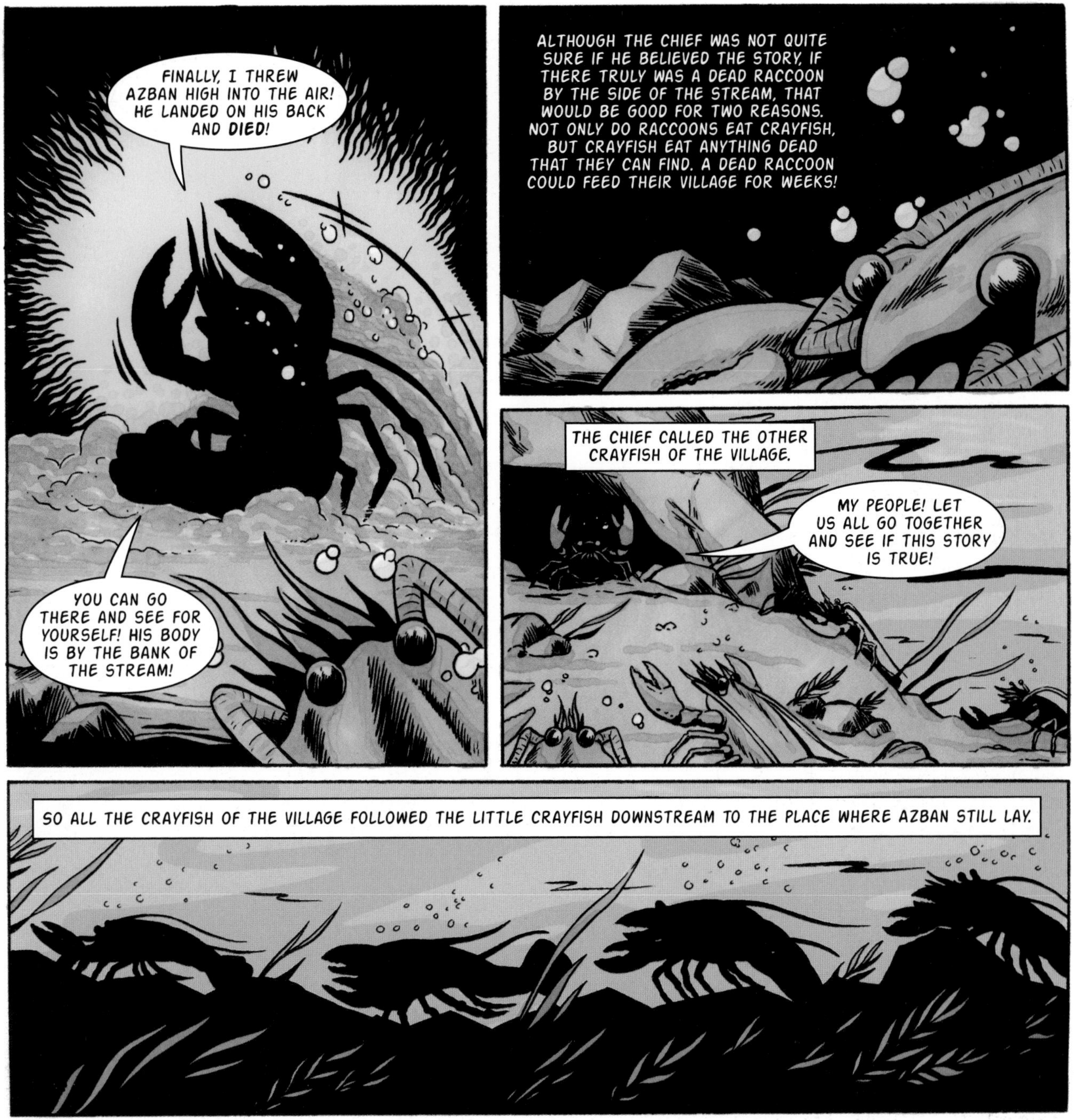
FINALLY, I THREW AZBAN HIGH INTO THE AIR! HE LANDED ON HIS BACK AND **DIED!**
YOU CAN GO THERE AND SEE FOR YOURSELF! HIS BODY IS BY THE BANK OF THE STREAM!
ALTHOUGH THE CHIEF WAS NOT QUITE SURE IF HE BELIEVED THE STORY, IF THERE TRULY WAS A DEAD RACCOON BY THE SIDE OF THE STREAM, THAT WOULD BE GOOD FOR TWO REASONS. NOT ONLY DO RACCOONS EAT CRAYFISH, BUT CRAYFISH EAT ANYTHING DEAD THAT THEY CAN FIND. A DEAD RACCOON COULD FEED THEIR VILLAGE FOR WEEKS!
THE CHIEF CALLED THE OTHER CRAYFISH OF THE VILLAGE.
MY PEOPLE! LET US ALL GO TOGETHER AND SEE IF THIS STORY IS TRUE!
SO ALL THE CRAYFISH OF THE VILLAGE FOLLOWED THE LITTLE CRAYFISH DOWNSTREAM TO THE PLACE WHERE AZBAN STILL LAY.

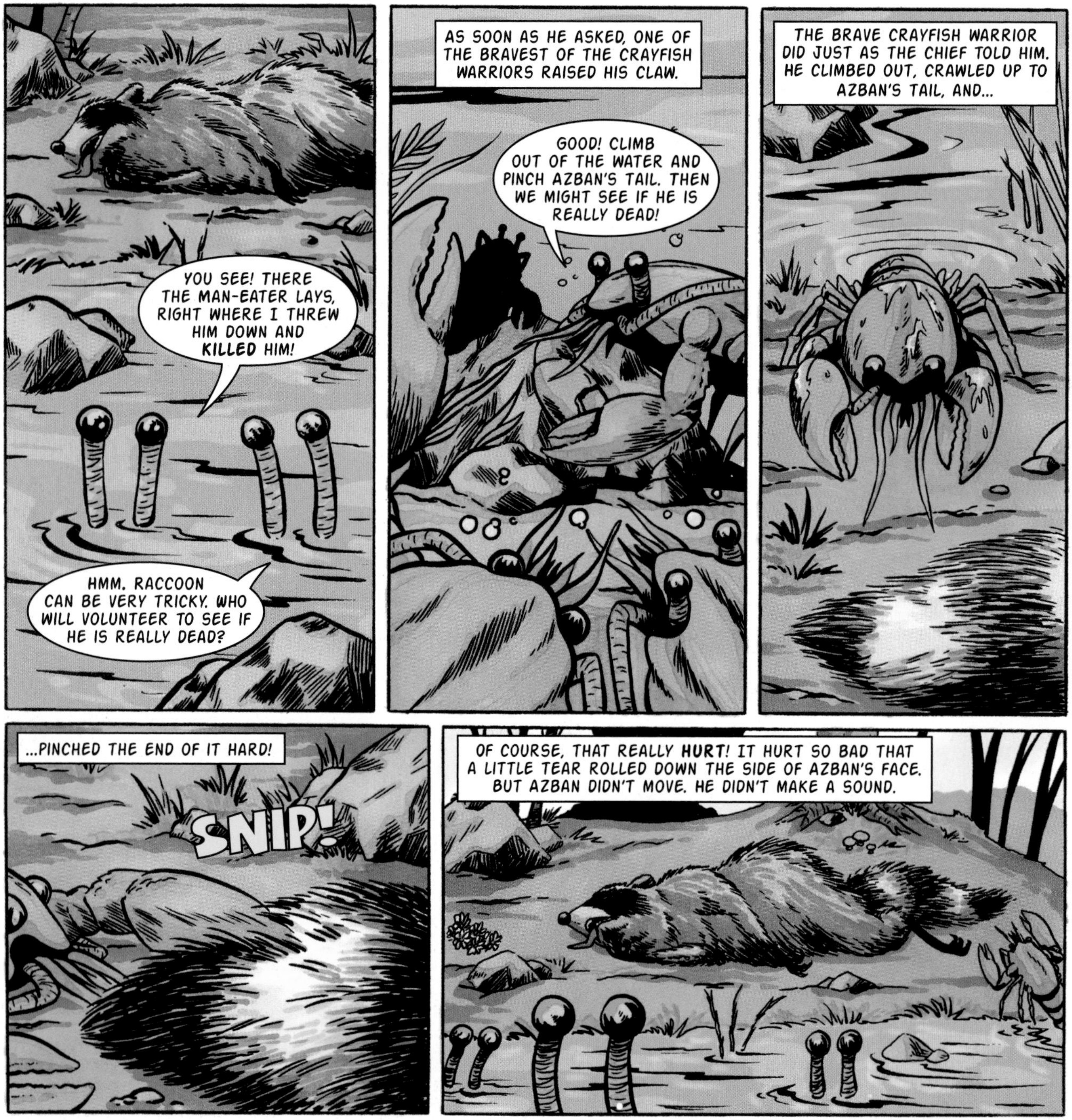

YOU SEE! THERE THE MAN-EATER LAYS, RIGHT WHERE I THREW HIM DOWN AND **KILLED** HIM!
HMM. RACCOON CAN BE VERY TRICKY. WHO WILL VOLUNTEER TO SEE IF HE IS REALLY DEAD?
AS SOON AS HE ASKED, ONE OF THE BRAVEST OF THE CRAYFISH WARRIORS RAISED HIS CLAW.
GOOD! CLIMB OUT OF THE WATER AND PINCH AZBAN'S TAIL. THEN WE MIGHT SEE IF HE IS REALLY DEAD!
THE BRAVE CRAYFISH WARRIOR DID JUST AS THE CHIEF TOLD HIM. HE CLIMBED OUT, CRAWLED UP TO AZBAN'S TAIL, AND...
...PINCHED THE END OF IT HARD!
SNIP!
OF COURSE, THAT REALLY **HURT**! IT HURT SO BAD THAT A LITTLE TEAR ROLLED DOWN THE SIDE OF AZBAN'S FACE. BUT AZBAN DIDN'T MOVE. HE DIDN'T MAKE A SOUND.

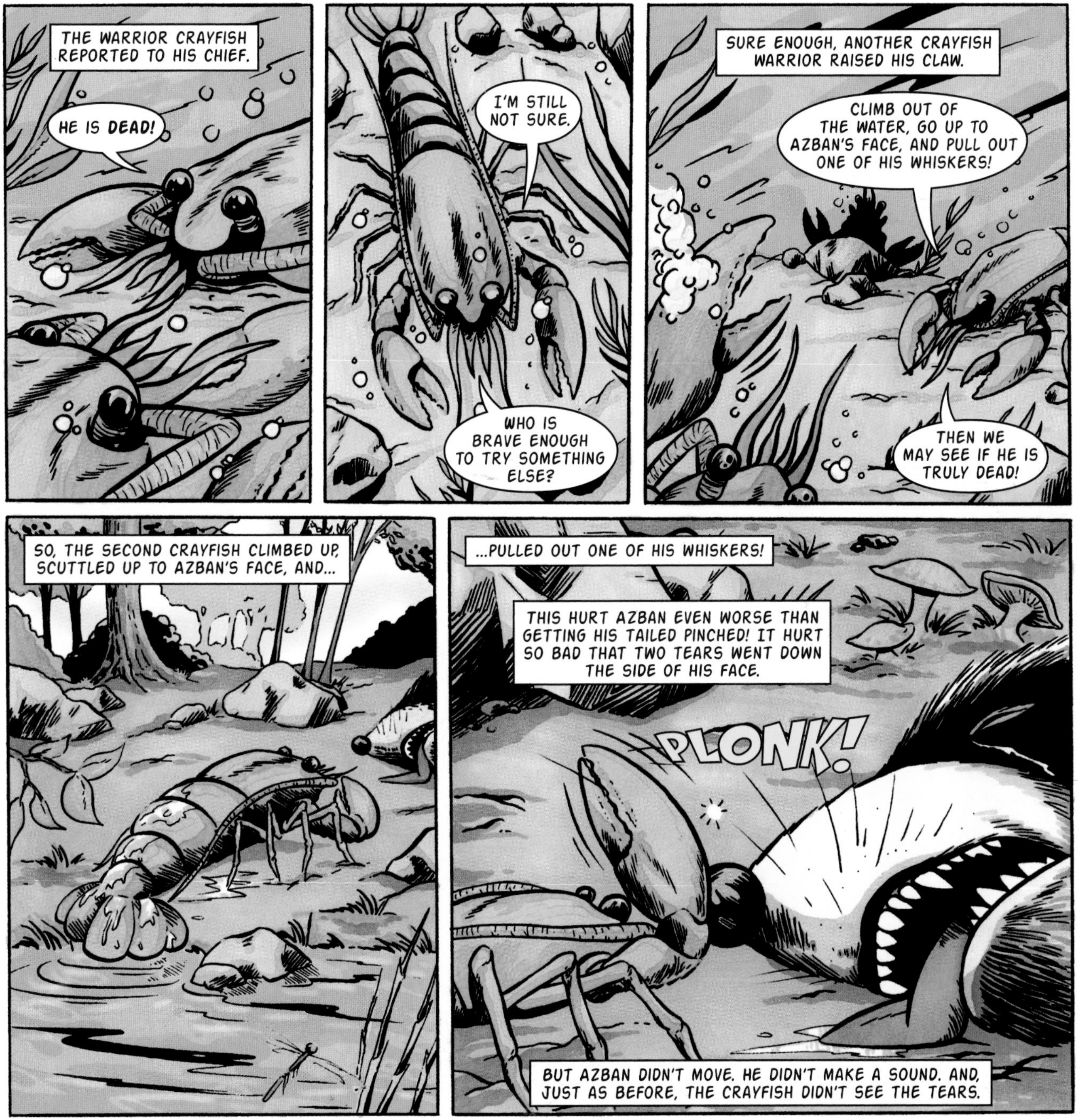
THE WARRIOR CRAYFISH REPORTED TO HIS CHIEF.
HE IS DEAD!
I'M STILL NOT SURE.
WHO IS BRAVE ENOUGH TO TRY SOMETHING ELSE?
SURE ENOUGH, ANOTHER CRAYFISH WARRIOR RAISED HIS CLAW.
CLIMB OUT OF THE WATER, GO UP TO AZBAN'S FACE, AND PULL OUT ONE OF HIS WHISKERS!
THEN WE MAY SEE IF HE IS TRULY DEAD!
SO, THE SECOND CRAYFISH CLIMBED UP, SCUTTLED UP TO AZBAN'S FACE, AND...
...PULLED OUT ONE OF HIS WHISKERS!
THIS HURT AZBAN EVEN WORSE THAN GETTING HIS TAILED PINCHED! IT HURT SO BAD THAT TWO TEARS WENT DOWN THE SIDE OF HIS FACE.
PLONK!
BUT AZBAN DIDN'T MOVE. HE DIDN'T MAKE A SOUND. AND, JUST AS BEFORE, THE CRAYFISH DIDN'T SEE THE TEARS.

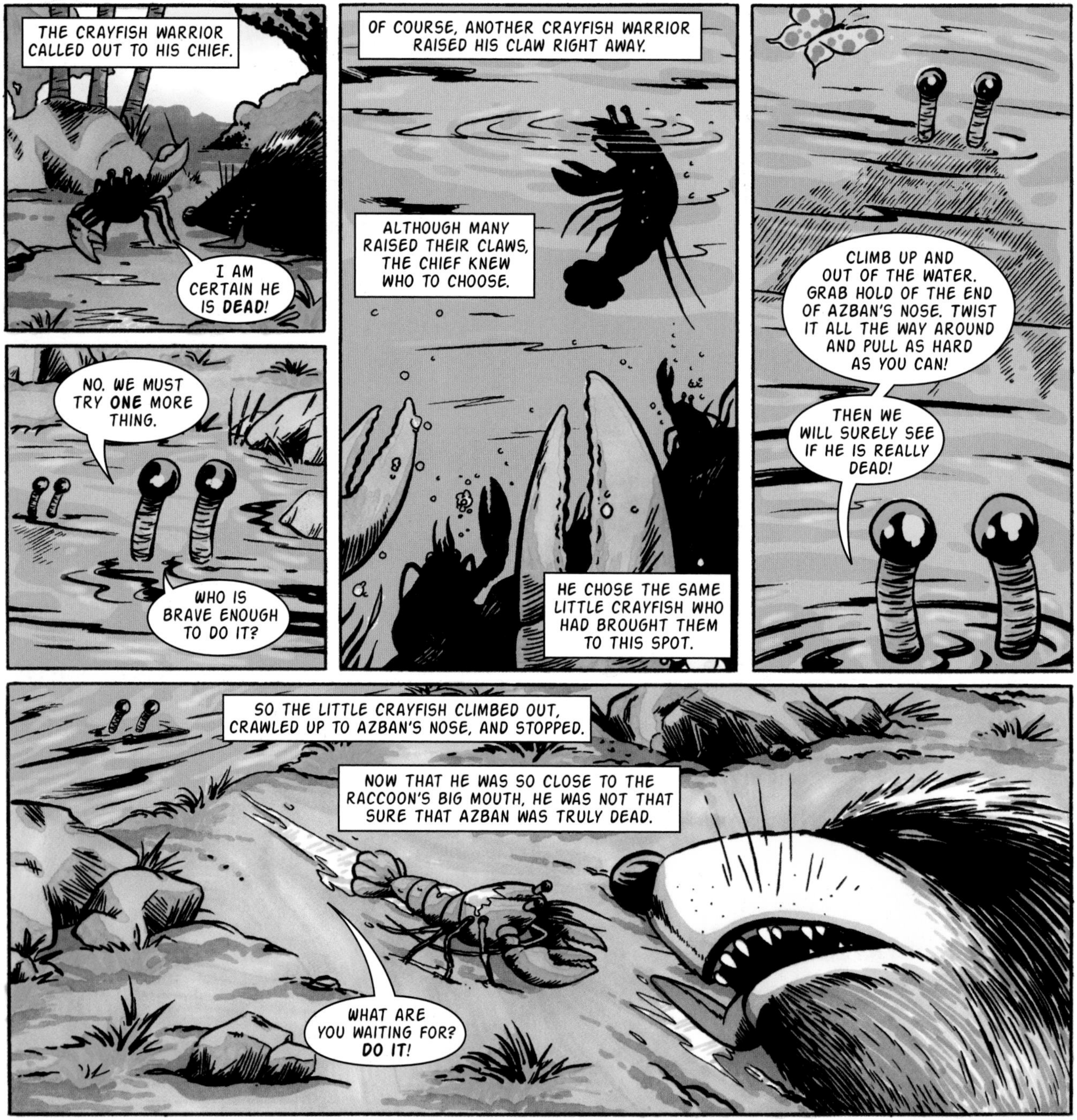
THE CRAYFISH WARRIOR CALLED OUT TO HIS CHIEF.
I AM CERTAIN HE IS **DEAD**!
NO. WE MUST TRY **ONE** MORE THING.
WHO IS BRAVE ENOUGH TO DO IT?
OF COURSE, ANOTHER CRAYFISH WARRIOR RAISED HIS CLAW RIGHT AWAY.
ALTHOUGH MANY RAISED THEIR CLAWS, THE CHIEF KNEW WHO TO CHOOSE.
HE CHOSE THE SAME LITTLE CRAYFISH WHO HAD BROUGHT THEM TO THIS SPOT.
CLIMB UP AND OUT OF THE WATER. GRAB HOLD OF THE END OF AZBAN'S NOSE. TWIST IT ALL THE WAY AROUND AND PULL AS HARD AS YOU CAN!
THEN WE WILL SURELY SEE IF HE IS REALLY DEAD!
SO THE LITTLE CRAYFISH CLIMBED OUT, CRAWLED UP TO AZBAN'S NOSE, AND STOPPED.
NOW THAT HE WAS SO CLOSE TO THE RACCOON'S BIG MOUTH, HE WAS NOT THAT SURE THAT AZBAN WAS TRULY DEAD.
WHAT ARE YOU WAITING FOR? **DO IT**!

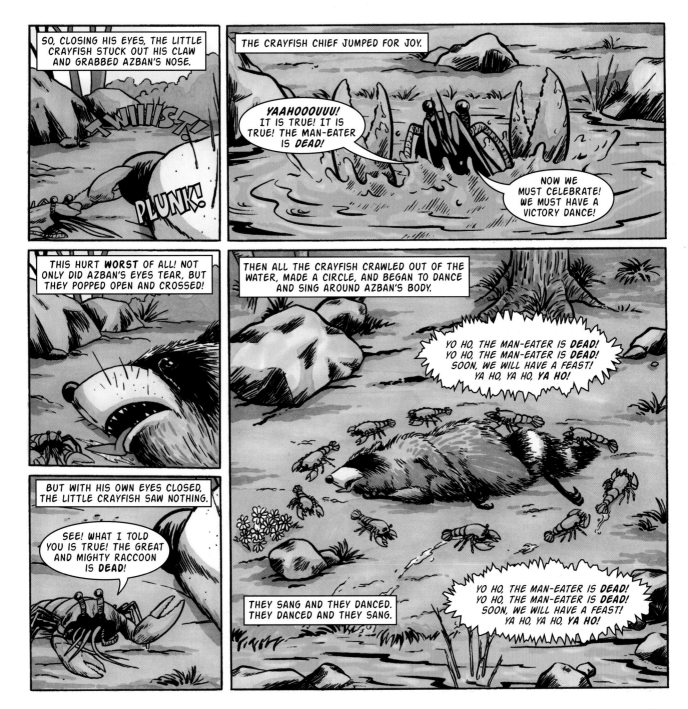

SO, CLOSING HIS EYES, THE LITTLE CRAYFISH STUCK OUT HIS CLAW AND GRABBED AZBAN'S NOSE.

TWIIIIST!

PLUNK!

THE CRAYFISH CHIEF JUMPED FOR JOY.

YAAHOOOUUU! IT IS TRUE! IT IS TRUE! THE MAN-EATER IS *DEAD*!

NOW WE MUST CELEBRATE! WE MUST HAVE A VICTORY DANCE!

THIS HURT **WORST** OF ALL! NOT ONLY DID AZBAN'S EYES TEAR, BUT THEY POPPED OPEN AND CROSSED!

BUT WITH HIS OWN EYES CLOSED, THE LITTLE CRAYFISH SAW NOTHING.

SEE! WHAT I TOLD YOU IS TRUE! THE GREAT AND MIGHTY RACCOON IS *DEAD*!

THEN ALL THE CRAYFISH CRAWLED OUT OF THE WATER, MADE A CIRCLE, AND BEGAN TO DANCE AND SING AROUND AZBAN'S BODY.

YO HO, THE MAN-EATER IS *DEAD*! YO HO, THE MAN-EATER IS *DEAD*! SOON, WE WILL HAVE A FEAST! YA HO, YA HO, *YA HO*!

YO HO, THE MAN-EATER IS *DEAD*! YO HO, THE MAN-EATER IS *DEAD*! SOON, WE WILL HAVE A FEAST! YA HO, YA HO, *YA HO*!

THEY SANG AND THEY DANCED. THEY DANCED AND THEY SANG.

45

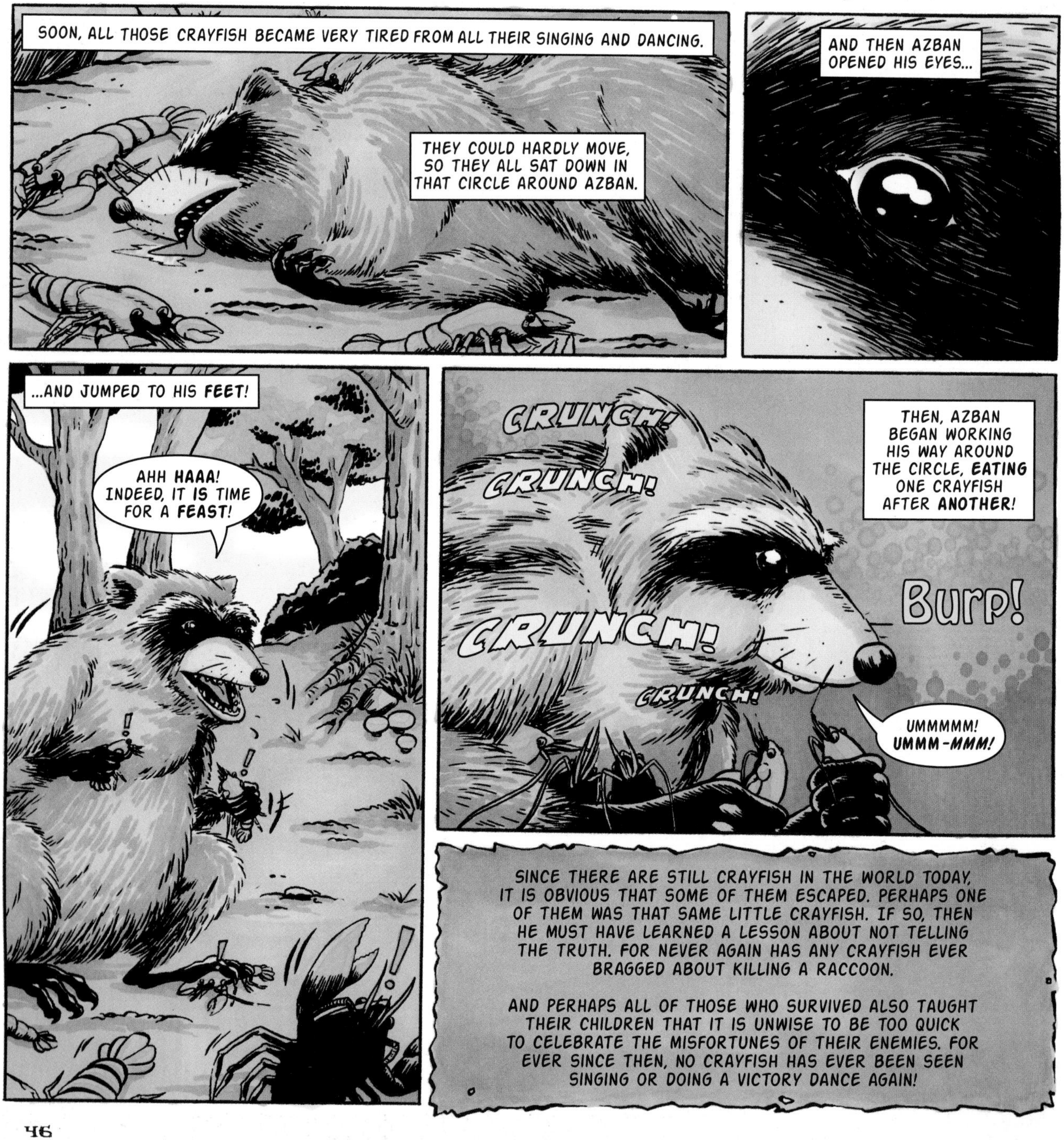
SOON, ALL THOSE CRAYFISH BECAME VERY TIRED FROM ALL THEIR SINGING AND DANCING.
THEY COULD HARDLY MOVE, SO THEY ALL SAT DOWN IN THAT CIRCLE AROUND AZBAN.
AND THEN AZBAN OPENED HIS EYES...
...AND JUMPED TO HIS FEET!
AHH HAAA! INDEED, IT IS TIME FOR A FEAST!
!
!
!
CRUNCH!
CRUNCH!
THEN, AZBAN BEGAN WORKING HIS WAY AROUND THE CIRCLE, EATING ONE CRAYFISH AFTER ANOTHER!
CRUNCH!
Burp!
CRUNCH!
UMMMMM! UMMM-MMM!
SINCE THERE ARE STILL CRAYFISH IN THE WORLD TODAY, IT IS OBVIOUS THAT SOME OF THEM ESCAPED. PERHAPS ONE OF THEM WAS THAT SAME LITTLE CRAYFISH. IF SO, THEN HE MUST HAVE LEARNED A LESSON ABOUT NOT TELLING THE TRUTH. FOR NEVER AGAIN HAS ANY CRAYFISH EVER BRAGGED ABOUT KILLING A RACCOON.
AND PERHAPS ALL OF THOSE WHO SURVIVED ALSO TAUGHT THEIR CHILDREN THAT IT IS UNWISE TO BE TOO QUICK TO CELEBRATE THE MISFORTUNES OF THEIR ENEMIES. FOR EVER SINCE THEN, NO CRAYFISH HAS EVER BEEN SEEN SINGING OR DOING A VICTORY DANCE AGAIN!

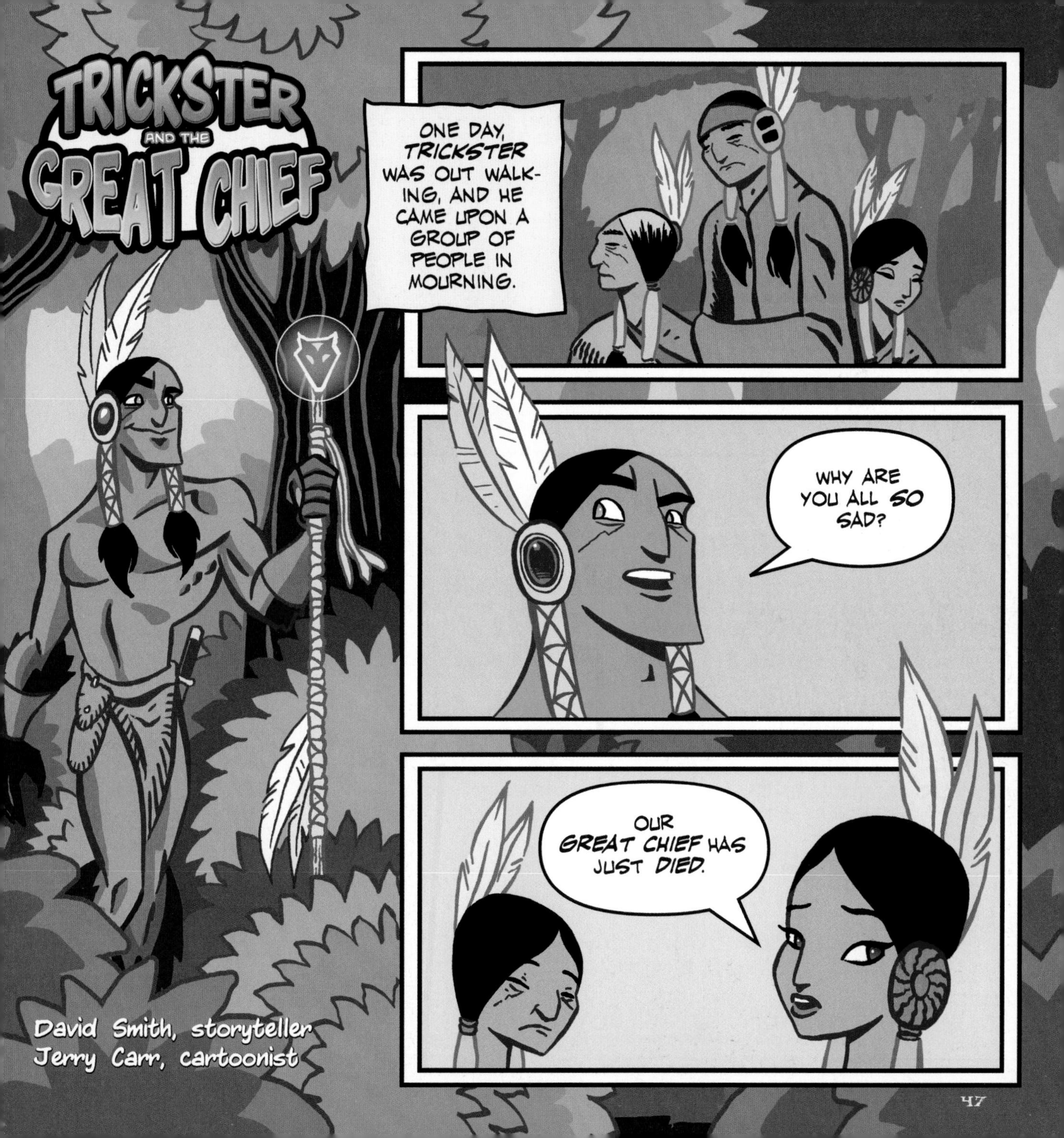
TRICKSTER AND THE GREAT CHIEF
ONE DAY, TRICKSTER WAS OUT WALKING, AND HE CAME UPON A GROUP OF PEOPLE IN MOURNING.
WHY ARE YOU ALL SO SAD?
OUR GREAT CHIEF HAS JUST DIED.
David Smith, storyteller
Jerry Carr, cartoonist

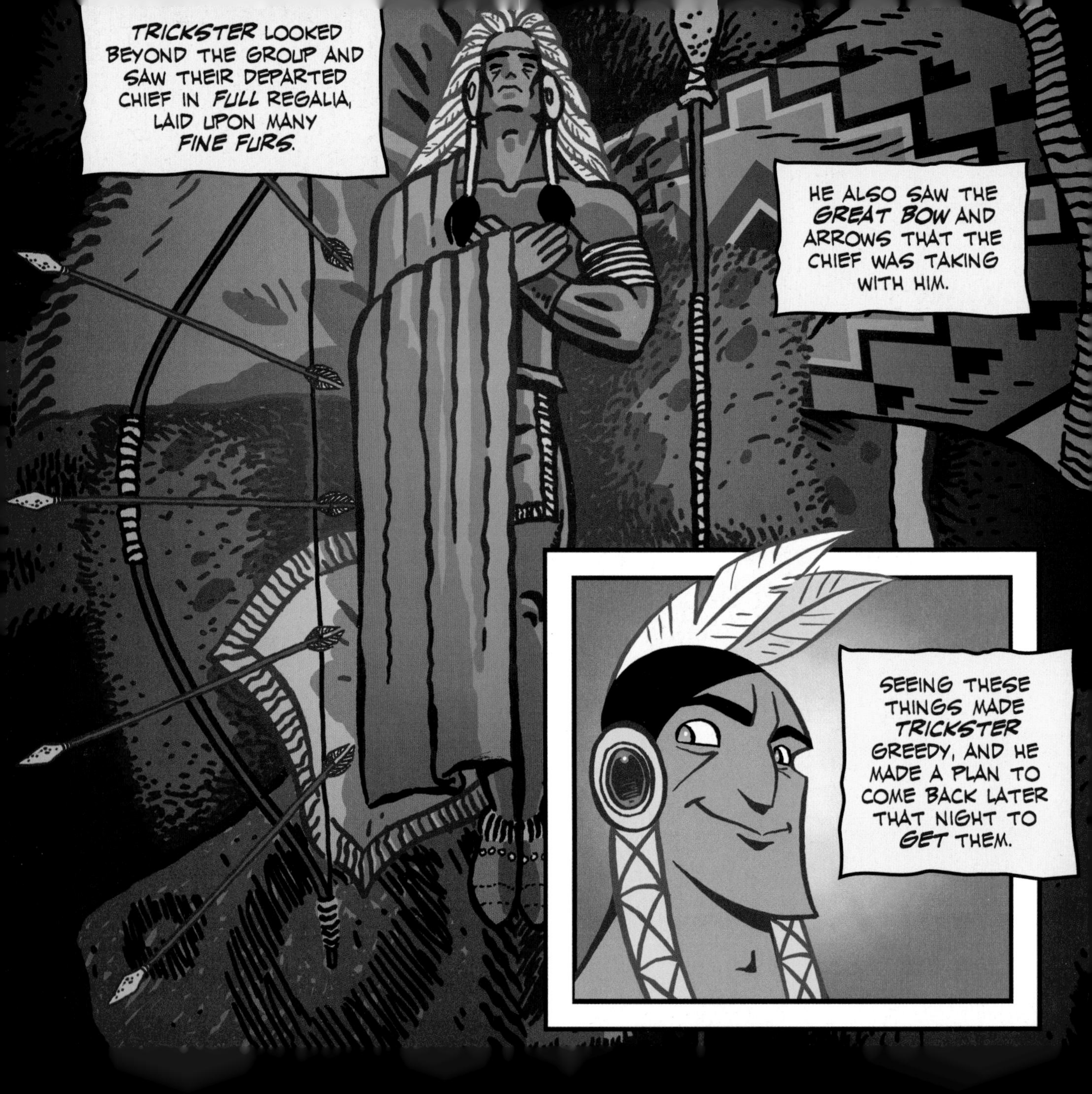
TRICKSTER LOOKED BEYOND THE GROUP AND SAW THEIR DEPARTED CHIEF IN FULL REGALIA, LAID UPON MANY FINE FURS.
HE ALSO SAW THE GREAT BOW AND ARROWS THAT THE CHIEF WAS TAKING WITH HIM.
SEEING THESE THINGS MADE TRICKSTER GREEDY, AND HE MADE A PLAN TO COME BACK LATER THAT NIGHT TO GET THEM.

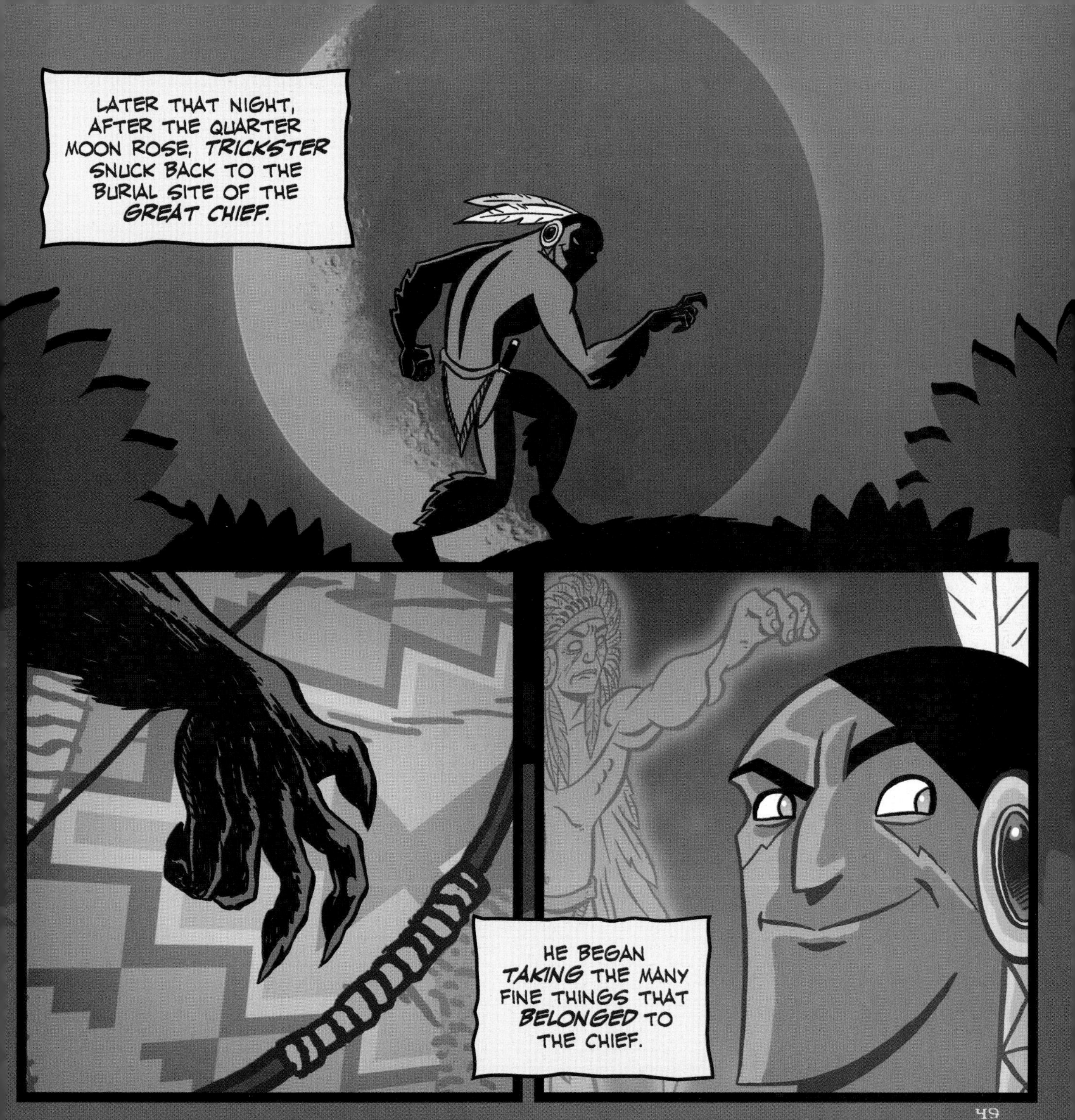
LATER THAT NIGHT, AFTER THE QUARTER MOON ROSE, TRICKSTER SNUCK BACK TO THE BURIAL SITE OF THE GREAT CHIEF.
HE BEGAN TAKING THE MANY FINE THINGS THAT BELONGED TO THE CHIEF.

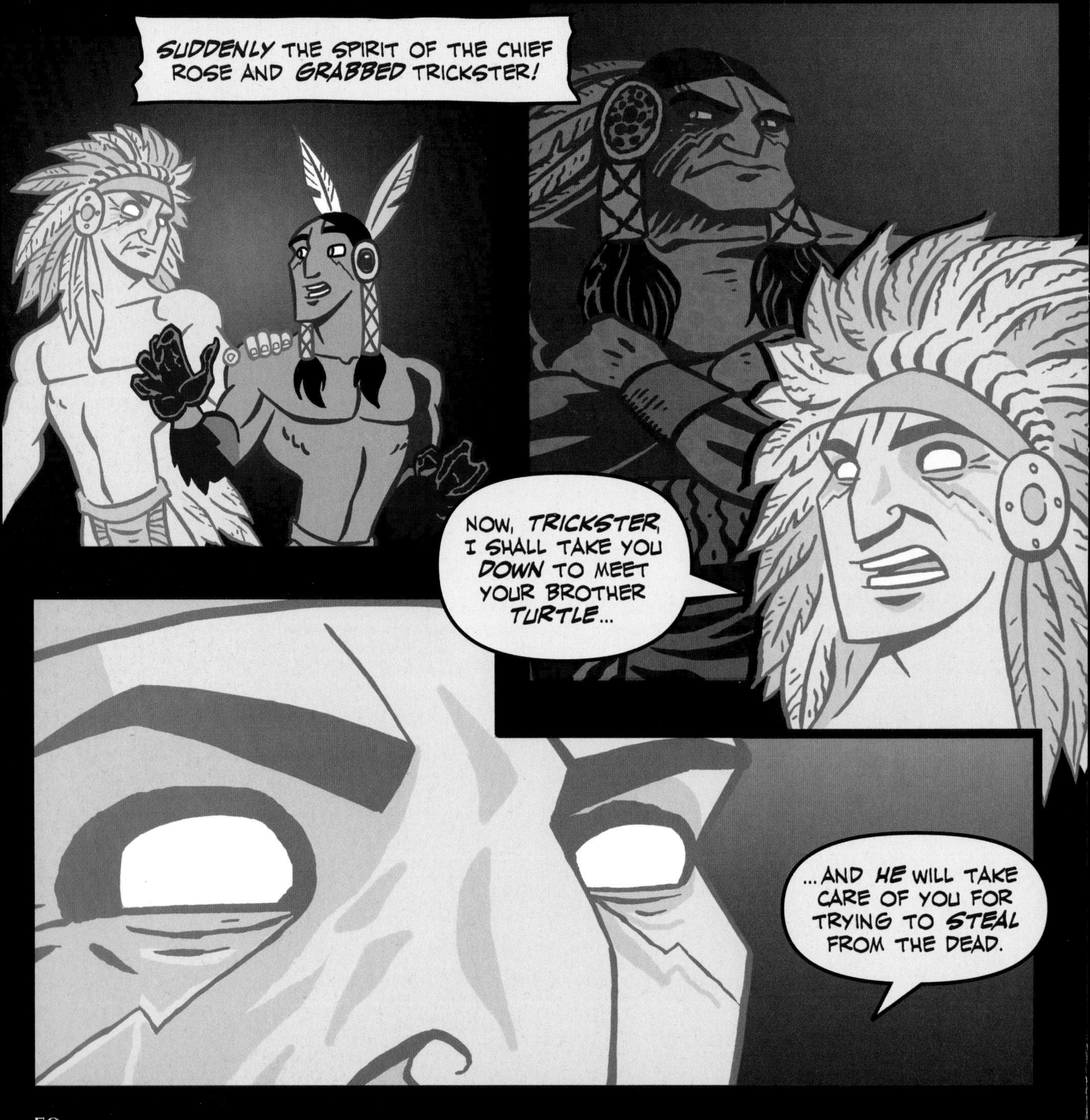
SUDDENLY THE SPIRIT OF THE CHIEF ROSE AND GRABBED TRICKSTER!
NOW, TRICKSTER, I SHALL TAKE YOU DOWN TO MEET YOUR BROTHER TURTLE...
...AND HE WILL TAKE CARE OF YOU FOR TRYING TO STEAL FROM THE DEAD.

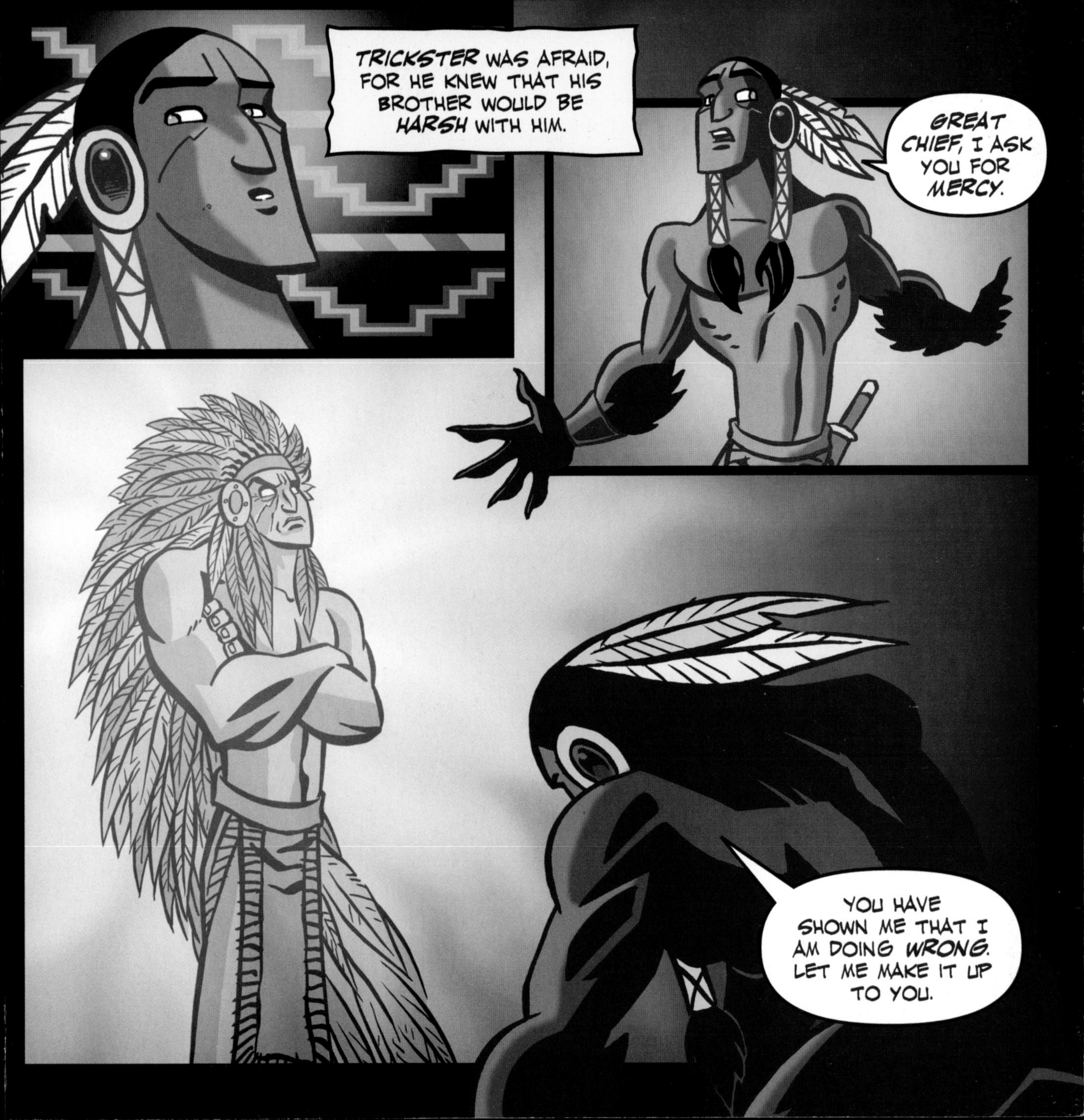
TRICKSTER WAS AFRAID, FOR HE KNEW THAT HIS BROTHER WOULD BE HARSH WITH HIM.
GREAT CHIEF, I ASK YOU FOR MERCY.
YOU HAVE SHOWN ME THAT I AM DOING WRONG. LET ME MAKE IT UP TO YOU.

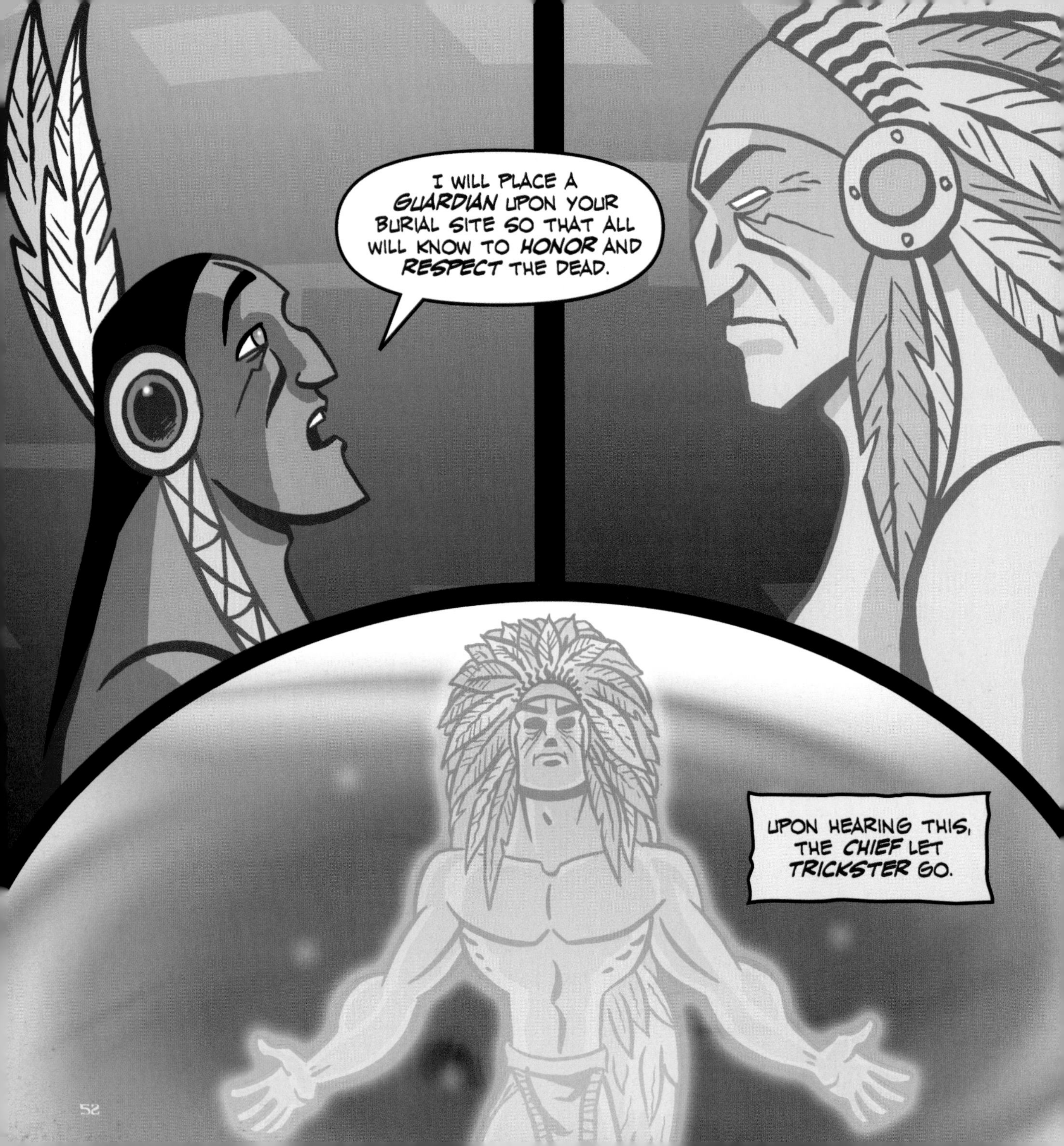
I WILL PLACE A GUARDIAN UPON YOUR BURIAL SITE SO THAT ALL WILL KNOW TO HONOR AND RESPECT THE DEAD.
UPON HEARING THIS, THE CHIEF LET TRICKSTER GO.

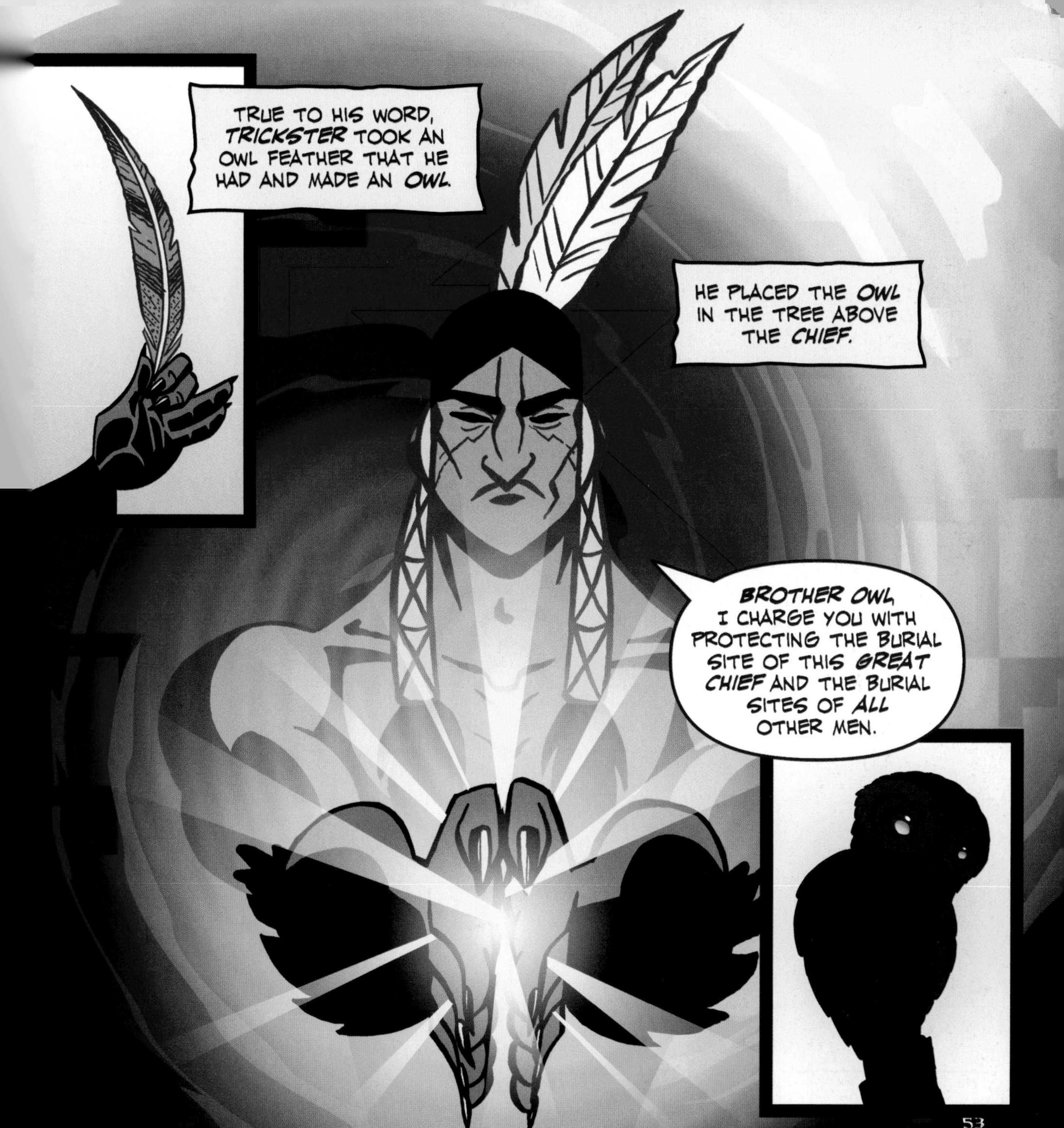
TRUE TO HIS WORD, TRICKSTER TOOK AN OWL FEATHER THAT HE HAD AND MADE AN OWL.
HE PLACED THE OWL IN THE TREE ABOVE THE CHIEF.
BROTHER OWL, I CHARGE YOU WITH PROTECTING THE BURIAL SITE OF THIS GREAT CHIEF AND THE BURIAL SITES OF ALL OTHER MEN.

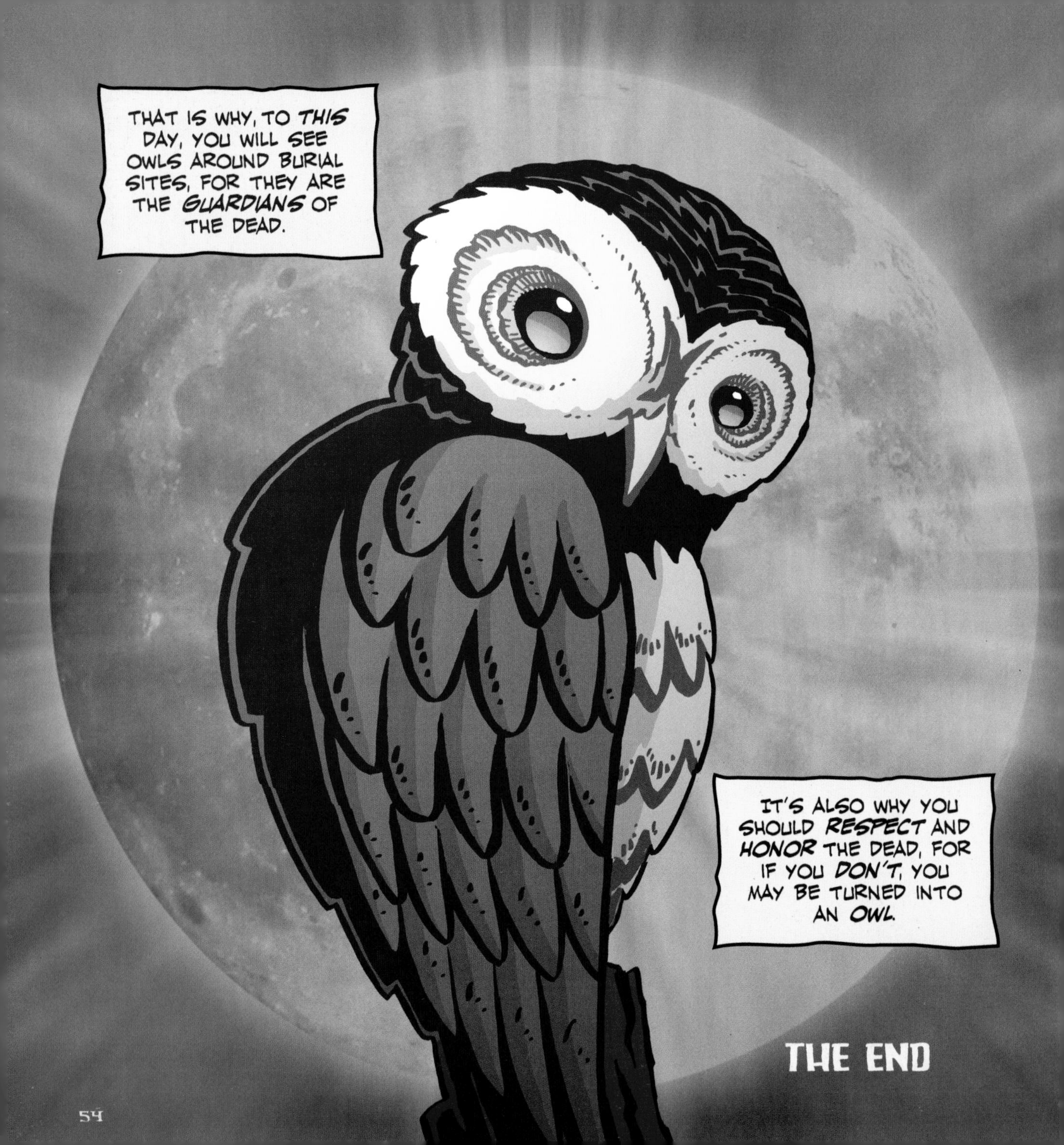
THAT IS WHY, TO THIS DAY, YOU WILL SEE OWLS AROUND BURIAL SITES, FOR THEY ARE THE GUARDIANS OF THE DEAD.
IT'S ALSO WHY YOU SHOULD RESPECT AND HONOR THE DEAD, FOR IF YOU DON'T, YOU MAY BE TURNED INTO AN OWL.
THE END

HORNED TOAD LADY & COYOTE

Retold by
Eldrena Douma

Illustrated by
Roy Boney Jr.

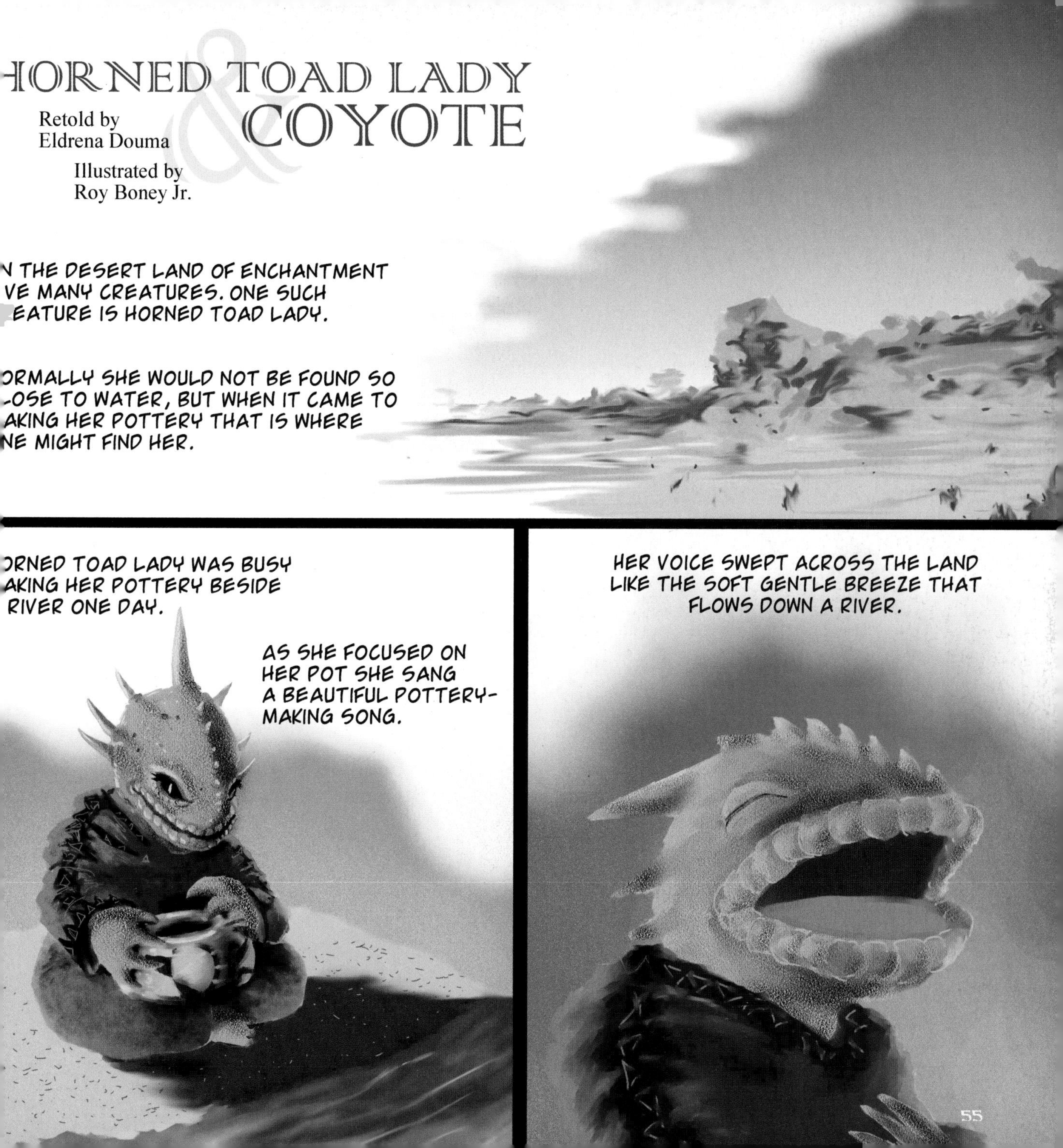

N THE DESERT LAND OF ENCHANTMENT VE MANY CREATURES. ONE SUCH EATURE IS HORNED TOAD LADY.
ORMALLY SHE WOULD NOT BE FOUND SO OSE TO WATER, BUT WHEN IT CAME TO AKING HER POTTERY THAT IS WHERE NE MIGHT FIND HER.
ORNED TOAD LADY WAS BUSY AKING HER POTTERY BESIDE RIVER ONE DAY.
AS SHE FOCUSED ON HER POT SHE SANG A BEAUTIFUL POTTERY-MAKING SONG.
HER VOICE SWEPT ACROSS THE LAND LIKE THE SOFT GENTLE BREEZE THAT FLOWS DOWN A RIVER.

IT HAPPENED THAT COYOTE OLD MAN WAS ON HIS WAY HOME WHEN HE HEARD THE BEAUTIFUL SONG HORNED TOAD LADY WAS SINGING.

AS HE FOLLOWED THE SONG BACK TO THE SINGER, HE STOPPED LONG ENOUGH TO ENJOY THE FULLNESS OF IT.

COYOTE HAS ALWAYS BEEN A COLLECTOR OF SONGS AND THIS WAS A SONG HE WANTED TO ADD TO HIS COLLECTION.

BUT HE KNEW HE WOULD FIRST HAVE TO ASK FOR PERMISSION.

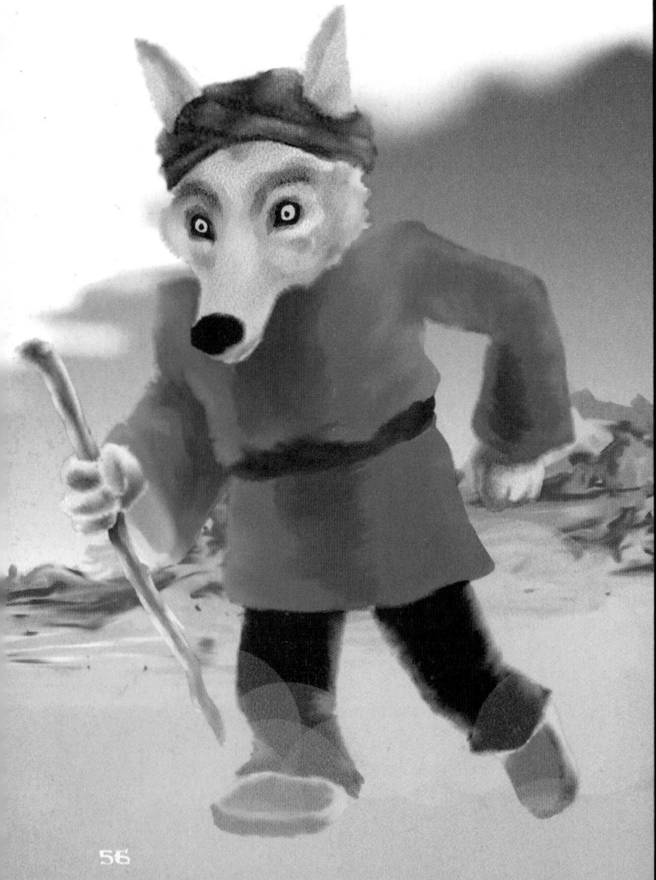

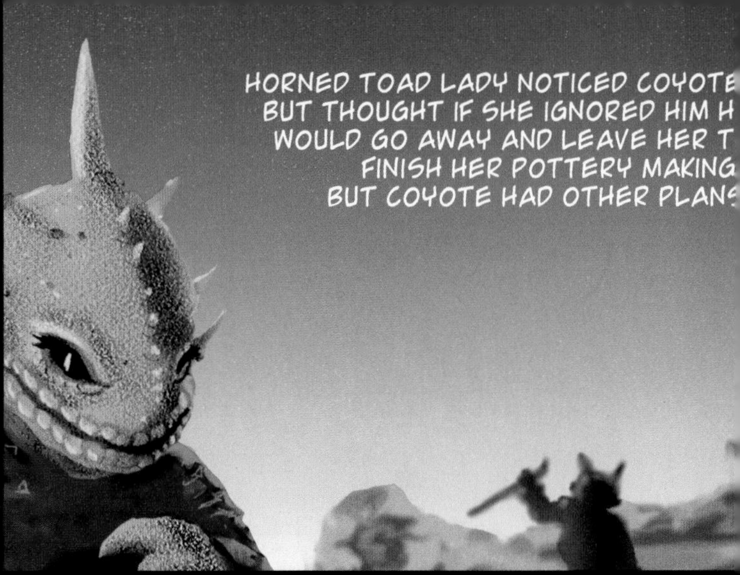
HORNED TOAD LADY NOTICED COYOTE
BUT THOUGHT IF SHE IGNORED HIM H
WOULD GO AWAY AND LEAVE HER T
FINISH HER POTTERY MAKING
BUT COYOTE HAD OTHER PLAN

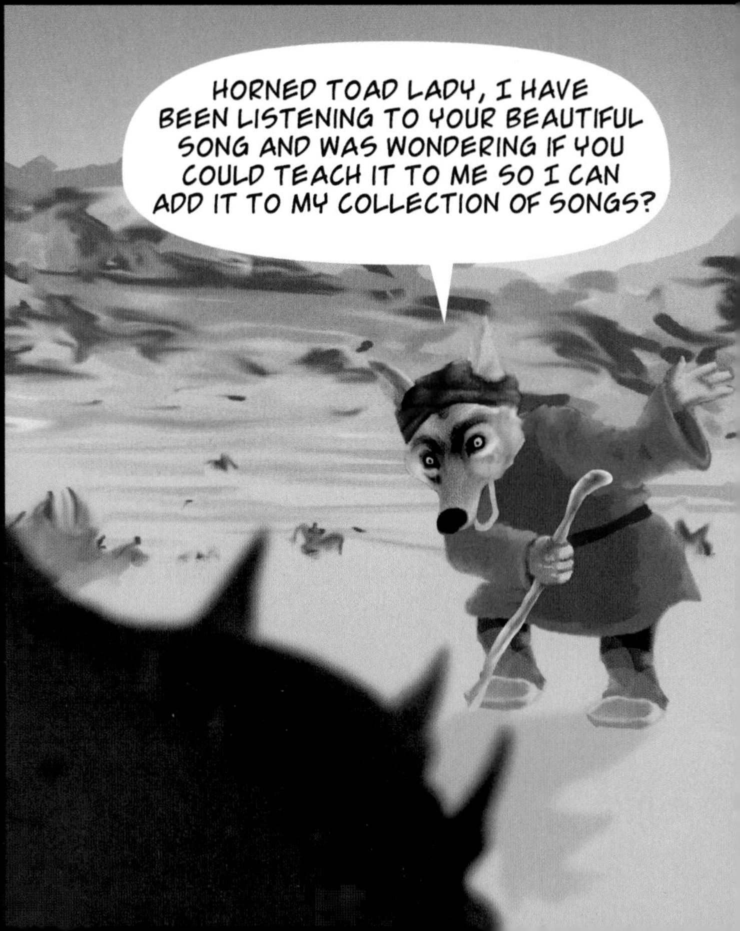
HORNED TOAD LADY, I HAVE BEEN LISTENING TO YOUR BEAUTIFUL SONG AND WAS WONDERING IF YOU COULD TEACH IT TO ME SO I CAN ADD IT TO MY COLLECTION OF SONGS?

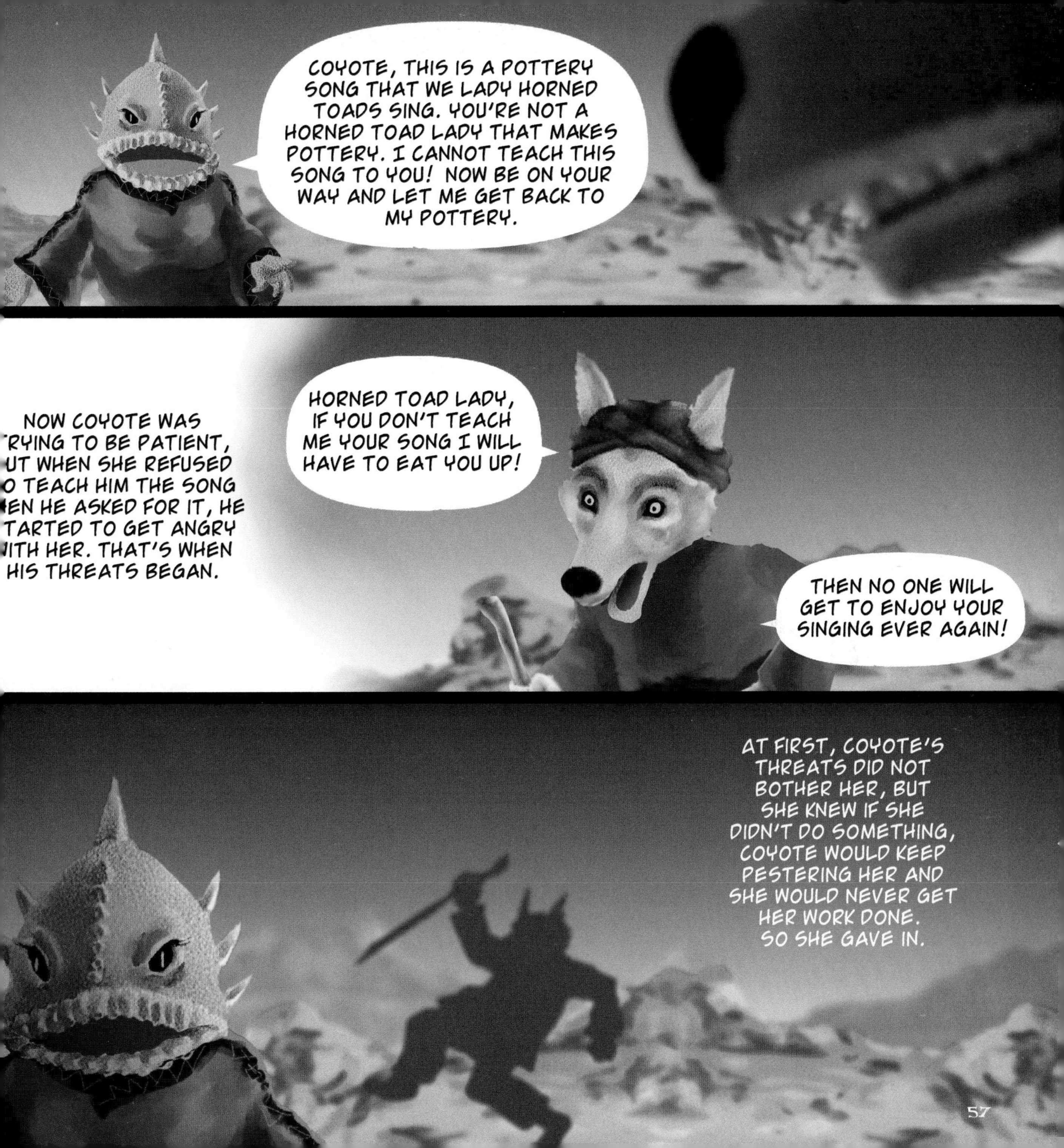
COYOTE, THIS IS A POTTERY SONG THAT WE LADY HORNED TOADS SING. YOU'RE NOT A HORNED TOAD LADY THAT MAKES POTTERY. I CANNOT TEACH THIS SONG TO YOU! NOW BE ON YOUR WAY AND LET ME GET BACK TO MY POTTERY.
NOW COYOTE WAS RYING TO BE PATIENT, UT WHEN SHE REFUSED O TEACH HIM THE SONG EN HE ASKED FOR IT, HE TARTED TO GET ANGRY ITH HER. THAT'S WHEN HIS THREATS BEGAN.
HORNED TOAD LADY, IF YOU DON'T TEACH ME YOUR SONG I WILL HAVE TO EAT YOU UP!
THEN NO ONE WILL GET TO ENJOY YOUR SINGING EVER AGAIN!
AT FIRST, COYOTE'S THREATS DID NOT BOTHER HER, BUT SHE KNEW IF SHE DIDN'T DO SOMETHING, COYOTE WOULD KEEP PESTERING HER AND SHE WOULD NEVER GET HER WORK DONE. SO SHE GAVE IN.

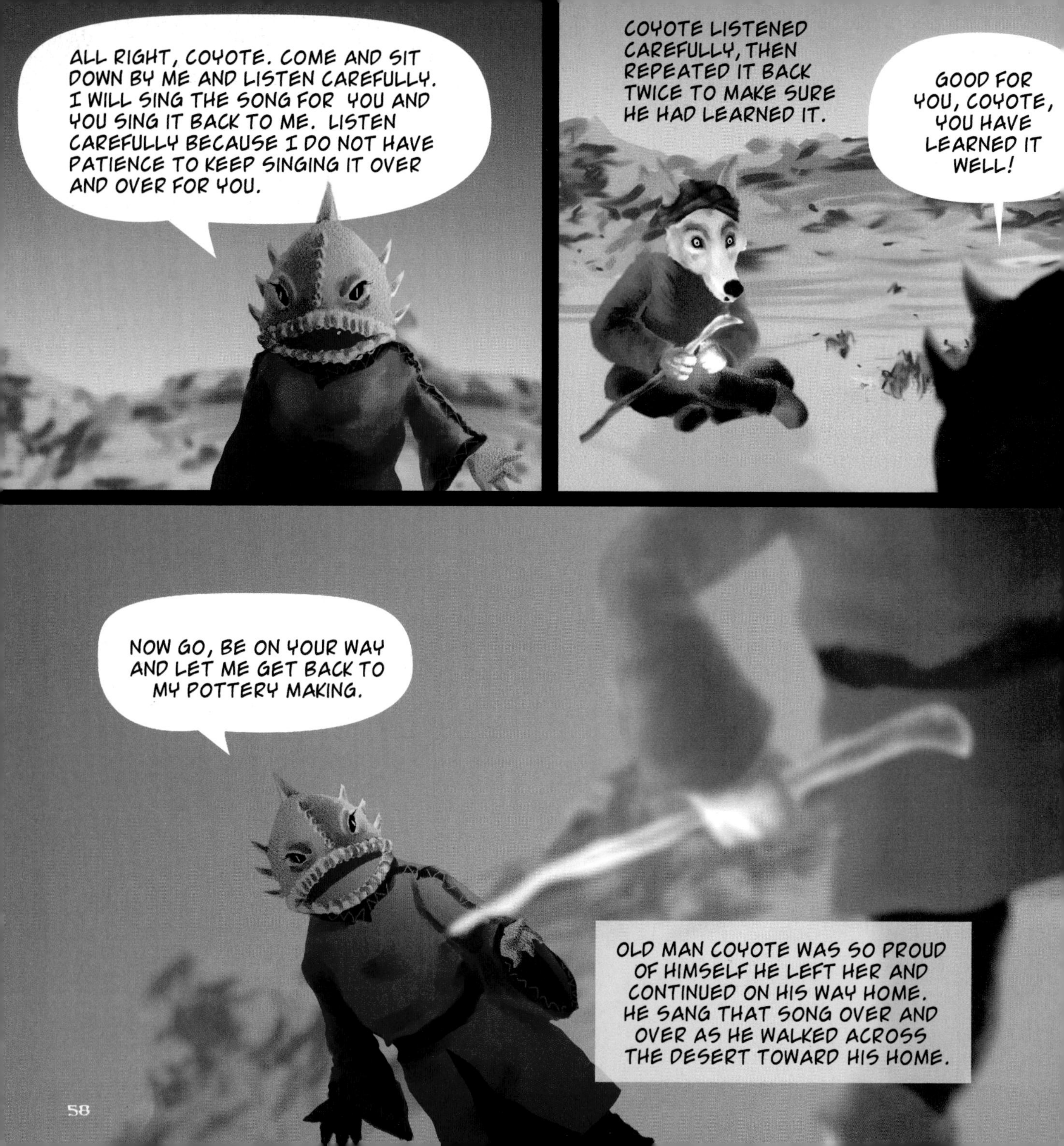
ALL RIGHT, COYOTE. COME AND SIT DOWN BY ME AND LISTEN CAREFULLY. I WILL SING THE SONG FOR YOU AND YOU SING IT BACK TO ME. LISTEN CAREFULLY BECAUSE I DO NOT HAVE PATIENCE TO KEEP SINGING IT OVER AND OVER FOR YOU.
COYOTE LISTENED CAREFULLY, THEN REPEATED IT BACK TWICE TO MAKE SURE HE HAD LEARNED IT.
GOOD FOR YOU, COYOTE, YOU HAVE LEARNED IT WELL!
NOW GO, BE ON YOUR WAY AND LET ME GET BACK TO MY POTTERY MAKING.
OLD MAN COYOTE WAS SO PROUD OF HIMSELF HE LEFT HER AND CONTINUED ON HIS WAY HOME. HE SANG THAT SONG OVER AND OVER AS HE WALKED ACROSS THE DESERT TOWARD HIS HOME.

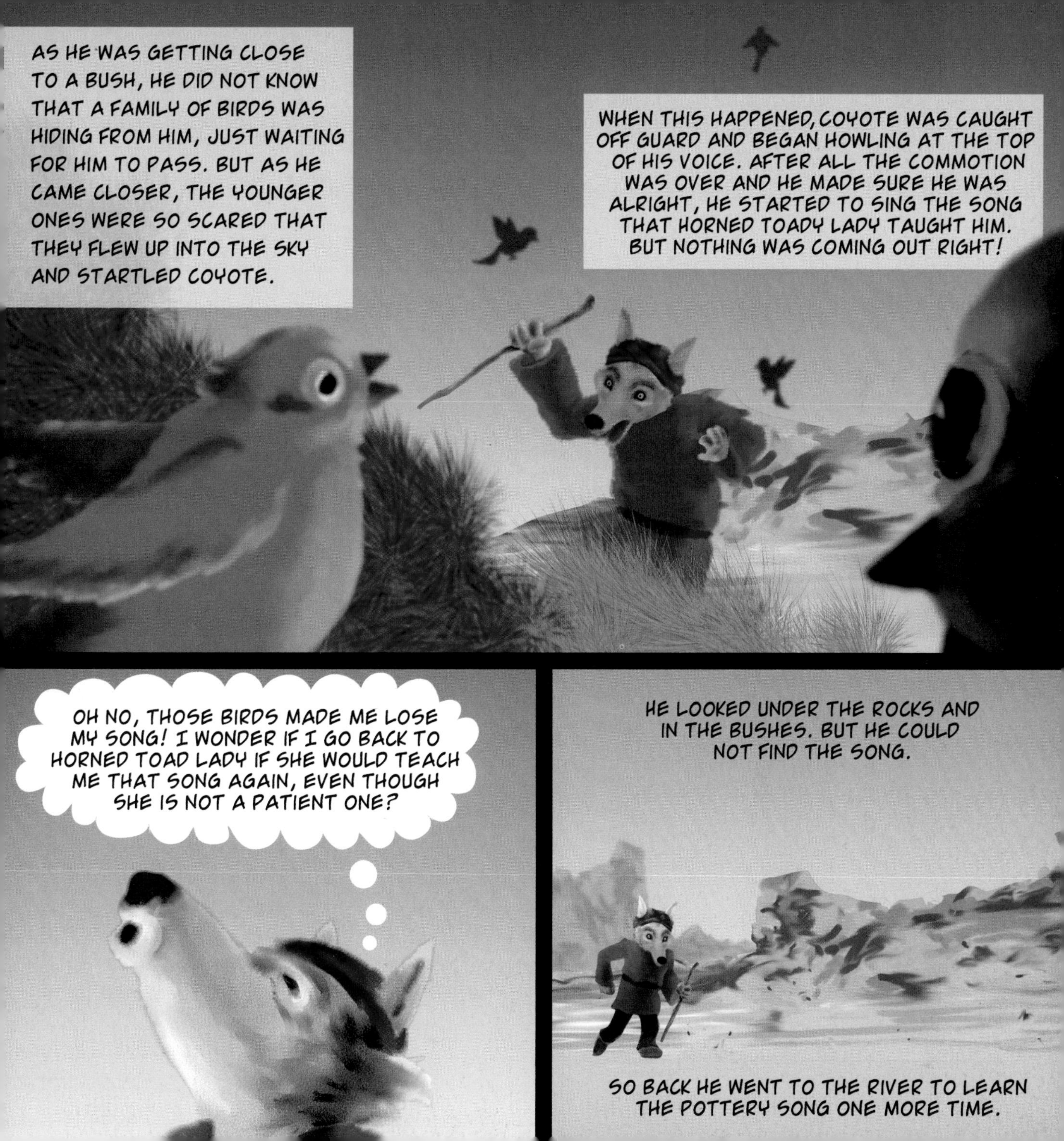
AS HE WAS GETTING CLOSE TO A BUSH, HE DID NOT KNOW THAT A FAMILY OF BIRDS WAS HIDING FROM HIM, JUST WAITING FOR HIM TO PASS. BUT AS HE CAME CLOSER, THE YOUNGER ONES WERE SO SCARED THAT THEY FLEW UP INTO THE SKY AND STARTLED COYOTE.
WHEN THIS HAPPENED, COYOTE WAS CAUGHT OFF GUARD AND BEGAN HOWLING AT THE TOP OF HIS VOICE. AFTER ALL THE COMMOTION WAS OVER AND HE MADE SURE HE WAS ALRIGHT, HE STARTED TO SING THE SONG THAT HORNED TOADY LADY TAUGHT HIM. BUT NOTHING WAS COMING OUT RIGHT!
OH NO, THOSE BIRDS MADE ME LOSE MY SONG! I WONDER IF I GO BACK TO HORNED TOAD LADY IF SHE WOULD TEACH ME THAT SONG AGAIN, EVEN THOUGH SHE IS NOT A PATIENT ONE?
HE LOOKED UNDER THE ROCKS AND IN THE BUSHES. BUT HE COULD NOT FIND THE SONG.
SO BACK HE WENT TO THE RIVER TO LEARN THE POTTERY SONG ONE MORE TIME.

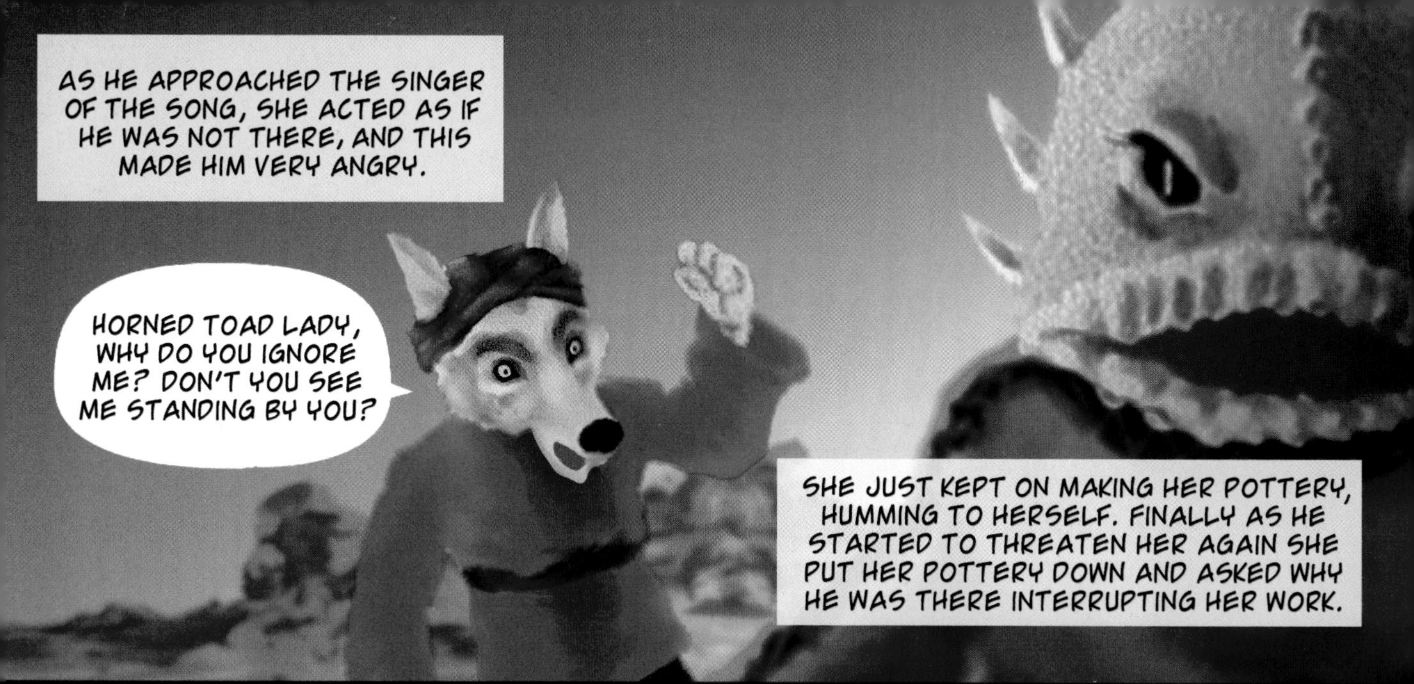
AS HE APPROACHED THE SINGER OF THE SONG, SHE ACTED AS IF HE WAS NOT THERE, AND THIS MADE HIM VERY ANGRY.
HORNED TOAD LADY, WHY DO YOU IGNORE ME? DON'T YOU SEE ME STANDING BY YOU?
SHE JUST KEPT ON MAKING HER POTTERY, HUMMING TO HERSELF. FINALLY AS HE STARTED TO THREATEN HER AGAIN SHE PUT HER POTTERY DOWN AND ASKED WHY HE WAS THERE INTERRUPTING HER WORK.

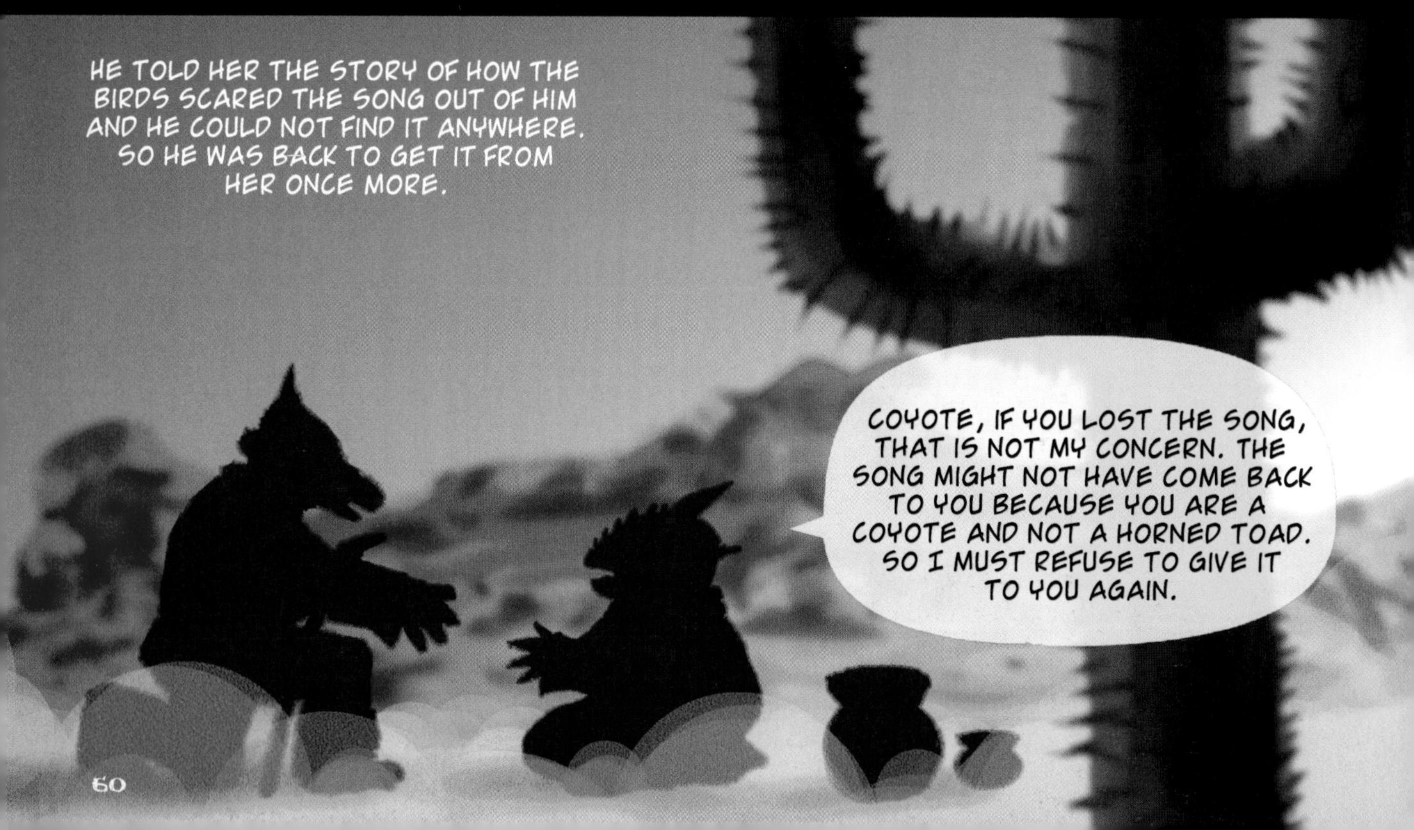
HE TOLD HER THE STORY OF HOW THE BIRDS SCARED THE SONG OUT OF HIM AND HE COULD NOT FIND IT ANYWHERE. SO HE WAS BACK TO GET IT FROM HER ONCE MORE.
COYOTE, IF YOU LOST THE SONG, THAT IS NOT MY CONCERN. THE SONG MIGHT NOT HAVE COME BACK TO YOU BECAUSE YOU ARE A COYOTE AND NOT A HORNED TOAD. SO I MUST REFUSE TO GIVE IT TO YOU AGAIN.

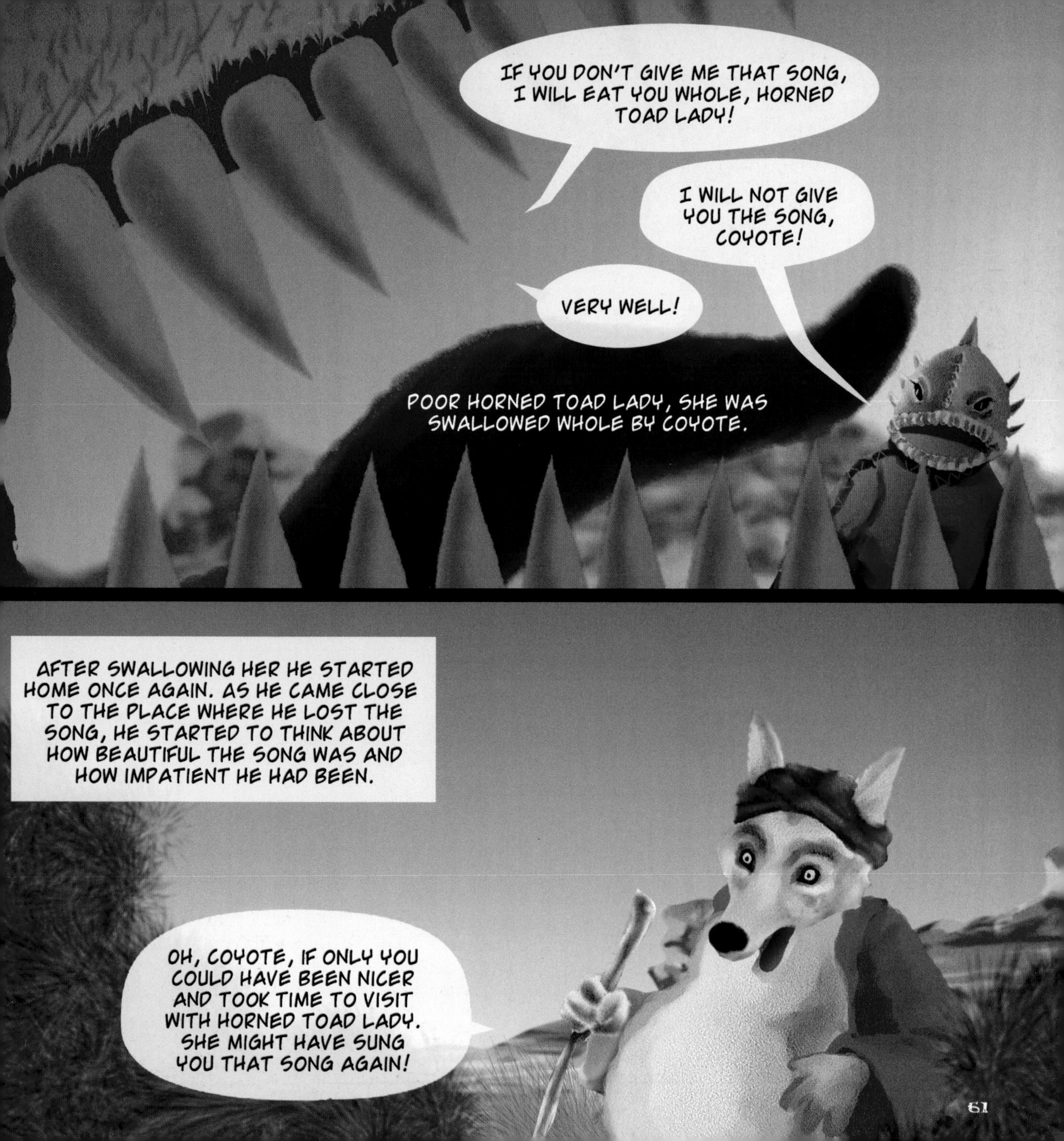
IF YOU DON'T GIVE ME THAT SONG, I WILL EAT YOU WHOLE, HORNED TOAD LADY!
I WILL NOT GIVE YOU THE SONG, COYOTE!
VERY WELL!
POOR HORNED TOAD LADY, SHE WAS SWALLOWED WHOLE BY COYOTE.
AFTER SWALLOWING HER HE STARTED HOME ONCE AGAIN. AS HE CAME CLOSE TO THE PLACE WHERE HE LOST THE SONG, HE STARTED TO THINK ABOUT HOW BEAUTIFUL THE SONG WAS AND HOW IMPATIENT HE HAD BEEN.
OH, COYOTE, IF ONLY YOU COULD HAVE BEEN NICER AND TOOK TIME TO VISIT WITH HORNED TOAD LADY. SHE MIGHT HAVE SUNG YOU THAT SONG AGAIN!

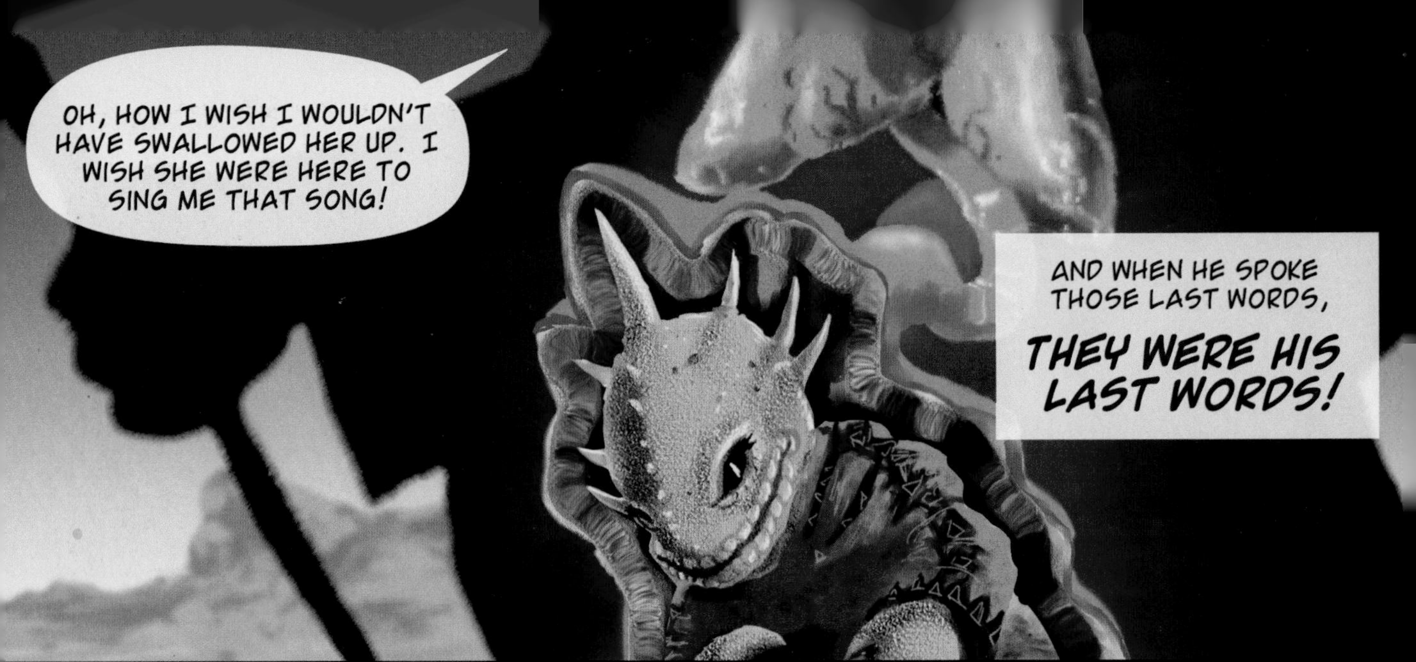
OH, HOW I WISH I WOULDN'T HAVE SWALLOWED HER UP. I WISH SHE WERE HERE TO SING ME THAT SONG!
AND WHEN HE SPOKE THOSE LAST WORDS, THEY WERE HIS LAST WORDS!

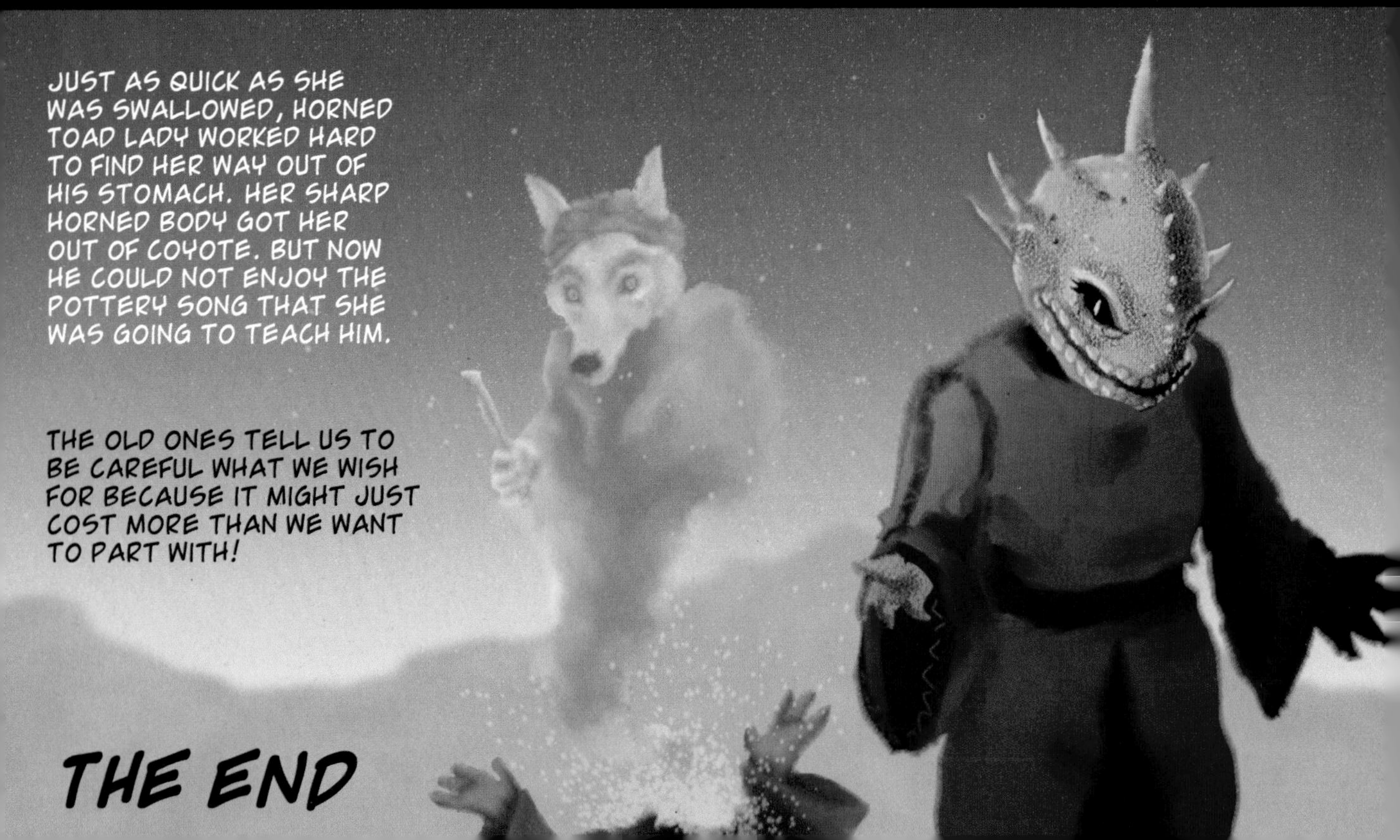
JUST AS QUICK AS SHE WAS SWALLOWED, HORNED TOAD LADY WORKED HARD TO FIND HER WAY OUT OF HIS STOMACH. HER SHARP HORNED BODY GOT HER OUT OF COYOTE. BUT NOW HE COULD NOT ENJOY THE POTTERY SONG THAT SHE WAS GOING TO TEACH HIM.
THE OLD ONES TELL US TO BE CAREFUL WHAT WE WISH FOR BECAUSE IT MIGHT JUST COST MORE THAN WE WANT TO PART WITH!
THE END

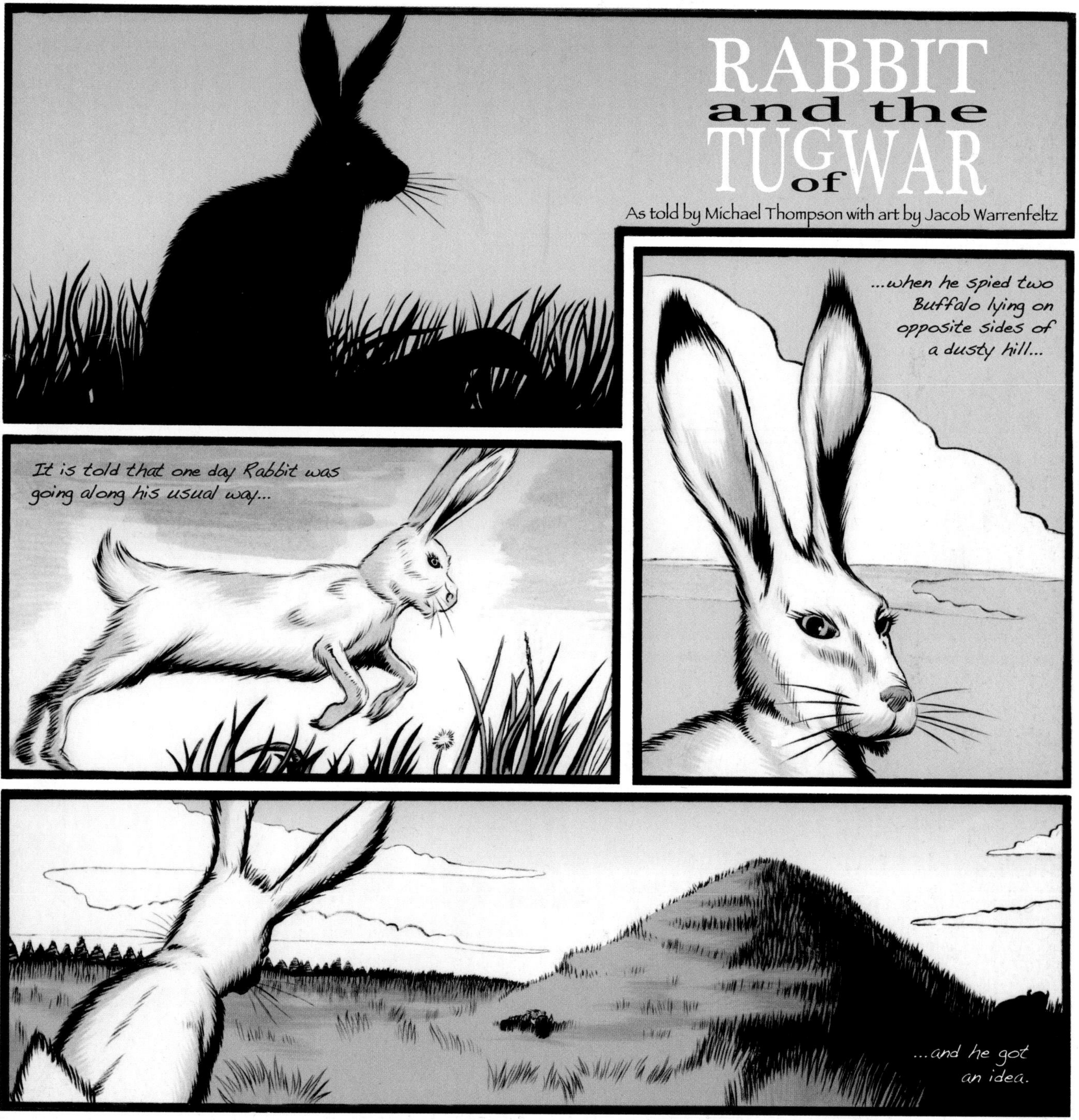
RABBIT and the TUG of WAR
As told by Michael Thompson with art by Jacob Warrenfeltz
It is told that one day Rabbit was going along his usual way...
...when he spied two Buffalo lying on opposite sides of a dusty hill...
...and he got an idea.

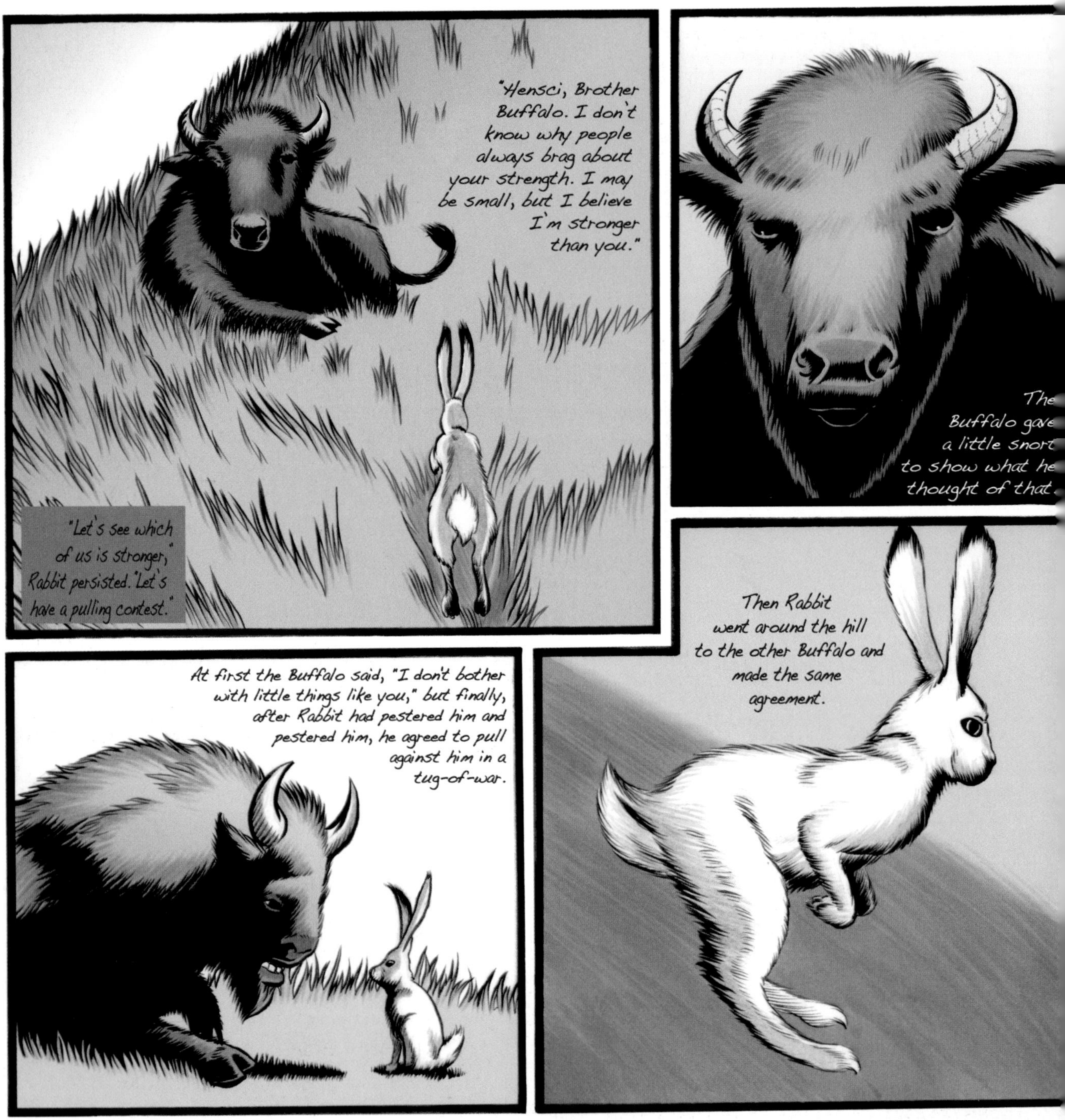
"Hensci, Brother Buffalo. I don't know why people always brag about your strength. I may be small, but I believe I'm stronger than you."
"Let's see which of us is stronger," Rabbit persisted. "Let's have a pulling contest."
The Buffalo gave a little snort to show what he thought of that.
At first the Buffalo said, "I don't bother with little things like you," but finally, after Rabbit had pestered him and pestered him, he agreed to pull against him in a tug-of-war.
Then Rabbit went around the hill to the other Buffalo and made the same agreement.

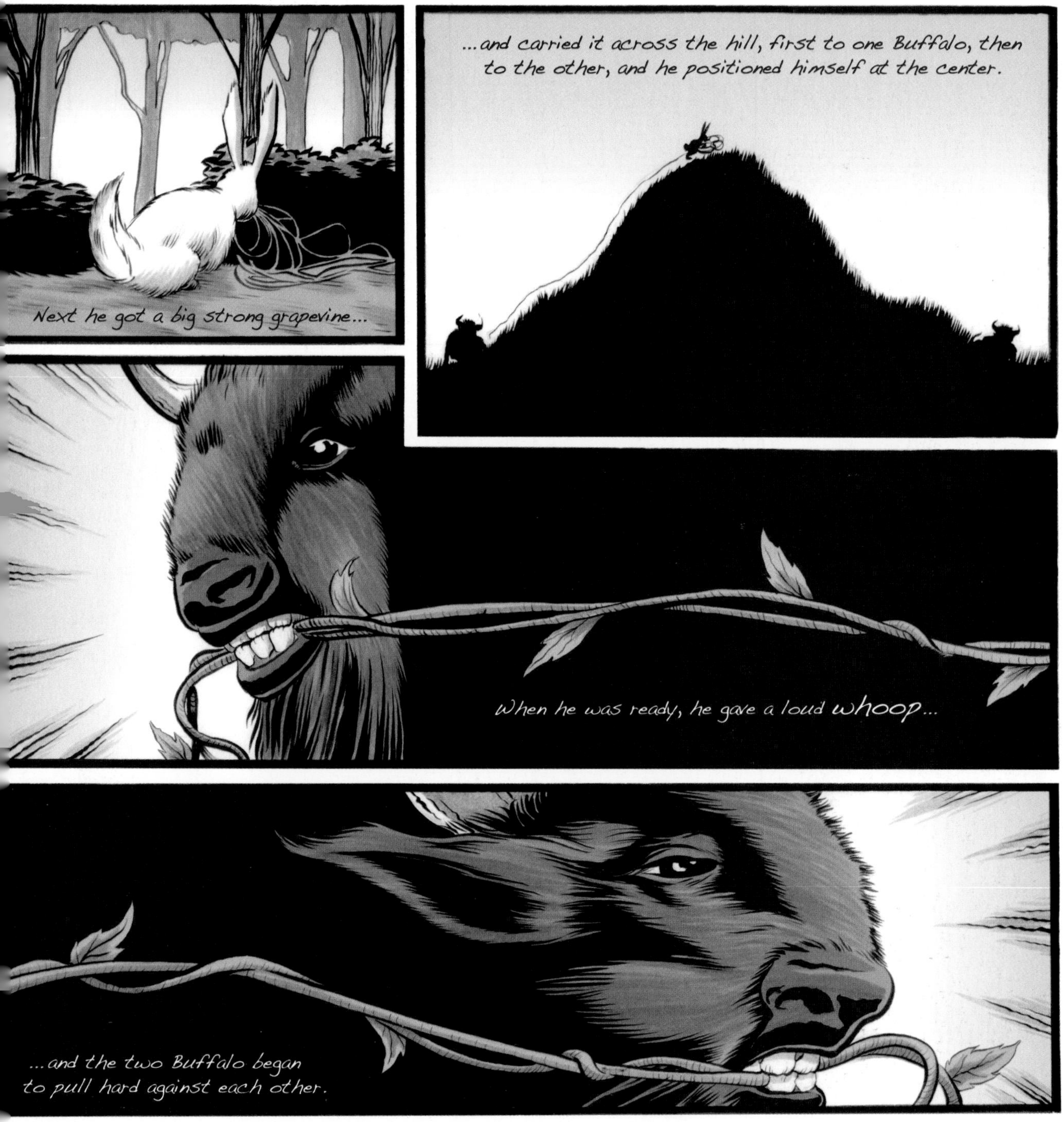

Next he got a big strong grapevine...
...and carried it across the hill, first to one Buffalo, then to the other, and he positioned himself at the center.
When he was ready, he gave a loud whoop...
...and the two Buffalo began to pull hard against each other.

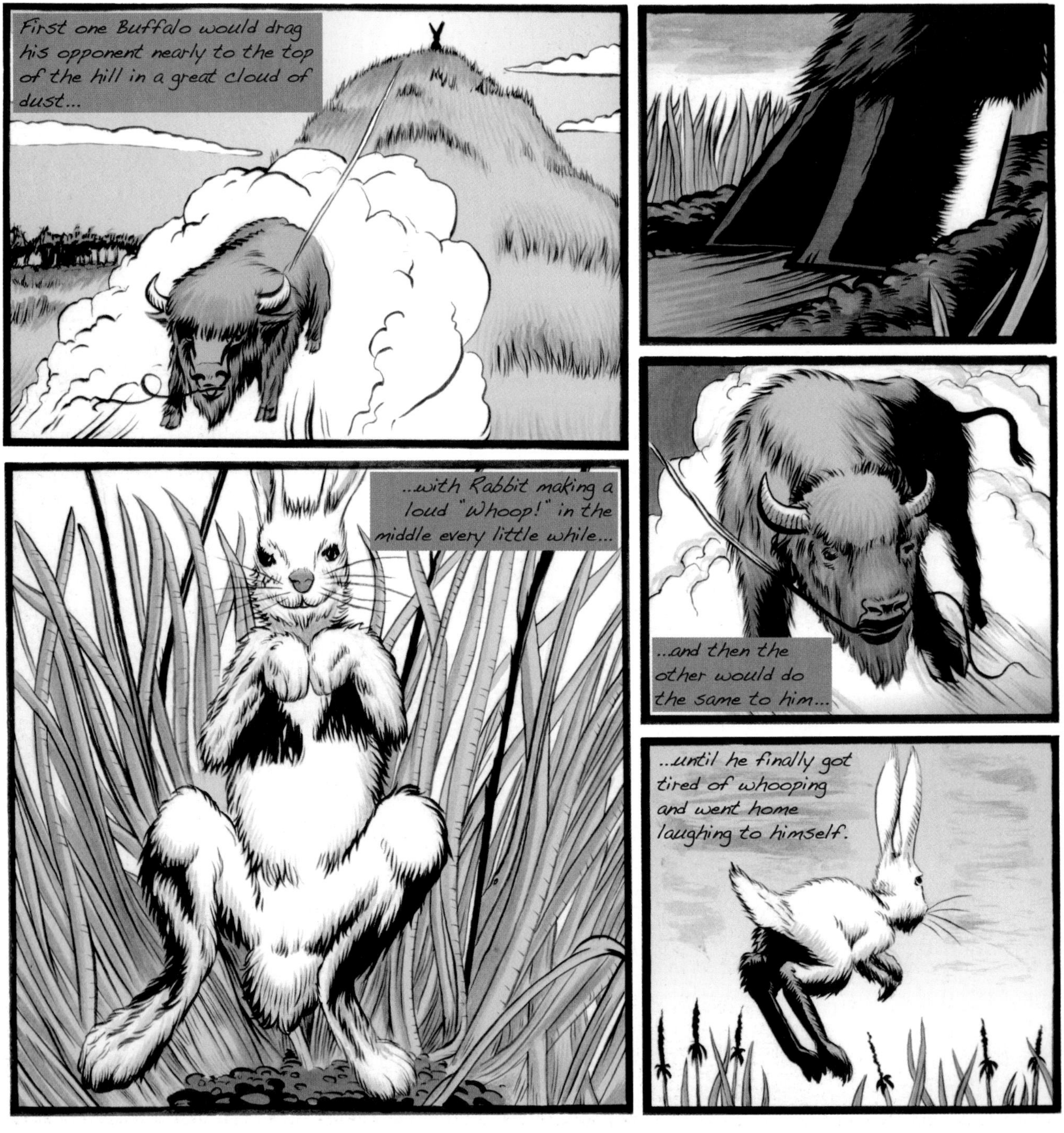
First one Buffalo would drag his opponent nearly to the top of the hill in a great cloud of dust...
...with Rabbit making a loud "Whoop!" in the middle every little while...
...and then the other would do the same to him...
...until he finally got tired of whooping and went home laughing to himself.

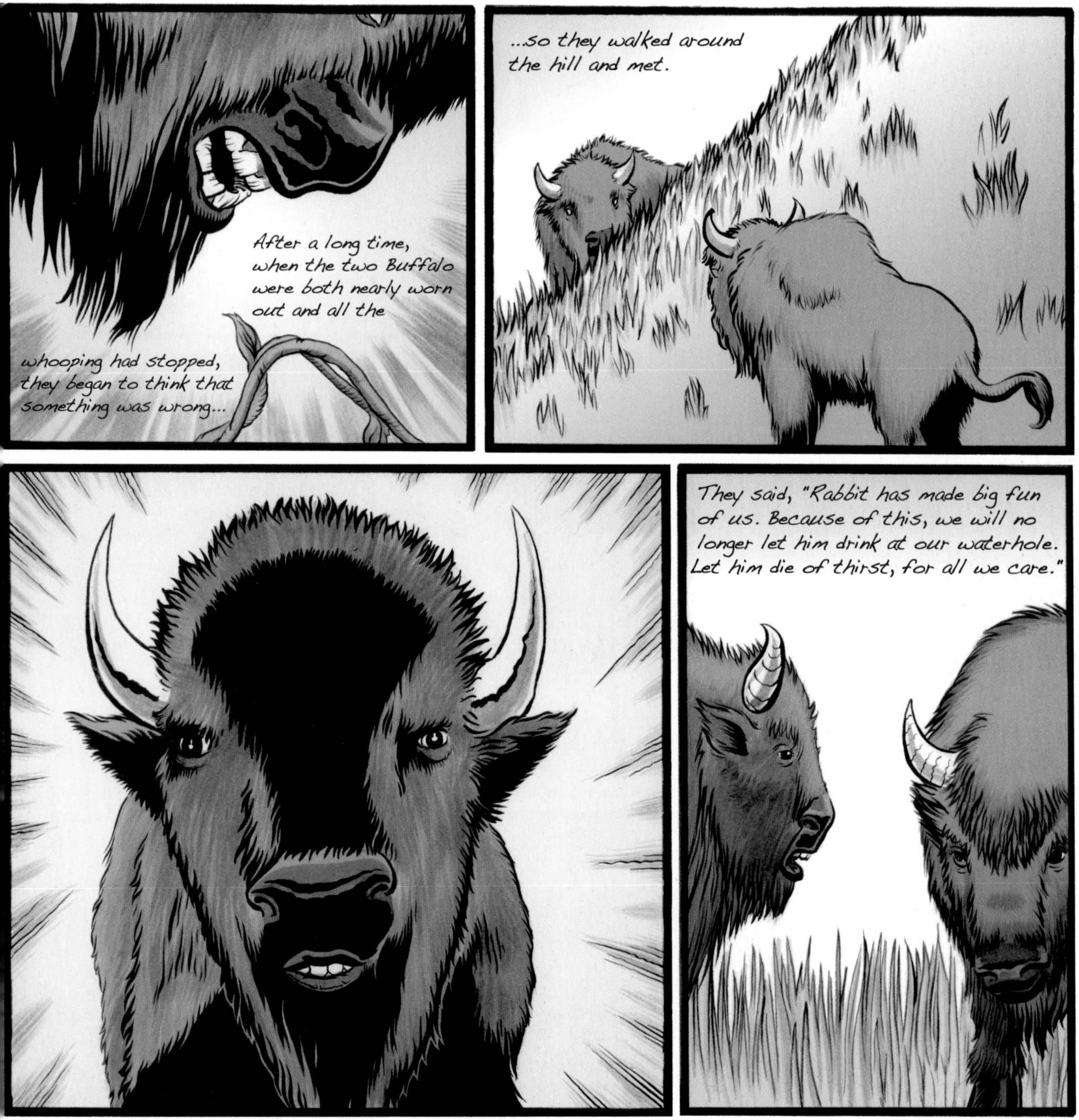
After a long time, when the two Buffalo were both nearly worn out and all the
whooping had stopped, they began to think that something was wrong...
...so they walked around the hill and met.
They said, "Rabbit has made big fun of us. Because of this, we will no longer let him drink at our waterhole. Let him die of thirst, for all we care."

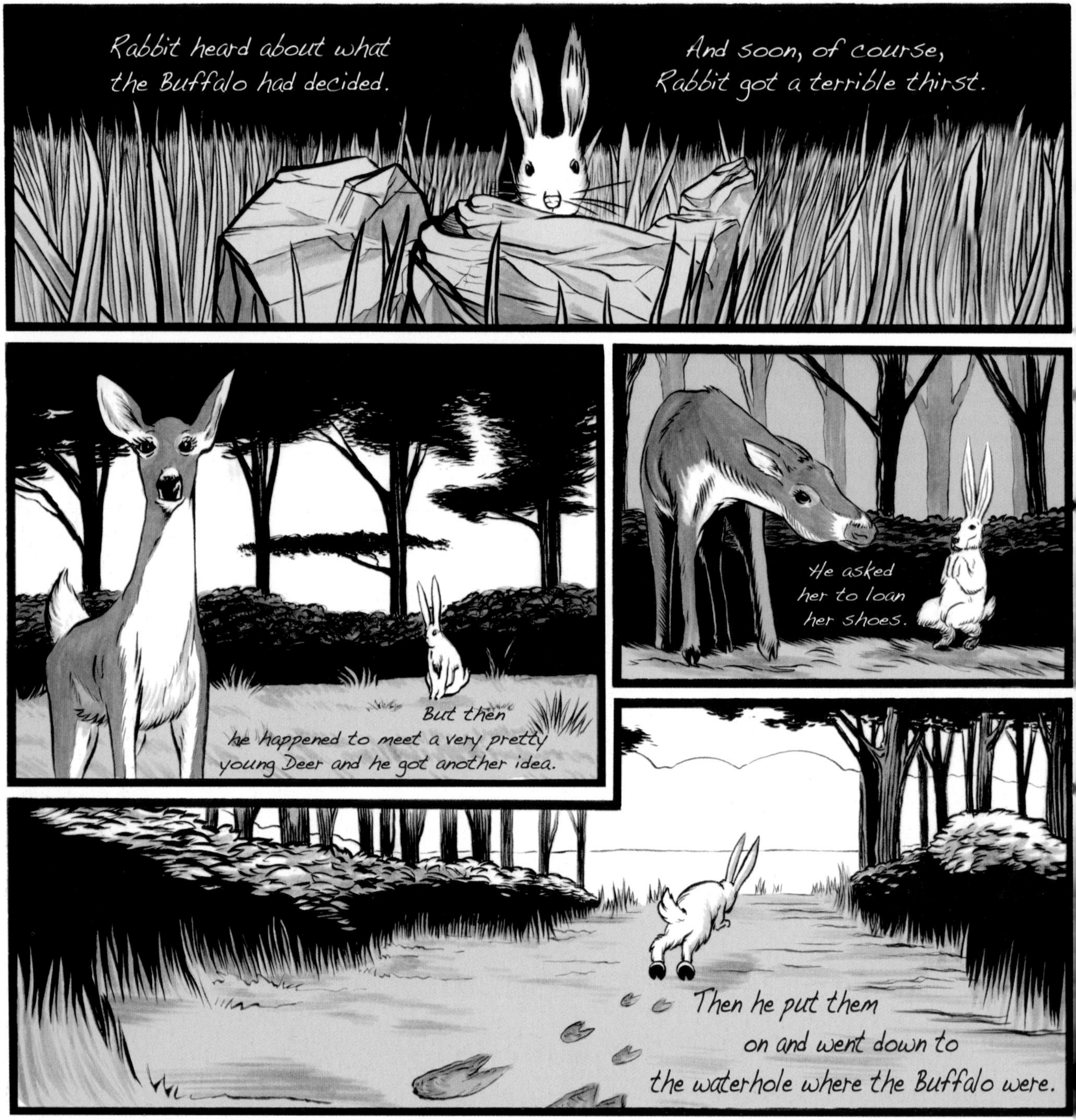
Rabbit heard about what the Buffalo had decided.
And soon, of course, Rabbit got a terrible thirst.
But then he happened to meet a very pretty young Deer and he got another idea.
He asked her to loan her shoes.
Then he put them on and went down to the waterhole where the Buffalo were.

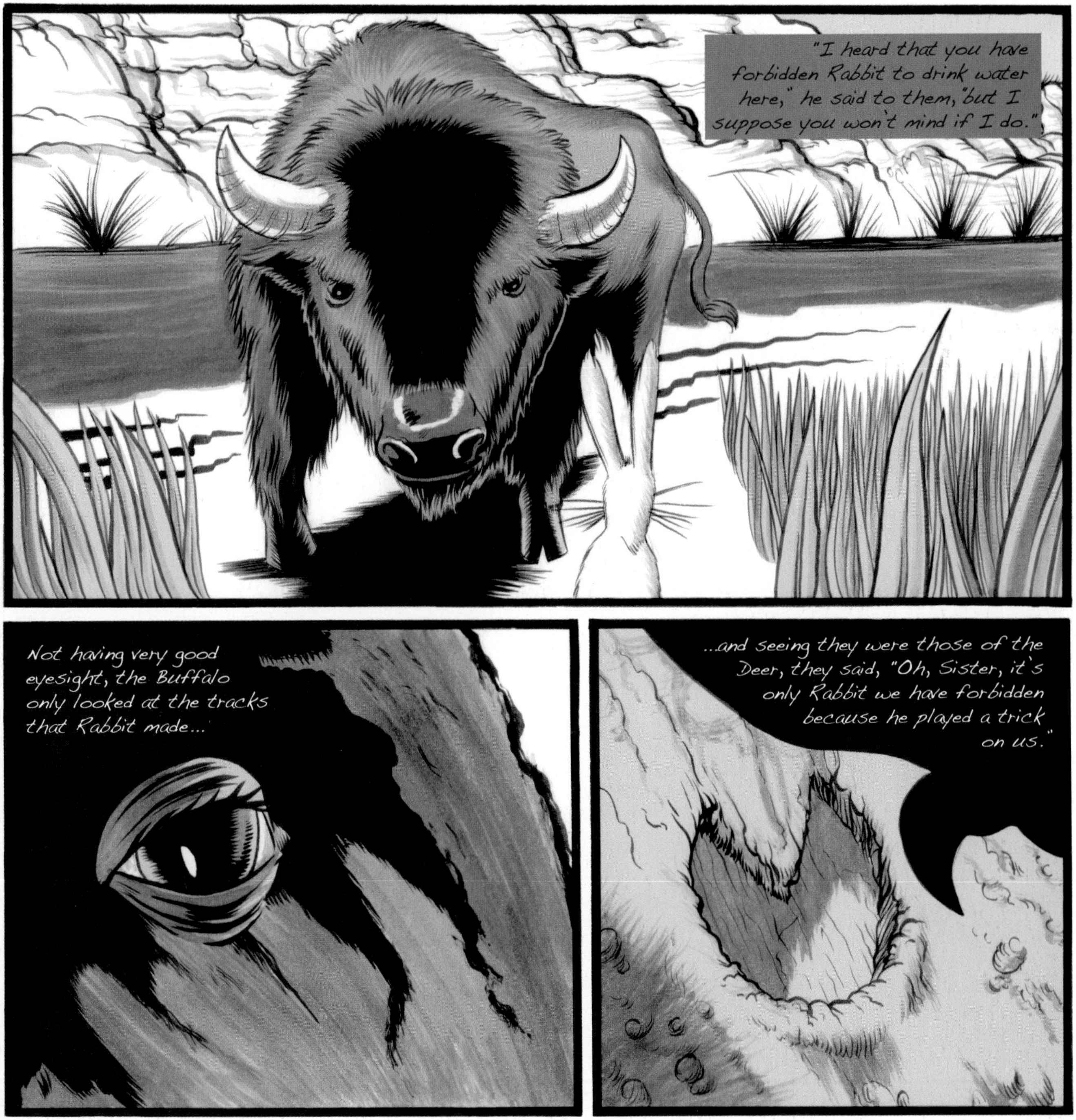
"I heard that you have forbidden Rabbit to drink water here," he said to them, "but I suppose you won't mind if I do."
Not having very good eyesight, the Buffalo only looked at the tracks that Rabbit made...
...and seeing they were those of the Deer, they said, "Oh, Sister, it's only Rabbit we have forbidden because he played a trick on us."

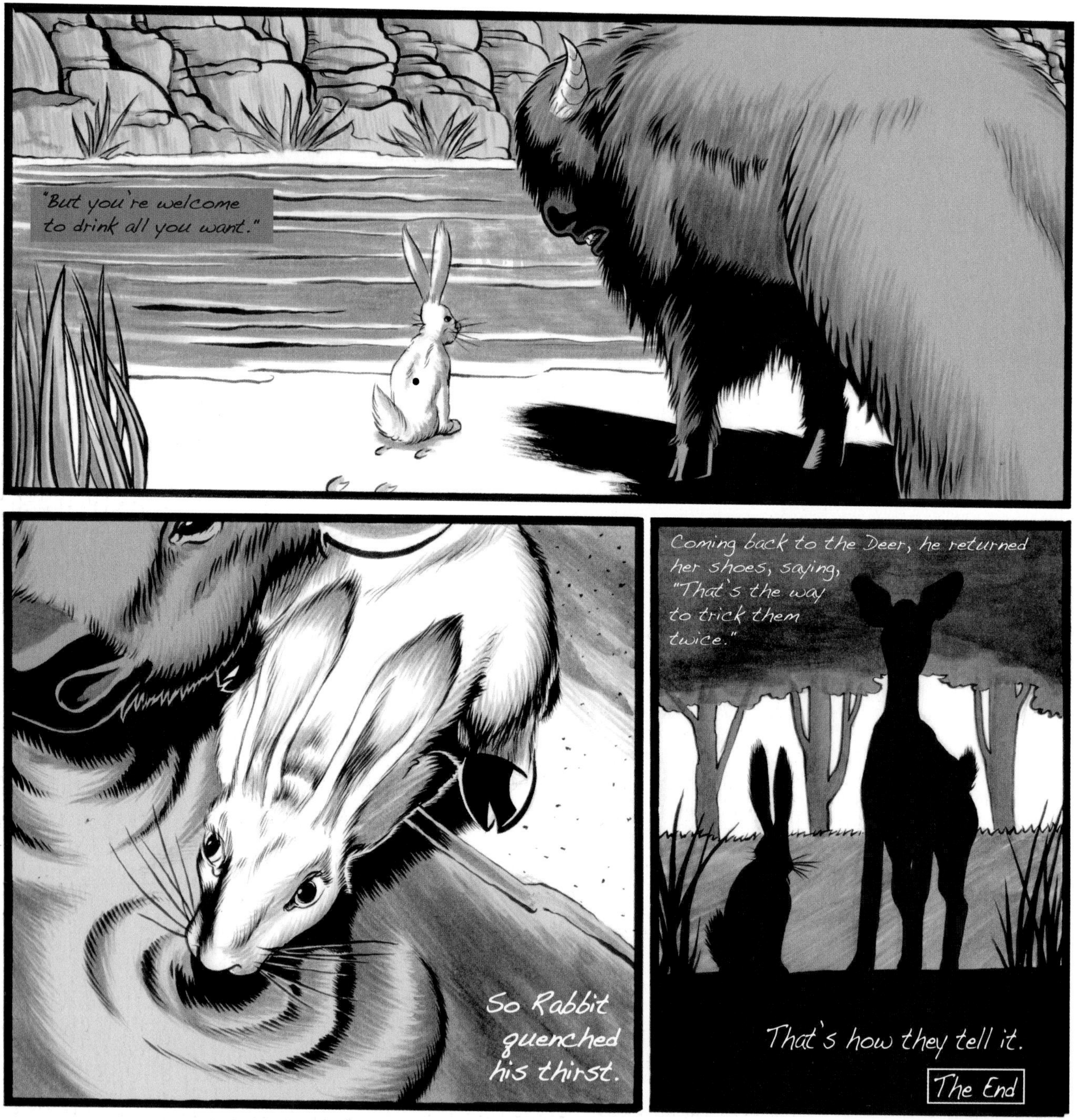
"But you're welcome to drink all you want."
So Rabbit quenched his thirst.
Coming back to the Deer, he returned her shoes, saying, "That's the way to trick them twice."
That's how they tell it.
The End

MOSHUP'S BRIDGE

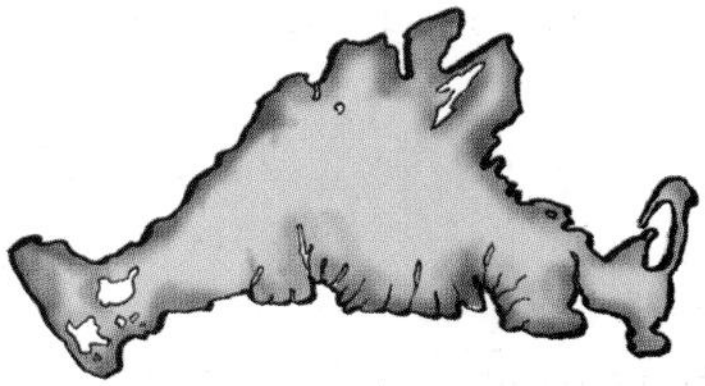

As told by Jonathan Perry, with art by Chris Piers & colors by Scott White

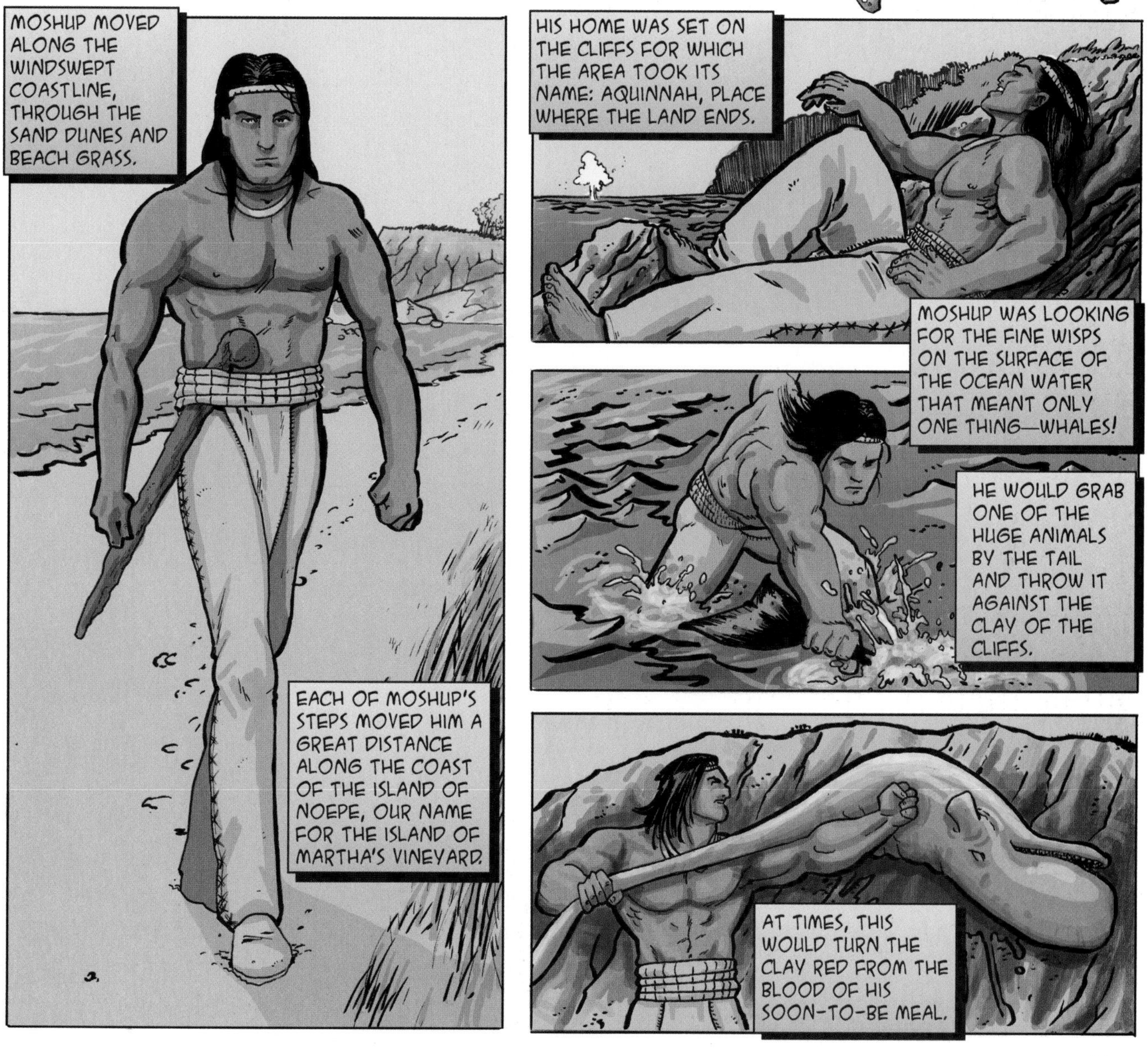
MOSHUP MOVED ALONG THE WINDSWEPT COASTLINE, THROUGH THE SAND DUNES AND BEACH GRASS.
EACH OF MOSHUP'S STEPS MOVED HIM A GREAT DISTANCE ALONG THE COAST OF THE ISLAND OF NOEPE, OUR NAME FOR THE ISLAND OF MARTHA'S VINEYARD.
HIS HOME WAS SET ON THE CLIFFS FOR WHICH THE AREA TOOK ITS NAME: AQUINNAH, PLACE WHERE THE LAND ENDS.
MOSHUP WAS LOOKING FOR THE FINE WISPS ON THE SURFACE OF THE OCEAN WATER THAT MEANT ONLY ONE THING—WHALES!
HE WOULD GRAB ONE OF THE HUGE ANIMALS BY THE TAIL AND THROW IT AGAINST THE CLAY OF THE CLIFFS.
AT TIMES, THIS WOULD TURN THE CLAY RED FROM THE BLOOD OF HIS SOON-TO-BE MEAL.

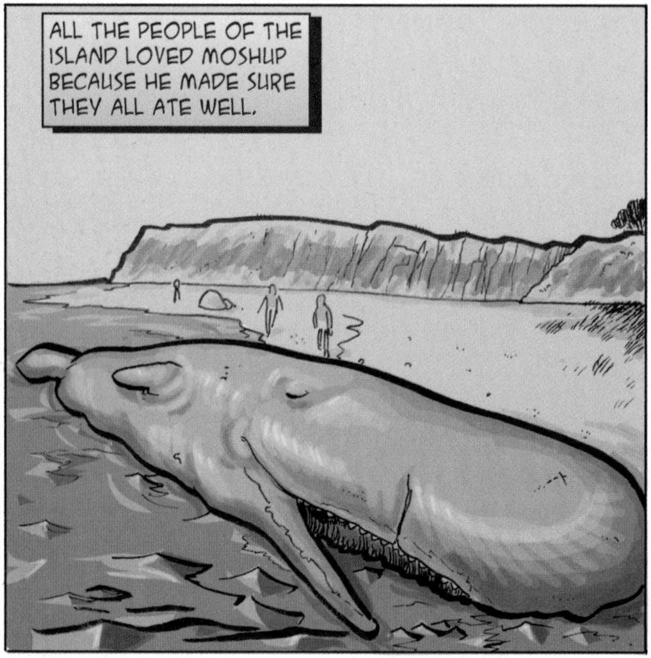
ALL THE PEOPLE OF THE ISLAND LOVED MOSHUP BECAUSE HE MADE SURE THEY ALL ATE WELL.

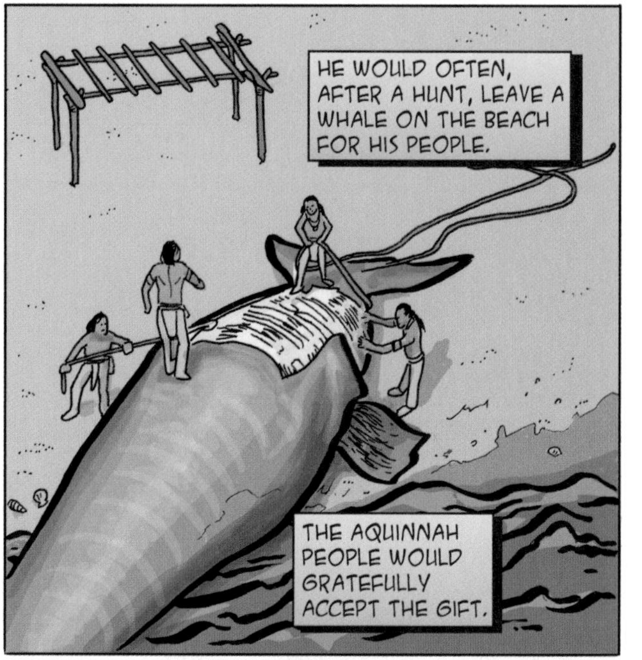
HE WOULD OFTEN, AFTER A HUNT, LEAVE A WHALE ON THE BEACH FOR HIS PEOPLE.
THE AQUINNAH PEOPLE WOULD GRATEFULLY ACCEPT THE GIFT.

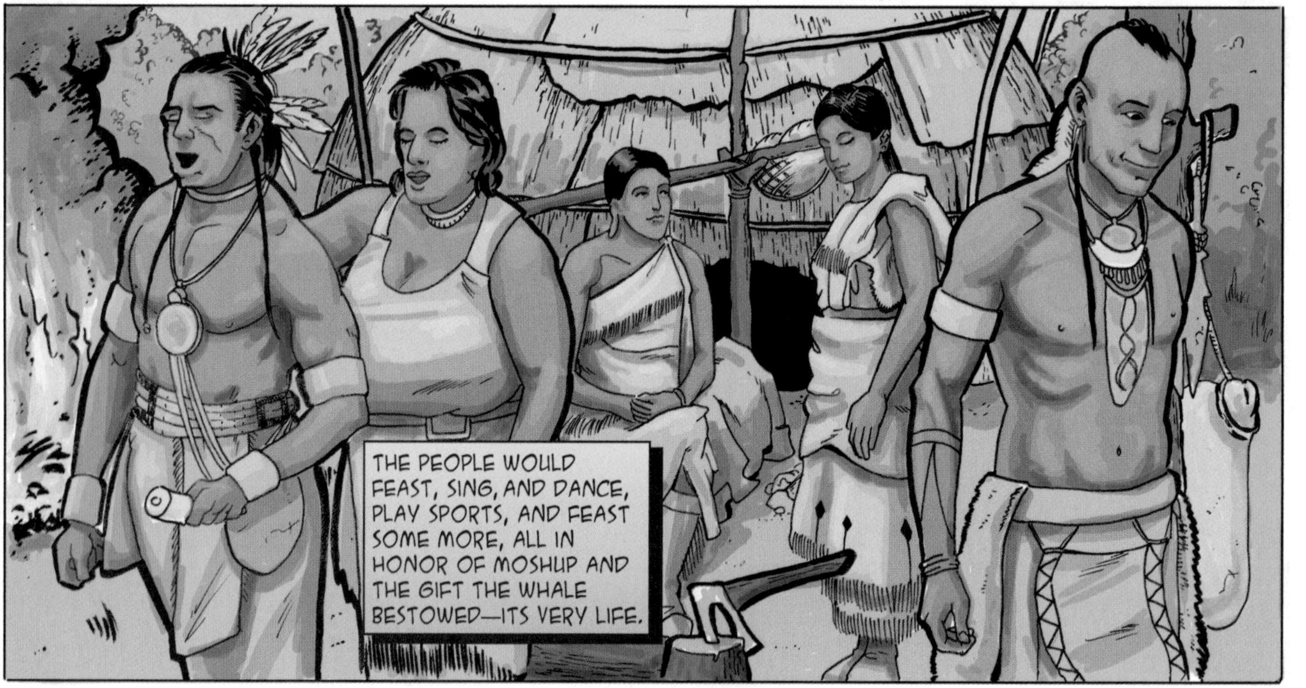
THE PEOPLE WOULD FEAST, SING, AND DANCE, PLAY SPORTS, AND FEAST SOME MORE, ALL IN HONOR OF MOSHUP AND THE GIFT THE WHALE BESTOWED—ITS VERY LIFE.

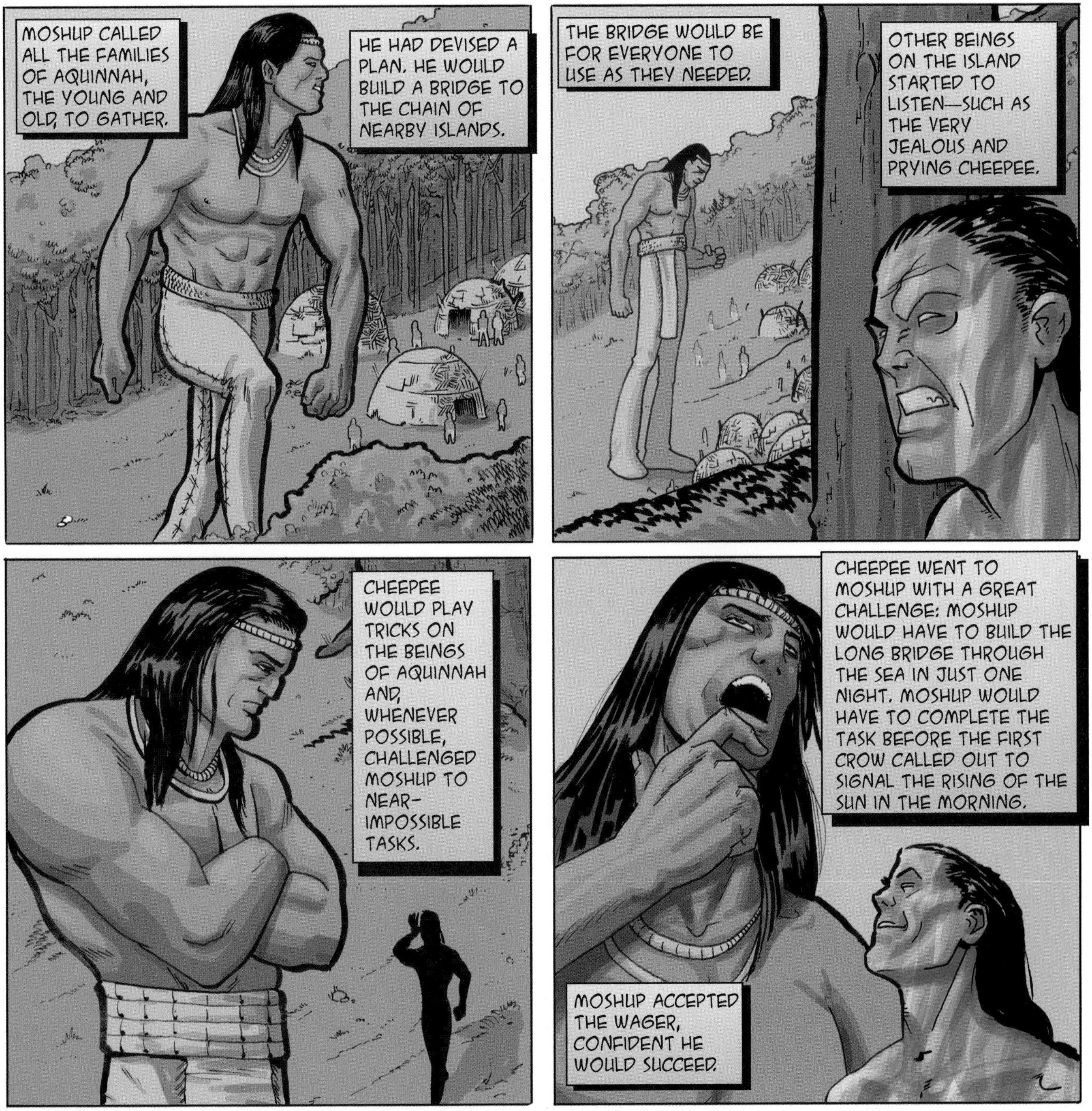
MOSHUP CALLED ALL THE FAMILIES OF AQUINNAH, THE YOUNG AND OLD, TO GATHER.
HE HAD DEVISED A PLAN. HE WOULD BUILD A BRIDGE TO THE CHAIN OF NEARBY ISLANDS.
THE BRIDGE WOULD BE FOR EVERYONE TO USE AS THEY NEEDED.
OTHER BEINGS ON THE ISLAND STARTED TO LISTEN—SUCH AS THE VERY JEALOUS AND PRYING CHEEPEE.
CHEEPEE WOULD PLAY TRICKS ON THE BEINGS OF AQUINNAH AND, WHENEVER POSSIBLE, CHALLENGED MOSHUP TO NEAR-IMPOSSIBLE TASKS.
CHEEPEE WENT TO MOSHUP WITH A GREAT CHALLENGE: MOSHUP WOULD HAVE TO BUILD THE LONG BRIDGE THROUGH THE SEA IN JUST ONE NIGHT. MOSHUP WOULD HAVE TO COMPLETE THE TASK BEFORE THE FIRST CROW CALLED OUT TO SIGNAL THE RISING OF THE SUN IN THE MORNING.
MOSHUP ACCEPTED THE WAGER, CONFIDENT HE WOULD SUCCEED.

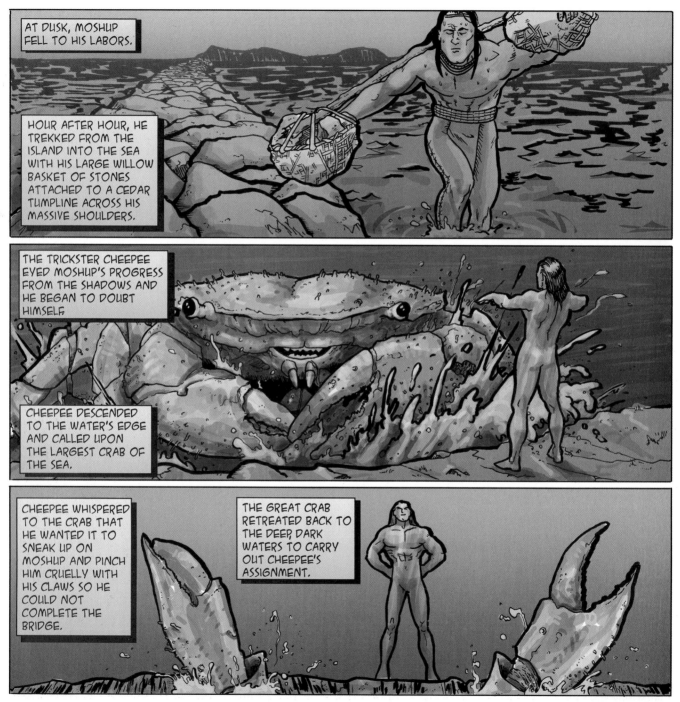

AT DUSK, MOSHUP FELL TO HIS LABORS.

HOUR AFTER HOUR, HE TREKKED FROM THE ISLAND INTO THE SEA WITH HIS LARGE WILLOW BASKET OF STONES ATTACHED TO A CEDAR TUMPLINE ACROSS HIS MASSIVE SHOULDERS.

THE TRICKSTER CHEEPEE EYED MOSHUP'S PROGRESS FROM THE SHADOWS AND HE BEGAN TO DOUBT HIMSELF.

CHEEPEE DESCENDED TO THE WATER'S EDGE AND CALLED UPON THE LARGEST CRAB OF THE SEA.

CHEEPEE WHISPERED TO THE CRAB THAT HE WANTED IT TO SNEAK UP ON MOSHUP AND PINCH HIM CRUELLY WITH HIS CLAWS SO HE COULD NOT COMPLETE THE BRIDGE.

THE GREAT CRAB RETREATED BACK TO THE DEEP, DARK WATERS TO CARRY OUT CHEEPEE'S ASSIGNMENT.

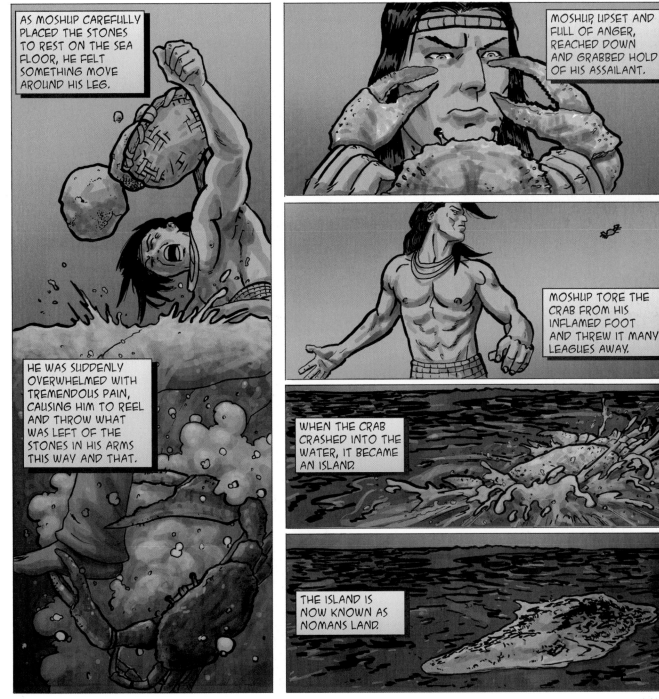

AS MOSHUP CAREFULLY PLACED THE STONES TO REST ON THE SEA FLOOR, HE FELT SOMETHING MOVE AROUND HIS LEG.

HE WAS SUDDENLY OVERWHELMED WITH TREMENDOUS PAIN, CAUSING HIM TO REEL AND THROW WHAT WAS LEFT OF THE STONES IN HIS ARMS THIS WAY AND THAT.

MOSHUP, UPSET AND FULL OF ANGER, REACHED DOWN AND GRABBED HOLD OF HIS ASSAILANT.

MOSHUP TORE THE CRAB FROM HIS INFLAMED FOOT AND THREW IT MANY LEAGUES AWAY.

WHEN THE CRAB CRASHED INTO THE WATER, IT BECAME AN ISLAND.

THE ISLAND IS NOW KNOWN AS NOMANS LAND.

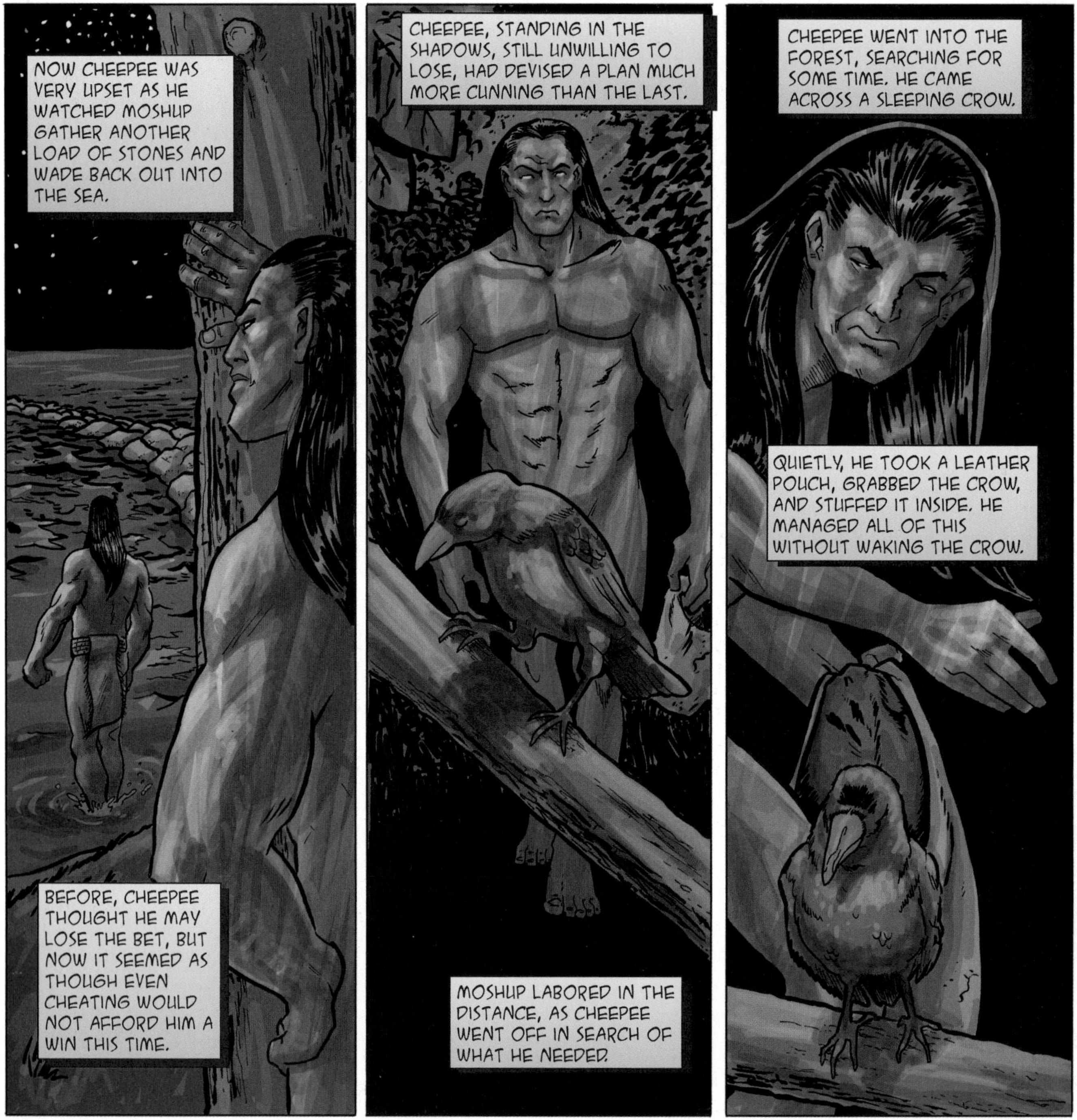

NOW CHEEPEE WAS VERY UPSET AS HE WATCHED MOSHUP GATHER ANOTHER LOAD OF STONES AND WADE BACK OUT INTO THE SEA.
BEFORE, CHEEPEE THOUGHT HE MAY LOSE THE BET, BUT NOW IT SEEMED AS THOUGH EVEN CHEATING WOULD NOT AFFORD HIM A WIN THIS TIME.
CHEEPEE, STANDING IN THE SHADOWS, STILL UNWILLING TO LOSE, HAD DEVISED A PLAN MUCH MORE CUNNING THAN THE LAST.
MOSHUP LABORED IN THE DISTANCE, AS CHEEPEE WENT OFF IN SEARCH OF WHAT HE NEEDED.
CHEEPEE WENT INTO THE FOREST, SEARCHING FOR SOME TIME. HE CAME ACROSS A SLEEPING CROW.
QUIETLY, HE TOOK A LEATHER POUCH, GRABBED THE CROW, AND STUFFED IT INSIDE. HE MANAGED ALL OF THIS WITHOUT WAKING THE CROW.

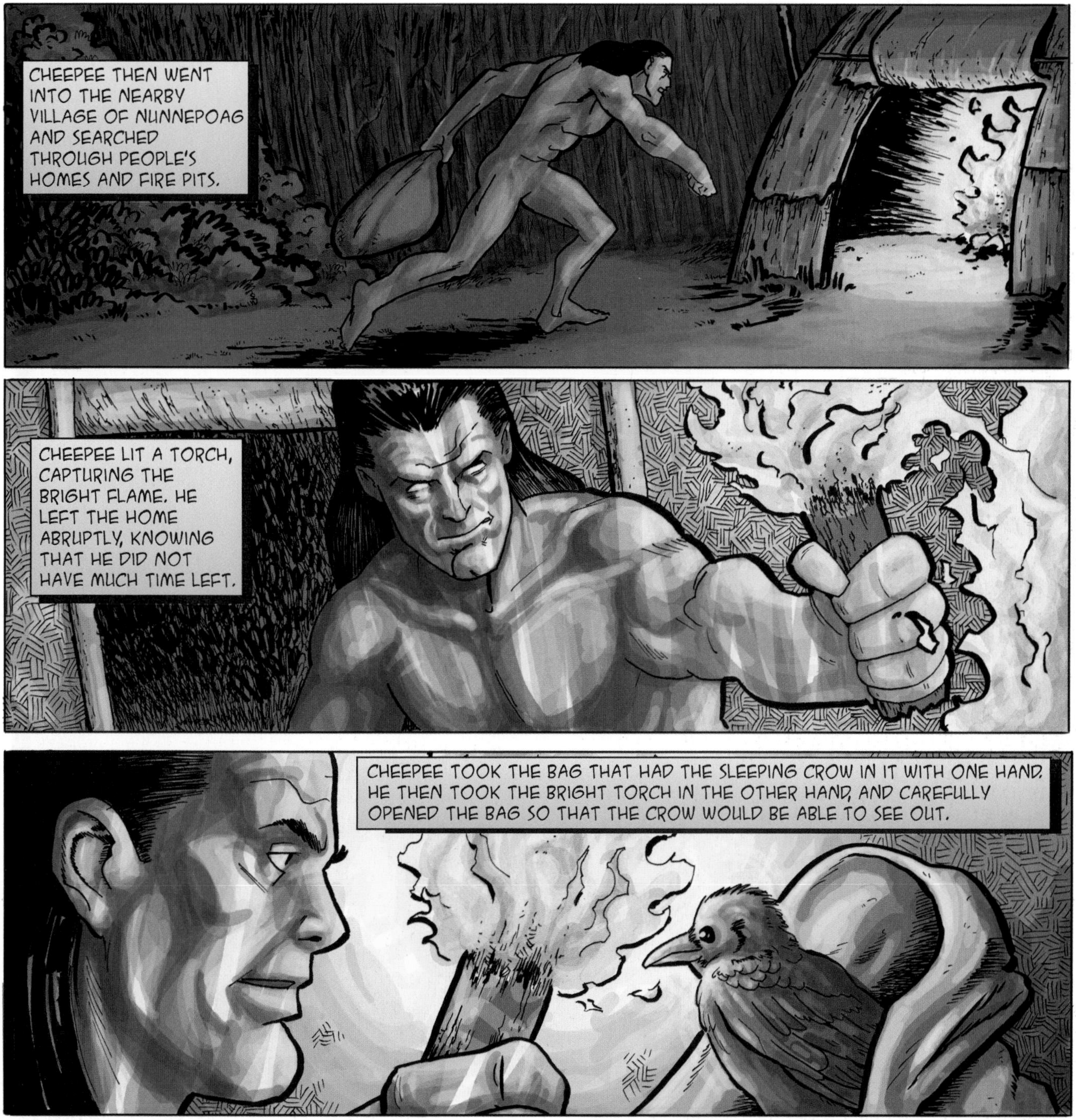
CHEEPEE THEN WENT INTO THE NEARBY VILLAGE OF NUNNEPOAG AND SEARCHED THROUGH PEOPLE'S HOMES AND FIRE PITS.
CHEEPEE LIT A TORCH, CAPTURING THE BRIGHT FLAME. HE LEFT THE HOME ABRUPTLY, KNOWING THAT HE DID NOT HAVE MUCH TIME LEFT.
CHEEPEE TOOK THE BAG THAT HAD THE SLEEPING CROW IN IT WITH ONE HAND. HE THEN TOOK THE BRIGHT TORCH IN THE OTHER HAND, AND CAREFULLY OPENED THE BAG SO THAT THE CROW WOULD BE ABLE TO SEE OUT.

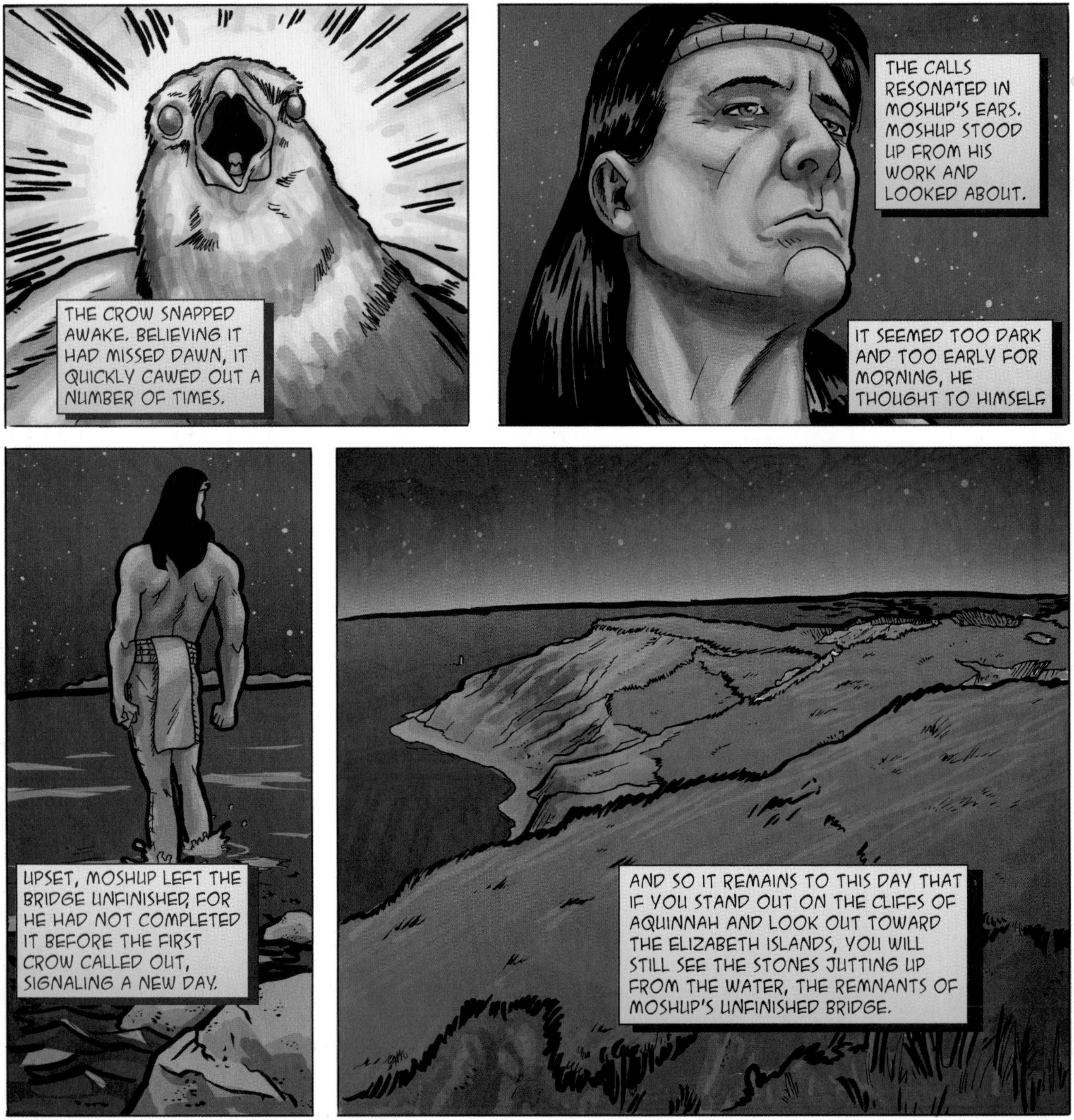
THE CROW SNAPPED AWAKE. BELIEVING IT HAD MISSED DAWN, IT QUICKLY CAWED OUT A NUMBER OF TIMES.
THE CALLS RESONATED IN MOSHUP'S EARS. MOSHUP STOOD UP FROM HIS WORK AND LOOKED ABOUT.
IT SEEMED TOO DARK AND TOO EARLY FOR MORNING, HE THOUGHT TO HIMSELF.
UPSET, MOSHUP LEFT THE BRIDGE UNFINISHED, FOR HE HAD NOT COMPLETED IT BEFORE THE FIRST CROW CALLED OUT, SIGNALING A NEW DAY.
AND SO IT REMAINS TO THIS DAY THAT IF YOU STAND OUT ON THE CLIFFS OF AQUINNAH AND LOOK OUT TOWARD THE ELIZABETH ISLANDS, YOU WILL STILL SEE THE STONES JUTTING UP FROM THE WATER, THE REMNANTS OF MOSHUP'S UNFINISHED BRIDGE.

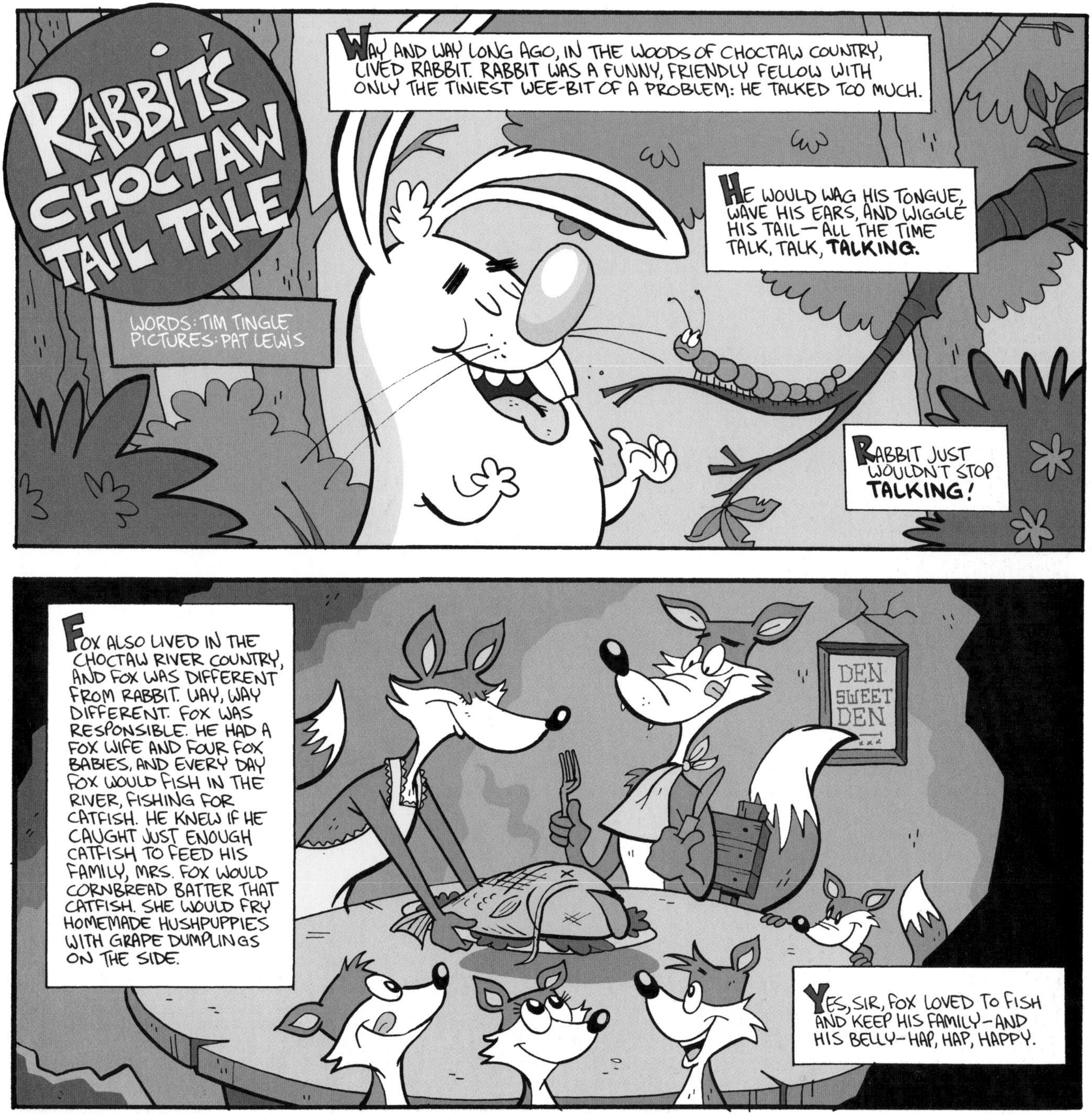
RABBIT'S CHOCTAW TAIL TALE
WORDS: TIM TINGLE
PICTURES: PAT LEWIS
WAY AND WAY LONG AGO, IN THE WOODS OF CHOCTAW COUNTRY, LIVED RABBIT. RABBIT WAS A FUNNY, FRIENDLY FELLOW WITH ONLY THE TINIEST WEE-BIT OF A PROBLEM: HE TALKED TOO MUCH.
HE WOULD WAG HIS TONGUE, WAVE HIS EARS, AND WIGGLE HIS TAIL—ALL THE TIME TALK, TALK, **TALKING.**
RABBIT JUST WOULDN'T STOP **TALKING!**
FOX ALSO LIVED IN THE CHOCTAW RIVER COUNTRY, AND FOX WAS DIFFERENT FROM RABBIT. WAY, WAY DIFFERENT. FOX WAS RESPONSIBLE. HE HAD A FOX WIFE AND FOUR FOX BABIES, AND EVERY DAY FOX WOULD FISH IN THE RIVER, FISHING FOR CATFISH. HE KNEW IF HE CAUGHT JUST ENOUGH CATFISH TO FEED HIS FAMILY, MRS. FOX WOULD CORNBREAD BATTER THAT CATFISH. SHE WOULD FRY HOMEMADE HUSHPUPPIES WITH GRAPE DUMPLINGS ON THE SIDE.
DEN SWEET DEN
YES, SIR, FOX LOVED TO FISH AND KEEP HIS FAMILY—AND HIS BELLY—HAP, HAP, HAPPY.

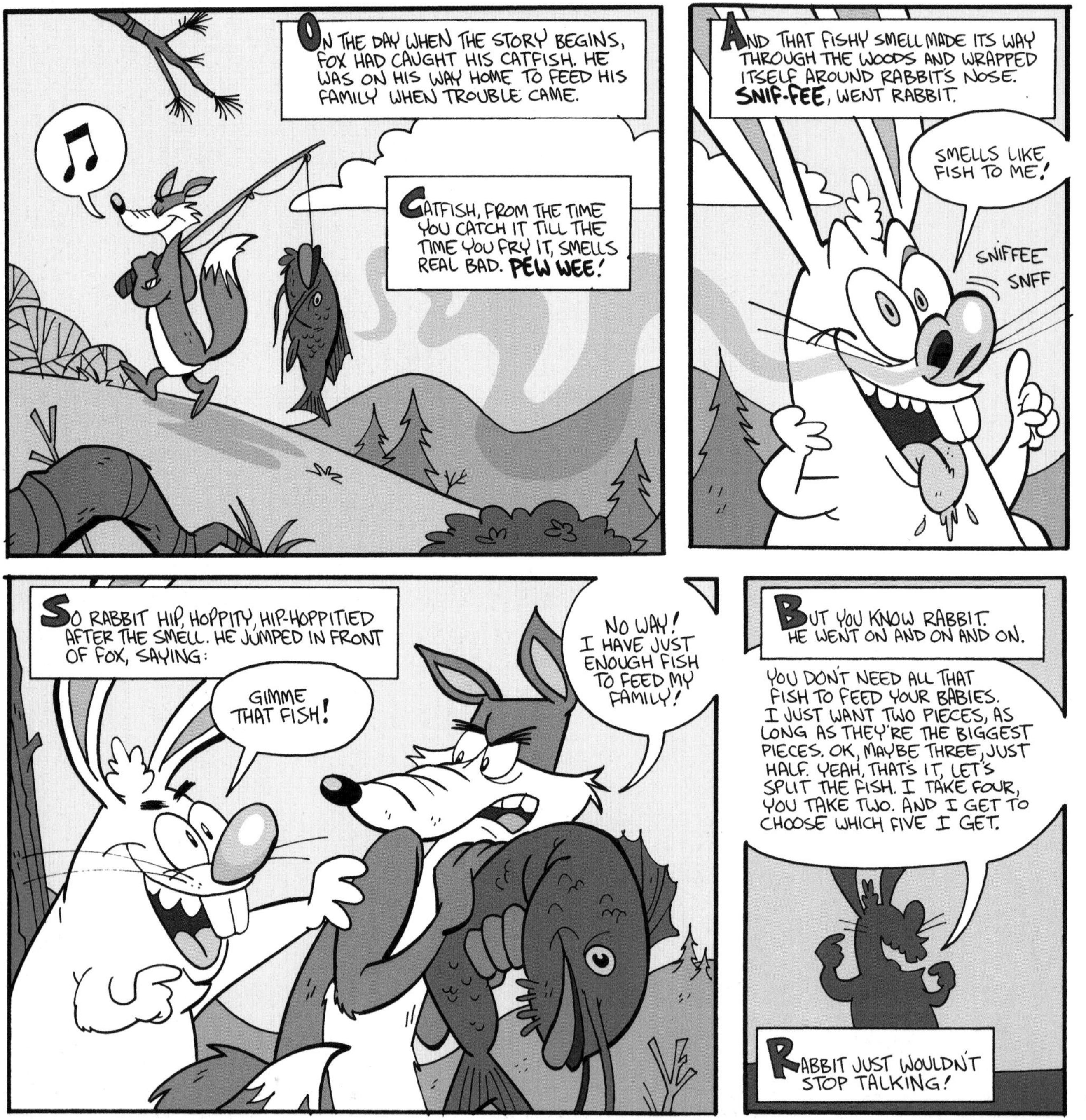
ON THE DAY WHEN THE STORY BEGINS, FOX HAD CAUGHT HIS CATFISH. HE WAS ON HIS WAY HOME TO FEED HIS FAMILY WHEN TROUBLE CAME.
♫
CATFISH, FROM THE TIME YOU CATCH IT TILL THE TIME YOU FRY IT, SMELLS REAL BAD. PEW WEE!
AND THAT FISHY SMELL MADE ITS WAY THROUGH THE WOODS AND WRAPPED ITSELF AROUND RABBIT'S NOSE. SNIF-FEE, WENT RABBIT.
SMELLS LIKE FISH TO ME!
SNIFFEE
SNFF
SO RABBIT HIP, HOPPITY, HIP-HOPPITIED AFTER THE SMELL. HE JUMPED IN FRONT OF FOX, SAYING:
GIMME THAT FISH!
NO WAY! I HAVE JUST ENOUGH FISH TO FEED MY FAMILY!
BUT YOU KNOW RABBIT. HE WENT ON AND ON AND ON.
YOU DON'T NEED ALL THAT FISH TO FEED YOUR BABIES. I JUST WANT TWO PIECES, AS LONG AS THEY'RE THE BIGGEST PIECES. OK, MAYBE THREE, JUST HALF. YEAH, THAT'S IT, LET'S SPLIT THE FISH. I TAKE FOUR, YOU TAKE TWO. AND I GET TO CHOOSE WHICH FIVE I GET.
RABBIT JUST WOULDN'T STOP TALKING!

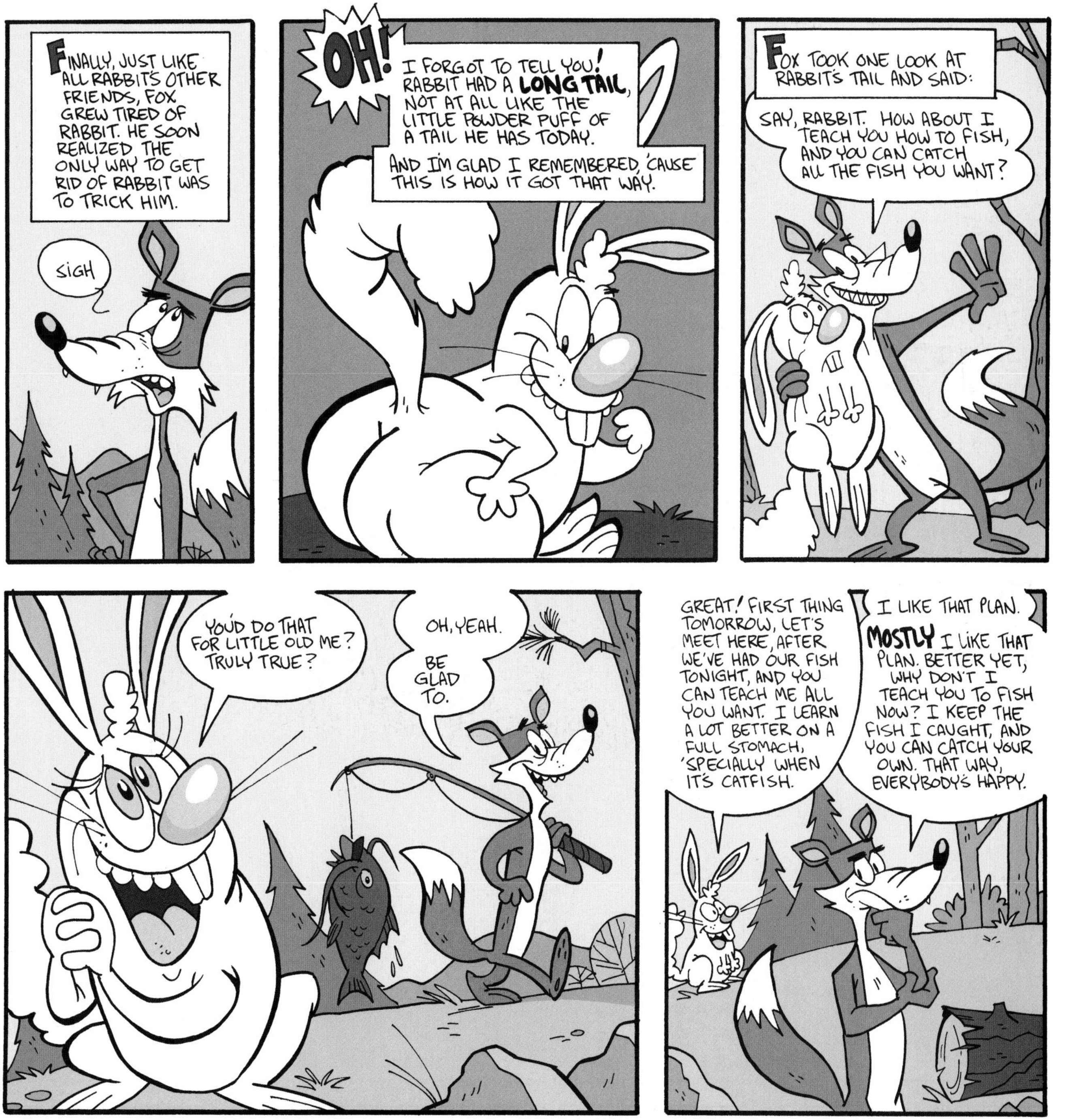

FINALLY, JUST LIKE ALL RABBIT'S OTHER FRIENDS, FOX GREW TIRED OF RABBIT. HE SOON REALIZED THE ONLY WAY TO GET RID OF RABBIT WAS TO TRICK HIM.
SIGH
OH!
I FORGOT TO TELL YOU! RABBIT HAD A LONG TAIL, NOT AT ALL LIKE THE LITTLE POWDER PUFF OF A TAIL HE HAS TODAY.
AND I'M GLAD I REMEMBERED, 'CAUSE THIS IS HOW IT GOT THAT WAY.
FOX TOOK ONE LOOK AT RABBIT'S TAIL AND SAID:
SAY, RABBIT. HOW ABOUT I TEACH YOU HOW TO FISH, AND YOU CAN CATCH ALL THE FISH YOU WANT?
YOU'D DO THAT FOR LITTLE OLD ME? TRULY TRUE?
OH, YEAH.
BE GLAD TO.
I LIKE THAT PLAN.
MOSTLY I LIKE THAT PLAN. BETTER YET, WHY DON'T I TEACH YOU TO FISH NOW? I KEEP THE FISH I CAUGHT, AND YOU CAN CATCH YOUR OWN. THAT WAY, EVERYBODY'S HAPPY.
GREAT! FIRST THING TOMORROW, LET'S MEET HERE, AFTER WE'VE HAD OUR FISH TONIGHT, AND YOU CAN TEACH ME ALL YOU WANT. I LEARN A LOT BETTER ON A FULL STOMACH, 'SPECIALLY WHEN IT'S CATFISH.

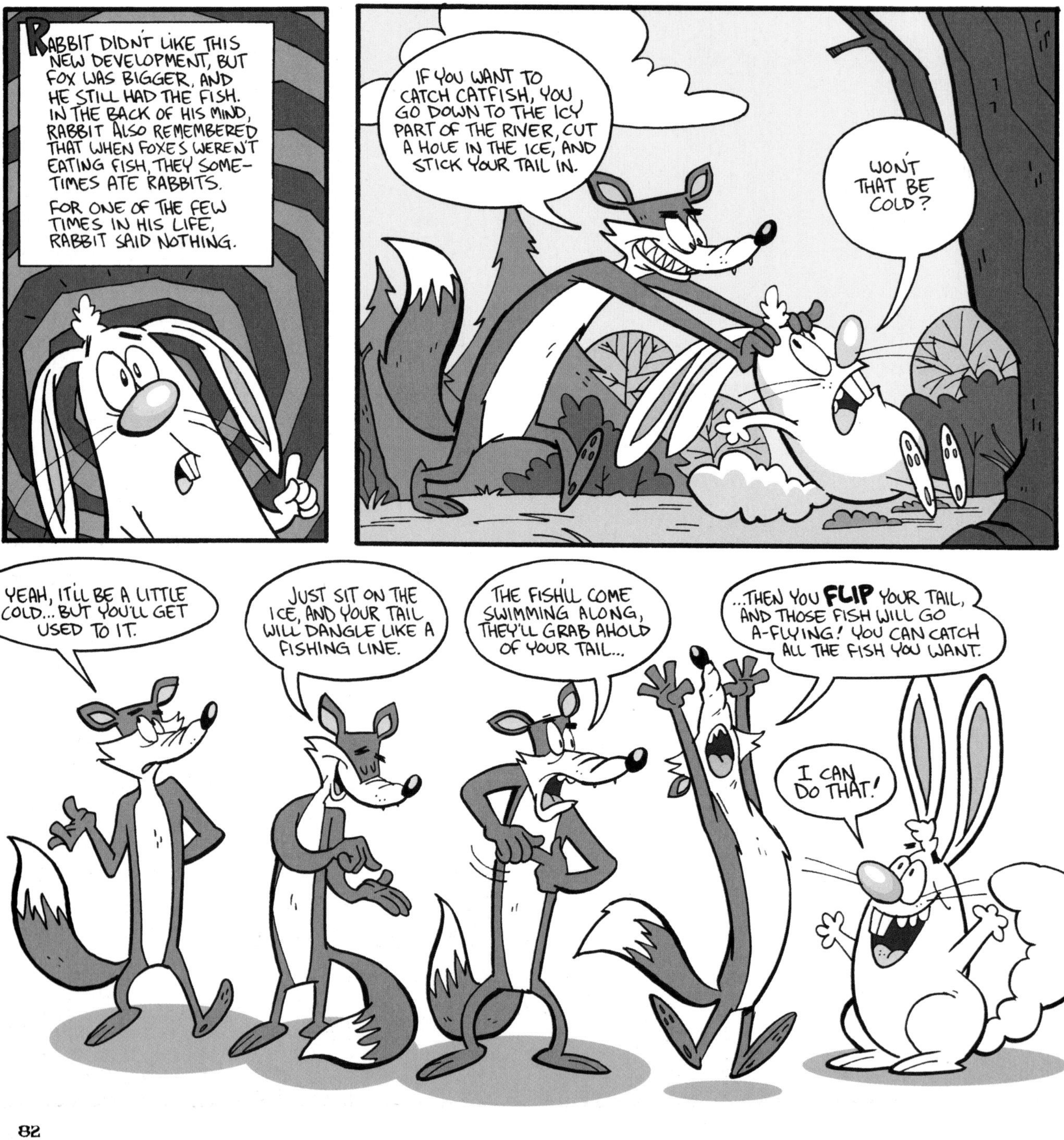
RABBIT DIDN'T LIKE THIS NEW DEVELOPMENT, BUT FOX WAS BIGGER, AND HE STILL HAD THE FISH. IN THE BACK OF HIS MIND, RABBIT ALSO REMEMBERED THAT WHEN FOXES WEREN'T EATING FISH, THEY SOMETIMES ATE RABBITS.
FOR ONE OF THE FEW TIMES IN HIS LIFE, RABBIT SAID NOTHING.
IF YOU WANT TO CATCH CATFISH, YOU GO DOWN TO THE ICY PART OF THE RIVER, CUT A HOLE IN THE ICE, AND STICK YOUR TAIL IN.
WON'T THAT BE COLD?
YEAH, IT'LL BE A LITTLE COLD... BUT YOU'LL GET USED TO IT.
JUST SIT ON THE ICE, AND YOUR TAIL WILL DANGLE LIKE A FISHING LINE.
THE FISH'LL COME SWIMMING ALONG, THEY'LL GRAB AHOLD OF YOUR TAIL...
...THEN YOU **FLIP** YOUR TAIL, AND THOSE FISH WILL GO A-FLYING! YOU CAN CATCH ALL THE FISH YOU WANT.
I CAN DO THAT!

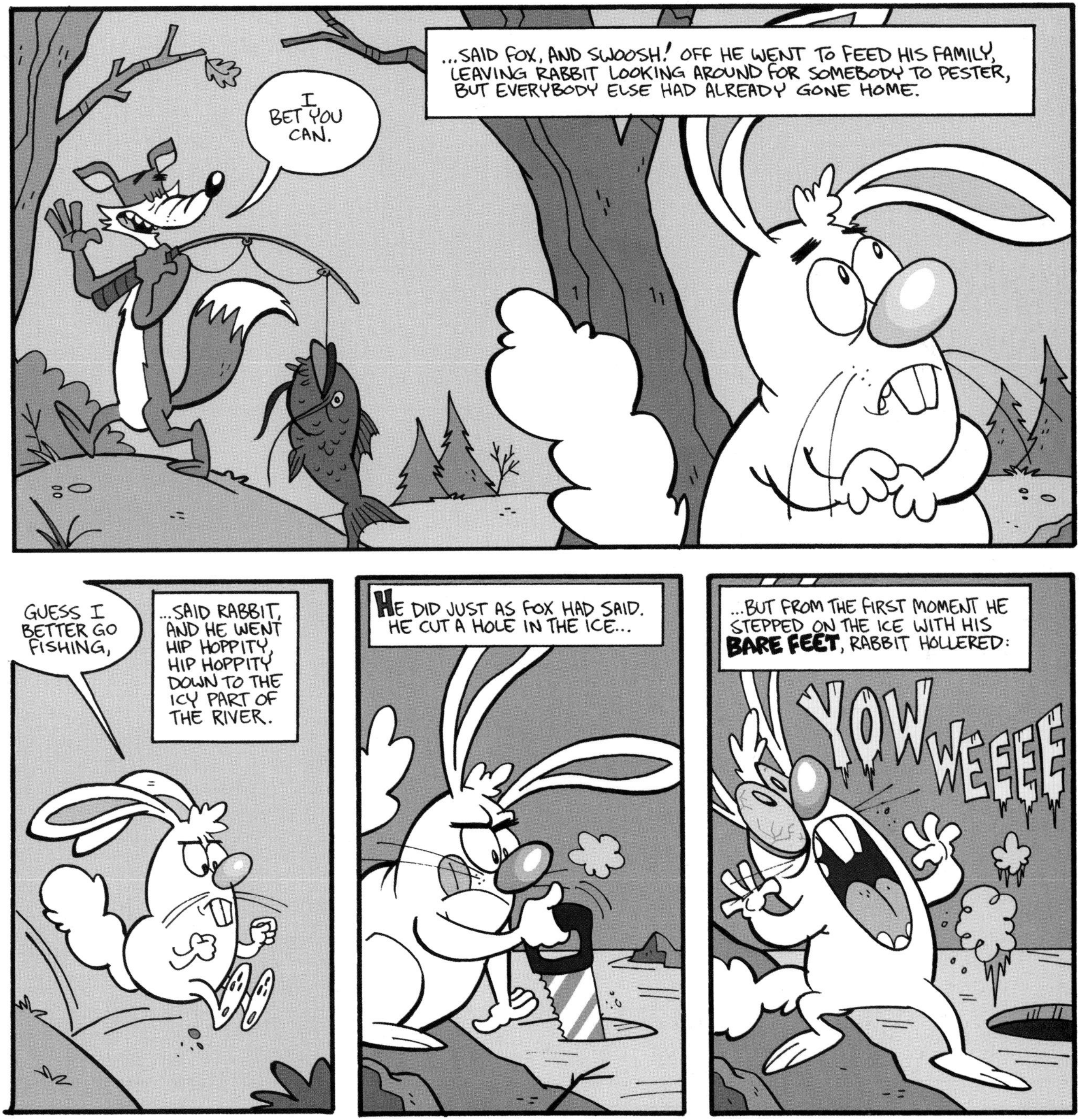
I BET YOU CAN.
...SAID FOX, AND SWOOSH! OFF HE WENT TO FEED HIS FAMILY, LEAVING RABBIT LOOKING AROUND FOR SOMEBODY TO PESTER, BUT EVERYBODY ELSE HAD ALREADY GONE HOME.
GUESS I BETTER GO FISHING,
...SAID RABBIT, AND HE WENT HIP HOPPITY, HIP HOPPITY DOWN TO THE ICY PART OF THE RIVER.
HE DID JUST AS FOX HAD SAID. HE CUT A HOLE IN THE ICE...
...BUT FROM THE FIRST MOMENT HE STEPPED ON THE ICE WITH HIS BARE FEET, RABBIT HOLLERED:
YOWWEEEE

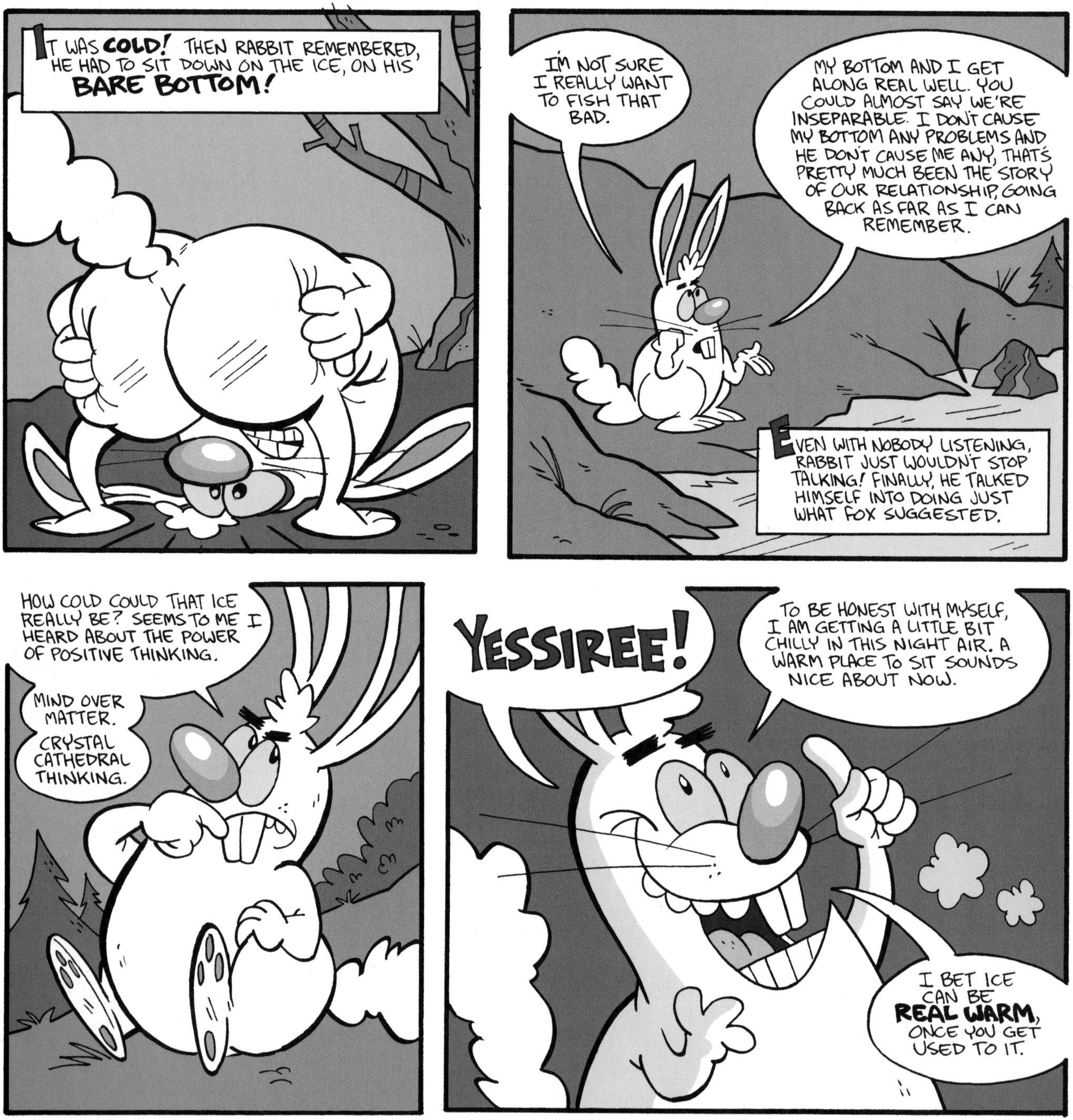
IT WAS COLD! THEN RABBIT REMEMBERED, HE HAD TO SIT DOWN ON THE ICE, ON HIS BARE BOTTOM!
I'M NOT SURE I REALLY WANT TO FISH THAT BAD.
MY BOTTOM AND I GET ALONG REAL WELL. YOU COULD ALMOST SAY WE'RE INSEPARABLE. I DON'T CAUSE MY BOTTOM ANY PROBLEMS AND HE DON'T CAUSE ME ANY, THAT'S PRETTY MUCH BEEN THE STORY OF OUR RELATIONSHIP, GOING BACK AS FAR AS I CAN REMEMBER.
EVEN WITH NOBODY LISTENING, RABBIT JUST WOULDN'T STOP TALKING! FINALLY, HE TALKED HIMSELF INTO DOING JUST WHAT FOX SUGGESTED.
HOW COLD COULD THAT ICE REALLY BE? SEEMS TO ME I HEARD ABOUT THE POWER OF POSITIVE THINKING.
MIND OVER MATTER. CRYSTAL CATHEDRAL THINKING.
YESSIREE!
TO BE HONEST WITH MYSELF, I AM GETTING A LITTLE BIT CHILLY IN THIS NIGHT AIR. A WARM PLACE TO SIT SOUNDS NICE ABOUT NOW.
I BET ICE CAN BE REAL WARM, ONCE YOU GET USED TO IT.

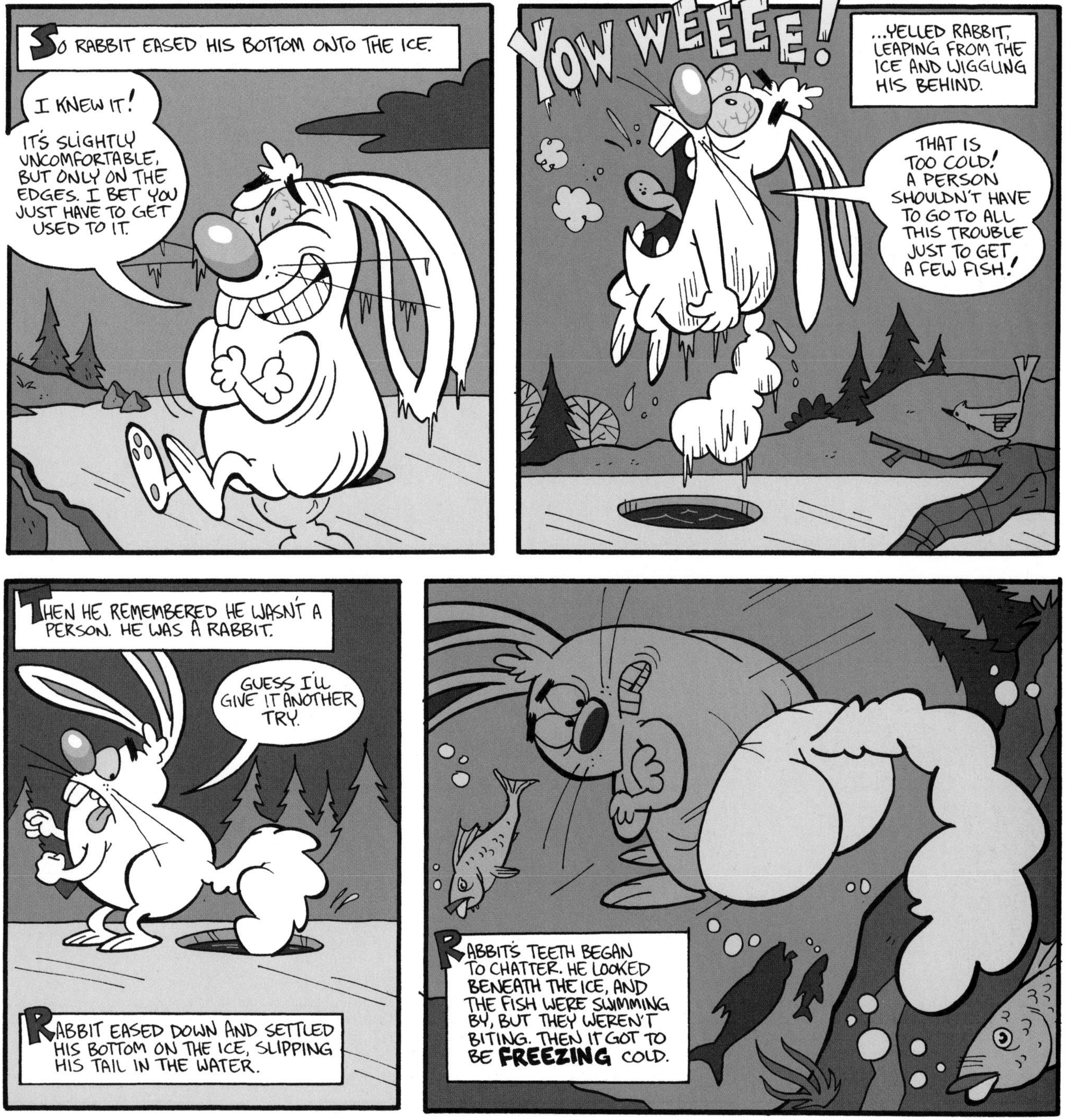
SO RABBIT EASED HIS BOTTOM ONTO THE ICE.
I KNEW IT! IT'S SLIGHTLY UNCOMFORTABLE, BUT ONLY ON THE EDGES. I BET YOU JUST HAVE TO GET USED TO IT.
YOW WEEEE!
...YELLED RABBIT, LEAPING FROM THE ICE AND WIGGLING HIS BEHIND.
THAT IS TOO COLD! A PERSON SHOULDN'T HAVE TO GO TO ALL THIS TROUBLE JUST TO GET A FEW FISH!
THEN HE REMEMBERED HE WASN'T A PERSON. HE WAS A RABBIT.
GUESS I'LL GIVE IT ANOTHER TRY.
RABBIT EASED DOWN AND SETTLED HIS BOTTOM ON THE ICE, SLIPPING HIS TAIL IN THE WATER.
RABBIT'S TEETH BEGAN TO CHATTER. HE LOOKED BENEATH THE ICE, AND THE FISH WERE SWIMMING BY, BUT THEY WEREN'T BITING. THEN IT GOT TO BE FREEZING COLD.

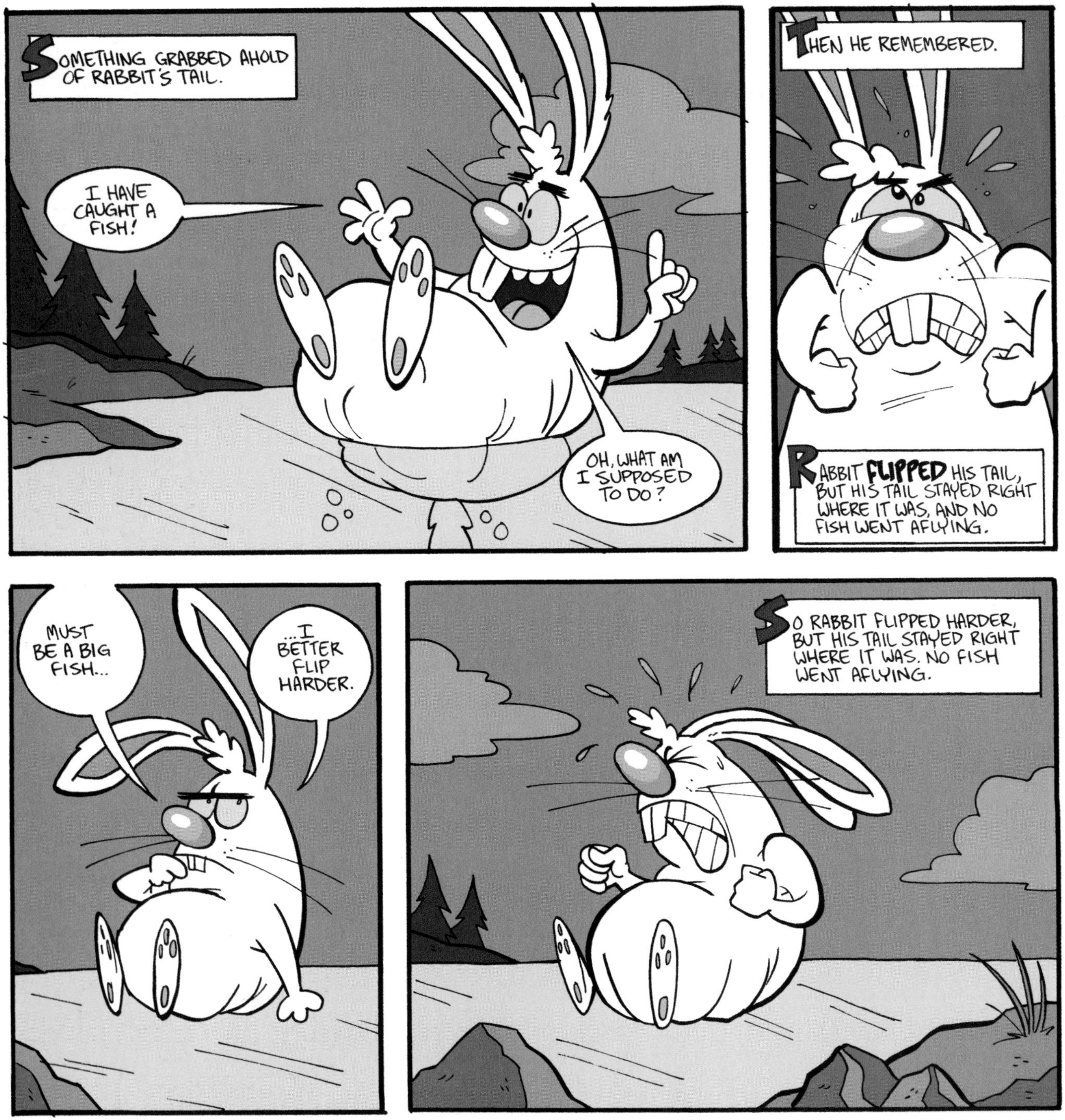
SOMETHING GRABBED AHOLD OF RABBIT'S TAIL.
I HAVE CAUGHT A FISH!
OH, WHAT AM I SUPPOSED TO DO?
THEN HE REMEMBERED.
RABBIT FLIPPED HIS TAIL, BUT HIS TAIL STAYED RIGHT WHERE IT WAS, AND NO FISH WENT AFLYING.
MUST BE A BIG FISH...
...I BETTER FLIP HARDER.
SO RABBIT FLIPPED HARDER, BUT HIS TAIL STAYED RIGHT WHERE IT WAS. NO FISH WENT AFLYING.

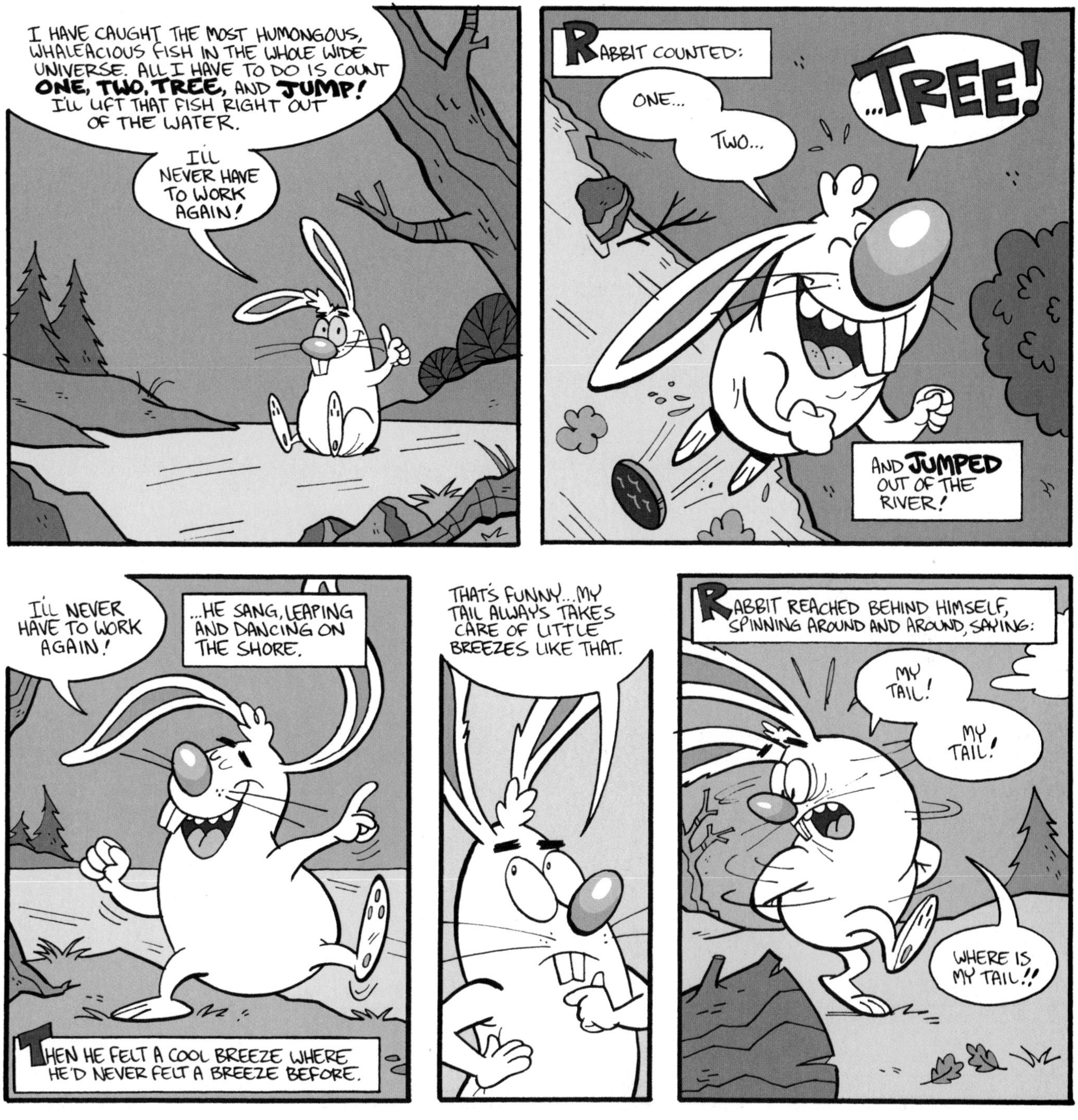

I HAVE CAUGHT THE MOST HUMONGOUS, WHALEACIOUS FISH IN THE WHOLE WIDE UNIVERSE. ALL I HAVE TO DO IS COUNT ONE, TWO, TREE, AND JUMP! I'LL LIFT THAT FISH RIGHT OUT OF THE WATER.
I'LL NEVER HAVE TO WORK AGAIN!
RABBIT COUNTED:
ONE...
TWO...
...TREE!
AND JUMPED OUT OF THE RIVER!
I'LL NEVER HAVE TO WORK AGAIN!
...HE SANG, LEAPING AND DANCING ON THE SHORE.
THEN HE FELT A COOL BREEZE WHERE HE'D NEVER FELT A BREEZE BEFORE.
THAT'S FUNNY... MY TAIL ALWAYS TAKES CARE OF LITTLE BREEZES LIKE THAT.
RABBIT REACHED BEHIND HIMSELF, SPINNING AROUND AND AROUND, SAYING:
MY TAIL!
MY TAIL!
WHERE IS MY TAIL!!

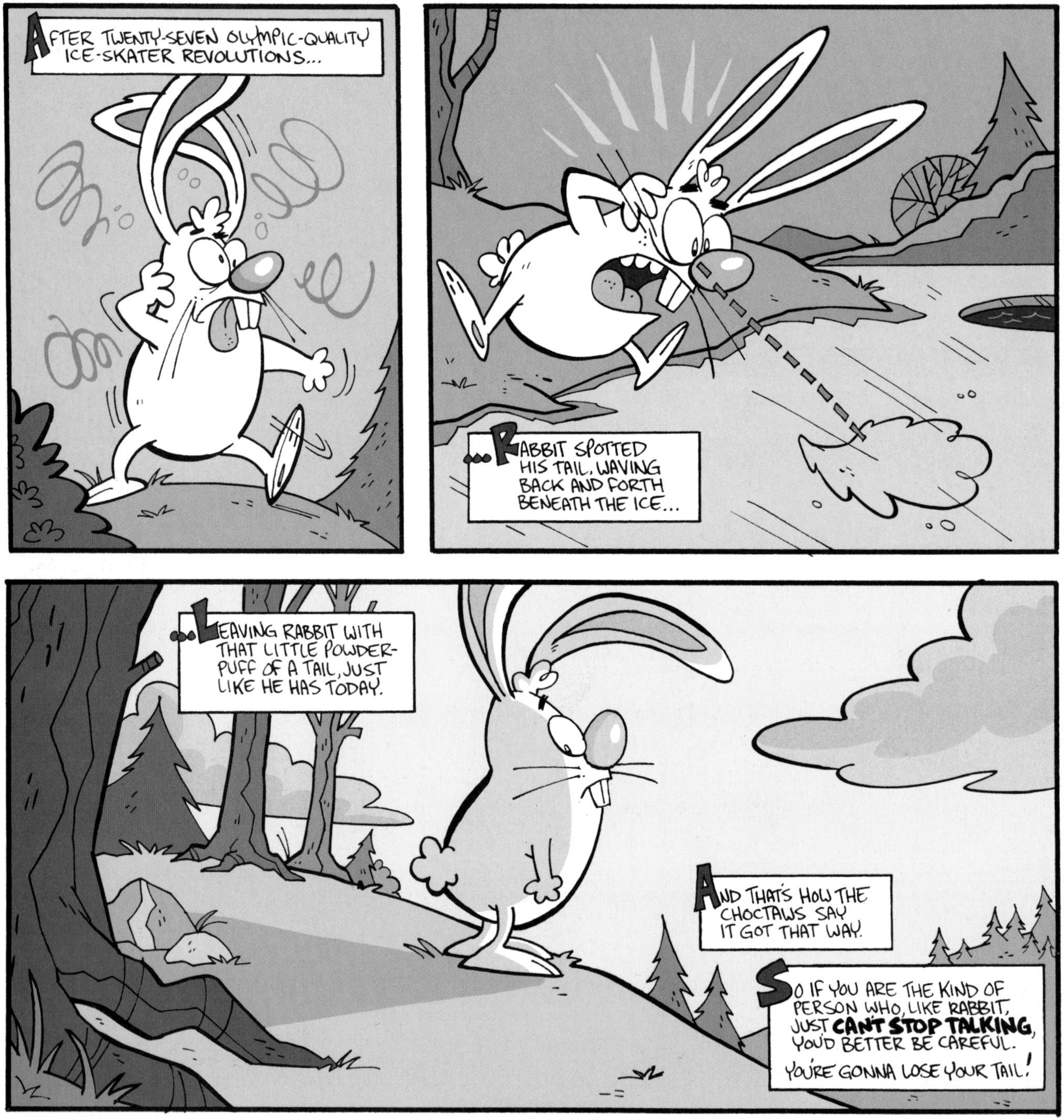
AFTER TWENTY-SEVEN OLYMPIC-QUALITY ICE-SKATER REVOLUTIONS...
...RABBIT SPOTTED HIS TAIL, WAVING BACK AND FORTH BENEATH THE ICE...
...LEAVING RABBIT WITH THAT LITTLE POWDER-PUFF OF A TAIL, JUST LIKE HE HAS TODAY.
AND THAT'S HOW THE CHOCTAWS SAY IT GOT THAT WAY.
SO IF YOU ARE THE KIND OF PERSON WHO, LIKE RABBIT, JUST CAN'T STOP TALKING, YOU'D BETTER BE CAREFUL.
YOU'RE GONNA LOSE YOUR TAIL!

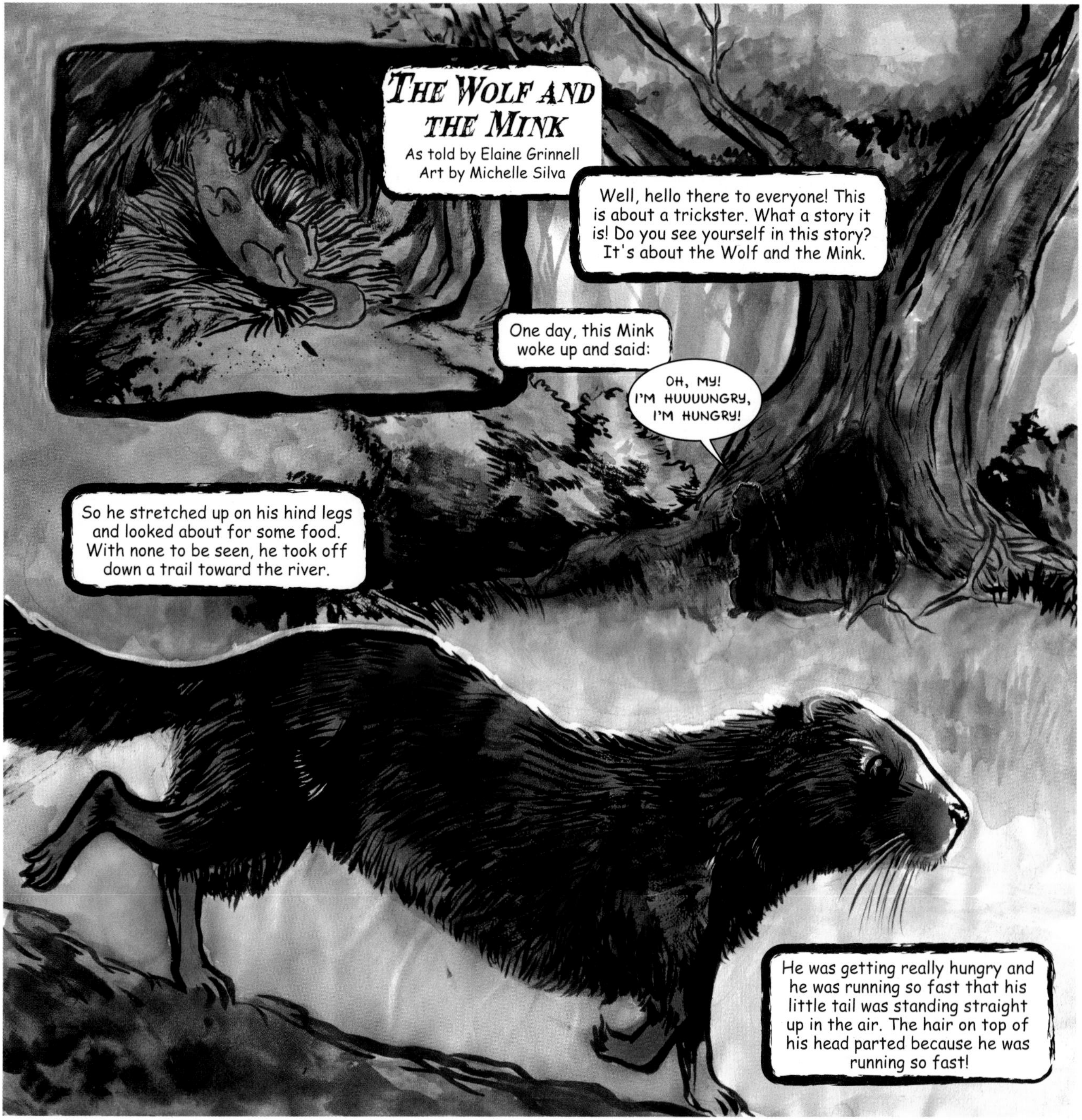
THE WOLF AND THE MINK
As told by Elaine Grinnell
Art by Michelle Silva
Well, hello there to everyone! This is about a trickster. What a story it is! Do you see yourself in this story? It's about the Wolf and the Mink.
One day, this Mink woke up and said:
OH, MY! I'M HUUUUNGRY, I'M HUNGRY!
So he stretched up on his hind legs and looked about for some food. With none to be seen, he took off down a trail toward the river.
He was getting really hungry and he was running so fast that his little tail was standing straight up in the air. The hair on top of his head parted because he was running so fast!

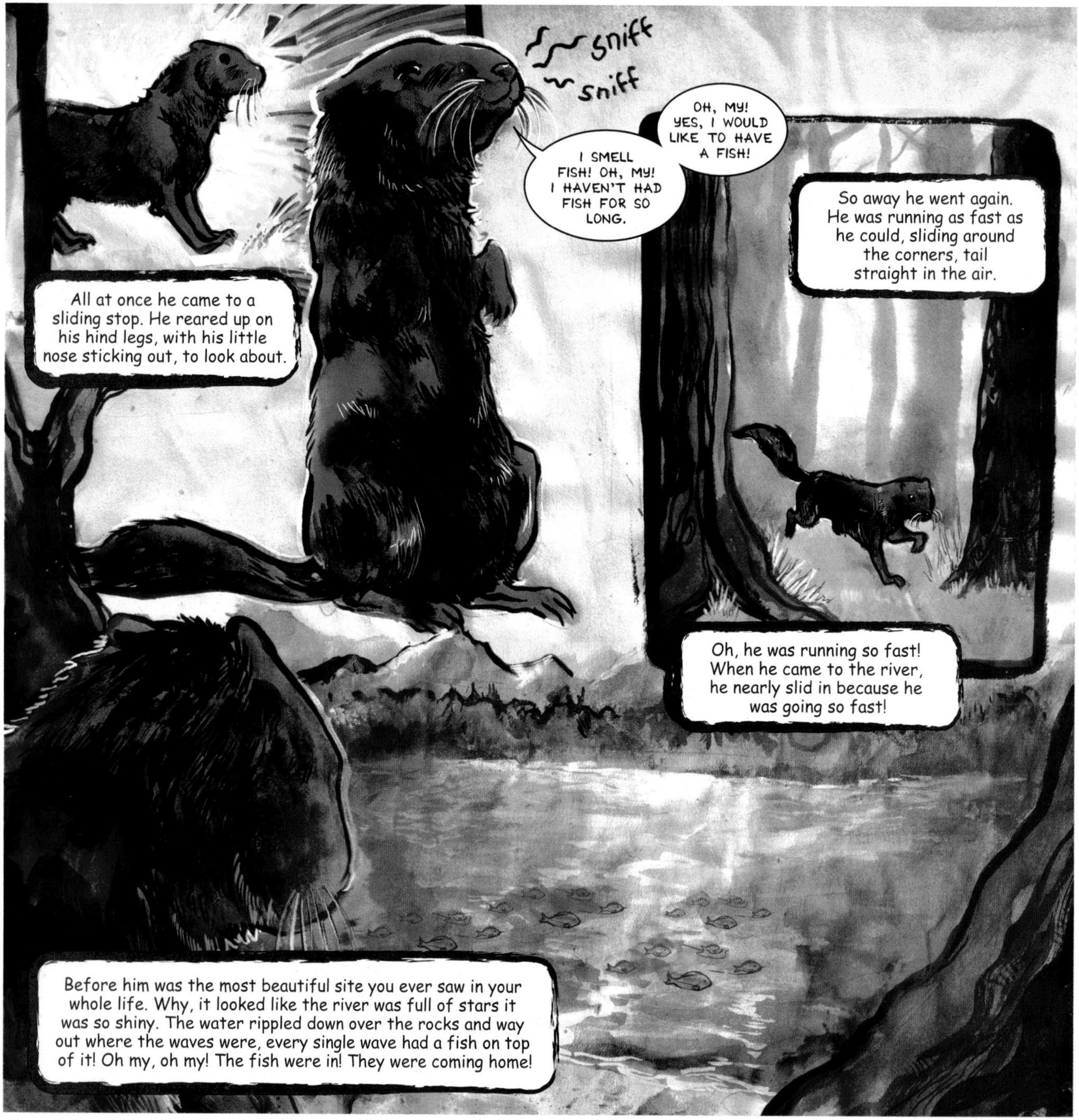
sniff
sniff
I SMELL FISH! OH, MY! I HAVEN'T HAD FISH FOR SO LONG.
OH, MY! YES, I WOULD LIKE TO HAVE A FISH!
All at once he came to a sliding stop. He reared up on his hind legs, with his little nose sticking out, to look about.
So away he went again. He was running as fast as he could, sliding around the corners, tail straight in the air.
Oh, he was running so fast! When he came to the river, he nearly slid in because he was going so fast!
Before him was the most beautiful site you ever saw in your whole life. Why, it looked like the river was full of stars it was so shiny. The water rippled down over the rocks and way out where the waves were, every single wave had a fish on top of it! Oh my, oh my! The fish were in! They were coming home!

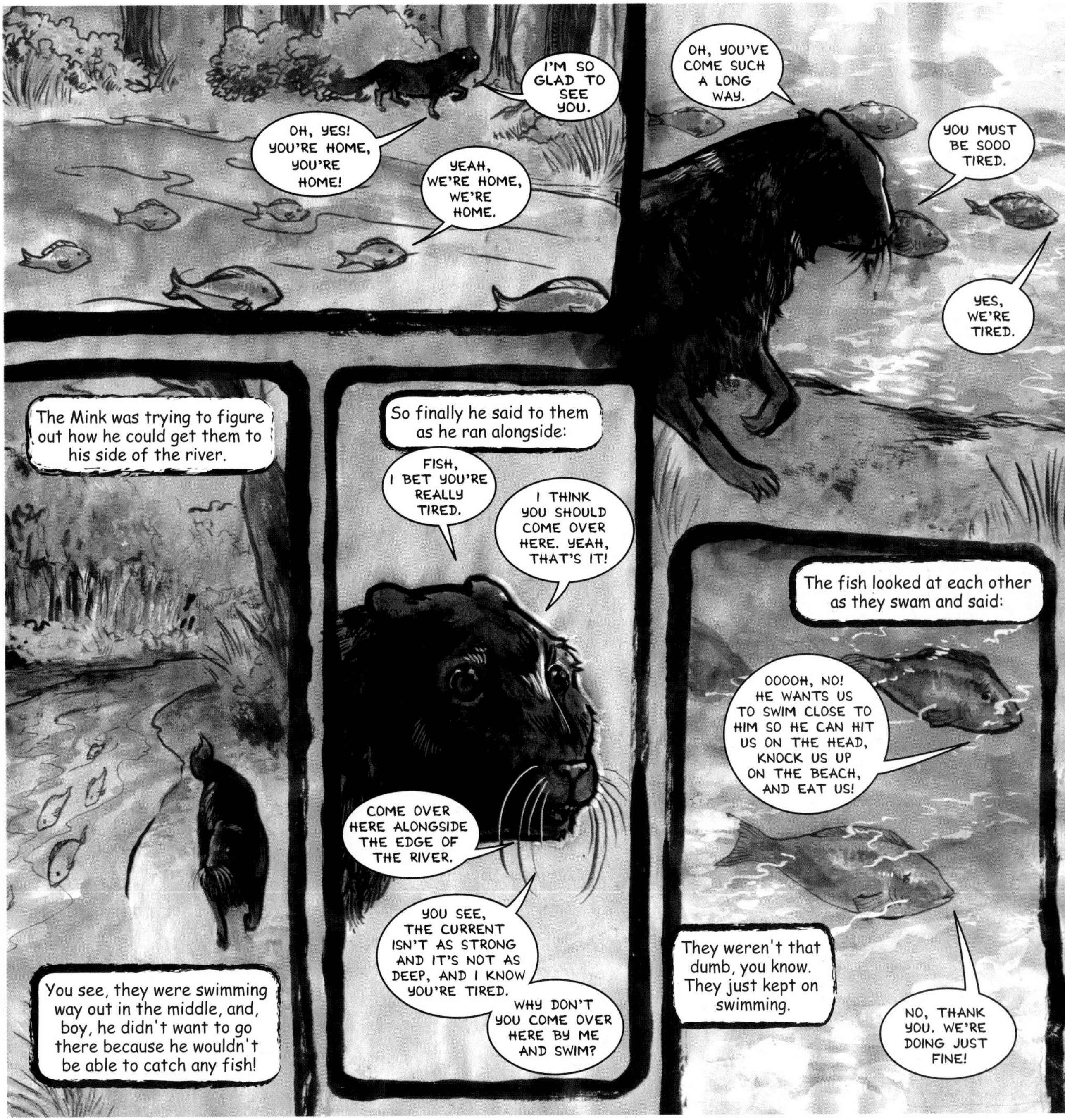
I'M SO GLAD TO SEE YOU.
OH, YES! YOU'RE HOME, YOU'RE HOME!
YEAH, WE'RE HOME, WE'RE HOME.
OH, YOU'VE COME SUCH A LONG WAY.
YOU MUST BE SOOO TIRED.
YES, WE'RE TIRED.
The Mink was trying to figure out how he could get them to his side of the river.
You see, they were swimming way out in the middle, and, boy, he didn't want to go there because he wouldn't be able to catch any fish!
So finally he said to them as he ran alongside:
FISH, I BET YOU'RE REALLY TIRED.
I THINK YOU SHOULD COME OVER HERE. YEAH, THAT'S IT!
COME OVER HERE ALONGSIDE THE EDGE OF THE RIVER.
YOU SEE, THE CURRENT ISN'T AS STRONG AND IT'S NOT AS DEEP, AND I KNOW YOU'RE TIRED.
WHY DON'T YOU COME OVER HERE BY ME AND SWIM?
The fish looked at each other as they swam and said:
OOOOH, NO! HE WANTS US TO SWIM CLOSE TO HIM SO HE CAN HIT US ON THE HEAD, KNOCK US UP ON THE BEACH, AND EAT US!
They weren't that dumb, you know. They just kept on swimming.
NO, THANK YOU. WE'RE DOING JUST FINE!

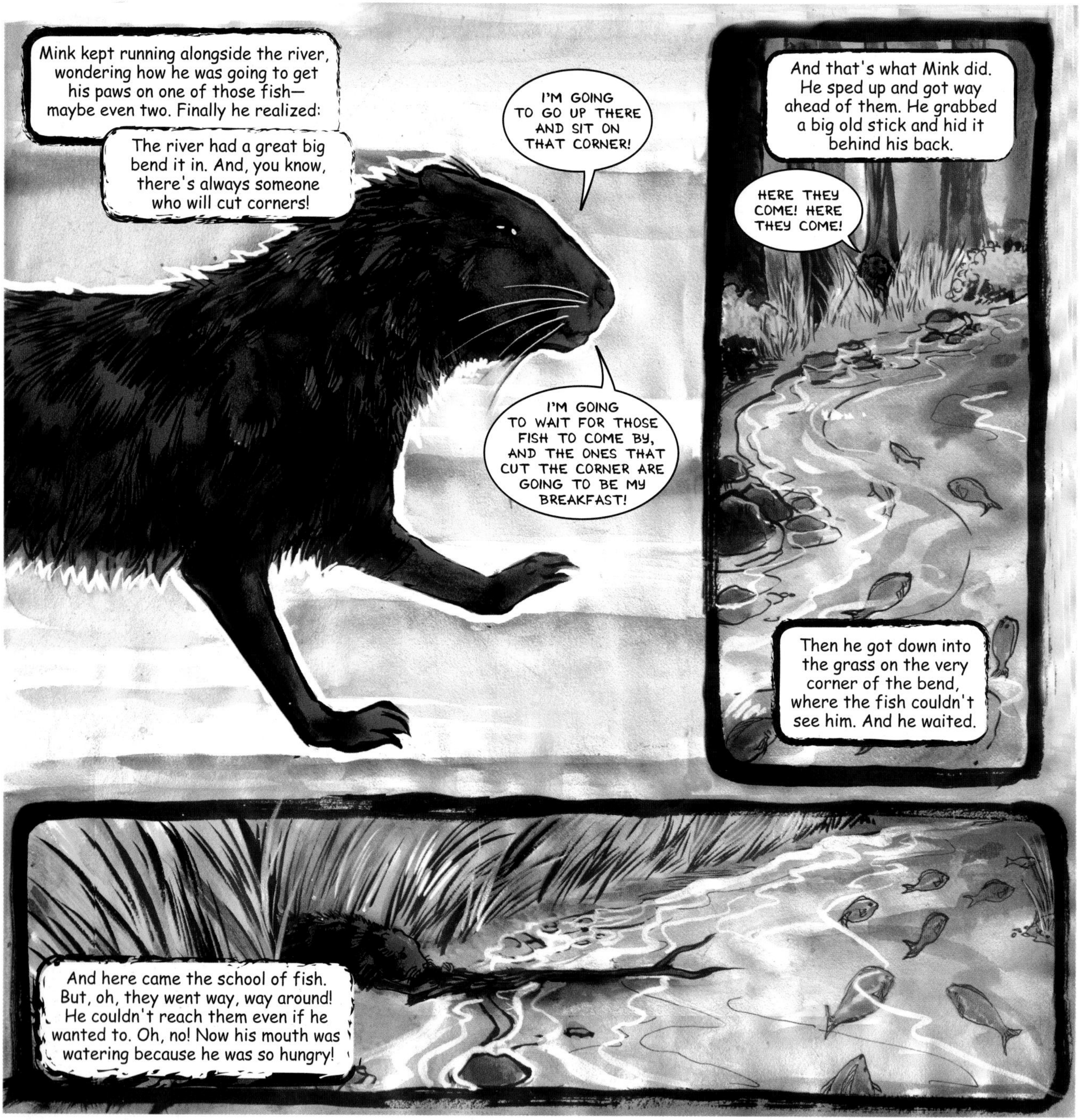

Mink kept running alongside the river, wondering how he was going to get his paws on one of those fish—maybe even two. Finally he realized:
The river had a great big bend it in. And, you know, there's always someone who will cut corners!
I'M GOING TO GO UP THERE AND SIT ON THAT CORNER!
I'M GOING TO WAIT FOR THOSE FISH TO COME BY, AND THE ONES THAT CUT THE CORNER ARE GOING TO BE MY BREAKFAST!
And that's what Mink did. He sped up and got way ahead of them. He grabbed a big old stick and hid it behind his back.
HERE THEY COME! HERE THEY COME!
Then he got down into the grass on the very corner of the bend, where the fish couldn't see him. And he waited.
And here came the school of fish. But, oh, they went way, way around! He couldn't reach them even if he wanted to. Oh, no! Now his mouth was watering because he was so hungry!

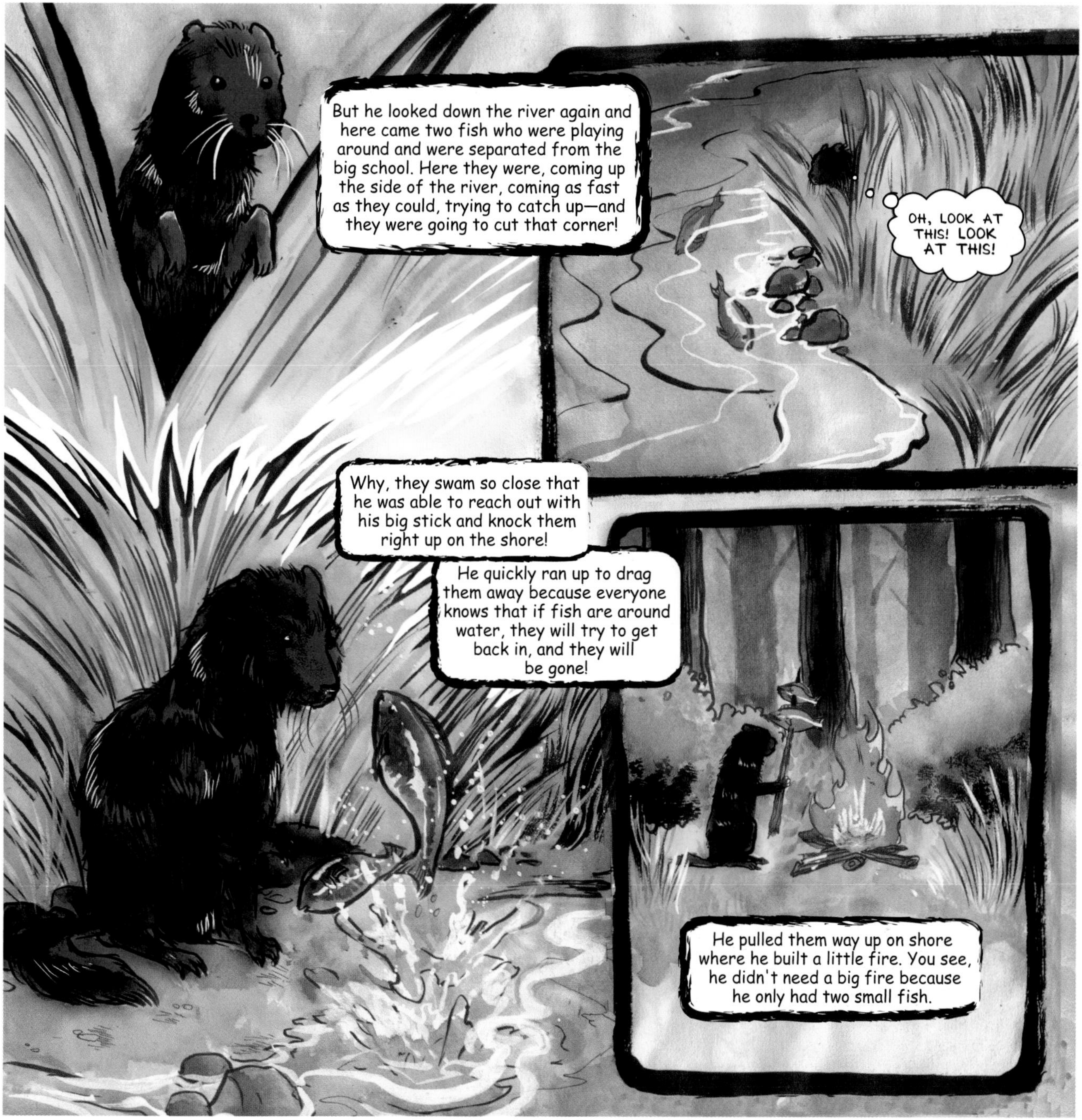
But he looked down the river again and here came two fish who were playing around and were separated from the big school. Here they were, coming up the side of the river, coming as fast as they could, trying to catch up—and they were going to cut that corner!
OH, LOOK AT THIS! LOOK AT THIS!
Why, they swam so close that he was able to reach out with his big stick and knock them right up on the shore!
He quickly ran up to drag them away because everyone knows that if fish are around water, they will try to get back in, and they will be gone!
He pulled them way up on shore where he built a little fire. You see, he didn't need a big fire because he only had two small fish.

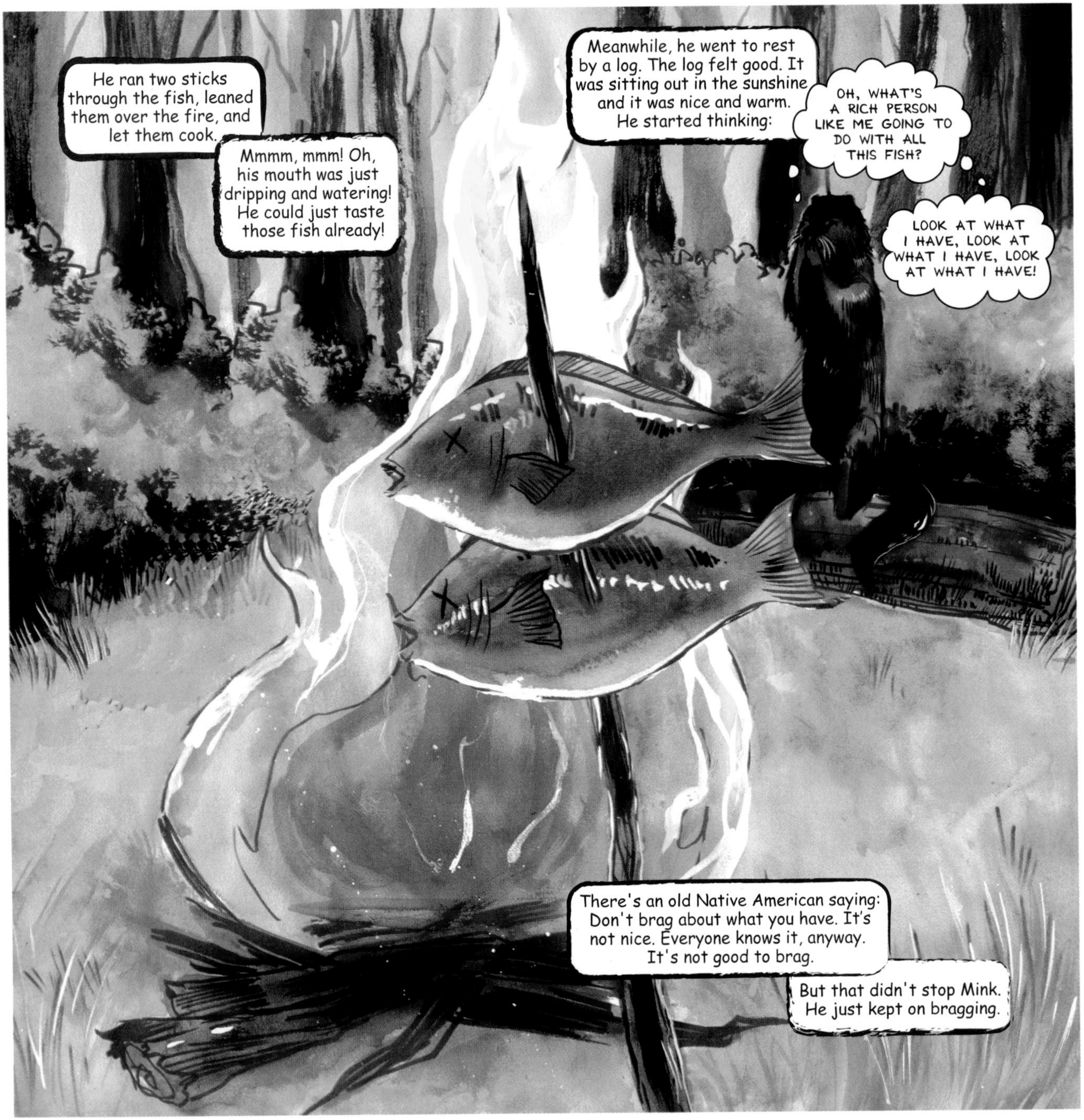
He ran two sticks through the fish, leaned them over the fire, and let them cook.
Mmmm, mmm! Oh, his mouth was just dripping and watering! He could just taste those fish already!
Meanwhile, he went to rest by a log. The log felt good. It was sitting out in the sunshine and it was nice and warm. He started thinking:
OH, WHAT'S A RICH PERSON LIKE ME GOING TO DO WITH ALL THIS FISH?
LOOK AT WHAT I HAVE, LOOK AT WHAT I HAVE, LOOK AT WHAT I HAVE!
There's an old Native American saying: Don't brag about what you have. It's not nice. Everyone knows it, anyway. It's not good to brag.
But that didn't stop Mink. He just kept on bragging.

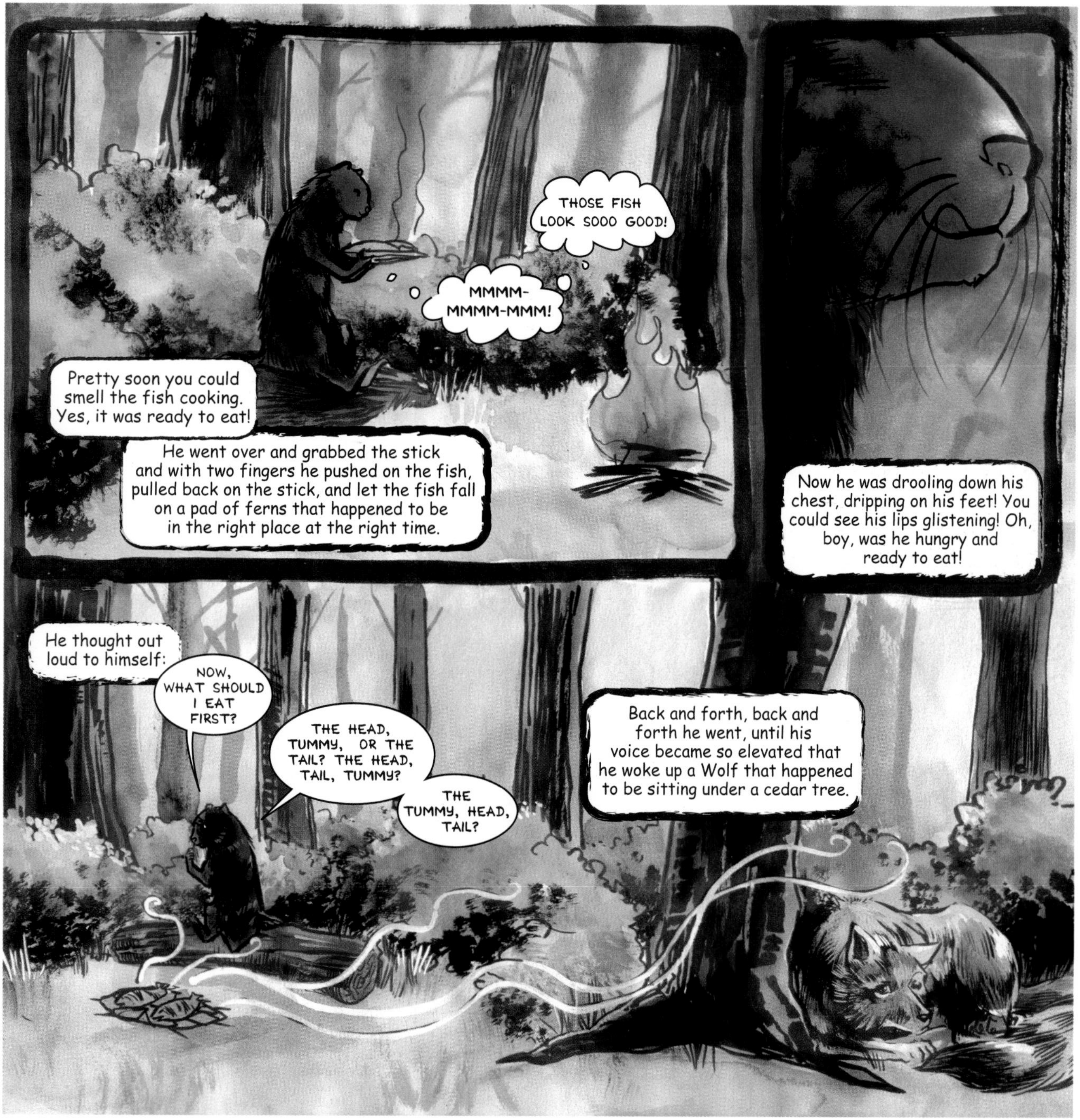
Pretty soon you could smell the fish cooking. Yes, it was ready to eat!
MMMM-MMMM-MMM!
THOSE FISH LOOK SOOO GOOD!
He went over and grabbed the stick and with two fingers he pushed on the fish, pulled back on the stick, and let the fish fall on a pad of ferns that happened to be in the right place at the right time.
Now he was drooling down his chest, dripping on his feet! You could see his lips glistening! Oh, boy, was he hungry and ready to eat!
He thought out loud to himself:
NOW, WHAT SHOULD I EAT FIRST?
THE HEAD, TUMMY, OR THE TAIL? THE HEAD, TAIL, TUMMY?
THE TUMMY, HEAD, TAIL?
Back and forth, back and forth he went, until his voice became so elevated that he woke up a Wolf that happened to be sitting under a cedar tree.

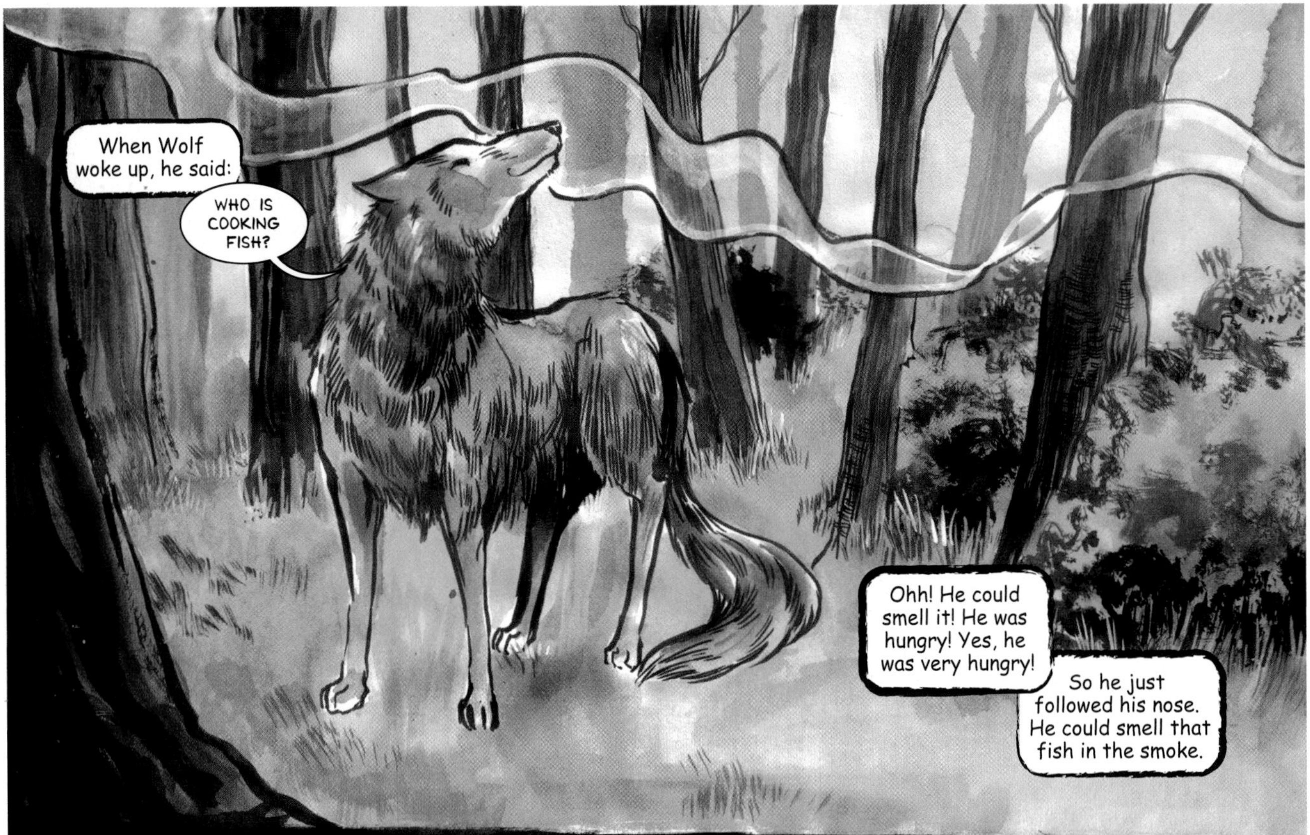
When Wolf woke up, he said:
WHO IS COOKING FISH?
Ohh! He could smell it! He was hungry! Yes, he was very hungry!
So he just followed his nose. He could smell that fish in the smoke.

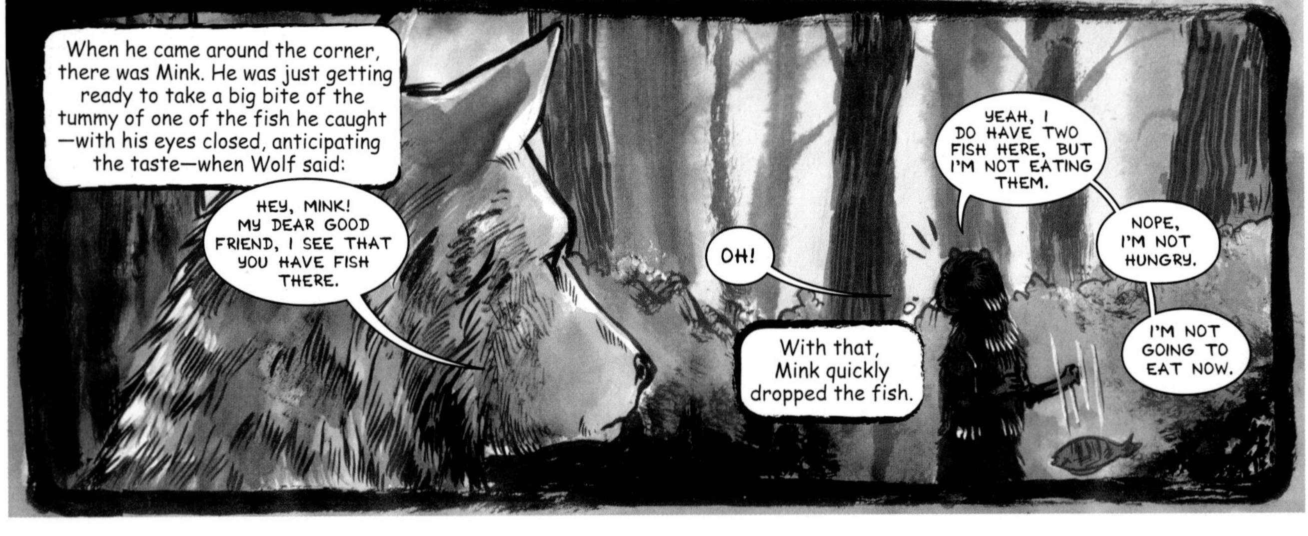
When he came around the corner, there was Mink. He was just getting ready to take a big bite of the tummy of one of the fish he caught—with his eyes closed, anticipating the taste—when Wolf said:
HEY, MINK! MY DEAR GOOD FRIEND, I SEE THAT YOU HAVE FISH THERE.
OH!
With that, Mink quickly dropped the fish.
YEAH, I DO HAVE TWO FISH HERE, BUT I'M NOT EATING THEM.
NOPE, I'M NOT HUNGRY.
I'M NOT GOING TO EAT NOW.

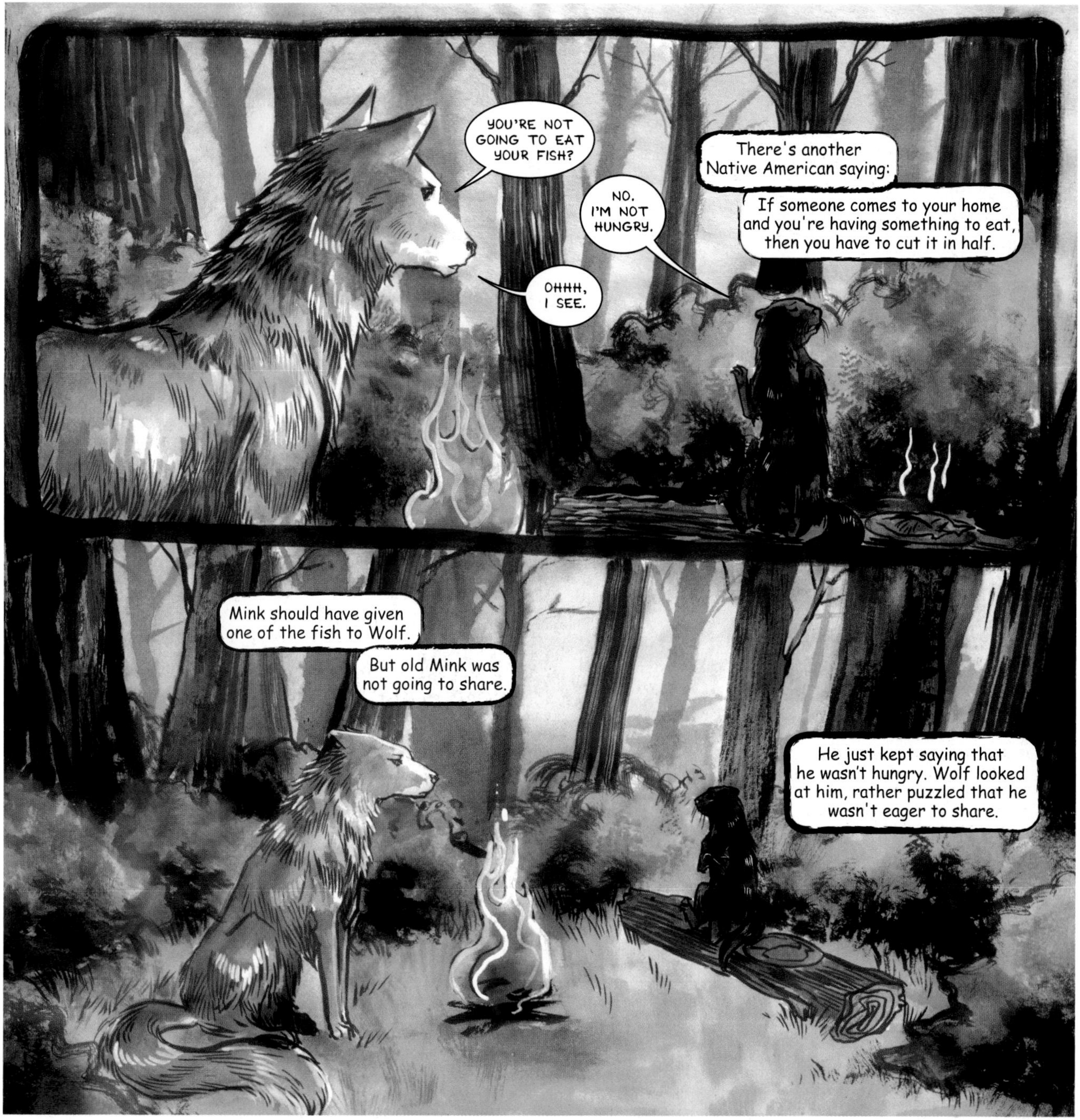
YOU'RE NOT GOING TO EAT YOUR FISH?
NO. I'M NOT HUNGRY.
OHHH, I SEE.
There's another Native American saying:
If someone comes to your home and you're having something to eat, then you have to cut it in half.
Mink should have given one of the fish to Wolf.
But old Mink was not going to share.
He just kept saying that he wasn't hungry. Wolf looked at him, rather puzzled that he wasn't eager to share.

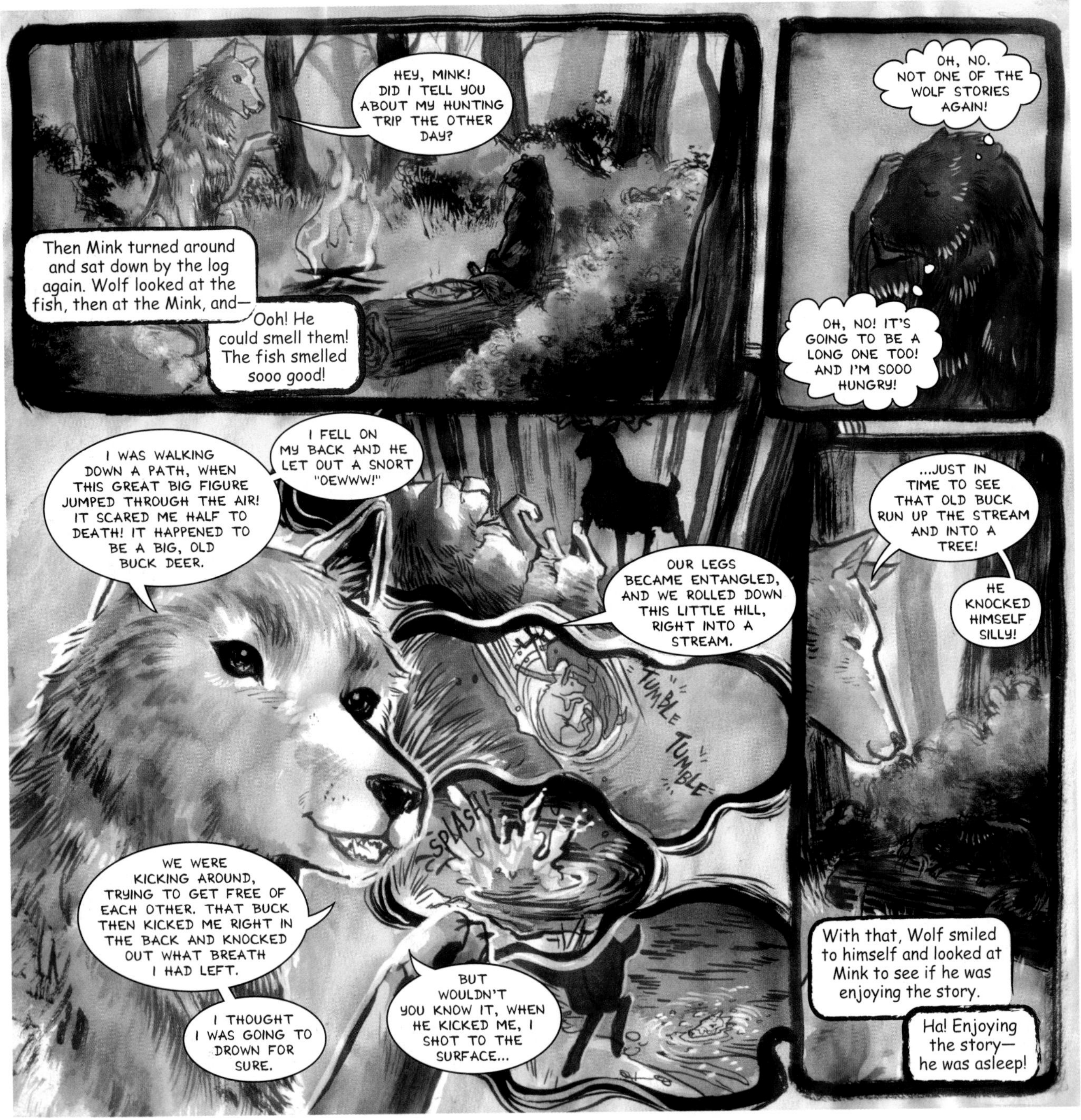
HEY, MINK! DID I TELL YOU ABOUT MY HUNTING TRIP THE OTHER DAY?
Then Mink turned around and sat down by the log again. Wolf looked at the fish, then at the Mink, and—
Ooh! He could smell them! The fish smelled sooo good!
OH, NO. NOT ONE OF THE WOLF STORIES AGAIN!
OH, NO! IT'S GOING TO BE A LONG ONE TOO! AND I'M SOOO HUNGRY!
I WAS WALKING DOWN A PATH, WHEN THIS GREAT BIG FIGURE JUMPED THROUGH THE AIR! IT SCARED ME HALF TO DEATH! IT HAPPENED TO BE A BIG, OLD BUCK DEER.
I FELL ON MY BACK AND HE LET OUT A SNORT "OEWWW!"
OUR LEGS BECAME ENTANGLED, AND WE ROLLED DOWN THIS LITTLE HILL, RIGHT INTO A STREAM.
TUMBLE TUMBLE TUMBLE
SPLASH!
WE WERE KICKING AROUND, TRYING TO GET FREE OF EACH OTHER. THAT BUCK THEN KICKED ME RIGHT IN THE BACK AND KNOCKED OUT WHAT BREATH I HAD LEFT.
I THOUGHT I WAS GOING TO DROWN FOR SURE.
BUT WOULDN'T YOU KNOW IT, WHEN HE KICKED ME, I SHOT TO THE SURFACE...
...JUST IN TIME TO SEE THAT OLD BUCK RUN UP THE STREAM AND INTO A TREE!
HE KNOCKED HIMSELF SILLY!
With that, Wolf smiled to himself and looked at Mink to see if he was enjoying the story.
Ha! Enjoying the story— he was asleep!

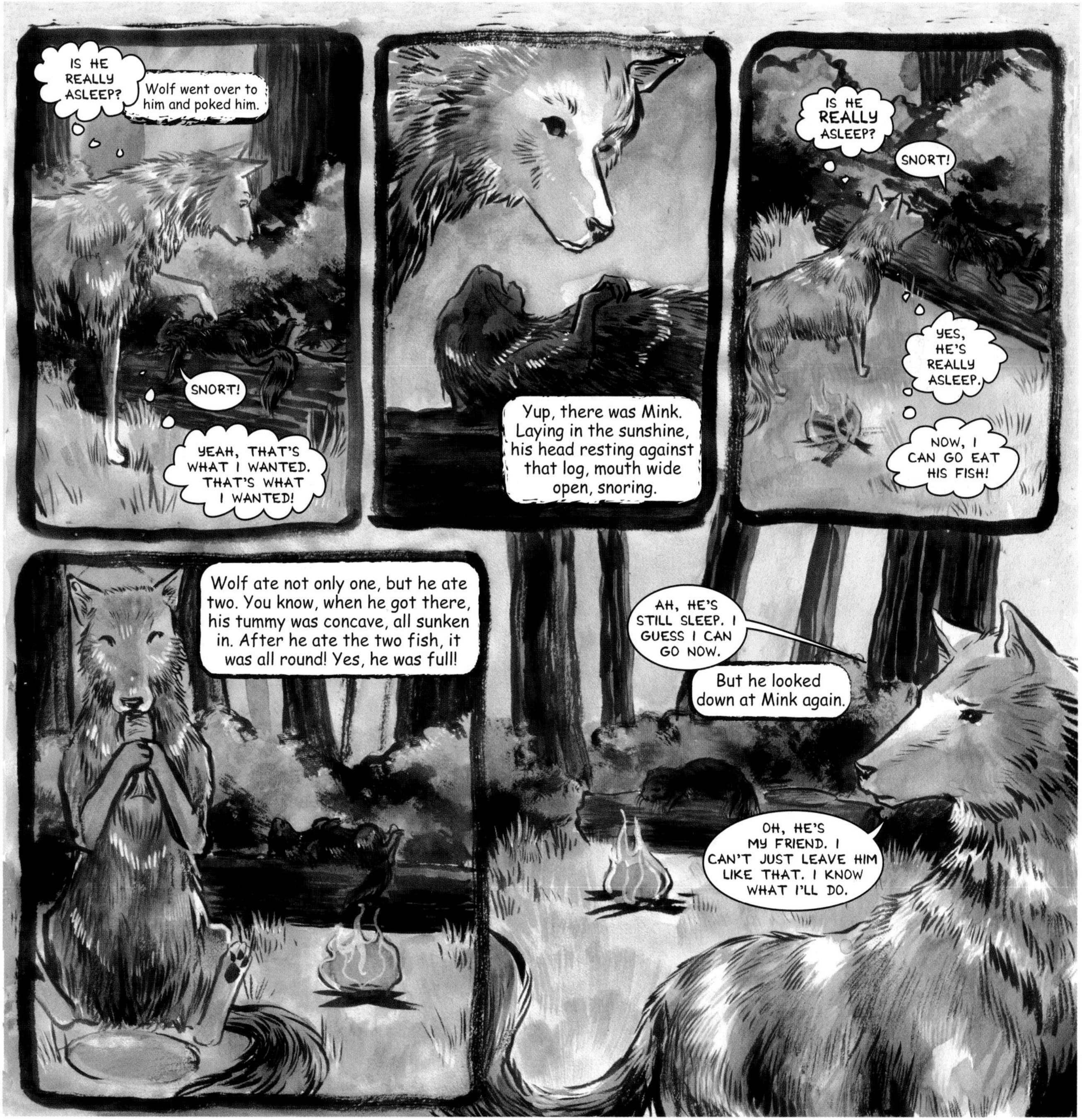
IS HE REALLY ASLEEP?
Wolf went over to him and poked him.
SNORT!
YEAH, THAT'S WHAT I WANTED. THAT'S WHAT I WANTED!
Yup, there was Mink. Laying in the sunshine, his head resting against that log, mouth wide open, snoring.
IS HE REALLY ASLEEP?
SNORT!
YES, HE'S REALLY ASLEEP.
NOW, I CAN GO EAT HIS FISH!
Wolf ate not only one, but he ate two. You know, when he got there, his tummy was concave, all sunken in. After he ate the two fish, it was all round! Yes, he was full!
AH, HE'S STILL SLEEP. I GUESS I CAN GO NOW.
But he looked down at Mink again.
OH, HE'S MY FRIEND. I CAN'T JUST LEAVE HIM LIKE THAT. I KNOW WHAT I'LL DO.

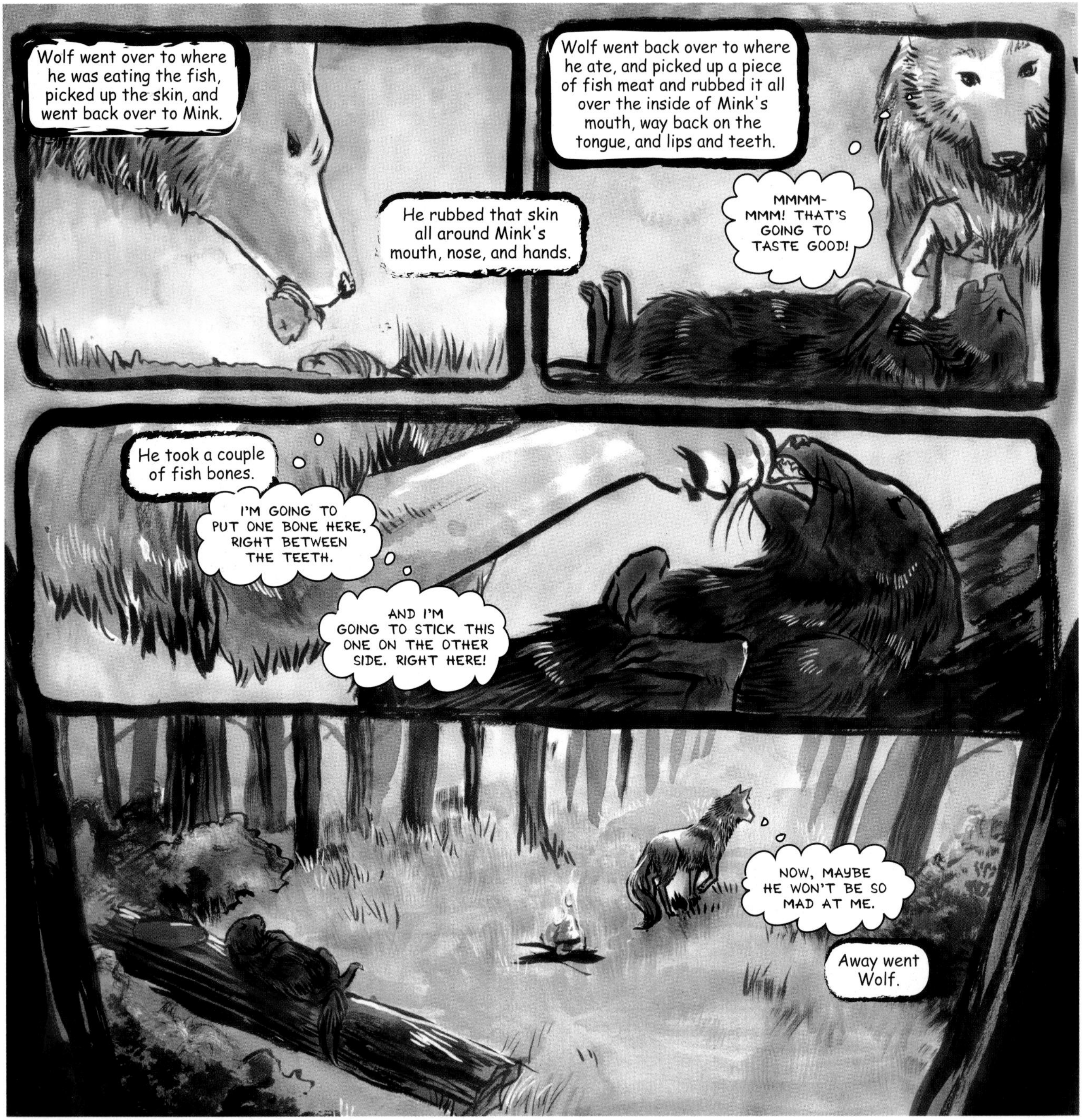
Wolf went over to where he was eating the fish, picked up the skin, and went back over to Mink.
He rubbed that skin all around Mink's mouth, nose, and hands.
Wolf went back over to where he ate, and picked up a piece of fish meat and rubbed it all over the inside of Mink's mouth, way back on the tongue, and lips and teeth.
MMMM-MMM! THAT'S GOING TO TASTE GOOD!
He took a couple of fish bones.
I'M GOING TO PUT ONE BONE HERE, RIGHT BETWEEN THE TEETH.
AND I'M GOING TO STICK THIS ONE ON THE OTHER SIDE. RIGHT HERE!
NOW, MAYBE HE WON'T BE SO MAD AT ME.
Away went Wolf.

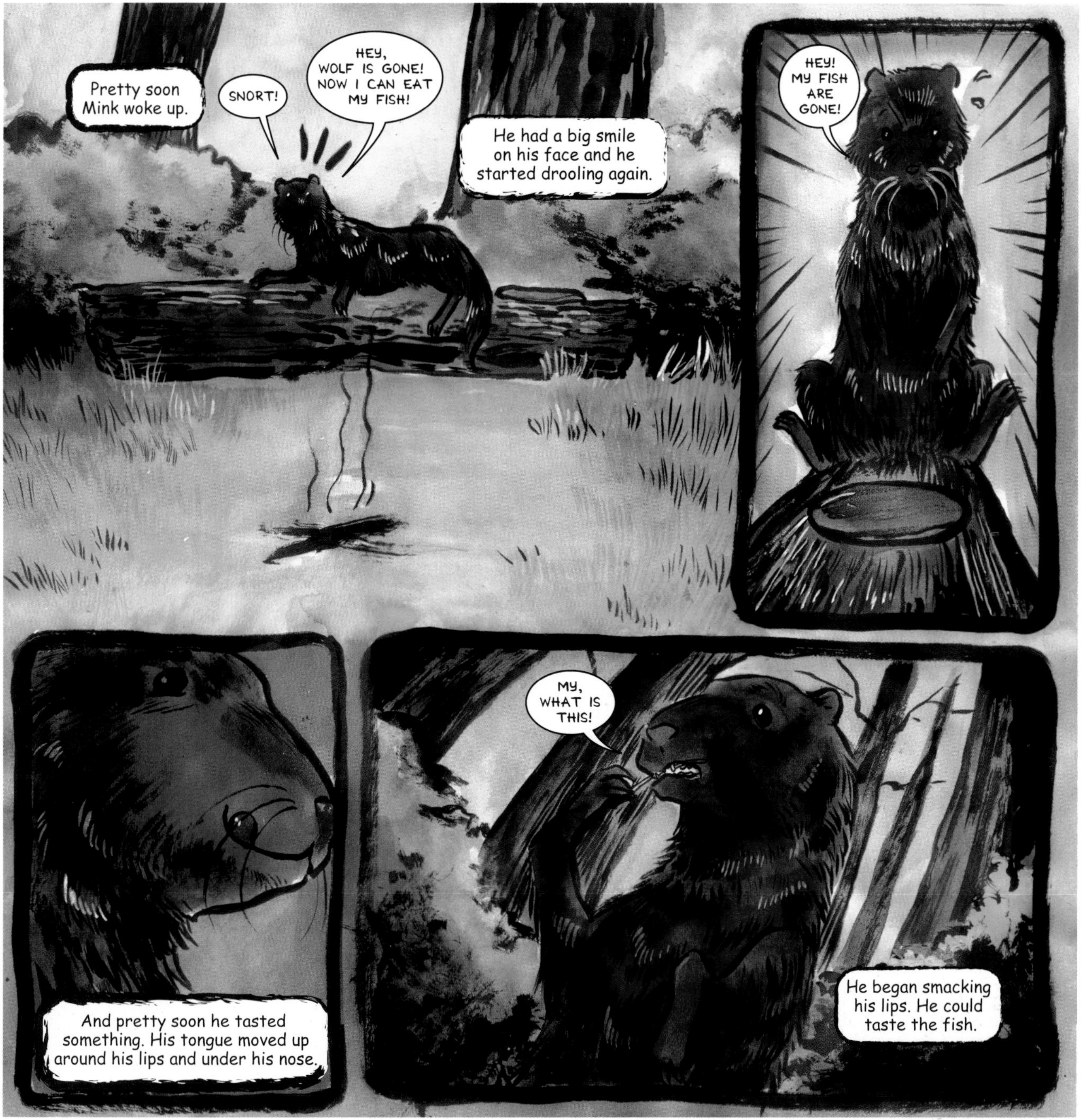
Pretty soon Mink woke up.
SNORT!
HEY, WOLF IS GONE! NOW I CAN EAT MY FISH!
He had a big smile on his face and he started drooling again.
HEY! MY FISH ARE GONE!
And pretty soon he tasted something. His tongue moved up around his lips and under his nose.
MY, WHAT IS THIS!
He began smacking his lips. He could taste the fish.

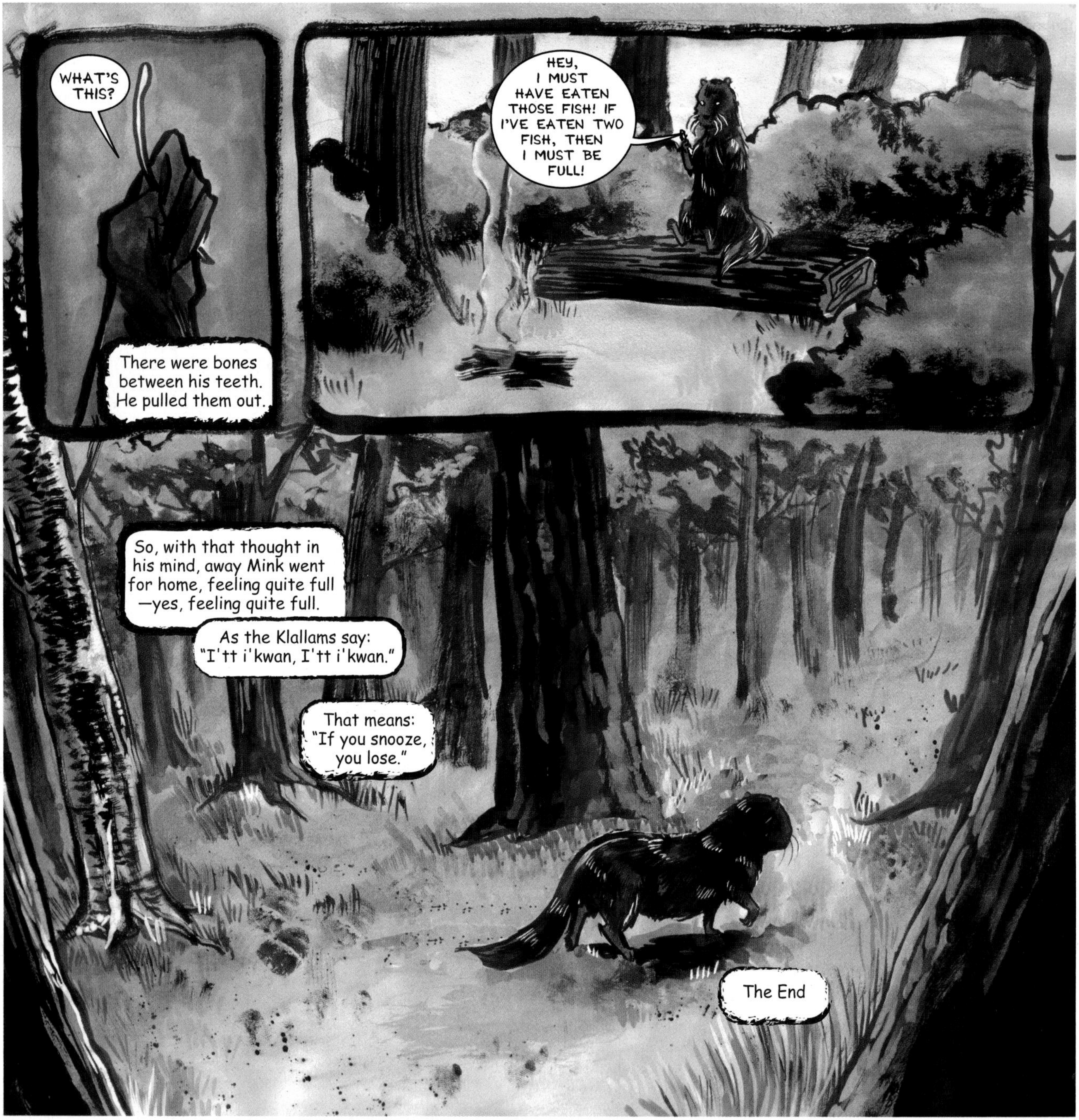

WHAT'S THIS?
There were bones between his teeth. He pulled them out.
HEY, I MUST HAVE EATEN THOSE FISH! IF I'VE EATEN TWO FISH, THEN I MUST BE FULL!
So, with that thought in his mind, away Mink went for home, feeling quite full —yes, feeling quite full.
As the Klallams say: "I'tt i'kwan, I'tt i'kwan."
That means: "If you snooze, you lose."
The End

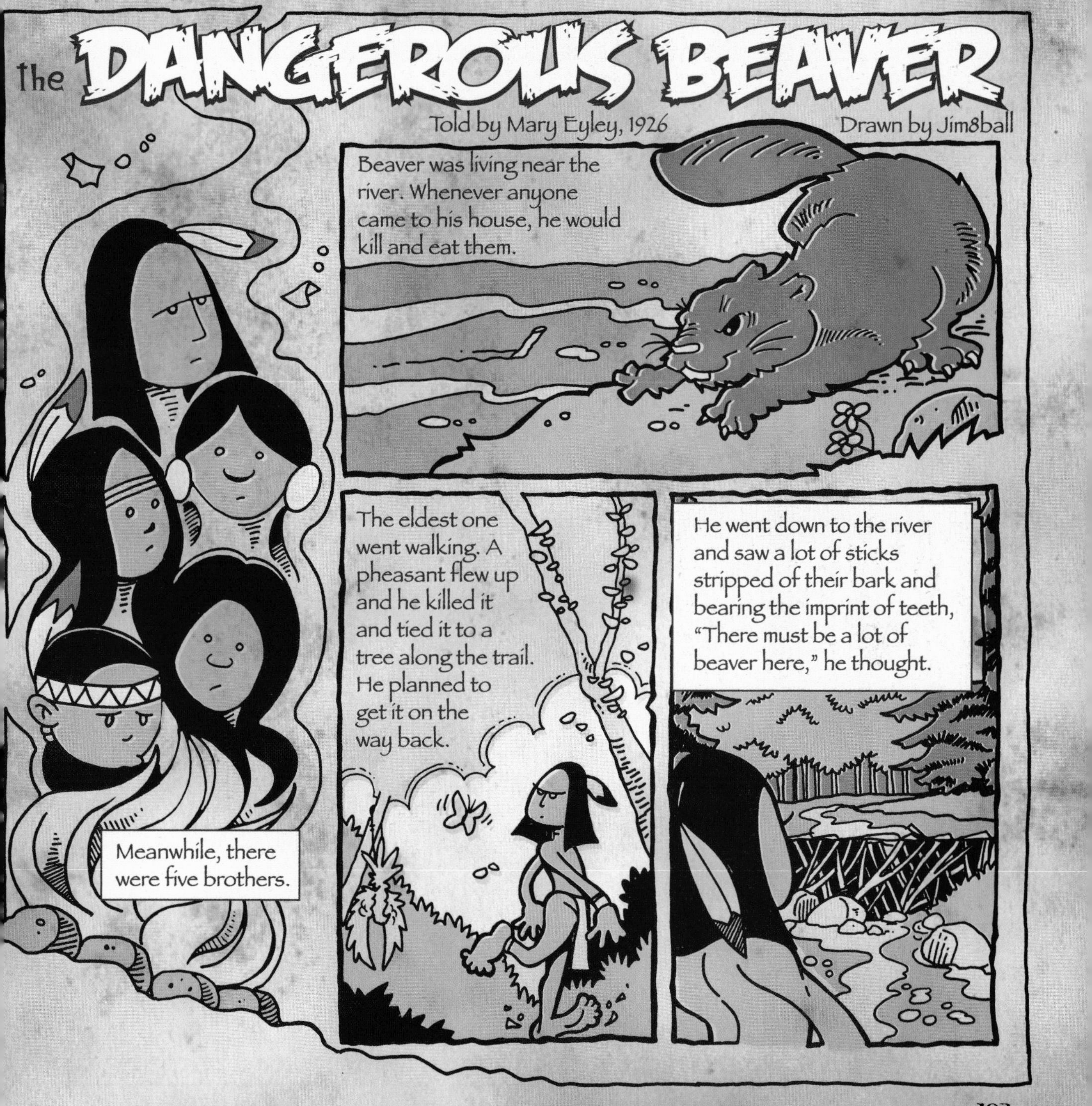
the DANGEROUS BEAVER
Told by Mary Eyley, 1926
Drawn by Jim8ball
Meanwhile, there were five brothers.
Beaver was living near the river. Whenever anyone came to his house, he would kill and eat them.
The eldest one went walking. A pheasant flew up and he killed it and tied it to a tree along the trail. He planned to get it on the way back.
He went down to the river and saw a lot of sticks stripped of their bark and bearing the imprint of teeth, "There must be a lot of beaver here," he thought.

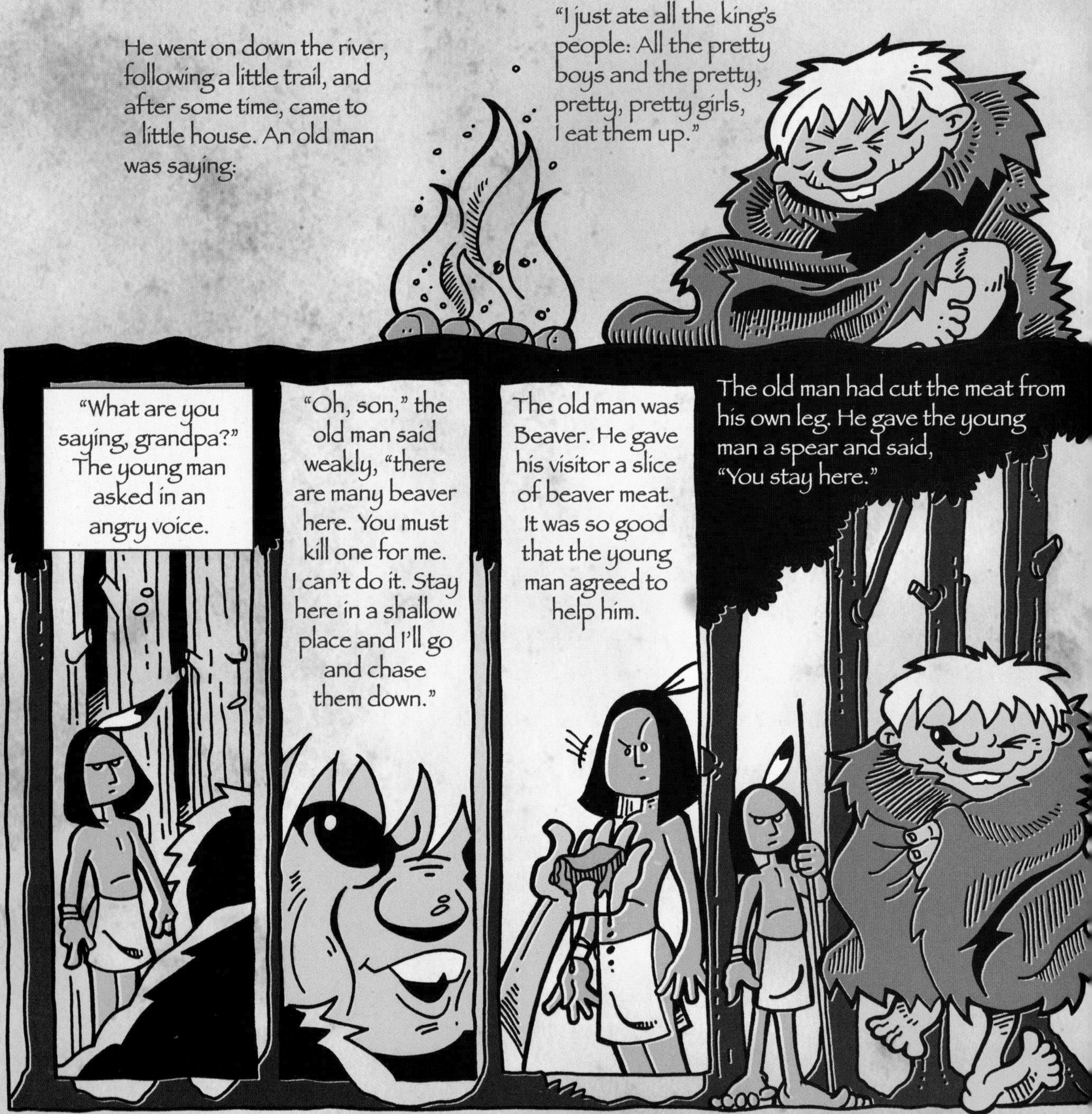
He went on down the river, following a little trail, and after some time, came to a little house. An old man was saying:
"I just ate all the king's people: All the pretty boys and the pretty, pretty, pretty girls, I eat them up."
"What are you saying, grandpa?" The young man asked in an angry voice.
"Oh, son," the old man said weakly, "there are many beaver here. You must kill one for me. I can't do it. Stay here in a shallow place and I'll go and chase them down."
The old man was Beaver. He gave his visitor a slice of beaver meat. It was so good that the young man agreed to help him.
The old man had cut the meat from his own leg. He gave the young man a spear and said, "You stay here."

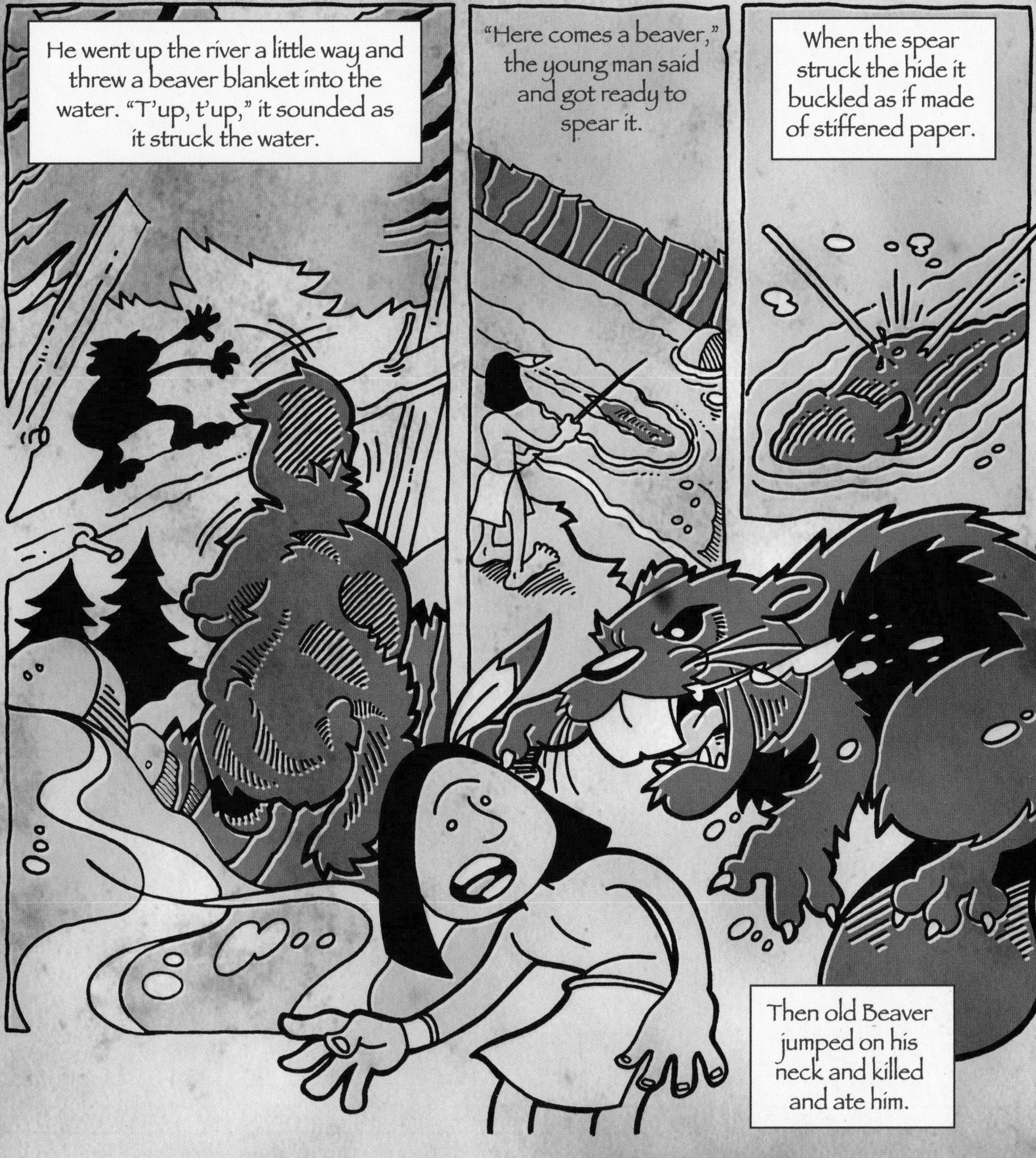
He went up the river a little way and threw a beaver blanket into the water. "T'up, t'up," it sounded as it struck the water.
"Here comes a beaver," the young man said and got ready to spear it.
When the spear struck the hide it buckled as if made of stiffened paper.
Then old Beaver jumped on his neck and killed and ate him.

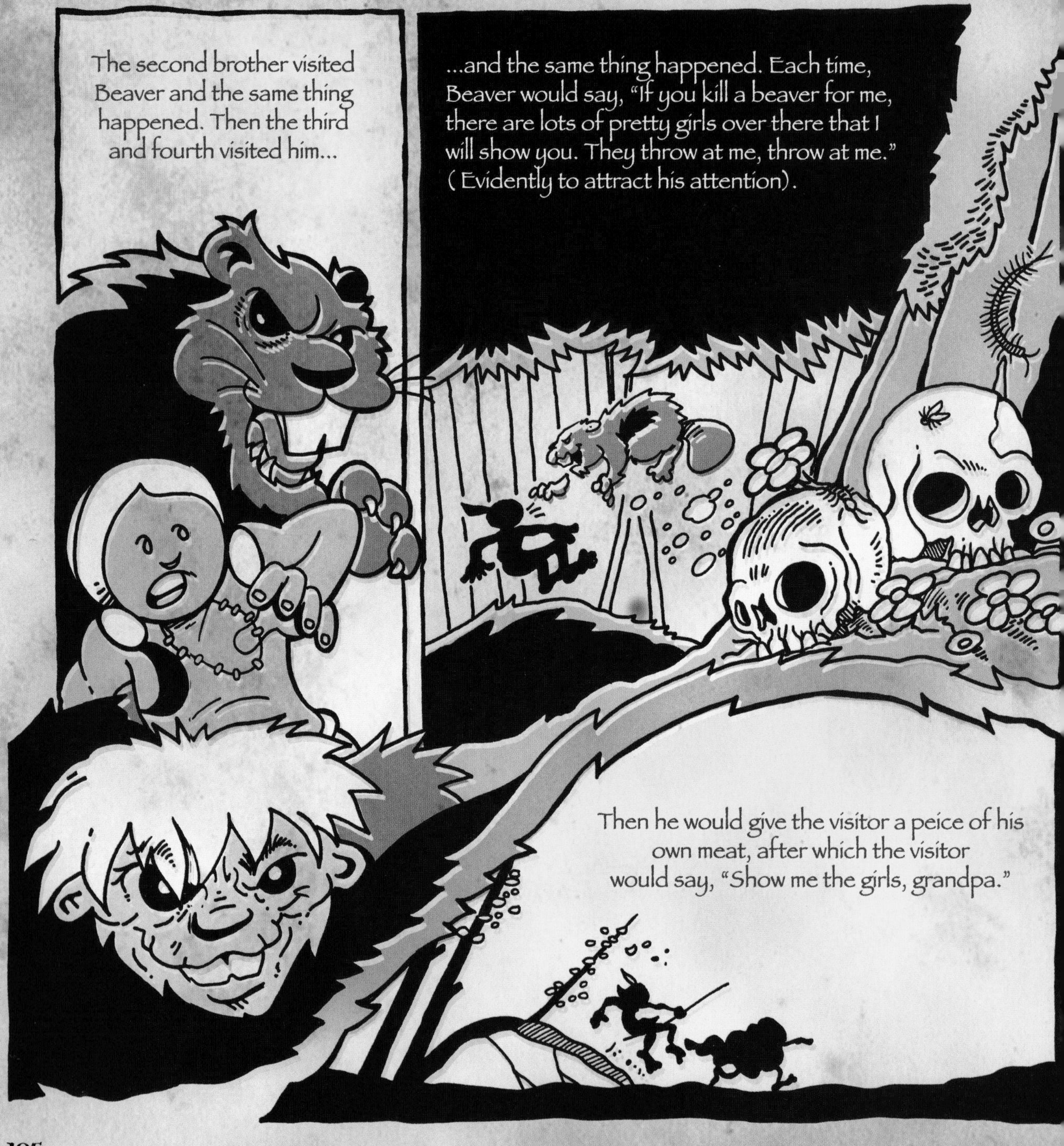
The second brother visited Beaver and the same thing happened. Then the third and fourth visited him...
...and the same thing happened. Each time, Beaver would say, "If you kill a beaver for me, there are lots of pretty girls over there that I will show you. They throw at me, throw at me." (Evidently to attract his attention).
Then he would give the visitor a peice of his own meat, after which the visitor would say, "Show me the girls, grandpa."

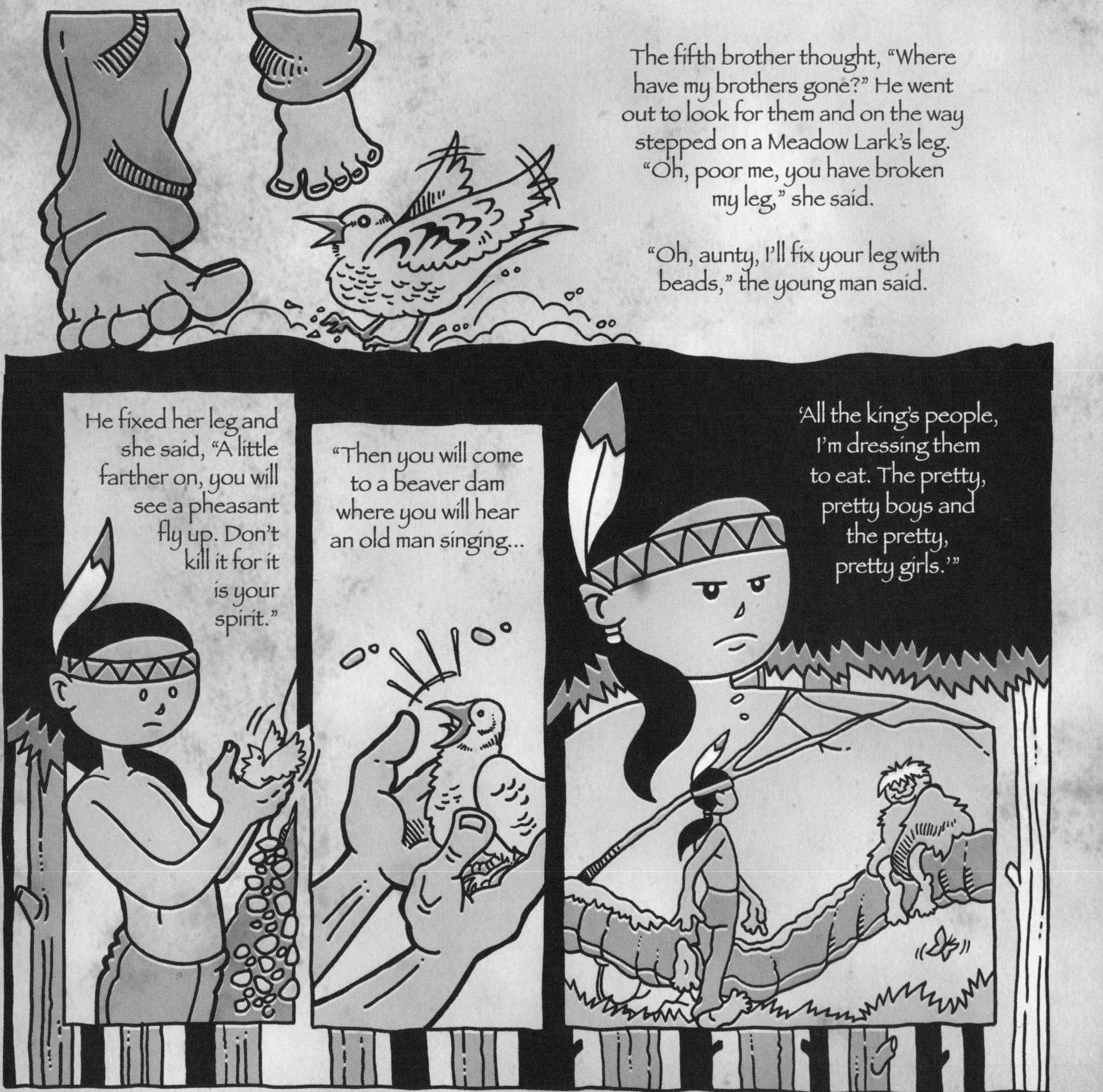
The fifth brother thought, "Where have my brothers gone?" He went out to look for them and on the way stepped on a Meadow Lark's leg. "Oh, poor me, you have broken my leg," she said.
"Oh, aunty, I'll fix your leg with beads," the young man said.
He fixed her leg and she said, "A little farther on, you will see a pheasant fly up. Don't kill it for it is your spirit."
"Then you will come to a beaver dam where you will hear an old man singing...
'All the king's people, I'm dressing them to eat. The pretty, pretty boys and the pretty, pretty girls.'"

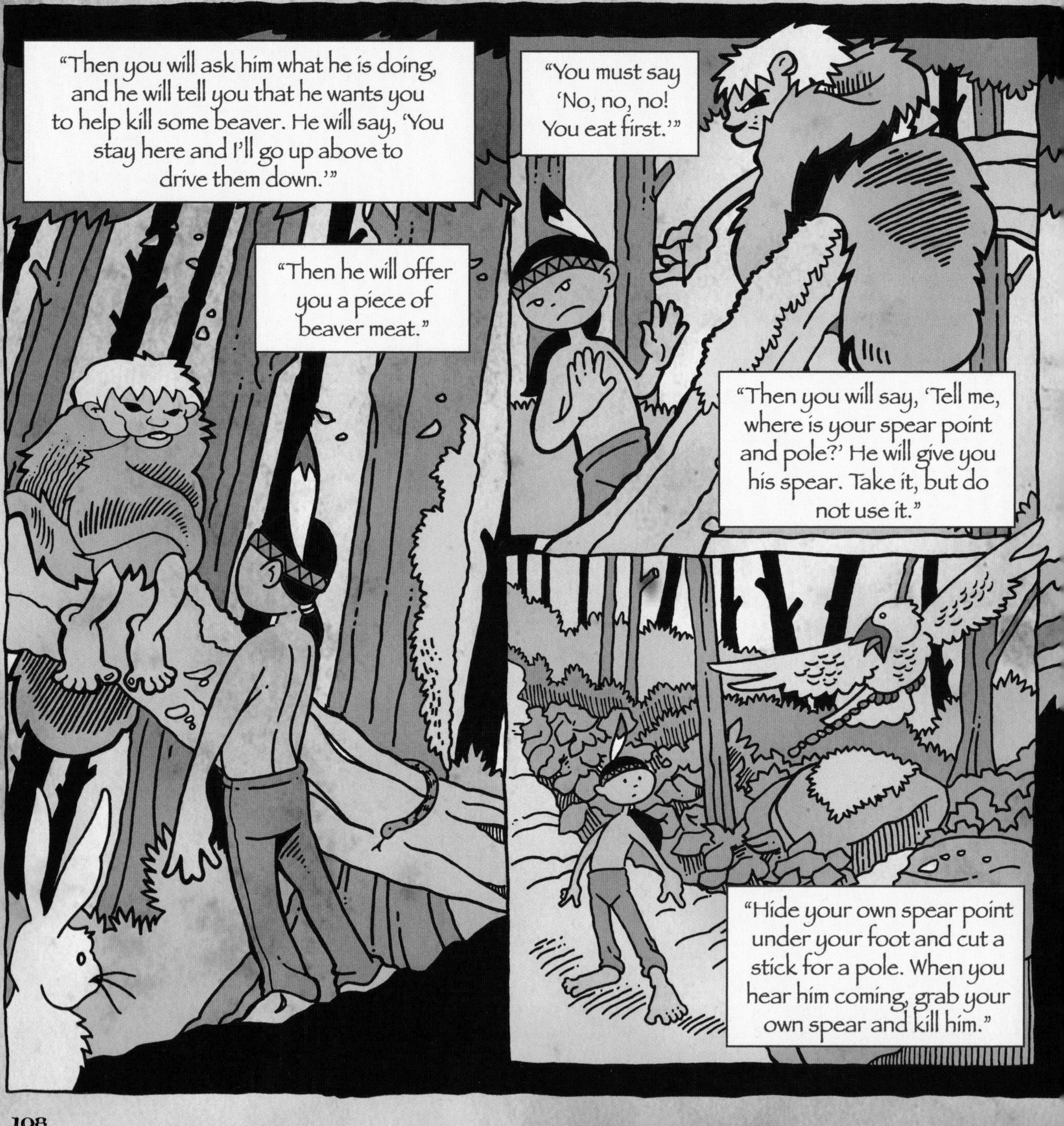
"Then you will ask him what he is doing, and he will tell you that he wants you to help kill some beaver. He will say, 'You stay here and I'll go up above to drive them down.'"
"Then he will offer you a piece of beaver meat."
"You must say 'No, no, no! You eat first.'"
"Then you will say, 'Tell me, where is your spear point and pole?' He will give you his spear. Take it, but do not use it."
"Hide your own spear point under your foot and cut a stick for a pole. When you hear him coming, grab your own spear and kill him."

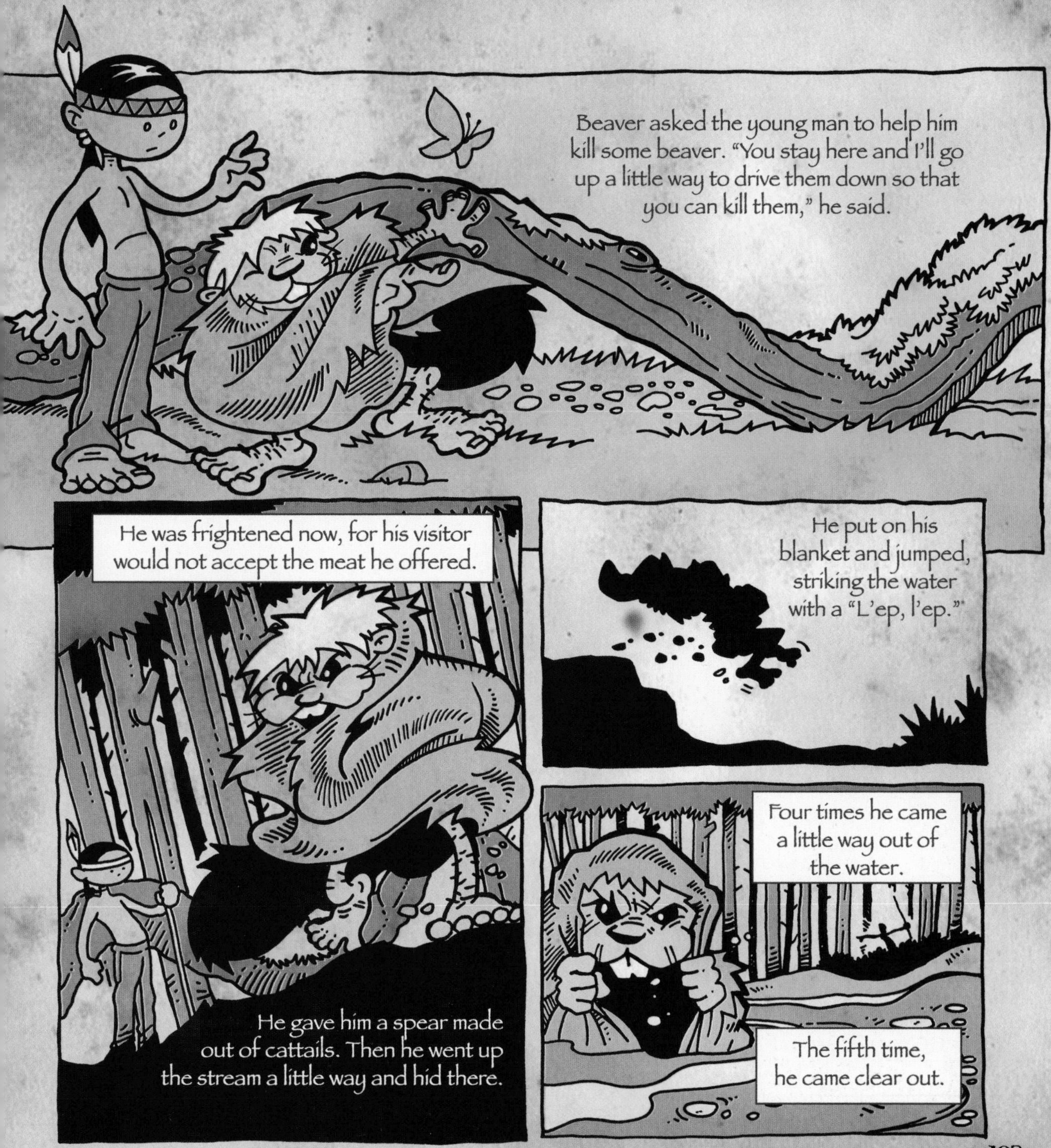
Beaver asked the young man to help him kill some beaver. "You stay here and I'll go up a little way to drive them down so that you can kill them," he said.
He was frightened now, for his visitor would not accept the meat he offered.
He gave him a spear made out of cattails. Then he went up the stream a little way and hid there.
He put on his blanket and jumped, striking the water with a "L'ep, l'ep."
Four times he came a little way out of the water.
The fifth time, he came clear out.

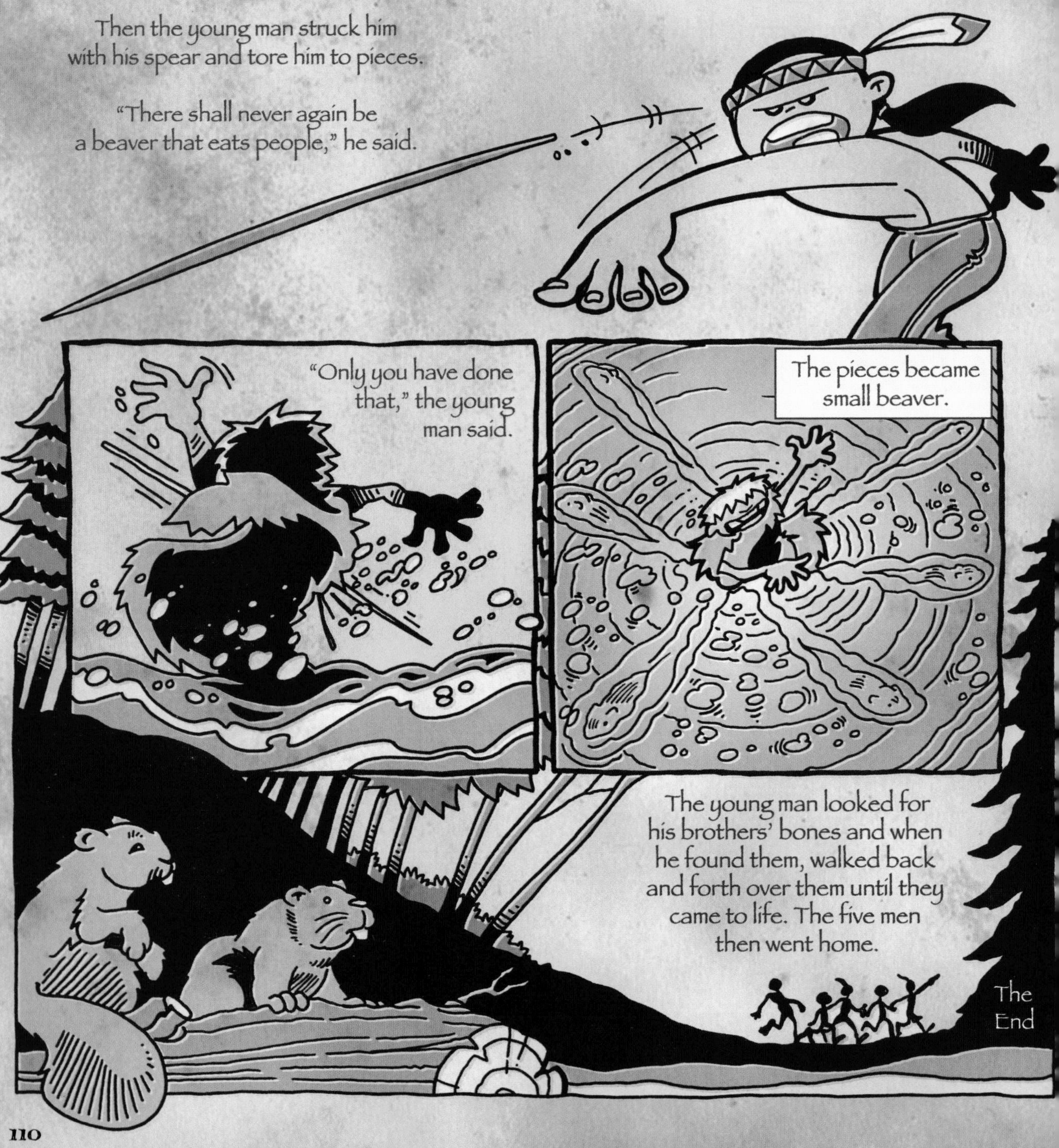
Then the young man struck him with his spear and tore him to pieces.
"There shall never again be a beaver that eats people," he said.
"Only you have done that," the young man said.
The pieces became small beaver.
The young man looked for his brothers' bones and when he found them, walked back and forth over them until they came to life. The five men then went home.
The End

GIDDY UP, WOLFIE

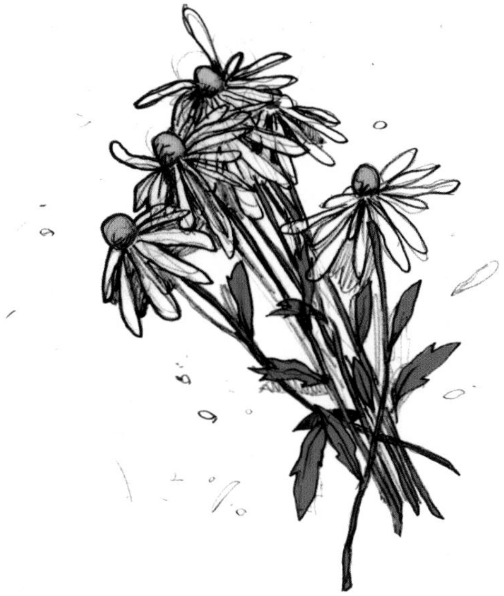

BY
GREG RODGERS
AND
MIKE SHORT

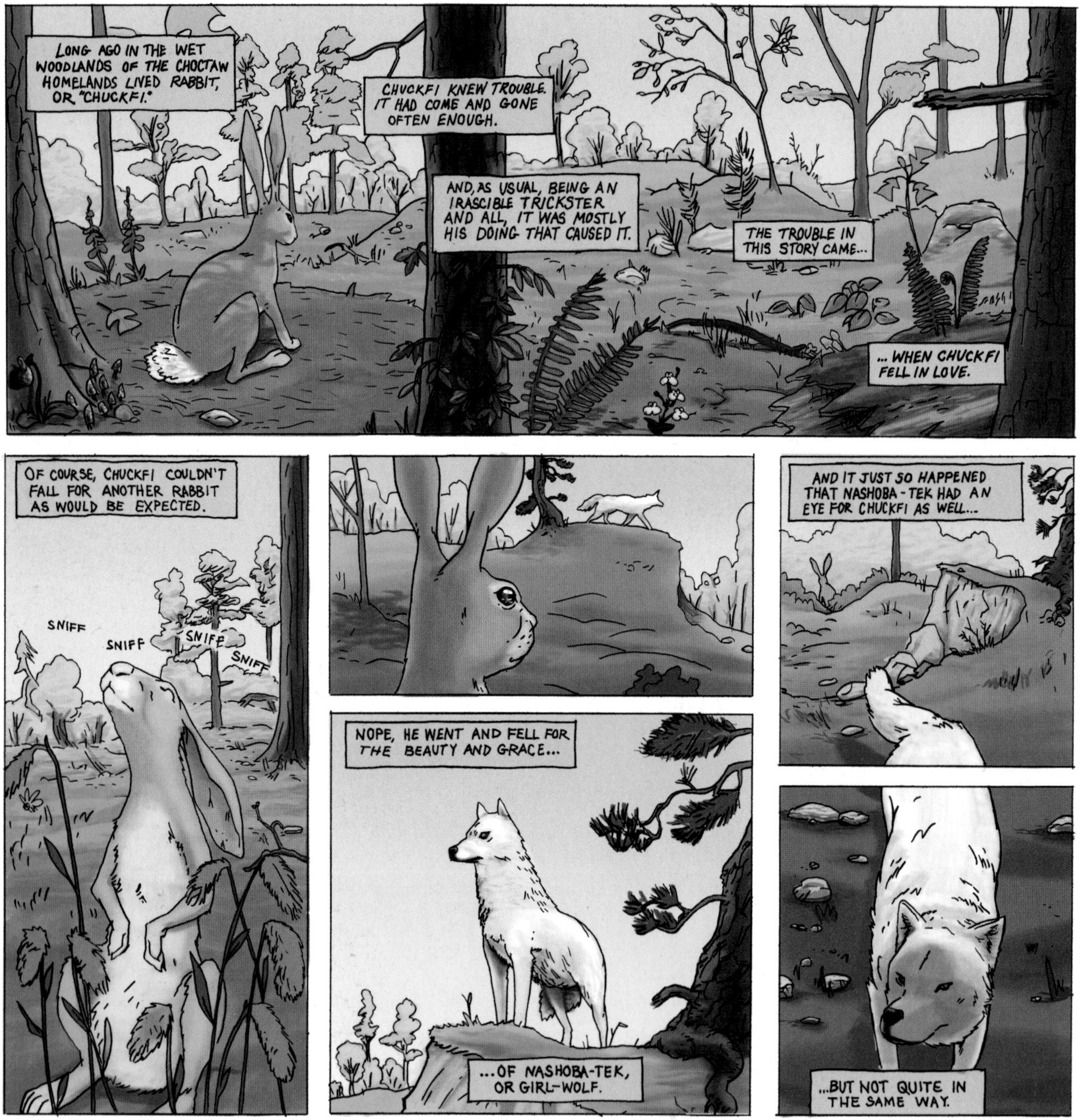
LONG AGO IN THE WET WOODLANDS OF THE CHOCTAW HOMELANDS LIVED RABBIT, OR "CHUCKFI."
CHUCKFI KNEW TROUBLE. IT HAD COME AND GONE OFTEN ENOUGH.
AND, AS USUAL, BEING AN IRASCIBLE TRICKSTER AND ALL, IT WAS MOSTLY HIS DOING THAT CAUSED IT.
THE TROUBLE IN THIS STORY CAME...
... WHEN CHUCKFI FELL IN LOVE.
OF COURSE, CHUCKFI COULDN'T FALL FOR ANOTHER RABBIT AS WOULD BE EXPECTED.
SNIFF
SNIFF
SNIFF
SNIFF
NOPE, HE WENT AND FELL FOR THE BEAUTY AND GRACE...
...OF NASHOBA-TEK, OR GIRL-WOLF.
AND IT JUST SO HAPPENED THAT NASHOBA-TEK HAD AN EYE FOR CHUCKFI AS WELL...
...BUT NOT QUITE IN THE SAME WAY.

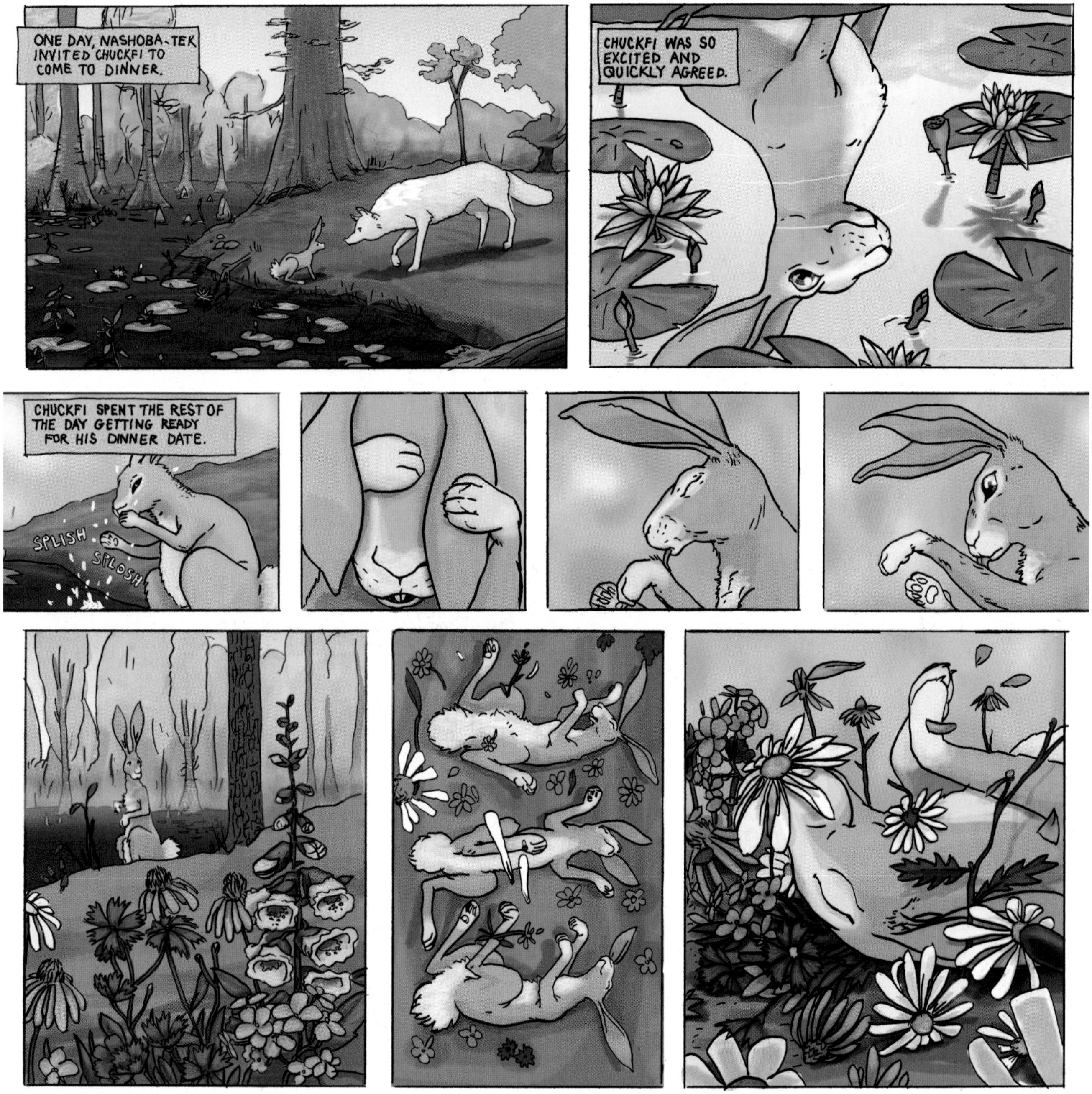

ONE DAY, NASHOBA-TEK INVITED CHUCKFI TO COME TO DINNER.
CHUCKFI WAS SO EXCITED AND QUICKLY AGREED.
CHUCKFI SPENT THE REST OF THE DAY GETTING READY FOR HIS DINNER DATE.
SPLISH
SPLOSH

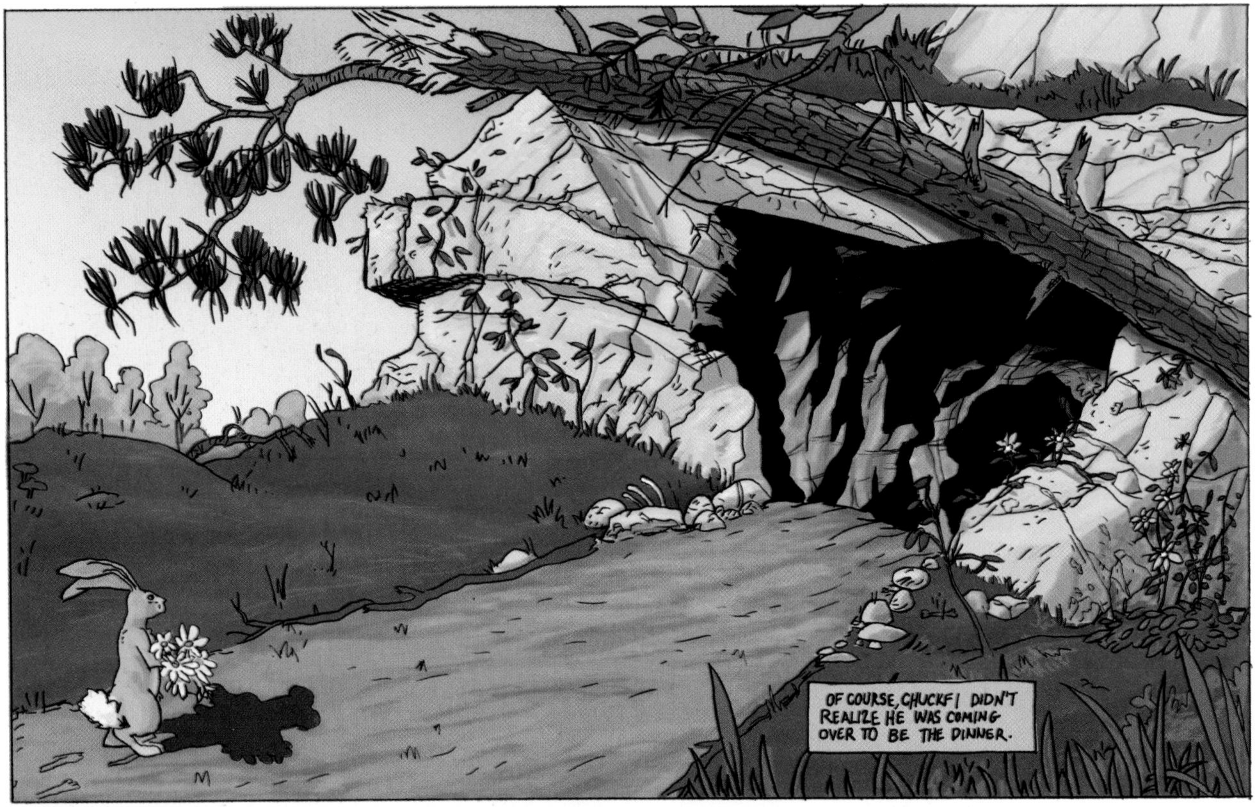
OF COURSE, CHUCKF I DIDN'T REALIZE HE WAS COMING OVER TO BE THE DINNER.

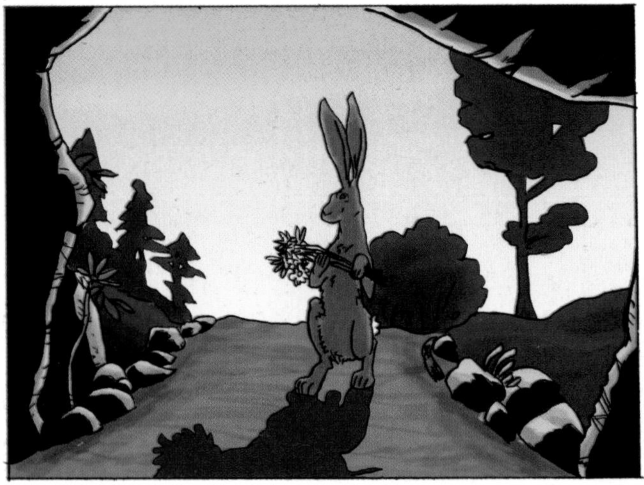

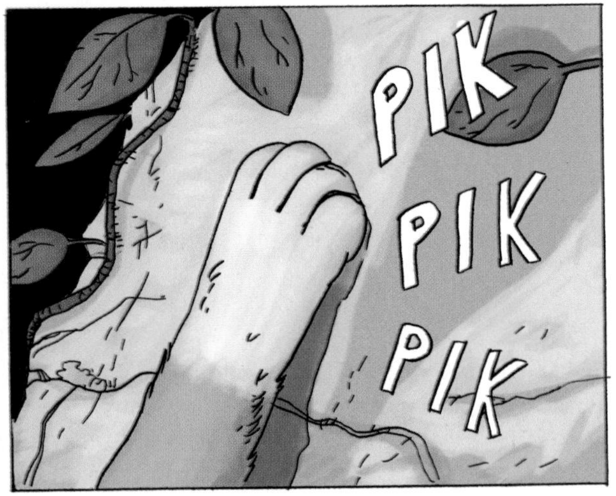
PIK
PIK
PIK

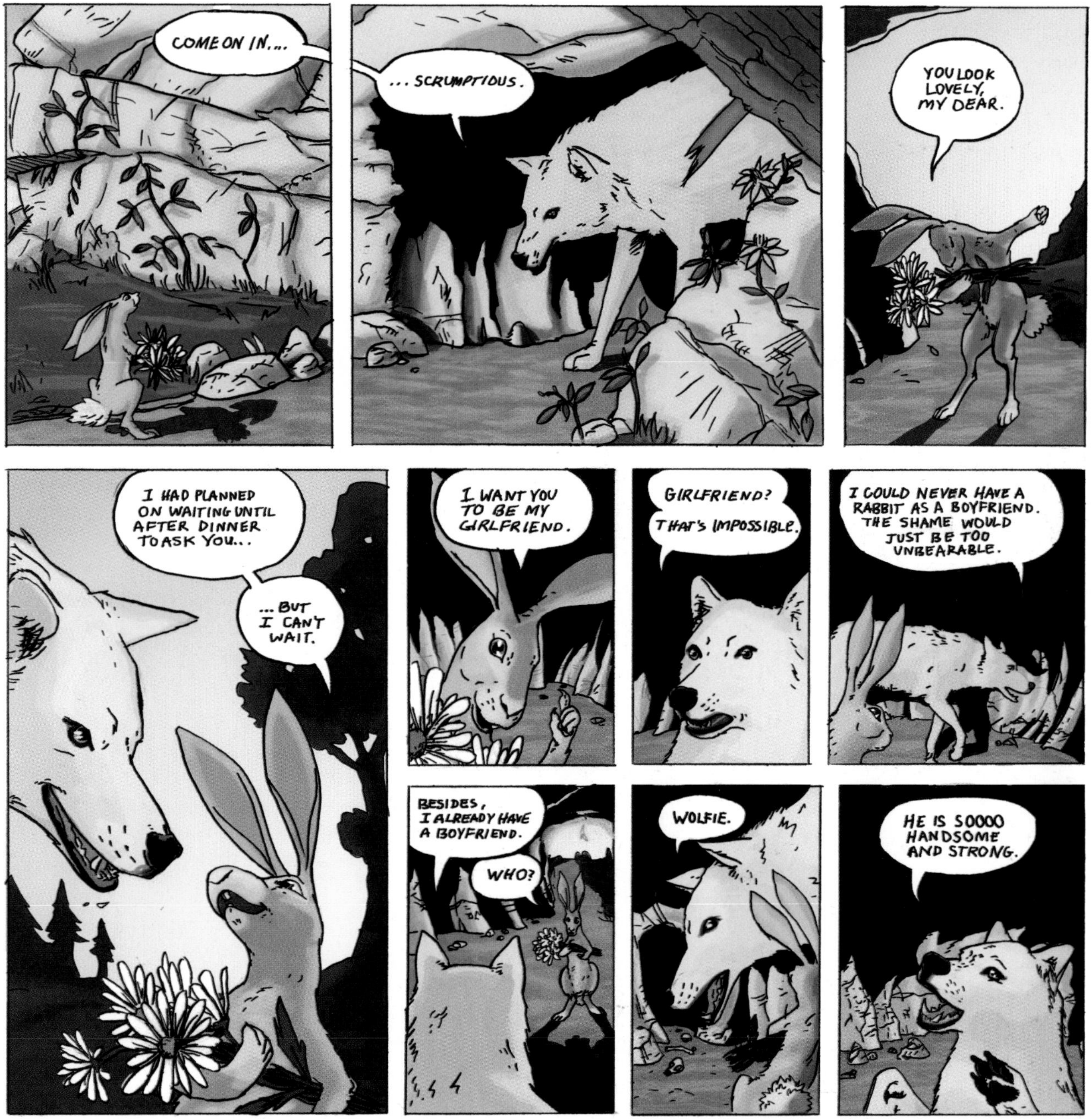
COME ON IN....
... SCRUMPTIOUS.
YOU LOOK LOVELY, MY DEAR.
I HAD PLANNED ON WAITING UNTIL AFTER DINNER TO ASK YOU...
... BUT I CAN'T WAIT.
I WANT YOU TO BE MY GIRLFRIEND.
GIRLFRIEND?
THAT'S IMPOSSIBLE.
I COULD NEVER HAVE A RABBIT AS A BOYFRIEND. THE SHAME WOULD JUST BE TOO UNBEARABLE.
BESIDES, I ALREADY HAVE A BOYFRIEND.
WHO?
WOLFIE.
HE IS SOOOO HANDSOME AND STRONG.

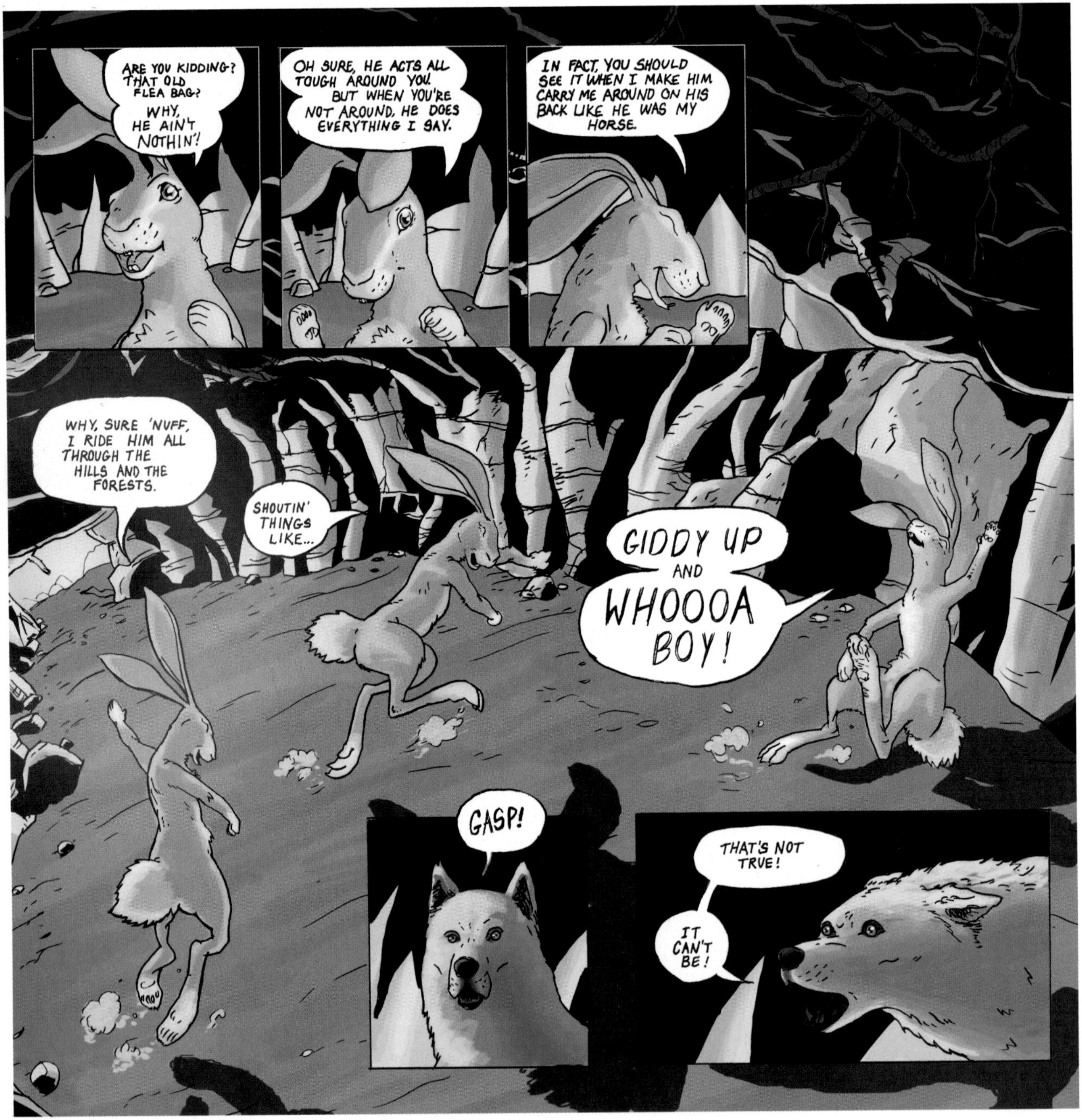
ARE YOU KIDDING? THAT OLD FLEA BAG?
WHY, HE AIN'T NOTHIN'!
OH SURE, HE ACTS ALL TOUGH AROUND YOU. BUT WHEN YOU'RE NOT AROUND, HE DOES EVERYTHING I SAY.
IN FACT, YOU SHOULD SEE IT WHEN I MAKE HIM CARRY ME AROUND ON HIS BACK LIKE HE WAS MY HORSE.
WHY, SURE 'NUFF, I RIDE HIM ALL THROUGH THE HILLS AND THE FORESTS.
SHOUTIN' THINGS LIKE...
GIDDY UP AND WHOOOA BOY!
GASP!
THAT'S NOT TRUE!
IT CAN'T BE!

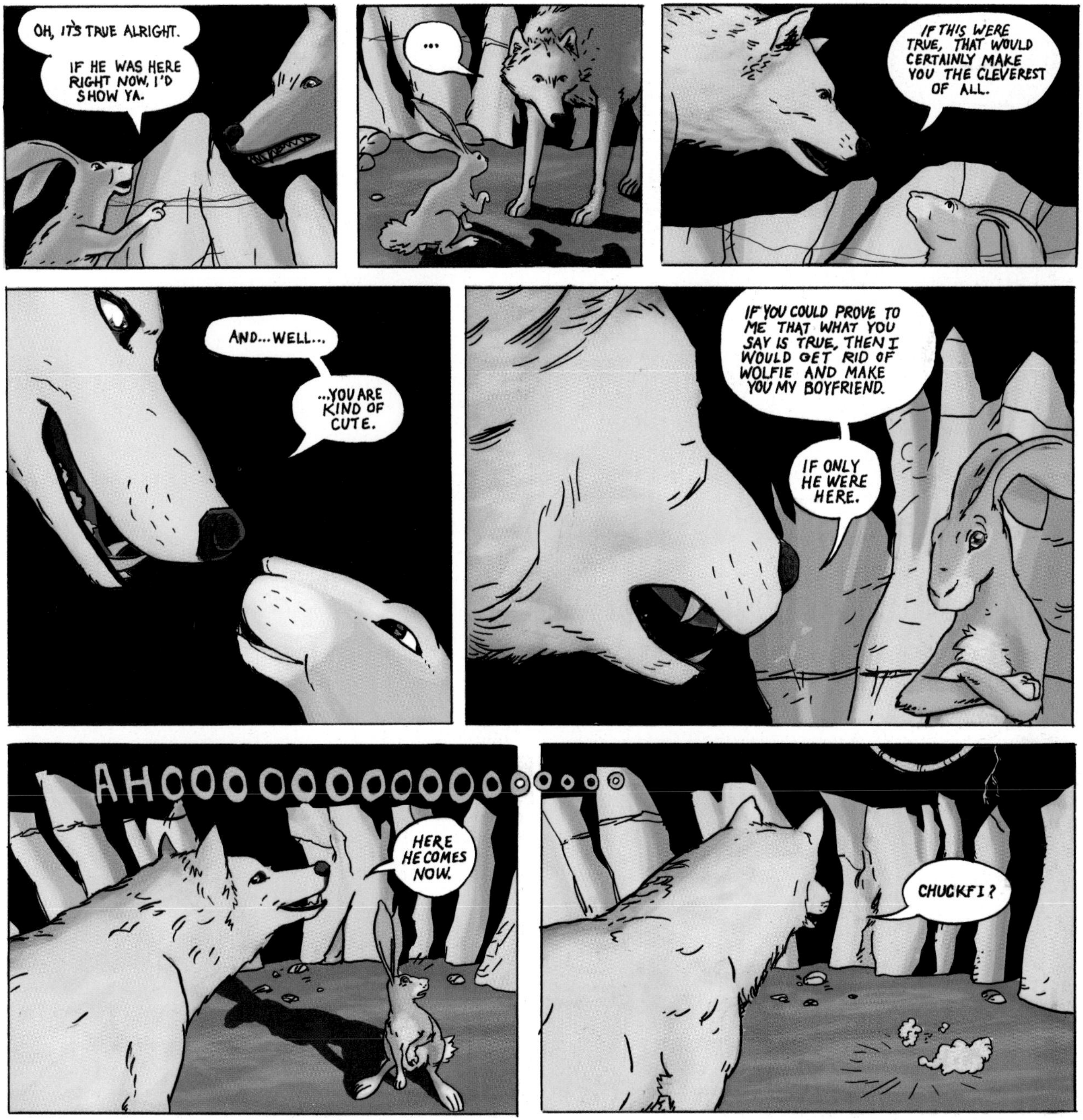
OH, IT'S TRUE ALRIGHT.
IF HE WAS HERE RIGHT NOW, I'D SHOW YA.
...
IF THIS WERE TRUE, THAT WOULD CERTAINLY MAKE YOU THE CLEVEREST OF ALL.
AND... WELL...
...YOU ARE KIND OF CUTE.
IF YOU COULD PROVE TO ME THAT WHAT YOU SAY IS TRUE, THEN I WOULD GET RID OF WOLFIE AND MAKE YOU MY BOYFRIEND.
IF ONLY HE WERE HERE.
AHOOOOOOOOOOOOOOOO
HERE HE COMES NOW.
CHUCKFI?

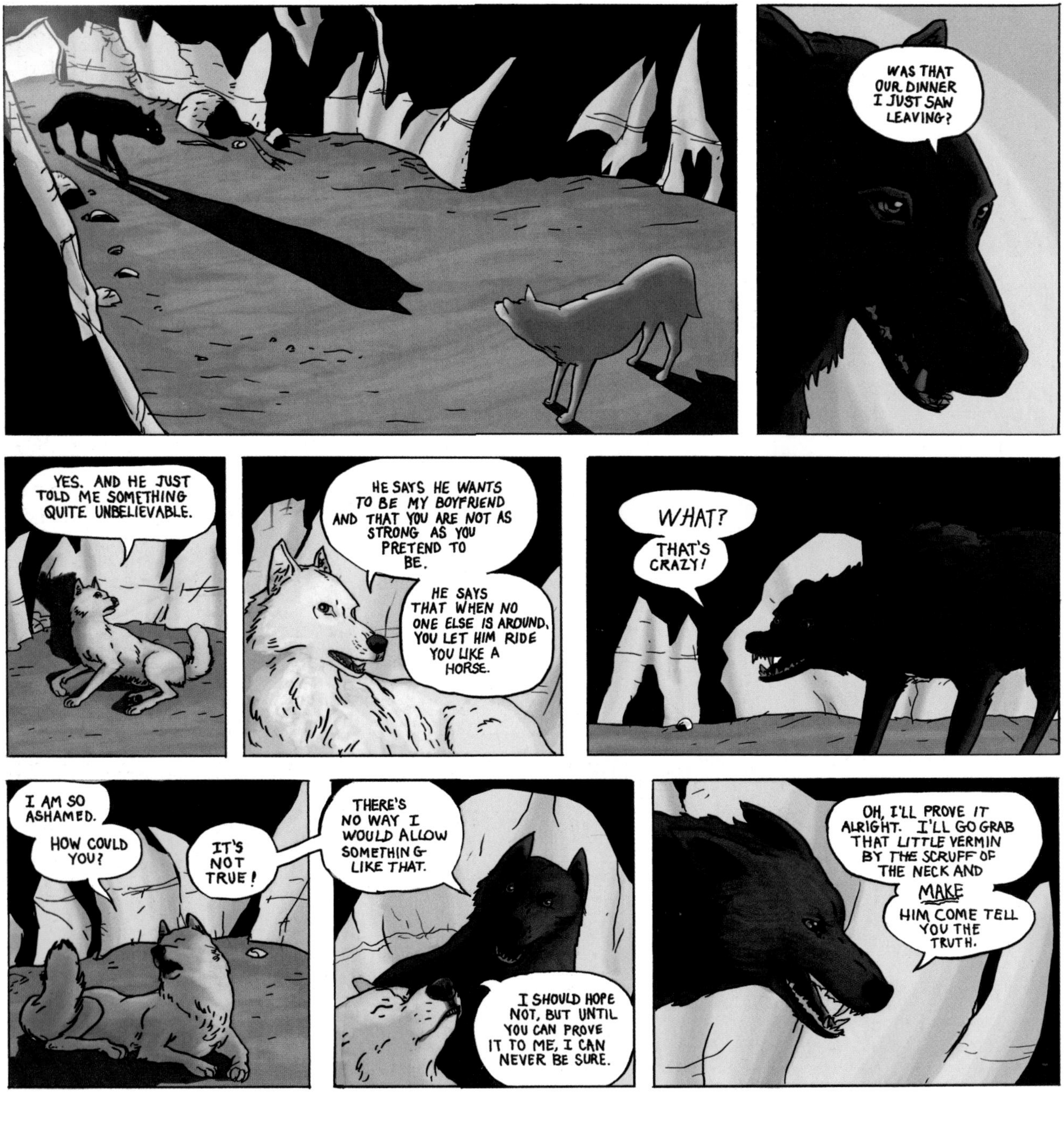
WAS THAT OUR DINNER I JUST SAW LEAVING?
YES. AND HE JUST TOLD ME SOMETHING QUITE UNBELIEVABLE.
HE SAYS HE WANTS TO BE MY BOYFRIEND AND THAT YOU ARE NOT AS STRONG AS YOU PRETEND TO BE.
HE SAYS THAT WHEN NO ONE ELSE IS AROUND, YOU LET HIM RIDE YOU LIKE A HORSE.
WHAT?
THAT'S CRAZY!
I AM SO ASHAMED.
HOW COULD YOU?
IT'S NOT TRUE!
THERE'S NO WAY I WOULD ALLOW SOMETHING LIKE THAT.
I SHOULD HOPE NOT, BUT UNTIL YOU CAN PROVE IT TO ME, I CAN NEVER BE SURE.
OH, I'LL PROVE IT ALRIGHT. I'LL GO GRAB THAT LITTLE VERMIN BY THE SCRUFF OF THE NECK AND MAKE HIM COME TELL YOU THE TRUTH.

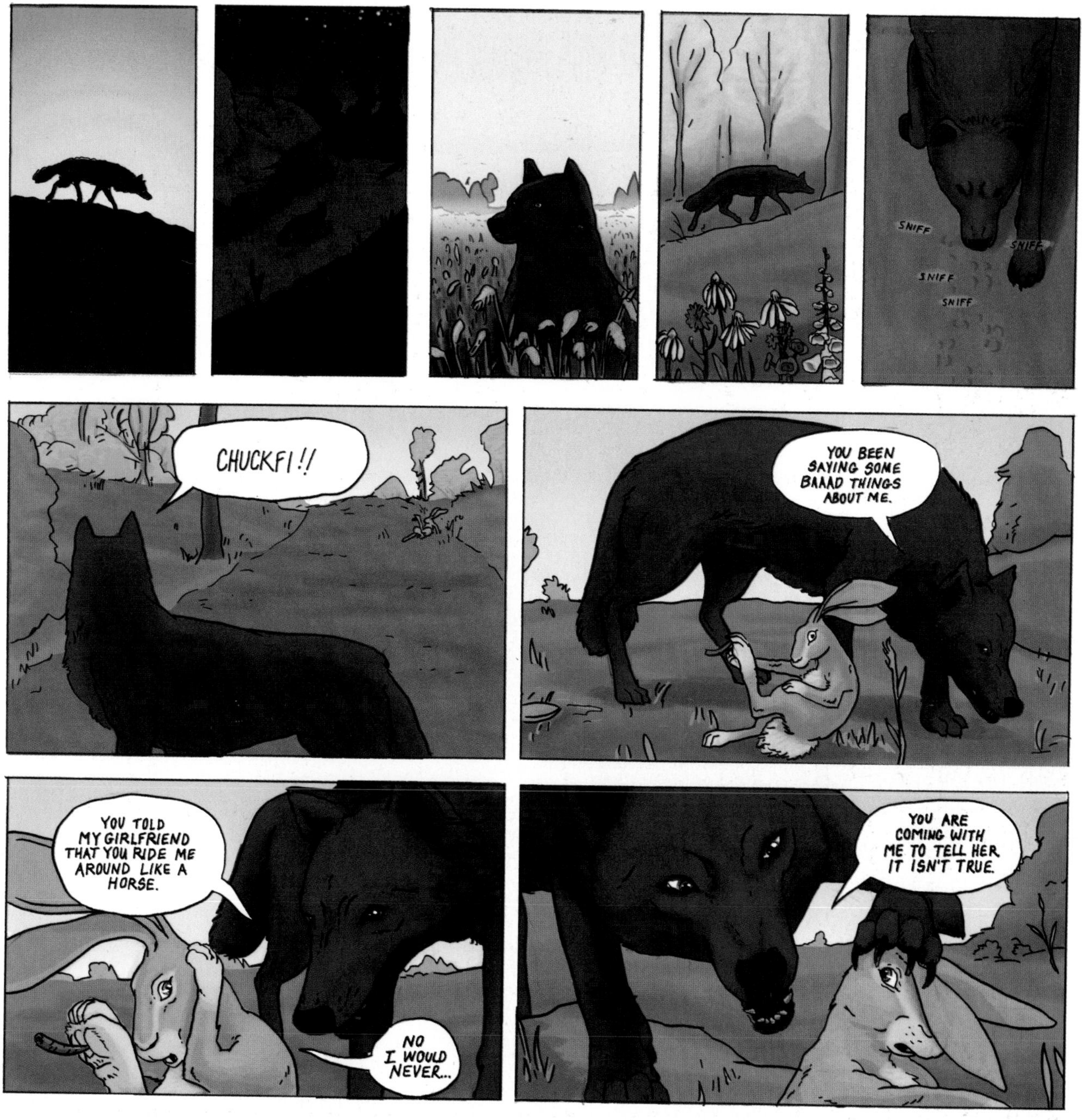
SNIFF
SNIFF
SNIFF
SNIFF
CHUCKFI!!
YOU BEEN SAYING SOME BAAAD THINGS ABOUT ME.
YOU TOLD MY GIRLFRIEND THAT YOU RIDE ME AROUND LIKE A HORSE.
NO I WOULD NEVER...
YOU ARE COMING WITH ME TO TELL HER IT ISN'T TRUE.

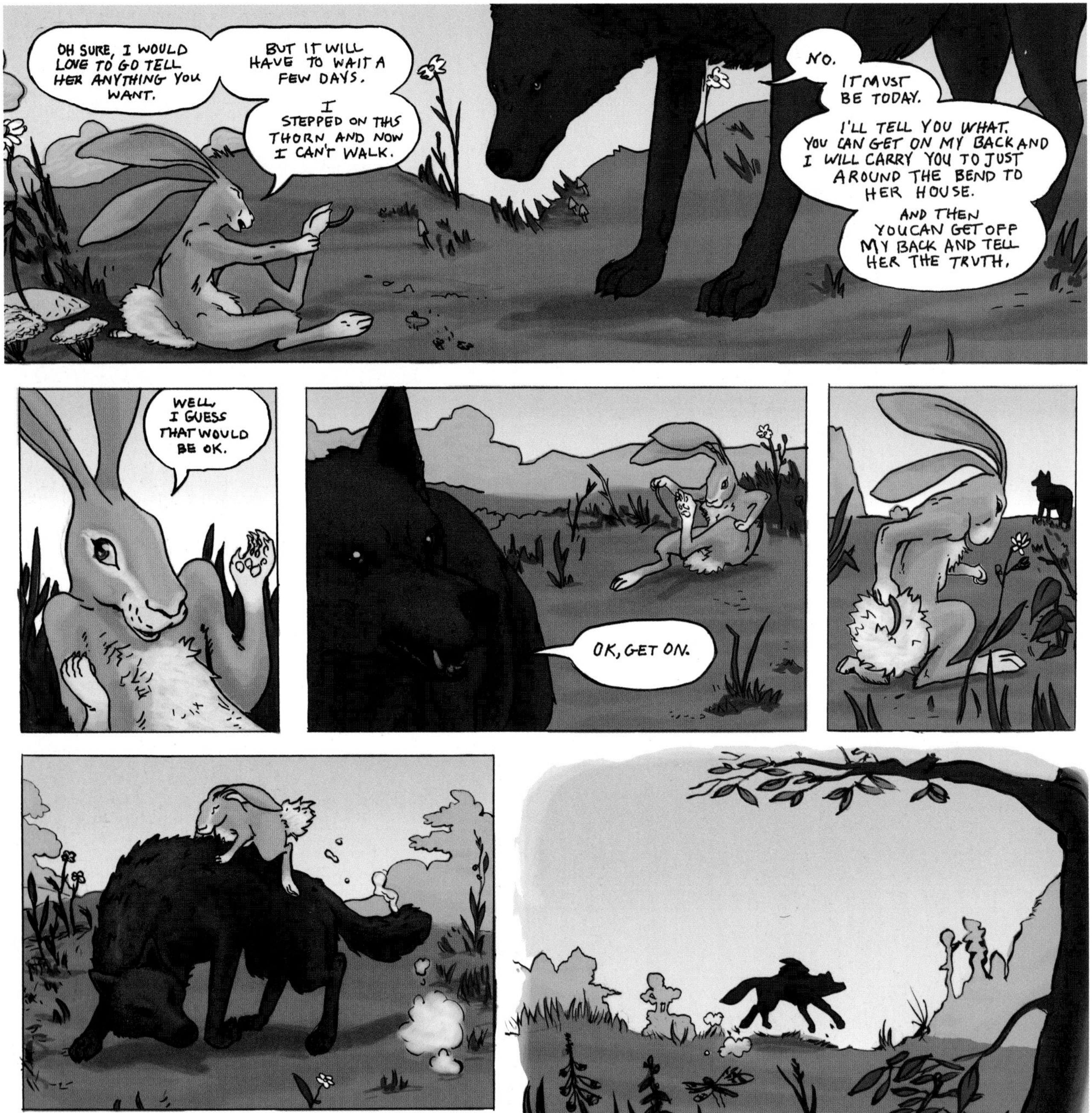
OH SURE, I WOULD LOVE TO GO TELL HER ANYTHING YOU WANT.
BUT IT WILL HAVE TO WAIT A FEW DAYS.
I STEPPED ON THIS THORN AND NOW I CAN'T WALK.
NO.
IT MUST BE TODAY.
I'LL TELL YOU WHAT. YOU CAN GET ON MY BACK AND I WILL CARRY YOU TO JUST AROUND THE BEND TO HER HOUSE.
AND THEN YOU CAN GET OFF MY BACK AND TELL HER THE TRUTH.
WELL, I GUESS THAT WOULD BE OK.
OK, GET ON.

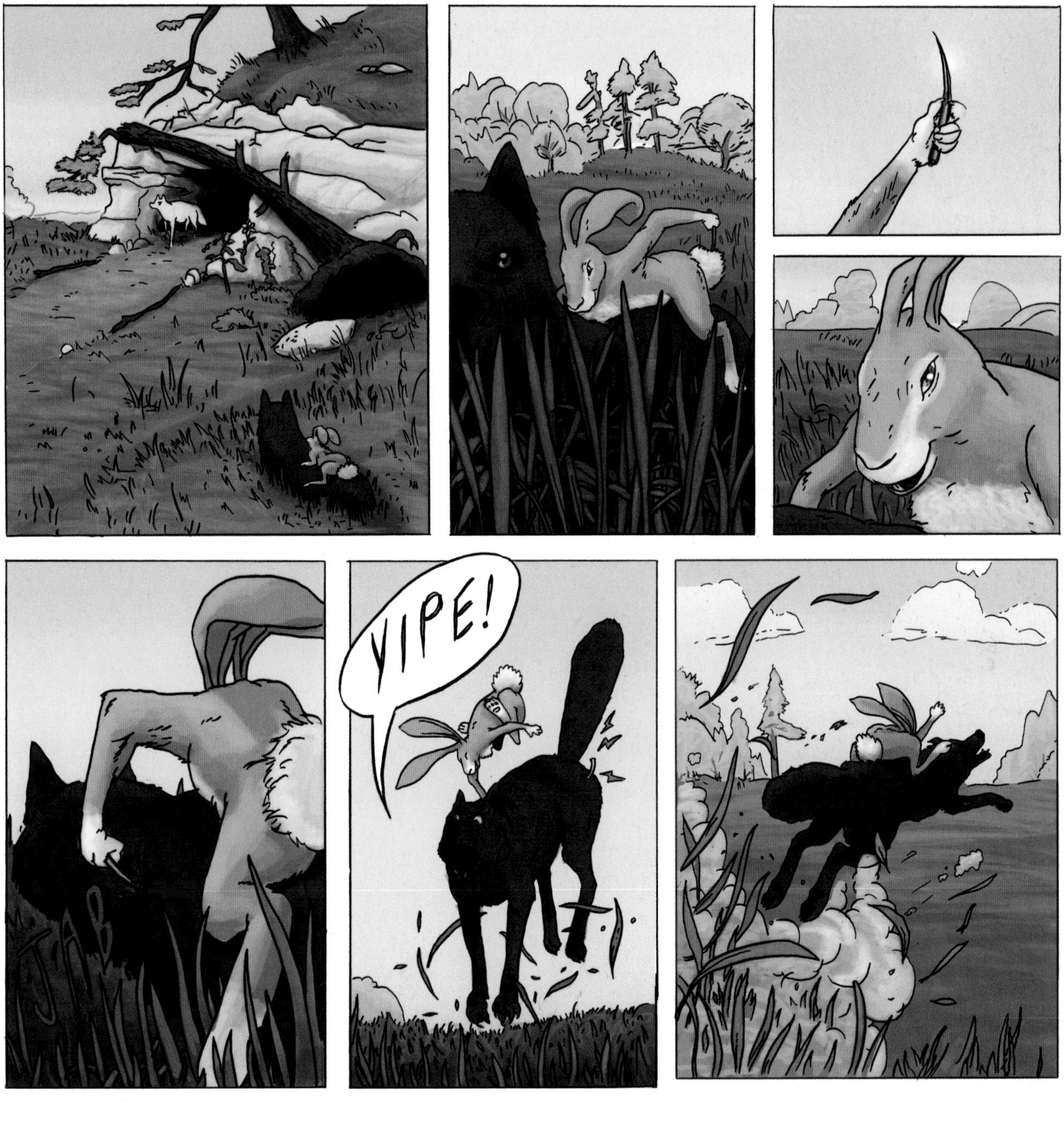
JAB
YIPE!

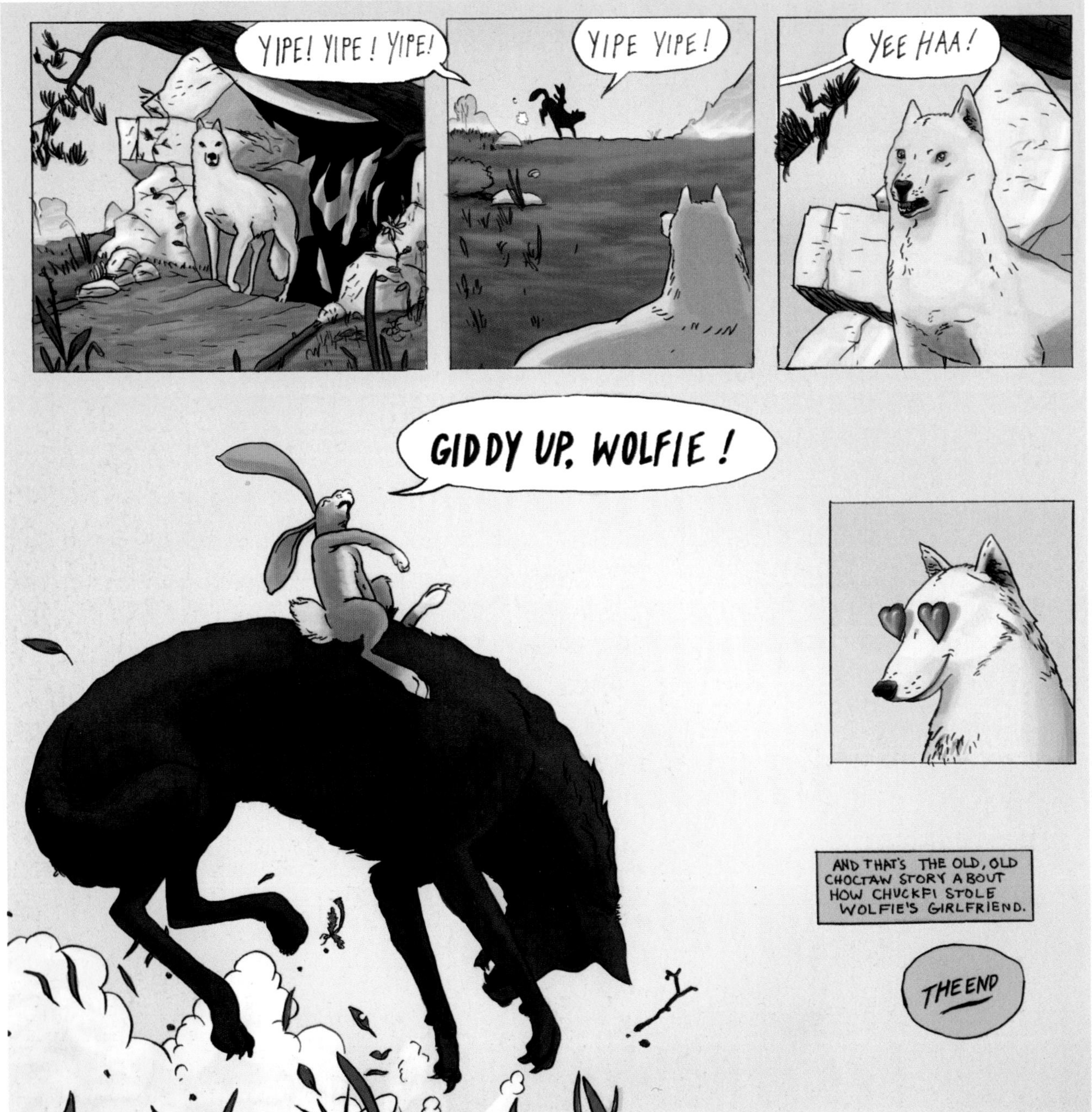
YIPE! YIPE! YIPE!
YIPE YIPE!
YEE HAA!
GIDDY UP, WOLFIE!
AND THAT'S THE OLD, OLD CHOCTAW STORY ABOUT HOW CHUCKFI STOLE WOLFIE'S GIRLFRIEND.
THE END

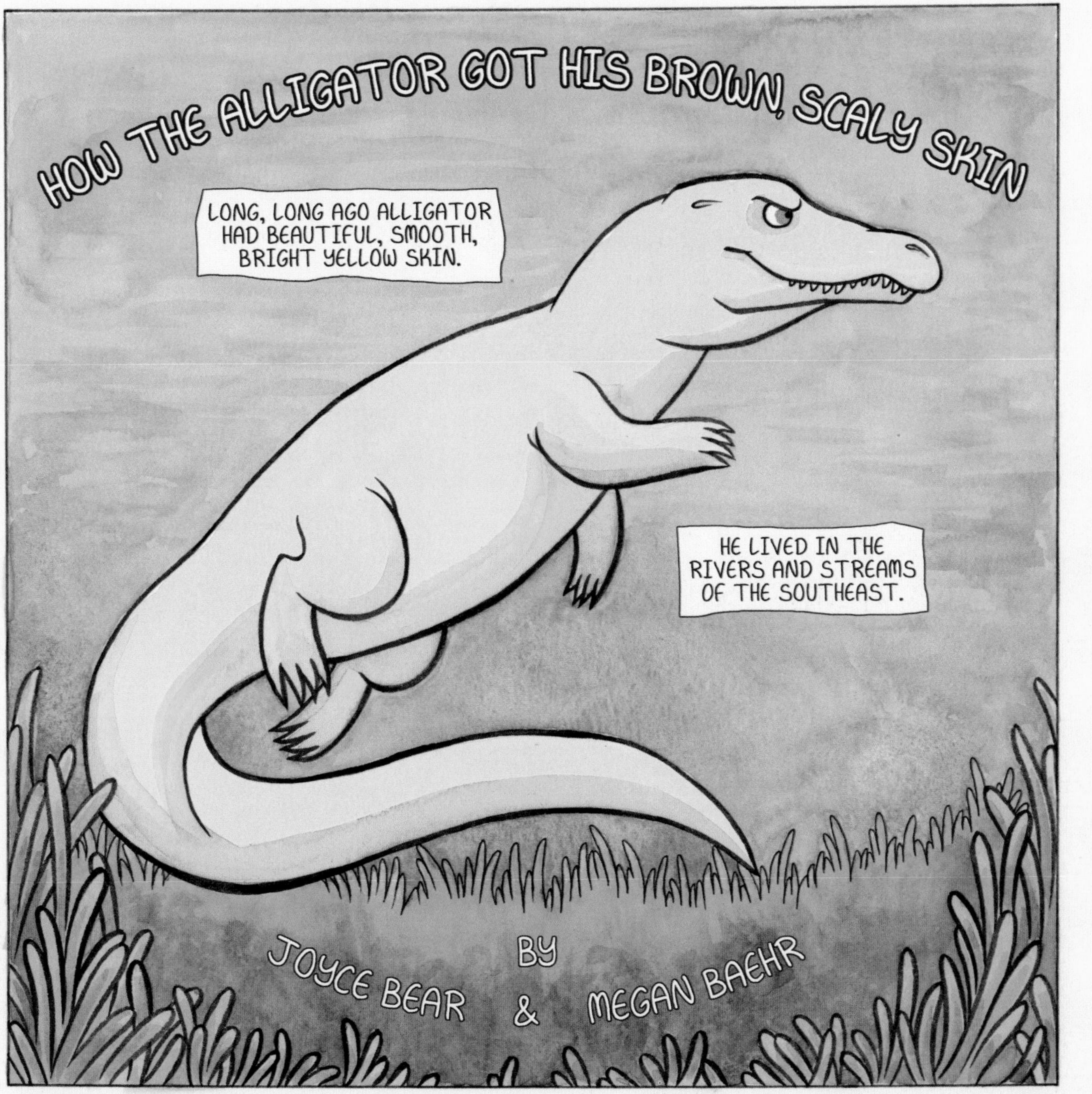
HOW THE ALLIGATOR GOT HIS BROWN, SCALY SKIN
LONG, LONG AGO ALLIGATOR HAD BEAUTIFUL, SMOOTH, BRIGHT YELLOW SKIN.
HE LIVED IN THE RIVERS AND STREAMS OF THE SOUTHEAST.
BY
JOYCE BEAR & MEGAN BAEHR

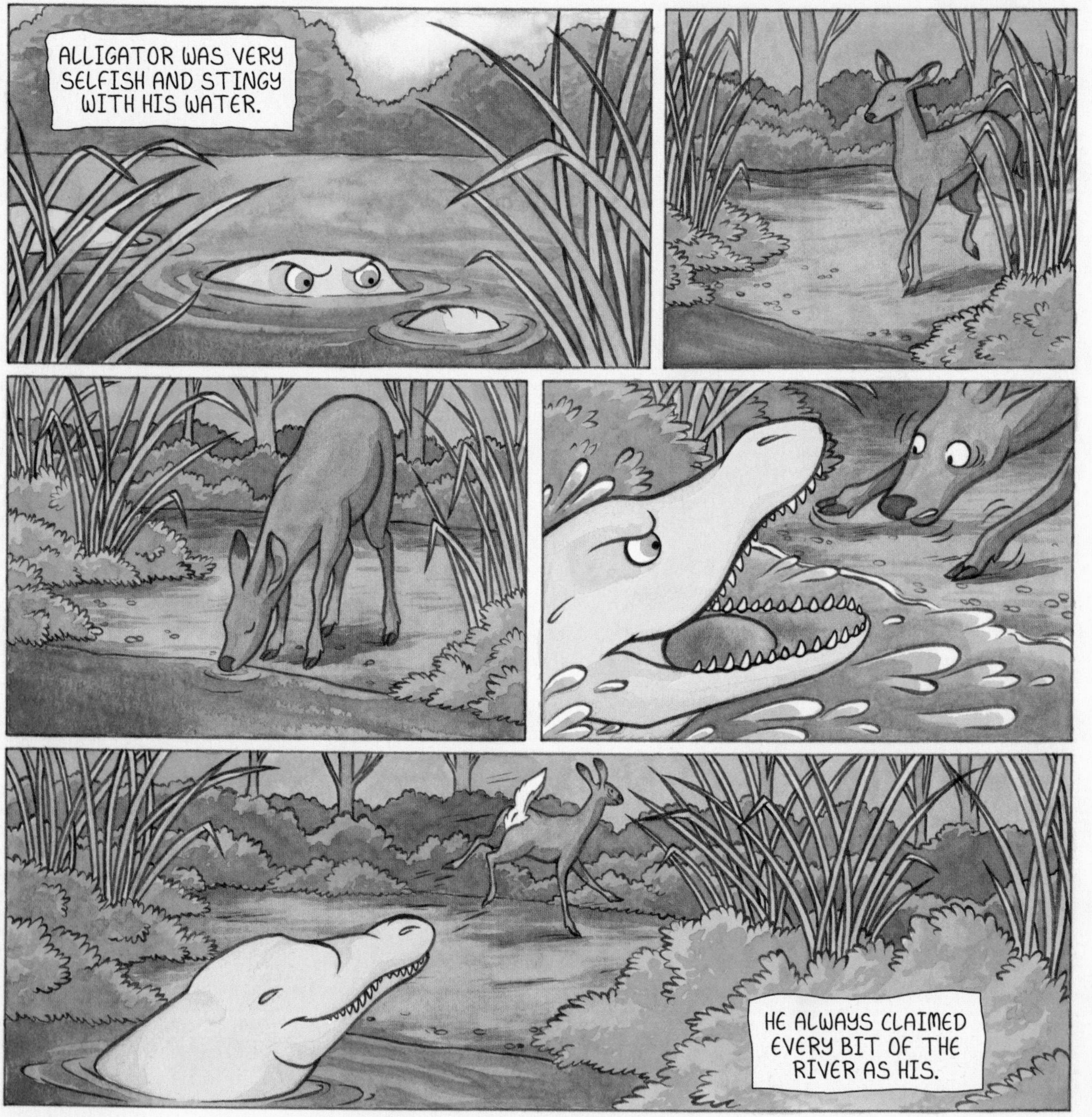
ALLIGATOR WAS VERY SELFISH AND STINGY WITH HIS WATER.
HE ALWAYS CLAIMED EVERY BIT OF THE RIVER AS HIS.

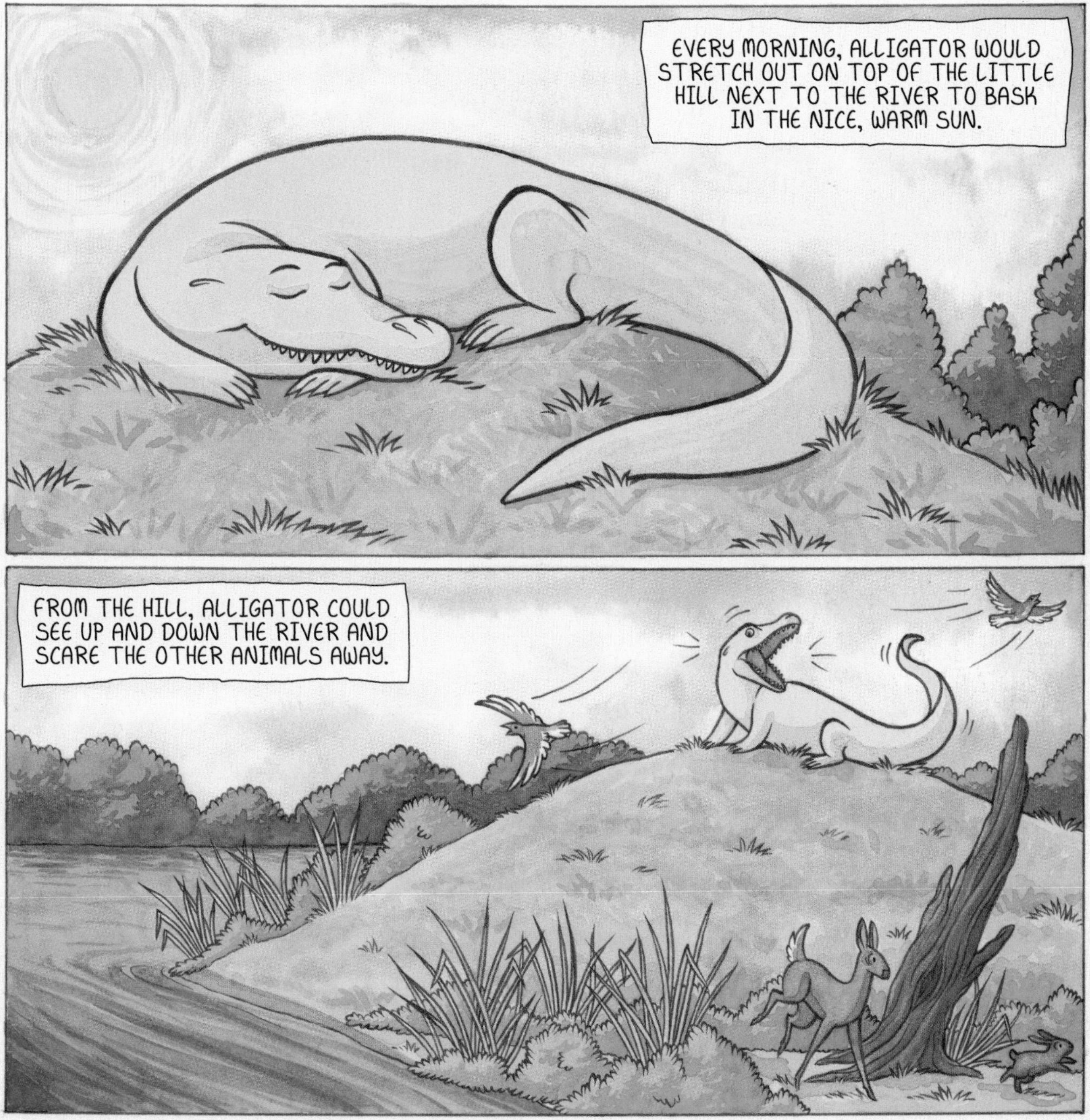
EVERY MORNING, ALLIGATOR WOULD STRETCH OUT ON TOP OF THE LITTLE HILL NEXT TO THE RIVER TO BASK IN THE NICE, WARM SUN.
FROM THE HILL, ALLIGATOR COULD SEE UP AND DOWN THE RIVER AND SCARE THE OTHER ANIMALS AWAY.

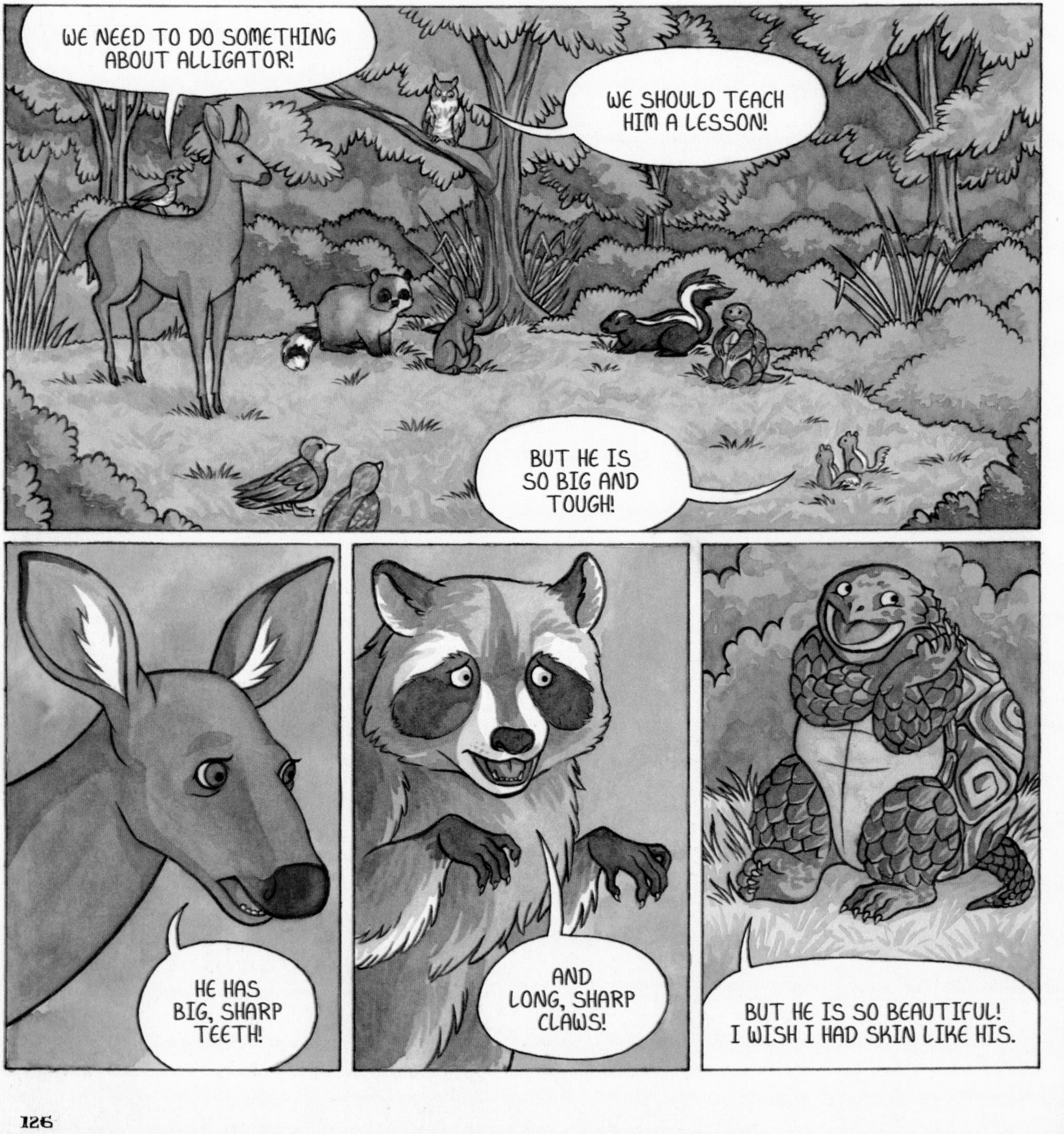
WE NEED TO DO SOMETHING ABOUT ALLIGATOR!
WE SHOULD TEACH HIM A LESSON!
BUT HE IS SO BIG AND TOUGH!
HE HAS BIG, SHARP TEETH!
AND LONG, SHARP CLAWS!
BUT HE IS SO BEAUTIFUL! I WISH I HAD SKIN LIKE HIS.

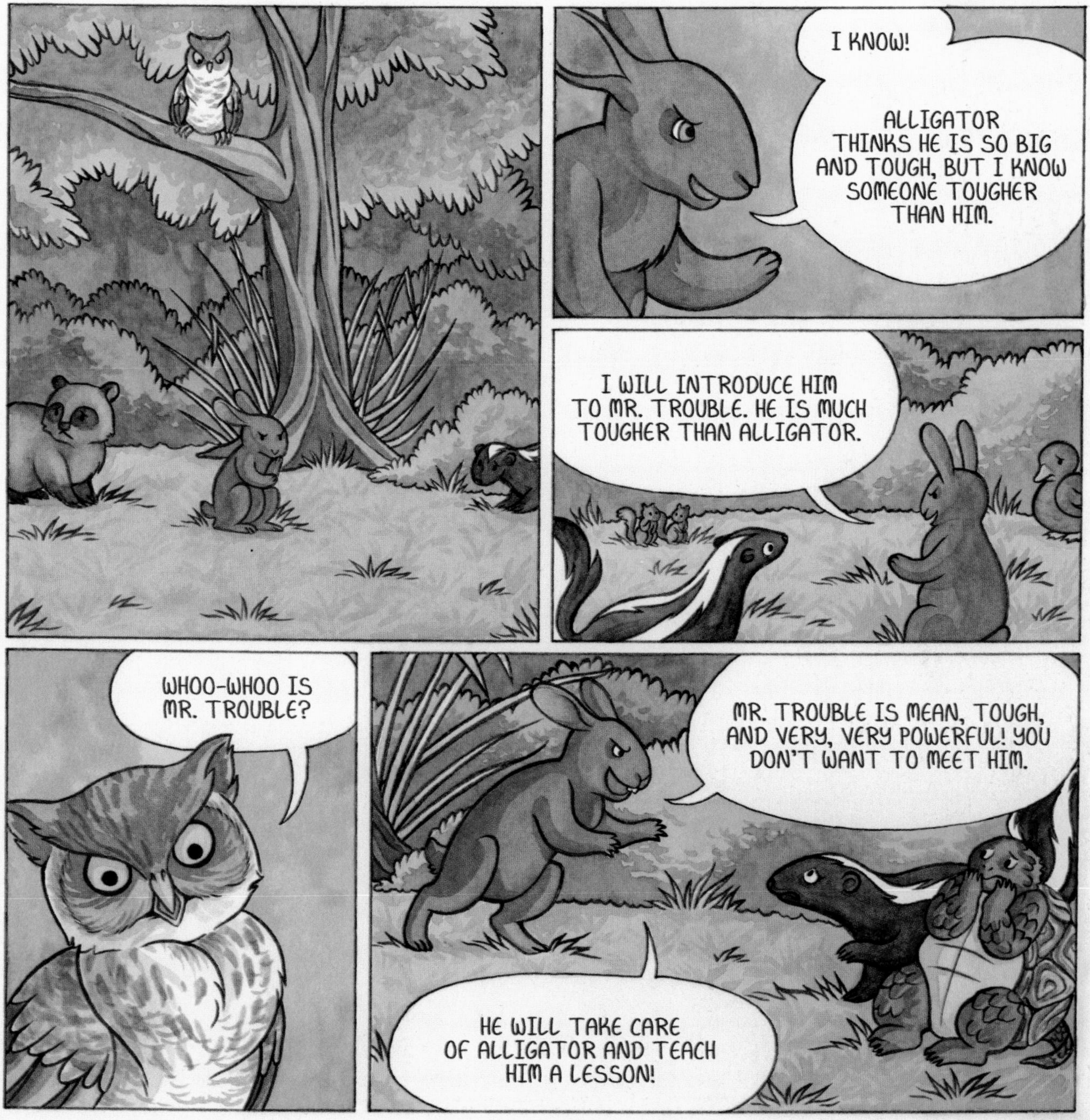
I KNOW!
ALLIGATOR THINKS HE IS SO BIG AND TOUGH, BUT I KNOW SOMEONE TOUGHER THAN HIM.
I WILL INTRODUCE HIM TO MR. TROUBLE. HE IS MUCH TOUGHER THAN ALLIGATOR.
WHOO-WHOO IS MR. TROUBLE?
MR. TROUBLE IS MEAN, TOUGH, AND VERY, VERY POWERFUL! YOU DON'T WANT TO MEET HIM.
HE WILL TAKE CARE OF ALLIGATOR AND TEACH HIM A LESSON!

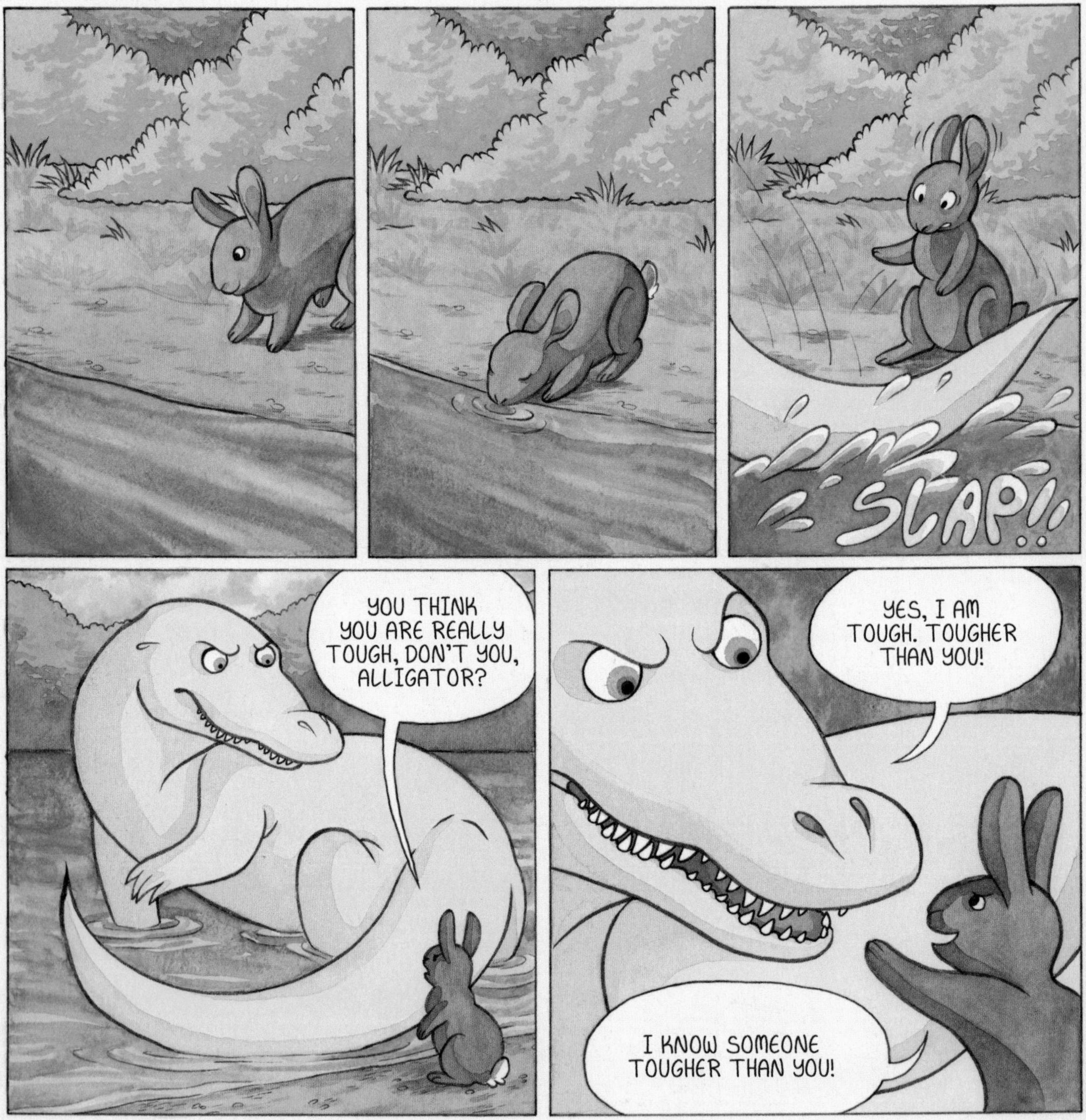
SLAP!!
YOU THINK YOU ARE REALLY TOUGH, DON'T YOU, ALLIGATOR?
YES, I AM TOUGH. TOUGHER THAN YOU!
I KNOW SOMEONE TOUGHER THAN YOU!

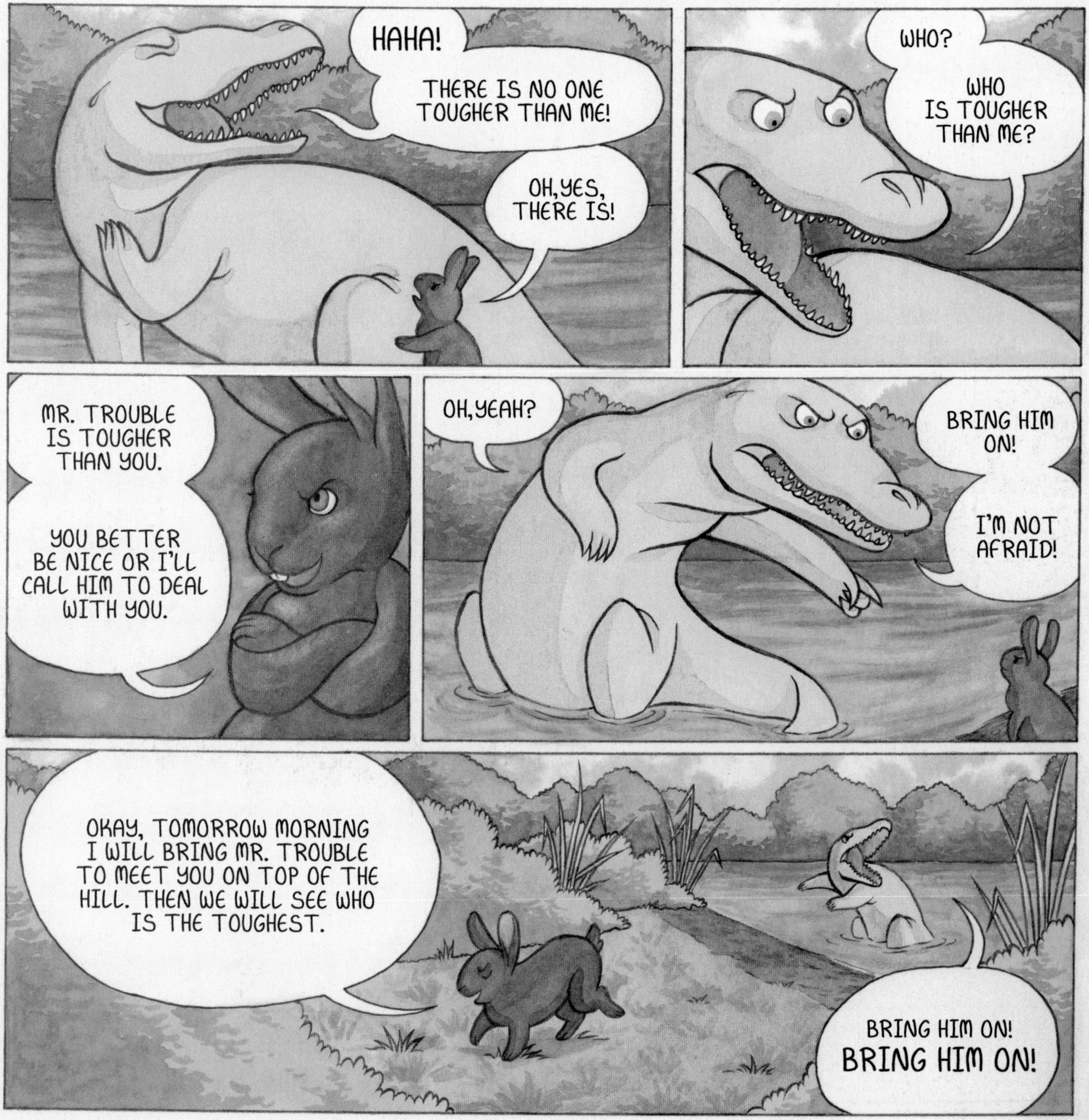
HAHA!
THERE IS NO ONE TOUGHER THAN ME!
OH, YES, THERE IS!
WHO?
WHO IS TOUGHER THAN ME?
MR. TROUBLE IS TOUGHER THAN YOU.
YOU BETTER BE NICE OR I'LL CALL HIM TO DEAL WITH YOU.
OH, YEAH?
BRING HIM ON!
I'M NOT AFRAID!
OKAY, TOMORROW MORNING I WILL BRING MR. TROUBLE TO MEET YOU ON TOP OF THE HILL. THEN WE WILL SEE WHO IS THE TOUGHEST.
BRING HIM ON!
BRING HIM ON!

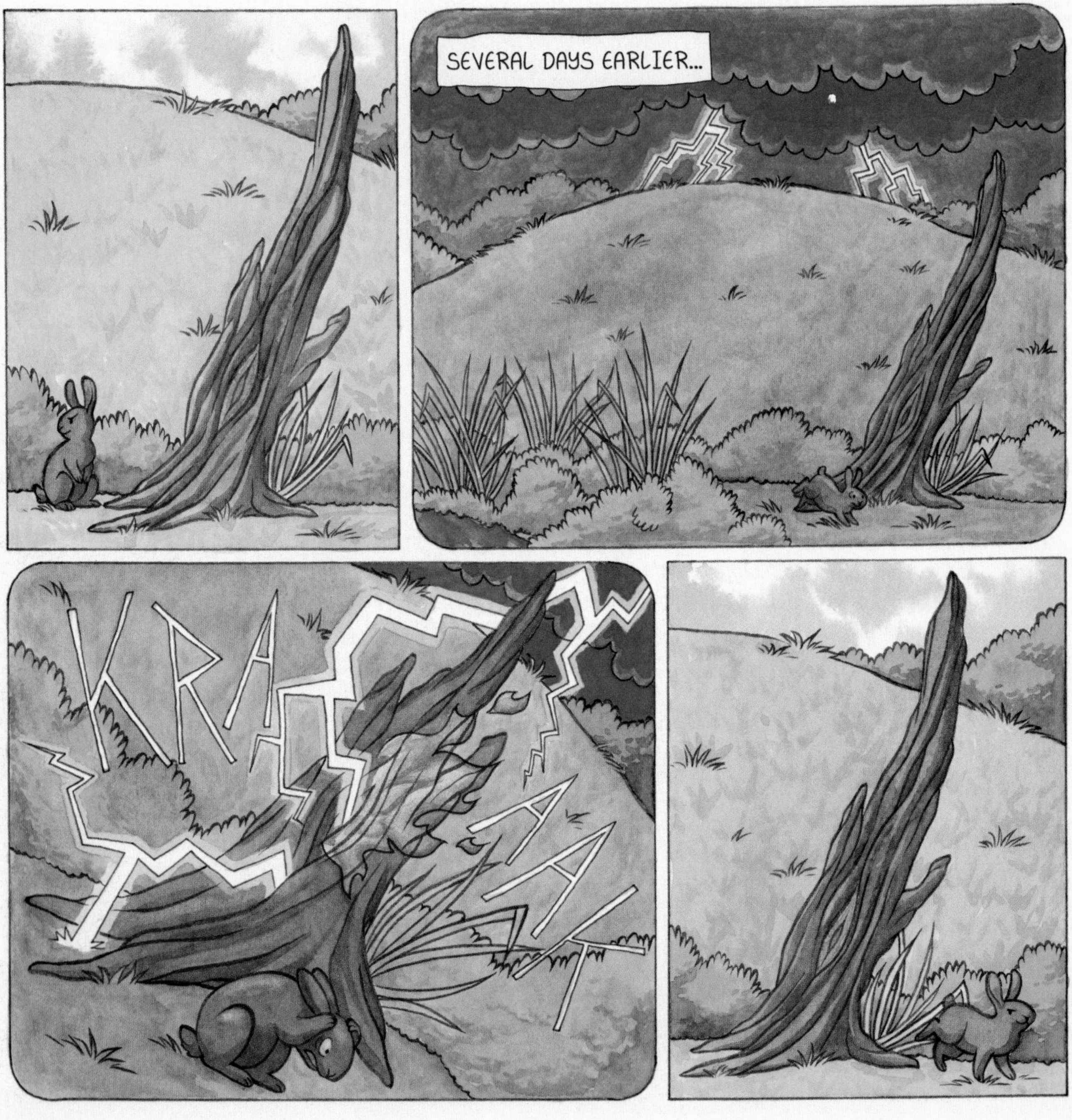
SEVERAL DAYS EARLIER...
KRAAAAT

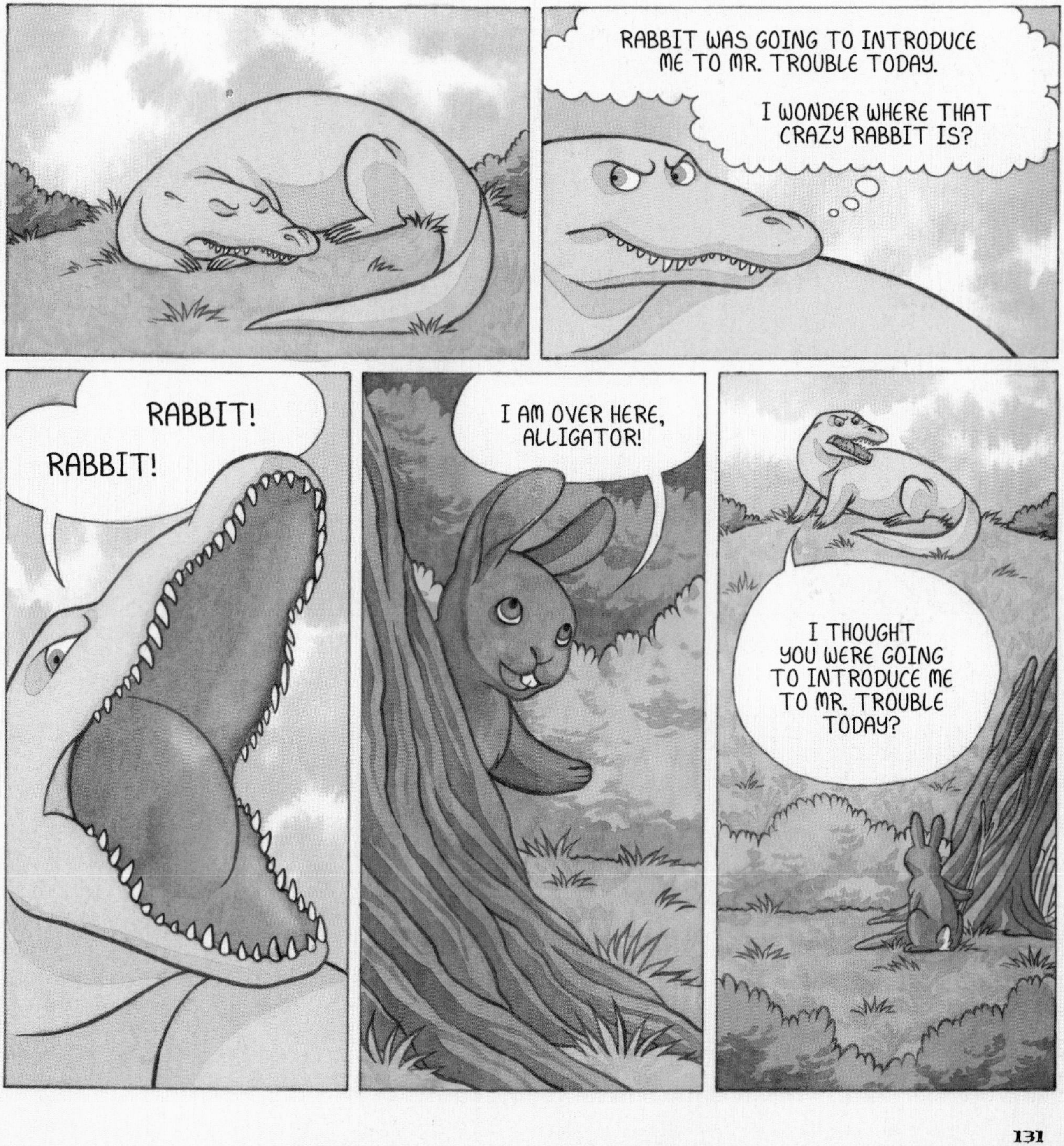
RABBIT WAS GOING TO INTRODUCE ME TO MR. TROUBLE TODAY.
I WONDER WHERE THAT CRAZY RABBIT IS?
RABBIT!
RABBIT!
I AM OVER HERE, ALLIGATOR!
I THOUGHT YOU WERE GOING TO INTRODUCE ME TO MR. TROUBLE TODAY?

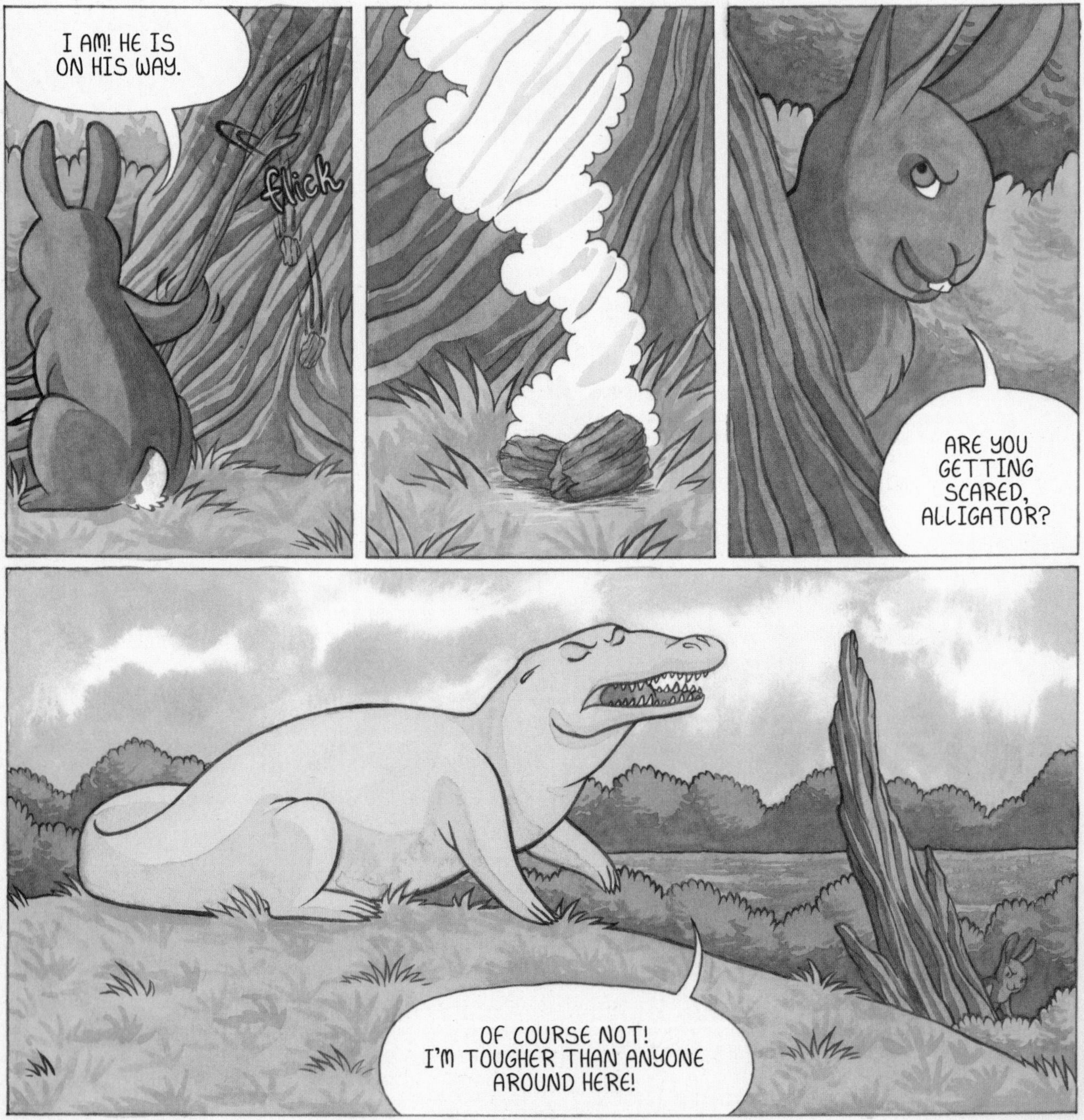
I AM! HE IS ON HIS WAY.
flick
ARE YOU GETTING SCARED, ALLIGATOR?
OF COURSE NOT! I'M TOUGHER THAN ANYONE AROUND HERE!

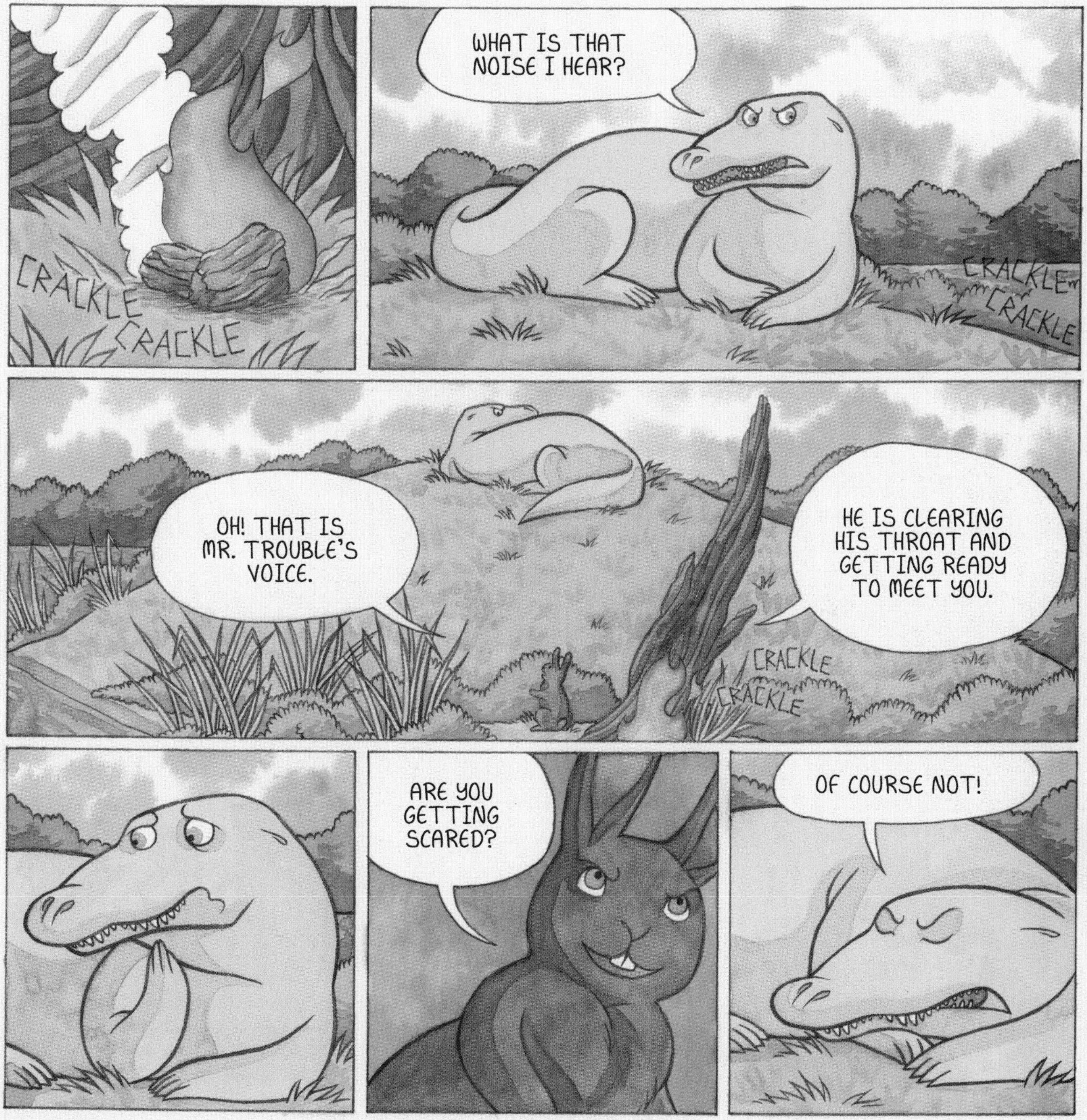
CRACKLE
CRACKLE
WHAT IS THAT NOISE I HEAR?
CRACKLE
CRACKLE
OH! THAT IS MR. TROUBLE'S VOICE.
HE IS CLEARING HIS THROAT AND GETTING READY TO MEET YOU.
CRACKLE
CRACKLE
ARE YOU GETTING SCARED?
OF COURSE NOT!

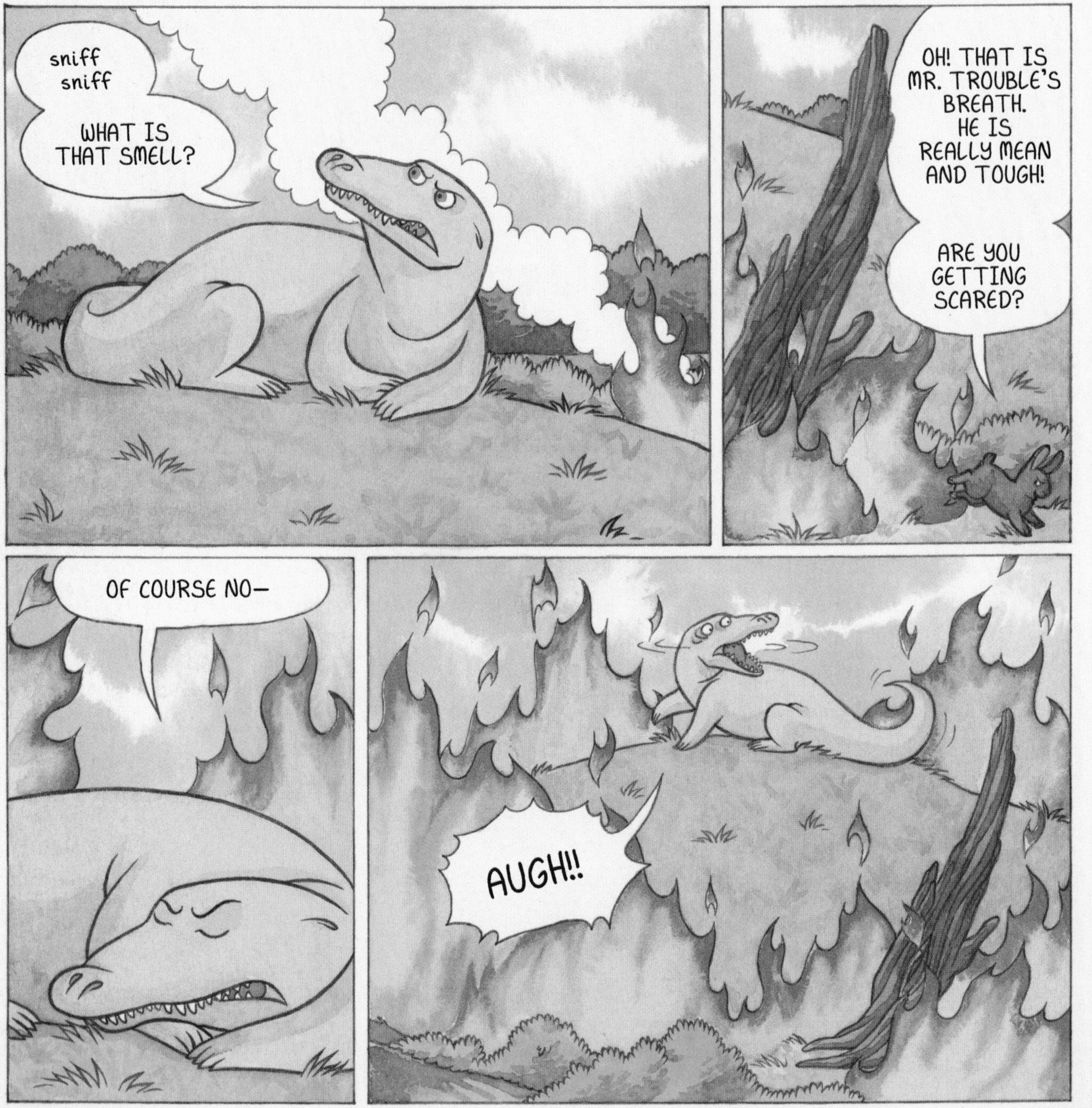
sniff sniff
WHAT IS THAT SMELL?
OH! THAT IS MR. TROUBLE'S BREATH. HE IS REALLY MEAN AND TOUGH!
ARE YOU GETTING SCARED?
OF COURSE NO—
AUGH!!

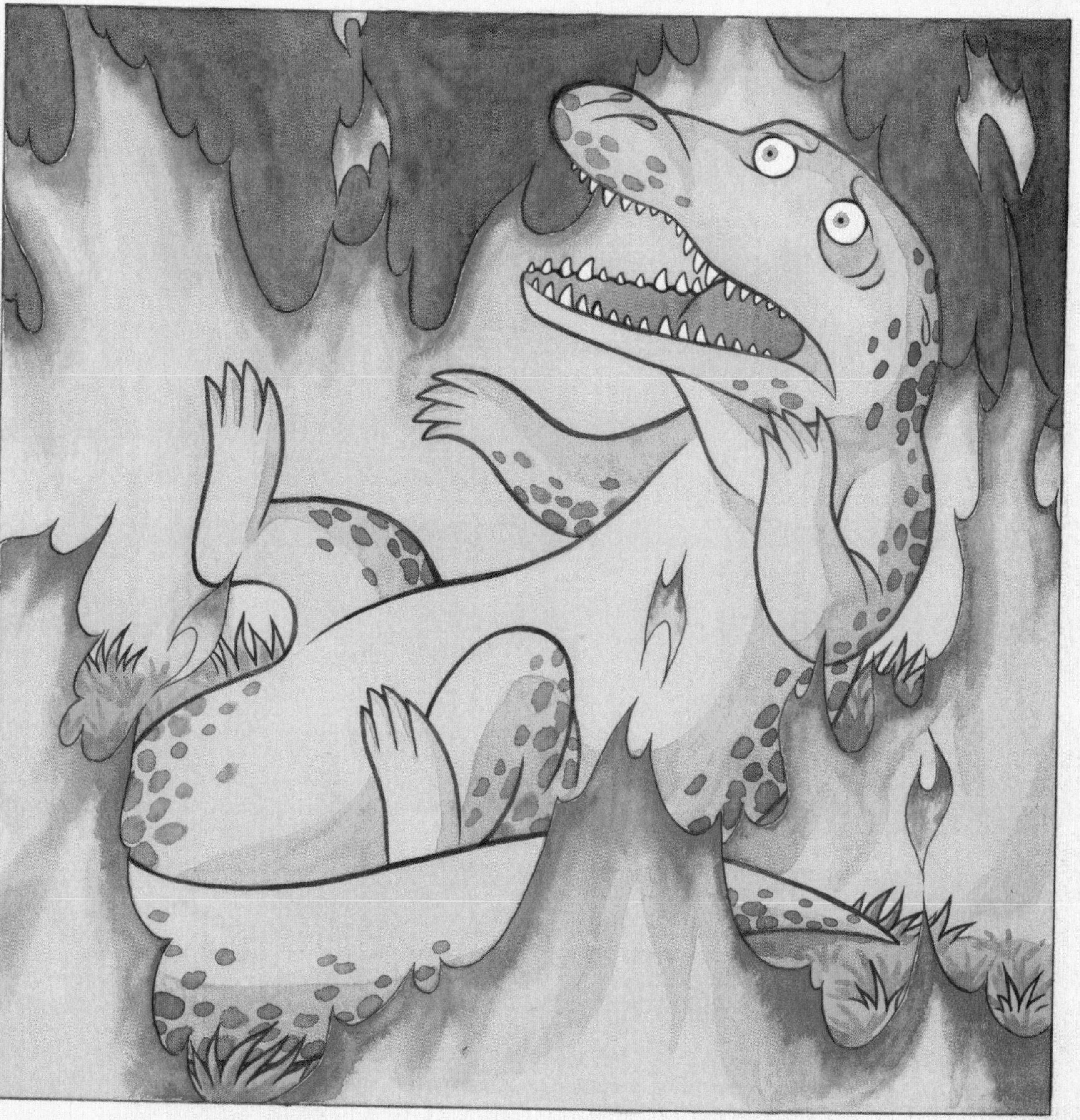

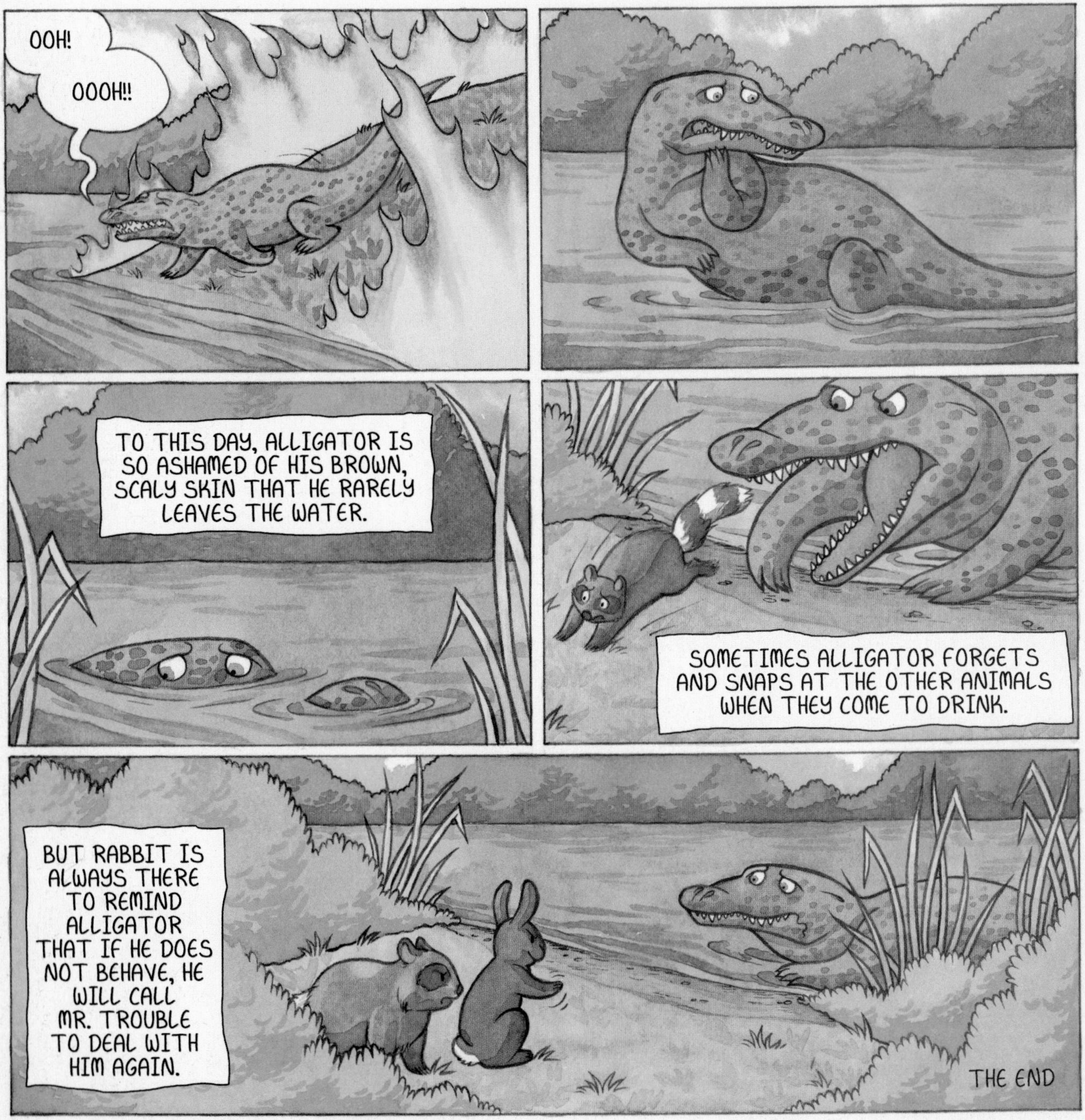
OOH!
OOOH!!
TO THIS DAY, ALLIGATOR IS SO ASHAMED OF HIS BROWN, SCALY SKIN THAT HE RARELY LEAVES THE WATER.
SOMETIMES ALLIGATOR FORGETS AND SNAPS AT THE OTHER ANIMALS WHEN THEY COME TO DRINK.
BUT RABBIT IS ALWAYS THERE TO REMIND ALLIGATOR THAT IF HE DOES NOT BEHAVE, HE WILL CALL MR. TROUBLE TO DEAL WITH HIM AGAIN.
THE END

The YEHASURI the Little Wild Indians

AS TOLD BY BECKEE GARRIS
ART BY ANDREW COHEN

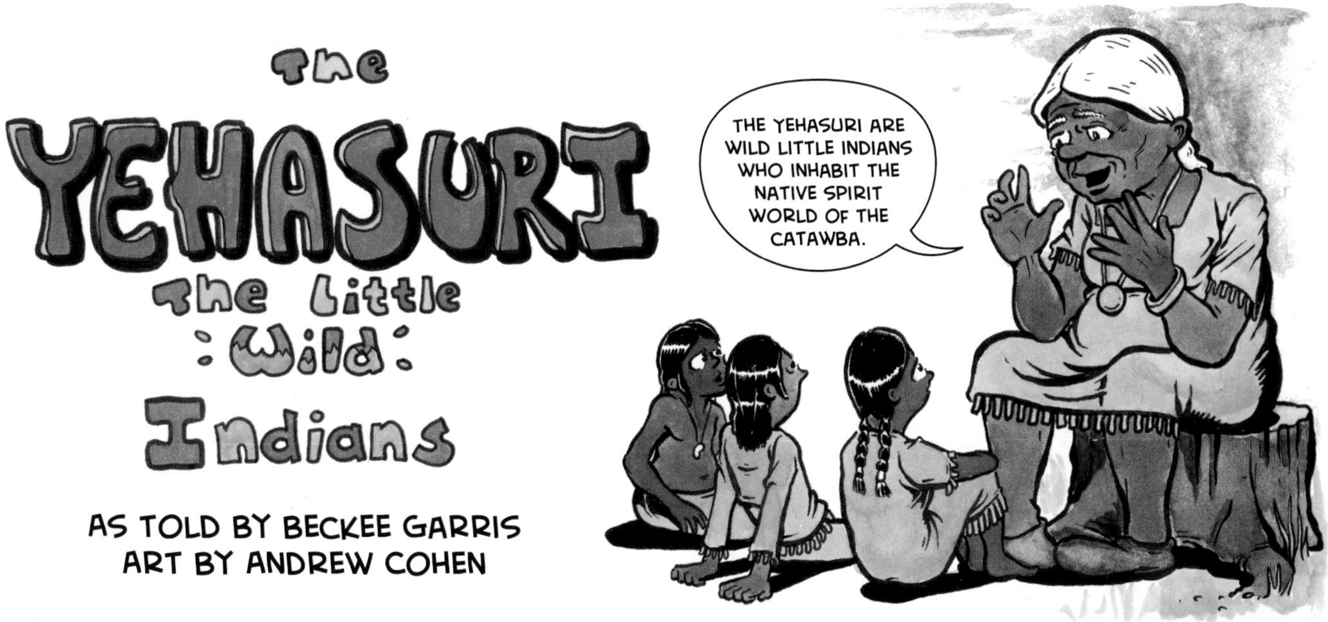
THE YEHASURI ARE WILD LITTLE INDIANS WHO INHABIT THE NATIVE SPIRIT WORLD OF THE CATAWBA.

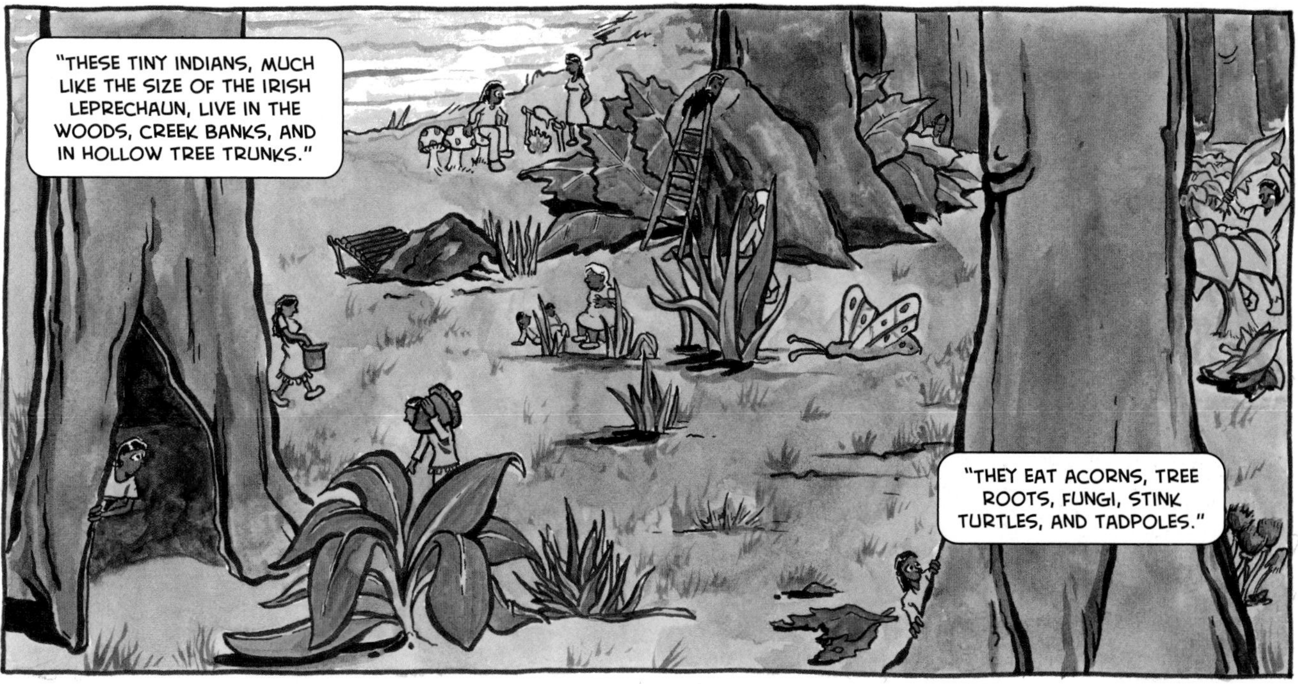
"THESE TINY INDIANS, MUCH LIKE THE SIZE OF THE IRISH LEPRECHAUN, LIVE IN THE WOODS, CREEK BANKS, AND IN HOLLOW TREE TRUNKS."
"THEY EAT ACORNS, TREE ROOTS, FUNGI, STINK TURTLES, AND TADPOLES."

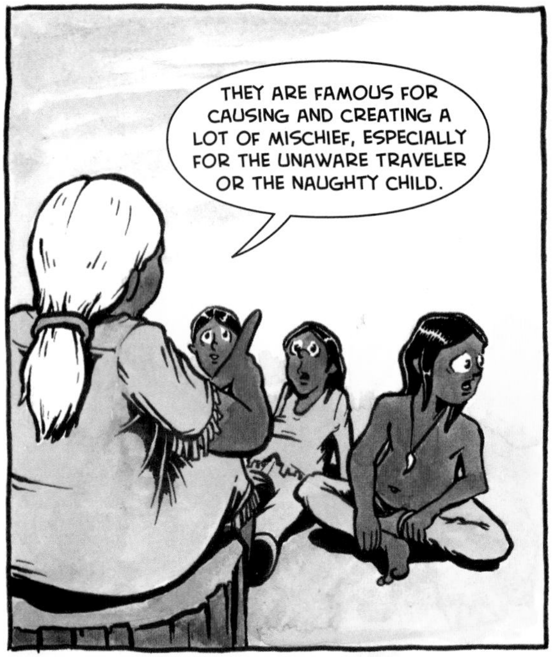
THEY ARE FAMOUS FOR CAUSING AND CREATING A LOT OF MISCHIEF, ESPECIALLY FOR THE UNAWARE TRAVELER OR THE NAUGHTY CHILD.

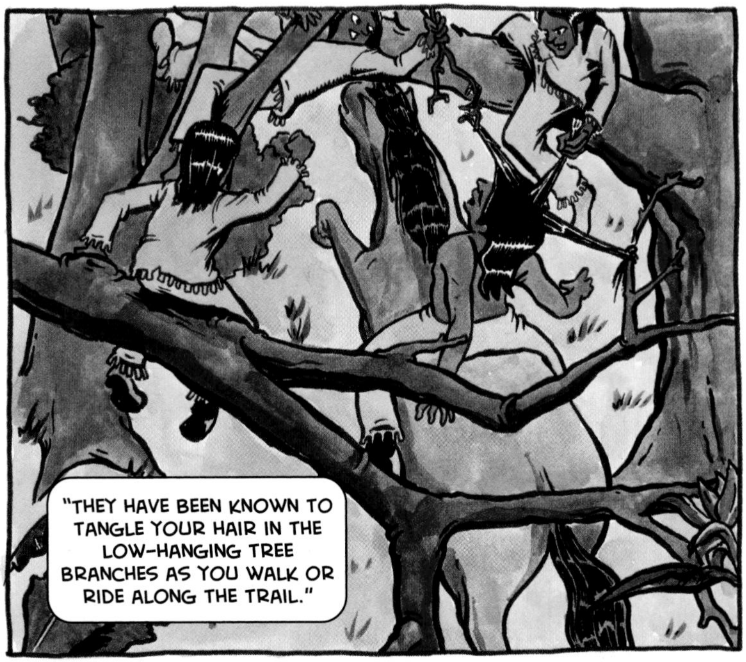
"THEY HAVE BEEN KNOWN TO TANGLE YOUR HAIR IN THE LOW-HANGING TREE BRANCHES AS YOU WALK OR RIDE ALONG THE TRAIL."

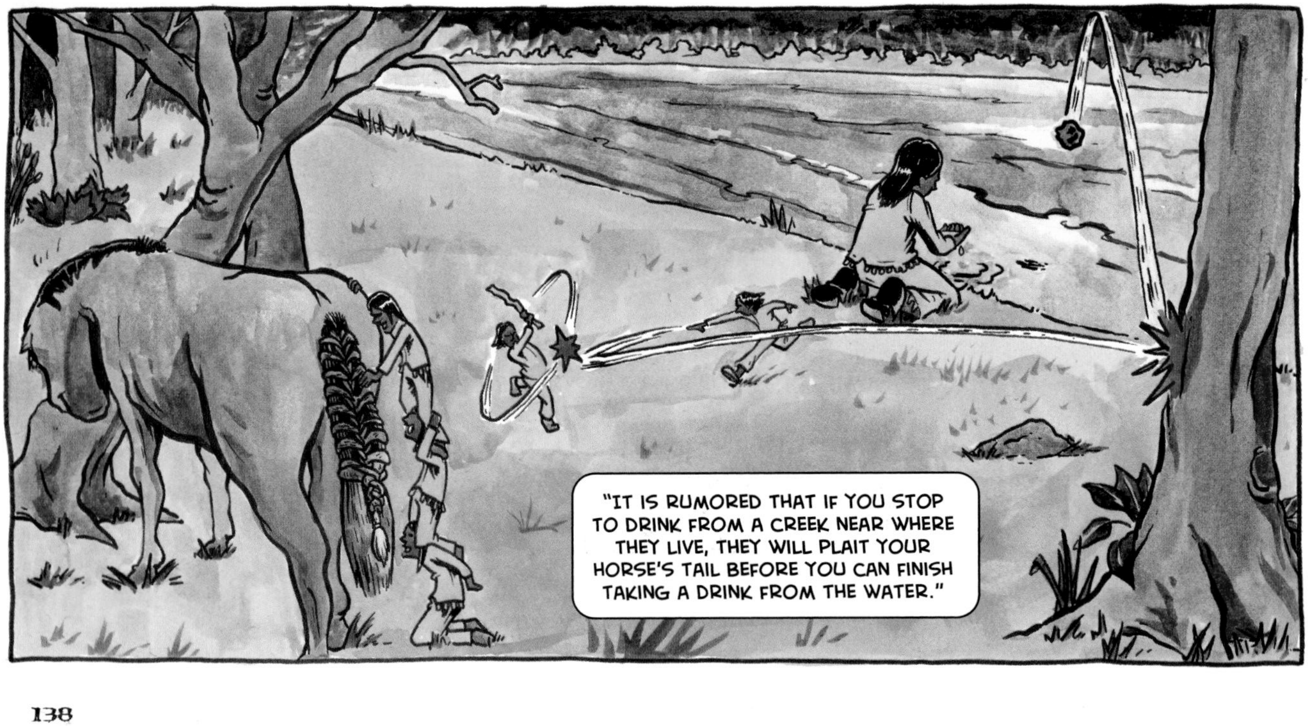
"IT IS RUMORED THAT IF YOU STOP TO DRINK FROM A CREEK NEAR WHERE THEY LIVE, THEY WILL PLAIT YOUR HORSE'S TAIL BEFORE YOU CAN FINISH TAKING A DRINK FROM THE WATER."

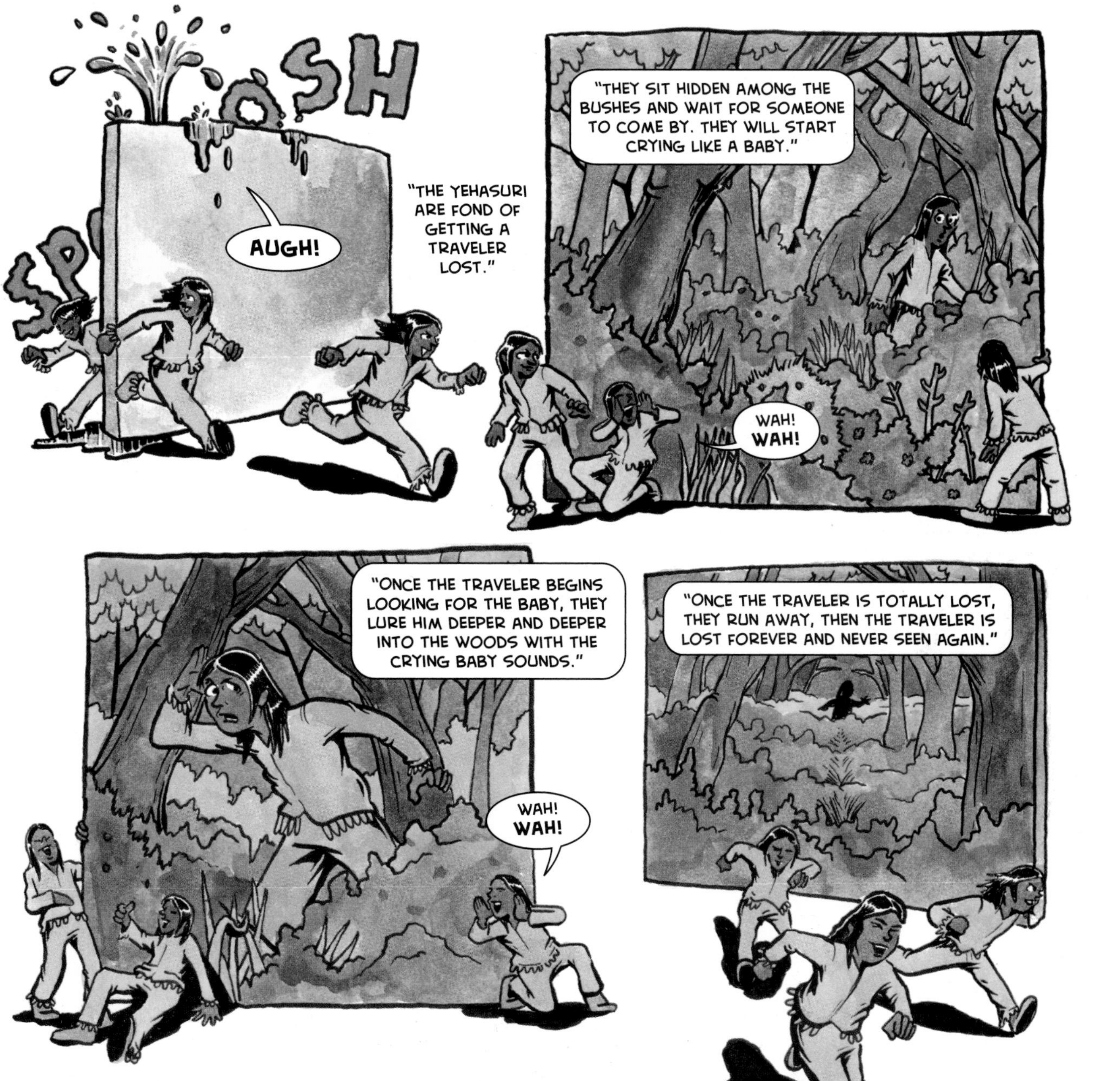
SPLOOSH
AUGH!
"THE YEHASURI ARE FOND OF GETTING A TRAVELER LOST."
"THEY SIT HIDDEN AMONG THE BUSHES AND WAIT FOR SOMEONE TO COME BY. THEY WILL START CRYING LIKE A BABY."
WAH! WAH!
"ONCE THE TRAVELER BEGINS LOOKING FOR THE BABY, THEY LURE HIM DEEPER AND DEEPER INTO THE WOODS WITH THE CRYING BABY SOUNDS."
WAH! WAH!
"ONCE THE TRAVELER IS TOTALLY LOST, THEY RUN AWAY, THEN THE TRAVELER IS LOST FOREVER AND NEVER SEEN AGAIN."

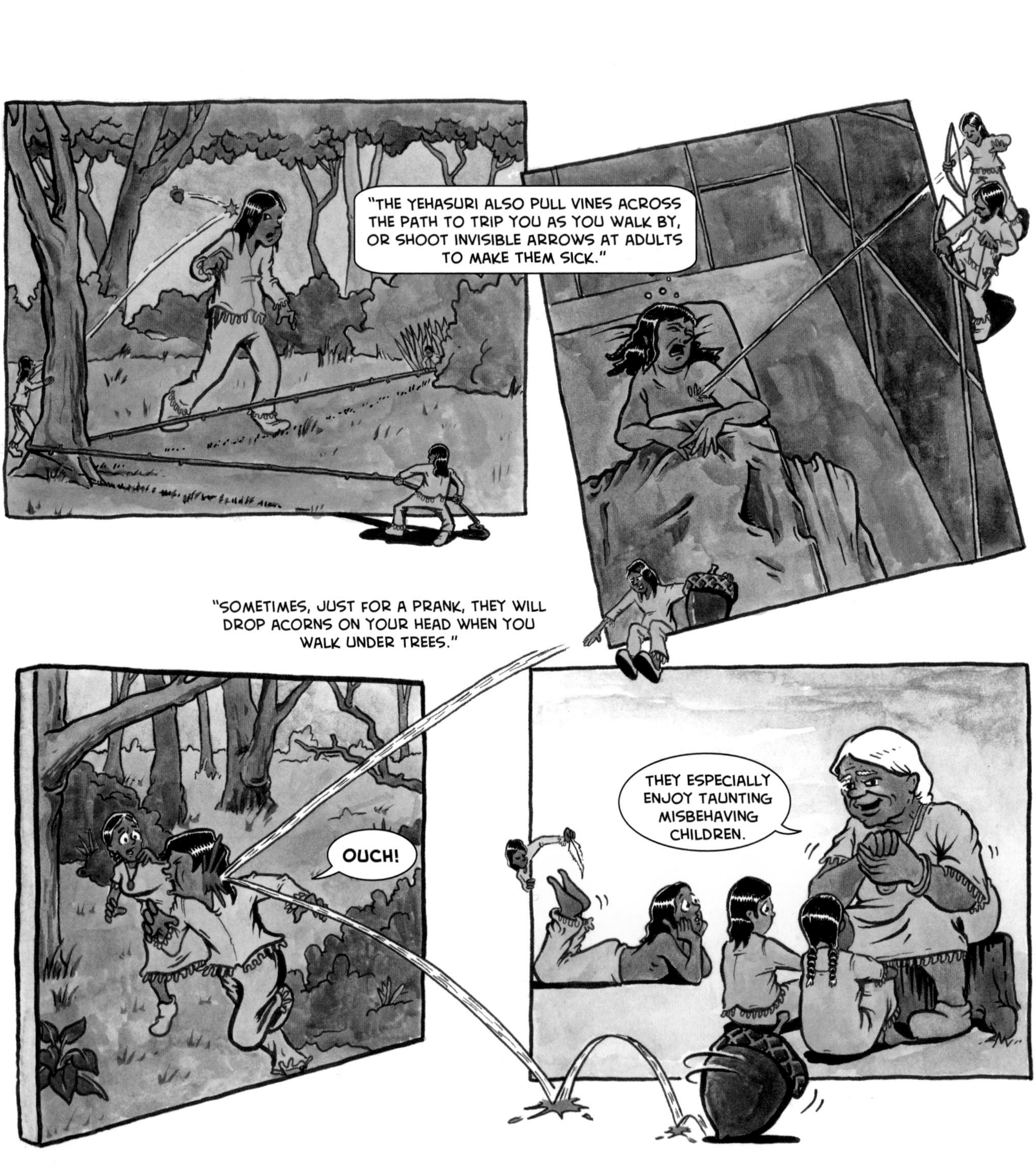
"THE YEHASURI ALSO PULL VINES ACROSS THE PATH TO TRIP YOU AS YOU WALK BY, OR SHOOT INVISIBLE ARROWS AT ADULTS TO MAKE THEM SICK."
"SOMETIMES, JUST FOR A PRANK, THEY WILL DROP ACORNS ON YOUR HEAD WHEN YOU WALK UNDER TREES."
OUCH!
THEY ESPECIALLY ENJOY TAUNTING MISBEHAVING CHILDREN.

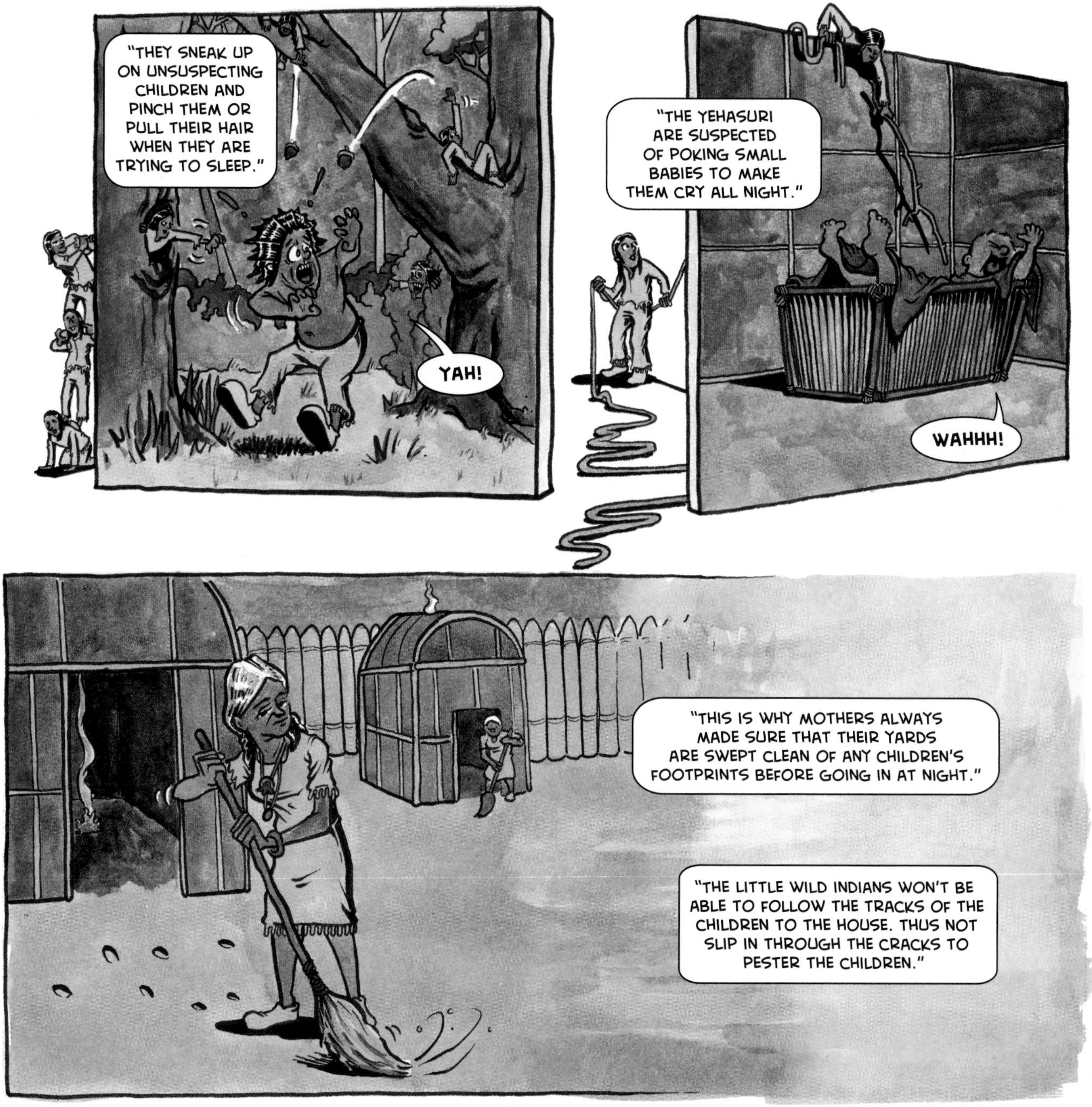
"THEY SNEAK UP ON UNSUSPECTING CHILDREN AND PINCH THEM OR PULL THEIR HAIR WHEN THEY ARE TRYING TO SLEEP."
YAH!
"THE YEHASURI ARE SUSPECTED OF POKING SMALL BABIES TO MAKE THEM CRY ALL NIGHT."
WAHHH!
"THIS IS WHY MOTHERS ALWAYS MADE SURE THAT THEIR YARDS ARE SWEPT CLEAN OF ANY CHILDREN'S FOOTPRINTS BEFORE GOING IN AT NIGHT."
"THE LITTLE WILD INDIANS WON'T BE ABLE TO FOLLOW THE TRACKS OF THE CHILDREN TO THE HOUSE. THUS NOT SLIP IN THROUGH THE CRACKS TO PESTER THE CHILDREN."

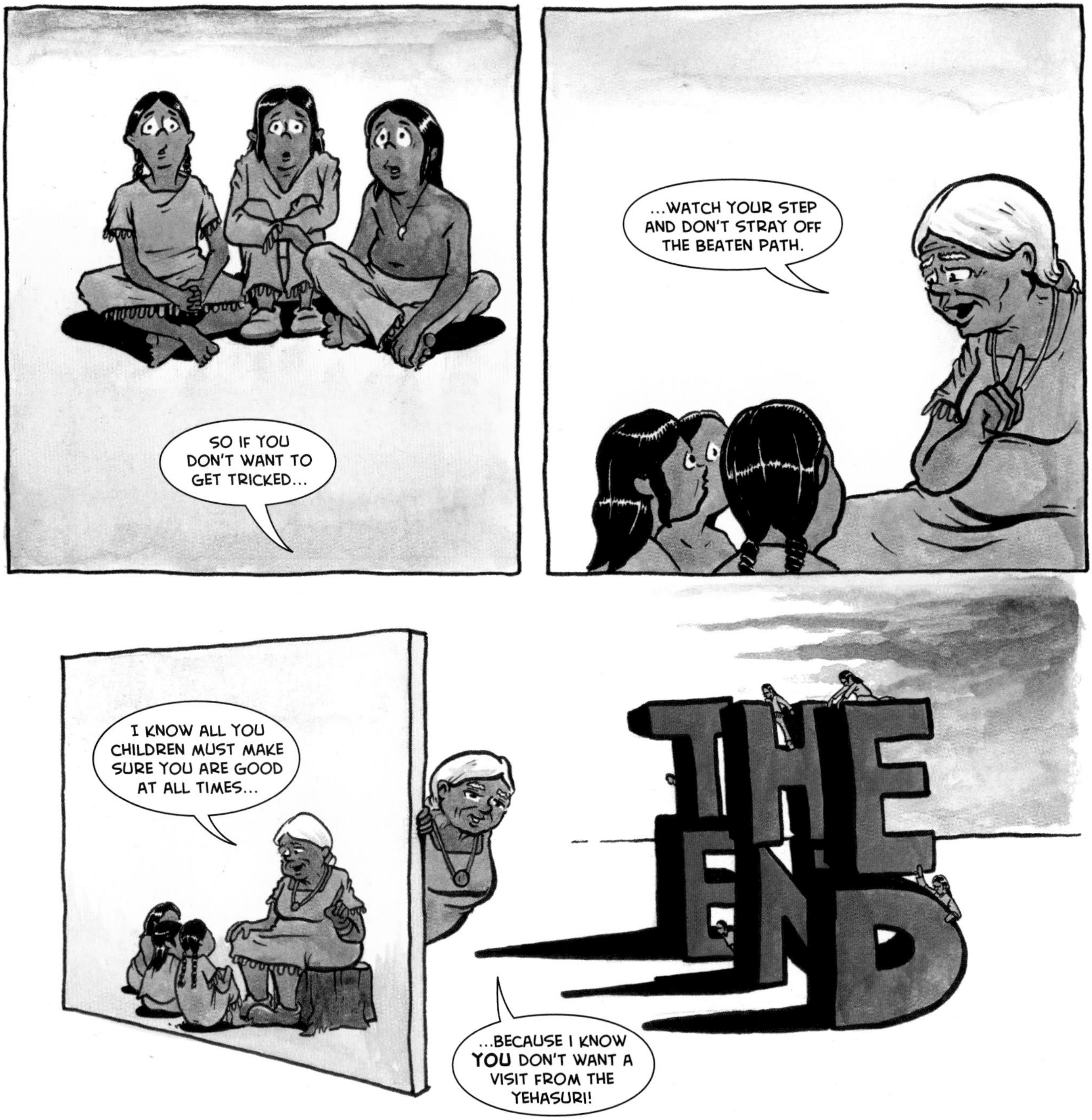
SO IF YOU DON'T WANT TO GET TRICKED...
...WATCH YOUR STEP AND DON'T STRAY OFF THE BEATEN PATH.
I KNOW ALL YOU CHILDREN MUST MAKE SURE YOU ARE GOOD AT ALL TIMES...
THE END
...BECAUSE I KNOW **YOU** DON'T WANT A VISIT FROM THE YEHASURI!

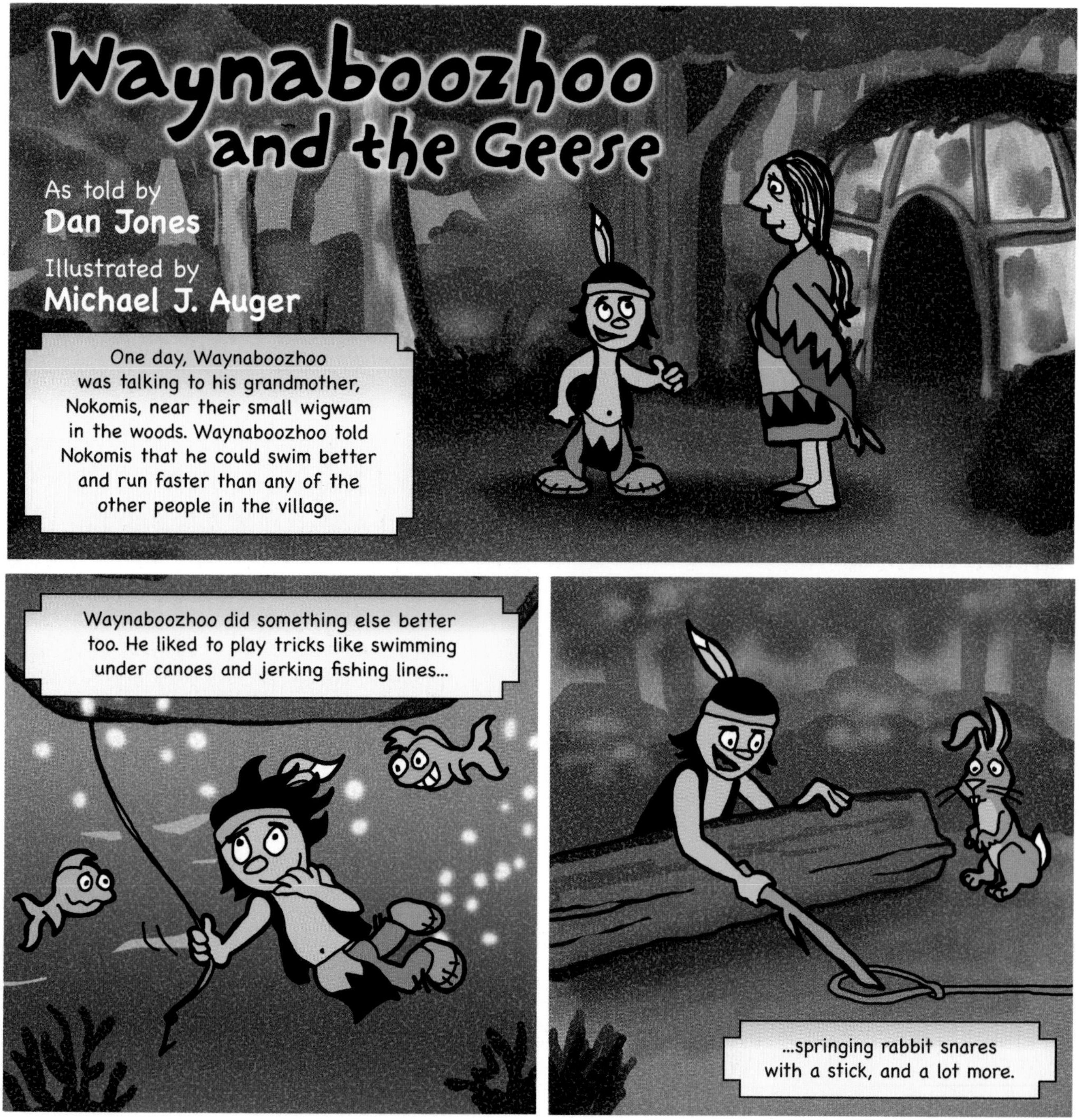
Waynaboozhoo and the Geese
As told by
Dan Jones
Illustrated by
Michael J. Auger
One day, Waynaboozhoo was talking to his grandmother, Nokomis, near their small wigwam in the woods. Waynaboozhoo told Nokomis that he could swim better and run faster than any of the other people in the village.
Waynaboozhoo did something else better too. He liked to play tricks like swimming under canoes and jerking fishing lines...
...springing rabbit snares with a stick, and a lot more.

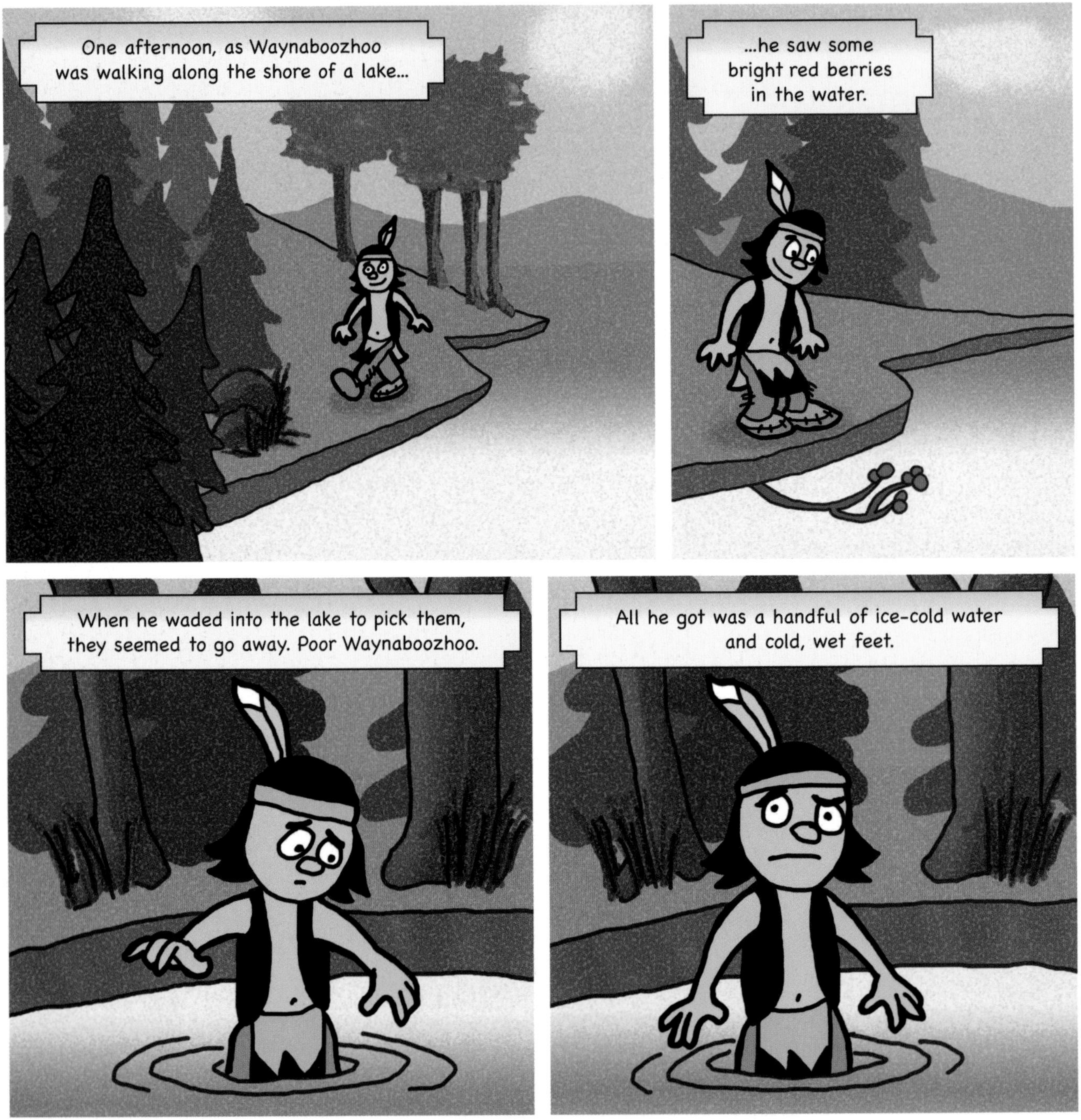
One afternoon, as Waynaboozhoo was walking along the shore of a lake...
...he saw some bright red berries in the water.
When he waded into the lake to pick them, they seemed to go away. Poor Waynaboozhoo.
All he got was a handful of ice-cold water and cold, wet feet.

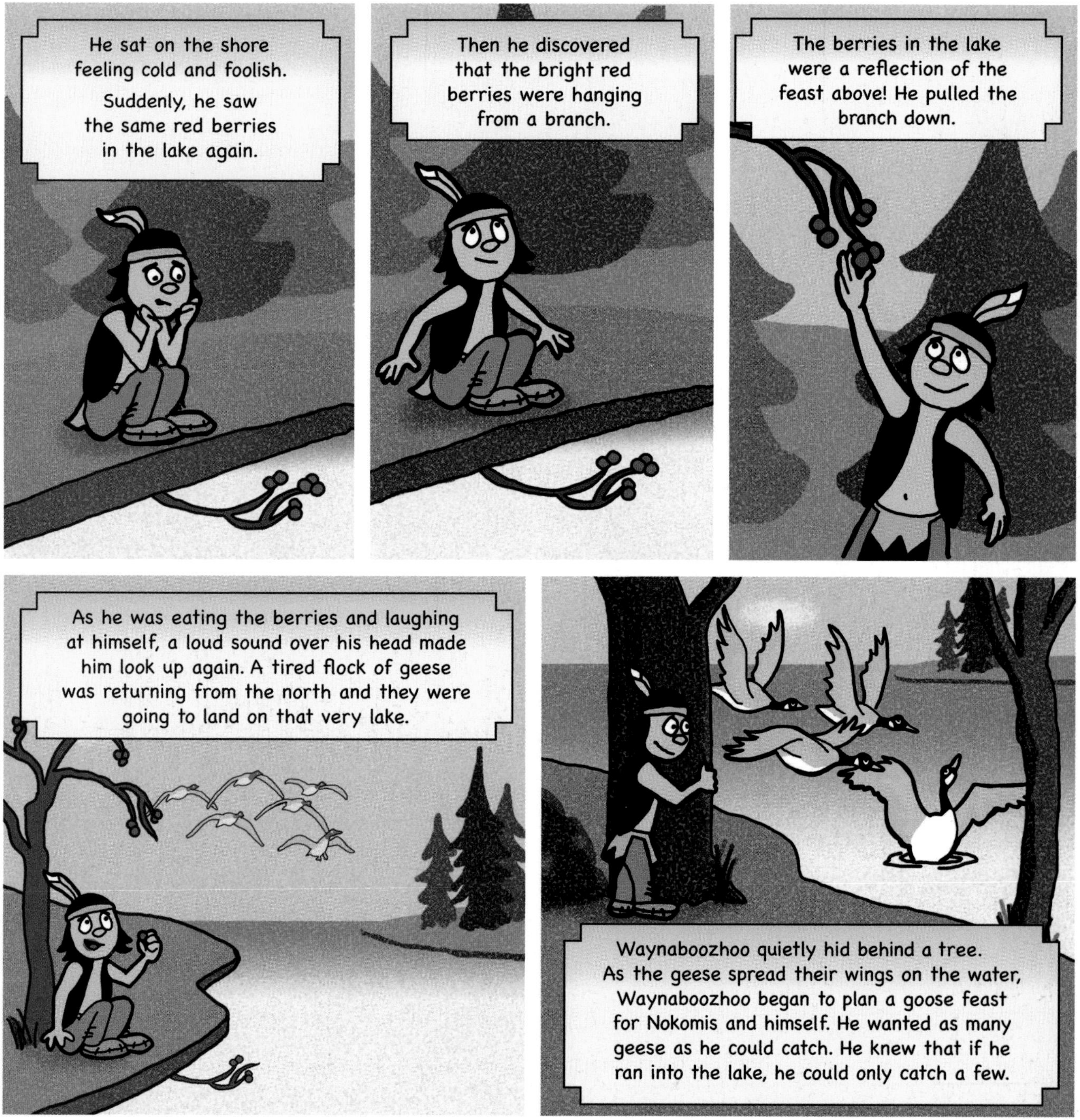
He sat on the shore feeling cold and foolish.
Suddenly, he saw the same red berries in the lake again.
Then he discovered that the bright red berries were hanging from a branch.
The berries in the lake were a reflection of the feast above! He pulled the branch down.
As he was eating the berries and laughing at himself, a loud sound over his head made him look up again. A tired flock of geese was returning from the north and they were going to land on that very lake.
Waynaboozhoo quietly hid behind a tree. As the geese spread their wings on the water, Waynaboozhoo began to plan a goose feast for Nokomis and himself. He wanted as many geese as he could catch. He knew that if he ran into the lake, he could only catch a few.

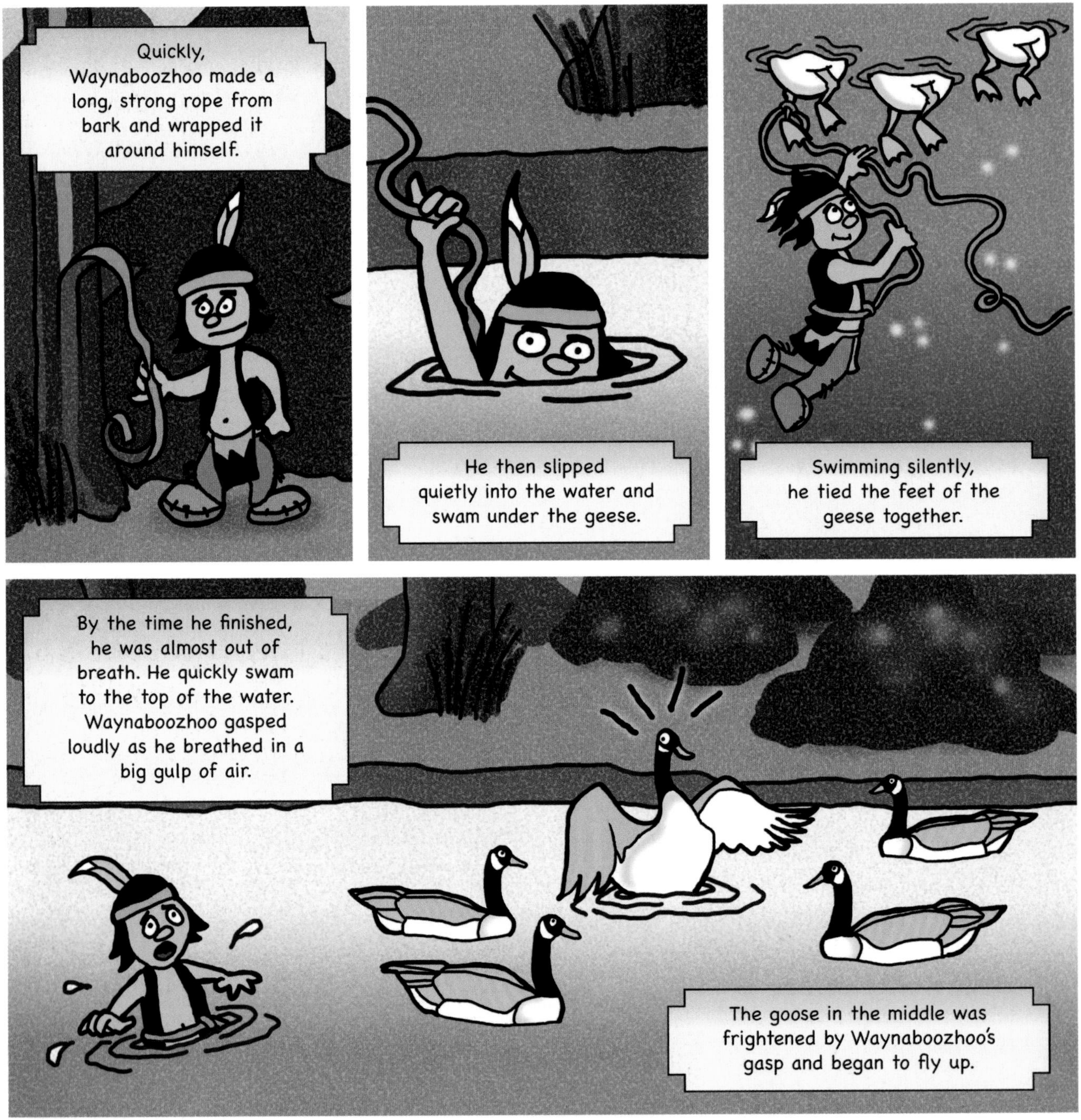
Quickly, Waynaboozhoo made a long, strong rope from bark and wrapped it around himself.
He then slipped quietly into the water and swam under the geese.
Swimming silently, he tied the feet of the geese together.
By the time he finished, he was almost out of breath. He quickly swam to the top of the water. Waynaboozhoo gasped loudly as he breathed in a big gulp of air.
The goose in the middle was frightened by Waynaboozhoo's gasp and began to fly up.

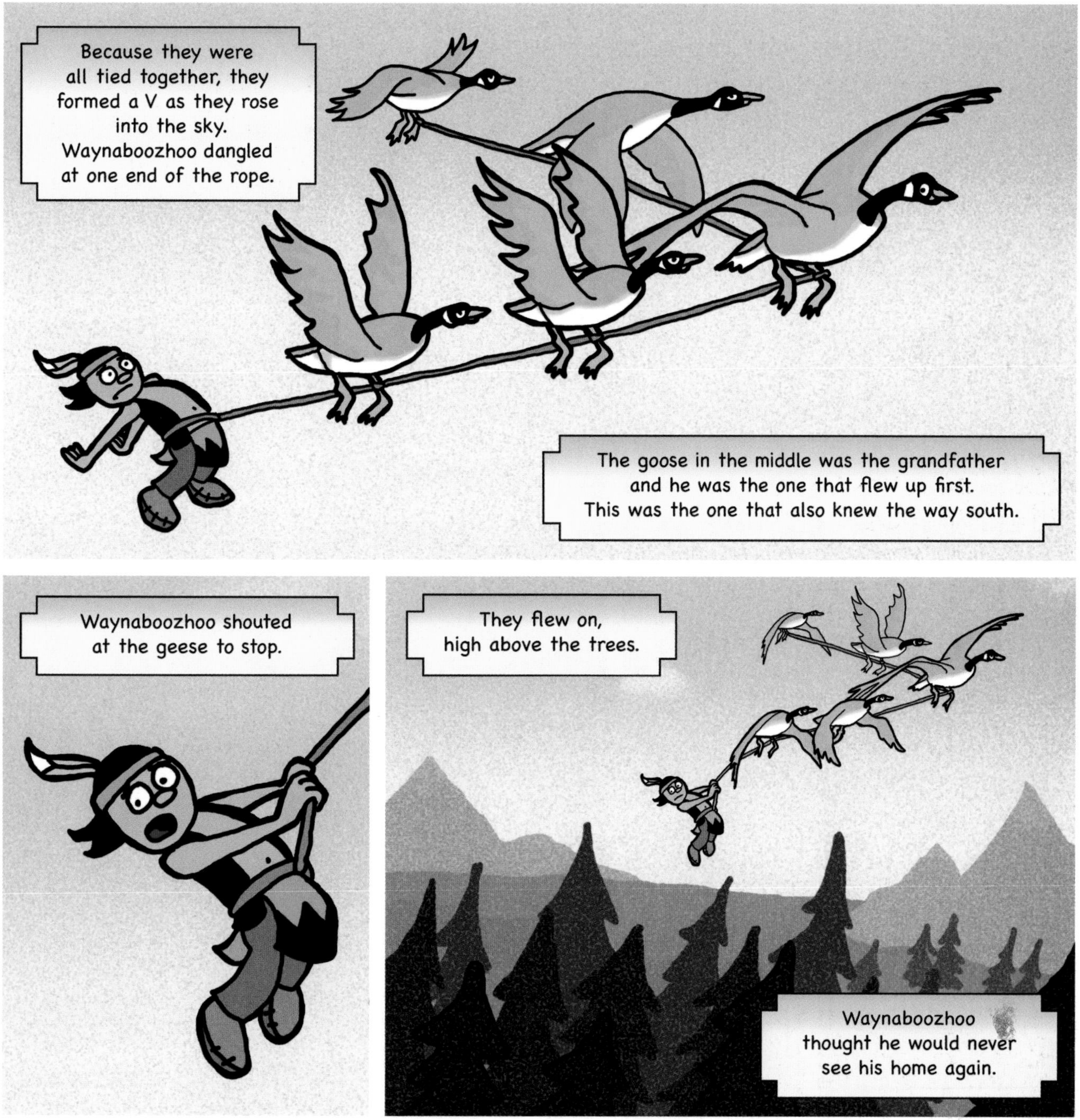

Because they were all tied together, they formed a V as they rose into the sky. Waynaboozhoo dangled at one end of the rope.
The goose in the middle was the grandfather and he was the one that flew up first. This was the one that also knew the way south.
Waynaboozhoo shouted at the geese to stop.
They flew on, high above the trees.
Waynaboozhoo thought he would never see his home again.

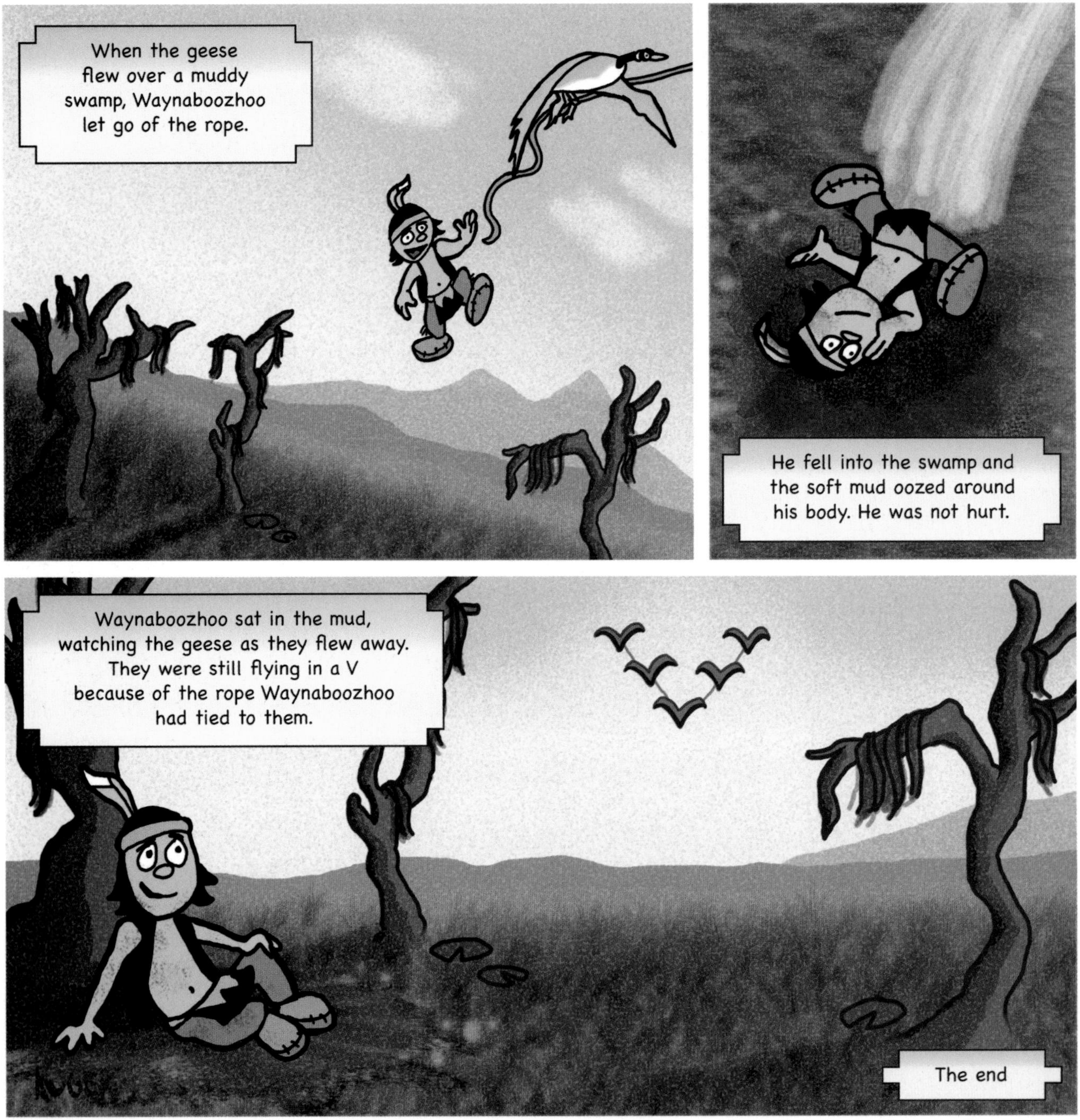
When the geese flew over a muddy swamp, Waynaboozhoo let go of the rope.
He fell into the swamp and the soft mud oozed around his body. He was not hurt.
Waynaboozhoo sat in the mud, watching the geese as they flew away. They were still flying in a V because of the rope Waynaboozhoo had tied to them.
The end

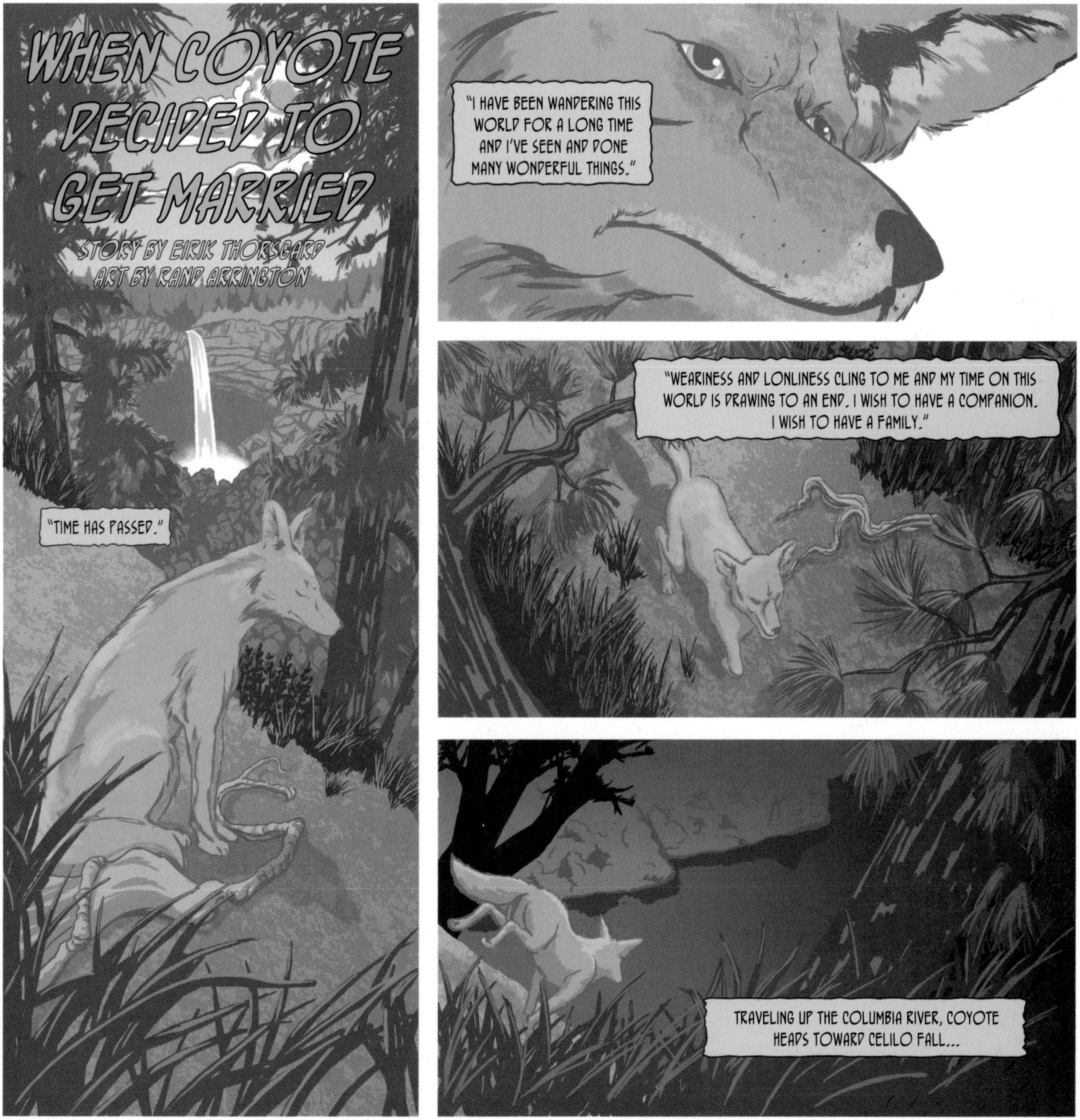
WHEN COYOTE DECIDED TO GET MARRIED
STORY BY EIRIK THORSGARD
ART BY RAND ARRINGTON
"TIME HAS PASSED."
"I HAVE BEEN WANDERING THIS WORLD FOR A LONG TIME AND I'VE SEEN AND DONE MANY WONDERFUL THINGS."
"WEARINESS AND LONLINESS CLING TO ME AND MY TIME ON THIS WORLD IS DRAWING TO AN END. I WISH TO HAVE A COMPANION. I WISH TO HAVE A FAMILY."
TRAVELING UP THE COLUMBIA RIVER, COYOTE HEADS TOWARD CELILO FALL...

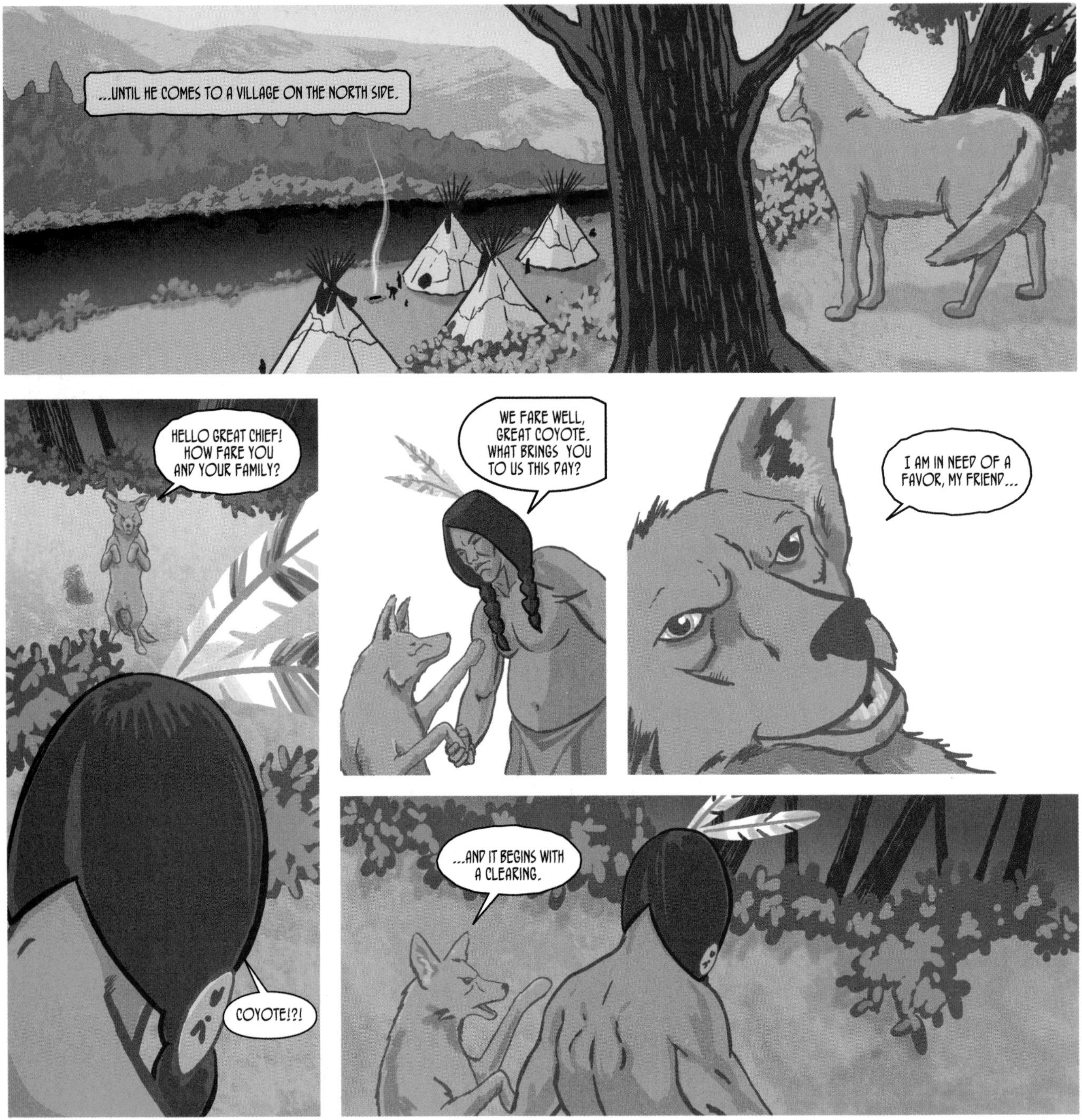
...UNTIL HE COMES TO A VILLAGE ON THE NORTH SIDE.
HELLO GREAT CHIEF! HOW FARE YOU AND YOUR FAMILY?
COYOTE!?!
WE FARE WELL, GREAT COYOTE. WHAT BRINGS YOU TO US THIS DAY?
I AM IN NEED OF A FAVOR, MY FRIEND...
...AND IT BEGINS WITH A CLEARING.

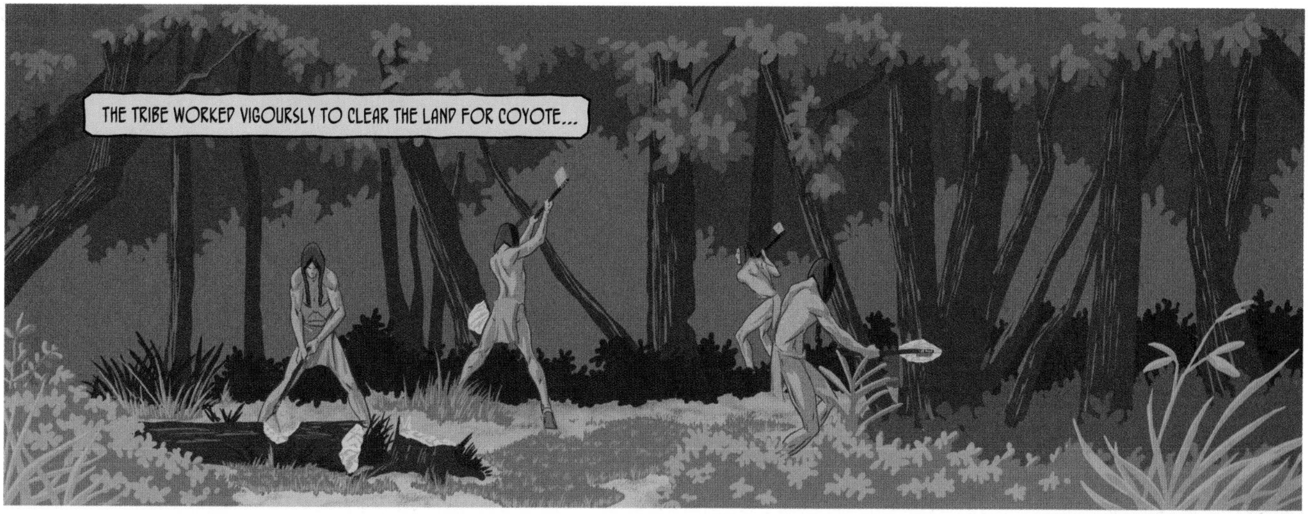
THE TRIBE WORKED VIGOURSLY TO CLEAR THE LAND FOR COYOTE...

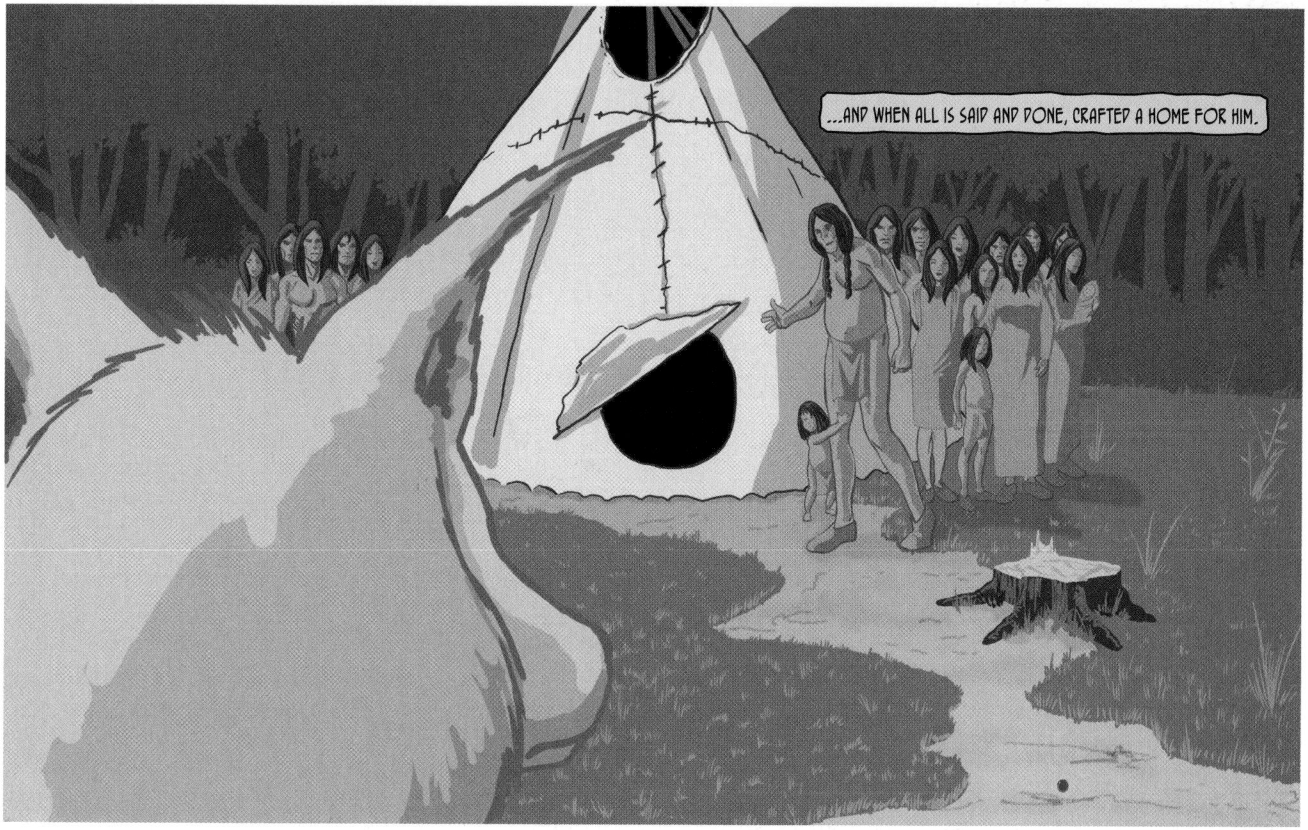
...AND WHEN ALL IS SAID AND DONE, CRAFTED A HOME FOR HIM.

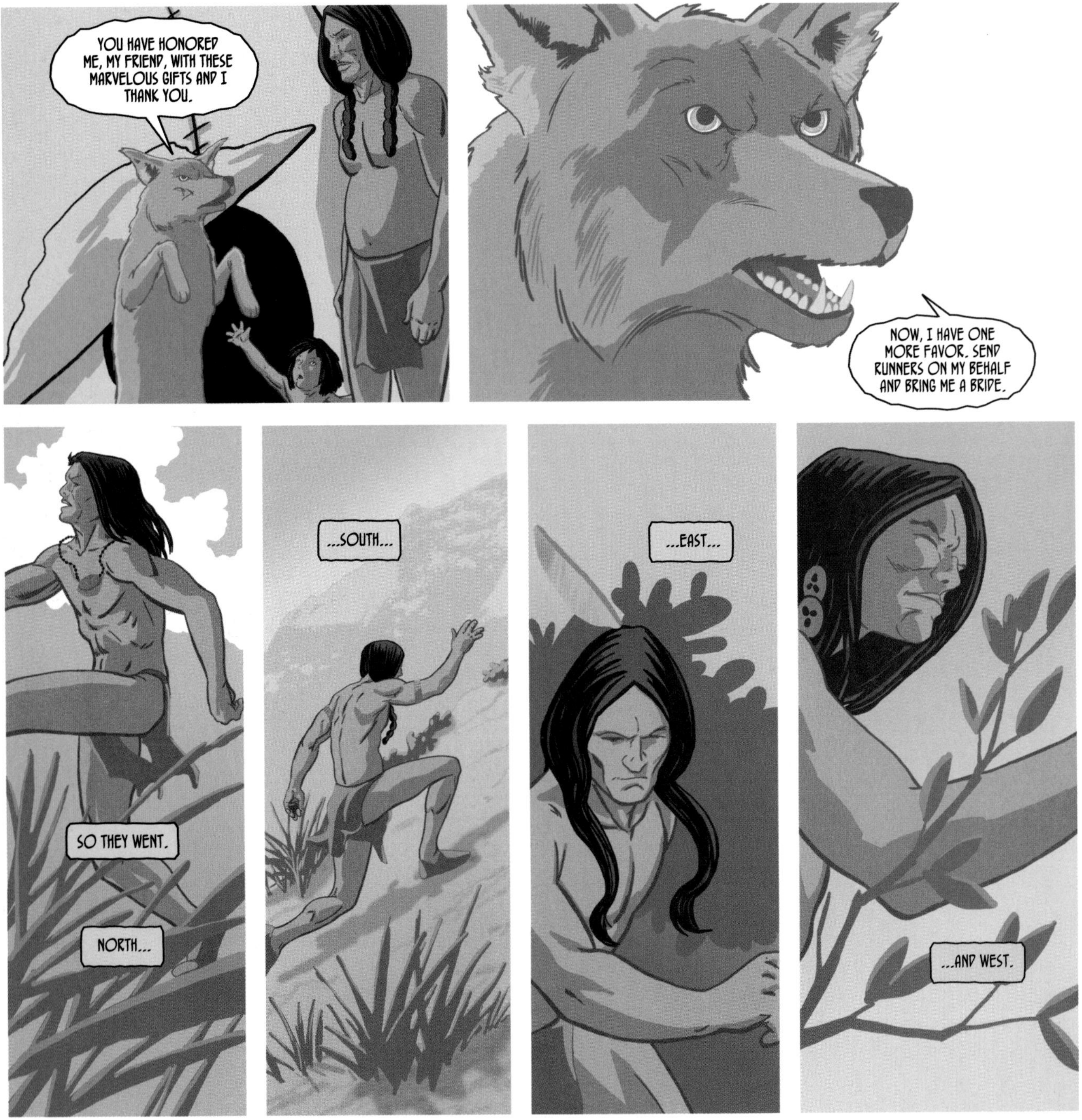
YOU HAVE HONORED ME, MY FRIEND, WITH THESE MARVELOUS GIFTS AND I THANK YOU.
NOW, I HAVE ONE MORE FAVOR. SEND RUNNERS ON MY BEHALF AND BRING ME A BRIDE.
SO THEY WENT.
NORTH...
...SOUTH...
...EAST...
...AND WEST.

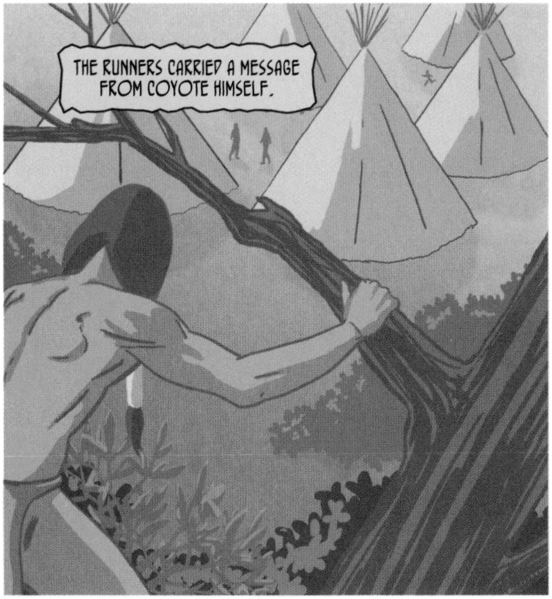
THE RUNNERS CARRIED A MESSAGE FROM COYOTE HIMSELF.

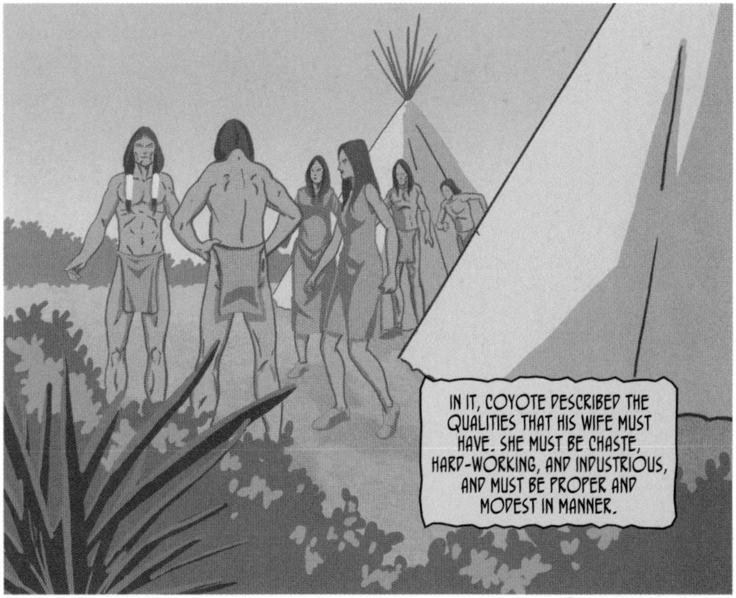
IN IT, COYOTE DESCRIBED THE QUALITIES THAT HIS WIFE MUST HAVE. SHE MUST BE CHASTE, HARD-WORKING, AND INDUSTRIOUS, AND MUST BE PROPER AND MODEST IN MANNER.

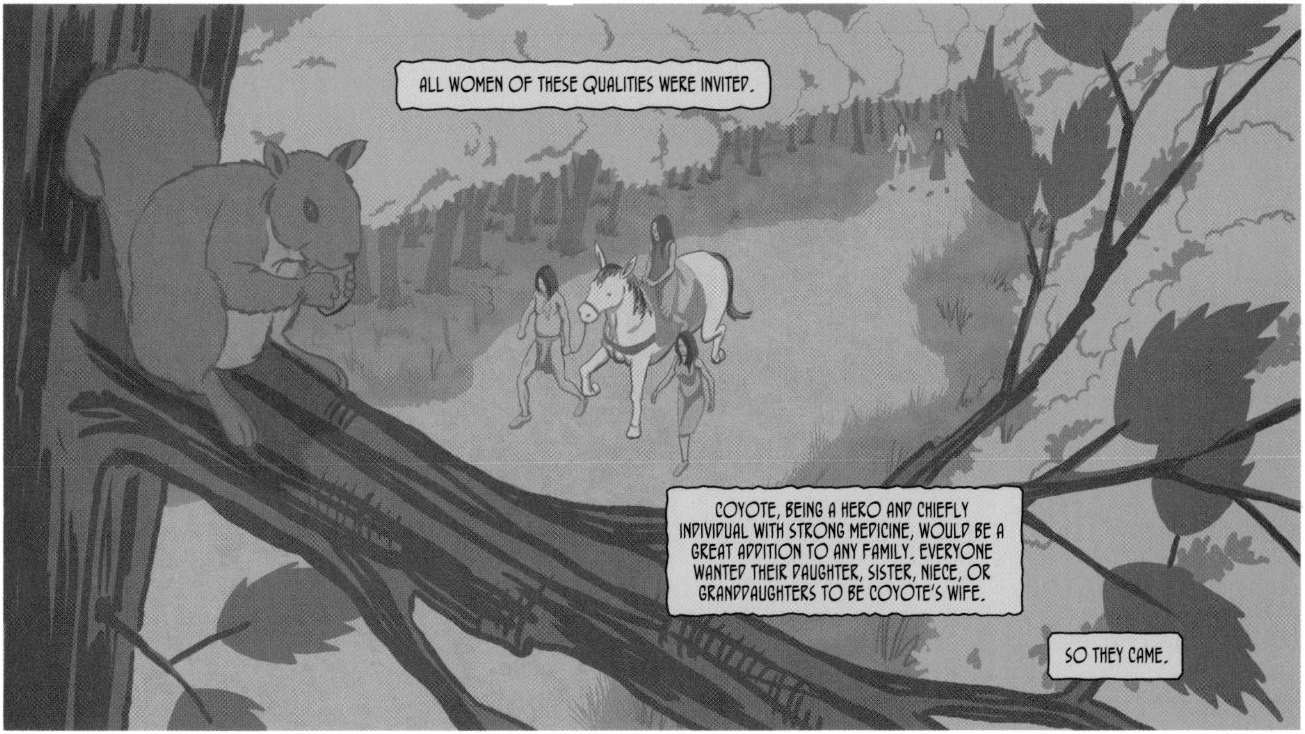
ALL WOMEN OF THESE QUALITIES WERE INVITED.
COYOTE, BEING A HERO AND CHIEFLY INDIVIDUAL WITH STRONG MEDICINE, WOULD BE A GREAT ADDITION TO ANY FAMILY. EVERYONE WANTED THEIR DAUGHTER, SISTER, NIECE, OR GRANDDAUGHTERS TO BE COYOTE'S WIFE.
SO THEY CAME.

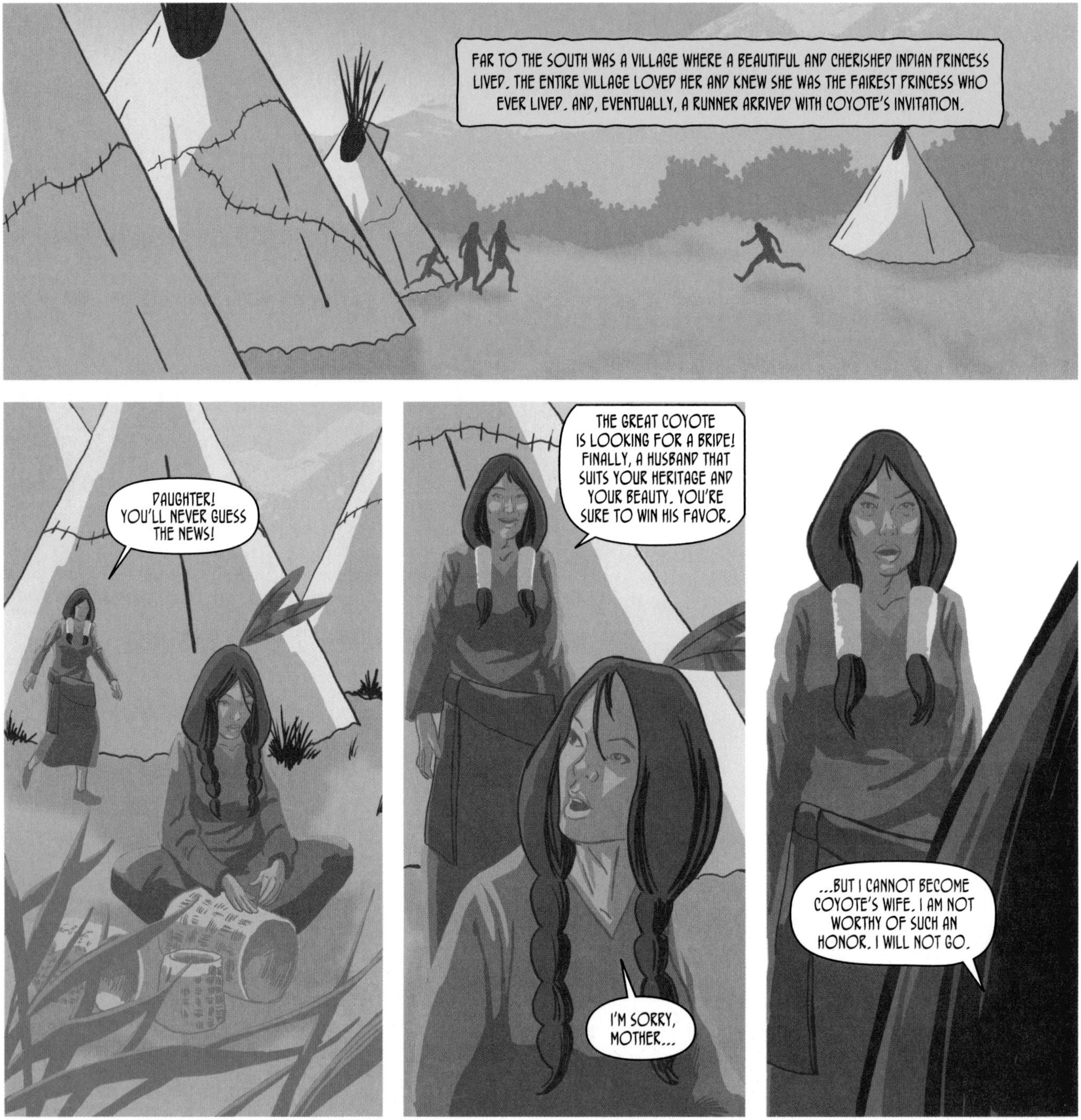
FAR TO THE SOUTH WAS A VILLAGE WHERE A BEAUTIFUL AND CHERISHED INDIAN PRINCESS LIVED. THE ENTIRE VILLAGE LOVED HER AND KNEW SHE WAS THE FAIREST PRINCESS WHO EVER LIVED. AND, EVENTUALLY, A RUNNER ARRIVED WITH COYOTE'S INVITATION.
DAUGHTER! YOU'LL NEVER GUESS THE NEWS!
THE GREAT COYOTE IS LOOKING FOR A BRIDE! FINALLY, A HUSBAND THAT SUITS YOUR HERITAGE AND YOUR BEAUTY. YOU'RE SURE TO WIN HIS FAVOR.
I'M SORRY, MOTHER...
...BUT I CANNOT BECOME COYOTE'S WIFE. I AM NOT WORTHY OF SUCH AN HONOR. I WILL NOT GO.

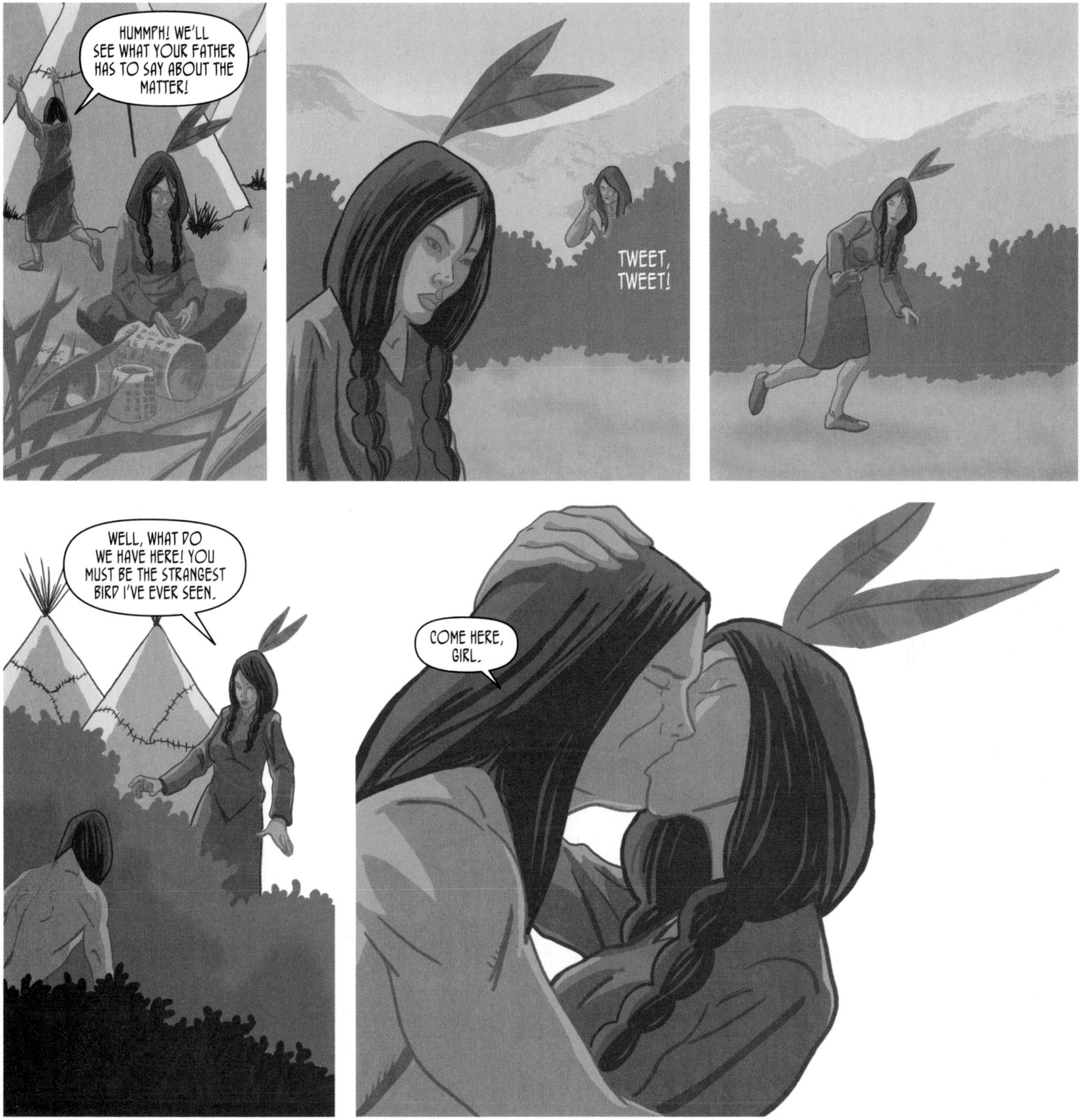
HUMMPH! WE'LL SEE WHAT YOUR FATHER HAS TO SAY ABOUT THE MATTER!
TWEET, TWEET!
WELL, WHAT DO WE HAVE HERE! YOU MUST BE THE STRANGEST BIRD I'VE EVER SEEN.
COME HERE, GIRL.

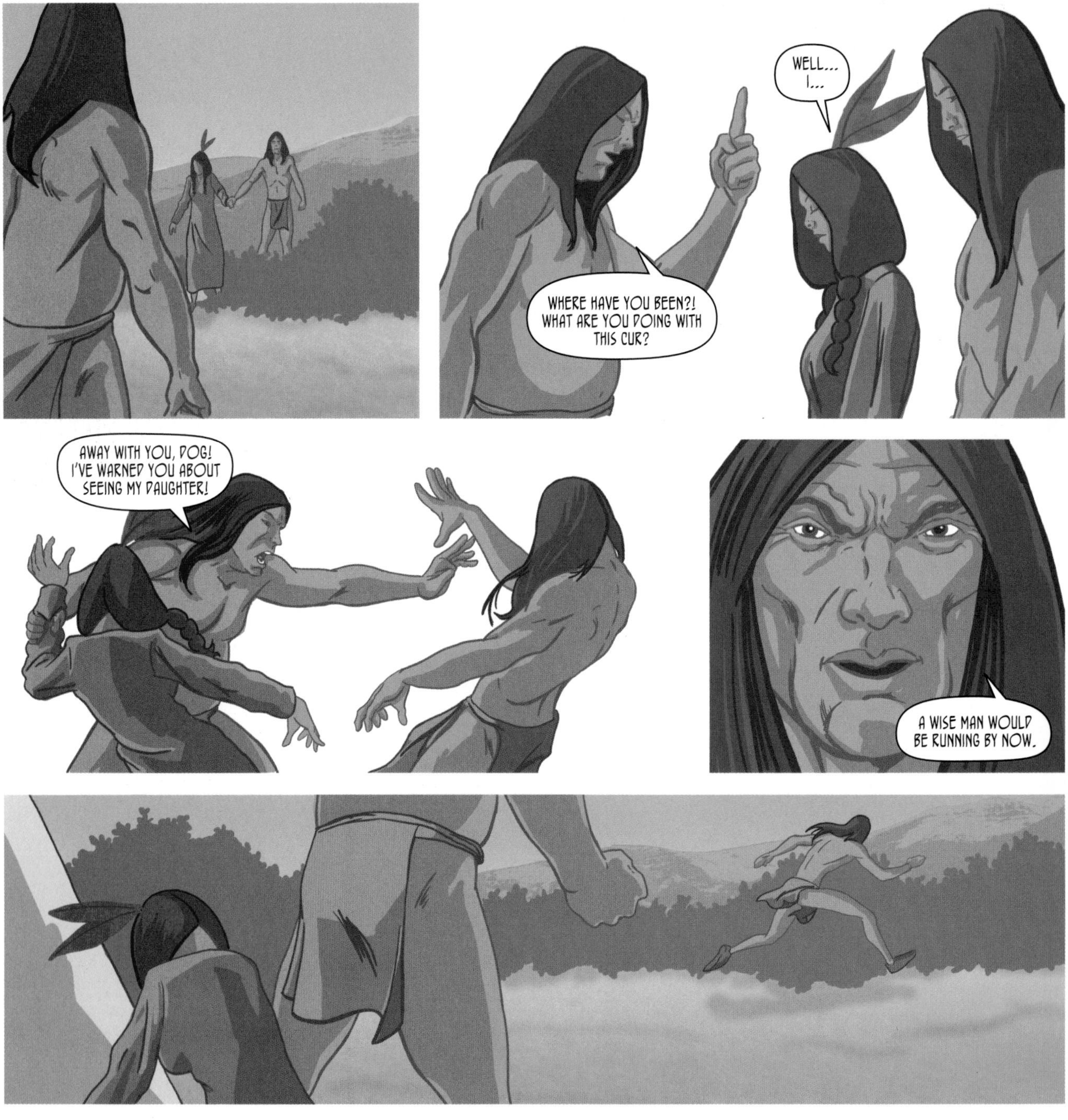
WHERE HAVE YOU BEEN?! WHAT ARE YOU DOING WITH THIS CUR?
WELL... I...
AWAY WITH YOU, DOG! I'VE WARNED YOU ABOUT SEEING MY DAUGHTER!
A WISE MAN WOULD BE RUNNING BY NOW.

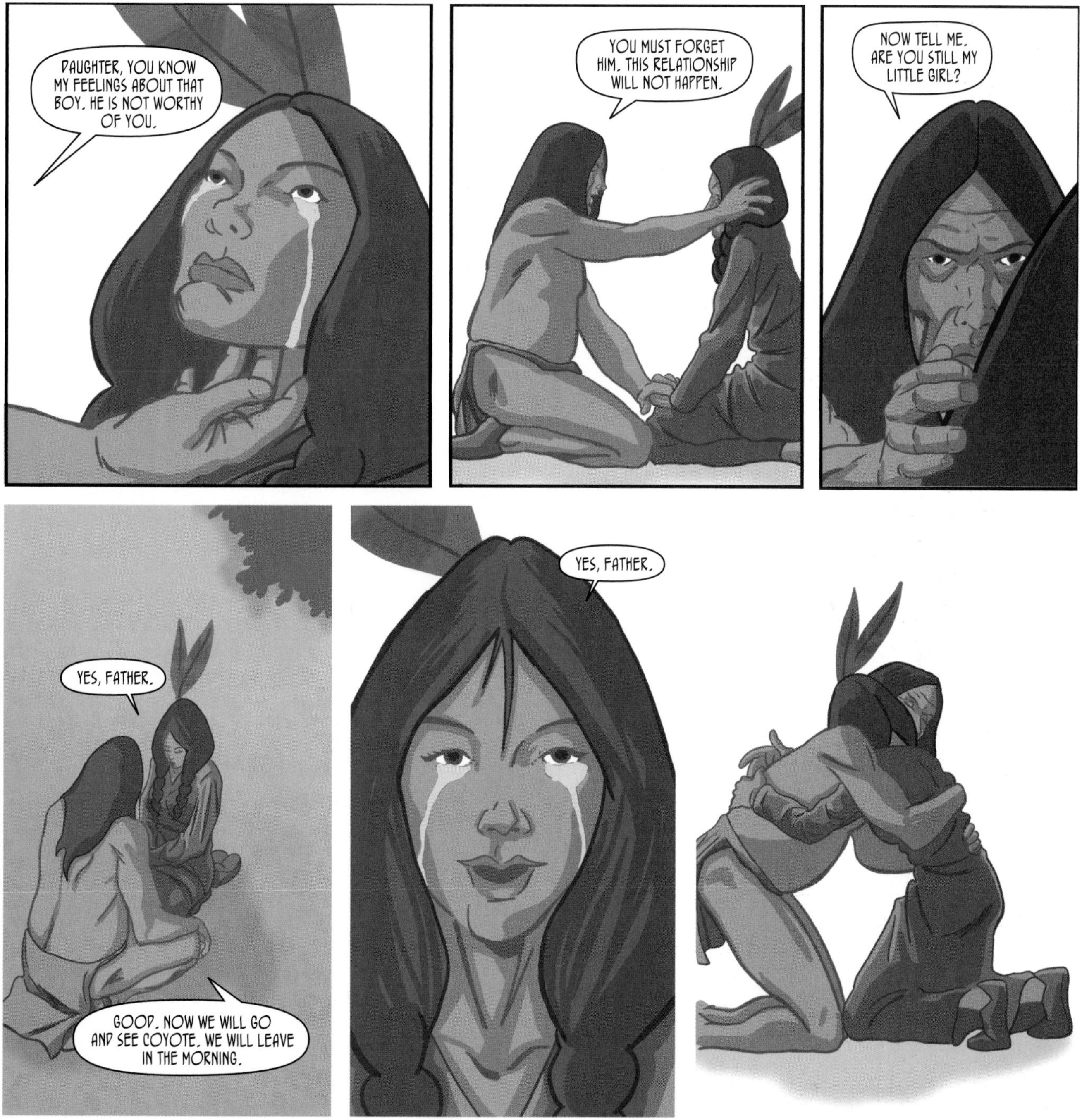
DAUGHTER, YOU KNOW MY FEELINGS ABOUT THAT BOY. HE IS NOT WORTHY OF YOU.
YOU MUST FORGET HIM. THIS RELATIONSHIP WILL NOT HAPPEN.
NOW TELL ME. ARE YOU STILL MY LITTLE GIRL?
YES, FATHER.
GOOD. NOW WE WILL GO AND SEE COYOTE. WE WILL LEAVE IN THE MORNING.
YES, FATHER.

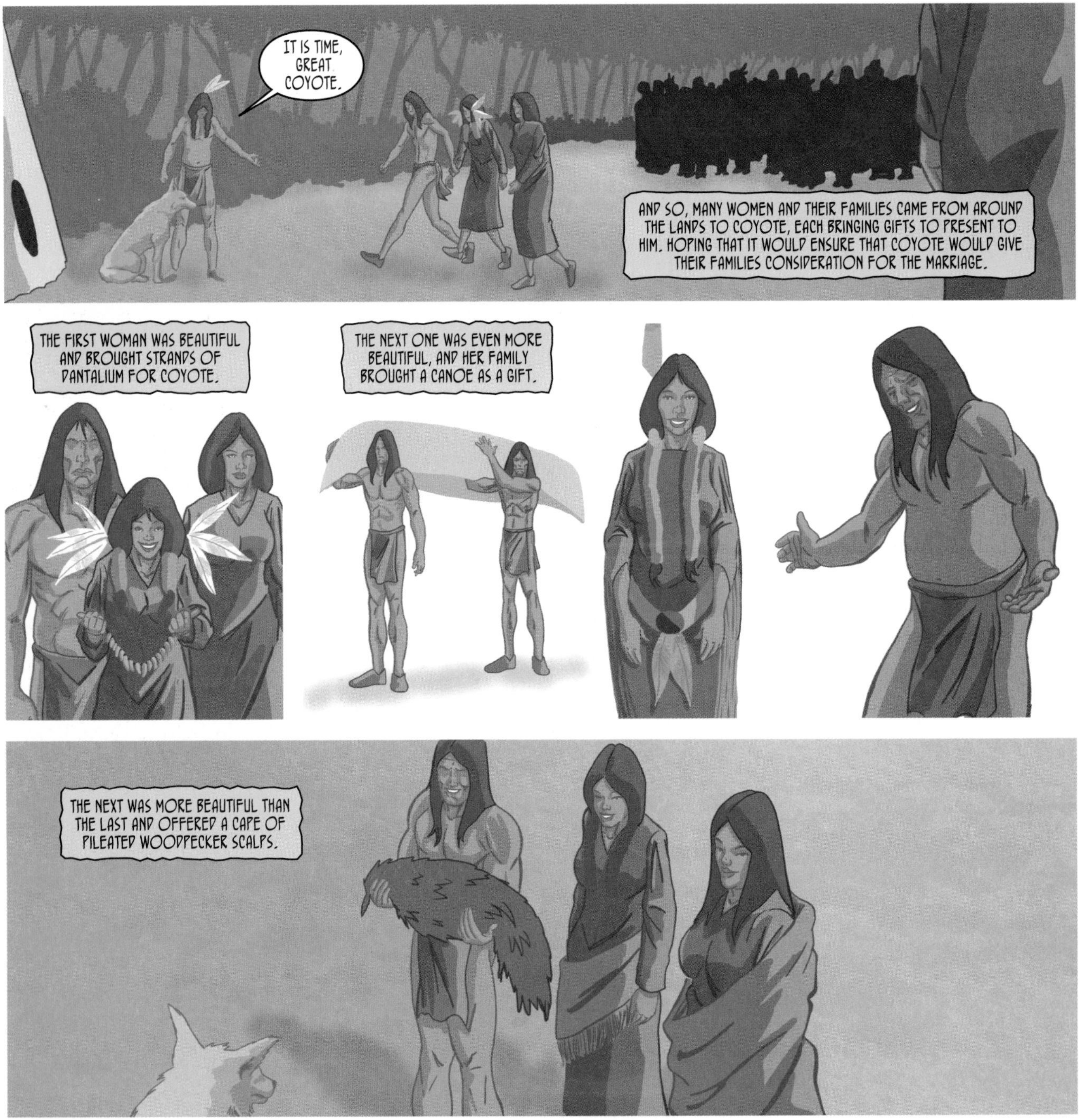
IT IS TIME, GREAT COYOTE.
AND SO, MANY WOMEN AND THEIR FAMILIES CAME FROM AROUND THE LANDS TO COYOTE, EACH BRINGING GIFTS TO PRESENT TO HIM. HOPING THAT IT WOULD ENSURE THAT COYOTE WOULD GIVE THEIR FAMILIES CONSIDERATION FOR THE MARRIAGE.
THE FIRST WOMAN WAS BEAUTIFUL AND BROUGHT STRANDS OF DANTALIUM FOR COYOTE.
THE NEXT ONE WAS EVEN MORE BEAUTIFUL, AND HER FAMILY BROUGHT A CANOE AS A GIFT.
THE NEXT WAS MORE BEAUTIFUL THAN THE LAST AND OFFERED A CAPE OF PILEATED WOODPECKER SCALPS.

AND STILL THEY CAME.

MORE BEAUTIFUL AND MORE PERFECT...

...THAN THE ONE BEFORE.

EACH BRINGING A GREATER GIFT THAN THE OTHER.

BUT COYOTE GREW BORED.

THEN THE WOMAN OF THE SOUTH CAME FORWARD, AND COYOTE TOOK GREAT INTEREST IN HER.

I PRESENT MY DAUGHTER TO YOU, O GREAT COYOTE. SHE COMES BEFORE YOU IN GREAT MODESTY, CHOOSING TO WEAR THE SIMPLEST AND OLDEST DRESS, AND BRAIDING HER HAIR CROOKED. SHE IS THE MOST INDUSTRIOUS WOMAN I HAVE EVER KNOWN. SHE WORKS QUICKLY, WITH GREAT SKILL AND DRIVEN EFFORT.

COYOTE LOOKED DEEPLY INTO THIS WOMAN. HE COULD SEE SHE TRULY WAS THE MOST BEAUTIFUL, HARD-WORKING, AND MODEST OF THE WOMEN THERE. BUT HE ALSO SAW MORE.

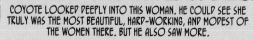

HOW COULD YOU BRING A WOMAN HERE TO ME THAT IS NOT PURE? I CAN SEE THIS IN HER!

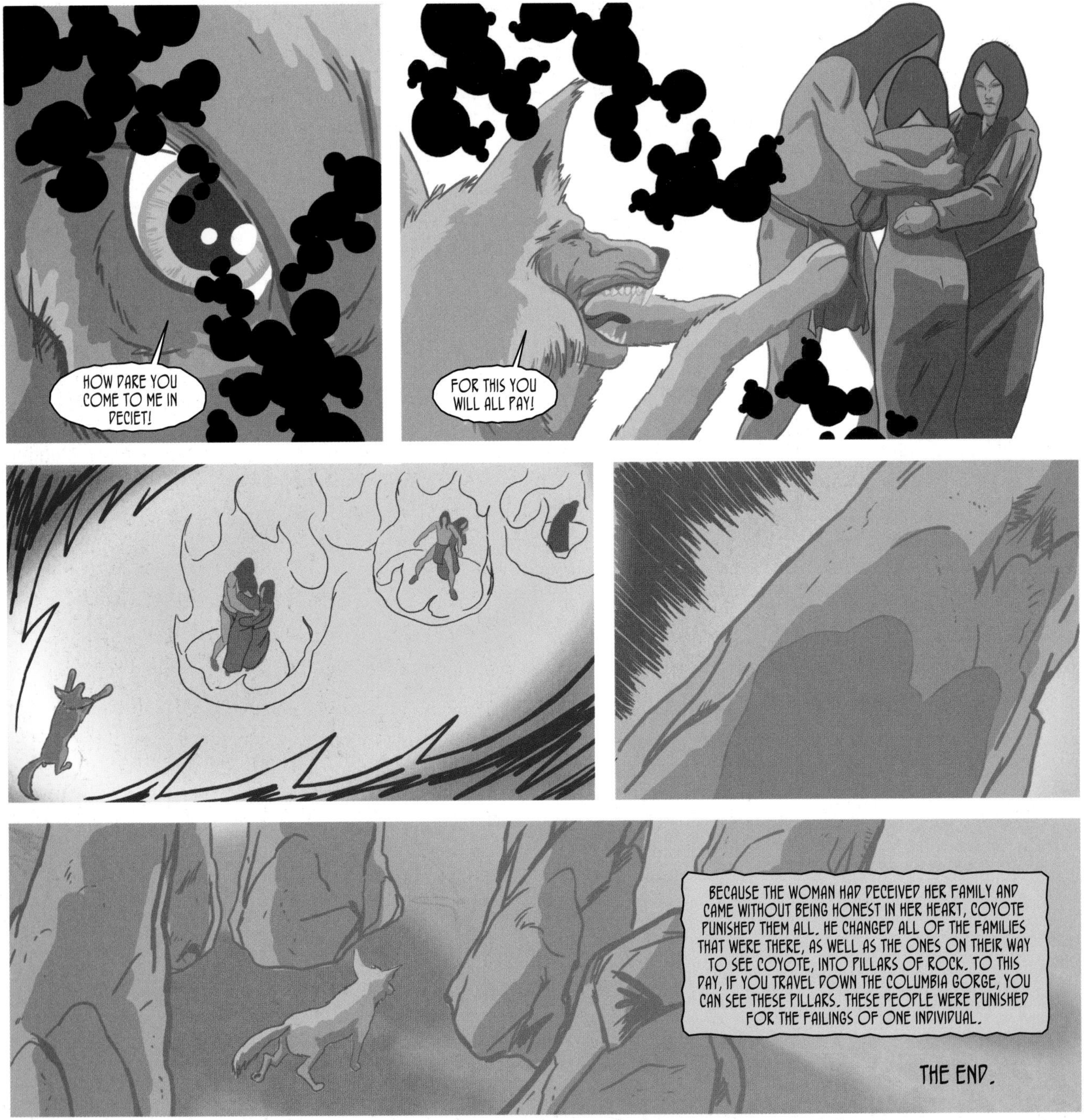
HOW DARE YOU COME TO ME IN DECIET!
FOR THIS YOU WILL ALL PAY!
BECAUSE THE WOMAN HAD DECEIVED HER FAMILY AND CAME WITHOUT BEING HONEST IN HER HEART, COYOTE PUNISHED THEM ALL. HE CHANGED ALL OF THE FAMILIES THAT WERE THERE, AS WELL AS THE ONES ON THEIR WAY TO SEE COYOTE, INTO PILLARS OF ROCK. TO THIS DAY, IF YOU TRAVEL DOWN THE COLUMBIA GORGE, YOU CAN SEE THESE PILLARS. THESE PEOPLE WERE PUNISHED FOR THE FAILINGS OF ONE INDIVIDUAL.
THE END.

PUAPUALENALENA
WIZARD DOG OF WAIPI'O VALLEY
STORY BY THOMAS C. CUMMINGS, JR. - ILLUSTRATION BY PAUL ZDEPSKI
Impossible! Who would dare steal my sacred 'AWA?!! Watch the 'awa field. Capture and bring the thief to me.
... If not, you both will DIE!!
It was the guards who reported the theft. And while enduring the tirade, the two trembled, eyes shut tight, keeping a safe distance from High Chief Kiha, whose family had ruled the Waipi'o Valley kingdom for hundreds of years.

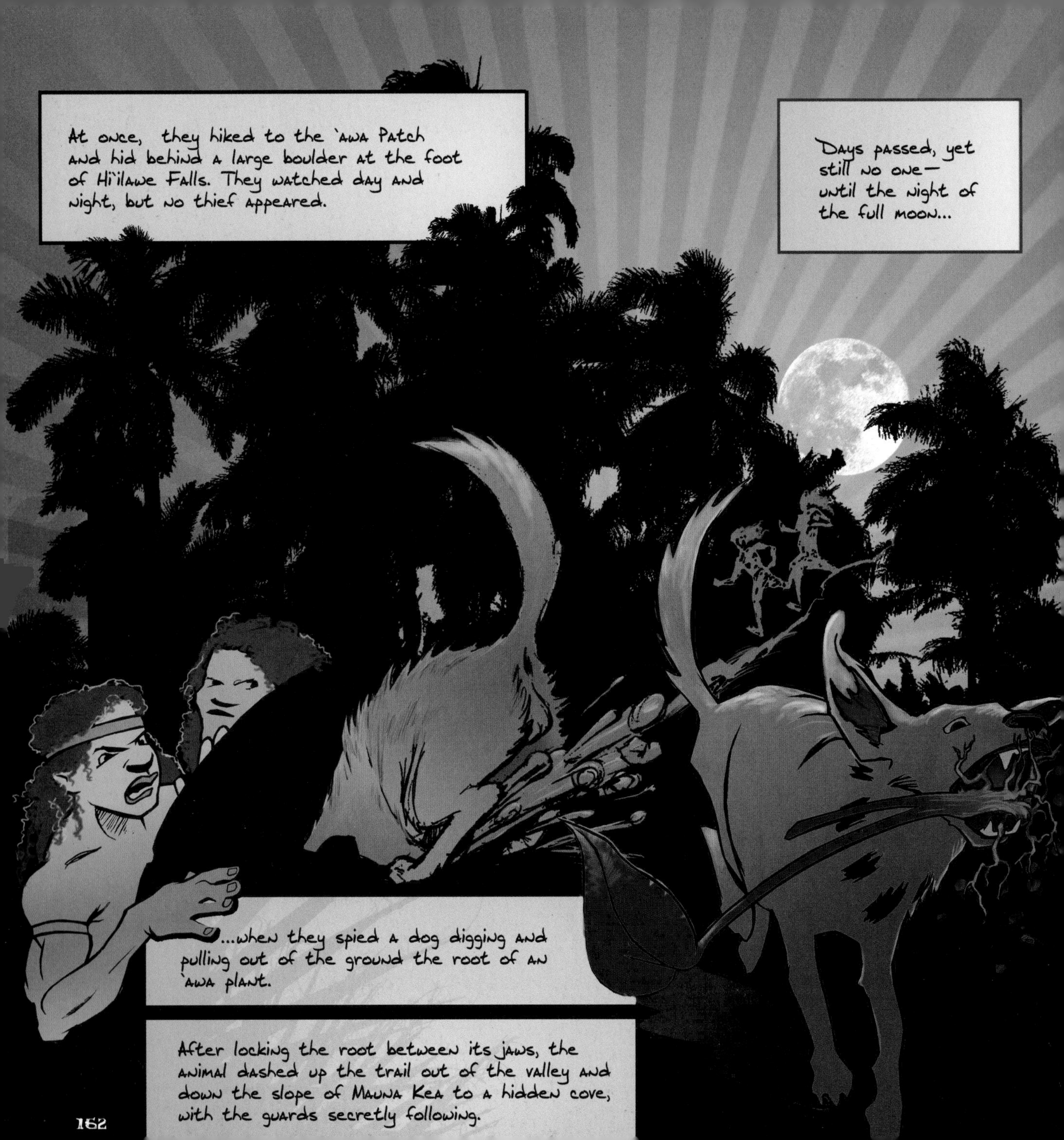
At once, they hiked to the `awa Patch and hid behind a large boulder at the foot of Hi`ilawe Falls. They watched day and night, but no thief appeared.
Days passed, yet still no one— until the night of the full moon...
...when they spied a dog digging and pulling out of the ground the root of an `awa plant.
After locking the root between its jaws, the animal dashed up the trail out of the valley and down the slope of Mauna Kea to a hidden cove, with the guards secretly following.

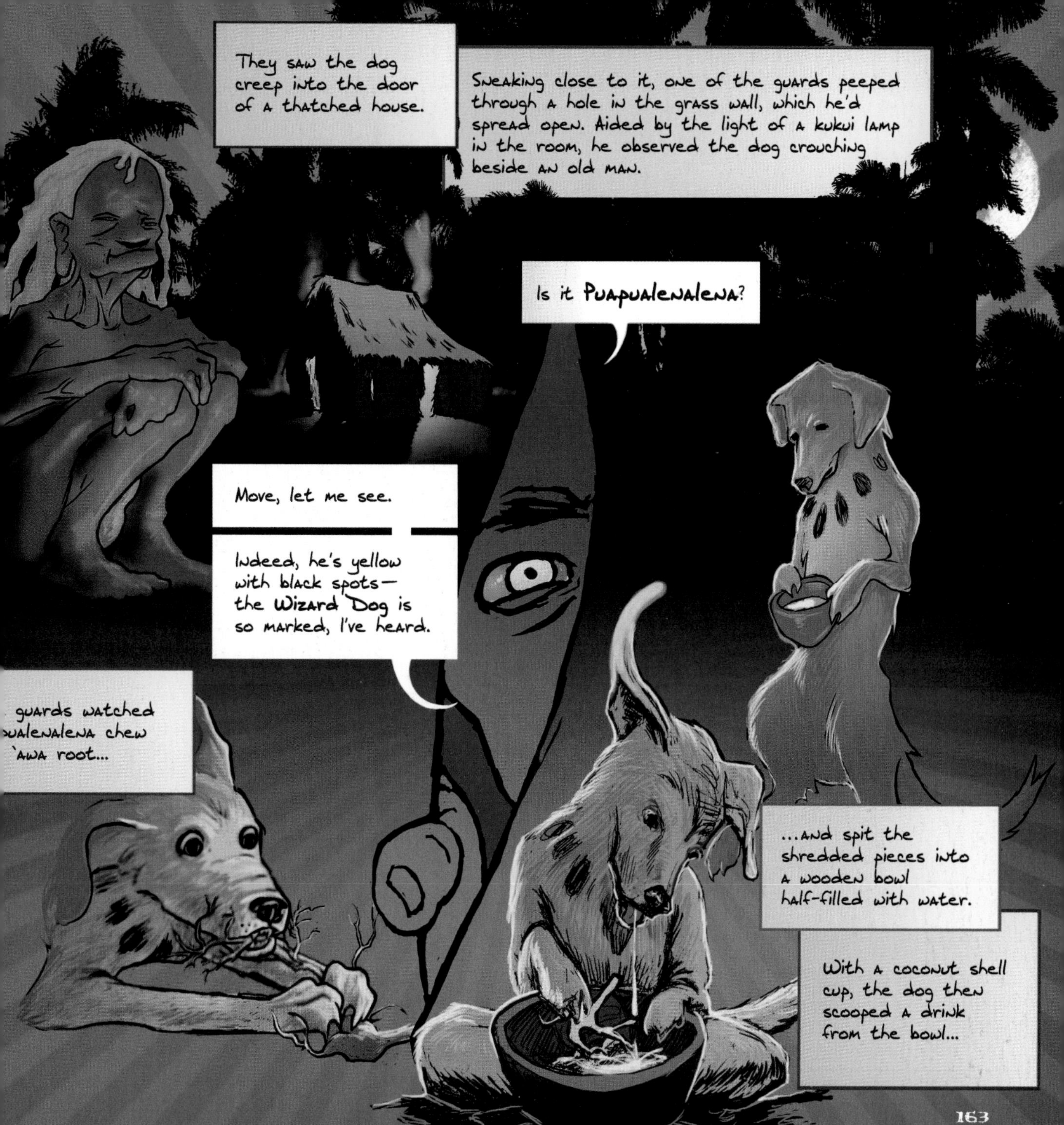
They saw the dog creep into the door of a thatched house.
Sneaking close to it, one of the guards peeped through a hole in the grass wall, which he'd spread open. Aided by the light of a kukui lamp in the room, he observed the dog crouching beside an old man.
Is it **Puapualenalena**?
Move, let me see.
Indeed, he's yellow with black spots— the **Wizard Dog** is so marked, I've heard.
guards watched
ualenalena chew
`awa root...
...and spit the shredded pieces into a wooden bowl half-filled with water.
With a coconut shell cup, the dog then scooped a drink from the bowl...

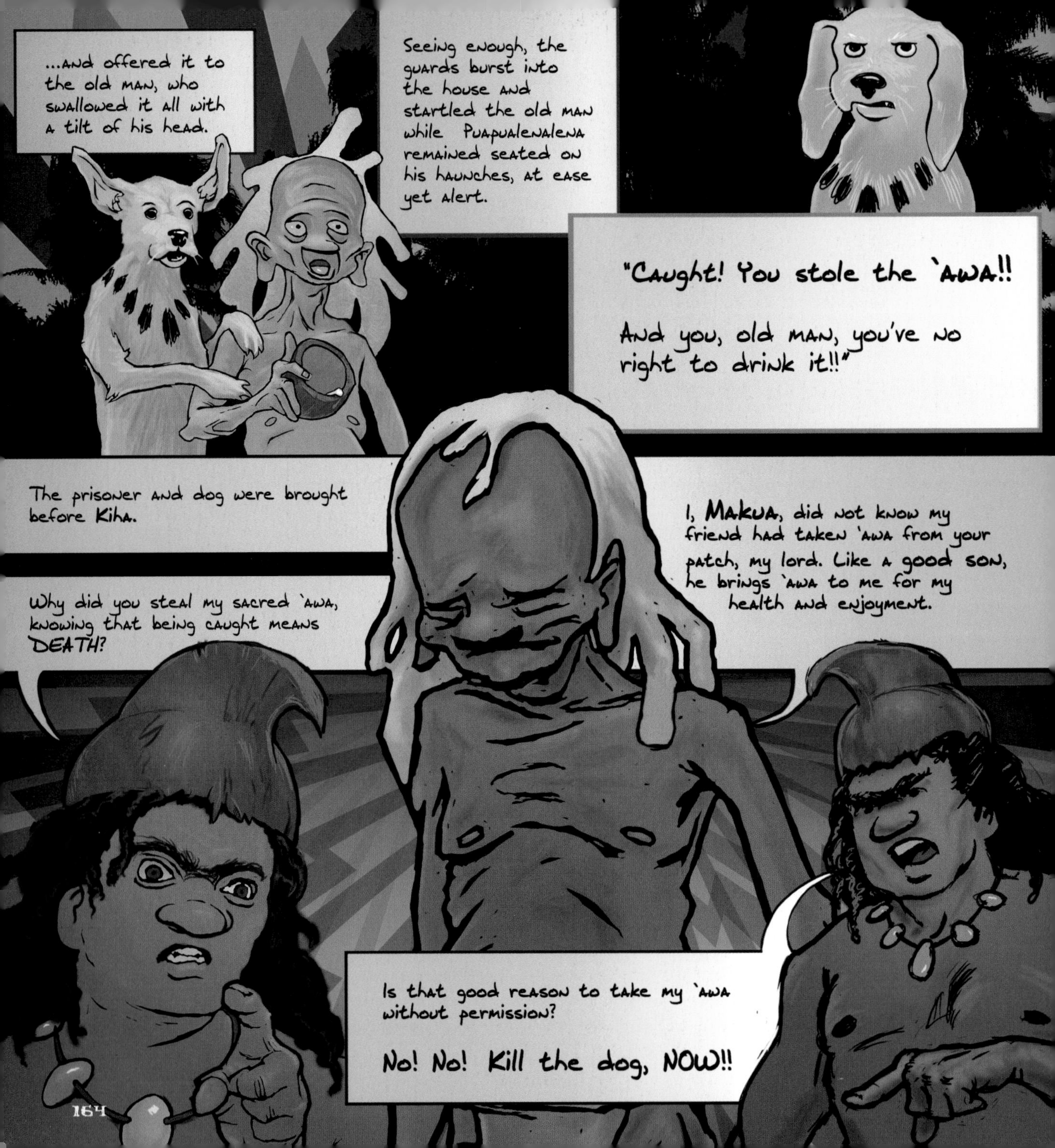

...and offered it to the old man, who swallowed it all with a tilt of his head.
Seeing enough, the guards burst into the house and startled the old man while Puapualenalena remained seated on his haunches, at ease yet alert.
"Caught! You stole the `awa!!
And you, old man, you've no right to drink it!!"
The prisoner and dog were brought before Kiha.
I, Makua, did not know my friend had taken `awa from your patch, my lord. Like a good son, he brings `awa to me for my health and enjoyment.
Why did you steal my sacred `awa, knowing that being caught means DEATH?
Is that good reason to take my `awa without permission?
No! No! Kill the dog, NOW!!

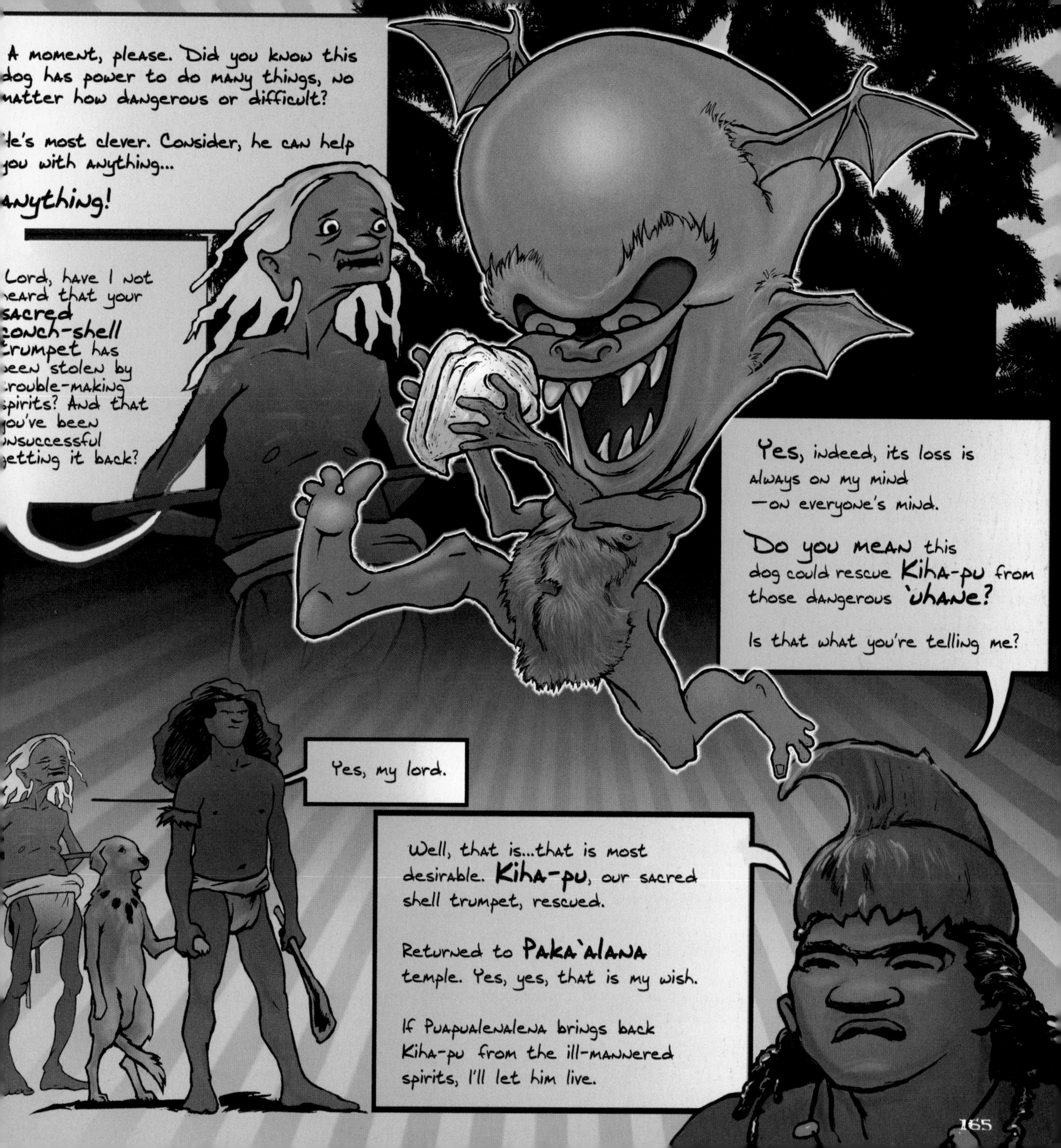
A moment, please. Did you know this dog has power to do many things, no natter how dangerous or difficult?
le's most clever. Consider, he can help you with anything...
anything!
Lord, have I not neard that your sacred conch-shell trumpet has been stolen by trouble-making spirits? And that you've been unsuccessful getting it back?
Yes, indeed, its loss is always on my mind —on everyone's mind.
Do you mean this dog could rescue Kiha-pu from those dangerous `uhane?
Is that what you're telling me?
Yes, my lord.
Well, that is...that is most desirable. Kiha-pu, our sacred shell trumpet, rescued.
Returned to Paka`alana temple. Yes, yes, that is my wish.
If Puapualenalena brings back Kiha-pu from the ill-mannered spirits, I'll let him live.

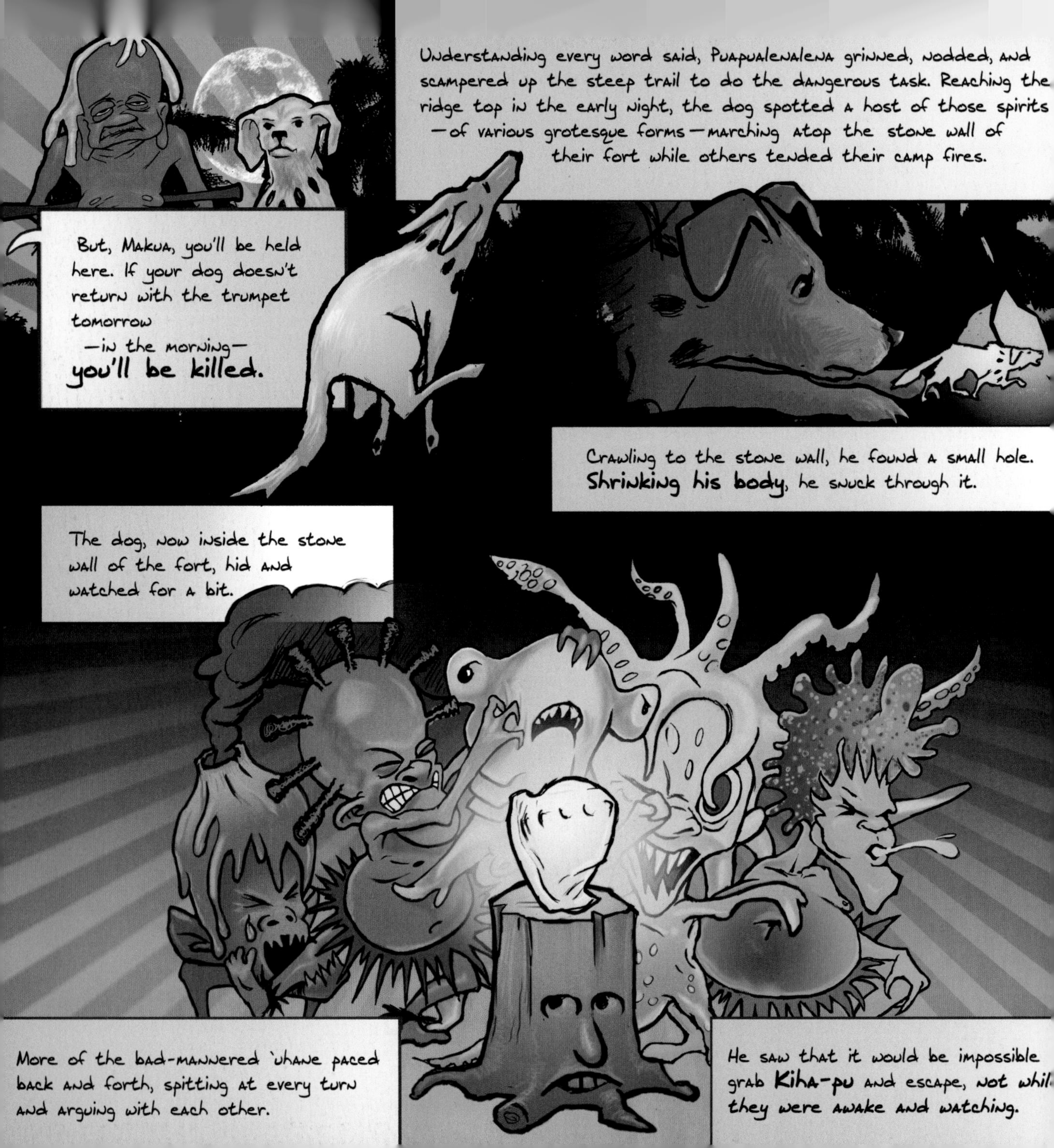
Understanding every word said, Puapualenalena grinned, nodded, and scampered up the steep trail to do the dangerous task. Reaching the ridge top in the early night, the dog spotted a host of those spirits —of various grotesque forms—marching atop the stone wall of their fort while others tended their camp fires.
But, Makua, you'll be held here. If your dog doesn't return with the trumpet tomorrow —in the morning— **you'll be killed.**
Crawling to the stone wall, he found a small hole. **Shrinking his body**, he snuck through it.
The dog, now inside the stone wall of the fort, hid and watched for a bit.
More of the bad-mannered `uhane paced back and forth, spitting at every turn and arguing with each other.
He saw that it would be impossible grab **Kiha-pu** and escape, **not whil they were awake and watching.**

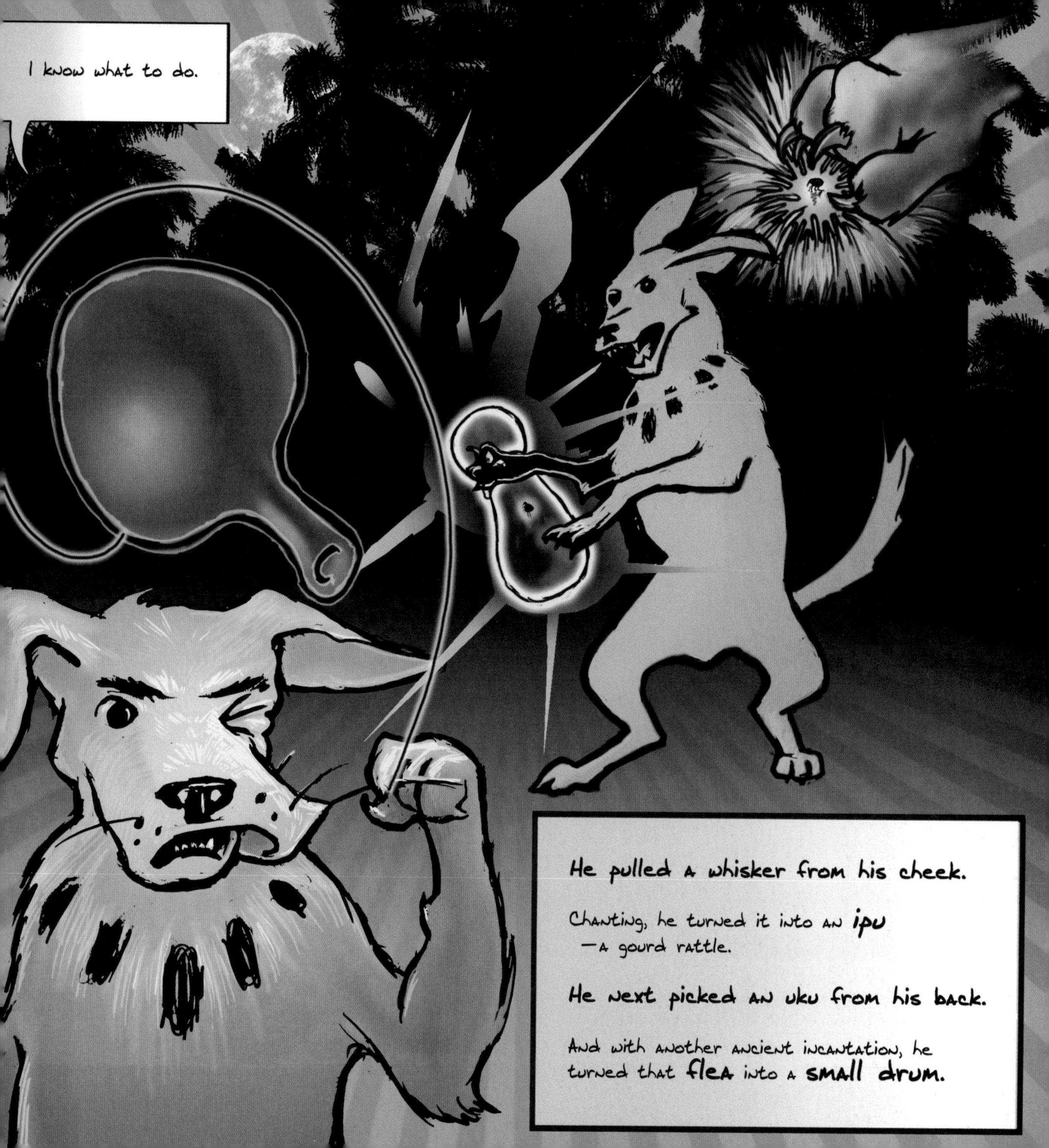

I know what to do.
He pulled a whisker from his cheek.
Chanting, he turned it into an ipu —a gourd rattle.
He next picked an uku from his back.
And with another ancient incantation, he turned that flea into a small drum.

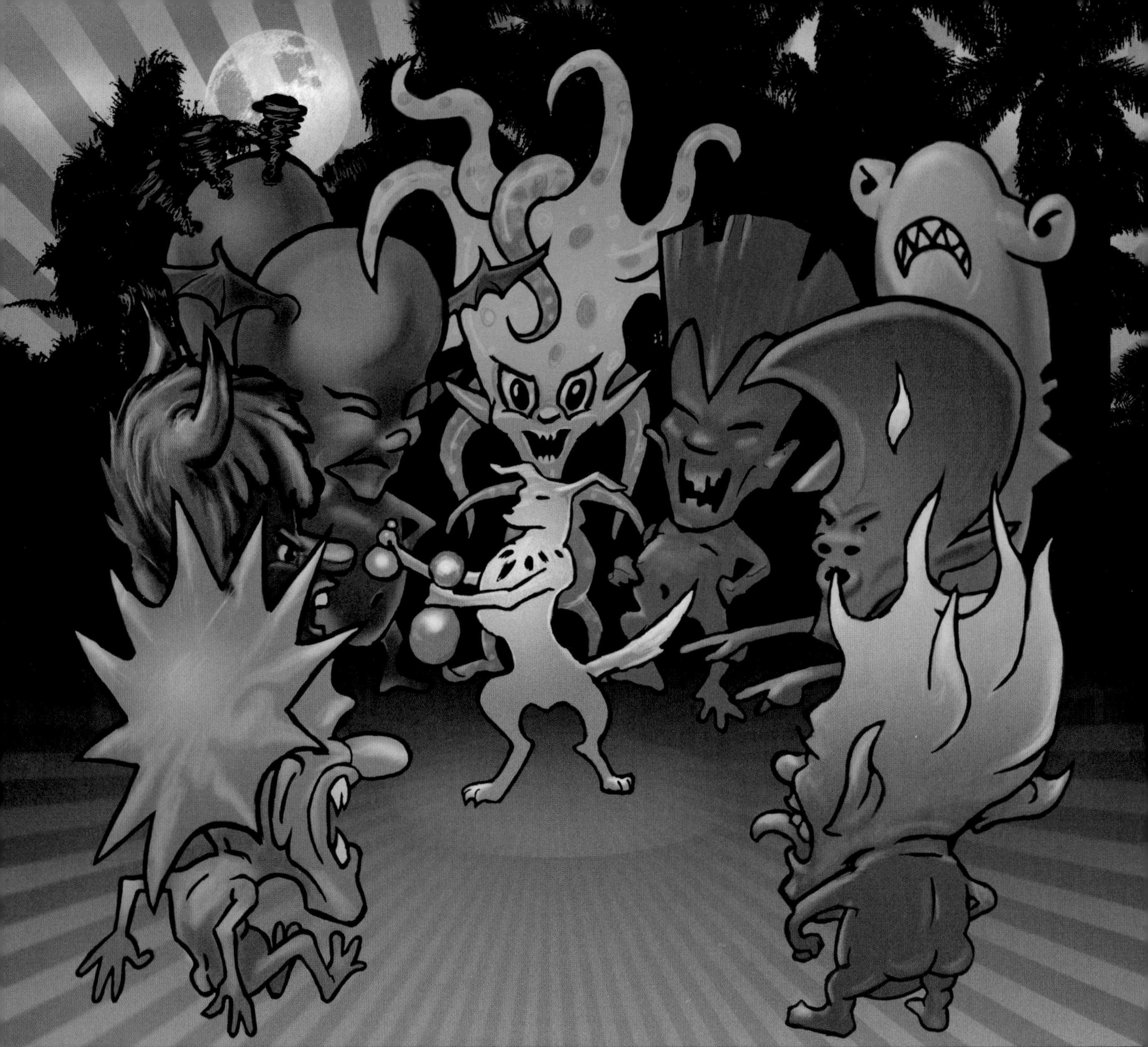

Then, fast-stepping to the middle of the fort floor, he danced, shaking the rattle with his right front paw. At intervals he beat the drum with his left front paw while swirling in circles, howling, barking, growling, emitting sounds only a dog of magical powers can. Shocked at seeing a dog in their midst —dancing and chanting, no less— the bare-chested spirits shrieked in ridicule.

hey were so unimpressed with apualenalena's performance that the spot they composed a dog egrading ditty:

"He looks so ugly,
He sounds too shrilly,
He dances poorly,
Truly, truly."

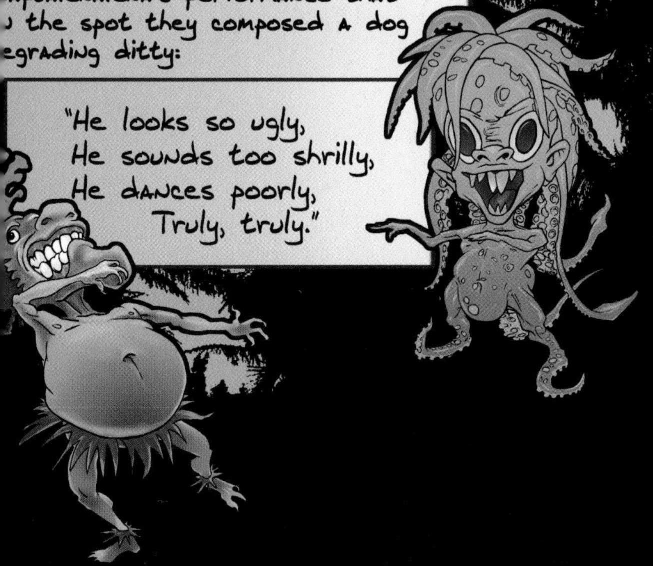

We'll chant as well, but quite, quite sweetly,
We'll show him how we dance right fleetly,
We'll know he'll know we're very neatly,
he best at chant and dance completely."

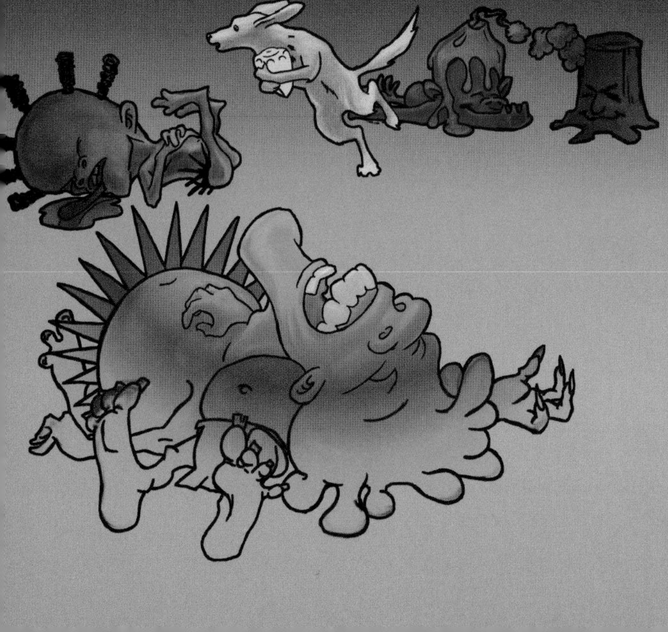

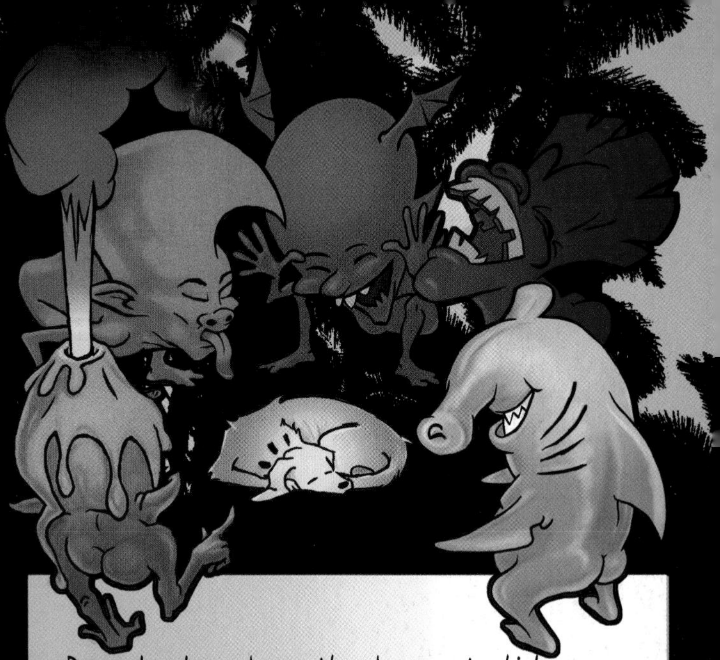

Puapualenalena drove the demons to higher levels of mad gyrations and incantations by magically doing a little better than they did. By the late part of the night, the dog slowed his frolicking, which moved the spirits to mock him with vulgar words—even bending over and wagging their naked backsides at him.

Then, when he curled into a ball and fell asleep, the demons soared to happy hysterics.

"Continue, **HULA MAKOU**, dance on. Let's show that dog we're better," cackled the demon leader. So, through the rest of the night, at the same fast pace and high pitch, all the spirits stayed in constant motion, showing extreme emotion. They seemed tireless, full of energy.

But then, as the sun was about to break out of the sea, they slumped to the ground, layered with sweat and out of breath. All at once, completely exhausted, they fell asleep, smiling.

Waiting for that moment, Puapualenalena rose from his pretended sleep, stepped so carefully over the snoring spirit bodies, and snatched Kiha-pu from the platform.

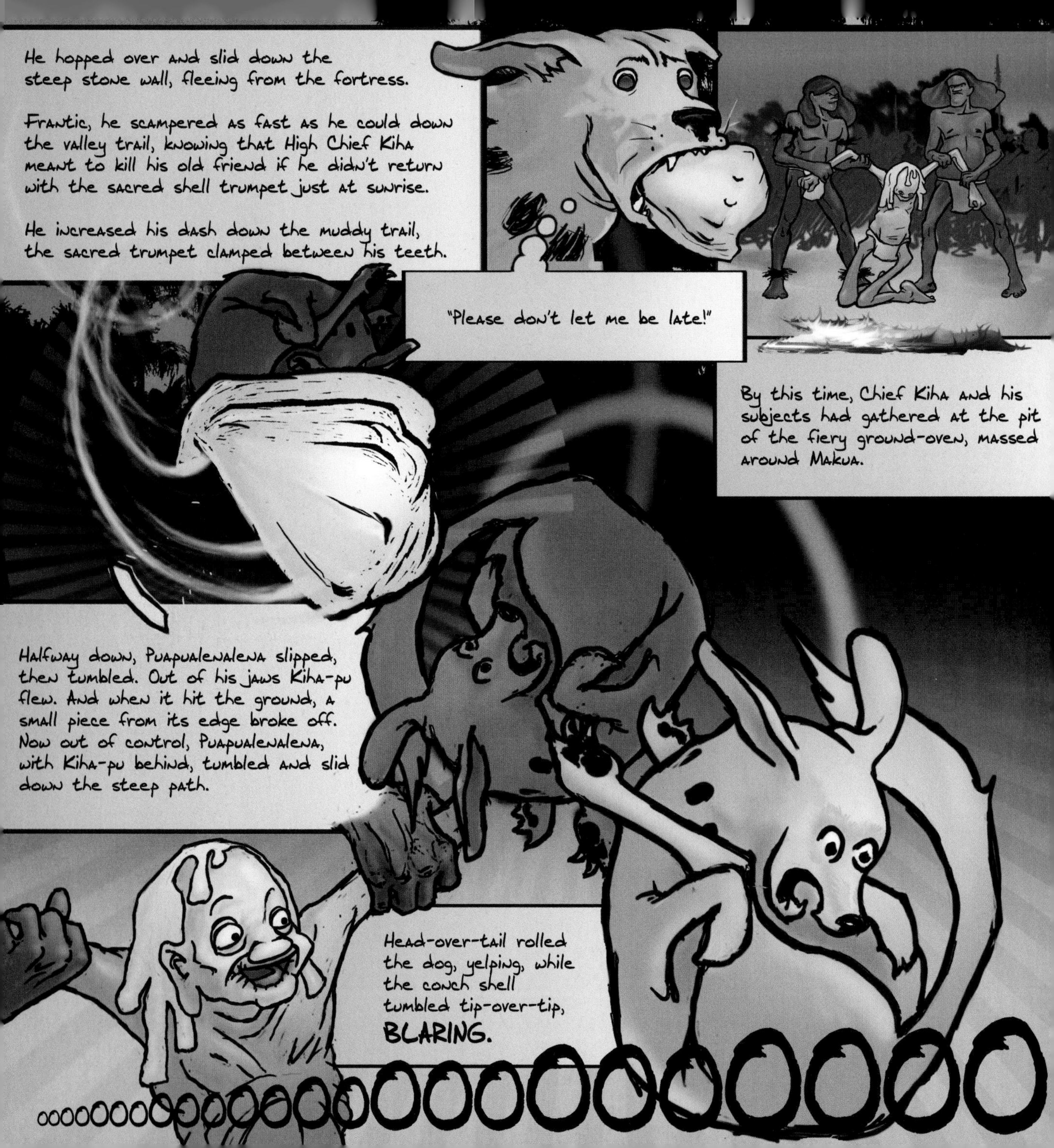
He hopped over and slid down the steep stone wall, fleeing from the fortress.
Frantic, he scampered as fast as he could down the valley trail, knowing that High Chief Kiha meant to kill his old friend if he didn't return with the sacred shell trumpet just at sunrise.
He increased his dash down the muddy trail, the sacred trumpet clamped between his teeth.
"Please don't let me be late!"
By this time, Chief Kiha and his subjects had gathered at the pit of the fiery ground-oven, massed around Makua.
Halfway down, Puapualenalena slipped, then tumbled. Out of his jaws Kiha-pu flew. And when it hit the ground, a small piece from its edge broke off. Now out of control, Puapualenalena, with Kiha-pu behind, tumbled and slid down the steep path.
Head-over-tail rolled the dog, yelping, while the conch shell tumbled tip-over-tip, BLARING.
oooooooooooooooooOOOOOOOOOOOOO

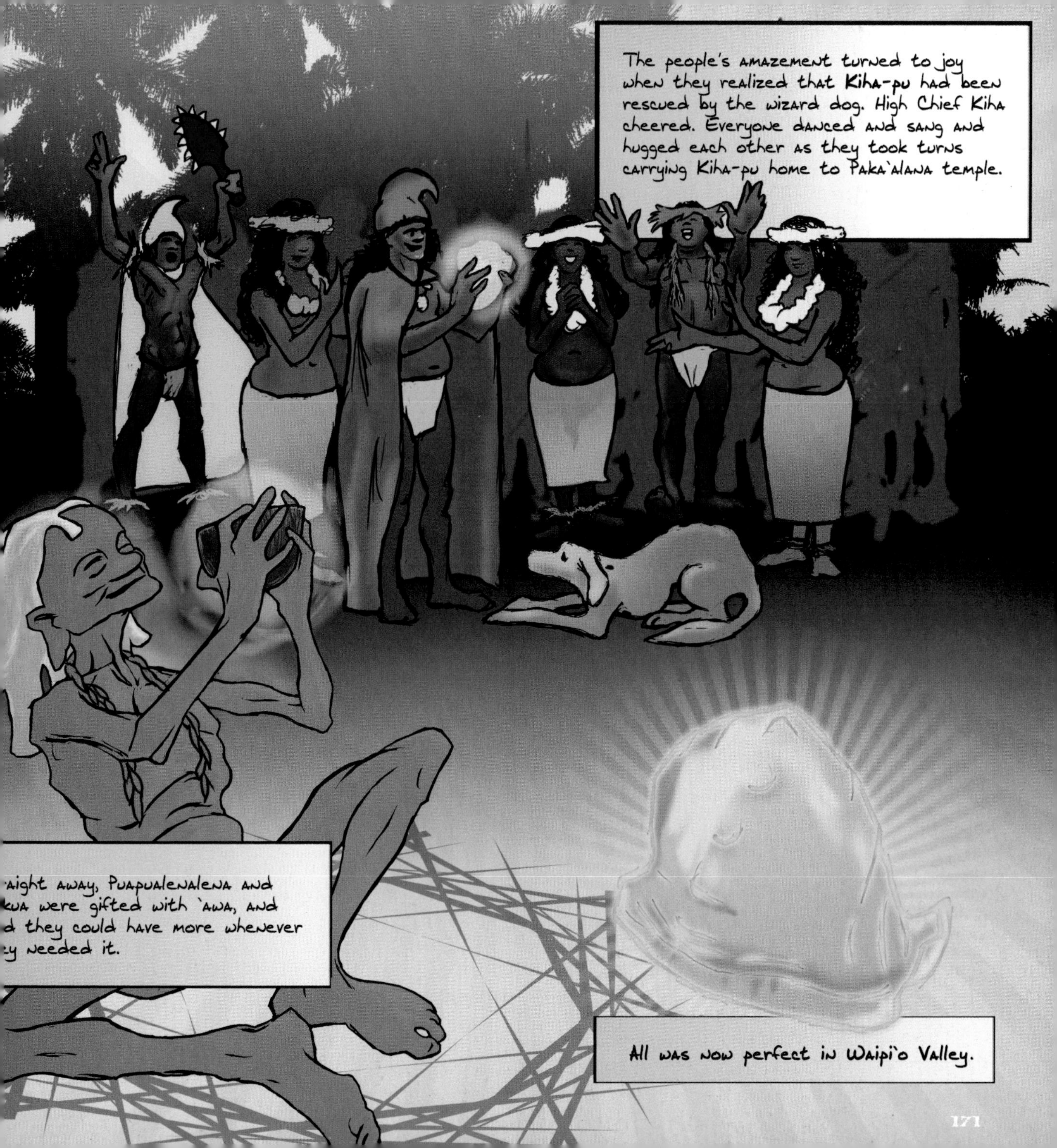

The people's amazement turned to joy when they realized that Kiha-pu had been rescued by the wizard dog. High Chief Kiha cheered. Everyone danced and sang and hugged each other as they took turns carrying Kiha-pu home to Paka`alana temple.
aight away, Puapualenalena and
kua were gifted with `awa, and
d they could have more whenever
y needed it.
All was now perfect in Waipi`o Valley.

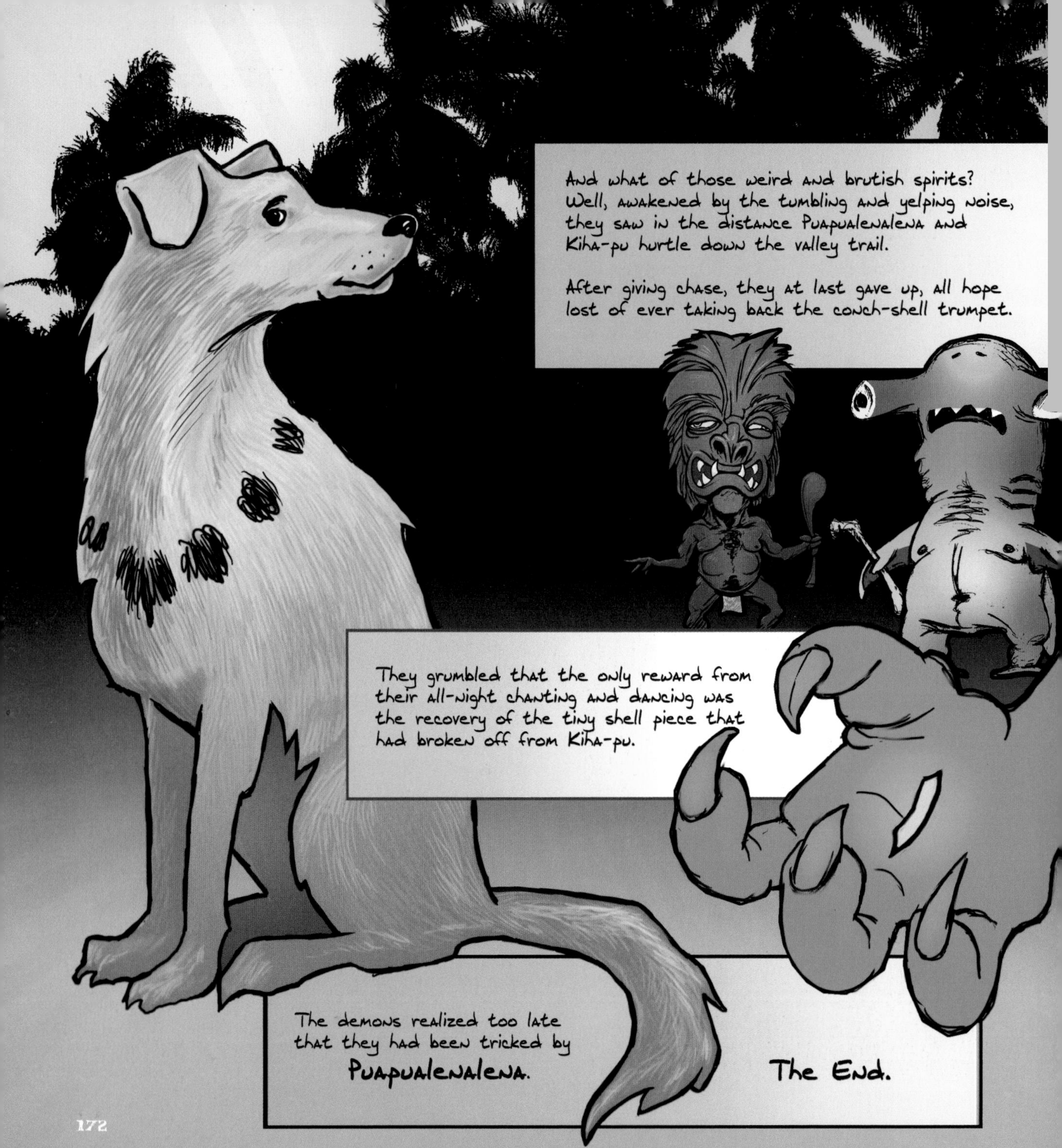
And what of those weird and brutish spirits? Well, awakened by the tumbling and yelping noise, they saw in the distance Puapualenalena and Kiha-pu hurtle down the valley trail.
After giving chase, they at last gave up, all hope lost of ever taking back the conch-shell trumpet.
They grumbled that the only reward from their all-night chanting and dancing was the recovery of the tiny shell piece that had broken off from Kiha-pu.
The demons realized too late that they had been tricked by Puapualenalena.
The End.

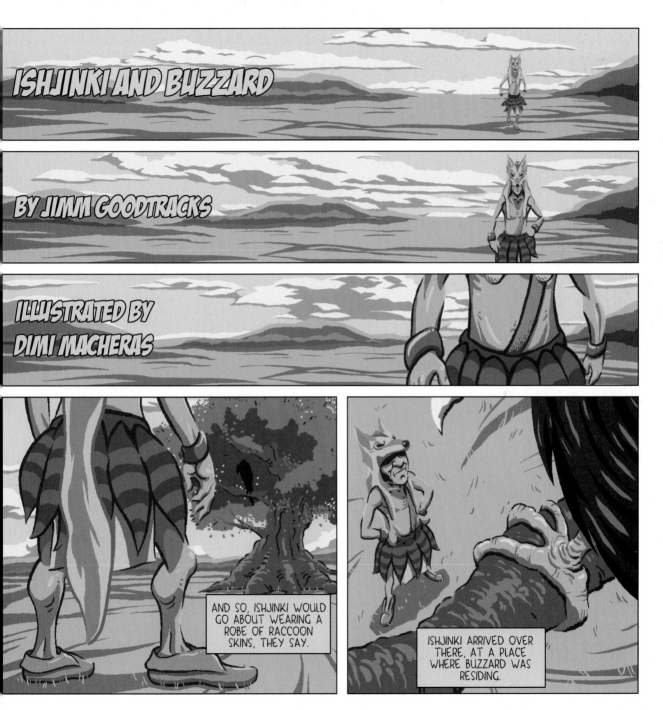

ISHJINKI AND BUZZARD

BY JIMM GOODTRACKS

ILLUSTRATED BY DIMI MACHERAS

AND SO, ISHJINKI WOULD GO ABOUT WEARING A ROBE OF RACCOON SKINS, THEY SAY.

ISHJINKI ARRIVED OVER THERE, AT A PLACE WHERE BUZZARD WAS RESIDING.

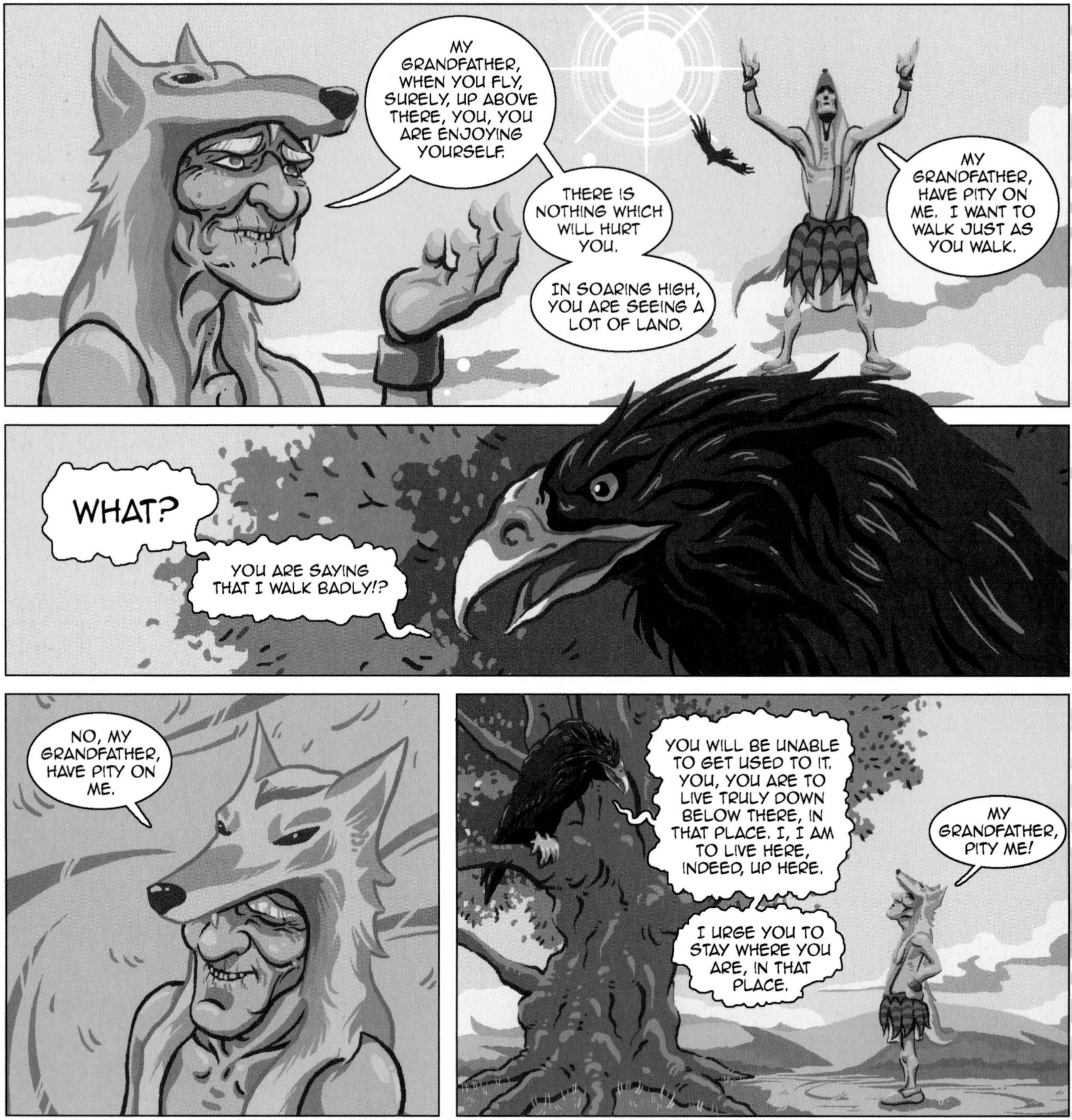
MY GRANDFATHER, WHEN YOU FLY, SURELY, UP ABOVE THERE, YOU, YOU ARE ENJOYING YOURSELF.
THERE IS NOTHING WHICH WILL HURT YOU.
IN SOARING HIGH, YOU ARE SEEING A LOT OF LAND.
MY GRANDFATHER, HAVE PITY ON ME. I WANT TO WALK JUST AS YOU WALK.
WHAT?
YOU ARE SAYING THAT I WALK BADLY!?
NO, MY GRANDFATHER, HAVE PITY ON ME.
YOU WILL BE UNABLE TO GET USED TO IT. YOU, YOU ARE TO LIVE TRULY DOWN BELOW THERE, IN THAT PLACE. I, I AM TO LIVE HERE, INDEED, UP HERE.
I URGE YOU TO STAY WHERE YOU ARE, IN THAT PLACE.
MY GRANDFATHER, PITY ME!

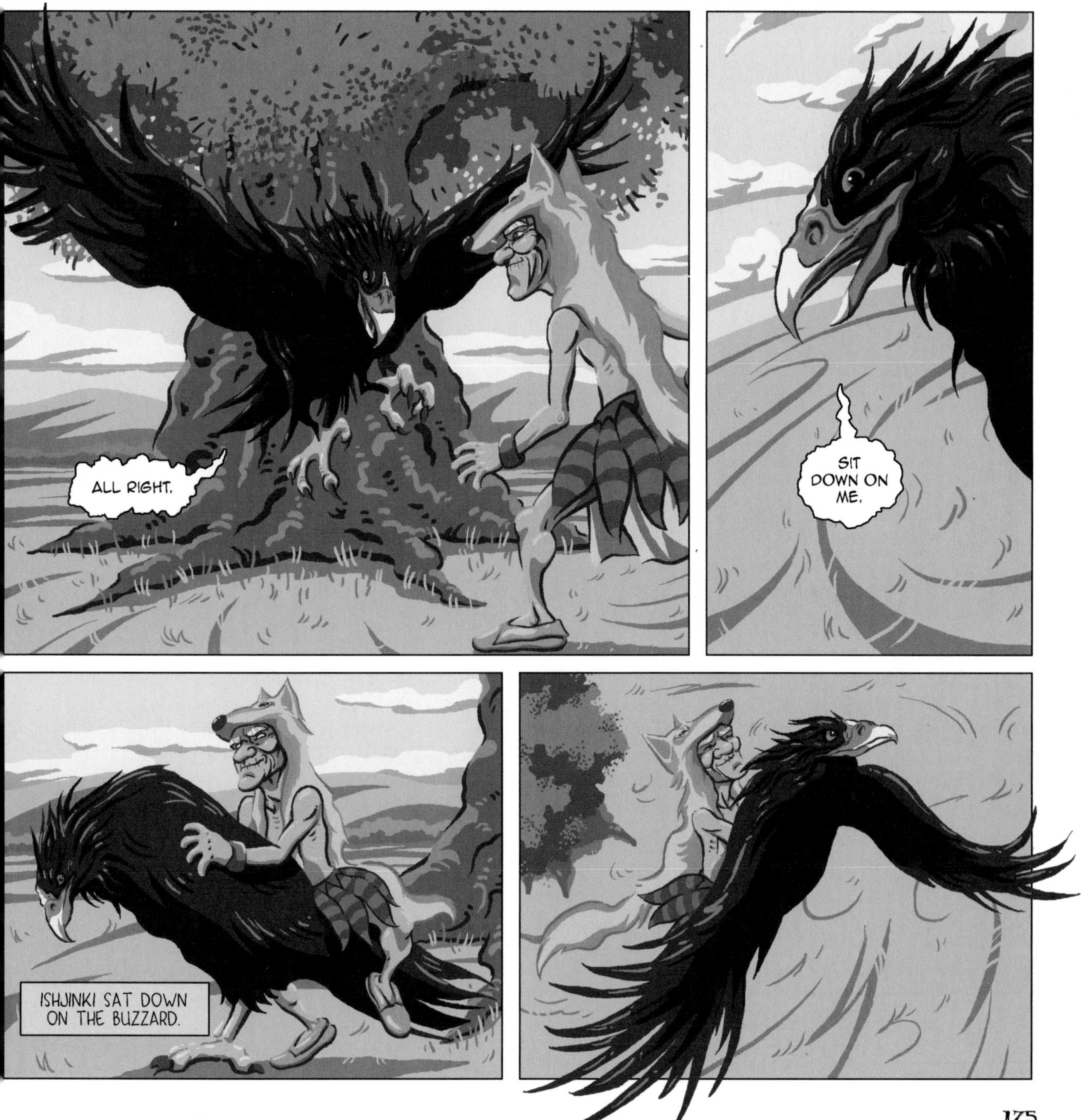
ALL RIGHT.
SIT DOWN ON ME.
ISHJINKI SAT DOWN ON THE BUZZARD.

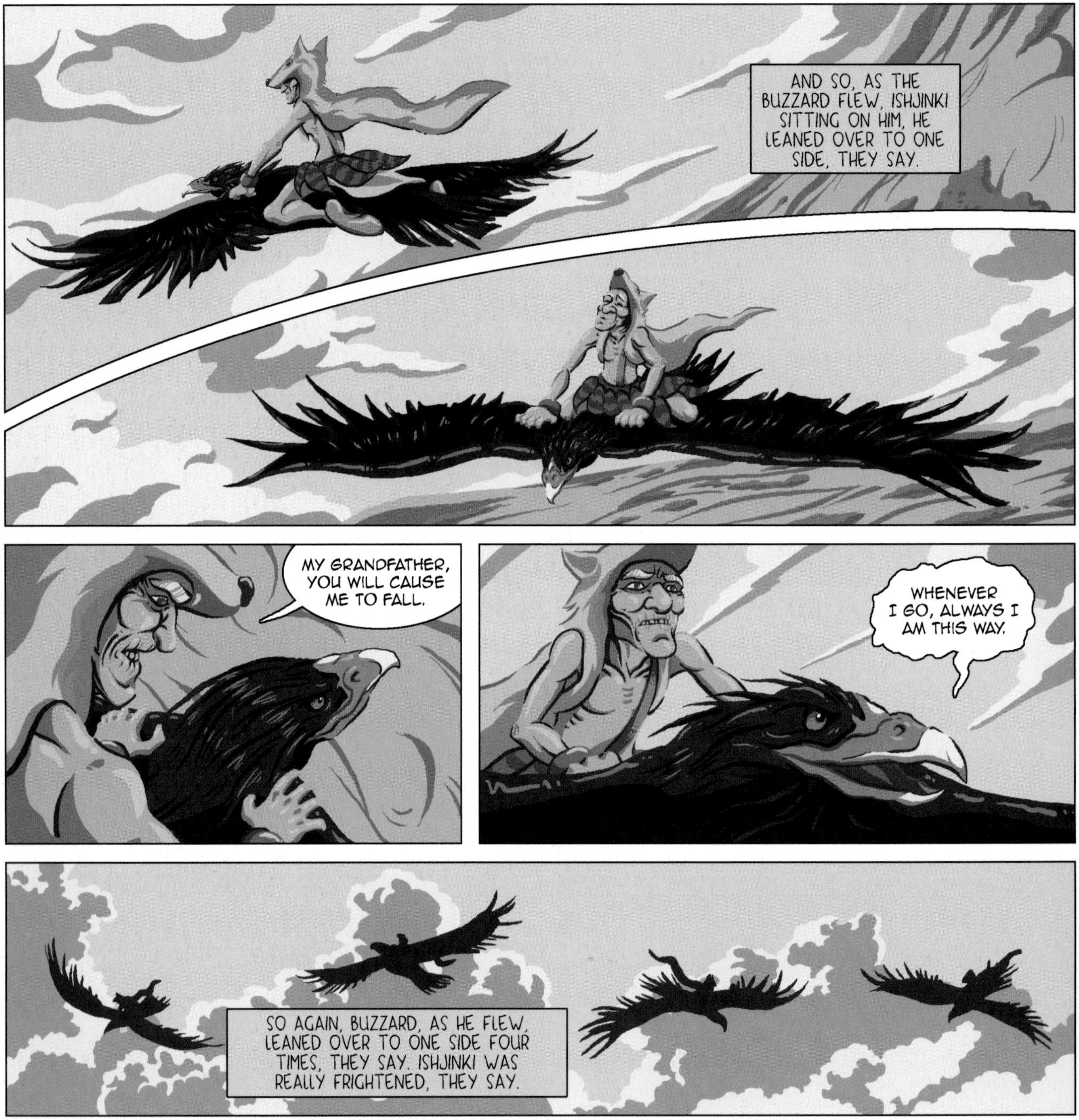
AND SO, AS THE BUZZARD FLEW, ISHJINKI SITTING ON HIM, HE LEANED OVER TO ONE SIDE, THEY SAY.
MY GRANDFATHER, YOU WILL CAUSE ME TO FALL.
WHENEVER I GO, ALWAYS I AM THIS WAY.
SO AGAIN, BUZZARD, AS HE FLEW, LEANED OVER TO ONE SIDE FOUR TIMES, THEY SAY. ISHJINKI WAS REALLY FRIGHTENED, THEY SAY.

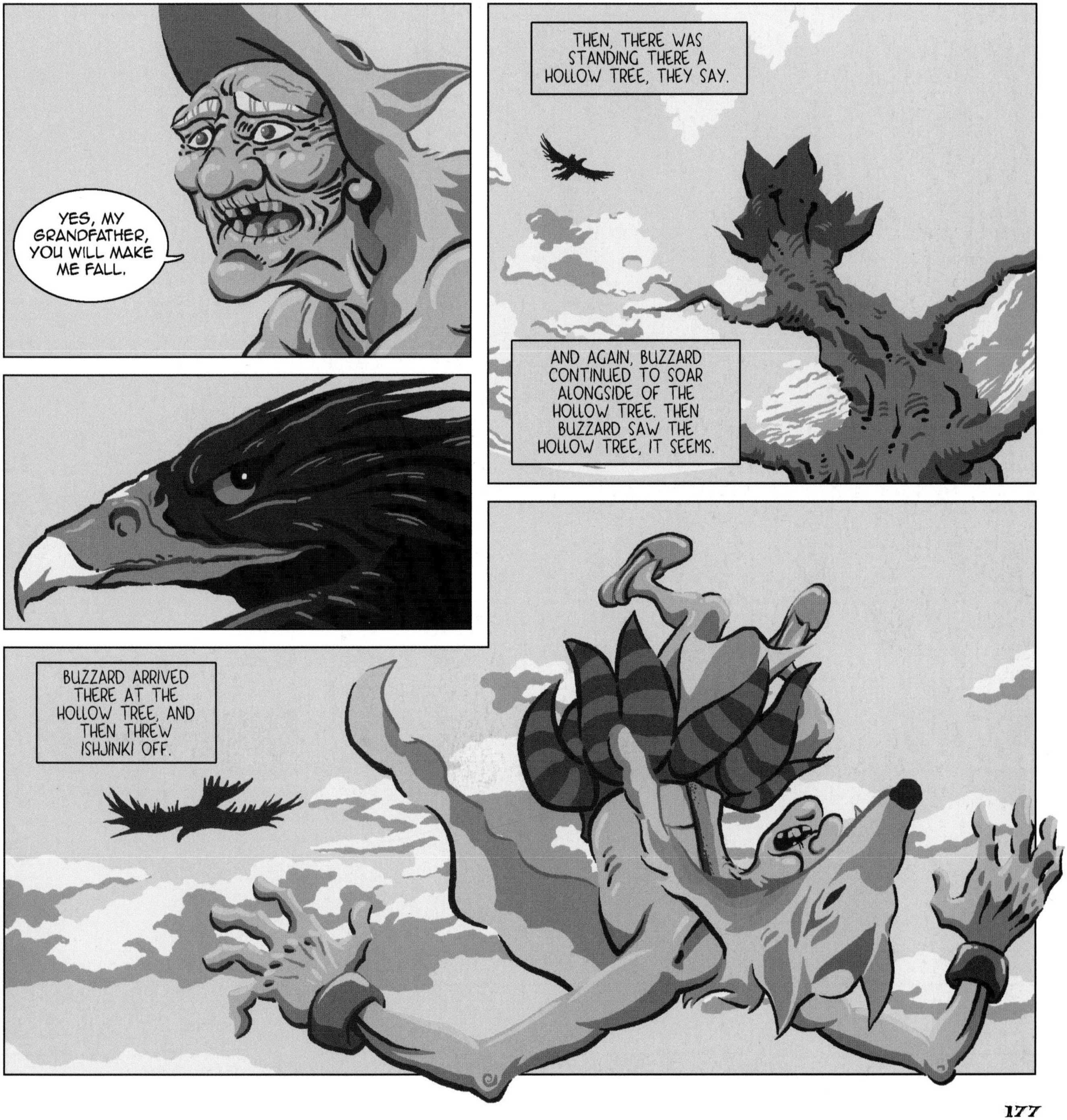
YES, MY GRANDFATHER, YOU WILL MAKE ME FALL.
THEN, THERE WAS STANDING THERE A HOLLOW TREE, THEY SAY.
AND AGAIN, BUZZARD CONTINUED TO SOAR ALONGSIDE OF THE HOLLOW TREE. THEN BUZZARD SAW THE HOLLOW TREE, IT SEEMS.
BUZZARD ARRIVED THERE AT THE HOLLOW TREE, AND THEN THREW ISHJINKI OFF.

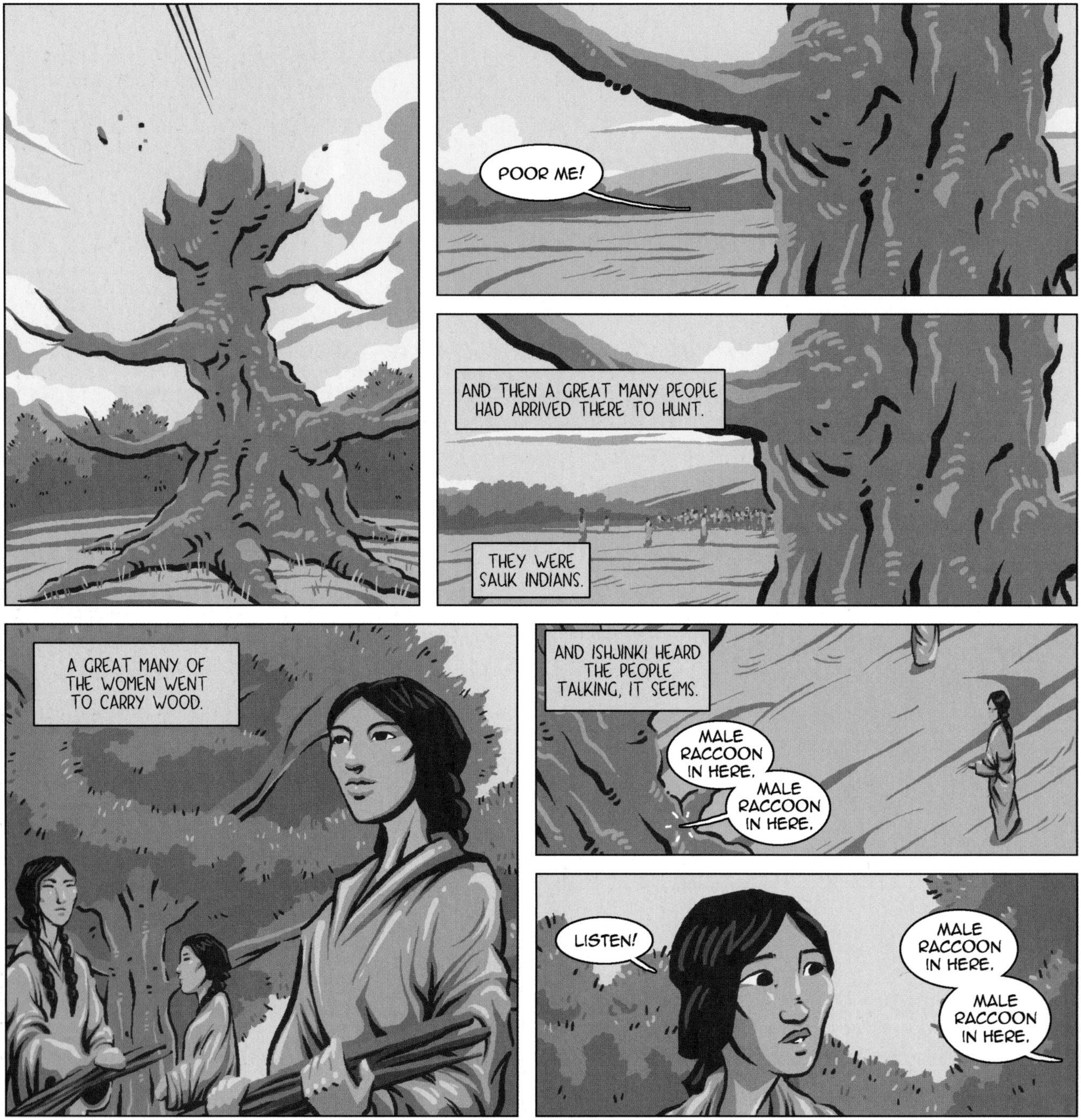

POOR ME!
AND THEN A GREAT MANY PEOPLE HAD ARRIVED THERE TO HUNT.
THEY WERE SAUK INDIANS.
A GREAT MANY OF THE WOMEN WENT TO CARRY WOOD.
AND ISHJINKI HEARD THE PEOPLE TALKING, IT SEEMS.
MALE RACCOON IN HERE.
MALE RACCOON IN HERE.
LISTEN!
MALE RACCOON IN HERE.
MALE RACCOON IN HERE.

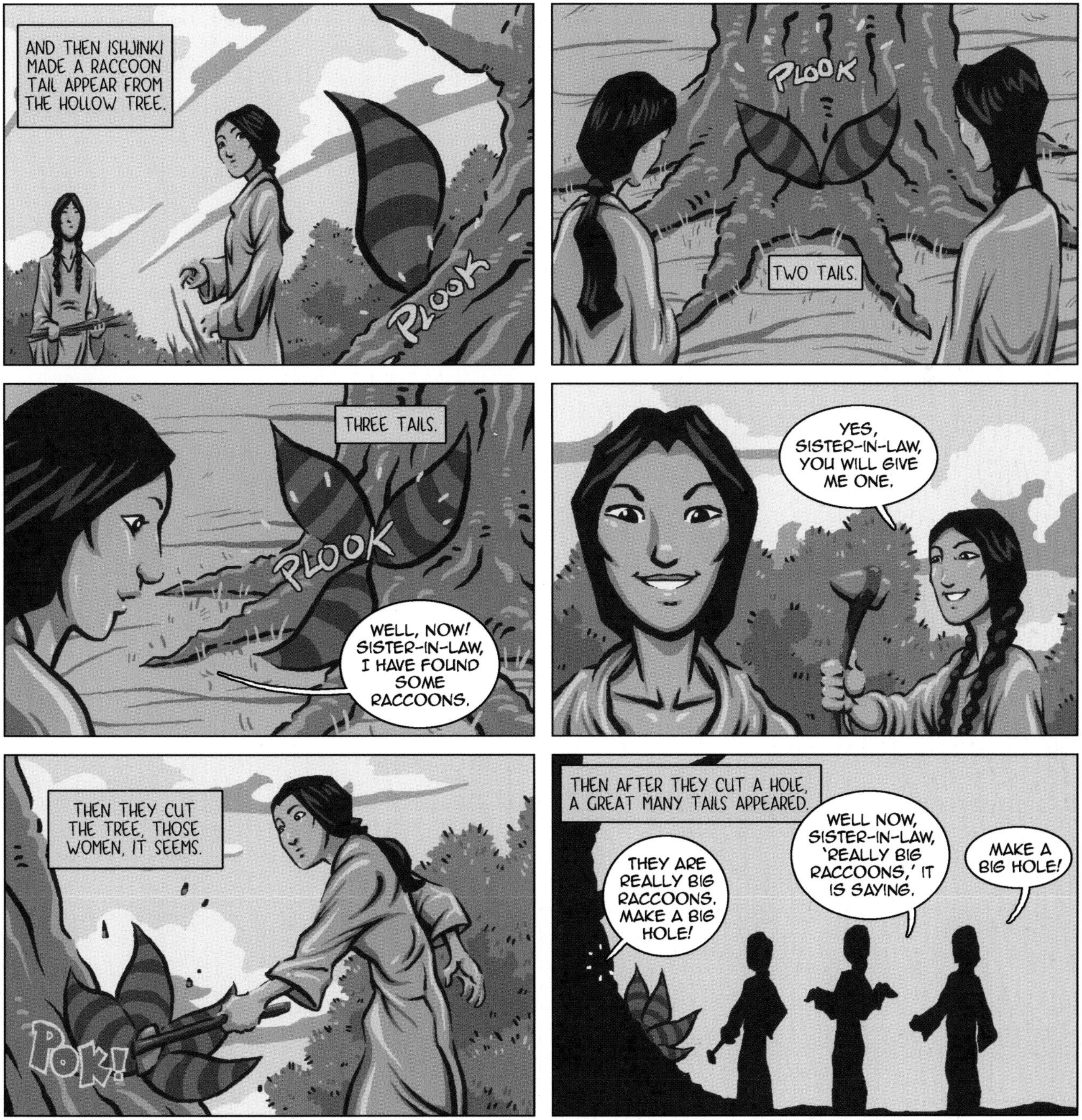
AND THEN ISHJINKI MADE A RACCOON TAIL APPEAR FROM THE HOLLOW TREE.
PLOOK
PLOOK
TWO TAILS.
THREE TAILS.
PLOOK
WELL, NOW! SISTER-IN-LAW, I HAVE FOUND SOME RACCOONS.
YES, SISTER-IN-LAW, YOU WILL GIVE ME ONE.
THEN THEY CUT THE TREE, THOSE WOMEN, IT SEEMS.
POK!
THEN AFTER THEY CUT A HOLE, A GREAT MANY TAILS APPEARED.
THEY ARE REALLY BIG RACCOONS. MAKE A BIG HOLE!
WELL NOW, SISTER-IN-LAW, 'REALLY BIG RACCOONS,' IT IS SAYING.
MAKE A BIG HOLE!

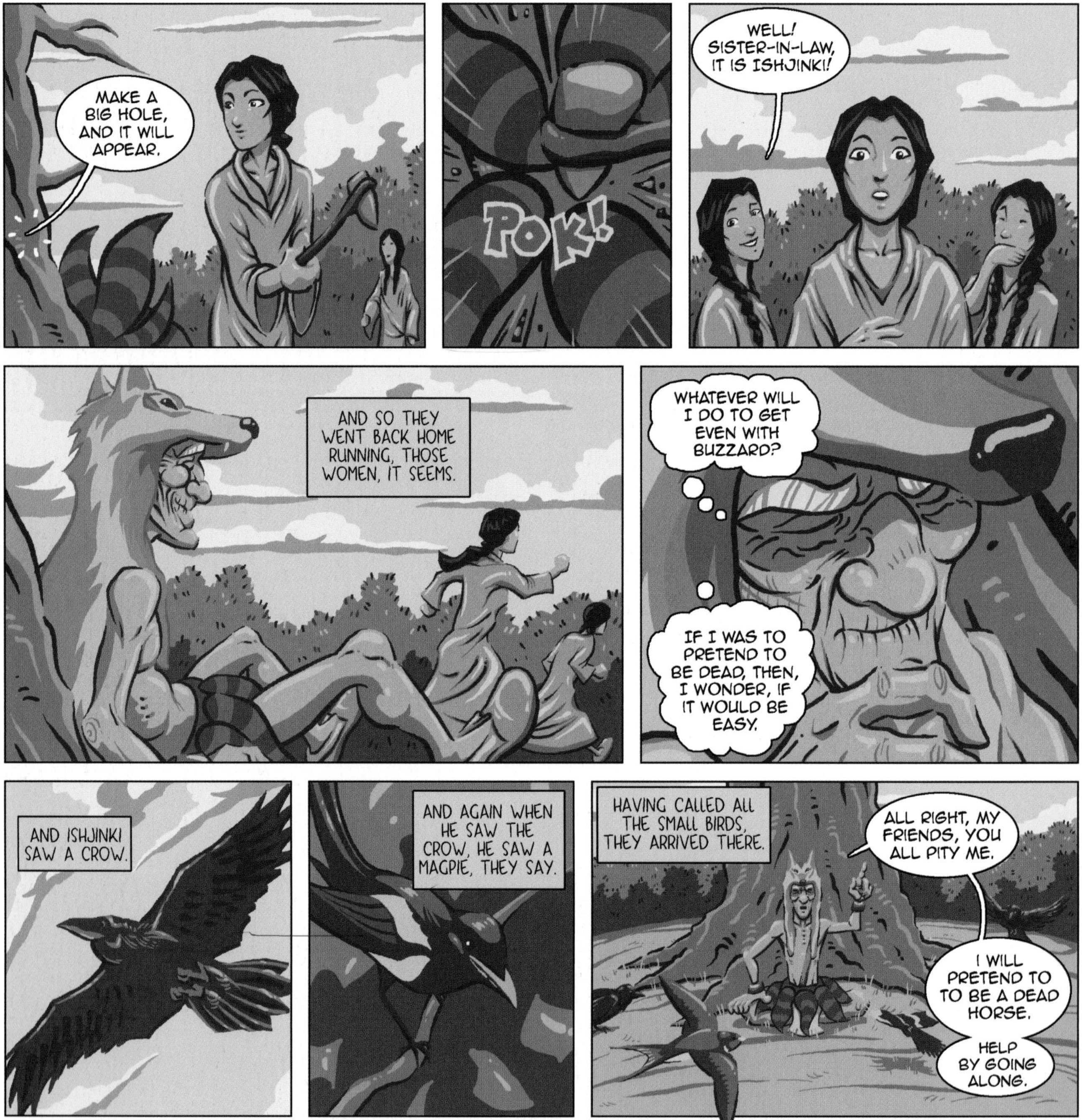
MAKE A BIG HOLE, AND IT WILL APPEAR.
POK!
WELL! SISTER-IN-LAW, IT IS ISHJINKI!
AND SO THEY WENT BACK HOME RUNNING, THOSE WOMEN, IT SEEMS.
WHATEVER WILL I DO TO GET EVEN WITH BUZZARD?
IF I WAS TO PRETEND TO BE DEAD, THEN, I WONDER, IF IT WOULD BE EASY.
AND ISHJINKI SAW A CROW.
AND AGAIN WHEN HE SAW THE CROW, HE SAW A MAGPIE, THEY SAY.
HAVING CALLED ALL THE SMALL BIRDS, THEY ARRIVED THERE.
ALL RIGHT, MY FRIENDS, YOU ALL PITY ME.
I WILL PRETEND TO TO BE A DEAD HORSE.
HELP BY GOING ALONG.

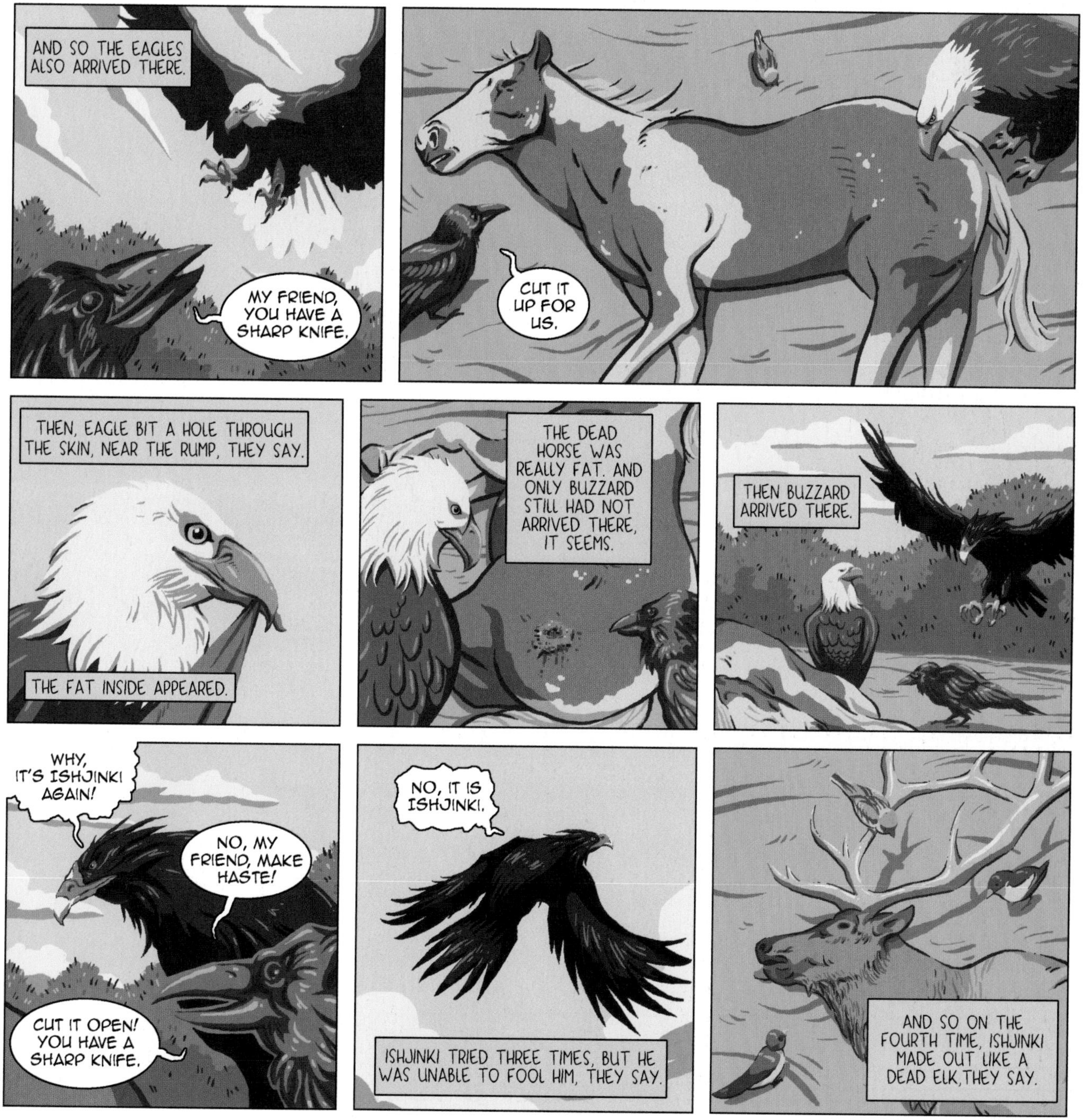
AND SO THE EAGLES ALSO ARRIVED THERE.
MY FRIEND, YOU HAVE A SHARP KNIFE.
CUT IT UP FOR US.
THEN, EAGLE BIT A HOLE THROUGH THE SKIN, NEAR THE RUMP, THEY SAY.
THE FAT INSIDE APPEARED.
THE DEAD HORSE WAS REALLY FAT. AND ONLY BUZZARD STILL HAD NOT ARRIVED THERE, IT SEEMS.
THEN BUZZARD ARRIVED THERE.
WHY, IT'S ISHJINKI AGAIN!
NO, MY FRIEND, MAKE HASTE!
CUT IT OPEN! YOU HAVE A SHARP KNIFE.
NO, IT IS ISHJINKI.
ISHJINKI TRIED THREE TIMES, BUT HE WAS UNABLE TO FOOL HIM, THEY SAY.
AND SO ON THE FOURTH TIME, ISHJINKI MADE OUT LIKE A DEAD ELK, THEY SAY.

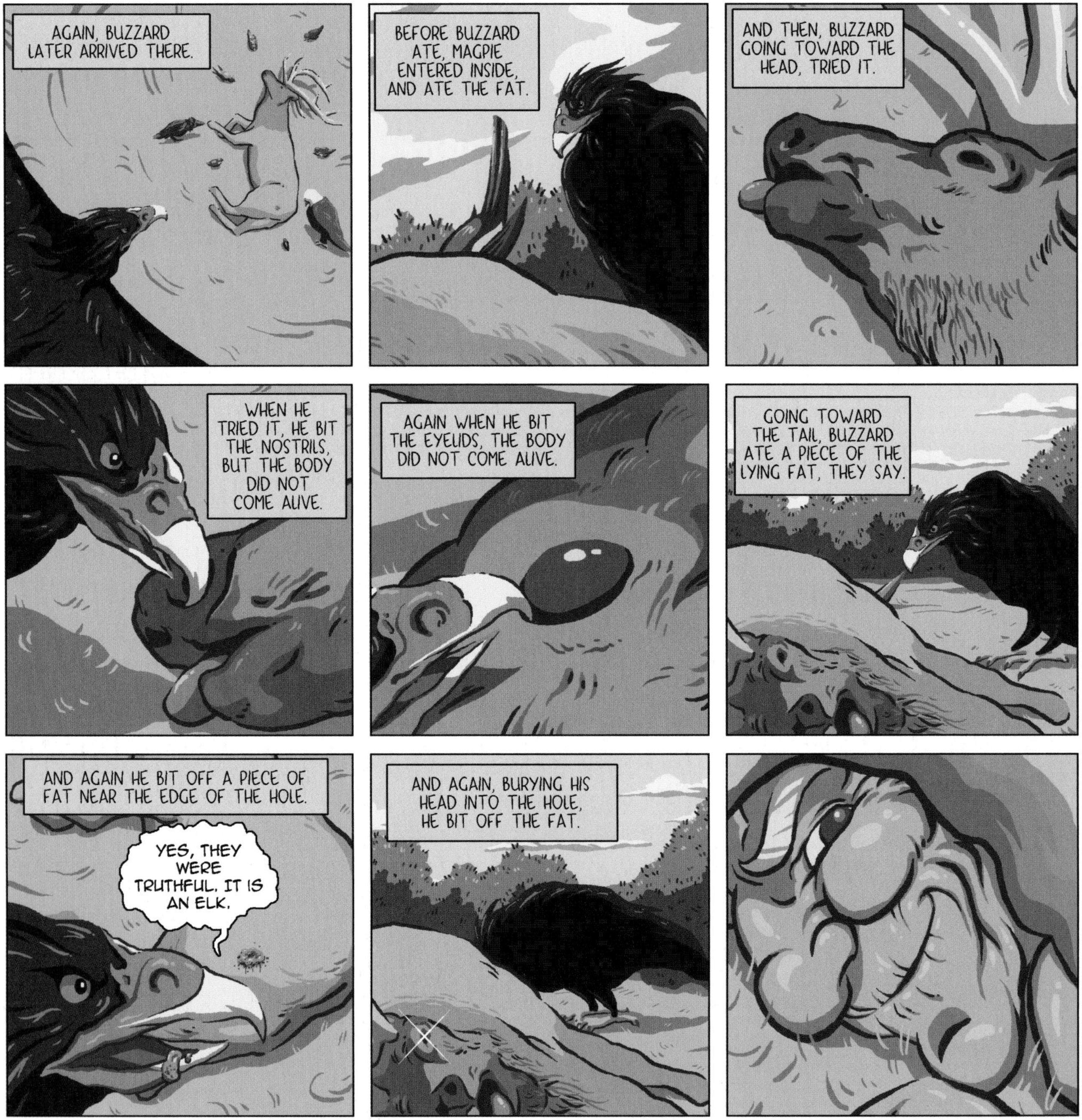
AGAIN, BUZZARD LATER ARRIVED THERE.
BEFORE BUZZARD ATE, MAGPIE ENTERED INSIDE, AND ATE THE FAT.
AND THEN, BUZZARD GOING TOWARD THE HEAD, TRIED IT.
WHEN HE TRIED IT, HE BIT THE NOSTRILS, BUT THE BODY DID NOT COME ALIVE.
AGAIN WHEN HE BIT THE EYELIDS, THE BODY DID NOT COME ALIVE.
GOING TOWARD THE TAIL, BUZZARD ATE A PIECE OF THE LYING FAT, THEY SAY.
AND AGAIN HE BIT OFF A PIECE OF FAT NEAR THE EDGE OF THE HOLE.
YES, THEY WERE TRUTHFUL. IT IS AN ELK.
AND AGAIN, BURYING HIS HEAD INTO THE HOLE, HE BIT OFF THE FAT.

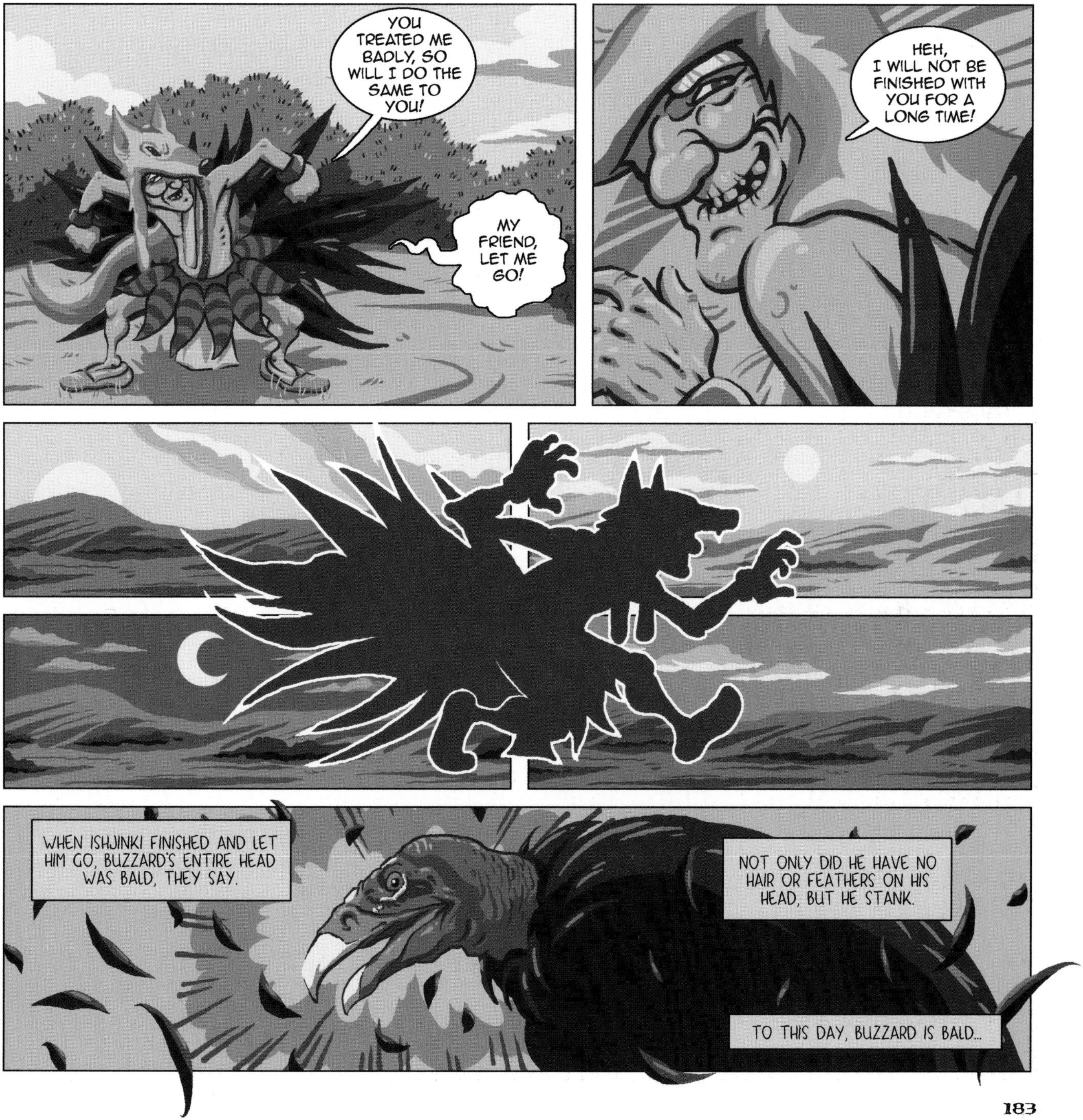
YOU TREATED ME BADLY, SO WILL I DO THE SAME TO YOU!
MY FRIEND, LET ME GO!
HEH, I WILL NOT BE FINISHED WITH YOU FOR A LONG TIME!
WHEN ISHJINKI FINISHED AND LET HIM GO, BUZZARD'S ENTIRE HEAD WAS BALD, THEY SAY.
NOT ONLY DID HE HAVE NO HAIR OR FEATHERS ON HIS HEAD, BUT HE STANK.
TO THIS DAY, BUZZARD IS BALD...

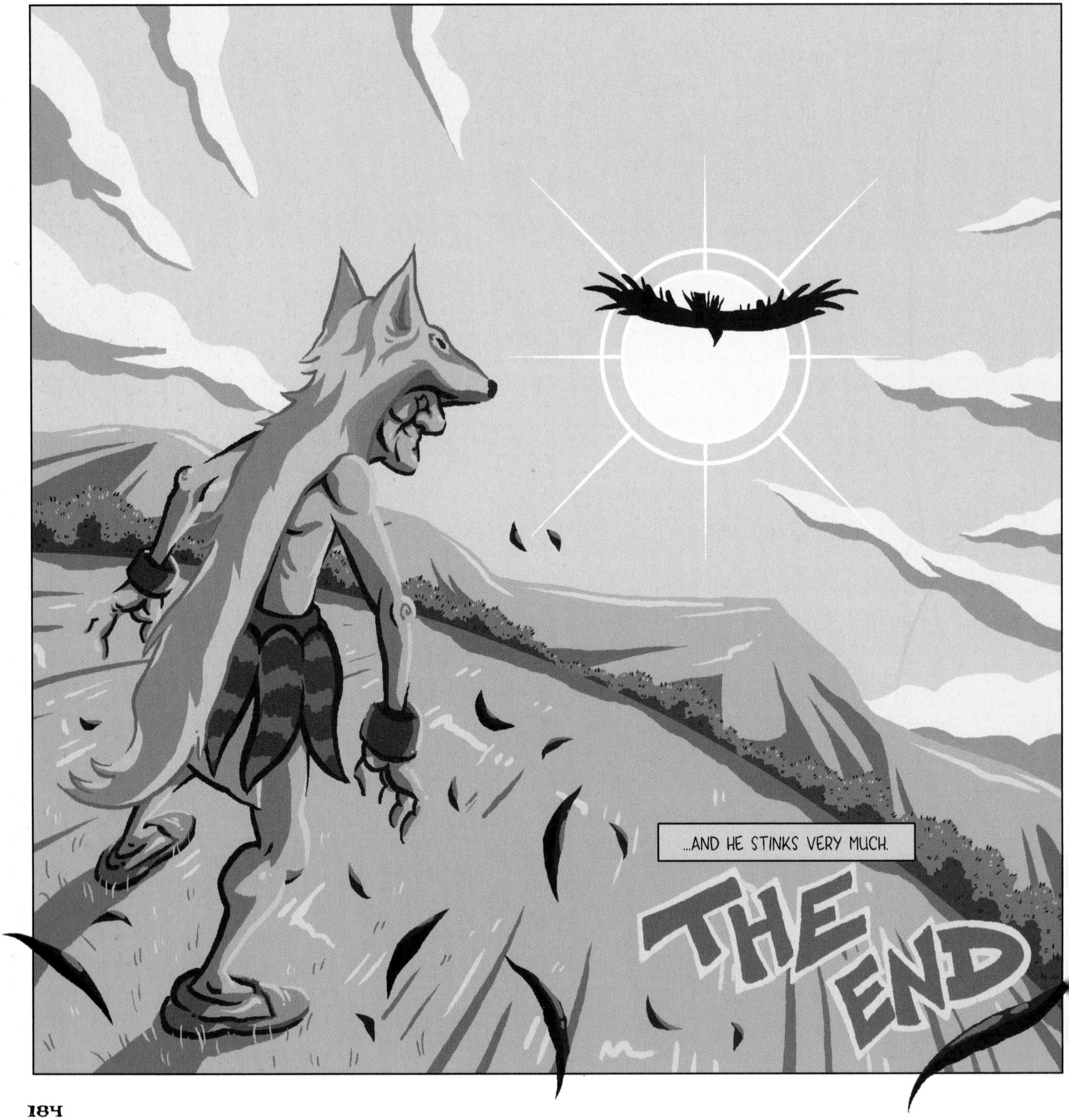
...AND HE STINKS VERY MUCH.
THE END

THE BEAR WHO STOLE THE CHINOOK

Song Lyrics by Jack Gladstone Art by Evan Keeling

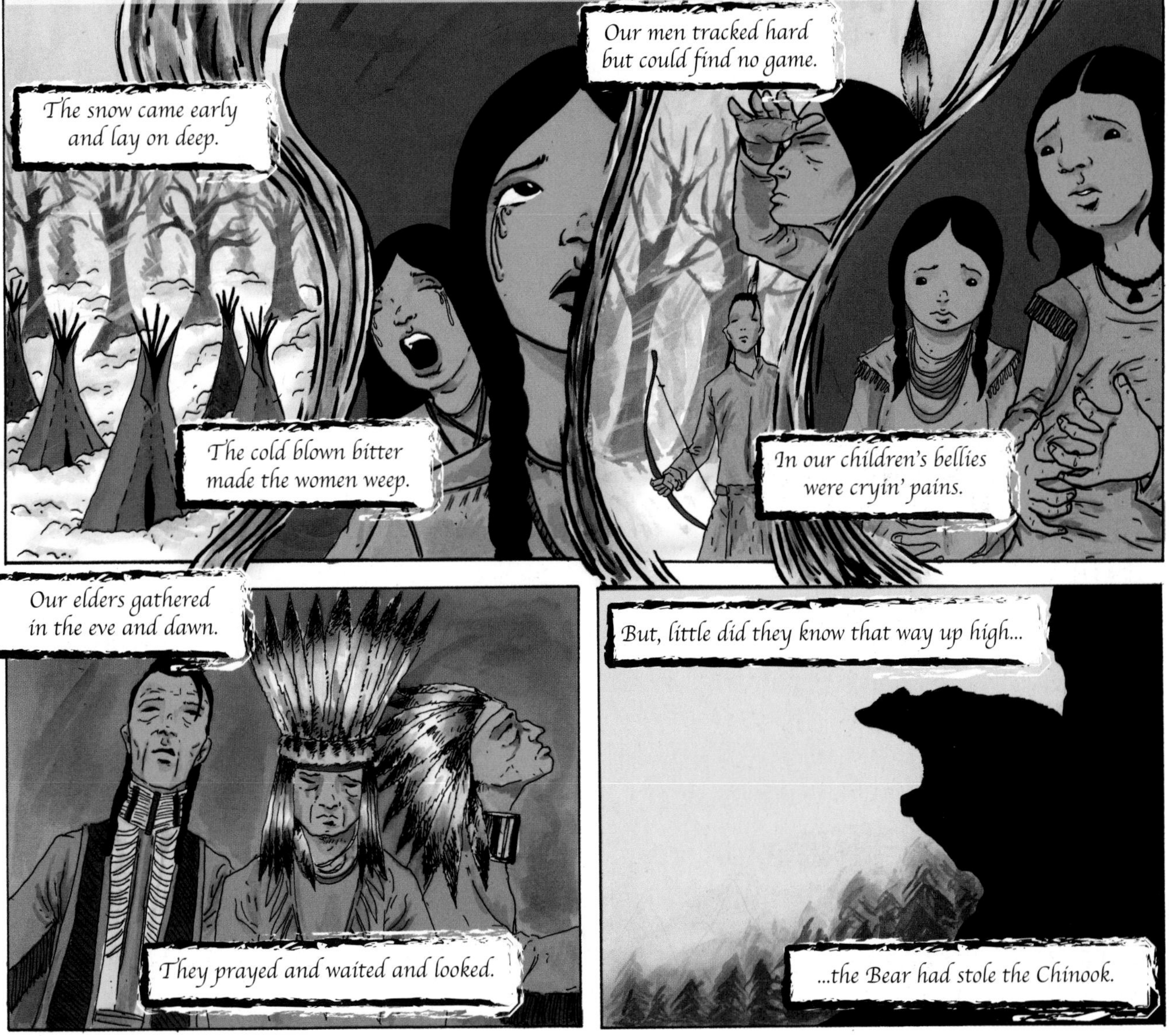

The snow came early and lay on deep.
The cold blown bitter made the women weep.
Our men tracked hard but could find no game.
In our children's bellies were cryin' pains.
Our elders gathered in the eve and dawn.
They prayed and waited and looked.
But, little did they know that way up high...
...the Bear had stole the Chinook.

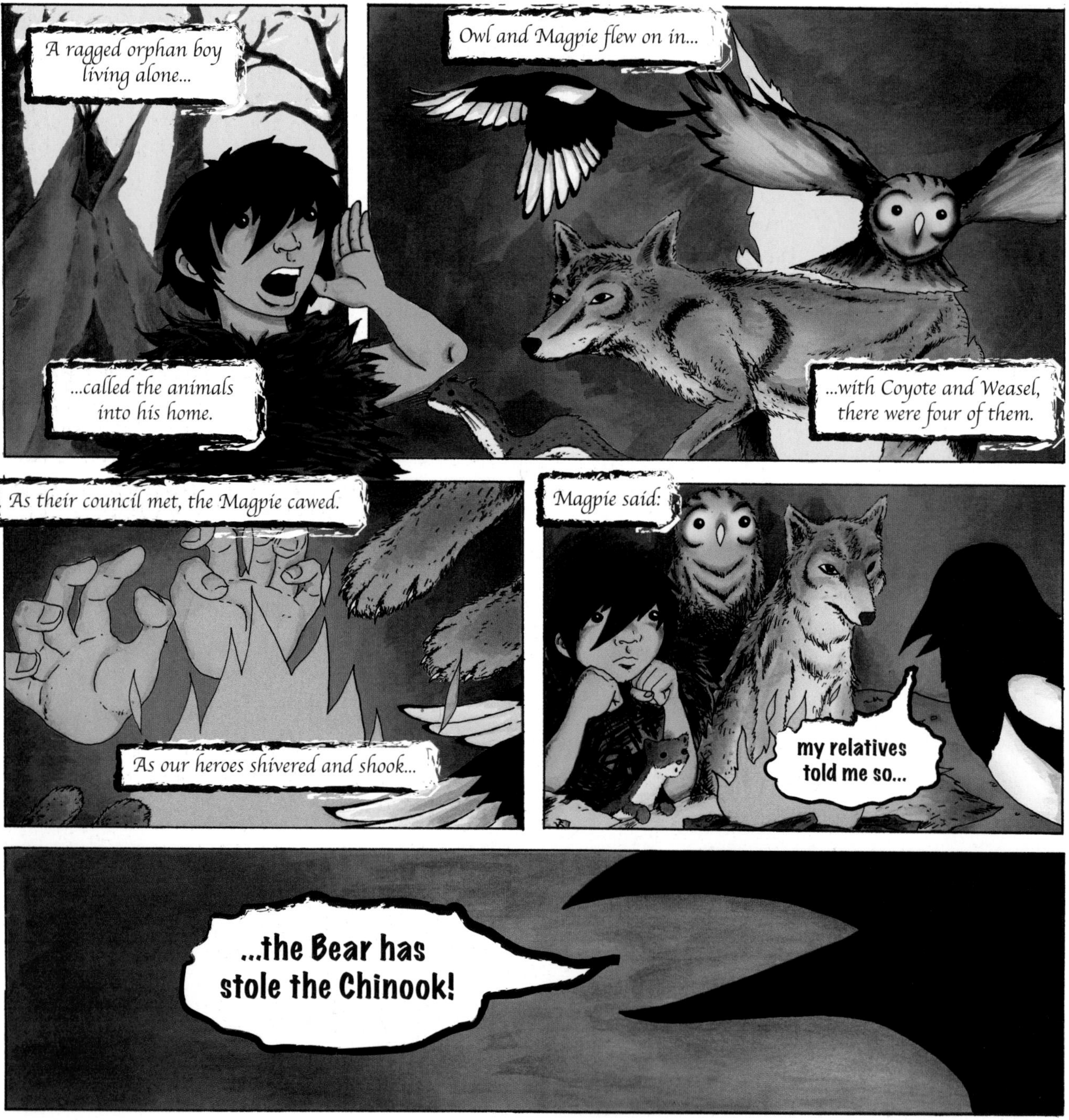
A ragged orphan boy living alone...
...called the animals into his home.
Owl and Magpie flew on in...
...with Coyote and Weasel, there were four of them.
As their council met, the Magpie cawed.
As our heroes shivered and shook...
Magpie said:
my relatives told me so...
...the Bear has stole the Chinook!

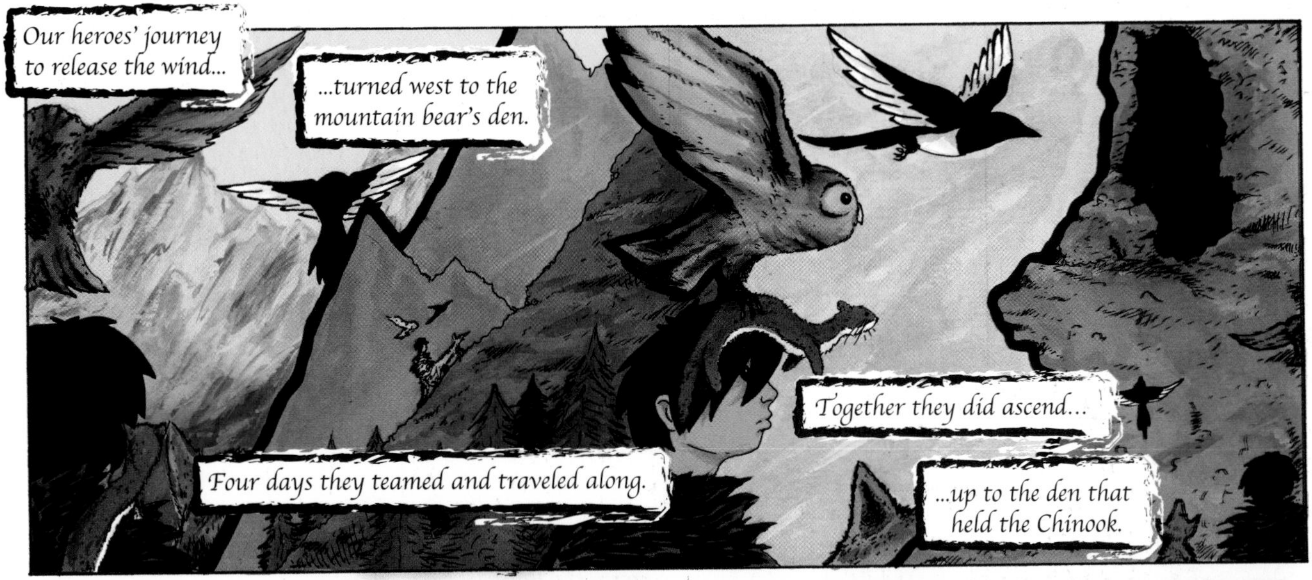

Our heroes' journey to release the wind...
...turned west to the mountain bear's den.
Four days they teamed and traveled along.
Together they did ascend...
...up to the den that held the Chinook.

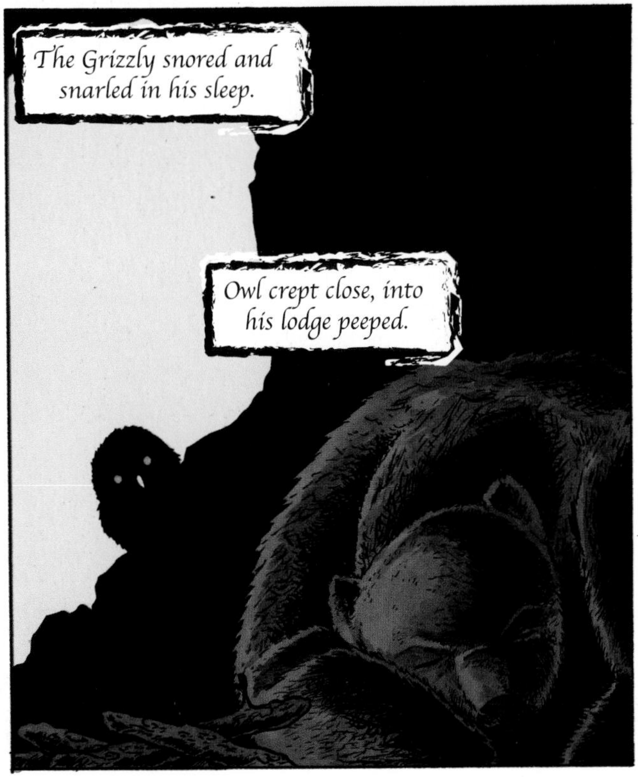

The Grizzly snored and snarled in his sleep.
Owl crept close, into his lodge peeped.

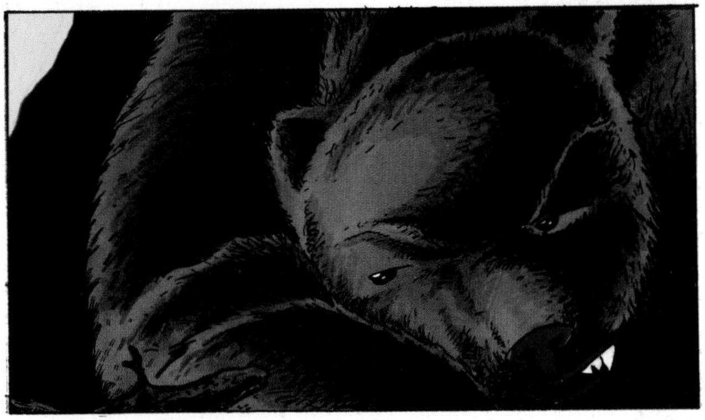

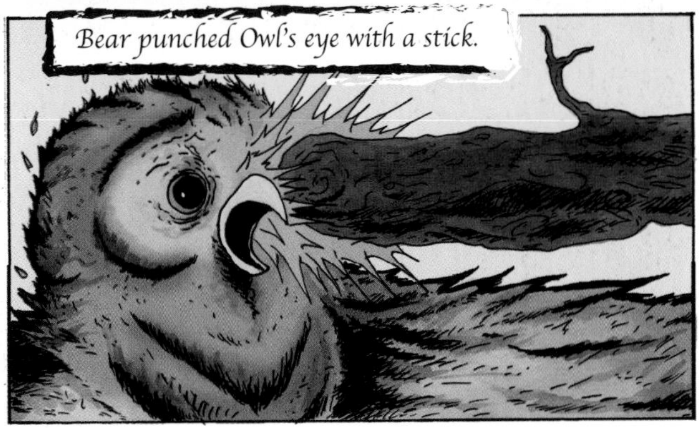

Bear punched Owl's eye with a stick.

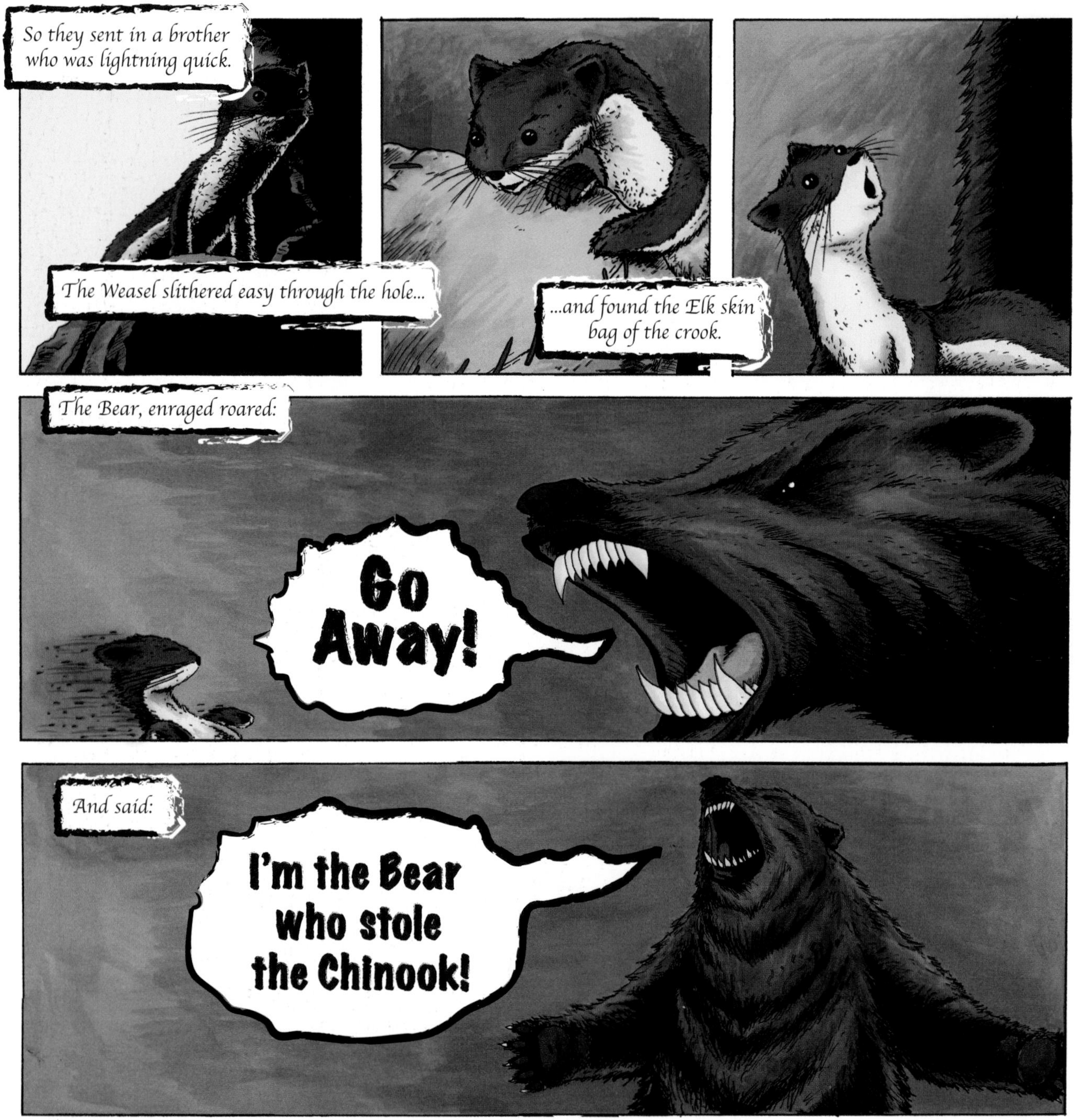
So they sent in a brother who was lightning quick.
The Weasel slithered easy through the hole...
...and found the Elk skin bag of the crook.
The Bear, enraged roared:
Go Away!
And said:
I'm the Bear who stole the Chinook!

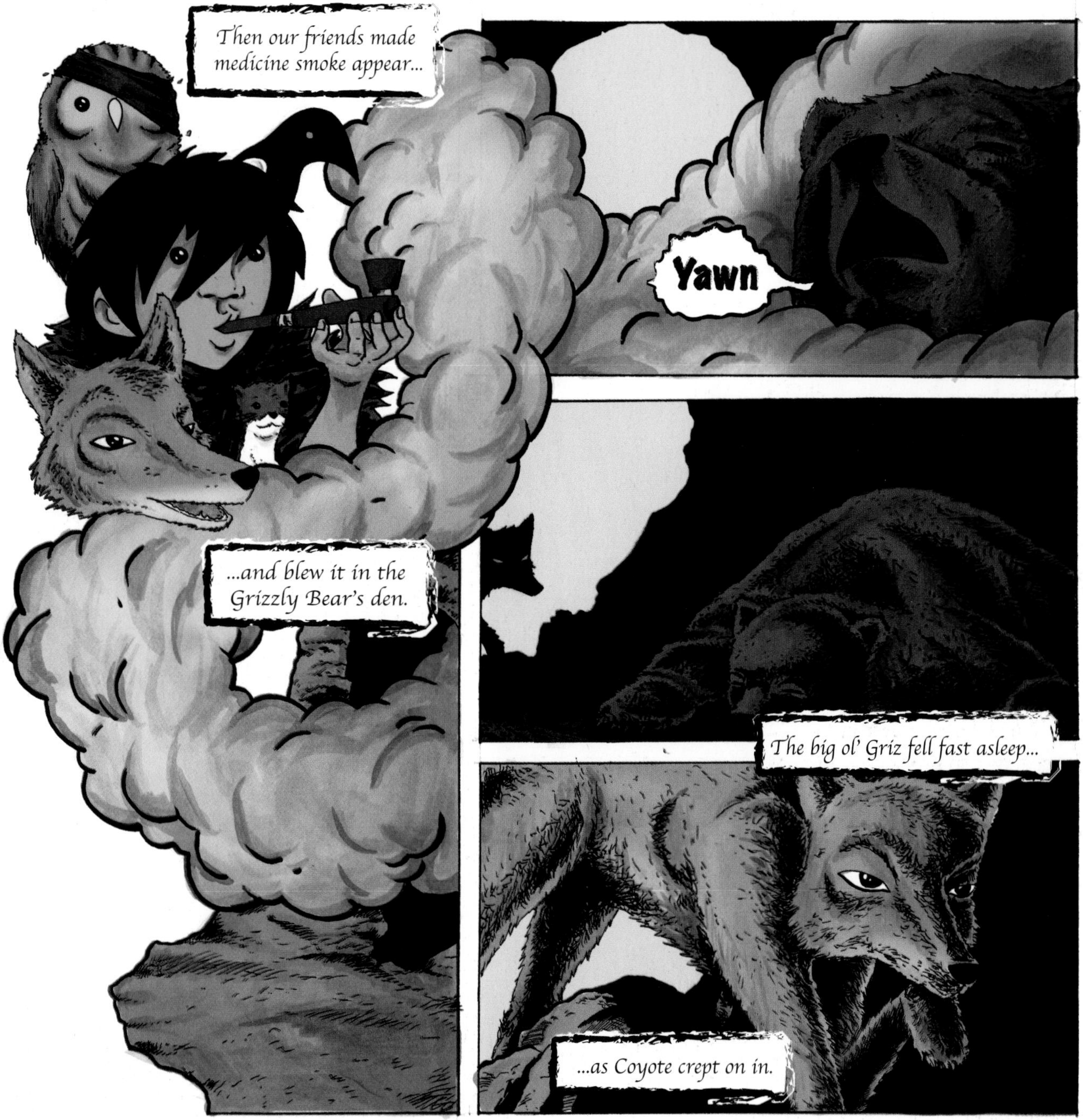
Then our friends made medicine smoke appear...
Yawn
...and blew it in the Grizzly Bear's den.
The big ol' Griz fell fast asleep...
...as Coyote crept on in.

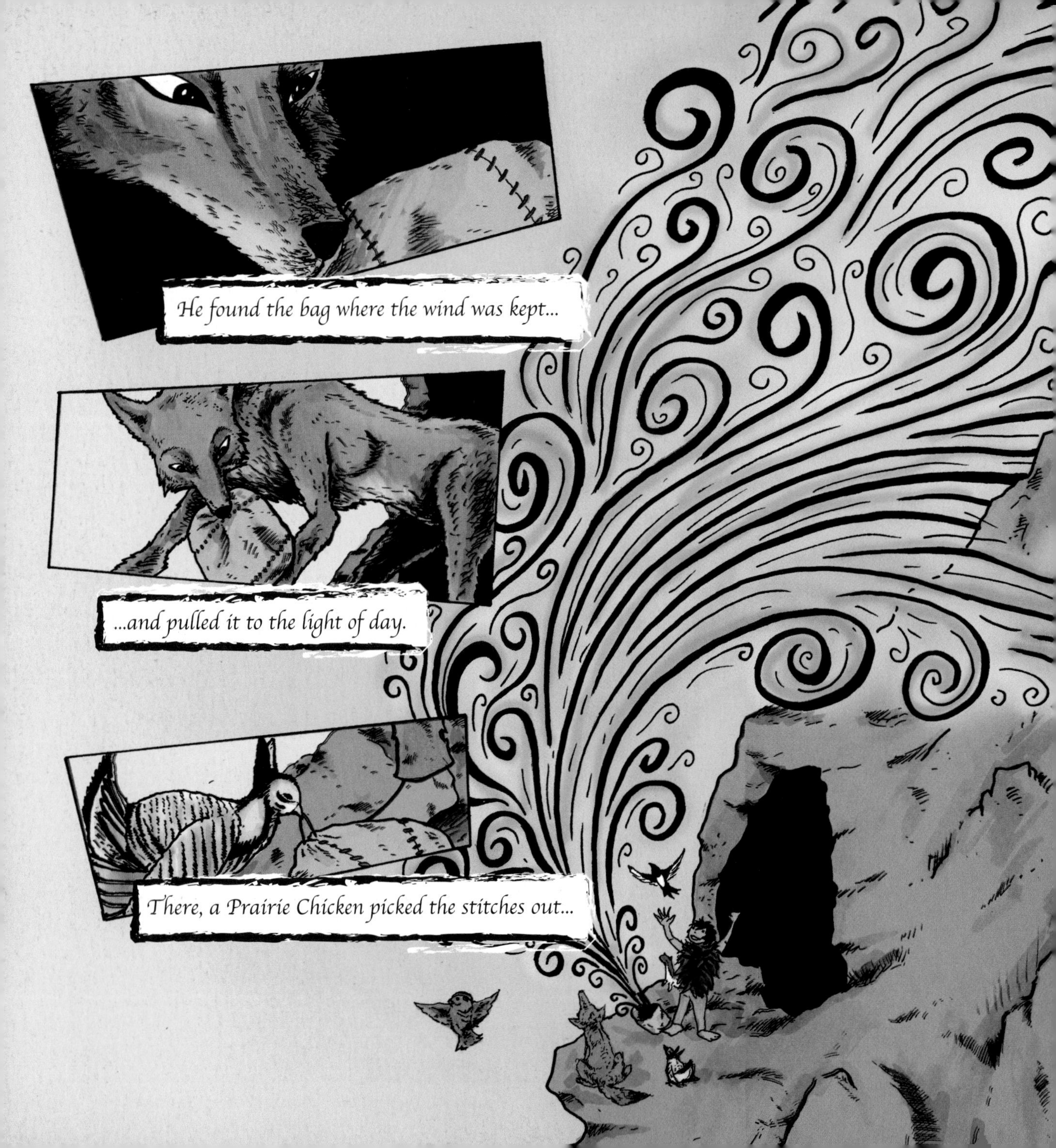
He found the bag where the wind was kept...
...and pulled it to the light of day.
There, a Prairie Chicken picked the stitches out...

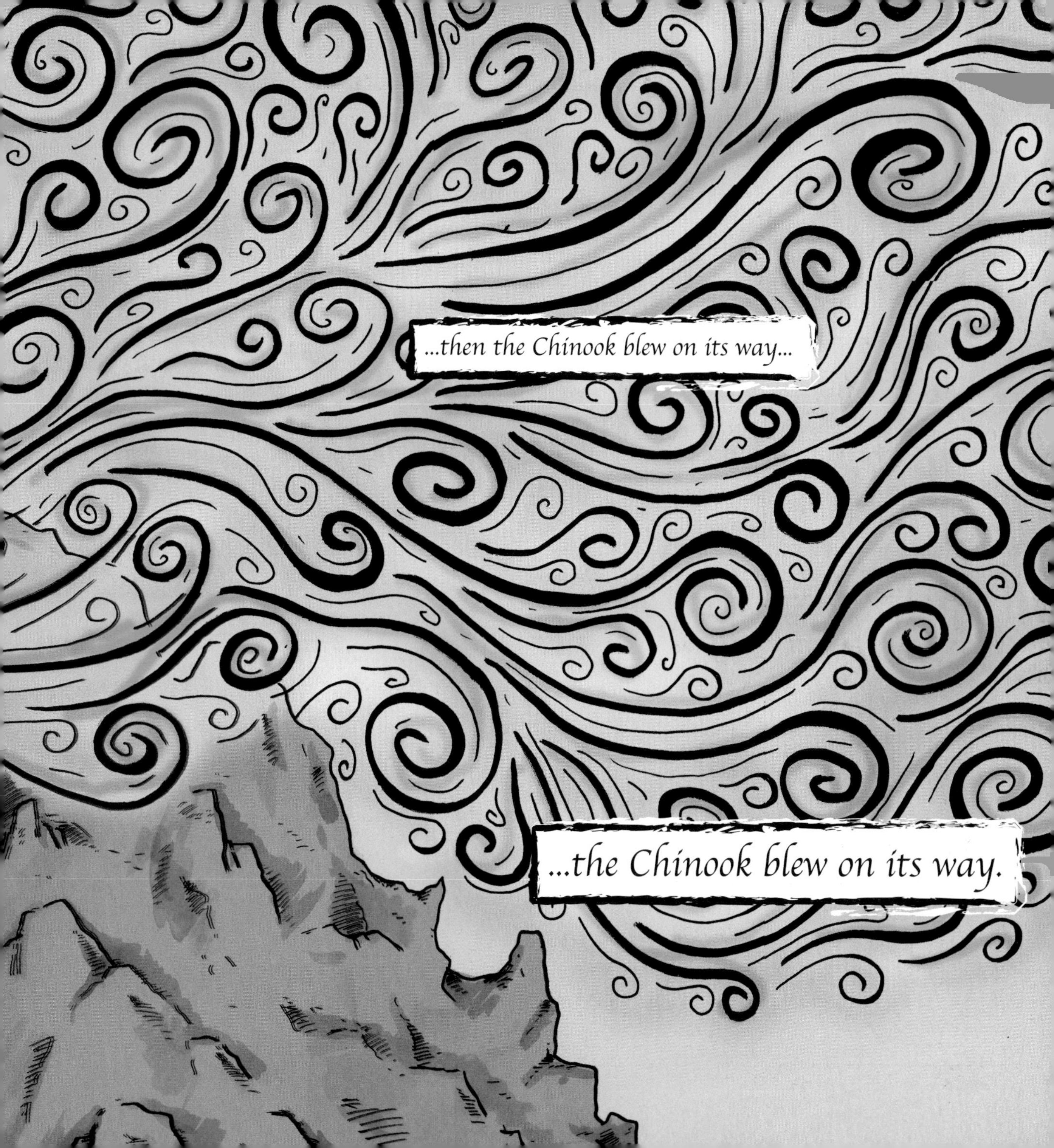
...then the Chinook blew on its way...
...the Chinook blew on its way.

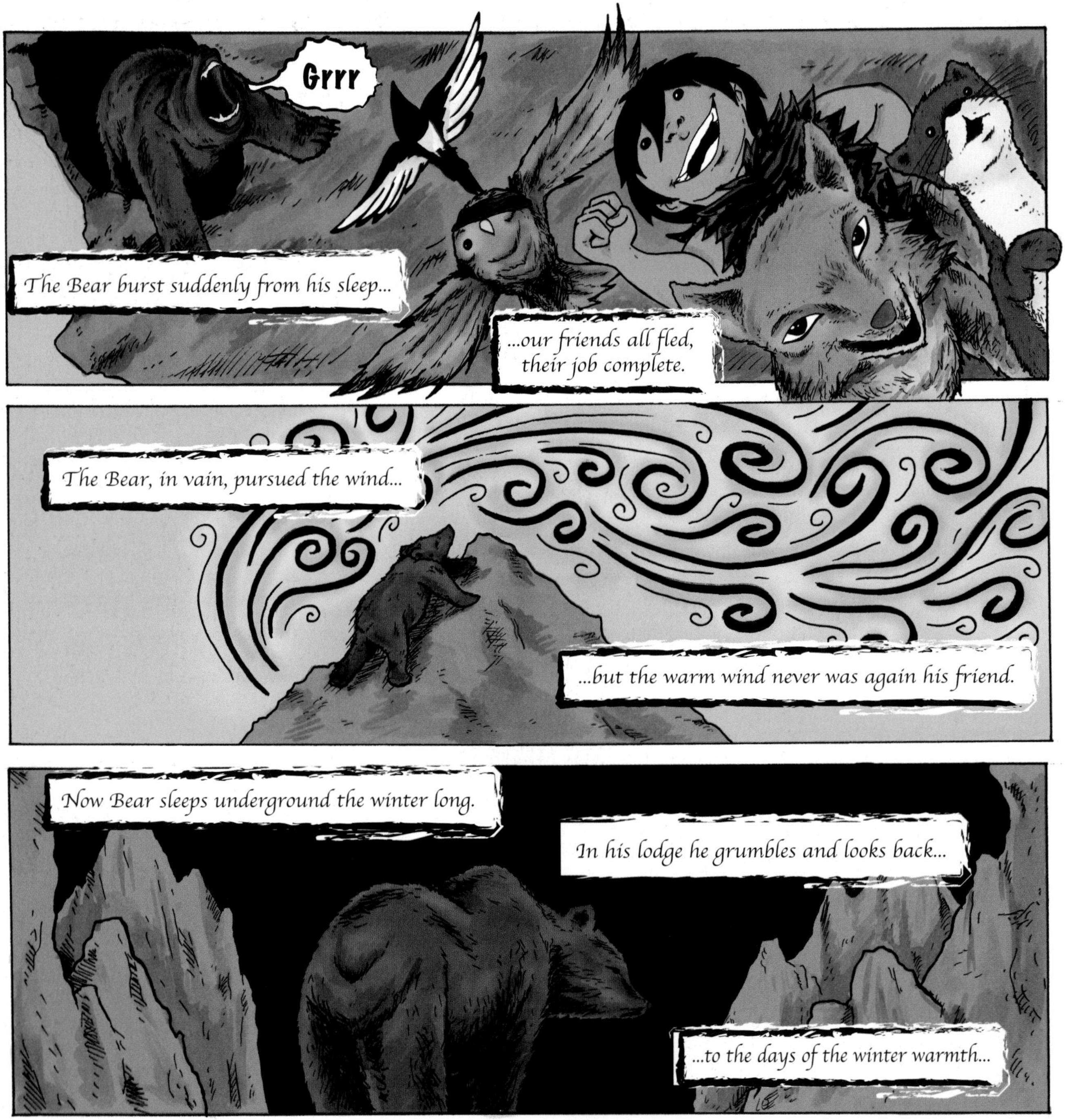
Grrr
The Bear burst suddenly from his sleep...
...our friends all fled, their job complete.
The Bear, in vain, pursued the wind...
...but the warm wind never was again his friend.
Now Bear sleeps underground the winter long.
In his lodge he grumbles and looks back...
...to the days of the winter warmth...

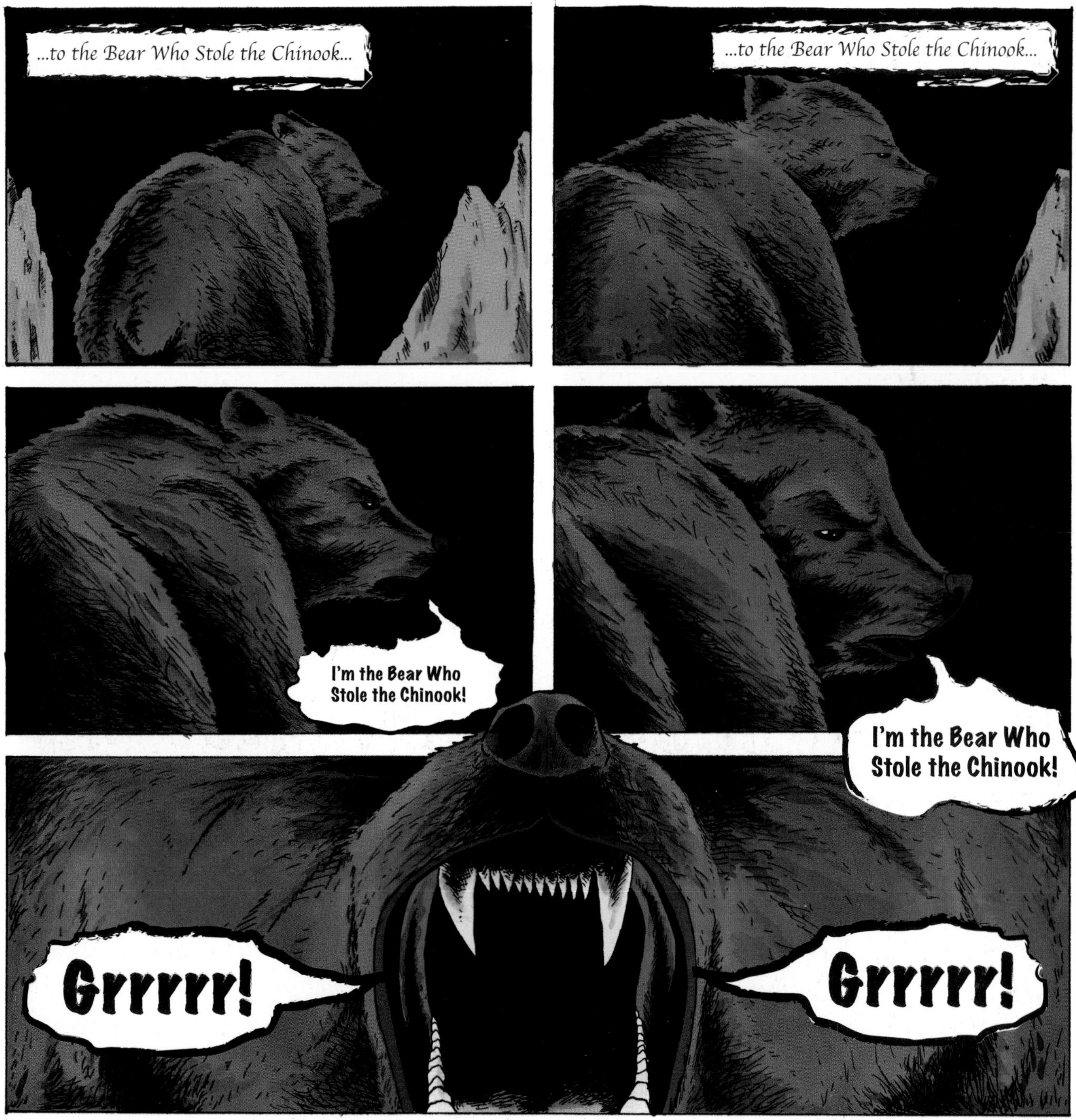

...to the Bear Who Stole the Chinook...
...to the Bear Who Stole the Chinook...
I'm the Bear Who Stole the Chinook!
I'm the Bear Who Stole the Chinook!
Grrrrr!
Grrrrr!

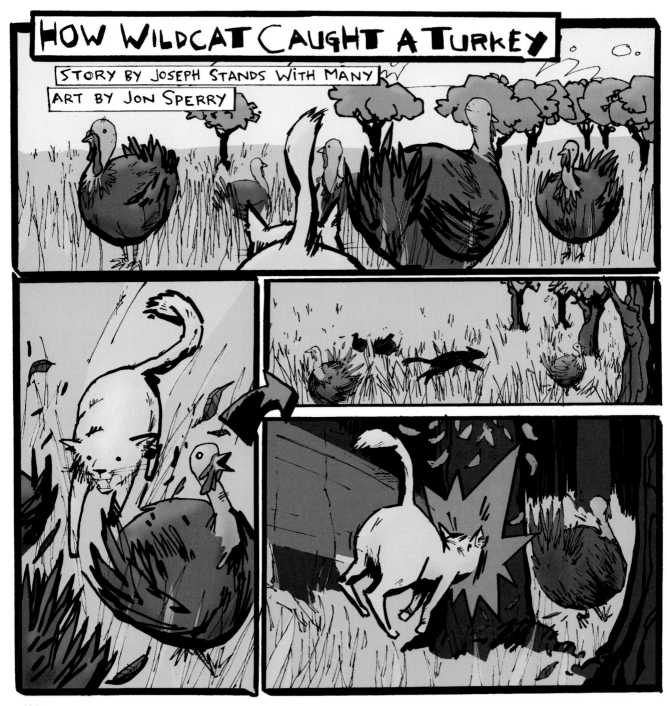

HOW WILDCAT CAUGHT A TURKEY

STORY BY JOSEPH STANDS WITH MANY

ART BY JON SPERRY

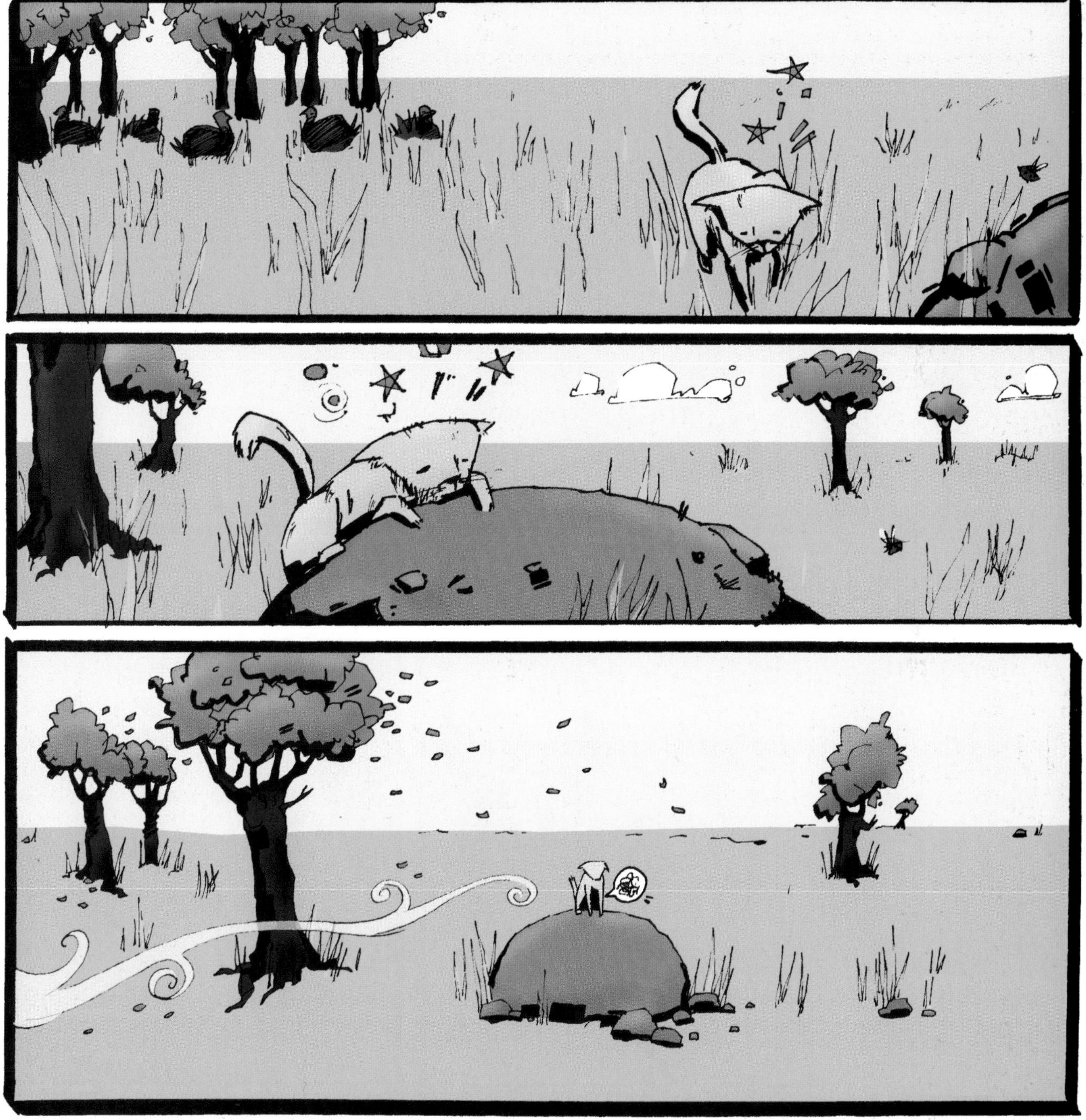

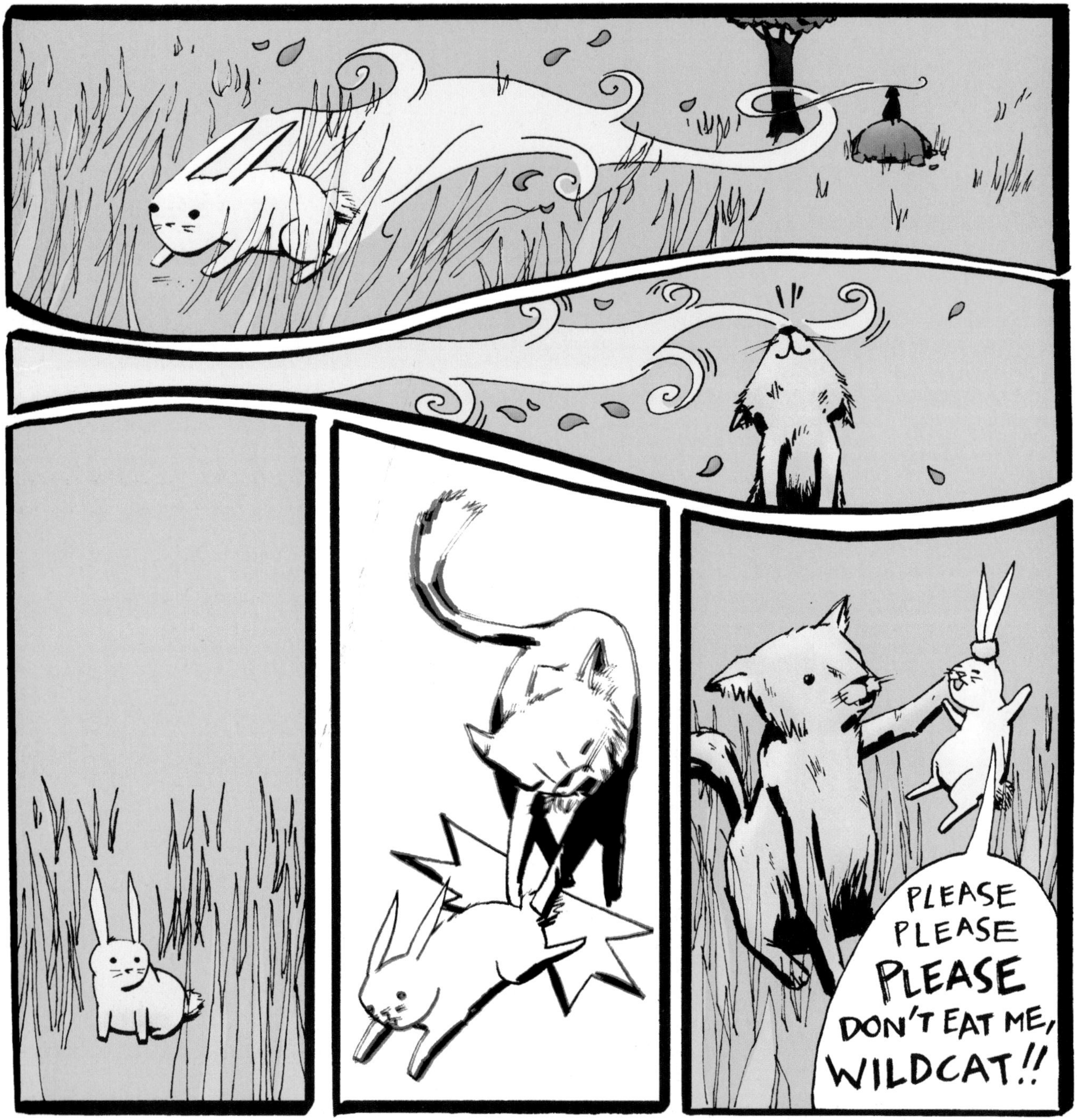
PLEASE
PLEASE
PLEASE
DON'T EAT ME,
WILDCAT!!

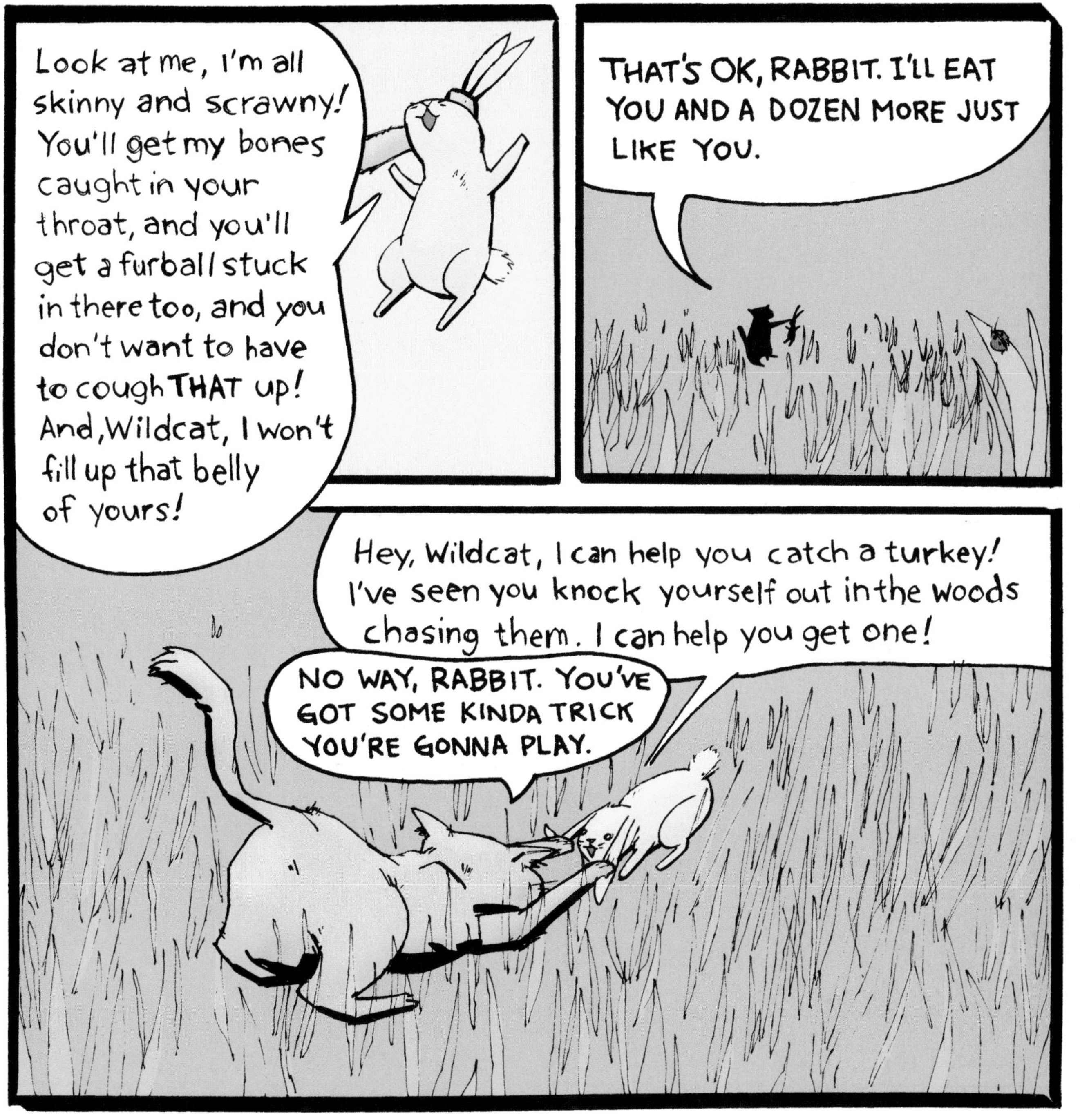
Look at me, I'm all skinny and scrawny! You'll get my bones caught in your throat, and you'll get a furball stuck in there too, and you don't want to have to cough THAT up! And, Wildcat, I won't fill up that belly of yours!
THAT'S OK, RABBIT. I'LL EAT YOU AND A DOZEN MORE JUST LIKE YOU.
Hey, Wildcat, I can help you catch a turkey! I've seen you knock yourself out in the woods chasing them. I can help you get one!
NO WAY, RABBIT. YOU'VE GOT SOME KINDA TRICK YOU'RE GONNA PLAY.

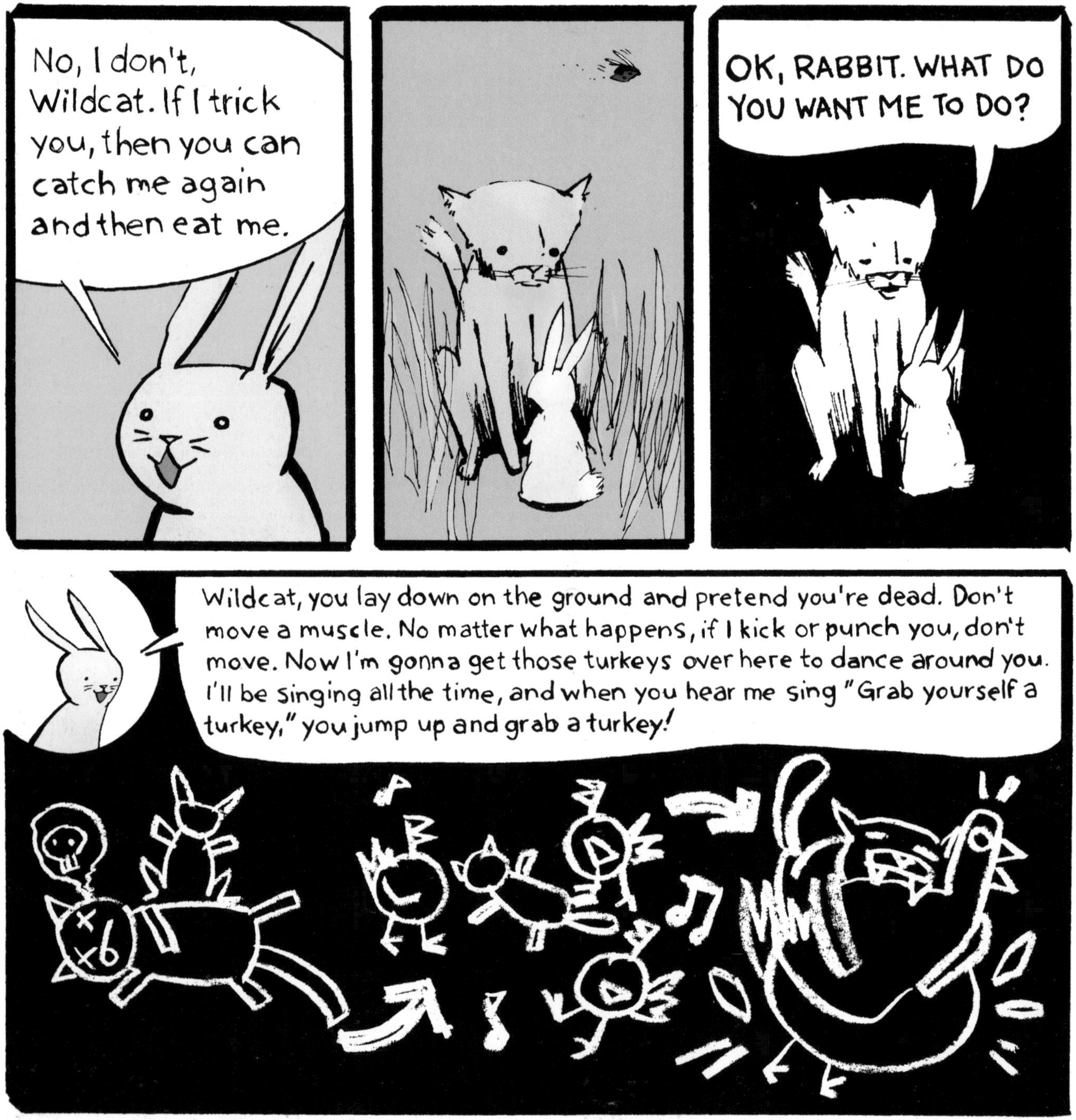
No, I don't, Wildcat. If I trick you, then you can catch me again and then eat me.
OK, RABBIT. WHAT DO YOU WANT ME TO DO?
Wildcat, you lay down on the ground and pretend you're dead. Don't move a muscle. No matter what happens, if I kick or punch you, don't move. Now I'm gonna get those turkeys over here to dance around you. I'll be singing all the time, and when you hear me sing "Grab yourself a turkey," you jump up and grab a turkey!

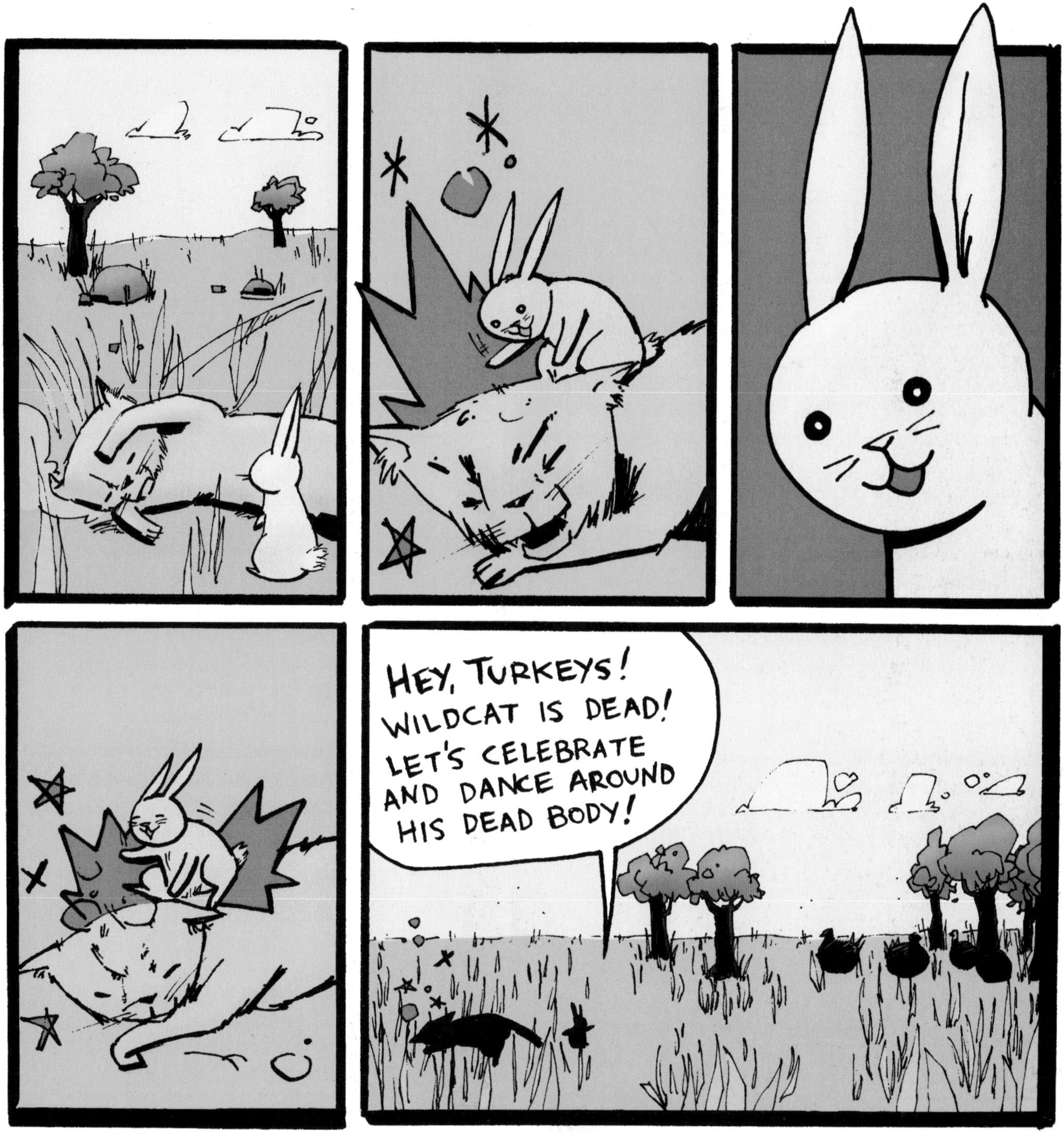
HEY, TURKEYS! WILDCAT IS DEAD! LET'S CELEBRATE AND DANCE AROUND HIS DEAD BODY!

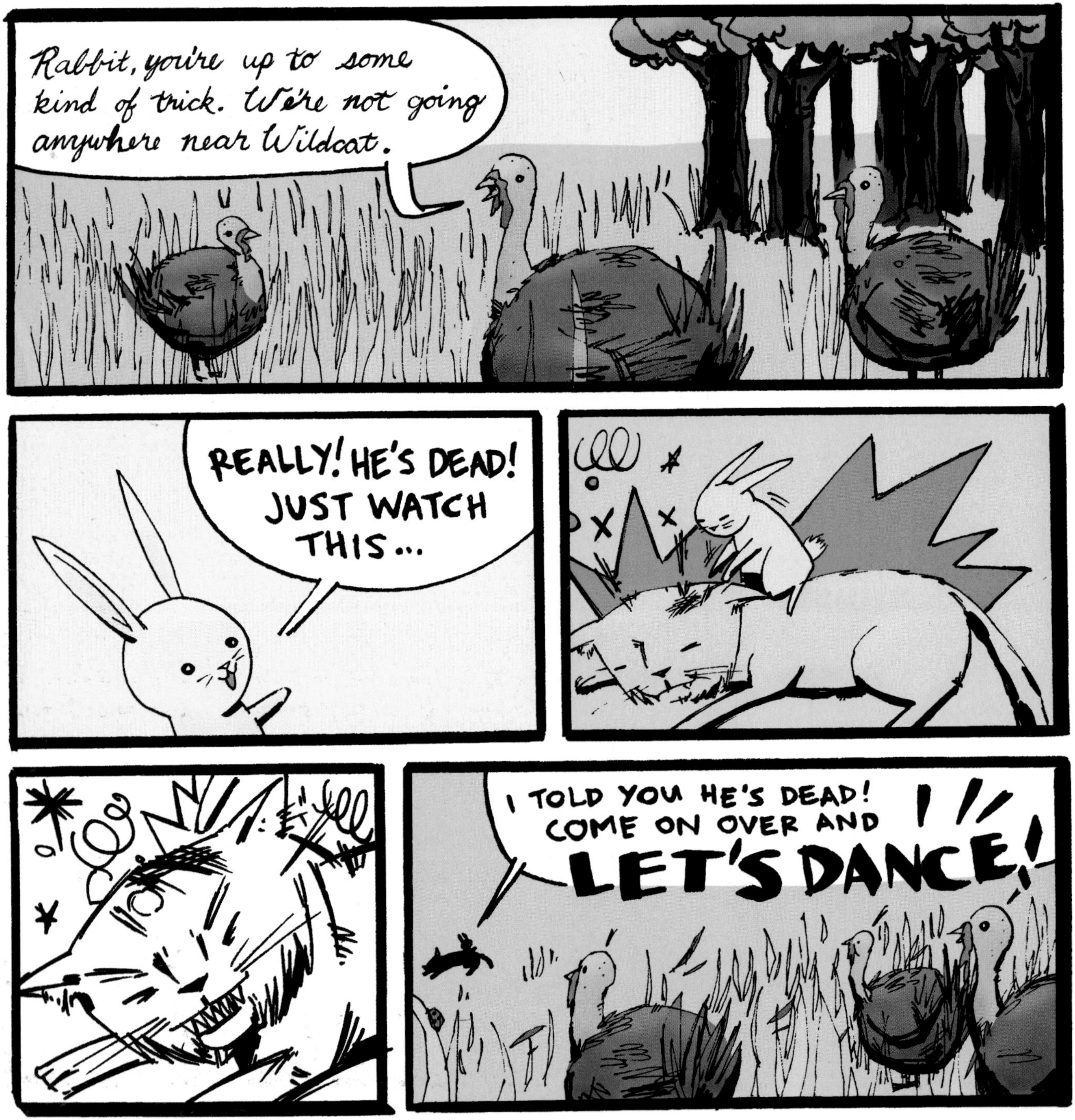
Rabbit, you're up to some kind of trick. We're not going anywhere near Wildcat.
REALLY! HE'S DEAD! JUST WATCH THIS...
I TOLD YOU HE'S DEAD! COME ON OVER AND LET'S DANCE!

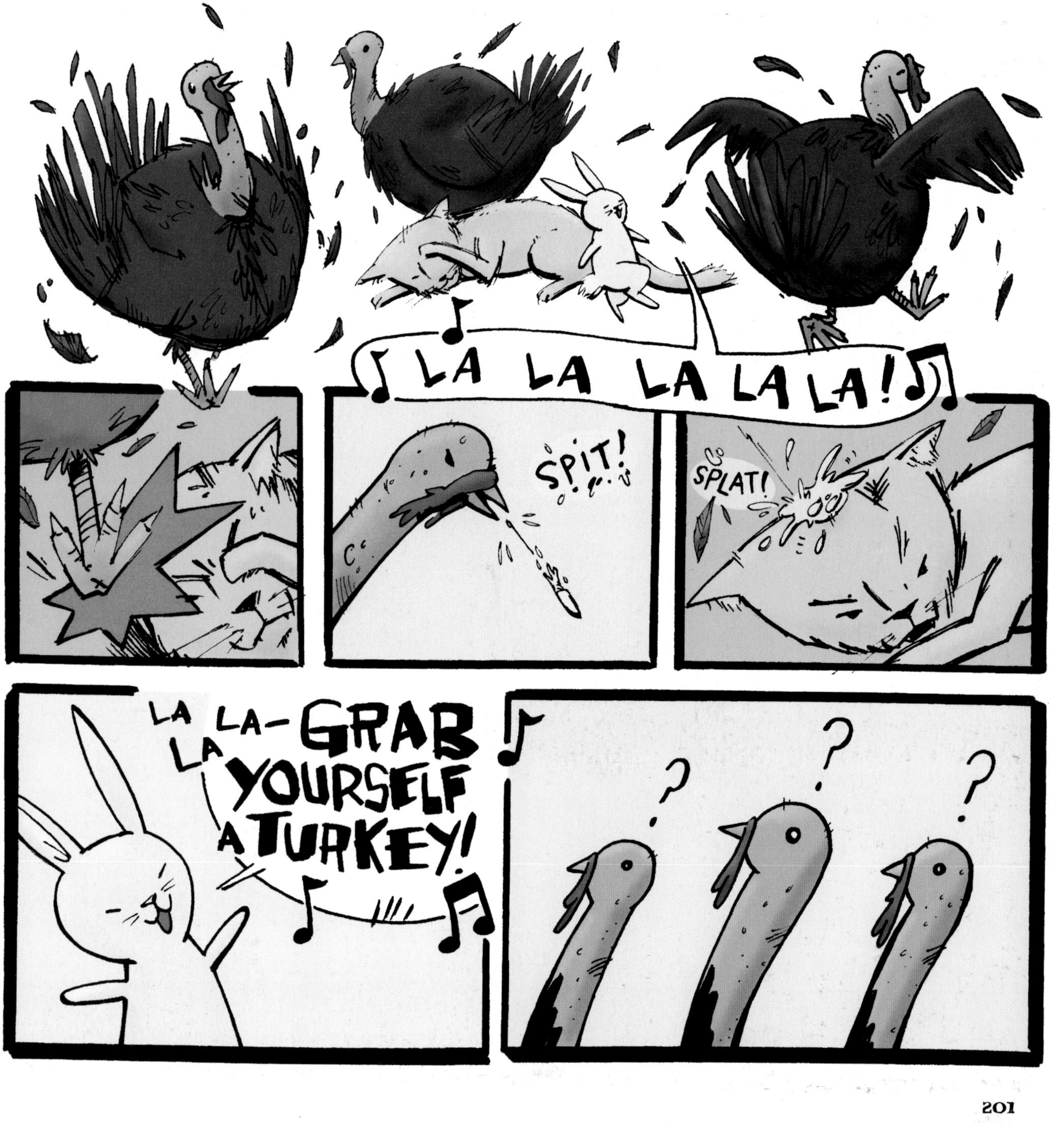
LA LA LA LA LA!
SPIT!
SPLAT!
LA LA LA-GRAB YOURSELF A TURKEY!
?
?
?

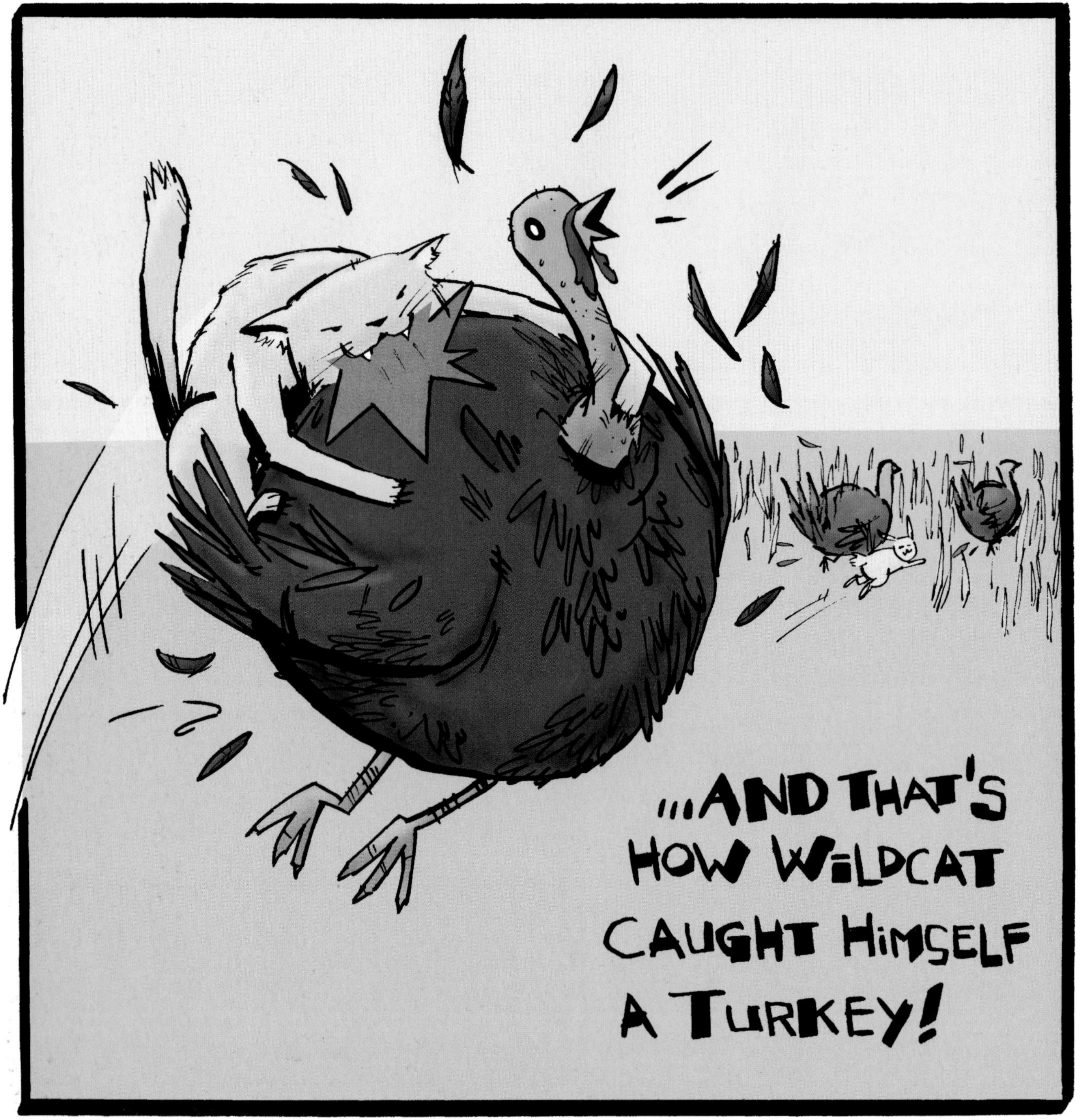
...AND THAT'S HOW WILDCAT CAUGHT HIMSELF A TURKEY!

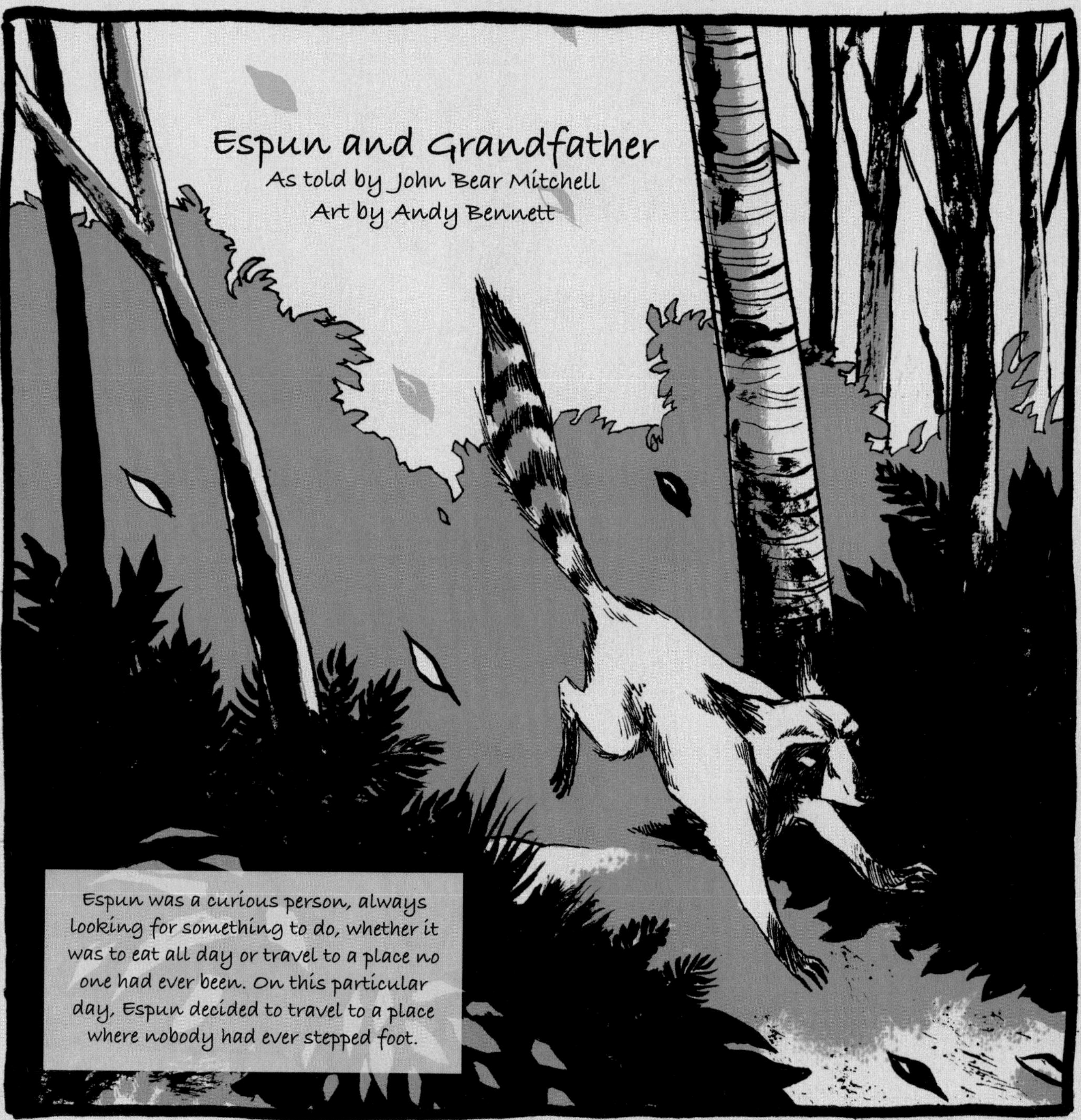
Espun and Grandfather
As told by John Bear Mitchell
Art by Andy Bennett
Espun was a curious person, always looking for something to do, whether it was to eat all day or travel to a place no one had ever been. On this particular day, Espun decided to travel to a place where nobody had ever stepped foot.

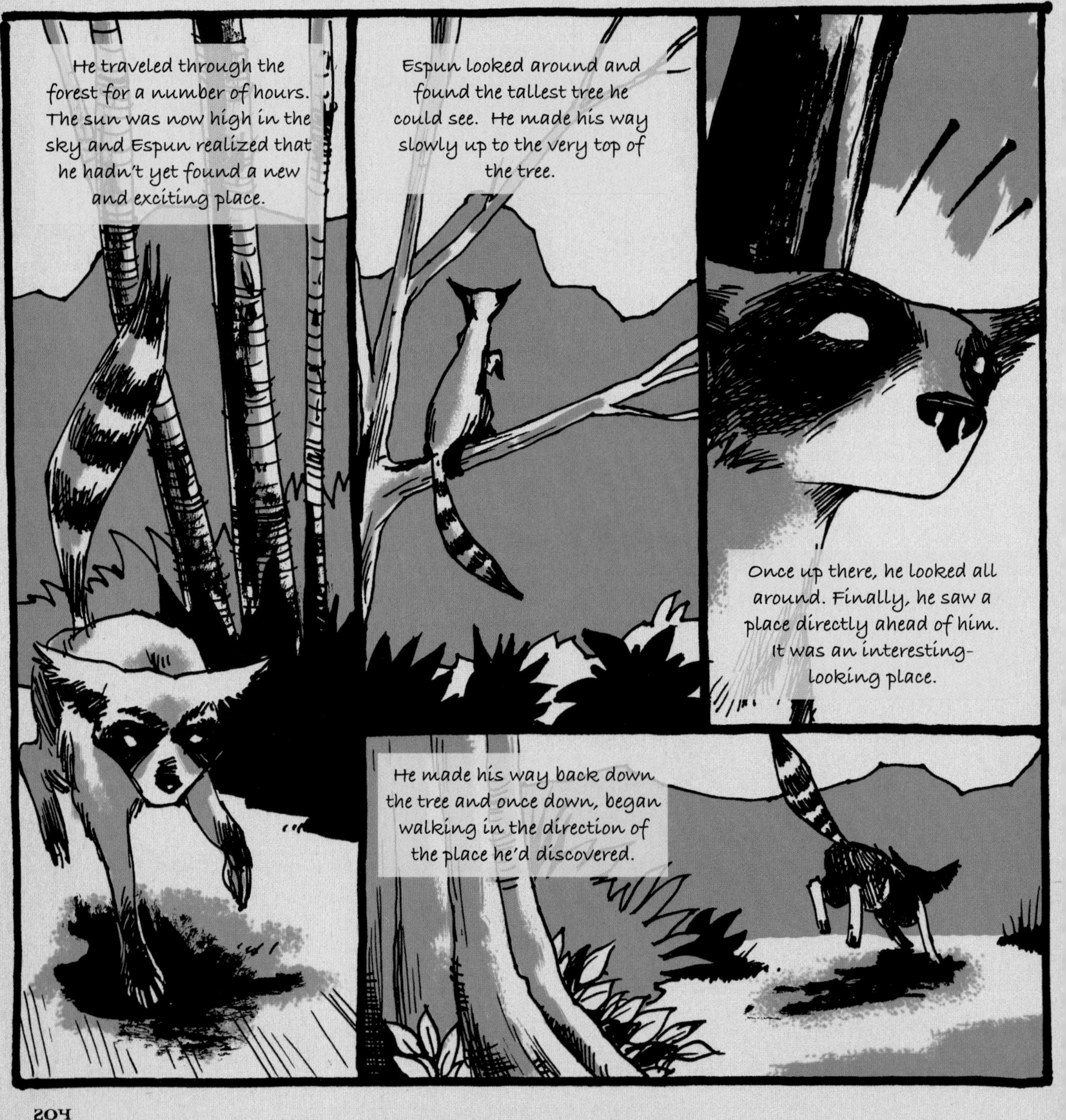
He traveled through the forest for a number of hours. The sun was now high in the sky and Espun realized that he hadn't yet found a new and exciting place.
Espun looked around and found the tallest tree he could see. He made his way slowly up to the very top of the tree.
Once up there, he looked all around. Finally, he saw a place directly ahead of him. It was an interesting-looking place.
He made his way back down the tree and once down, began walking in the direction of the place he'd discovered.

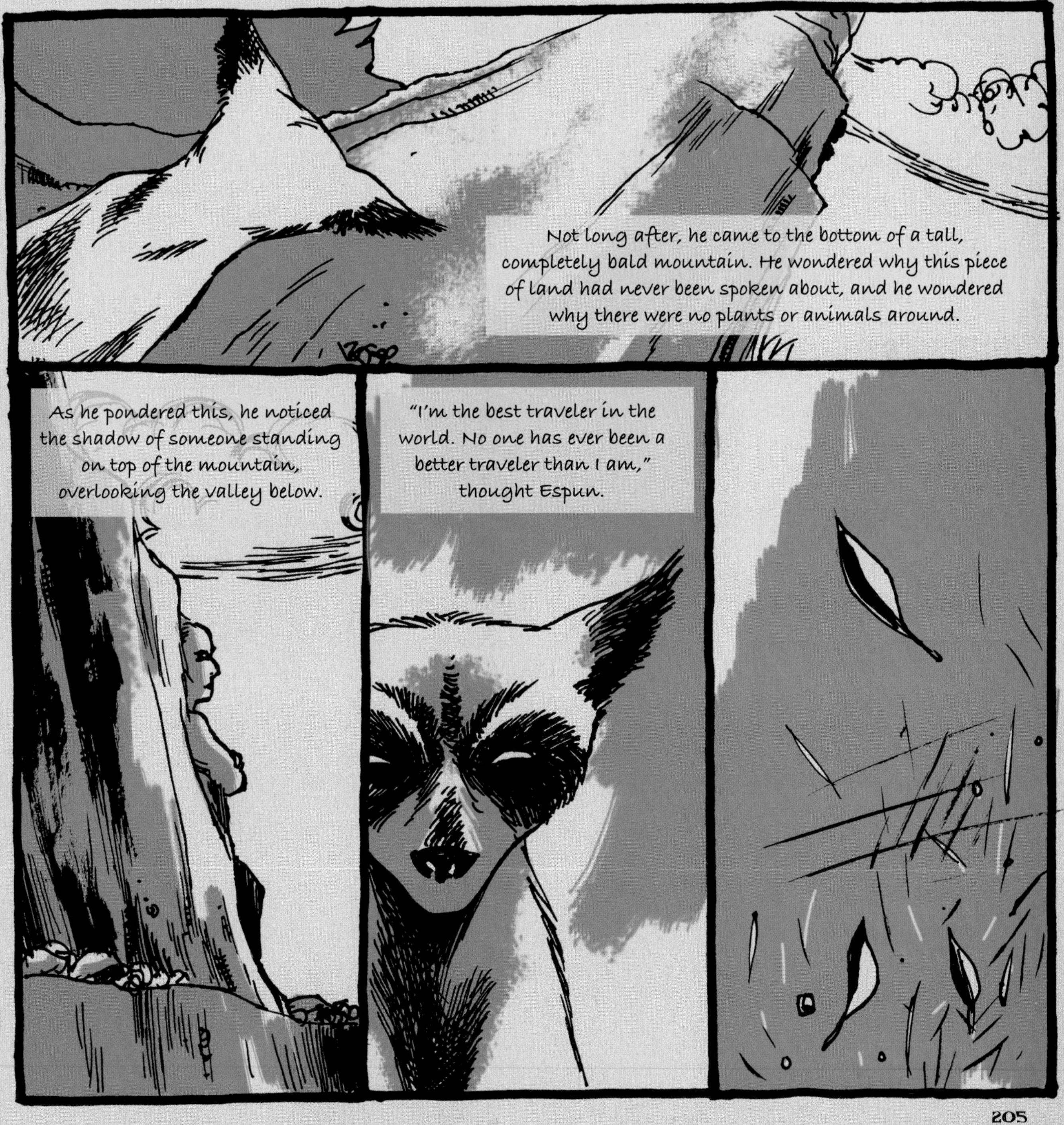
Not long after, he came to the bottom of a tall, completely bald mountain. He wondered why this piece of land had never been spoken about, and he wondered why there were no plants or animals around.
As he pondered this, he noticed the shadow of someone standing on top of the mountain, overlooking the valley below.
"I'm the best traveler in the world. No one has ever been a better traveler than I am," thought Espun.

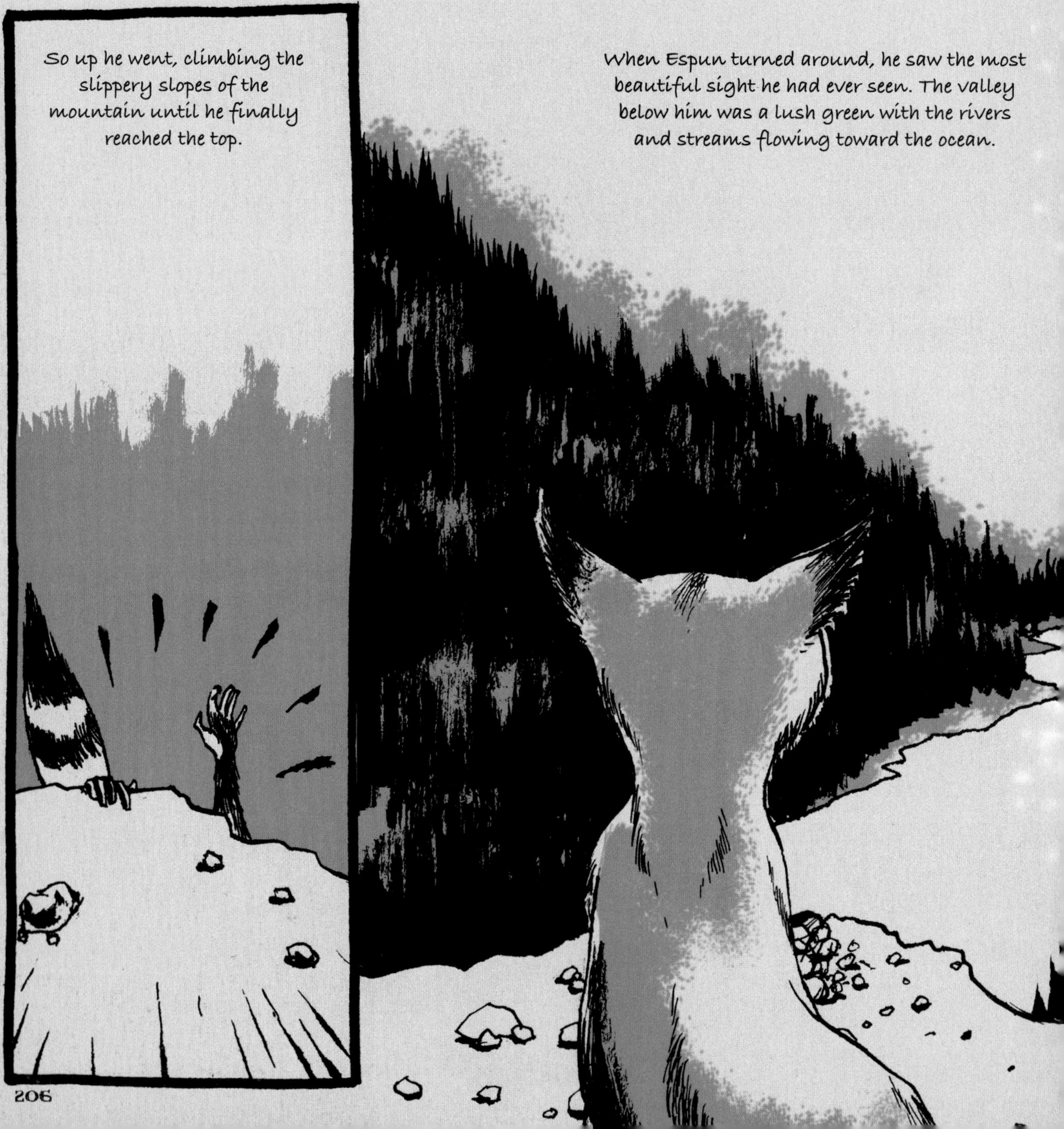
So up he went, climbing the slippery slopes of the mountain until he finally reached the top.
When Espun turned around, he saw the most beautiful sight he had ever seen. The valley below him was a lush green with the rivers and streams flowing toward the ocean.

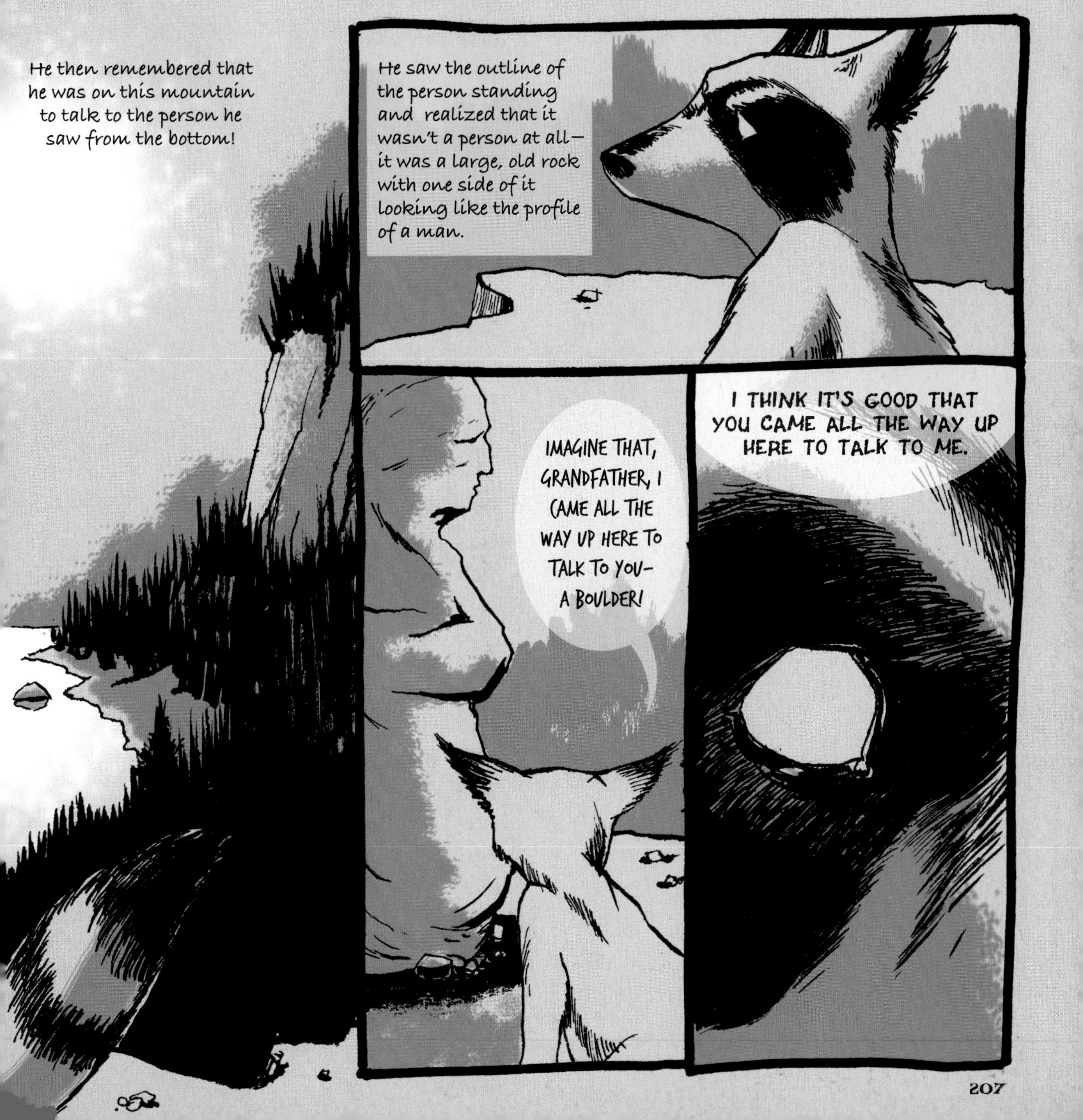
He then remembered that he was on this mountain to talk to the person he saw from the bottom!
He saw the outline of the person standing and realized that it wasn't a person at all—it was a large, old rock with one side of it looking like the profile of a man.
IMAGINE THAT, GRANDFATHER, I CAME ALL THE WAY UP HERE TO TALK TO YOU—A BOULDER!
I THINK IT'S GOOD THAT YOU CAME ALL THE WAY UP HERE TO TALK TO ME.

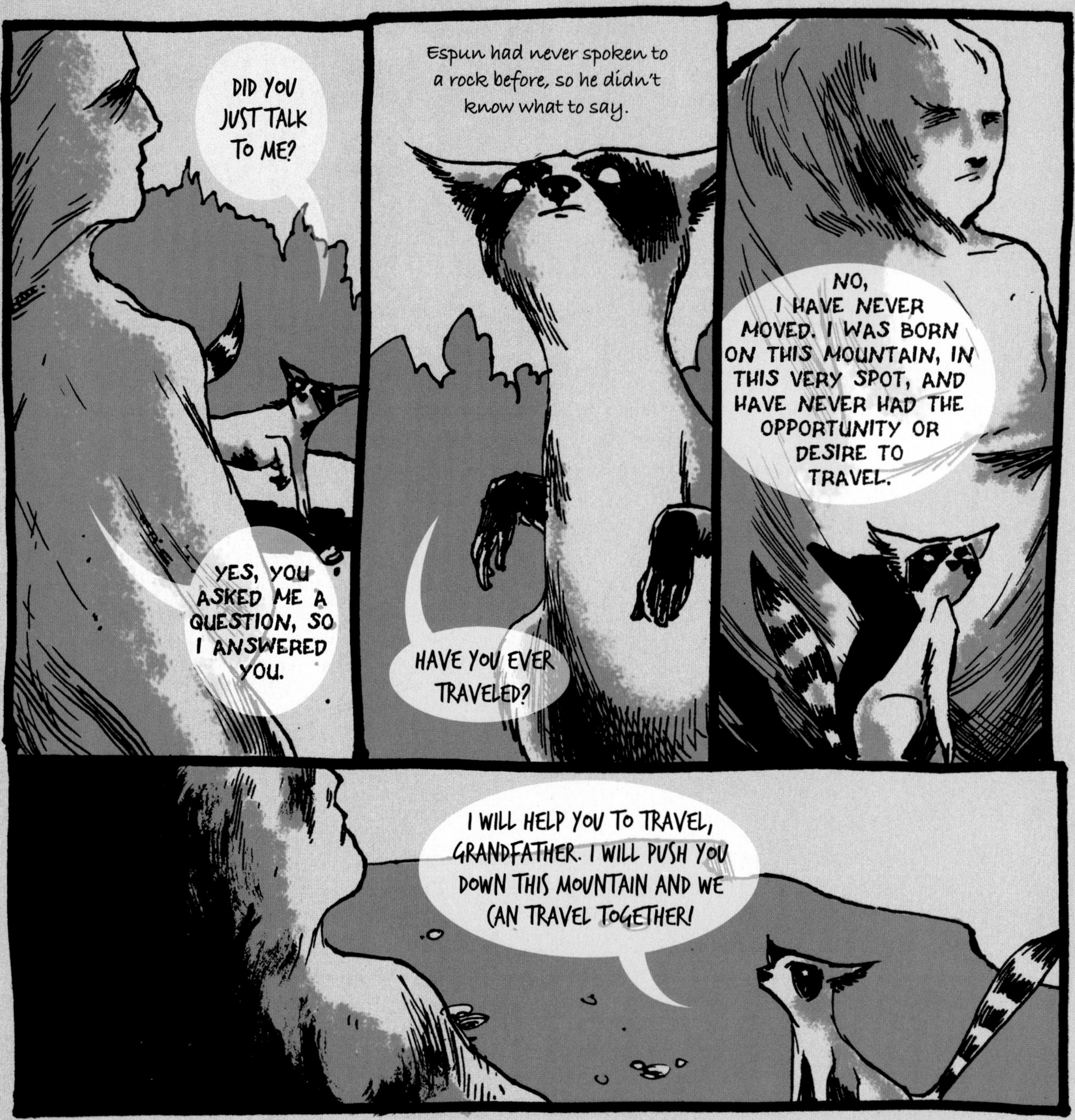
DID YOU JUST TALK TO ME?
YES, YOU ASKED ME A QUESTION, SO I ANSWERED YOU.
Espun had never spoken to a rock before, so he didn't know what to say.
HAVE YOU EVER TRAVELED?
NO, I HAVE NEVER MOVED. I WAS BORN ON THIS MOUNTAIN, IN THIS VERY SPOT, AND HAVE NEVER HAD THE OPPORTUNITY OR DESIRE TO TRAVEL.
I WILL HELP YOU TO TRAVEL, GRANDFATHER. I WILL PUSH YOU DOWN THIS MOUNTAIN AND WE CAN TRAVEL TOGETHER!

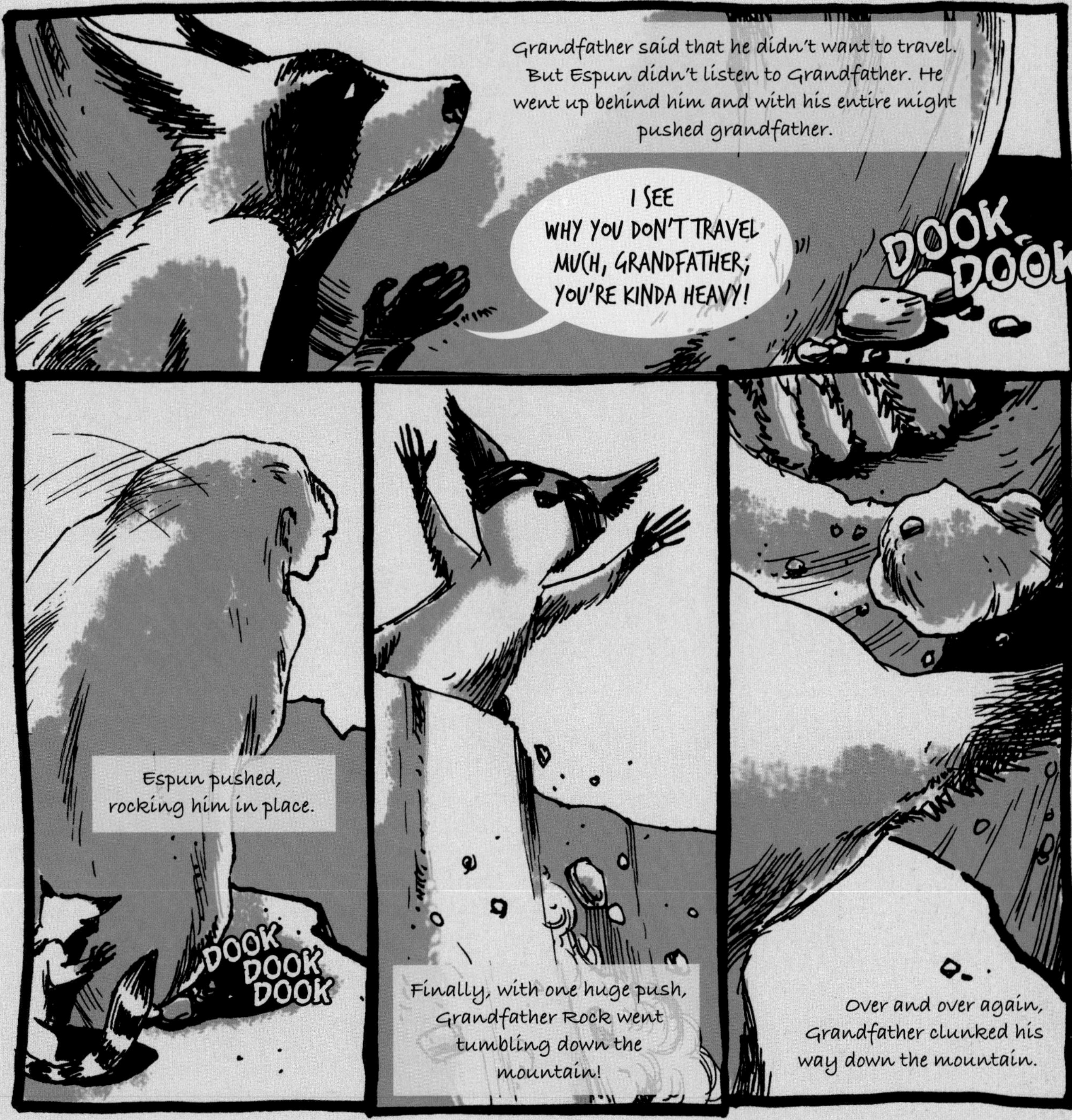
Grandfather said that he didn't want to travel. But Espun didn't listen to Grandfather. He went up behind him and with his entire might pushed grandfather.
I SEE WHY YOU DON'T TRAVEL MUCH, GRANDFATHER; YOU'RE KINDA HEAVY!
DOOK DOOK
Espun pushed, rocking him in place.
DOOK DOOK DOOK
Finally, with one huge push, Grandfather Rock went tumbling down the mountain!
Over and over again, Grandfather clunked his way down the mountain.

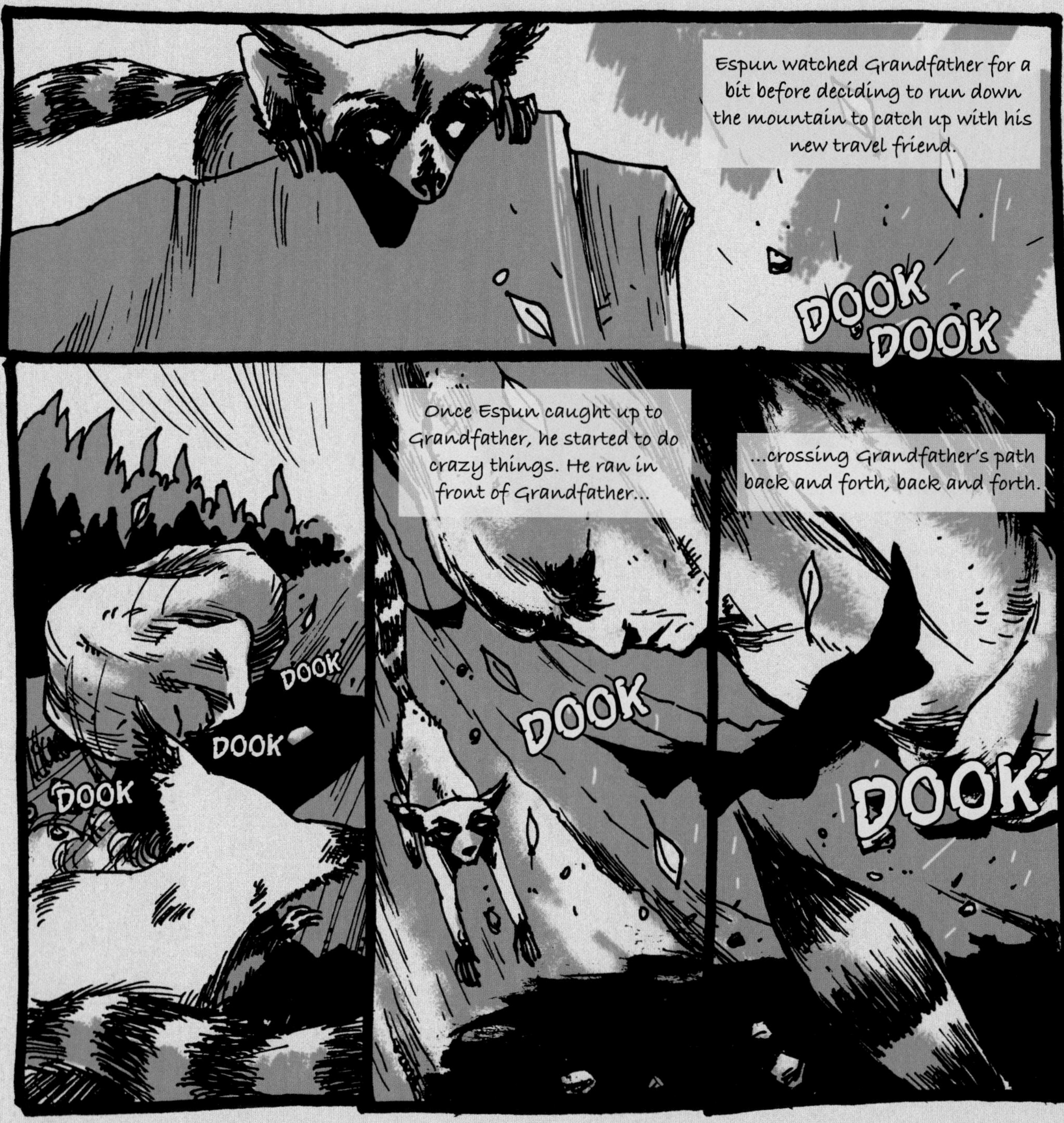
Espun watched Grandfather for a bit before deciding to run down the mountain to catch up with his new travel friend.
DOOK
DOOK
DOOK
DOOK
DOOK
Once Espun caught up to Grandfather, he started to do crazy things. He ran in front of Grandfather...
DOOK
...crossing Grandfather's path back and forth, back and forth.
DOOK

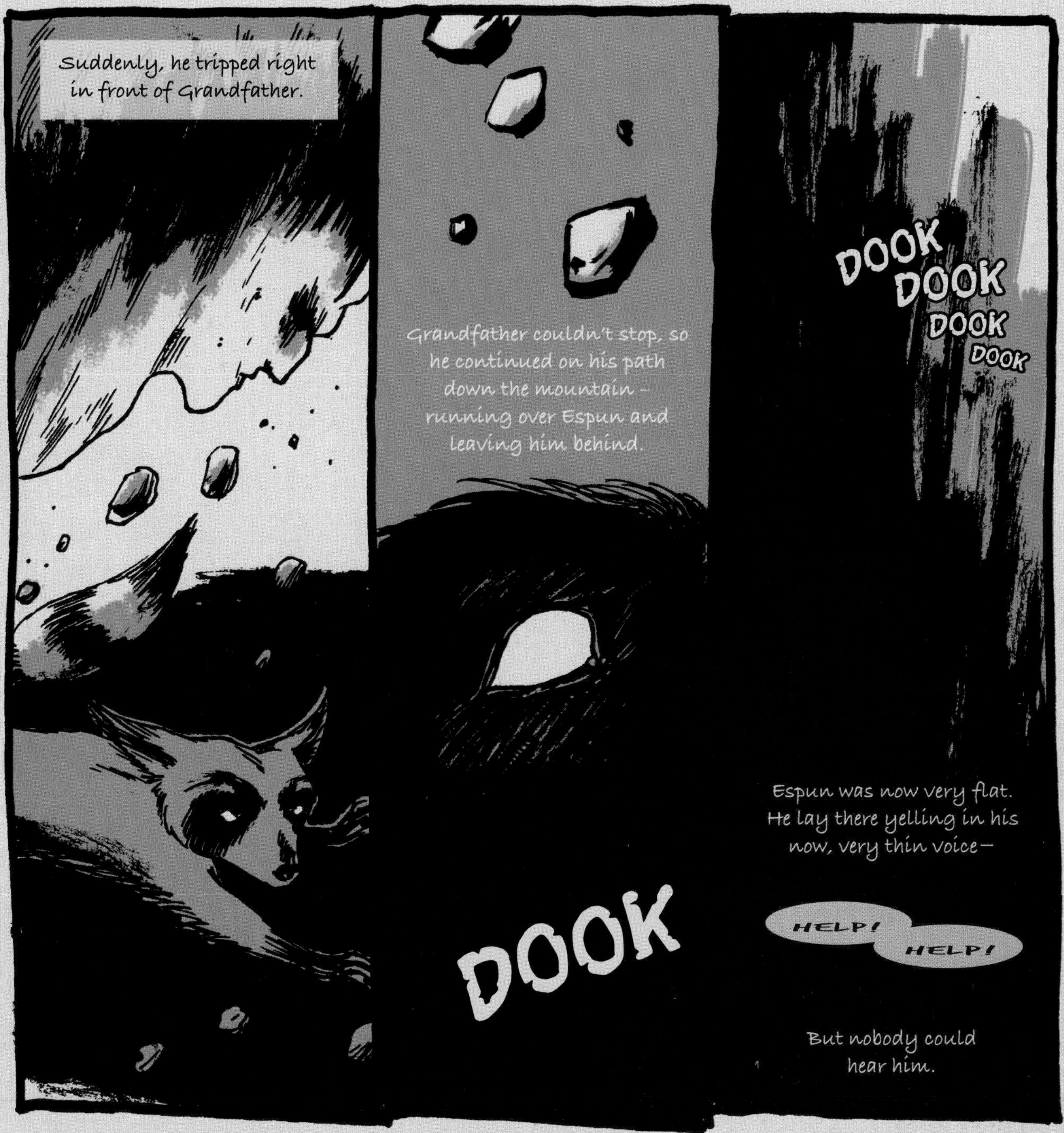
Suddenly, he tripped right in front of Grandfather.
Grandfather couldn't stop, so he continued on his path down the mountain – running over Espun and leaving him behind.
DOOK
DOOK
DOOK
DOOK
DOOK
Espun was now very flat. He lay there yelling in his now, very thin voice—
HELP!
HELP!
But nobody could hear him.

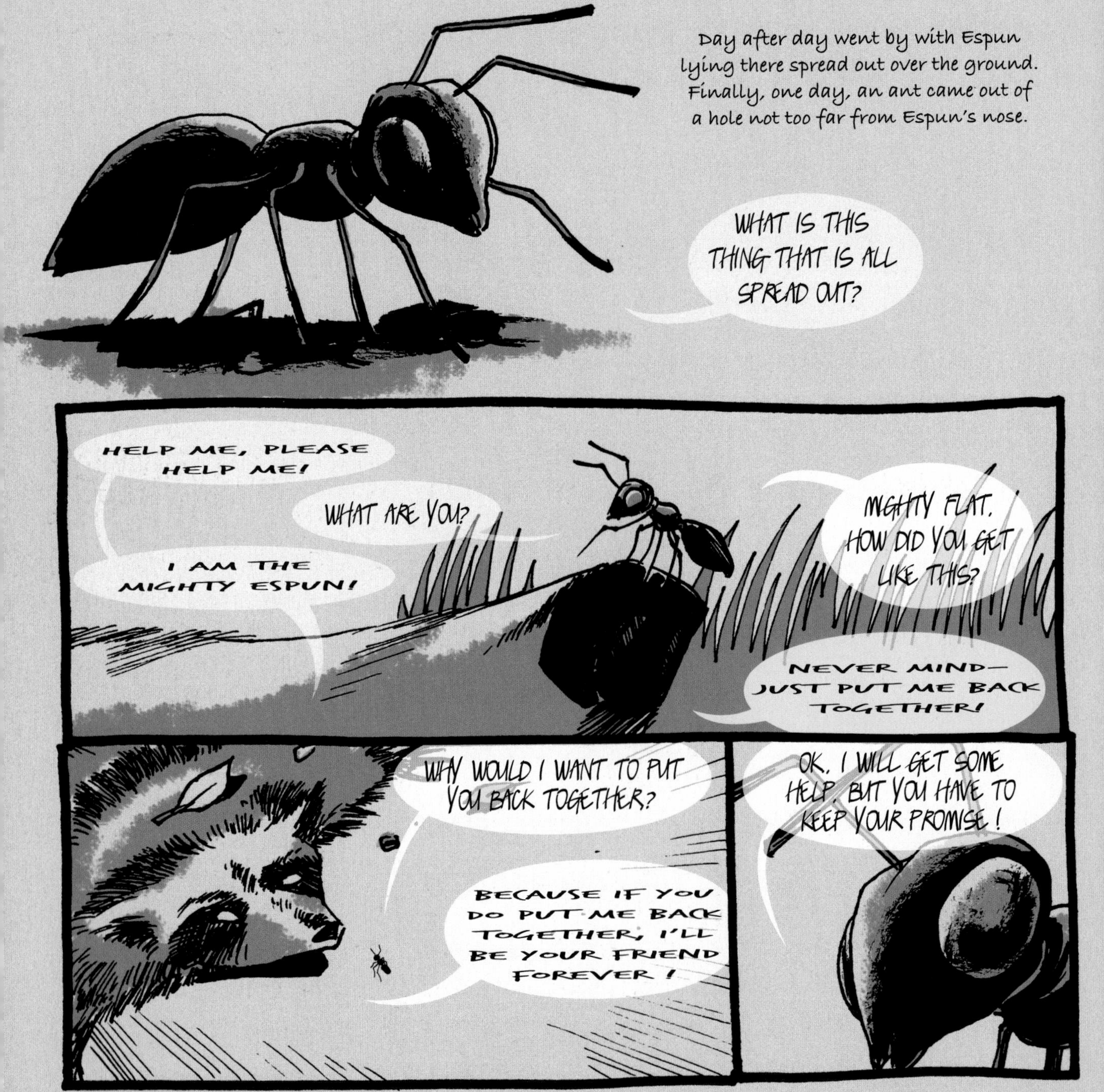
Day after day went by with Espun lying there spread out over the ground. Finally, one day, an ant came out of a hole not too far from Espun's nose.
WHAT IS THIS THING THAT IS ALL SPREAD OUT?
HELP ME, PLEASE HELP ME!
WHAT ARE YOU?
I AM THE MIGHTY ESPUN!
MIGHTY FLAT. HOW DID YOU GET LIKE THIS?
NEVER MIND— JUST PUT ME BACK TOGETHER!
WHY WOULD I WANT TO PUT YOU BACK TOGETHER?
BECAUSE IF YOU DO PUT ME BACK TOGETHER, I'LL BE YOUR FRIEND FOREVER!
OK, I WILL GET SOME HELP. BUT YOU HAVE TO KEEP YOUR PROMISE!

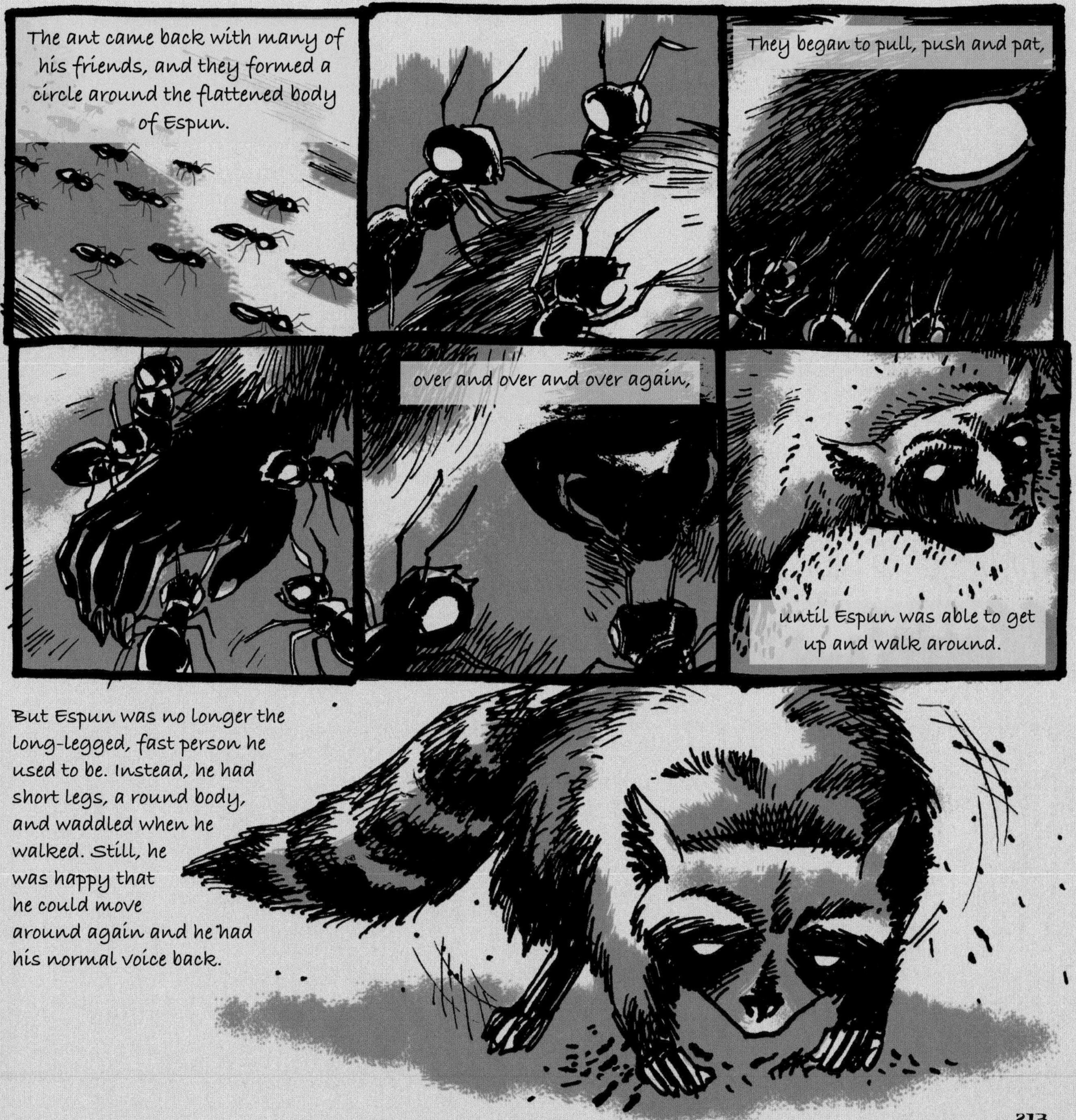
The ant came back with many of his friends, and they formed a circle around the flattened body of Espun.
They began to pull, push and pat,
over and over and over again,
until Espun was able to get up and walk around.
But Espun was no longer the long-legged, fast person he used to be. Instead, he had short legs, a round body, and waddled when he walked. Still, he was happy that he could move around again and he had his normal voice back.

With that, Espun began his trek home, brushing the ants off from his body as he went. The ants stood behind, watching him walk away.

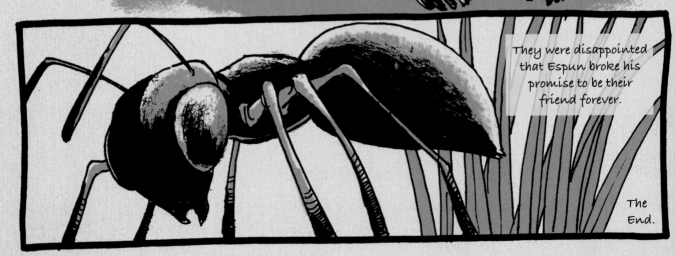

They were disappointed that Espun broke his promise to be their friend forever.

The End.

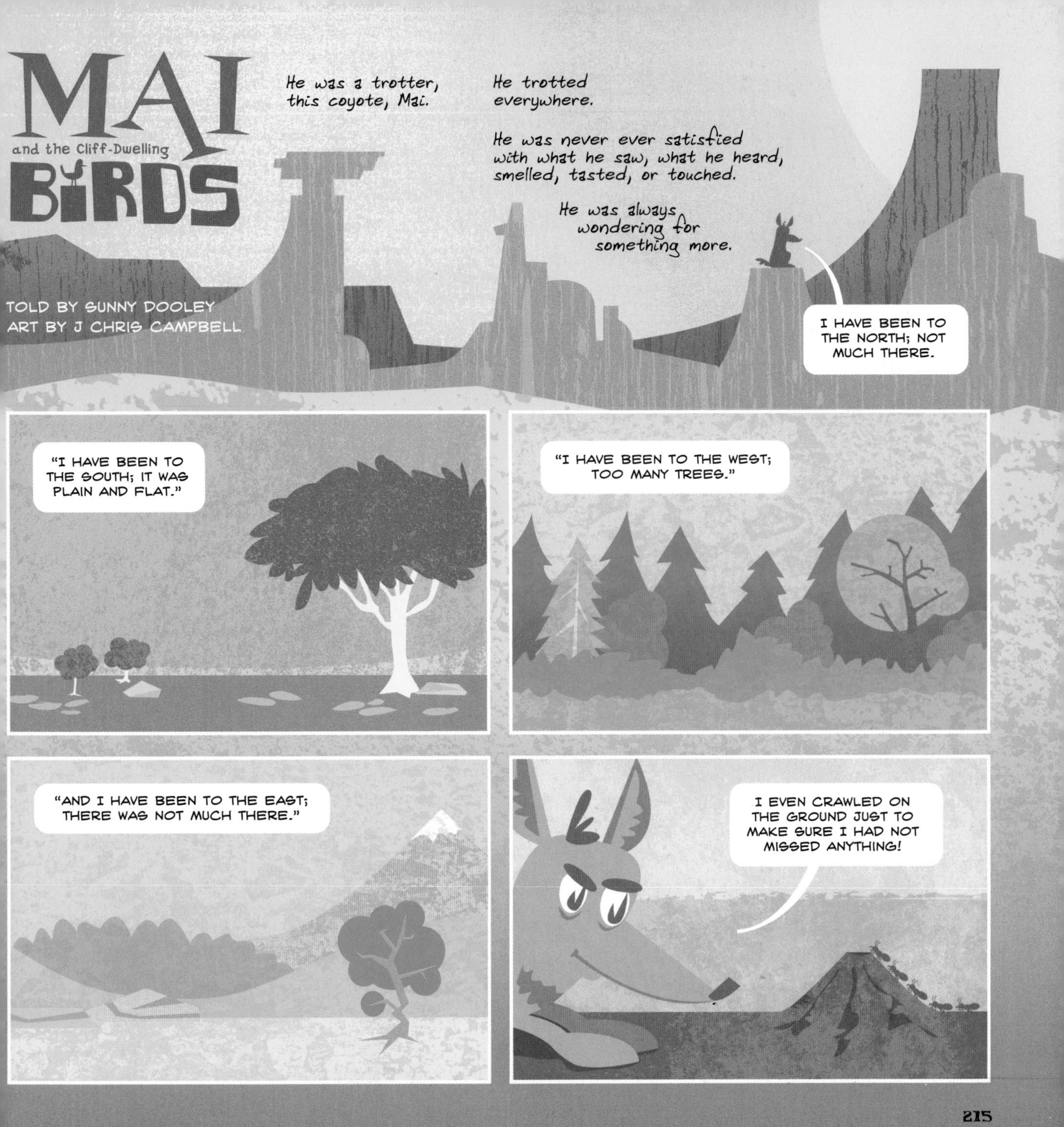
MAI
and the Cliff-Dwelling
BIRDS
TOLD BY SUNNY DOOLEY
ART BY J CHRIS CAMPBELL
He was a trotter, this coyote, Mai.
He trotted everywhere.
He was never ever satisfied with what he saw, what he heard, smelled, tasted, or touched.
He was always wondering for something more.
I HAVE BEEN TO THE NORTH; NOT MUCH THERE.
"I HAVE BEEN TO THE SOUTH; IT WAS PLAIN AND FLAT."
"I HAVE BEEN TO THE WEST; TOO MANY TREES."
"AND I HAVE BEEN TO THE EAST; THERE WAS NOT MUCH THERE."
I EVEN CRAWLED ON THE GROUND JUST TO MAKE SURE I HAD NOT MISSED ANYTHING!

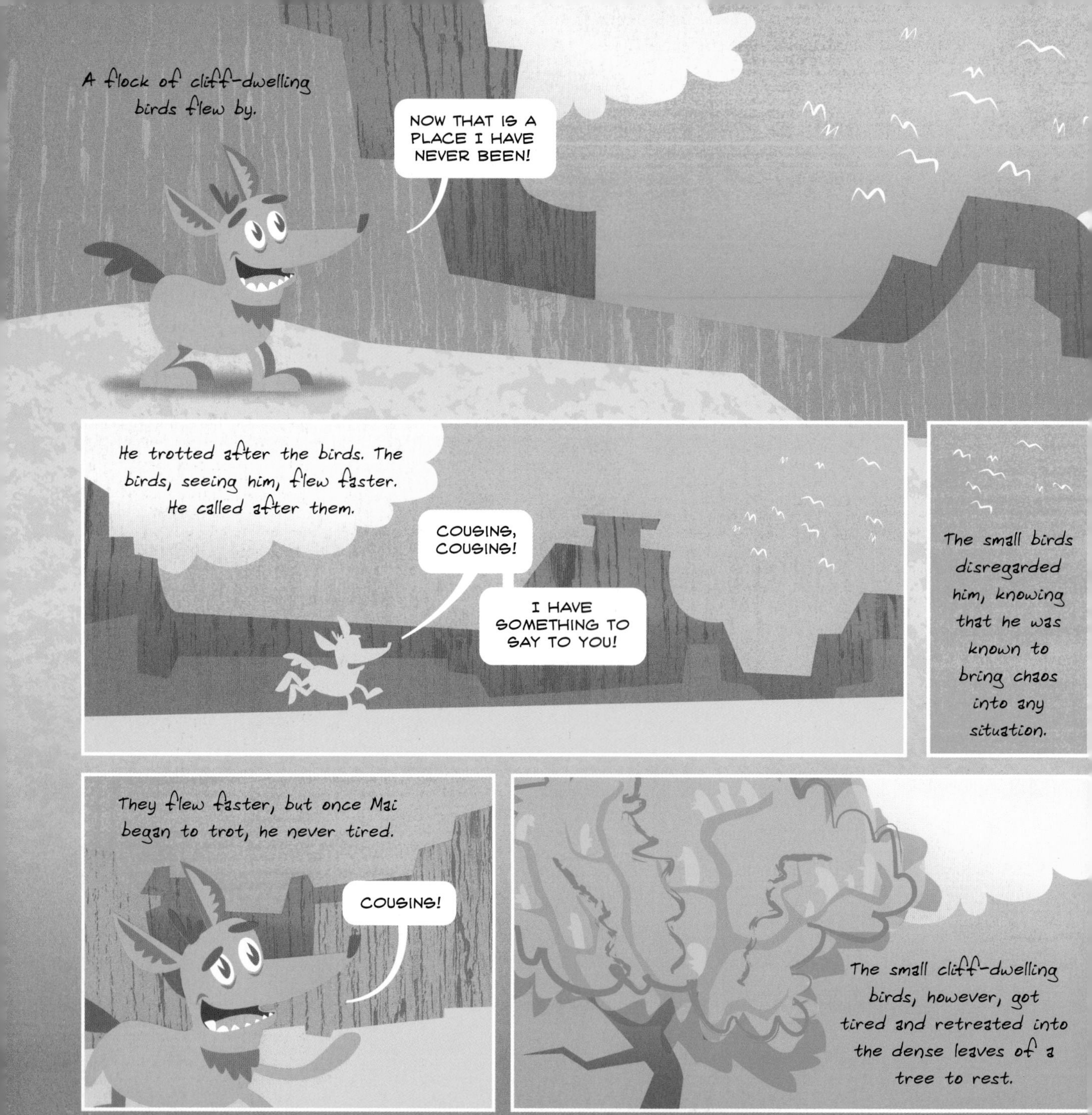
A flock of cliff-dwelling birds flew by.
NOW THAT IS A PLACE I HAVE NEVER BEEN!
He trotted after the birds. The birds, seeing him, flew faster. He called after them.
COUSINS, COUSINS!
I HAVE SOMETHING TO SAY TO YOU!
The small birds disregarded him, knowing that he was known to bring chaos into any situation.
They flew faster, but once Mai began to trot, he never tired.
COUSINS!
The small cliff-dwelling birds, however, got tired and retreated into the dense leaves of a tree to rest.

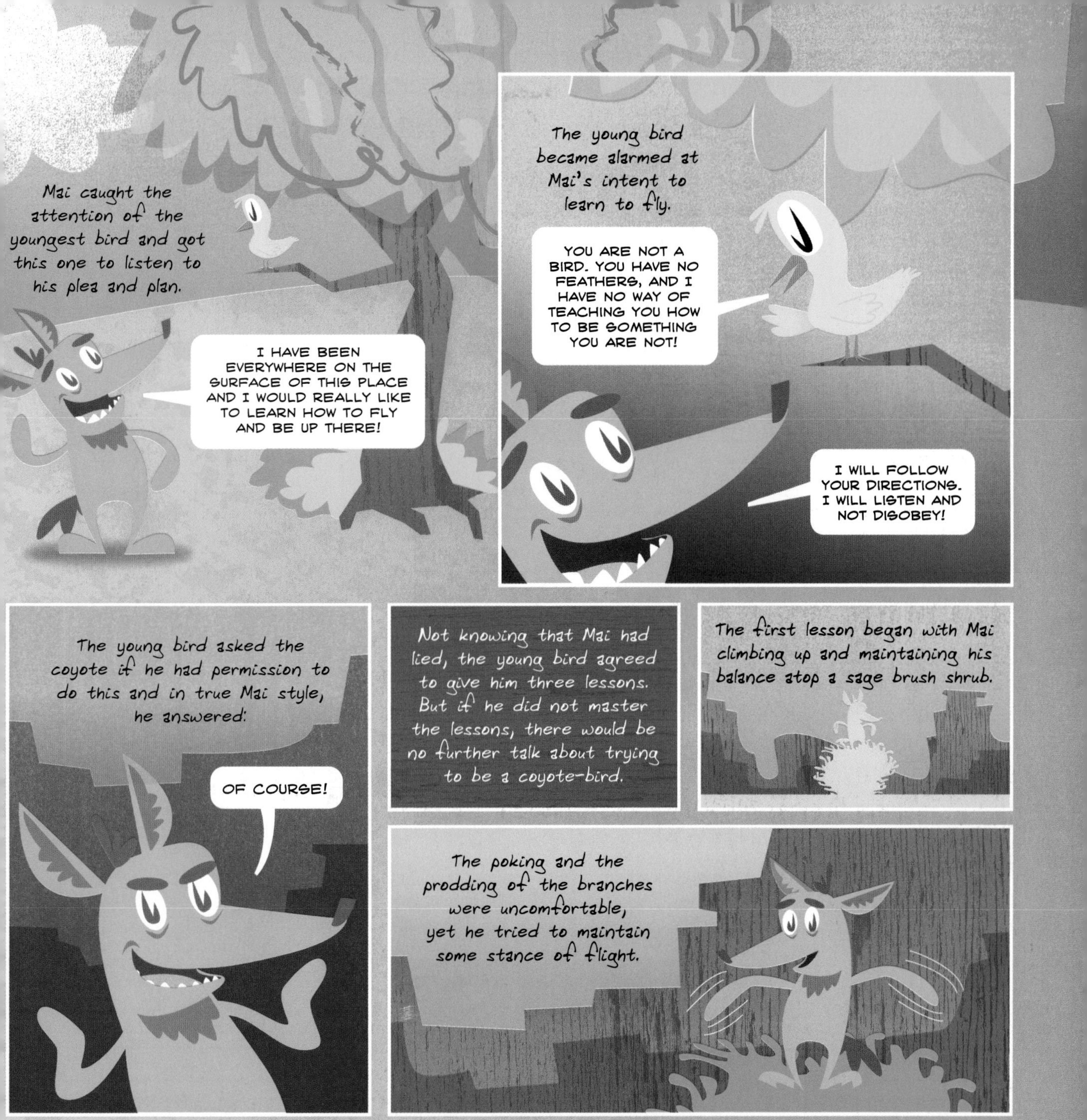
Mai caught the attention of the youngest bird and got this one to listen to his plea and plan.
I HAVE BEEN EVERYWHERE ON THE SURFACE OF THIS PLACE AND I WOULD REALLY LIKE TO LEARN HOW TO FLY AND BE UP THERE!
The young bird became alarmed at Mai's intent to learn to fly.
YOU ARE NOT A BIRD. YOU HAVE NO FEATHERS, AND I HAVE NO WAY OF TEACHING YOU HOW TO BE SOMETHING YOU ARE NOT!
I WILL FOLLOW YOUR DIRECTIONS. I WILL LISTEN AND NOT DISOBEY!
The young bird asked the coyote if he had permission to do this and in true Mai style, he answered:
OF COURSE!
Not knowing that Mai had lied, the young bird agreed to give him three lessons. But if he did not master the lessons, there would be no further talk about trying to be a coyote-bird.
The first lesson began with Mai climbing up and maintaining his balance atop a sage brush shrub.
The poking and the prodding of the branches were uncomfortable, yet he tried to maintain some stance of flight.

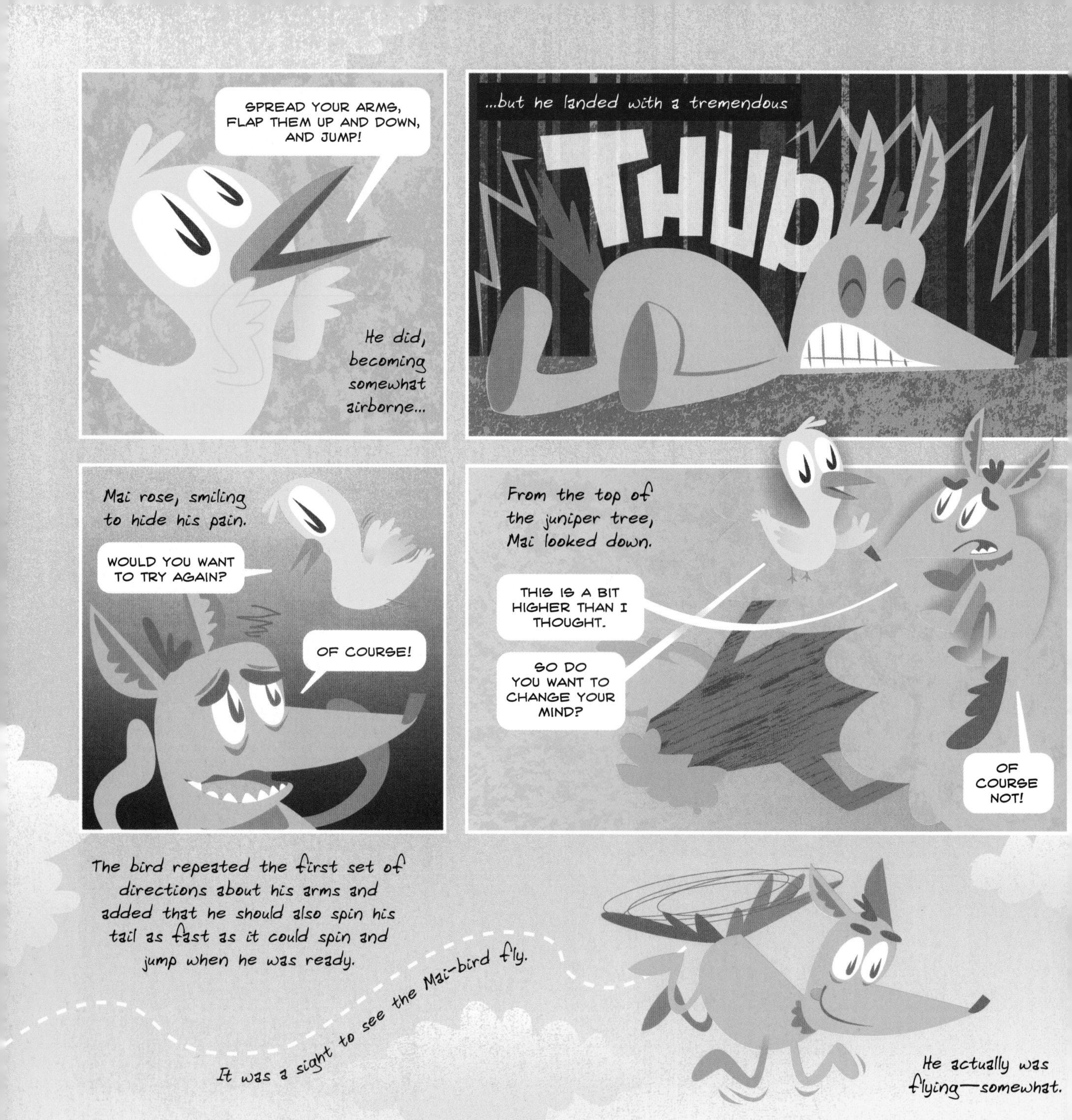
SPREAD YOUR ARMS, FLAP THEM UP AND DOWN, AND JUMP!
He did, becoming somewhat airborne...
...but he landed with a tremendous
THUD
Mai rose, smiling to hide his pain.
WOULD YOU WANT TO TRY AGAIN?
OF COURSE!
From the top of the juniper tree, Mai looked down.
THIS IS A BIT HIGHER THAN I THOUGHT.
SO DO YOU WANT TO CHANGE YOUR MIND?
OF COURSE NOT!
The bird repeated the first set of directions about his arms and added that he should also spin his tail as fast as it could spin and jump when he was ready.
It was a sight to see the Mai-bird fly.
He actually was flying—somewhat.

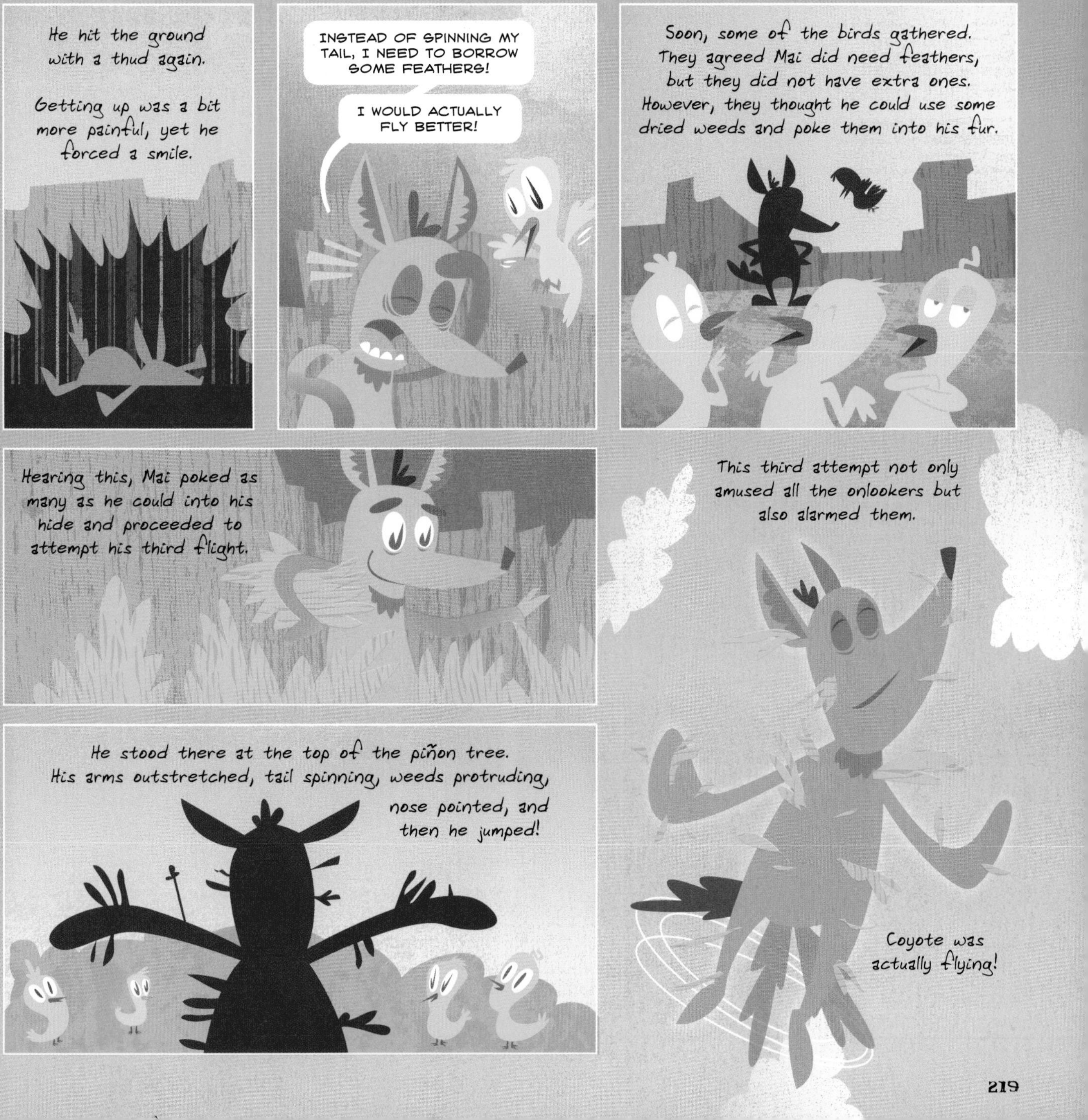
He hit the ground with a thud again.
Getting up was a bit more painful, yet he forced a smile.
INSTEAD OF SPINNING MY TAIL, I NEED TO BORROW SOME FEATHERS!
I WOULD ACTUALLY FLY BETTER!
Soon, some of the birds gathered. They agreed Mai did need feathers, but they did not have extra ones. However, they thought he could use some dried weeds and poke them into his fur.
Hearing this, Mai poked as many as he could into his hide and proceeded to attempt his third flight.
This third attempt not only amused all the onlookers but also alarmed them.
He stood there at the top of the piñon tree. His arms outstretched, tail spinning, weeds protruding, nose pointed, and then he jumped!
Coyote was actually flying!

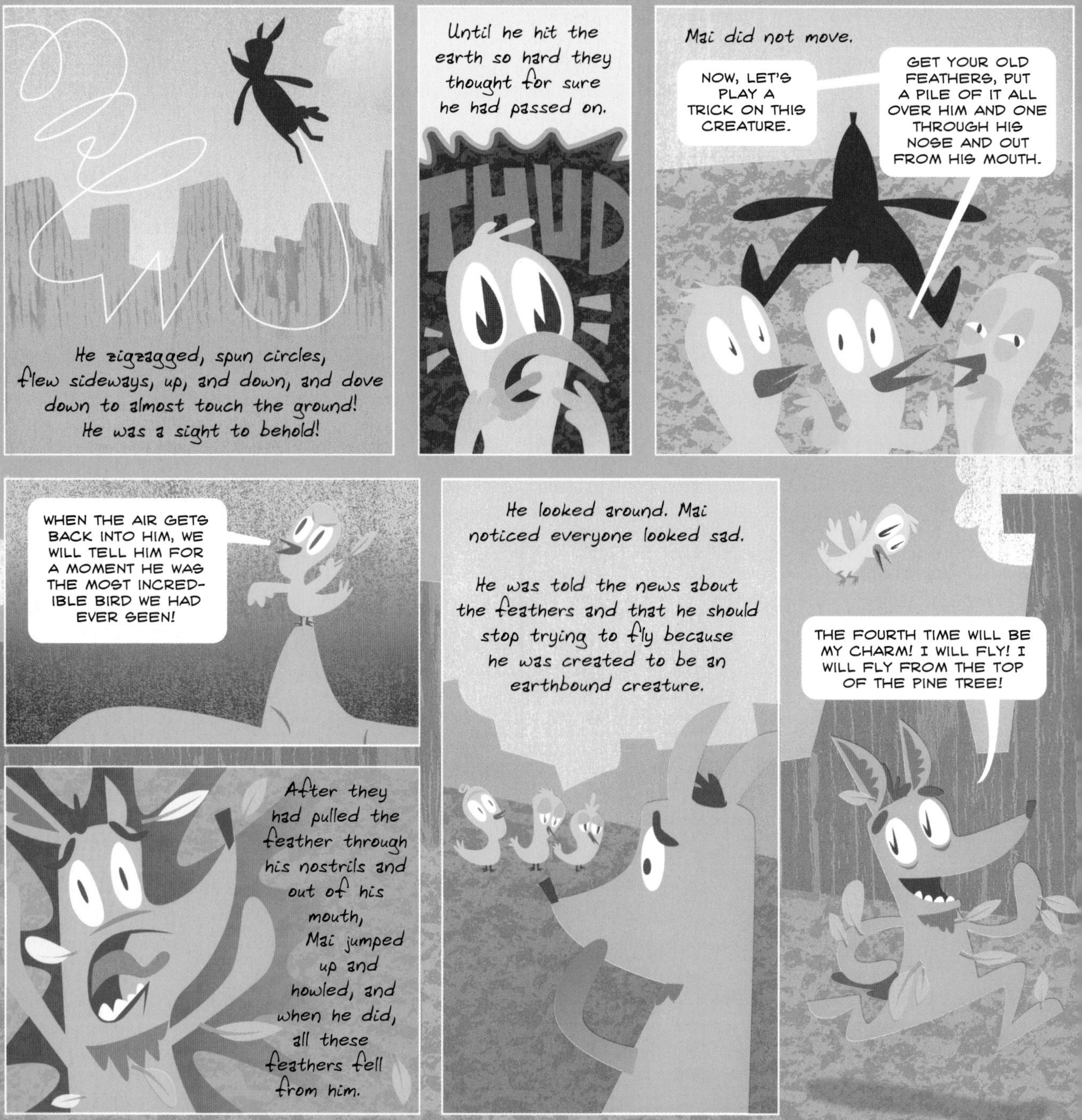
He zigzagged, spun circles, flew sideways, up, and down, and dove down to almost touch the ground! He was a sight to behold!
Until he hit the earth so hard they thought for sure he had passed on.
THUD
Mai did not move.
NOW, LET'S PLAY A TRICK ON THIS CREATURE.
GET YOUR OLD FEATHERS, PUT A PILE OF IT ALL OVER HIM AND ONE THROUGH HIS NOSE AND OUT FROM HIS MOUTH.
WHEN THE AIR GETS BACK INTO HIM, WE WILL TELL HIM FOR A MOMENT HE WAS THE MOST INCREDIBLE BIRD WE HAD EVER SEEN!
After they had pulled the feather through his nostrils and out of his mouth, Mai jumped up and howled, and when he did, all these feathers fell from him.
He looked around. Mai noticed everyone looked sad.
He was told the news about the feathers and that he should stop trying to fly because he was created to be an earthbound creature.
THE FOURTH TIME WILL BE MY CHARM! I WILL FLY! I WILL FLY FROM THE TOP OF THE PINE TREE!

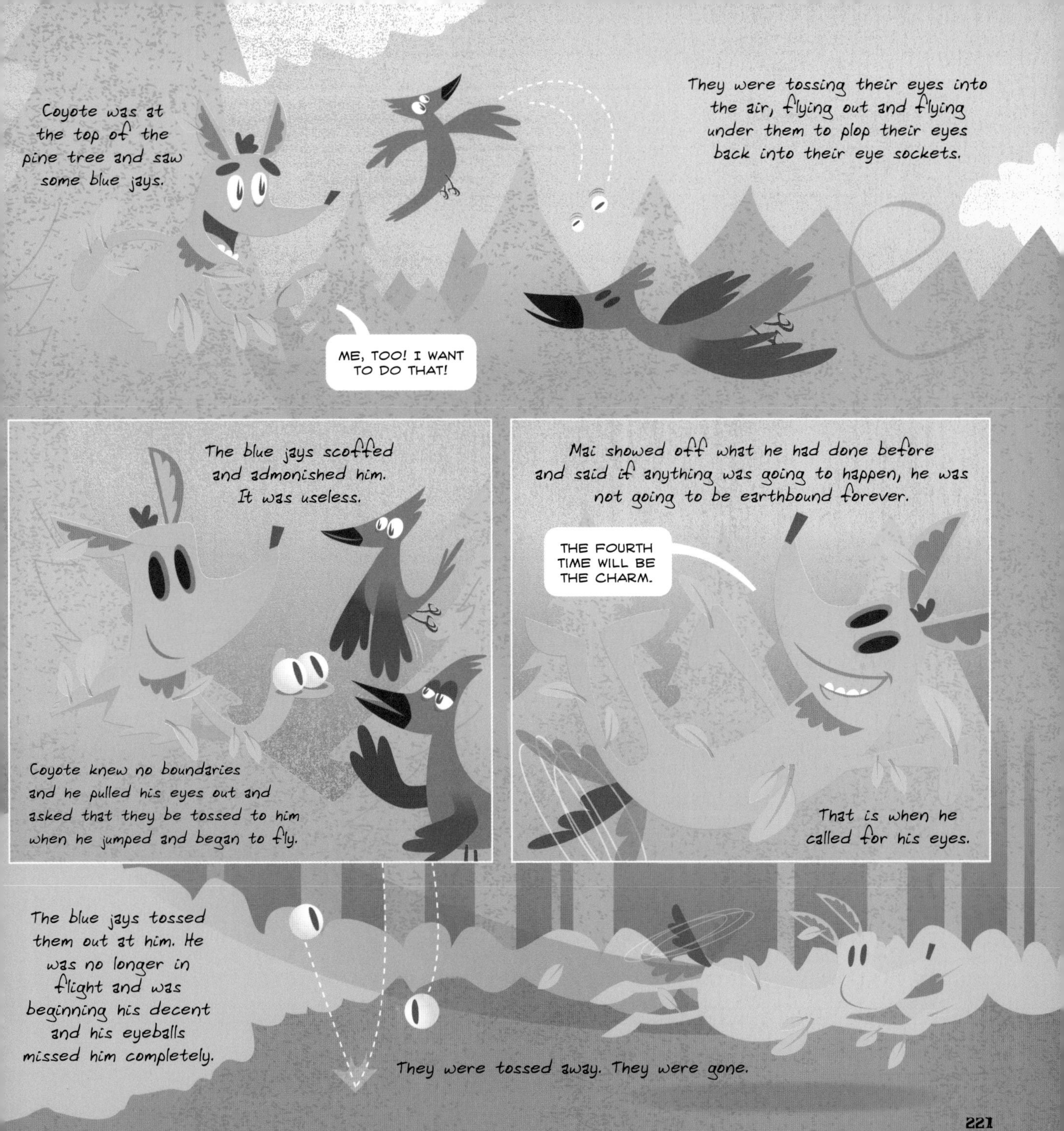
Coyote was at the top of the pine tree and saw some blue jays.
They were tossing their eyes into the air, flying out and flying under them to plop their eyes back into their eye sockets.
ME, TOO! I WANT TO DO THAT!
The blue jays scoffed and admonished him. It was useless.
Coyote knew no boundaries and he pulled his eyes out and asked that they be tossed to him when he jumped and began to fly.
Mai showed off what he had done before and said if anything was going to happen, he was not going to be earthbound forever.
THE FOURTH TIME WILL BE THE CHARM.
That is when he called for his eyes.
The blue jays tossed them out at him. He was no longer in flight and was beginning his decent and his eyeballs missed him completely.
They were tossed away. They were gone.

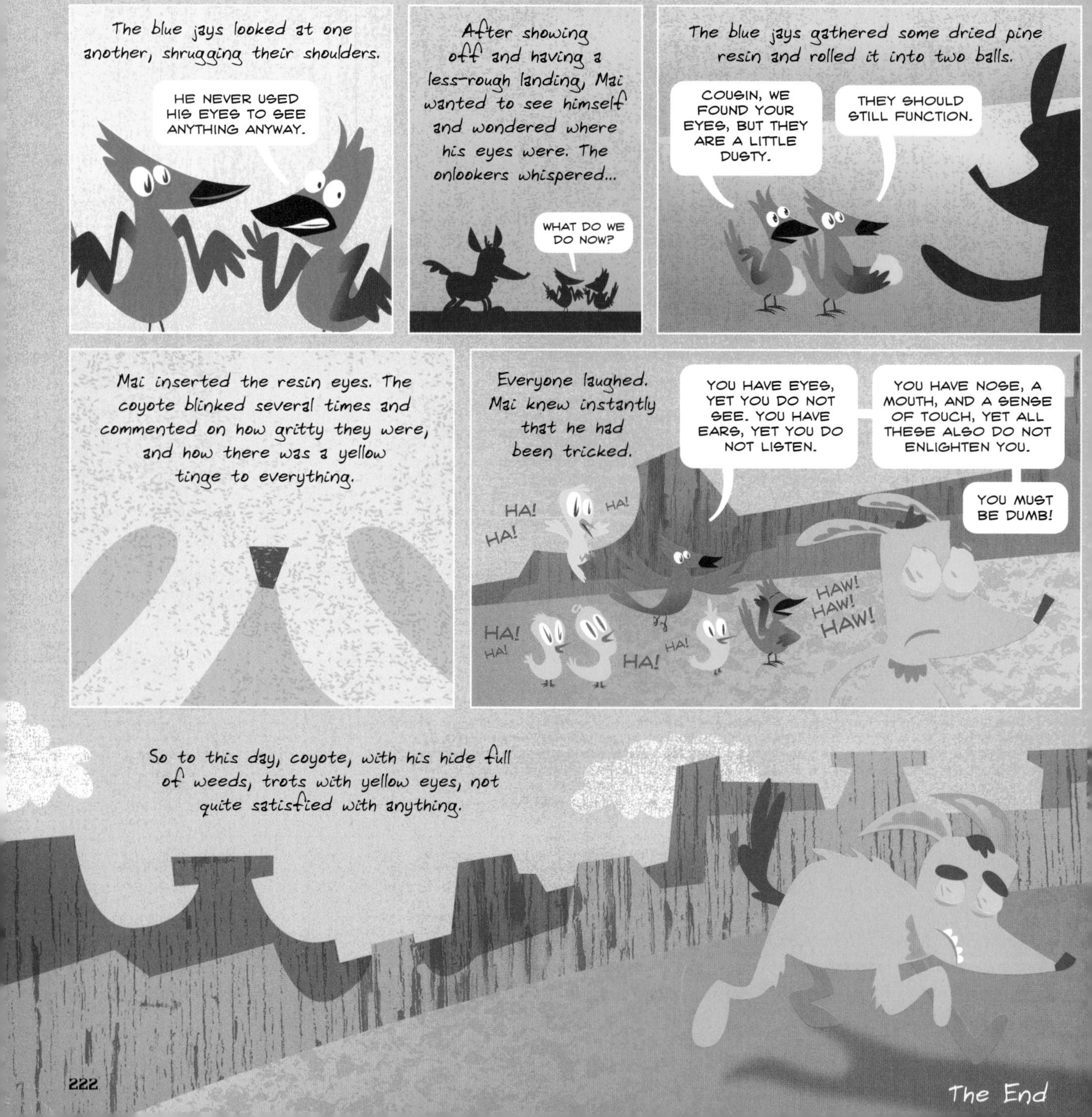
The blue jays looked at one another, shrugging their shoulders.
HE NEVER USED HIS EYES TO SEE ANYTHING ANYWAY.
After showing off and having a less-rough landing, Mai wanted to see himself and wondered where his eyes were. The onlookers whispered...
WHAT DO WE DO NOW?
The blue jays gathered some dried pine resin and rolled it into two balls.
COUSIN, WE FOUND YOUR EYES, BUT THEY ARE A LITTLE DUSTY.
THEY SHOULD STILL FUNCTION.
Mai inserted the resin eyes. The coyote blinked several times and commented on how gritty they were, and how there was a yellow tinge to everything.
Everyone laughed. Mai knew instantly that he had been tricked.
YOU HAVE EYES, YET YOU DO NOT SEE. YOU HAVE EARS, YET YOU DO NOT LISTEN.
YOU HAVE NOSE, A MOUTH, AND A SENSE OF TOUCH, YET ALL THESE ALSO DO NOT ENLIGHTEN YOU.
YOU MUST BE DUMB!
HA! HA! HA!
HA! HA! HA! HA! HA!
HAW! HAW! HAW!
So to this day, coyote, with his hide full of weeds, trots with yellow eyes, not quite satisfied with anything.
The End

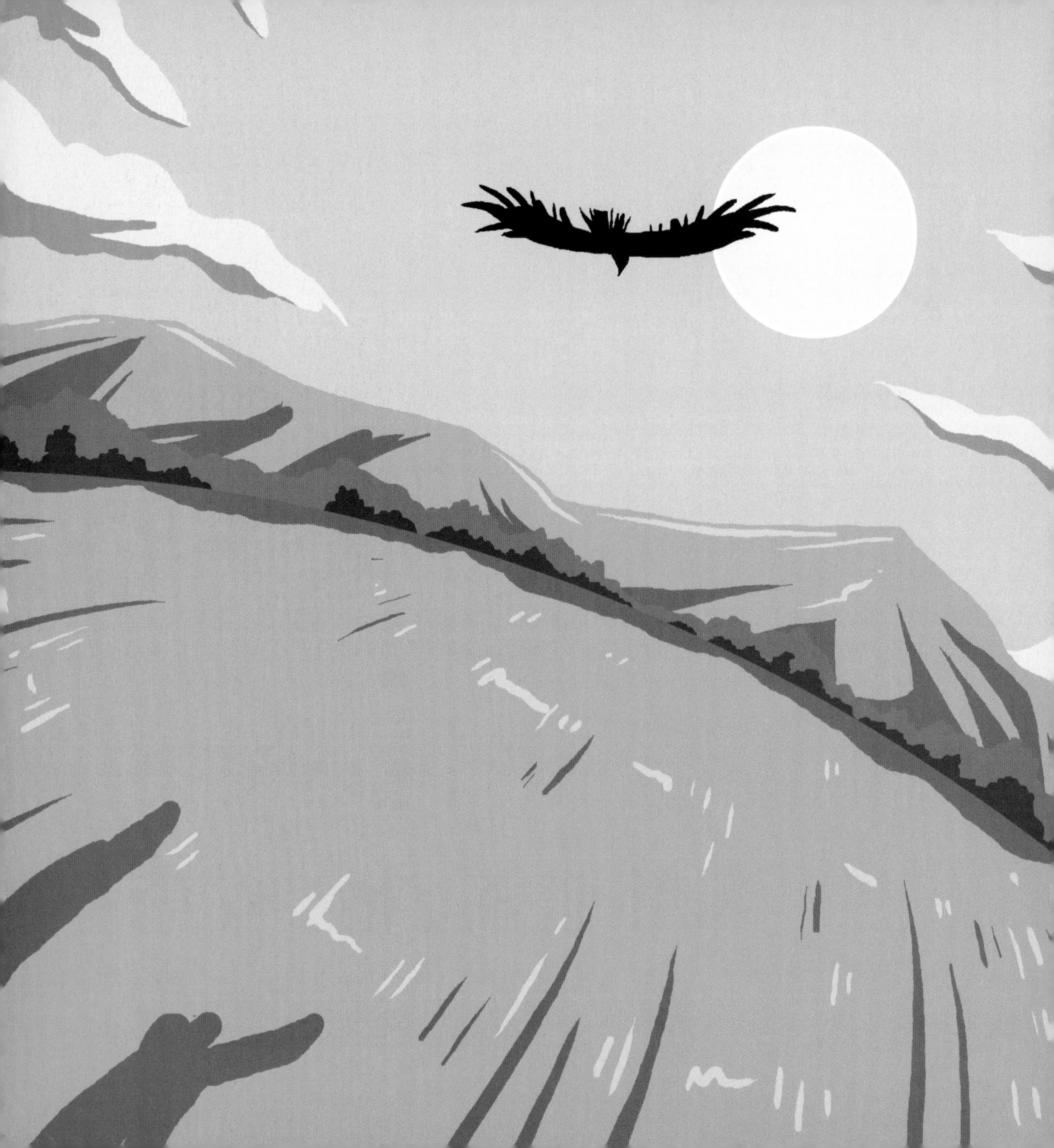

From the Editor

I WAS CASUALLY THUMBING THROUGH BOOKS AT OUR LOCAL LIBRARY WHEN I CAME ACROSS *AMERICAN INDIAN TRICKSTER TALES* BY ALFONSO ORTIZ AND RICHARD ERDOES. I WAS FAMILIAR WITH THE TYPICAL EUROPEAN MYTHS AND TALES AND A FEW ASIAN ONES, BUT I HAD NEVER READ A NATIVE AMERICAN TRICKSTER TALE.

MY INTEREST WAS PIQUED. GLANCING THROUGH THE BOOK, I SAW THAT IT HAD A WONDERFUL RANGE OF STORIES AND WAS PEPPERED WITH POWERFUL NATIVE AMERICAN-STYLE ILLUSTRATIONS OF COYOTES, RABBITS, SHAPE-SHIFTERS, AND OTHER CRITTERS AND BEINGS. THE STORIES WERE SERIOUS, FUNNY, MISCHIEVOUS, NAUGHTY, ALLEGORICAL. I WAS HOOKED; I COULDN'T PUT THE BOOK DOWN. WHEN I FINISHED, I REALIZED HOW LITTLE I KNEW ABOUT NATIVE AMERICAN CULTURE. HERE I AM—AN AMERICAN—AND, PROBABLY LIKE MOST OF US, I DIDN'T KNOW ABOUT THE CULTURE OF THE PEOPLE WHO LIVED HERE FOR THOUSANDS OF YEARS PRIOR TO EUROPEAN SETTLEMENT AND WESTERN EXPANSION. WHEN I TRAVEL ABROAD, I OFTEN THINK ABOUT THE PEOPLE WHO LIVED IN THAT PLACE HUNDREDS AND THOUSANDS OF YEARS AGO. I THINK ABOUT THE RULING ROYALTY, THE MARCHING ARMIES, AND THE PEOPLE WHO TILLED THE SOIL. BUT, FOR SOME REASON, I'D NEVER THOUGHT THAT WAY WHEN I STOOD ON AMERICAN SOIL.

AS A COMIC BOOK CREATOR AND SOMEONE WHO APPRECIATES NATURE, I MULLED OVER THE APPEAL OF PRODUCING NATIVE AMERICAN TRICKSTER STORIES IN A SEQUENTIAL FORMAT. A LITTLE RESEARCH REVEALED THAT SUCH A BOOK DIDN'T EXIST. FOR THIS BOOK, I WANTED THE STORIES TO BE AUTHENTIC, MEANING THEY WOULD HAVE TO BE WRITTEN BY NATIVE AMERICAN STORYTELLERS. FINDING WILLING STORYTELLERS WASN'T THAT EASY; AFTER ALL, THERE'S SOME HEAVY HISTORICAL BAGGAGE BETWEEN NATIVE AMERICANS AND WHITES, AND SEVERAL PEOPLE I APPROACHED ABOUT THE PROJECT WERE UNSURE OF MY INTENTIONS.

EVENTUALLY I GAINED THE SUPPORT OF FEW KEY PEOPLE, WHO IN TURN HELPED ME FIND OTHER PARTICIPANTS, AND PRETTY SOON THE BALL WAS ROLLING. TO ENSURE A PROPER FIT BETWEEN THE WRITTEN STORIES AND THE ILLUSTRATIONS, THE STORYTELLERS EACH SELECTED AN ARTIST FROM A POOL OF CONTRIBUTING TALENTS TO RENDER THEIR STORIES. ADDITIONALLY, THE STORYTELLERS APPROVED THE STORYBOARDS. IN TERMS OF EDITING, TEXT WAS CHANGED ONLY WHEN PANEL SPACE WAS AN ISSUE AND ONLY WITH THE APPROVAL OF THE STORYTELLER. THE POINT WASN'T TO WESTERNIZE THE STORIES FOR GENERAL CONSUMPTION, BUT RATHER TO PROVIDE AN OPPORTUNITY TO EXPERIENCE AUTHENTIC NATIVE AMERICAN STORIES, EVEN IF IT SOMETIMES MEANT CLASHING WITH WESTERN VERNACULAR.

I HOPE THIS BOOK SERVES AS A BRIDGE FOR READERS TO LEARN MORE ABOUT THE ORIGINAL PEOPLE OF THIS LAND AND TO FOSTER A GREATER APPRECIATION AND UNDERSTANDING AMONG ALL INHABITANTS.

—MATT DEMBICKI

CONTRIBUTORS

JOHN ACTIVE IS A FIFTY-NINE-YEAR-OLD YUP'IK ESKIMO FROM WESTERN ALASKA. HE WAS RAISED BY HIS GRANDMOTHER, WHO USED TO TELL HIM TRADITIONAL YUP'IK STORIES AT BEDTIME. WHEN HE GREW UP, HE BECAME A STORYTELLER AND IS A *YUP'IK NEWS* REPORTER FOR PUBLIC AM RADIO STATION KYUK IN BETHEL, ALASKA, WHERE HE HAS WORKED FOR MORE THAN TWENTY-FIVE YEARS.

BORN DEEP IN THE APPALACHIAN MOUNTAINS IN 1969, **RAND ARRINGTON** WAS ALWAYS FASCINATED WITH COMICS. SOME OF HIS EARLIEST MEMORIES ARE OF PAGING THROUGH HIS OLDER BROTHER'S COMICS, ENTHRALLED BY THE DYNAMIC PICTURES. AFTER COLLEGE, HE JUMPED INTO THE WORLD OF PRINT AND DESIGN, FOLLOWED BY WEB DEVELOPMENT, WHERE HE HAS BEEN ACTIVELY PREPARING HIMSELF TO FOLLOW HIS LIFELONG PASSION OF CREATING COMIC BOOKS.

MICHAEL J. AUGER IS A DEVIANT DABBLER IN COMICS. HE IS KNOWN FOR CREATING WHIMSICAL CHARACTERS WHO HAVE AN OFFBEAT QUALITY AND CHILDLIKE CHARM. HAVING DONE HIS TIME AT THE COLUMBUS COLLEGE OF ART AND DESIGN IN OHIO, HE CURRENTLY RESIDES IN THE WASHINGTON, DC, AREA. AUGER HAS CREATED ADS, ALBUM COVERS, BOOK ILLUSTRATIONS, CATALOGS, POSTERS, FLYERS, MURALS, AND OTHER PROJECTS FOR A VARIETY OF CLIENTS. SEE HIS SAMPLES AT WWW.ARTY4EVER.COM.

MEGAN BAEHR RECENTLY GRADUATED FROM THE SCHOOL OF VISUAL ARTS IN NEW YORK. SHE LIVES IN SOUTHERN VERMONT, WHERE SHE HAS LEAPT INTO HER CARTOONING CAREER WITH GREAT ENTHUSIASM. BAEHR IS MAKING COMICS, TEACHING COMICS TO YOUNG PEOPLE AT LOCAL SCHOOLS, AND DABBLING IN OTHER CREATIVE ENDEAVORS. SHE HOPES TO ACCELERATE THE CREATION OF HER FIRST GRAPHIC NOVEL IN THE COMING YEAR. VISIT HER WORK AT WWW.FRIEDWONTONS.COM.

JOYCE (CHILDERS) BEAR IS FROM LUCHAPOKA (WHAT IS TODAY KNOWN AS TULSA, OKLAHOMA). SINCE 1996 SHE HAS MANAGED THE CULTURE PRESERVATION DEPARTMENT FOR THE MUSCOGEE (CREEK) NATION. SHE ALSO SERVES AS A CONSULTANT TO STATE AND FEDERAL AGENCIES AND IS THE CURRENT CHAIRPERSON OF THE CULTURAL PRESERVATION COMMITTEE FOR THE INTER-TRIBAL COUNCIL OF THE FIVE CIVILIZED TRIBES.

ANDY BENNETT IS AN ARTIST FROM COLUMBUS, OHIO, WHO IS A LONGTIME MEMBER OF THE PANEL COMICS COLLECTIVE. HIS WORK CAN BE SEEN IN MOONSTONE BOOKS'S VAMPIRE THE MASQUERADE SERIES OF GRAPHIC NOVELS, AS WELL AS THE *AVENGER CHRONICLES* AND *GHOST SONATA* COLLECTIONS AND *SAINT GERMAINE* FROM TRANSFUZION. VISIT WWW.B3NN3TT.COM.

ROY BONEY JR. IS A CHEROKEE NATION CITIZEN FROM TAHLEQUAH, OKLAHOMA. HE WORKS AS AN ANIMATOR AND GRAPHIC ARTIST FOR THE CHEROKEE NATION AND IS AN ADJUNCT INSTRUCTOR OF MULTIMEDIA. HE IS ALSO CO-OWNER OF CHEROKEE ROBOT, A MULTIMEDIA COMPANY THAT SPECIALIZES IN CREATING NATIVE LANGUAGE ANIMATIONS AND INTERACTIVE MEDIA. HIS PREVIOUS

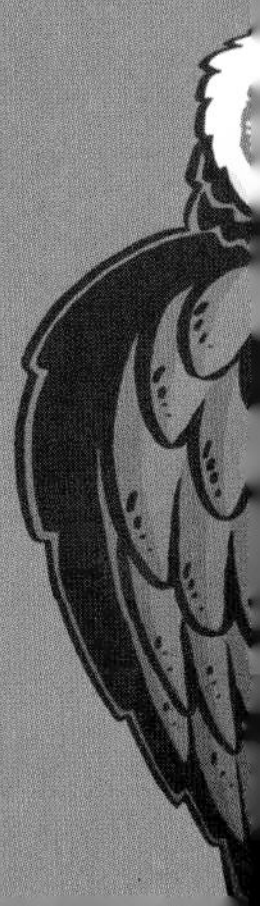

COMIC BOOK WORK INCLUDES *DEAD EYES OPEN* FROM SLAVE LABOR GRAPHICS.

JAMES BRUCHAC IS AN AWARD-WINNING AUTHOR, STORYTELLER, TRACKING EXPERT, AND WILDERNESS INSTRUCTOR AND GUIDE. RAISED IN GREENFIELD CENTER, NEW YORK, BRUCHAC IS THE ELDEST SON OF WORLD-RENOWNED ABENAKI INDIAN STORYTELLER AND AUTHOR JOSEPH BRUCHAC. BRUCHAC AND HIS FATHER WERE AWARDED A 2005 CONSERVATION ACHIEVEMENT AWARD FROM THE NATIONAL WILDLIFE FEDERATION. AS A STORYTELLER, BRUCHAC HAS OFFERED PROGRAMS FOR SCHOOLS AND COLLEGES ACROSS THE COUNTRY AS WELL AS FOR NUMEROUS LIBRARIES, MUSEUMS, AND STORYTELLING FESTIVALS.

JOSEPH BRUCHAC IS A WRITER WHOSE POEMS, STORIES, AND ESSAYS HAVE BEEN WIDELY PUBLISHED OVER THE PAST THIRTY YEARS. HE'S AUTHORED MORE THAN 120 BOOKS, TWO OF WHICH ARE FORTHCOMING GRAPHIC NOVELS FROM FIRST SECOND BOOKS. HIS WORK OFTEN REFLECTS HIS ABENAKI ANCESTRY AND HIS DEEP DEBT TO TRADITIONAL STORIES—ESPECIALLY THE TRICKSTER TALES THAT KEEP REMINDING HIM NOT TO TAKE HIMSELF OR ANY OF HIS ACCOMPLISHMENTS TOO SERIOUSLY.

SOMETIME IN THE 1800S, A FULL-BLOODED CHEROKEE LADY WALKED INTO PENDLETON, SOUTH CAROLINA, LEADING A MILK COW. SHE WAS THE GREAT-GREAT-GRANDMOTHER OF ARTIST **J CHRIS CAMPBELL**. IN 1998 CAMPBELL MOVED INTO THE SUBDIVISION OF INDIAN HILLS, ONTO A STREET NAMED AFTER THE CHICKASAW TRIBE, WHERE HE DRAWS COMICS ON HIS COMPUTER, NONE OF WHICH HAVE EVER HAD ANYTHING TO DO WITH NATIVE AMERICANS, UNTIL NOW. VISIT WWW .JCHRISCAMPBELL.COM.

JERRY CARR WAS BORN IN THE WILDS OF SOUTHERN VIRGINIA, A SELF-PROCLAIMED MUTANT OFFSPRING TO NORMAL PARENTS. HIS TRAVELS EVENTUALLY LED HIM TO INSIGHT STUDIOS, WHERE HE DEVELOPED THE POPULAR ALL-AGES ROMP CRYPTOZOO CREW GRAPHIC NOVEL SERIES WITH WRITER ALLAN GROSS. HE RECENTLY FINISHED COLORING THE ONLINE STRIP *MIGHTY MOTOR SAPIENS* FOR ROWDY.COM WITH MARK WHEATLEY AND CRAIG TALLIFER.

ANDREW COHEN DOES THE COMICS *HOWZIT FUNNIES*, *LAW MONGER*, AND WEB-COMIC-TURNED-GRAPHIC NOVEL *SPADEFOOT*. HE LIVES IN WASHINGTON, DC.

JASON COPLAND GRADUATED FROM THE EMILY CARR INSTITUTE OF ART AND DESIGN. HE COLLABORATED WITH MATT DEMBICKI FOR HIS STORY "SEND LOUIS HIS UNDERWEAR," WHICH APPEARED IN *POSTCARDS*, AN EISNER-NOMINATED ANTHOLOGY FROM VILLARD. COPLAND LIVES IN VANCOUVER, CANADA, WITH HIS WIFE AND THEIR SON. WHEN HE'S NOT DRAWING, YOU CAN FIND HIM GUARDING THE NET FOR HIS LOCAL RECREATIONAL HOCKEY TEAM.

THOMAS C. CUMMINGS JR. HAS BEEN A STORYTELLER FOR MORE THAN FORTY YEARS. HE WAS RAISED IN HAWAI'I BY HIS GRANDPARENTS, WHO SHOWED HIM HAWAIIAN CUSTOMS, INCLUDING CHANT AND HULA, WHICH ARE ALSO FORMS OF STORYTELLING. THROUGH HIS DECADES AS AN EDUCATOR—AT ONE TIME IN THE CLASSROOM, NOW AS A CULTURAL SPECIALIST AT THE BISHOP MUSEUM—HIS STORIES REFLECT HIS LOVE FOR HAWAI'I AND THE WORLDVIEW AND VALUES OF HAWAIIANS AND OTHER POLYNESIANS.

MATT DEMBICKI IS A COMICS CREATOR IN THE WASHINGTON, DC, AREA. HE ENJOYS SELF-PUBLISHING

BUT ON OCCASION HE CONTRIBUTES TO OTHER PROJECTS. HIS NATURE PARABLE *MR. BIG* RECEIVED THE 2007 HOWARD E. DAY MEMORIAL PRIZE FOR SMALL PRESS COMICS. HE IS ALSO A FOUNDING MEMBER OF DC CONSPIRACY, A LOCAL COMICS CREATORS' COLLABORATIVE. VISIT HIM AT HTTP://MATT-DEMBICKI.BLOGSPOT.COM.

SUNNY DOOLEY IS A NATIVE DINÉ (NAVAJO) STORYTELLER FROM A NEW MEXICO COMMUNITY CALLED CHI CHIL' TAH (WHERE THE OAKS GROW). THE STORIES SHE TELLS HAVE BEEN TOLD FOR GENERATIONS FROM HER MATRILINEAL CLAN OF THE SALTWATER PEOPLE. WITH DIN□ AS HER FIRST LANGUAGE, SUNNY INTERPRETS MANY OF THE STORIES SHE TELLS INTO ENGLISH, COMPLETE WITH THEIR RICH CULTURAL, TRADITIONAL, AND HISTORICAL CONTEXT.

ELDRENA DOUMA IS A PUEBLO INDIAN WHOSE LOVE OF TRIBAL STORIES BEGAN AS A YOUNG GIRL ON BOTH THE LAGUNA AND HOPI RESERVATIONS. SHE LISTENED TO FAMILY MEMBERS AND TRIBAL ELDERS TELL THEIR STORIES AND TRIBAL HISTORIES. THROUGH HER SIYA ("GRANDMOTHER" IN TEWA), DOUMA GAINED A MORE PERSONAL APPRECIATION FOR THE ORAL TRADITION OF TELLING STORIES AND FOLKTALES. DOUMA TRAVELS THROUGHOUT THE UNITED STATES TELLING TRIBAL STORIES AS WELL AS STORIES SHE HAS WRITTEN.

DAYTON EDMONDS, A MEMBER OF THE CADDO NATION, HAS DEVELOPED A DIVERSE MINISTRY, LIFESTYLE, AND ARTISTRY. HE IS RETIRED, BUT FOR TWENTY-FIVE YEARS HE SERVED AS A PROFESSIONAL COMMUNITY DEVELOPER IN SOUTHERN OREGON AND NORTH-CENTRAL WASHINGTON. EDMONDS'S ART FORMS—DRAWING, PAINTING, SCULPTURE, PRINTMAKING, AND PUPPETRY—BLEND WITH HIS STORYTELLING AND HELP HIM WEAVE THOUGHT-PROVOKING PICTURES. VISIT HIS WEBSITE AT WWW.DAYTONEDMONDS.NET.

MARY EYLEY WAS A COWLITZ ELDER WHO LIVED IN NESIKA, WASHINGTON, ON THE UPPER COWLITZ RIVER. HER STORIES AND OTHERS WERE COMPILED IN A COLLECTION, *LEGENDS OF THE COWLITZ INDIAN TRIBE*, BY ROY WILSON, AN ENROLLED COWLITZ MEMBER WHO ALSO SERVED AS CHAIRMAN OF THE TRIBAL COUNCIL. THE STORY IS USED WITH HIS PERMISSION.

MICAH FARRITOR HAS BEEN IN COMICS SINCE 2004. HIS ILLUSTRATED WORKS INCLUDE THE SCIENCE-FICTION ADVENTURE *WHITE PICKET FENCES* BY MATT ANDERSON AND ERIC HUTCHINS AND "HOMESICK" BY JOSHUA FIALKOV IN THE ANTHOLOGY *POSTCARDS*. IT WAS A PLEASURE TO BE IN SUCH GREAT AND CREATIVE COMPANY AS A PART OF THE *TRICKSTER* ANTHOLOGY.

BECKEE GARRIS WAS BORN AND RAISED ON THE CATAWBA INDIAN RESERVATION IN ROCK HILL, SOUTH CAROLINA. SHE RETIRED IN 1999 IN ORDER TO DEDICATE HERSELF TO LEARNING THE PROPER WAY OF MAKING CATAWBA POTTERY AND TO PURSUE A DEGREE IN NATIVE AMERICAN STUDIES AT THE UNIVERSITY OF SOUTH CAROLINA. SHARING HER KNOWLEDGE ABOUT HER CATAWBA HERITAGE WITH OTHERS THROUGH LANGUAGE, POTTERY, STORYTELLING, DRUMMING, AND DANCING PROGRAMS IS HER PASSION.

JACK GLADSTONE IS A NATIVE POET-SINGER AND LECTURER FROM THE BLACKFEET INDIAN NATION OF MONTANA. REGARDED AS A CULTURAL BRIDGE BUILDER, HE DELIVERS PROGRAMS NATIONALLY ON AMERICAN INDIAN MYTHOLOGY AND HISTORY. IN A

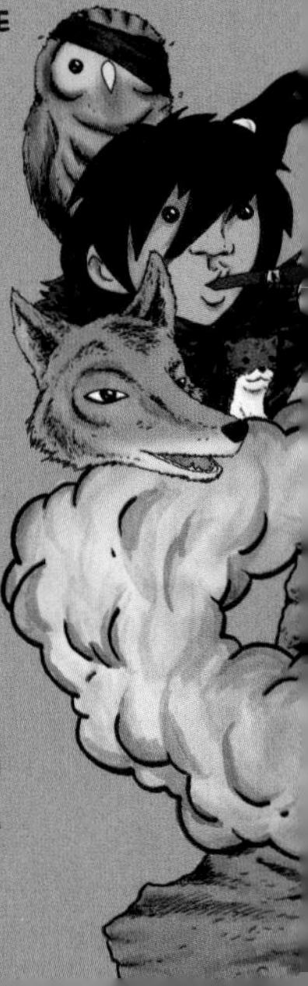

CAREER SPANNING TWO DECADES, GLADSTONE HAS PRODUCED A DOZEN CRITICALLY ACCLAIMED CDS. A FORMER COLLEGE INSTRUCTOR, HE HAS BEEN FEATURED ON THE TRAVEL CHANNEL AND IN *USA TODAY* MAGAZINE.

JIMM GOODTRACKS IS IOWAY/OTOE AND WORKS TO RESEARCH AND PRESERVE THE IOWAY/OTOE-MISSOURIA LANGUAGE (BA'XOJE JIWE'RE-NU'T^ACHI), ORAL TRADITION, HISTORY, AND CUSTOMS. HE COMPOSED THE IOWAY/OTOE-MISSOURIA DICTIONARY, WITH MORE THAN 9,000 ENTRIES, WHICH IS USED BY LINGUISTS AND EDUCATORS AS A RESOURCE FOR COMPARATIVE WORK WITH OTHER SIOUAN LANGUAGES. GOODTRACKS WISHES TO CREATE A KNOWLEDGE RESOURCE IN PRINT FOR THE YOUNGER GENERATIONS SO THEY CAN LEARN ABOUT THEIR HERITAGE AND LANGUAGE.

ELAINE GRINNELL IS AN ELDER IN THE JAMESTOWN S'KLALLAM TRIBE AND LIVES IN SEQUIM, WASHINGTON. GRINNELL'S GRANDFATHER, WHO WITH HER GRANDMOTHER RAISED HER, WOULD HOOK UP A WAGON TO AN OLD TRACTOR TO TAKE THEM TO THE BEACH TO GET DEVILFISH, ALSO CALLED OCTOPUS. IN 2007 GRINNELL—A HISTORIAN, STORYTELLER, AND COOK—RECEIVED THE WASHINGTON STATE GOVERNOR'S HERITAGE AWARD FOR HELPING TO KEEP HER CULTURE ALIVE.

JIM8BALL, AKA **JIM COON**, HAS BEEN PUBLISHING HIS OWN COMICS AND MINICOMICS SINCE 1995. HE LIVES IN UPSTATE NEW YORK WITH HIS WIFE AND DAUGHTER. WHEN NOT WORKING AS A T-SHIRT DESIGNER FOR A LOCAL SCREEN PRINTING COMPANY, COON SPENDS HIS WEEKENDS AT CRAFT SHOWS AND FESTIVALS DRAWING CARICATURES. IN HIS SPARE TIME HE LIKES TO SLEEP. VISIT HIS BLOG AT WWW.JIM8BALL.BLOGSPOT.COM.

DAN JONES IS AN OJIBWE LANGUAGE PROFESSOR AT FOND DU LAC TRIBAL AND COMMUNITY COLLEGE IN MINNESOTA AND HAS MADE THE ANISHINAABE LANGUAGE HIS LIFE'S MISSION. JONES KNEW ONLY ANISHINAABE UNTIL HE WAS REMOVED FROM HIS HOME IN ONTARIO, CANADA, AT AGE FIVE AND SENT TO A RESIDENTIAL SCHOOL WHERE THE TEACHERS HIT HIS HANDS WITH A STICK IF HE SPOKE ANISHINAABE. IN ADDITION TO HIS REGULAR LANGUAGE CLASSES, HE TEACHES A WEEKLY LANGUAGE IMMERSION GROUP.

EVAN KEELING WORKS AT THE SMITHSONIAN INSTITUTION AND IS A FOUNDING MEMBER OF THE DC CONSPIRACY COMICS CREATORS' COLLABORATIVE. HIS PROJECTS HAVE INCLUDED WORKING ON GALLERIES FOR THE NATIONAL MUSEUM OF THE AMERICAN INDIAN IN WASHINGTON, DC. COMICS HE HAS CREATED INCLUDE *CRUMBSNATCHERS* AND *ATAXIA OVERDRIVE*. KEELING LIVES IN WASHINGTON, DC, WITH HIS WIFE.

PAT LEWIS IS A CARTOONIST AND ILLUSTRATOR FROM PITTSBURGH, PENNSYLVANIA. HIS FIRST BOOK, *THE CLAWS COME OUT*, FROM IDW PUBLISHING, IS CURRENTLY AVAILABLE IN STORES, AT AMAZON.COM, AND FROM LEWIS'S WEBSITE, WWW.LUNCHBREAKCOMICS.COM.

DIMI MACHERAS WAS BORN IN ALASKA AND IS A CHICKALOON VILLAGE TRIBAL MEMBER. HIS ART HAS BEEN INCLUDED IN SEVERAL CULTURAL PROJECTS, SUCH AS AN INTERACTIVE ATHABASCAN LANGUAGE COMPUTER PROGRAM AND CHILDREN'S STORYBOOKS, INCLUDING *YA NE DAH AH*, BASED ON CHICKALOON LEGENDS. MOST RECENTLY, HE ILLUSTRATED THE COMIC BOOK *STRONG MAN* FOR THE ASSOCIATION OF ALASKA SCHOOL BOARDS. HE LIVES IN SEATTLE AND IS WORKING TOWARD STARTING HIS OWN CREATOR-OWNED COMIC SERIES.

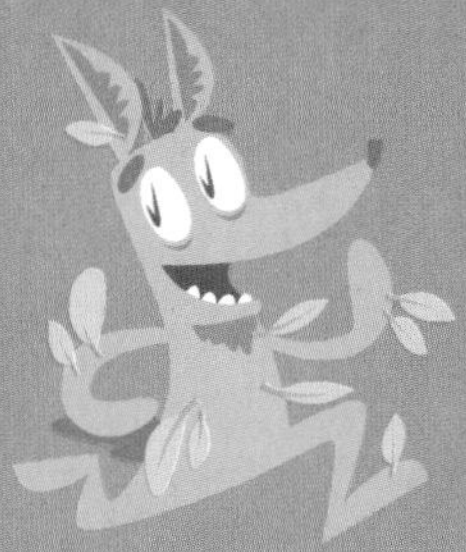

JOHN BEAR MITCHELL, A MEMBER OF THE PENOBSCOT NATION, IS ASSOCIATE DIRECTOR OF THE WABANAKI CENTER AT THE UNIVERSITY OF MAINE AND THE UNIVERSITY OF MAINE SYSTEM NATIVE PROGRAM WAIVER COORDINATOR. HE ALSO TEACHES COURSES ON WABANAKI HISTORY AND CONTEMPORARY ISSUES AT THE UNIVERSITY. WHILE WORKING HIS WAY THROUGH COLLEGE, MITCHELL TOURED WITH THE NATIVE AMERICAN STORYTELLERS OF NEW ENGLAND.

JONATHAN PERRY IS AN AQUINNAH WAMPANOAG ARTIST AND CULTURAL PRACTITIONER WHO TRAVELS EXTENSIVELY AS A SPEAKER, PRESENTER, PERFORMING ARTIST, AND VISUAL ARTIST. FEATURED IN A NUMBER OF DOCUMENTARY FILMS REPRESENTING INDIGENOUS PEOPLE OF THE EASTERN UNITED STATES, PERRY HAS APPEARED IN PRESS INTERVIEWS, TELEVISION COMMERCIALS, SPECIAL FEATURES, AND ON RADIO PROGRAMS. HE IS A LONG-TERM EMPLOYEE OF THE WAMPANOAG INDIGENOUS PROGRAM AT THE PLIMOTH PLANTATION IN MASSACHUSETTS.

CHRIS PIERS WAS BORN AND RAISED IN MASSACHUSETTS AND NOW LIVES IN ALEXANDRIA, VIRGINIA. HE HAS WRITTEN AND DRAWN STORIES IN THE SELF-PUBLISHED ARENA WITH THE DC CONSPIRACY COMICS CREATORS' COLLABORATIVE. HIS DAY JOB IS IN GRAPHIC DESIGN, AND HE TEACHES WRITING FOR COMICS AT A LOCAL WRITERS' CENTER AND COHOSTS THE WEEKLY PODCAST "TELEVISION ZOMBIES."

CHOCTAW/CHICKASAW WRITER AND STORYTELLER **GREG RODGERS** OF OKLAHOMA CITY TELLS STORIES AND PRESENTS WORKSHOPS AT FESTIVALS, SCHOOLS, LIBRARIES, AND TRIBAL EVENTS THROUGHOUT THE COUNTRY. RODGERS'S STORYTELLING REPERTOIRE INCLUDES BOTH TRADITIONAL AND CONTEMPORARY CHOCTAW STORIES, FAMILY STORIES, AND PERSONAL STORIES. HIS PERFORMANCES ARE A PUBLIC DEMONSTRATION OF HIS TRUE PASSION, THE COLLECTION AND RESPECTFUL PRESERVATION OF HIS PEOPLE'S MEMORIES—THE FOUNDATION OF THE CHOCTAW ORAL NARRATIVE. VISIT RODGERS AT WWW.GREGRODGERS.INFO.

MIKE SHORT LIVES IN LORTON, VIRGINIA, WHERE HE WATCHES DVDS WITH HIS WIFE, PLAYS WITH HIS KIDS, CHASES HIS RUNAWAY DOG, OR BURNS THE MIDNIGHT OIL DRAWING COMICS.

MICHELLE SILVA IS A TWENTY-TWO-YEAR-OLD WHO ATTENDS THE UNIVERSITY OF MINNESOTA, MAJORING IN GRAPHIC DESIGN AND ART. WHEN SHE'S NOT DOING HER HOMEWORK, SHE IS USUALLY FOUND LURKING AROUND HER COMPUTER, DRAWING COMICS. CHECK HER OUT AT HTTP://OBECOMINGX.DEVIANTART.COM/GALLERY.

JON SPERRY IS A FREELANCE ILLUSTRATOR, CARTOONIST, AND GRAPHIC DESIGNER. HE LIVES IN THE PORTLAND, OREGON, AREA WITH HIS WIFE AND HIS OWN LITTLE WILDCAT, MR. BOOTS, ESQ. YOU CAN VIEW MORE OF HIS WORK OR CONTACT HIM THROUGH HIS WEBSITE AT WWW.JONSPERRY.COM.

DAVID "TIM" SMITH HAS BEEN A VALUABLE ASSET TO THE WINNEBAGO TRIBE OF NEBRASKA FOR MANY YEARS. SMITH GRADUATED MORNINGSIDE COLLEGE WITH A DEGREE IN HISTORY AND EARNED HIS MASTER'S DEGREE IN HISTORY FROM THE UNIVERSITY OF CALIFORNIA AT LOS ANGELES. HE THEN RETURNED TO WINNEBAGO AS THE TRIBAL HISTORIAN. SMITH IS ALSO DIRECTOR OF INDIAN STUDIES AT LITTLE PRIEST TRIBAL COLLEGE. HE WROTE HIS FIRST BOOK, *FOLKLORE OF THE WINNEBAGO TRIBE*, IN 1998.

JOSEPH STANDS WITH MANY IS A CHEROKEE STORYTELLER, EDUCATOR, WRITER, AND POET. FOR THE PAST TEN YEARS, HE HAS PRESENTED HIS STORYTELLING PROGRAMS AT SCHOOLS, COLLEGES, UNIVERSITIES, GOVERNMENT AGENCIES, AND MUSEUMS. HE HAS ALSO PERFORMED, ALONE AND WITH HIS SON, AT THE SMITHSONIAN'S NATIONAL MUSEUM OF THE AMERICAN INDIAN IN WASHINGTON, DC. FOR MORE ABOUT STANDS WITH MANY, VISIT WWW.STANDSWITHMANY.COM.

MICHAEL THOMPSON (MVSKOKE CREEK) WAS BORN IN HOLDENVILLE, OKLAHOMA, AND RAISED ON A SOUTH GEORGIA CATTLE FARM ALONG THE FLINT RIVER. HE HAS BEEN A TEACHER, WRITER, AND OCCASIONAL COMMUNITY ACTIVIST IN SEVERAL STATES. HE AND HIS WIFE HAVE MADE NUMEROUS PRESENTATIONS ON CONTEMPORARY NATIVE LITERATURE AT STATE AND NATIONAL CONFERENCES. THE STORY HE PROVIDED WAS ADAPTED FROM THE W. O. TUGGLE COLLECTION OF STORIES COMPILED BY ETHNOGRAPHER JOHN SWANTON IN THE EARLY 1900S.

EIRIK THORSGARD IS AN ENROLLED MEMBER OF THE CONFEDERATED TRIBES OF THE GRAND RONDE COMMUNITY OF OREGON AND WORKS IN THEIR CULTURAL RESOURCES DEPARTMENT AS THE CULTURAL PROTECTION COORDINATOR. HE IS DESCENDED FROM SEVERAL TRIBES, INCLUDING SLAHALA, THAPPENISH, PAIUTE, THE TUMWATA BAND OF THE CLALLIWALLA, AND SHAWNEE. HE HAS A MASTER'S DEGREE IN APPLIED ANTHROPOLOGY AND IS PURSUING A DOCTORATE IN INDIGENOUS ARCHAEOLOGY WHILE WORKING AND RAISING FOUR CHILDREN WITH HIS WIFE.

TIM TINGLE IS AN OKLAHOMA CHOCTAW AND A TOURING STORYTELLER AND WRITER, SPEAKING AND PERFORMING AT TRIBAL GATHERINGS, UNIVERSITIES, FESTIVALS, AND WRITING CONFERENCES. TINGLE'S FIRST BOOK, *WALKING THE CHOCTAW ROAD*, AND HIS CHILDREN'S BOOK, *CROSSING BOK CHITTO*, ILLUSTRATED BY CHEROKEE ARTIST JEANNE ROREX-BRIGES, HAVE WON SEVERAL AWARDS. TINGLE WAS MENTORED BY REVERED CHOCTAW HISTORIAN AND STORYTELLER CHARLIE JONES, WHO OFTEN SHARED HIS VERSION OF "HOW RABBIT LOST HIS TAIL," WHICH TINGLE HAS REWRITTEN FOR THIS BOOK.

JACOB WARRENFELTZ LOVES COMIC BOOKS. HE DREAMS ABOUT COMICS HE'S YET TO DRAW, HE TOILS OVER COMICS HE HAS DRAWN, AND HE TALKS INCESSANTLY ABOUT COMICS HE'S CURRENTLY DRAWING. IF YOU'RE EVER IN TAKOMA PARK, MARYLAND, LOOK HIM UP AND HE'LL LIKELY TELL YOU ALL ABOUT HIS CURRENT PROJECT. IT WILL BE THE GREATEST SIX-HOUR CONVERSATION YOU'VE EVER HAD.

SCOTT WHITE, A GRADUATE OF SAVANNAH COLLEGE OF ART AND DESIGN, HAS CONTRIBUTED TO MANY COMICS ANTHOLOGIES, INCLUDING THE *2004 SMALL PRESS EXPO ANTHOLOGY* AND *LIQUID REVOLVER*. HE HAS ALSO DONE NUMEROUS DESIGNS FOR T-SHIRTS, BELTS, AND POSTERS.

PAUL ZDEPSKI'S ARTWORK CAN BE SEEN AT WWW.ZILLUSTRATION.COM. HE GIVES MANY THANKS TO THOMAS CUMMINGS JR., LEILEHUA YUEN, AND THE STAFF OF THE BISHOP MUSEUM FOR THEIR HELPFUL RESEARCH ON CULTURE, DRESS, AND LORE.

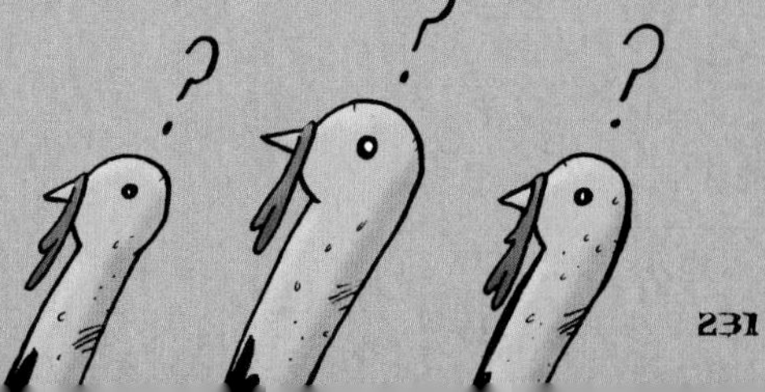

Special thanks

TO PETER KUPER AND RAFER ROBERTS FOR THEIR HELP. THIS BOOK WOULD NOT
HAVE BEEN POSSIBLE WITHOUT PETER'S INITIAL COVER ILLUSTRATION AND RAFER'S
PRELIMINARY BOOK DESIGN AND FORMATTING. I OWE YOU GUYS!